COLONY ONE

by T. L. Ford

To: Kristen, Enjoy! —T

(J. L. Ford)

Colony One
Copyright © by Theresa L. Ford
All rights reserved.

Cover's woman by subVersion, cover by Theresa L. Ford
Book design by Theresa L. Ford
Illustrations by Theresa L. Ford

Jerome Koger
Editor
Lucid Dream Editing
luciddreamediting@gmail.com

Roy M. Maier
Editor

Visit Mrs. Ford's website at www.Cattail.Nu .
Printed in the United States of America
First Published: December 2018
Independently Published, v.4
Cattail.Nu

Print version:
ISBN: 978-1-7905-8218-1

Acknowledgments

Ingi Ford, for love and giving me the opportunity to write.

Joan Lambert Bailey, for Japanese culture answers and cross-check.
Mary Bernhard, for cultural awareness and humor.
Dame, for motivation and feedback.
Lucas del Pino, for Argentina knowledge.
E. Engberts, for word smithing and publishing information.
Graham, for brainstorming help.
Jerome Koger, for editing.
Nick Kuhns, for word smithing and brainstorming assistance.
Roy M. Maier, for editing.
Dr. Steven Maier, for physics assistance.
Ian McAdams, for gun and ammunition information.
Charlene McBride Taylor, for edits and offering photo references.
Don Patterson, for his efforts on behalf of our military amputees, which inspired medical advances in this novel.
Lynn Ribeiro, for piano consultations.
Michelle Shaw, for listening to me mutter and correcting some errors.
Lynette Stanford, for fan fiction before the story was even finished that forced me to redo the timeline.
Daniel Stephens, onlineitalianclub.com, for Italian translation assistance.
subVersion, for that awesome woman artwork on the cover.
Felicity Weiss, for brainstorming and motivation.

Discord groups (**Alpha World, Author Dawn Chapman, LitRPG Forum, TSN Illuminati Division**), for brainstorming, answering random questions, motivation, and listening to me ramble about this book while I was writing it.
Southern Maryland Creative Writing Meetup, for feedback and proof-reading.

There are many others who also helped me. I'm blessed to have such a wonderful community of people who supported and assisted me through this process. Thank you all!

Table of Contents

Part 1

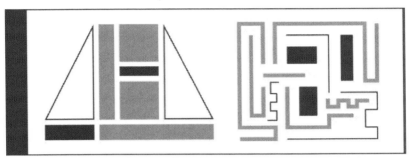

L minus 16:306:13:45   ~2π

It was her music, her gifted playing of the piano, that decided them. She wasn't a particularly beautiful young girl, despite her long yellowish-brown hair. They had prettier girls, but none with a talent like hers. This orphan, performing on stage, had no idea of the events that would cascade her into an entirely different life.

The adopting parents seemed perfect. All of the right background checks, the right home, the right location, resources to develop and grow a young prodigy. A perfect vision of a nice, upper-middle-class, childless couple that wanted to help a young girl. Perfect interviews. Even tentatively hopeful conversations between the prospective parents and the young girl, who willingly, happily, climbed into her new parents' car when the time came.

Everything was indeed perfect, even through the two month post-placement interview. Just after the interview, however, the façade vanished. The young girl was drugged during the evening meal and when she awoke, she was chained in a windowless, cement-floored room. The only things within reach were a bed, a lamp on a table, a piano, and a toilet. Across the dank basement room were a bookshelf, a fake window with curtains, a couple pretty, if strange, tapestries, a toy box filled with stuffed animals, and an old white-washed dresser with tiny pink flowers painted on. A spotlight fixed in a ceiling corner shone on the piano, and a security camera in the opposite corner was set for constant monitoring and recording.

She yelled and screamed and tried to break free, but her "father" merely came in, stabbed her with a drug-filled needle, and left again. Two things were in her favor. One, she could not play the piano while drugged and two, the older upright piano was wood. Despite panic and terror, her mind cleared. The

7

top of the piano was glued closed and any potential hazards removed, so she took to slamming the piano fallboard shut after playing and the old wood eventually split enough for her to snap off the tiniest wedge of wood. No longer than her finger; no wider than a pencil, but it was enough.

Her escape left her battered and covered in blood, more animal than human, viciously determined to survive by whatever means necessary, and unwilling to ever trust someone else with her fate again. She scavenged for food in trash cans and stayed out of sight until being taken in by a street gang.

People don't consider this beginning when they talk about the person responsible for Colony One, the space habitat that is the future of humanity. Most don't even know about it. Instead, they talk about her connection to the Marino family - the Italian Mafia - saying that this created the sharp, unforgiving edge to Colony One's legal system by which all people are now bound. Adapt and live by the rules or die. No prison system, no welfare, no crime.

My research suggests differently: the Marino family, Sal Marino in particular, was responsible for making the Founder human again. I had the privilege to interview her and this is what she told me - the real story of our space station's origin.

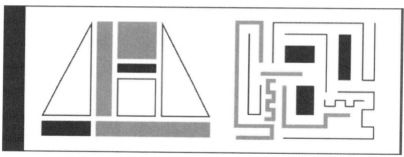

L minus 13:49:13:14   ~26π/15

The alley between the two high-rise buildings wasn't touched by the early evening sun. Piles of debris on either side had blown in and gotten stuck. Four street kids squatted between two large piles of trash, dividing their spoils.

The future Founder, the youngest at ten years old, held out the tiny crust of bread she'd found in the East Street Bakery dumpster. She wished she could have eaten it already. The empty grinding in her stomach could be felt clear to her throat. She would never get anything at all if she were so stupid as to forget her rank in the small group, which was the lowest. She was scrawny and her jeans and red top were falling apart, having long since been ruined by continuous use in outdoor weather. Her hair was brown with grime.

Mason, the oldest, and leader of their small gang, glared at her. "Is that all, Grub?" Mason was a tall, muscled boy who routinely made people cross the street in fear because of his hard glare and scowl. He snatched the bread from her and stuffed it in his mouth. In one swallow, the bite was gone.

Grub, for that was what the group called her, tried hard not to cry, but her eyes watered anyway. He might have hit her had she brought back nothing. She tried to convince herself that this was better. Training, he would call it, telling her that she needed to learn to pull her own weight and learn to scavenge properly. Grub nodded timidly and bit her lip, preparing to duck, if needed. Refusing to show weakness, she didn't wipe the water from her eyes. As much as she was scared of him, she was more scared of being alone. She'd already learned a lot about surviving on the street from him. If it cost a bite of bread, so be it.

Her hero, Caitlin, the second oldest, stepped in front of her. Caitlin, in her early teens, had the best clothes of all of them, dark blue jeans and a logo'd t-shirt; they'd gotten lucky in the last house they'd broken into. "Come on, Mason. Don't give her such a hard time," Caitlin implored. "She's just a little runt. Look, I got a great haul."

Grub quickly wiped her eyes while hidden behind Caitlin. One day, she wanted to grow up and be like Caitlin - strong, tough, and dangerous, yet still kind and good to her friends. She peeked around Caitlin to see what the older girl had found.

Caitlin handed over a styrofoam sandwich container which Mason opened, revealing a paper-wrapped, mostly uneaten sandwich in near pristine condition. Grub unconsciously wet her lips at this treasure, but she knew not to speak or reach.

Mason took his larger share of the sandwich and passed the styrofoam container back to Caitlin who crouched down next to their fourth member - a pale, thin boy with narrow lips and a broad nose who sat nearby. Caitlin handed him half of half a sandwich. Paul stuffed it in his mouth whole, picking a crumb off his threadbare t-shirt. Caitlin handed the container and the remaining inch of sandwich to Grub. Mason scowled disapprovingly, but did not comment and grabbed a box to sleep on for the night.

Grub stared up at Caitlin with wide eyes and asked, "Sure?" Caitlin had taken her into their small band three years earlier.

Caitlin nodded, glaring at Mason. "It's my share. Have it, Grub." She reached into her back pocket. "And I got you this." She handed Grub one of those pocket city guide books that someone had thrown out.

Grub didn't hesitate before shoving the rest of the sandwich into her mouth just like Paul had. It was almost enough to make her stomach feel full. She read the guide book with a similar gusto. She adored any books she could get her hands on. Printed material was a rare find. Most people only used their phones. Mason just rolled his eyes and sat down on his cardboard, leaning his back against the building wall, and closed his eyes.

When the other three curled up into a pile for the night, Grub snuggled against Caitlin for warmth, avoiding, as usual, anything that might annoy Mason.

Two days later, Grub sat in the alleyway, studying the city map in the pocket guide and then comparing her memory to it, while waiting on the others to return. They'd be a few more hours yet; she was early, sitting next to a full loaf of bread she'd stolen in a grocery parking lot while a woman returned her cart to the queue.

A small bird hopped nearby and Grub watched it intently, admiring the way it seemed delicately fragile and weightless, with its absolute stillness followed by quick, sudden movements. Birds knew how to avoid predators and Grub had tried mimicking that at the grocery. People busy with their own concerns hadn't noticed her scrunched down between the cars. This was risky, but she'd come up short on contributions the last two days.

Mason ran into the alley, scaring the bird away. He bent forward, leaning with his hands on his knees, trying to catch his breath. "Grub!" he wheezed, "The Fross brothers picked up Caitlin. Paul's watching the place right now, but we have to go get her or we'll lose her." He kneeled down next to a hole in the cement wall near a drainpipe. Without the usual prod with a stick for mice and spiders, he reached in and pulled out his spare shiv.

Grub felt panic squeeze her chest, tightening her lungs and making it hard to breathe. She shivered. The Fross brothers were an organized crime group that their small gang avoided. Grub had been warned to stay away at all costs. She knew what they did without having to be explicitly told.

"They got her in the house off Prescott Street, but she won't be there much longer and then we'll never see her again," Mason growled, reaching once again into the hole, deeper this time, and withdrew a waterproof plastic bag with two filled 9mm magazines and two boxes of bullets. Once more, and the gun came out also sealed in a plastic bag. Mason took the gun and a magazine out of their bags. To prevent any light from glinting on the gun's silver, they'd added a matte black finish and that seemed to suck away what little light reached the alley. "Remember when I showed you how to use this?"

Grub nodded, hesitantly, eyes wide. She'd been a good shot, the best of all of them, that day with the soda cans.

Mason shoved the gun and magazine into her hands. "Show me. Load it."

Grub swallowed and looked at the magazine. It was filled with 16 rounds.

"Faster, Grub!" Mason ordered sharply.

Her hands shook, but she closed her eyes and remembered the day she was standing in front of the targets. Her memory was crystal clear. The dank, abandoned warehouse with broken floors smelled like mice nests. This mixed with the odor of gunpowder and burnt carbon. Paul had just taken his turn and passed the gun to her. She saw her hands load the gun and then carefully aim. Mason had growled at her to exhale before shooting to keep the gun steady. Grub frowned and snapped out of the memory. The gun was empty. She checked that the top round was seated properly in the magazine before slamming it into the gun. She grabbed the back of the slide, pulled it and let it go, listening as it snapped forward, sending a round into the chamber. The gun felt heavy, solid in her hand.

Mason pulled at his hair. "There's a trash can across the street. You're going to hide behind that and shoot the guards when Paul distracts them. And then you shoot anyone else who comes out. Me and Paul will go in and get Caitlin. We'll prolly have to carry her. Don't come in. You don't need to see any of that stuff." Mason's eyes squinted at her and he said sternly, "You're going to have to kill people. It's them or us and Caitlin. You understand?"

Grub nodded again.

He narrowed his eyes at her. "And don't fire so fast you waste bullets. Check your aim. You'll only have those two magazines. 32 bullets." He looked like he was beginning to doubt his decision. "Promise you'll kill anyone that comes out. Blood promise, Grub." Mason took the gun and the other magazine and shoved them into a paper bag. He did not unload the gun.

Grub stood a little straighter and tried to look fierce. "For Caitlin." She took her shiv and sliced her palm, wincing at the sharp sting, but held her hand up to him, letting the blood drip anyway.

"Come on then." Mason shoved the other magazine at her and she put it in her pocket. He then handed the paper bag to her and started off at a brisk walk. "Should never have taken those clothes," Mason hissed.

Holding the bag very carefully so the gun would point away from her and hoping it wouldn't fire, Grub scurried after him. They couldn't afford to waste the bullet.

When Grub and Mason arrived at Paul's lookout, Paul reported that the Fross brothers hadn't returned yet. His lookout was a sunken stairwell a good distance from the Fross brothers' house on Prescott Street. They were likely out getting dinner somewhere, but could be back any minute. As nearly as he could tell, there were only the guards by the door, and he'd only seen one man go inside and not come out.

Paul held up a wad of newspaper he'd mashed into a soccer-sized ball, probably around some cardboard and other fillers. This was wrapped in a couple plastic grocery bags so it wouldn't fall apart.

Mason thumped him on the back. "That's good, Paul. Ok, you're both going to go down the street. Paul's going house-side, and Grub, you go across the street. He'll kick the ball down and chase it. You match him and call out that you want him to pass it to you. He's not going to. Instead..."

Paul interrupted, "I'm going to kick it right at them. Duck behind that trash can and as soon as I get past..." He nudged Grub in the ribs.

"You shoot them," Mason finished. "Got it?"

Grub clutched the paper bag with the gun. She nodded shakily.

Paul dropped the ball and began kicking it across the street. He angled sharply toward their target and Grub ran to keep up on her side.

As they got closer, Grub shouted, "Hey! It's my turn! Kick it over here!"

Paul yelled back, "In a minute! I almost beat my record!"

Grub's shoe caught on a broken sidewalk and she stumbled. She ran faster to keep up, ignoring the throbbing in her toe. The trash can approached too quickly and her heart pounded more from terror than running. The men were watching Paul. To distract them, she hollered, "You ain't got a record! Kick it to me!"

As soon as the two men standing in front of the building looked over at her, Paul kicked the ball directly at them and Grub ducked behind the trash can, pulling the gun from the paper bag. With a sharp inhale, she popped up and fired off a shot. It missed. She'd wasted a bullet. For the next shot, she aimed, exhaled and didn't inhale, to steady her hand, and fired twice. This time successfully.

The remaining man pulled a gun from the back of his pants and shot at Grub, but his first shots also missed. Grub aimed and fired two more times. The man fell back into the building's wall and slid downwards. Grub crouched down and waited. She heard the door open so she jumped up, and fired two bullets at the man who came out, counting and keeping track of how many bullets she'd have.

It was sheer chance, a bit of luck, that Grub saw movement on the building's roof. She darted back down, inhaling and exhaling quickly. She stood and shot the man on the roof; four shots to actually hit him. Three more men came out to that same fate. Two were not carrying guns. Customers.

Paul and Mason rushed in.

She thought her gun only had one bullet left and that would be chambered. Grub tilted the gun to find the magazine release, watching her finger press the small button. The magazine shot out and clattered to the ground. Grub slammed in the full magazine, and bent to pick up the empty one, before following Paul and Mason into the house. One of the men on the doorstep was still alive. She put the gun to his head and devoid of emotion, shot him. Grub stepped inside. The hallway was filled with cigarette smoke and perfume, and it nearly made her gag.

The first room she looked in was empty, a poker game still on the table. She pocketed the money in the pot and moved on. When she got to the first room that held a girl, she shook as the flashback overwhelmed her. This girl

wasn't chained or tied but stared up the ceiling light with glazed eyes. She
didn't even notice when Grub went up to her and put a bullet in her head.

Grub killed three more girls before Mason found her and stopped her. It
took all three of them to drag the drugged, limp Caitlin. They were out and
away before the first police sirens were heard.

Three days later, Grub found Caitlin laying in a lake of blood from her
slashed wrists. Grub stared at her own future for a long time, feeling the air
cool her throat as she inhaled, and listening to silent scream in her mind. She
didn't want to end up like this.

Grub turned and fled. She ran for a long time, not caring where she was
going, and eventually collapsed. When she woke up, she raided the nearest
dumpster for food, and gave serious thought to what she needed to do. Even if
she was smart, she'd inevitably blossom out into a young woman and her
options on the street were limited. She needed a different life path. She
headed south. Winters were always too dangerous this far north.

She broke into a house and stole new clothes, carefully choosing a shirt
and jeans that were already worn out and a few sizes too big. She almost
wished for the lookout Mason and Paul would have provided, or that at least
she had thought to steal the gun. Not wanting to be seen, she also broke into a
library and absorbed the wilderness survival books, easily memorizing things
with her avid need. She randomly grabbed a few other books and a couple
things from the employee kitchen, and took a backpack someone had left

behind that was in a basket labeled 'Lost and Found'. On her way out, she tossed the city guide Caitlin had given her. She didn't want anyone finding out where she'd come from.

Over the next two years, Grub relied on no one but herself. During the first summer, she stayed in Charlotte, North Carolina, and spent as much time as possible in libraries, scanning through books to keep her company through the winter. When school season arrived, she travelled southwest to the Chattahoochee National Forest where she stayed out of sight and used her new-found book knowledge to fish, hunt, and gather wild edible plants. She slept far from any human habitation in debris huts which she destroyed each day, until she found a small cave entrance which was obscured from view. She ousted the raccoons that were living there and moved her debris hut inside. Rather than return to Charlotte where she might be recognized, she pilfered more clothes, and headed farther south to Georgia, taking the name Alex Smith.

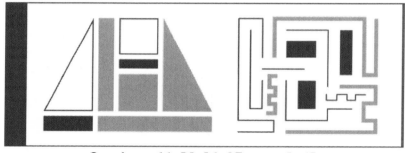

L minus 11:89:21:37   ~8π/5

The cold, torrential rain pelted Alex like tiny, sharp rocks. Alex could feel the static in the air. The deafening roars of thunder almost immediately followed the flashes of light. She needed shelter. The rough grey of the Atlanta city street had no overhangs, no covered bus benches, and the air smelled of dirt and wet pavement. The stolen, lightweight jacket offered no protection at all.

Lightning cracked nearby and every cell of her body was screaming danger. Alex dodged into the first store with an "Open" sign. A small bell jingled softly. Outside, hail began pounding the street. It sounded like gunfire.

Alex blinked around. She was dripping on a beautiful, slightly-faded oriental carpet in a small antiques shop. Low shelves made three aisles on the right, displaying figurines, statues, and vases. Exquisite furniture pieces, arranged to show their best features, were to the left. Large, beautiful paintings hung on the walls. The proprietor, an elderly gentleman in an immaculate grey suit, was sitting on a stool behind a glass display box toward the back.

"Quite the storm out there," the proprietor said, setting an open magazine he'd been reading down on the counter. He stood.

Alex glanced back out. The rain and hail had gotten so heavy the buildings across the street were obscured. She couldn't retreat. She yearned for one of the large stores where she could have remained anonymous, preferably one with a built-in mini-food cafeteria. "Can I wait here, just until it slows a bit?" she asked. Her throat was scratchy from disuse and she had to clear it midway through.

"Yes, wait there." The man went through a door behind the counter and returned a moment later carrying several small kitchen towels.

Alex stepped off the carpet and set her very worn backpack down with a dishearteningly wet splosh. "Thanks," she said, sopping up the worst of the water in her hair and clothes. Thinking of the family dynamics she'd seen while spying on campers, she added, "Sorry about your carpet." The unnatural words sounded hollow. She hoped the carpet wasn't ruined.

The slight nod he gave her suggested it was the right thing to say. He replied, "It'll dry, faster than you actually." He tilted his head to the side slightly, thinking, and then said, "I have something we can wrap you in, if you want to try drying your clothes in my oven?"

She hesitated with that terrified stillness of a wild animal. He didn't seem like the kind of person who would hurt her. Could she even justify the time it would take to dry her clothes when she needed to find food and shelter for the night? "What do I have to do for it?"

"Not freeze to death in my shop? Don't worry. You have nothing to fear from me."

Just at that moment, her whole body shook with uncontrollable shivers. She knew all too well the dangers of hypothermia. It's why she had come so far south. She nodded. She grabbed her bag and wrapped it in the soaked towels so it wouldn't drip as she carried it. She still left a trail of wet footprints on the smooth cement floor.

As she followed him back, she saw a small area in the back left of the shop had been set up as a diminutive living room. Four elegant and comfortable armchairs surrounded a round table. Two floor lights by the wall would brighten the area quite well if turned on. She automatically noticed things that might be sellable at a pawn shop. Maybe a couple of the vases, but nothing much of real value.

He led her through the door into a surprisingly large back room. Off to the right was a small kitchen, complete with stove, oven, microwave, sink, cabinets, and a small four person table. A door that was slightly ajar had a small office beyond that. Then the door to the bathroom. Most of the space was dedicated to boxes, varying in size from huge wooden crates to tiny cardboard boxes. The big ones had auction house inventory data sheets stapled to them.

He motioned for her to wait and went to the very back and retrieved two blue blankets. "Packing blankets," he explained. "Not too clean, but at least dry. Use one as a towel. I'll turn the oven on while you wrap up." He gestured to the bathroom.

The small bathroom was decorated nautically, in blues, with three small paintings, obviously from different artists. One ocean and beach with a sailboat, one sand and shells, and the last, a gorgeous lighthouse. The shell-shaped bar of soap was on a ceramic rendition of coiled rope, and the hand-napkins had beach houses on them. Alex, of course, didn't give any attention to these details, although she saw them and would remember later.

Her hands shook so badly she could barely get her clothes off. She couldn't regret leaving her winter clothes buried under rocks and hidden in the back of the cave she'd claimed as her own. Those were self-made from animals she'd hunted and eaten. Warm furs, most novice-stiff, wouldn't keep her quietly anonymous. She wrapped in the first dry blanket, even right over her head, and sat on the closed toilet until the shaking stopped. The blanket absorbed the water, and slightly warmer, she reversed the blanket so the dry side was toward her, and rubbed at her hair. When she finished, she did her best to dry her underwear and put them back on and then did the same with the threadbare t-shirt from her backpack.

She saw her fingertips were still blue and frowned at them disapprovingly. Traitors. Granted, she hadn't eaten in two days and that had been cold rain, but she needed her body to take better care of her. She promised her empty belly that she would fill it later that evening now that she was in a more commercial area and could find a suitable restaurant dumpster.

She yanked knots from her hair with her broken comb, staring at her unfamiliar reflection for a moment in confusion. The girl who looked back at her was much older and gaunt, with unevenly cut hair that was too long to be a boy's style and too short to be feminine with her face-shape. She was just starting that gangly-awkward teenage look, limbs slightly long for her too-thin body.

She blotted at her meager belongings and repacked them in the now damp backpack, keeping her knife out. She pulled the dry blanket around her shoulders and lifted the excess up around her waist so she could hold it closed with her off-hand that also hid her knife. She wrapped everything else in the other blanket, and carried it out to the small kitchen area. It was awkward while holding the dry blanket around her, but as soon as he saw her emerge, the shop's proprietor came to help her with the bundle.

In addition to turning the oven on its lowest setting, he'd also put a tea kettle on to heat, and Alex wondered if she could talk him into giving her a cup of hot tea. They put her clothes on a metal tray, leaving the oven door partly open to prevent it from getting too hot. Alex hovered next to the radiating heat.

"I haven't seen you around before," the man commented. Even though he continued to study the oven intently and didn't look directly at her, the seemingly casual tone was not casual at all.

"My mom and I just moved to the area. I thought today would be a good day to explore. I left early, before the rain." Alex shuddered convincingly. "My mistake." Her voice was still gritty and she decided she would definitely practice talking next winter to keep her voice active.

"Would you like to call her to tell her you are ok?"

"Naw. She's busy unpacking. If I call, she'll demand I come home and help." Caitlin had said Alex was the quickest, best liar she'd ever seen (once she'd given her a few lessons). "Truth be told, I snuck out while she was still sleeping and left her a note."

The man raised an eyebrow and chuckled. "Teenagers," he said. "I'm Sal Marino. You are?"

"Alex Smith. Would you prefer Sal or Mr. Marino?"

Sal's mouth opened slightly in startled bafflement. He touched his chin a moment, breathing in and studying her, and then answered, "Call me Sal." He removed two sturdy ceramic mugs from one of the cabinets. "Hot cocoa, tea, or herbal tea?"

As good as she remembered hot cocoa tasting, she knew the effects of sugar and caffeine on an empty stomach. "Herbal tea." She'd at least get some nutrients from that. She selected a packet labelled rose hips for the vitamin c from his collection of assorted herbal teas. He also chose one of the herbal teas.

Sal filled both mugs and carried them to the table. "Have a seat, young adventurer."

To prevent him from asking her probing questions, she took the lead. "Do you own the shop or work here?"

"Own."

"It looks like you sell some really nice stuff." Alex didn't wait for the tea bag to finish steeping. She sipped some of the hot-but-not-too-hot weak tea while the tea bag was still in the cup.

"Nice stuff, eh?" Sal sounded amused when he added, "I'll have you know, those are very expensive, very valuable collector's items."

Alex, concerned she'd insulted him accidentally, clarified, "I never thought much about antiques."

"Most people don't."

Alex definitely didn't want the conversation to turn toward her so she prompted, "What makes them valuable?"

"That's a complex question." Clearly going into a teacher-lecture mode, Sal elaborated, "Many factors go into the evaluation of an item. Authenticity, what kind, when it was made, what is it made out of, who made it and if it is marked and signed, how well it was maintained and if it was repaired or restored, who has owned it, who is collecting that type item."

Pleased that the man was content to talk and not pry, Alex asked, "So how do you know what's what?" She drank more of her tea and begged her stomach to be satisfied with the post-fast offering.

Sal lifted his cup to sip his tea and his sleeve dropped, revealing a beautiful gold watch with a sparkling black face that would have been a worthwhile sell at a pawn shop. He responded, "There are price guides and prior auction results, magazines and catalogs, as well as a strong antiques community that keeps track of things. If you know the buyers, you can get a nice profit buying low and selling at a reasonable price. You just have to be able to recognize things at the auctions and estate sales. It's a science."

Alex had a hard time focusing on what he was saying, but heard 'science', and inquired, "Are you any good at it?" Her mug was empty already. She wished she could eat the mug. She wondered if the tea bag was edible.

"Sometimes I like to think so." Sal stood up and brought the teapot over and refilled her mug. When he returned the pot to the stove, he paused to flip her clothes over in the oven. He stared at them for a moment.

"They're not burning, are they?" she asked, trying to quell her panic. She didn't have any others.

"No," he hesitated and then said, "Ah, I was just thinking about boosting the temperature a little. I think we should leave it." He came back over to the table and sat down. "Are you feeling warmer?"

"Yes, thank you." Alex swirled the tea bag around in the water, willing it to darken faster. "What's the most you've ever made on an antique?"

"On a single item, just about $233,000." He sat up straighter. "It was a particularly fine claw-foot couch."

Alex gasped. "That much? Why isn't everyone doing antiques?"

Sal smiled with amusement. "That's very rare and very lucky. Not too many people are lucky enough to both find and recognize the right things, and often, shows don't have any items of significant value."

"I suppose I'd have to be older anyway," Alex sighed. She gave up waiting on the tea bag and drank more.

"You'd also need money to invest in the purchases initially. All of the inventory sitting out there in the shop was paid for by me. Until someone buys it, there's no profit at all. Meanwhile, I have building fees and utilities."

So much money tied up in what appeared to be junk was daunting. Alex couldn't fathom why someone would do that. "So how do you stay in business?"

"I mostly sell to private collectors I know. They tell me what they are looking for and I try to locate it. The store itself is where I put things I find accidentally. The most interesting thing I ever found is that book out front in the glass display case. It's a religious book from the 16th century in Latin with exquisite artwork. Every now and then, I turn the page to prevent any one page from over-exposure to light. The glass case itself filters most light."

"Can you read it?"

"No, I don't know Latin. Every now and then I'll try to translate some of it but it takes a long time. The characters are different from current Latin and some things we don't have definitions for."

Alex continued to ask him questions about his antiques to deflect any inquiries about herself and he gladly talked and explained things. He was a natural teacher. Outside, the storm continued to rage even though the hail stopped. When her clothes were dry, she took them back into the bathroom and changed. The warm cloth cooled all too quickly, but was magnificent for a few moments at least. She carefully and neatly folded both packing blankets and set them on the toilet seat.

She supposed she should leave under the guise of heading home before he could ask her questions, but it was still raining. That would definitely defeat the purpose of drying her clothes. She went back out and found Sal back in the front of the shop, wiping down his counter.

"Still raining," he noted unnecessarily. "How are you at playing chess?"

"Uh, chess? I've heard of it."

"Good time to learn then." He went over to one of the shelves and took a beautiful wood box from it over to the round table surrounded by the armchairs.

Alex left her backpack on the floor next to the counter and came around to watch him set up the board with pieces that came from a small velvet-lined drawer. For the next twenty minutes, he described the different pieces and basic rules. As soon as the smell hit her, she couldn't concentrate on anything else. From the back of the shop, the mouth-watering scent of baking lasagne beckoned. Her stomach growled noisily.

Sal chuckled. "That'll be the lasagne, I suppose. It should be done heating fairly soon. That's why I've got the oven. A person should eat real food. I can't smell so well anymore - old nose," he tapped his nose sadly, "But the timer will go off. There's plenty for both of us."

"Really?" It was too much to hope for - actual food. Fresh, warm, solid food.

"Yes, really. It doesn't look like that rain is stopping soon and it's lunch time. I always have enough for several people anyway." He paused and then added, "I have someone making all my lunches. She definitely adheres to the idea that Italians should never have too little food on the table."

"Are you Italian?" Alex asked.

Again, his eyebrows scrunched together and he gave her a really odd look making her wonder how she'd erred. "Yes. Marino - it's an Italian name. Likely some ancestor into boats."

"I had a couple friends who were Mexican," she offered, trying to find something they had in common, that wouldn't make the conversation seem so one-sided, but would still prevent questions about herself.

The kitchen timer went off and they both returned to the kitchen. Alex could not believe her luck. She could skip foraging for the night and concentrate on finding a safe spot to sleep. She'd spotted a potentially good library a couple miles back.

Sal set out two exquisitely beautiful fine china plates and matching salad plates, silverware, and a water glass for her which he filled, and a wine glass for himself. She hovered eagerly, unable to stop herself. He took the lasagne from the oven, asked her to get the salad from the refrigerator, and got out serving utensils. He opened a bottle of wine from the cabinet and poured a beautiful red liquid into his glass. He also set out a pair of cloth napkins.

He indicated she should sit and he sat himself. He took some salad and passed the serving bowl to her. She mimicked his actions precisely, unwilling to risk being tossed out. It was all she could do not to pick up everything on the table and shove it into her mouth. When he took his fork and began to eat, so did she. It was a strange, silent meal, with Sal inconspicuously watching Alex eat and Alex observing Sal as discreetly as possible.

They moved on to the lasagne. Whenever Sal sipped his wine, Alex sipped her water. Alex suspected the slower pace was probably good for her empty stomach anyway, but she was really worried about doing something that would make him doubt her identity or worse, something to make him kick her out of the store, food uneaten. A long time ago, she'd overheard a discussion about the bad table manners of the orphans and how they needed to be taught better, but the group home had never implemented any training. She'd certainly never learned any manners out on the street.

She finished her serving before he did his probably due to taking larger bites. She set her fork back on her napkin, only to notice that his napkin was nowhere in sight. She rolled back through her memory and saw him slide it down onto his lap. Too late now; she couldn't correct it without making the blunder even more obvious.

"Have more," Sal said, taking the lasagne dish that was easily within reach of both of them, and handing it to her. She took a second serving and put the dish back on the table.

This time, he ran out before she did, but he simply put his silverware on his plate and folded his hands in his lap and waited for her to finish. She tried to continue the same pace, trying really hard not to twitch. When she finished and set her fork and knife on her plate, he stood and took the dishes over to the sink and rinsed them, setting them on the counter.

Sal handed Alex a towel. He meticulously washed each dish and handed it to her to dry and told her where to put it away again. He scraped the leftover lasagne into the garbage and Alex had to resist the urge to cry out and dive in after it. After cleaning the lasagne pan, he left that dish on the counter.

"Let's go play some chess," Sal said cheerily. "Do you remember how the pieces move?"

Alex nodded. "It seems like a lot of possible combinations of games."

His mouth twitched. "You might say that. I'll start. We'll do a simple test game to get you used to the moves."

As they played, Alex's ever-present gnawing hunger dissipated and she felt full for the first time since leaving the forest. It was a nice feeling. She began to be able to think about the chess pieces and actual strategy.

Sal described each move he made and why he moved that particular piece and commented on her potential moves. The game went very slowly at first and picked up as Alex started making moves on her own. Sal won. That was the last game Sal ever won against Alex.

While they played, Alex asked about the antiques around them and Sal described their history and how he came to own them and why each piece was special. When the rain stopped, neither of them noticed. They played five more games before Sal noticed the sun was starting to set. "It's gotten late on us, Alex."

Alex glanced out of the front window. "Is it night already?"

Sal glanced at his watch. "It's after 7 already. Your mom is probably going crazy with worry. You should call her."

"Nah, it's only a short hop away from here. It won't take me but a few minutes to get home."

"Alex, I've been thinking about hiring some help for the shop. Dusting, sweeping, unpacking, and helping me pack again. I'm not as young and spry as I used to be. Would you be interested?"

Alex's heart skipped a beat. Money! Real money. Possibly even more food.

"All under-the-table type work. I'm guessing you are underage for an actual job. Just some cash for a bit of help."

Alex had the sense to say, "I'll have to ask my mom and see if she thinks it's ok." That's what she'd overheard a pair of kids out camping say. When she'd been hiding and spying on people for entertainment, she hadn't realized it was training for future conversations.

Sal nodded. "Come by tomorrow or any time in the next week and let me know. I'm not in any particular hurry."

"Thank you for rescuing me from the hail and cold and for lunch, Sal. I really appreciate it. I owe you and I never forget when I owe someone something. I liked playing chess with you." Alex collected her still-damp backpack, waved, and left, turning away and walking down the street with confidence just in case he was looking.

Alex ducked into the very first alley. It was twilight so there was still a bit of light coming in from the sky, but very little. The streetlights had already flickered on and she needed to get off the street before the night-citizens came out. It was simply too dangerous in an unknown location. She shimmied up the very first building pipe she saw, and peered over the roof to make sure it

21

was uninhabited. No one was there and she didn't see any security cameras. She slipped over the edge. The roof was covered in small, sharp rocks. It's not that the builder had said, "Cover the roof with sharp rocks so no one will hang out there," but rather, "Put the cheapest something up there to protect the roof." It wasn't the best nest for the evening, but it would do.

She crouched down and made her way over to the corner as quietly as possible to prevent her footsteps from disturbing anyone below. In the corner, she peeked up over the building's railing and saw the street below. It was a good view and no lights shone in her direction to give her away. She only saw one person walking quickly down the street. She cleared the rocks from a spot big enough for her to sit and settled in and listened. Toward the restaurants a short way past the antiques store, she could hear people in groups talking and laughing, although they were too far away to actually understand.

She dozed off with her knife clutched in her hand on her lap and her pants damp from the still-wet roof. The sky was still overcast so she had no stars to judge the time, but she thought she slept for maybe an hour. She heard quiet voices below that were too soft for her to make out. She pulled her knees in closer to her chest and tried to shrink into the building. Through the night, the street seemed to have a lot of activity, especially considering the stores were closed. Several times, she looked over the wall at the street to see individuals and groups walking by. That was a bit scary, but she also didn't hear gunshots or screams, or sounds of people getting robbed or beat up.

The night passed uneventfully. When she judged it was around 3 a.m., she left the roof and headed toward the restaurants to scavenge for breakfast. She was raiding the third dumpster when she became aware she was being followed. She continued as if she didn't know it and slipped behind a solid stairway. When the man passed, she grabbed him and threw him against the wall and put her knife to his throat.

"Why are you following me?" she growled.

"Hey, hey, stay cool," he pleaded.

"Why?" she demanded. "Tell me or I'll bleed you out right here, right now. Move and I'll do the same."

"You're new in this area. You don't know how things go around here. It's my job to keep an eye on things. That's all. I'm not gonna hurt you."

"Who pays you?"

"The local mafia. I'm going to report you slept on the street and raided trash cans for food. They ain't gonna care at all. If you start vandalizing things or leaving stuff around, they'll care, though. Bag your refuse and throw it in the trash cans. This is a clean neighborhood. Any business you want to start, you'd better run it by them first, too."

Alex stepped back away from him, but did not relax. Thankfully, he made no sudden moves. He stood away from the wall and straightened his shirt.

"Passing through or staying?" he asked.

Alex pondered her options; she couldn't answer Sal until she knew if the area was safe, and if she stayed, she'd definitely take Sal up on his job offer. "Dunno yet. What kind of business does the mafia run?"

"Nothing of interest to a homeless kid."

"Safe neighborhood?"

"If you mind your own business and don't mess the place up."

"Law enforcement?"

"The family IS the law. Don't cross them."

Alex nodded her understanding and opened her hand with a slight wave to indicate he was free to go. He scampered off without hesitation.

Later that day, Alex was certain she wanted to stay in this neighborhood for the summer. The library was magnificent. In addition to a whole section of college-level textbooks, the library held current subscriptions to a large number of scientific journals. She would be able to memorize enough to last through the upcoming winter easily.

Even more useful was the mostly unused single bathroom on the lower level next to the magazines. She'd be able to wash there. If that man on the street hadn't been lying, the area was relatively safe. She'd just need to avoid the mafia family which shouldn't be a problem. She'd keep to herself, spend all her time at the library or the antiques store or in hiding. She had a nice selection of dumpsters with food in them and it was possible Sal might even pay her enough to supplement dumpster dives with fresh fruit and vegetables. It was an ideal location.

She made her way back to Sal's shop. The bell rang softly as she entered. Sal was again sitting behind his counter, reading what she now recognized as a catalog of antiques. "Hi, Sal. Is that offer of a job still open?"

"Alex, come in." He closed the catalog. "Did your mom say you could work here?"

"She did, well, provided it doesn't have too many hours. I think she's glad I wouldn't be randomly wandering around the streets while she's at work. She was a little annoyed yesterday."

"How does eight dollars per hour sound for the afternoons? Most of my shipments arrive in the afternoon, but because I don't know exactly when they'll be here, it would be good if you were here, even if we're just playing chess."

She answered, "You're going to pay me eight dollars an hour to play chess?"

"Sure. There's only so much sweeping and dusting that needs to be done.

23

You can even come early if you want and help me eat all that lunch Irene makes."

Alex shook his hand. "Deal."

"Excellent. Start tomorrow."

"Thank you, Sal." She left the store, practically skipping as she went in search of a better nighttime shelter midway between the restaurants and the library.

The next afternoon, Alex arrived just about exactly at noon, having left the library at 20 minutes until the hour. Lunch was a magnificent spaghetti with a very hearty meat sauce, with crusts of toasted bread and olive oil for dipping. They talked more antiques while they ate and Alex wasn't quite as timid through lunch, although she still very carefully mirrored his actions. This time, her napkin went into her lap.

After lunch, Alex pestered Sal about what he wanted done and exactly how he wanted those things done. She was a quick and careful study and did everything as well as she could. She did a thorough job cleaning out the packing materials area and organizing all of the supplies. She wiped down every surface in the kitchen and scoured the bathroom. Sal wouldn't let her sweep between the shelves. He did that himself, very careful not to bump anything. Alex did sweep the other half of the store where the furniture was. She also washed the front windows. She finished just about at closing time.

Sal handed her some cash, which Alex glanced at and said, "Sal, you can't pay me for time we spend eating lunch. It's not working."

"It's bad form to argue with your employer," he said lightly. "Noon to 6 p.m. daily. 6 hours times $8 equals $48. You do know basic arithmetic, yes?"

"I just don't want you deciding I'm too expensive and firing me," she countered, matching his tone.

Sal laughed at that. "More likely you'll quit because you've overworked yourself."

On her way back to her night-shelter (a mostly unused lean-to behind one of the residences), she stopped at a drug store and bought a toothbrush, toothpaste, shampoo, and bath soap. She wished she had enough money for scissors. She normally would have stolen such items, but she didn't want any reason at all for the local mafia to seek her out. She also bought an orange. She felt delightfully rich. She wondered if she saved enough money if she could buy a real winter coat. She'd never even thought that would ever be possible.

The next day Sal told her she'd worn him out the previous day and he demanded she just sit and keep him company for the afternoon. They played chess and Alex asked him about the paintings on the wall. That proved to be a boon. He loved art more than antiques and spoke about his favorite famous painters and styles and how the paintings were created. Again, they got distracted until well after dark which made them both laugh when they noticed.

24

Sal offered to drive her home and she declined, repeating that it was just a short way. On the way back to her lean-to, she bought a compact umbrella to prevent Sal from offering a ride when it rained.

A week later, three crates from an auction arrived and they spent the week unpacking, sorting, and repacking everything except the few items Sal wanted to keep for the shop, with Sal explaining everything in great detail. Alex loved to listen to him talk. It was like being in some kind of fantasy world where people didn't hurt each other and conversations didn't revolve around who could do what for, or to, whom, and where hunger and fear weren't daily companions. Sometimes she wished she could tell him that. Instead, she was thankful he didn't pry into her life.

Sometimes a customer would come in and Alex would serve them hot tea at the round table in the diminutive living room and then slip quietly into the back of the store out of sight. Sal would bring various pieces over to the table, where the bright light would show off the items. He'd sit and drink tea with the customer. If they had questions, he always had the answer, but he never pressed them and never tried to force them to buy. With several of the customers, they never even discussed the piece or the price, but instead talked about current events, sports, art, religion, kids, pets, or whatever the person seemed to want to discuss. Almost always, they bought something. As the least expensive item in the store was a figurine for $5,500, Sal was certainly making a profit. The most expensive was the Latin book, for $108,000.

While Alex still didn't let Sal win at chess, she at least took the nice long path to the victory so Sal could enjoy the game and think he might win for a while. "So you don't ever sell art?" she asked.

"No, it's a different class of buyer and I wouldn't be able to part with anything I liked. Antiques, I can look at and see their monetary value and the effort that went into making them, but art, I can look at and see part of the soul of the artist."

Alex glanced over at the painting on the wall doubtfully. "Projecting your own feelings, maybe. But it's just a painting." She knew that comment would rile him up. She grinned to let him know she wasn't serious.

"Just a painting!" Sal scolded in mock horror. "Sacrilege! When you stand at the foot of the great paintings and your insides cry and you can no longer look away, you'll understand."

"Now you really are kidding," she said.

"Haven't you ever been in an art gallery, young lady?" he asked indignantly.

"No?" Alex moved her knight strategically to give Sal an advantage.

Sal frowned. "What is school teaching you these days? Idiots, the lot of them. I'll take you this Saturday if you're free."

Alex had planned on getting through the rest of the scientific journals this weekend, but she supposed art also counted as education. "How much does it cost?"

Sal hesitated, pursing his lips suspiciously at the unguarded knight, and then took her knight with his bishop. "I'll cover the costs."

"You already pay me too much." She moved a pawn toward its inevitable promotion that would win her the game.

Sal blinked at that move but then relocated his bishop to safety. "I consider it an obligation to correct your ignorance."

Alex moved another chess piece. Sal would realize he was going to lose again in the next move or two. "Do I need anything?" Like photo I.D., which she didn't have?

"No, but you should leave your backpack home. The museum won't let you carry it in anyway. Meet me here at the shop at 8 a.m.?"

No way was she leaving her backpack anywhere on the street where someone would steal all of her cash. She simply nodded and moved the next piece.

Several moves later, he studied the board, frowned, and tipped his king over, sighing. "Again?"

They reset the board. He moved a piece.

"Don't move that one, Sal," Alex said. "You already know you lose if you move that one there." She knew his patterns and thought processes by now. That opening would only lead down one of 10 paths for him and all of them would lead to the end too quickly. He could certainly deviate from those, but he wouldn't. His eyebrows furrowed and he frowned at her a moment. Alex added, quite pleased with herself, "I consider it an obligation to correct your ignorance."

Sal growled amusedly, but he moved a different piece. He still lost and they didn't have enough time left for another game. They put the pieces and the board away.

Sal watched her pick up her backpack and said, "I'll beat you at chess tomorrow. I've been going too easy on you."

She laughed. "I hope so. See you tomorrow, Sal."

Alex was still grinning when she stopped to pick up her evening dinner - two perfectly ripe glorious oranges. In her entire life, she didn't think she'd ever felt so happy. She wasn't starving. She had energy. Her mental focus was outstanding. Most importantly, though, she thought she might be able to call Sal her friend, not someone who kept her around for what she could do, like the street gang had, or the adults that wanted to show off her piano playing before... well, before that.

Even her fellow group home kids and schoolmates before weren't her friends; they didn't understand most of what she'd talked about. Sure, Sal didn't know her history, but what was history that she was going to leave behind anyway? She could be anyone she chose. She just had to get through a few more years until she was old enough to be an adult and not be threatened by police and child services, and she could get a job, make some real money, and maybe even find something she really enjoyed doing. Maybe she'd run the antiques store for Sal when he got too old to run it himself?

Alex went to her lean-to and settled in for the night. She ate her oranges and listened to the evening birds and the city sounds. The sun set, although she couldn't see it because the buildings were too high, but the sky shifted darker. She started reviewing the physics journals she'd scanned earlier. She should probably wait until winter, but it looked curiously fascinating.

The articles from CERN on particle physics, complete with their data, and discussions were an incredible find. She rotated the data around in her head and just as an experiment, she decided to see if she could make both the underlying equations as well as the program that generated the data. The clarity from adequate nutrition was amazing.

She played with the data picture, visualizing the underlying chaos of particle movements, fit the data summaries to a raw data set, lost everything in one too many particle orbits and tried again. There was something not quite right. Something missing. Something that had to be there but wasn't. She walked down in size from a water molecule, carefully analyzing each constituent of the previous piece. She mirrored everything. There, the missing force, hiding in the mirror, with its missing field. Clear as daylight, she could see it all in her head.

"Hah," she thought with some wry amusement, "I shouldn't publish this. They'll just give the Nobel prize to some man anyway. What would it mean? What use is it?"

She tried to sleep, but her mind wouldn't let go. All the particles and data points swam together with their formulas and chaos, and taunted her with something she thought she should be getting. She skipped foraging in the morning and just bought herself a decent breakfast at one of the shops. She also skipped the library and instead, walked around the neighborhood, barely seeing anything except data rolling through her head screaming for a pattern or a grouping, bleeding for their formula.

Alex was a little late getting to the antiques store because she forgot to pay attention to the clocks, but her stomach growled on queue. She jogged to the shop and the bell rang softly as always.

Sal looked up from his catalog and smiled, "Good! You're here! I was beginning to worry. Lunch is already ready."

"Sorry I'm late. I forgot to look at the time."

"No problem," Sal said lightly, "The rush of customers will wait."

That made her laugh. He obviously wasn't upset at all. Lunch smelled divine and Alex followed Sal back to the kitchen. "What is that?" she asked peering over his shoulder as he removed a dish from the oven.

"Ossobuco alla milanese." Seeing her look of confusion, he translated, "Veal, in white wine, with vegetables. It's got lemon, garlic, and parsley."

"It smells wonderful. Your Irene is a really fantastic chef."

"I'll tell her you said so. I probably don't praise her enough."

"You should. She might stop cooking for you." Alex retrieved glasses and water for herself. "White or red?" He answered and she opened a new bottle of wine and poured for him.

Sal chuckled and sat down. "You're still coming to the art museum tomorrow, yes?"

She nodded, putting her napkin in her lap, again precisely mimicking him. She didn't feel she needed to anymore, but it had become something of a game. He would try to make her slip up on her copy. Wrong hand reaching for his drink, putting his fork back wrong, that kind of thing, and she'd try not to miss anything. He usually managed to catch her at something.

The particles again spun on their chaotic orbits and the formulas rearranged themselves dynamically to match. She needed a formula to rearrange the formula.

"Distracted today?" Sal asked, his voice rumbling with laughter.

"No," Alex answered, and then she looked around. He'd managed to reverse everything in front of him and drape his napkin across his wine glass. She chuckled and shook her head in amusement. "Uh, yeah, I guess."

"What is it?" Sal began rearranging his place setting back to the proper orientation.

Alex tapped her finger on the table, and asked, "Can I tell you a secret, Sal?"

"Sure." He put his folded napkin next to his plate.

"I'm pretty smart." Alex bit her lip and waited, watching his response carefully.

Sal grinned at her. "I know. People don't usually absorb and master chess in a couple games. I haven't been going easy on you."

Alex cringed. She hadn't even thought about that. For smart, she was easily tricked. "Well, then," she hesitated, "You wouldn't be surprised if I told you I've been working on a math problem."

Sal drank the last of his wine. "Of all the things I would have guessed you might say, I never would have come up with that."

Still speaking timidly, unsure how far to go, she continued, "I've been spending a lot of time in the library and I think I might have..." No, she knew she had it with absolute certainty, "a new piece of physics."

Sal nodded wisely. "Physics is a very complex field. You need a lot of ground knowledge first. I wouldn't be surprised if you managed to come up with one of the core principles though." His tone suggested he'd be a little surprised.

"You know physics?" Could she run the concept past him?

Sal chuckled. "I know art. I know antiques. Not exactly a mathematical wonder."

Alex stood and collected the dirty dishes to take over to the sink. "Do you mind if we skip chess today so I can keep working on the problem?"

"Not at all. I have new catalogs that came in this morning." Together, they washed and put away the dishes. While Alex tried to insist she could take care of them herself, he argued that he enjoyed the company.

For the afternoon, Sal sat at the counter with his magazines, mumbling to himself and taking notes, while Alex kept changing sitting locations, mumbling stuff to herself. An audio track of the store would have made a very strange song with the ending: "I can find that. Maybe if I move those over there? I'll need to send a note to Dan. That can't possibly work. Oh, I've seen that! Where did I see it? Holy shit." On the profanity, Sal turned to Alex, "None of that language. You're a young lady."

Alex winced guiltily. "Sorry, Sal, but holy shit, I think I have a use for it."

He raised his eyebrow and squinted at her.

She said, "I'll have to find a way to implement it, but I know how I'm going to get rich." She chewed on her knuckle and stood up to pace back and forth in front of the counter.

Sal watched her with an amused grin. "Not going to get rich on chess championships?"

Alex stumbled to a halt. "What?"

"Chess championships. Lots of money to be made in those." Sal set his magazine aside.

"I didn't know such a thing existed." Could someone actually make money doing that? For a moment, she dreamed about having enough money to buy a safe house somewhere. Maybe one of those campers she could move around?

Sal continued, "I've been thinking about it for some time. Getting you a real tutor, that is. I'm not the most qualified chess instructor."

Reality quashed her dream like a hand smacking a mosquito and Alex replied, "That sounds like something that would make a person famous."

He closed his magazine and set it neatly back on the pile of mail. "Sometimes. In your case, I'd say yes."

Alex shook her head. "I can't be famous, besides that wouldn't make me the richest person on the planet."

"Your idea will?" Sal stood up and stretched.

Alex replied, "It has potential. I'll have to think about it some more."

"You keep thinking then, but no more of that language." Sal moved to unlock the case with the Latin book to turn a page.

"Yeah, yeah," Alex went into the back to make tea. She brought him a cup also. He was back reading another one of his catalogs. As she set the tea down next to him, she leaned over and looked at the catalog. "The things you find interesting," she teased.

A man in a business suit came in. He was not a customer by his bearing and complete lack of interest in their wares. He looked dangerous. Sal put his hand on Alex's shoulder. "Go ahead and leave for the day, Alex. I'll see you tomorrow morning promptly."

"You sure you don't need me to stay?" she whispered as the strange man approached the counter. Sal subtly shook his head and tilted his head toward the back. So commanded, Alex left through the back door, looking with unease over her shoulder as she left. If the local mafia was going to harass an old man, she should have at least stayed and tried to deflect any attack toward herself. She was much sturdier than Sal was.

The next morning, Alex was relieved to find Sal unharmed and in a good mood. She'd spent the night too worried to concentrate on anything else. "Are you ok?" she asked, coming into the store.

"Oh, yeah," Sal answered with a casual hand-wave. "We just had some things to discuss."

Alex walked back to the counter. "Who was that guy?"

Sal squinted at her and then answered, "He's family."

She gazed directly at Sal, intent on saying what she'd decided last night. "I didn't tell you, but back when I first came into town, this guy told me there's a local mafia. If you think there's going to be any kind of trouble, don't send me away. I may not look like much, but I can help defend your store."

"Hmmm," Sal replied, frowning. "You don't need to worry about the local mafia." Then he looked beyond her, back out of the front of the store. "Our car is here. I thought you might get a kick out of riding in a limousine today. What do you think?"

Alex turned to look. The shiny black limousine sparkled as if brand new. "Wow! Really?"

"Yes." He glanced at her shoulder and said, "I thought you were leaving your backpack home?"

"Oh. I forgot," she lied. "I'm just so used to carrying it everywhere. How about I leave it here in the store?" If his security that was protecting a $108,000 book wasn't good enough to protect her stolen clothes and half-used toiletries, she wasn't sure what could. "I'll just leave it here." She set it behind the counter.

Sal reset the store's alarm and locked the front door on their way out. "I think we only have time to get to one museum today so I'm taking you to my favorite."

As she climbed into the limousine, she teased, "That a polite way of telling me to super-appreciate it and ohhh and ahhh a lot?" Alex reflected that it was nice to be able to joke with someone. She was living in a fantasy.

"Hah! You'll see!" he growled with faux-displeasure.

The driver closed the door after them and Alex stared around with wide eyes. The inside was spacious and meticulously clean. She wished she had had a chance to clean up that morning. The fine upholstery made her feel particularly grungy. There were buttons that begged to be pushed and cabinets and drawers with potential treasures. A shiny black and white marble counter even had a small sink with what looked like a refrigerator underneath. The cabin was separated from the driver by a closed-window wall with dark wood paneling.

Sal settled in opposite her. "It's not too bad, is it?" he remarked with a twinkle in his eye.

She ran her fingers across the counter's smooth marble. "How can you afford this? Your shop doesn't make this much money." Then she realized that wasn't the most tactful statement she could have said.

Luckily, the comment didn't seem to offend him. He answered, "I'm independently wealthy. I just dabble in the antiques to support my art habit, but I really don't need to work. I just like to buy expensive paintings. I have quite a few in my house."

Alex's eyes were huge as she looked around. She thought he was renting the limousine. Did his reply mean he owned it?

"Did you get a chance to eat breakfast?" Sal leaned forward and popped open the small refrigerator. He handed her a bottled orange juice and took one for himself.

Alex had prudently eaten a roll she'd bought specially to prevent the dire hunger pangs of a morning spent walking around. "I ate." She opened the orange juice and drank anyway.

"I figure we should go through the painting styles in historical order so you can see how they progress. The oil paintings of the Baroque period are my favorites. How the artists render silks and brocades is amazing." As the ride continued, Sal described the types of art she'd see and their historical

31

significance.

Alex didn't understand his enthusiasm until they were standing in front of one of Rembrandt van Rijn's paintings and she could not look away. "How'd he get the light to glow like that?" she whispered in awe. "It's amazing." She didn't want to just look and memorize to go over later if she needed it. She wanted to stand there and savor each small detail in the here and now. Sal had been right. She could see the soul of the artist, the immortalized moment of the subject, the years of practice needed to build up to that brush stroke, that particular blend of color.

A long time later, Sal said, "Told you so."

"I apologize for ever mocking you. I was so wrong." She still couldn't tear her eyes away from the painting.

Sal chuckled. "Come on. There's more to see." He led her on to another exhibit.

They ate lunch at the small restaurant in the museum. Alex winced at the prices, but Sal didn't seem overly concerned.

On the ride back to his shop, he asked, "What was your favorite?"

Alex thought carefully and replayed all of the paintings she'd seen in her mind's eye. "I don't think I could pick a favorite. I love the metal armors - how they do the silver with the shine highlights. I wasn't so fond of the modern art."

Sal nodded at that and passed her an apple juice from the refrigerator. "It has its place, but modern art isn't my favorite either."

When they arrived back, it was well after dark. Her backpack had been adjusted a little, just the top squished in a bit, but otherwise in the same spot. She verified that with her memory of how she'd left it. "Hey, Sal, might want to get a few mouse traps. My backpack's changed. Something jumped on it."

"You sure? We'd see other signs of mice if we had them. Maybe it just settled? I'll get mouse traps tomorrow just in case." Sal picked up a couple magazines to take home.

"I'll do a good sweep under the shelves and go through the cabinets on Monday." She put her backpack on. "Sal, thank you for taking me to the museum today."

"You sure you don't want me to drop you off at home?" He peered at her.

"Naw," she answered, "Mum would likely faint if she saw me getting out of that barge."

"Barge?! You dare call my car a barge!" He laughed and they each went their separate ways.

At the library the next day, Alex went through every art book. She concluded that art creation was a skill that required a decade or more of practice to master. Just the muscle memory alone would take quite a bit of effort in most of the mediums. She wondered if she could get Sal to take her to a sculpture exhibit, and then she laughed at the thought. Her, thinking about an activity other than survival. What had Sal done to her?

On Tuesday while they were unpacking another shipment, Sal said offhandedly, "I need to be late tomorrow and Thursday. Would you come open the shop? I'm not expecting any customers. Just sit here in case someone comes in and answer the phone and tell them I'll be around in the afternoon."

"Sure, Sal." Alex carefully unwrapped another vase and set it aside. She folded the wrapping paper and put it on the growing pile.

"Here's the back door key." Sal dug in his pocket and gave her a key. "The security combination for the alarm is 648522. Let me show you how to turn it off and on again." He also showed her the phone number for the security company in case there was a problem and gave her his own cell phone number.

Later that night, the wind picked up, blowing Alex's newspapers around. She chased them down and stuffed them inside her shirt and pants for warmth. While the overall temperature wasn't cold, the rain itself would be cold. The rain started and the wind continued to pick up. By midnight, the newspaper was dissolving and the wind was strong enough that it began to get scary. The large raindrops felt like tiny bullets. A plastic lawn chair rolled by and she huddled against the debris in the lean-to. It was the lightning that decided her. She didn't need to risk her life when she had somewhere to go.

She grabbed her backpack and went to the shop. She felt vaguely guilty, as if she were breaking a trust, but let herself in anyway. She turned off the alarm before it triggered an alert. Leaving the light off, she went into the bathroom and dried off as best she could. She switched to the slightly drier clothes from her backpack and then pondered what to do. She went back out into the shop's storage area, took several of the flattened boxes, and stacked them. She curled up on top of them with her backpack as a pillow and lay there in the dark wondering why she felt guilty. Outside the wind picked up and the loud howling of it between the buildings was unnerving. She was glad to be inside.

The storm was still raging outside in the early morning so Alex skipped going out to forage for breakfast. She made herself a pot of tea instead, and went into the bathroom and cleaned up. She had a moment of inspiration and went and got the shop's scissors and gave herself a haircut. She didn't take it too short, because the length would help keep her neck warm in the upcoming winter, but she thought she did a reasonable job getting it even.

Then, because she still had a few hours before the store should open, she took the opportunity to wash her spare clothes and dry them in the oven, and then she swapped to those, and did her main clothes. All the way down to her underwear. She felt more human, less of an animal. She made sure the bathroom was spotlessly clean and free of hair, and then she started cleaning the rest of the store. It was already clean from her previous efforts, but she made sure every surface was meticulous. With her newfound respect for art,

33

she even dusted the tops of the picture frames with extreme care. She now recognized the paintings in the store, even the bathroom, and knew they far out-valued even the book in the glass display case.

Alex went to the front window and stared out. The rain fell almost sideways in the gusts of wind. She watched until sunrise. The rain began lessening and eventually stopped. Promptly at 9 a.m., she unlocked the front door and stood looking out at the wet street until Sal arrived at 11:30, dropped off by what looked like the same limousine, and carrying lunch. She resisted the urge to tell him she'd come in during the night, but only just barely and because as far as he knew, she was living with her mom. She felt guilty though and that was an uncomfortable, new feeling, and she didn't care for it at all.

When she stopped to buy dinner that night, she saw the school supplies were featured. She was shocked. How had the time passed that quickly? She wasn't done in the library yet and she hadn't even begun to plan for the winter. In the morning she verified with a careful inquiry that school was indeed starting in two weeks. She had to leave immediately or risk not having enough food stored through winter. She left the library early and went shopping. She had enough money for a coat and a change of clothes, and joy, a new pair of shoes. Sal had certainly been generous. She pondered a new backpack, but thought she'd do better with some staple grains instead, which she'd get closer to the forest. Rice, barley, and oats would fill out the winter diet nicely.

Sal was sitting at his counter, reading a catalog. Alex paused at the door and watched him a moment before going in. "Hey, there," he greeted her cheerfully, closing his magazine.

"Hi, Sal."

"Look at you. New clothes! Very nice." He stood and came around the counter, pausing as he saw her expression. "What's wrong?"

"School's starting. My mom told me I have to stop working at the shop and focus on my studies."

"That's a good priority," he said after a moment. "You can still come by and visit."

"True." She faked a happier smile. She was afraid her eyes were still reflecting her sadness, so she stepped past him to ostensibly put her much puffier backpack behind the counter. She unzipped it and pulled out her new coat. "New coat," she said, holding it up for inspection. "Does it really get this cold down here?"

"It can."

She put the coat on top of her backpack, rather than stuff it back inside. She wanted her backpack to look normal.

The kitchen alarm went off. "That's lunch," Sal announced. "Pizza today. Not that nasty fast food stuff, but real Italian pizza."

The afternoon passed heartbreakingly pleasantly, with chess, and Alex asking Sal about his art collection at home. She watched the time, though,

34

because she couldn't risk waiting until dark. She pointed at the clock before they started another game.

Sal nodded, and together, they put away all the pieces and the board. "Do you have all your school supplies?" Sal asked.

"Not quite all of them yet. That's part of the reason Mom wants me to stop working here now. I've got to go over last year's books and get ready."

"Tell you what. I've really enjoyed having you work here this summer. Come by tomorrow afternoon, and as a thank you, I'll take you supply shopping?"

"Sal, you've already given me so much. I can't accept more."

"Of course you can. Humor an old man."

"Ok," she lied. "If Mom says I can." Once again that uncomfortable guilty feeling settled in her stomach. Sal was a nice man. She didn't like lying to him.

When she left, she kept walking all night long, headed with as much speed as she could muster, back to the forest and her cave. Unexpected tears fell from her eyes.

Winter was especially cold that year and Alex was glad to have her new coat. Her monthly cycle finally made an appearance, much to her annoyance, but she made do, as the prehistoric woman used to, with absorbent materials and washable leather liners. She worked through the library material she'd memorized and spent a whole month checking and verifying her new physics. She even figured out how she'd be able to create the very first perpetual energy battery using the knowledge. It would cost a lot initially, but once the first one was made, she could easily create others, because she could use the infinite energy source to shift matter around enough to make more. She could visualize all of the tools and configurations she'd need. Whenever she was mentally exhausted, she granted herself some time to remember her discussions with Sal and recall all the beautiful paintings in the museum.

As soon as she saw the first kids in the campground, she knew school was out. She secured her winter gear, even her coat, carefully hiding everything under the rocks at the back of her cave again. She was looking forward to seeing Sal again. It'd been a cold and lonely winter, and she'd exhausted all the books she'd memorized. She needed vegetables and fruits. The high protein winter diet left her more mentally fuzzy than she liked. She began her hike back to the city. Would Sal let her work in his store for the summer again?

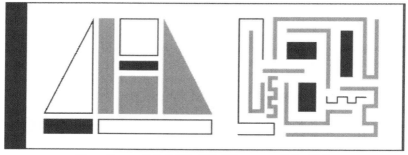

When she arrived at the antiques shop mid-afternoon, Alex opened the door and listened to the bell ring softly. Her tension melted away at the sound and she stepped into Sal's sanctuary. Sal was sitting behind his counter, reading a catalog, almost as if she'd never left. He looked older, with even more grey in his hair and new wrinkles around his eyes and chin. More hesitantly than she would have preferred, she inquired, "Mr. Marino, I was wondering if you were hiring this summer?"

Sal raised his eyes to her and his answering smile was all she'd hoped for. "Alex, you came back!"

"I missed you, Sal. It's been a long school year." Her cave meditations had certainly been long and insightful even though it couldn't be counted as school. Now that she knew what it was like to have an actual friend, she didn't care for solitude at all and that had made her especially lonely. Several times, she'd even gotten so depressed that she'd wondered if it would have been better to not know what having a friend was like.

"Yes, it has been a long school year. How were your grades?" Sal stood and came around the counter.

"I passed. I guess I move on?" She set her new (stolen) backpack down by the door and wandered through the aisles, noting things missing and things added. "You've had a profitable few months." She thought briefly on giving him a hug like she'd seen campers do when they greeted friends and family, but she didn't know how to go about doing that. He didn't come close enough immediately to make that part of their greeting anyway.

He waved her to follow him. "I have bought many new things. I'll tell you about them later. Come have some tea. I want to hear about your school year."

Alex accompanied him back to the kitchen. "Not much to tell. Lots of studying. Did more thinking on that physics thing." Alex got tea bags, cups, napkins, and spoons, while Sal added water to the kettle. It was as if she'd never left. "It's going to work if I can ever get a chance to implement it."

The stove snapped and popped as the gas lit underneath the kettle. Sal straightened and turned to her. "Yes? What do you need to do that?"

"I'm not asking you for money, Sal." Alex sat down in her old chair.

36

"Well, actually, I am, I'm asking for my job back. I was wondering if you could teach me everything I need to know to trade antiques and make a profit."

"Of course you can have your job back; same deal if you like." Sal sat in his chair also. "These old bones have surely missed your youthful strength unpacking and repacking. I don't mind imparting a bit of wisdom if you don't plan to open up a competing store across the street."

"Thank you! I would never, ever be your competition, Sal," Alex answered with so much earnestness that Sal laughed. She flushed. "So tell me about the new things you bought?" For the remainder of the work day, Sal went through each new item and told her its history, qualities, and potential buyers. Alex refused to take his money for the day, even though he tried to insist.

When Alex left the store, she was focused on finding the best night sleeping place and scavenging for dinner. She did not notice the car that pulled up next to her until two men in suits got out. "Boss wants to see you," the closer one said, pulling his jacket aside to show a very shiny holstered gun. "Get in."

Very briefly, Alex pondered running. Bullet or tackle, she had no doubt they could take her. She'd had precisely three cups of tea and some water from a hose within the last two days. She was already a little lightheaded and given the recent walking to get to Sal's store, more than a little exhausted. "No need to threaten me," she said softly, opening her hands, palms up. She got in the car, between the two of them, holding her backpack on her lap in front of her. Her heart thumped so fast, she felt they must surely hear it. Whenever it seemed like neither one was directly watching her, she moved the zipper on her pack. She might get a chance to get her knife from her pack into her jacket sleeve.

The car stopped at a restaurant named "Gente Di Mare". Alex had raided its dumpster in the past. They served fine Italian food, but there was rarely much left over, making the trash can not really worth the trouble. As they got out of the car, Alex managed to move her knife to her sleeve. She was pretty pleased with herself, until they took her backpack, patted her down, and confiscated her knife too. She merely shrugged unrepentantly, and said, "Self-defense." She watched morosely as they took her backpack into the restaurant. She waited outside with the man that had shown her his gun. She wondered if she'd be able to get either item back. What use would they possibly have for a change of clothes, a washcloth, some toiletries, feminine products, a couple plastic bags, and a somewhat dented camping knife?

When the man who had taken her things inside opened the door and gestured to them, Alex thought she might pass out, so badly frayed were her nerves. "Come on," the gunman ordered and having no choice at all, Alex obeyed.

The inside of the restaurant was beautifully atmospheric. Actual candles lit the tables, while soft yellow electric sconces provided enough light to see reasonably, if not brightly. White tablecloths overlay deep red ones at an angle. Dishes were nice china with real silverware, and the cloth napkins were a matching deep red. Customers didn't even look up as the three of them passed through to the private rooms in the back.

They brought her to a fairly large private office where a man that seemed vaguely familiar sat behind the dark wooden desk. She couldn't remember ever having seen him before, but she was so lightheaded that her memory wasn't working as it should. Her backpack and knife were nowhere to be seen. The men took up position on either side of her and she was not offered either of the two leather guest chairs.

The man behind the desk folded his hands on the desk and asked, "Who do you work for? Which family? The police?"

Alex didn't want to mention Sal's name and get him into trouble. "Nobody," she answered. It was technically true. She didn't start work for Sal until the next day officially.

The man sighed. "Do you speak Italian?"

"No, Sir." She hesitated and then offered, "I can learn it if you need me to. I'm a quick study."

"Hrm. Last year, I figured you were mostly harmless, but I was glad when you left. And here you are back again, as if disappearing and reappearing is normal. Surely your employers would have realized this would be suspicious. They set you up."

"I don't know what you are talking about, Sir? I don't have any employers. Honest. I was just off at school in the next county over and was too busy to come back here." She quickly tried to recall the map of Atlanta and figure out what the next county over might be, but she couldn't quite focus with fear tearing at her nerves.

The man said something in another language that Alex thought might be Italian. The two men took her arms and dragged her from the room. The gunman said something to her in that same language.

"I don't know Italian," she replied desperately. "English, please?"

They took her outside, behind the restaurant. There was a large plastic sheet already on the ground. That's when she panicked and tried to break free and run. Even if she hadn't been weakened from hunger and exhaustion, she wouldn't have been strong enough to get free. The men had muscles like iron under their suits. The non-gunman took some duct tape from his pocket and secured her hands behind her back.

Gunman said something else in Italian. The other man pushed her to her knees on the front of the plastic sheet.

"What do you want? I don't speak Italian," she pleaded. "Please."

Gunman took out his gun, checked its ammunition, cocked it, and put it to her forehead.

"Oh, please don't kill me," she sobbed. "I'm worth a small fortune. I can do lots of useful things."

He demanded something again in Italian.

"I know you know English. You spoke it earlier." She was crying. "Please let me go. You'll never see me again. I swear."

"Who do you work for?" Gunman growled.

"I don't work for anybody. Honest. I'm just a street kid. I came here because you have a nice library. That's all. I don't have to stay. I'm not a threat. Please don't shoot me." She would NOT give Sal's name. Some repayment that would be for his kindness.

"You an undercover cop?" Gunman asked, pressing the barrel into her forehead so hard that her head tilted backwards.

"No! Hell, no. I'm just a kid. I ain't nobody. Please, please, don't shoot me," she whispered. Her mouth was dry.

Gunman said something in Italian to non-gunman.

Alex kneeled there, shaking in terror, sobbing, and wondering what she'd done to come to their attention. "Please don't kill me," she pleaded, having a hard time speaking because her chin was trembling so badly.

Non-gunman answered in Italian. They spoke back and forth a couple more times. Alex continued to beg. They yelled at her in Italian, pushed the gun against her forehead, demanding something. Alex cried and continued to repeat that she didn't know what they were saying. This went on for several minutes that felt like an eternity.

Gunman pulled the gun back away from her head, uncocked it, and holstered it. "You don't ever cross the family, you understand?"

She nodded quickly. "Yeah. Yes. I understand. Never. I swear."

Non-gunman pulled a knife from his pocket and cut the duct tape holding her hands.

Gunman pointed back toward the door. "Get your backpack. You're free to go."

Alex hadn't even noticed her backpack when they'd brought her out. She didn't even remove the duct tape hanging from her left wrist. She scrambled to her backpack, took it, and ran. She found herself at the library and stepped into the outside stairwell that would go directly to the basement if someone dared to unlock it. She cowered in the corner by the door, shrinking back on herself, all the while, distantly registering all the symptoms of shock, as if she were floating outside herself looking back at a stranger weeping. She hadn't even realized she'd wet herself sometime during that confusing interrogation.

When Alex was able to move again, she got her other clothes from her backpack, noticing that the contents had been completely searched and rearranged. Nothing was missing. Her knife was in the front pocket. She changed into her other clothes and carefully rolled the soiled pants and socks inside the slightly cleaner shirt, before packing it.

Alex's stomach growled. She needed food. She pried herself up from the hard cement. She got lucky; the nearest trash can that was likely to have food, did - an entire half of a ham sandwich in relatively good condition, which she stuffed into her mouth and ate like an animal. The sky was already lightening with that pre-dawn blue. She made her way back to the library. She'd find an Italian-English dictionary and find out what they'd said to her. Maybe it would make sense? She wanted to say goodbye to Sal, too. He'd be expecting her at lunch time. She could be out of the neighborhood before sundown. She didn't know what she'd done to acquire the interest of the local mafia, but it endangered Sal, too, and possibly even his cook, Irene. She couldn't risk them getting hurt.

A few hours later, Alex sat in a quiet corner of the library with three Italian-English dictionaries. She first translated what the boss had said to her reply about school in the next county, "You dare lie to me," and then to his men, "Take her out back and if she doesn't tell you who she is working for, get rid of her."

The comment in the hallway was gunman telling her that she might as well give over her employer's name as they were going to find out eventually anyway.

Outside, gunman had repeated the boss' questions about her employers. He'd described what her brains would look like on the plastic sheet if she didn't talk. Alex felt nauseous just putting the words together.

"I think I believe she doesn't know our language," Gunman had said to non-gunman.

"Or she's a damn good actress," was the reply.

"I don't even think she knows who she's hanging out with."

"Hah. Probably really thinks he's just a store owner."

"How stupid can she be?"

"She really is just a terrified kid; look at her. Let her go."

Alex tapped her fingers on the English-Italian book and double-checked that she had the right translation. She was only 'hanging out' with Sal. What did they mean? Then it all snapped into place. The boss was clearly related to Sal; it's why he looked so familiar. Maybe brothers, even. A super-rich man with a small, inconspicuous store-front. Sal's comment about her not worrying about the local mafia. The clues, here and there, readily apparent if had she been paying attention.

Alex bent over the desk, rocking, and then let her head rest on her arms and cried silently. Sal had known. He had allowed it.

"Are you ok?" a soft, heavily-accented voice asked.

She looked up and saw the man who was always dressed in black with the odd hair curls on either side of his face. Last summer, she'd seen him at the library often but she'd never spoken with him.

"Yes, I'm fine." She wiped her eyes on her sleeve. "I just learned something is all."

He leaned forward slightly, glancing at her books. "Learning is not something to be afraid of."

Examples to be afraid of blazed through her brain like a forest fire. Carnal knowledge, street knowledge, and now, betrayal. "I suppose it depends on how you learn it," she replied quietly.

"Well, a book is hardly at fault," he conceded.

She stilled her fingers that were pounding the dictionary. "True, a book has never betrayed me." She tried smiling for his sake, but was sure she just looked ghastly. She shifted the conversation away from herself. "I've seen you here before. If I might be curious, not insulting, but your clothes and hair, are they significant?" Alex's voice sounded fake to herself, a habit of disguise and redirecting interest away from herself, not an actual inquiry.

"I remember you from last year. Yes, I'm a rabbi. I teach over at the yeshiva. I wish my students were as enthusiastic about this library as you?" he seemed to be fishing for more information about her.

Alex, refusing to let the conversation steer to herself, asked, "What do you teach?"

His mouth quirked up at the corners, but he answered, "Sciences, mostly. I have a special summer session on physics starting soon."

Even in her despair, Alex felt a moment of jealousy. What would it be like to actually sit in a physics class and have people who might understand her to talk with? She set that thought aside for later consideration, and tried to focus on the conversation and keeping it neutral. "I've always liked science. There's something amazing in absolute, undeniable, repeatable proof."

"Which type of science do you like the most?" he probed, yet again trying to turn the topic toward her.

"I've never really considered any subject a favorite. They're all pretty equal." He tilted his head curiously so she knew she'd blundered somehow. She quickly corrected, "Earth sciences, I think. There's so much yet that needs to be done." To keep the conversation neutral, she added, "Micro weather systems are fascinating. How can the weather on one side of a mountain be so different from on the other side on the same day and time, and how should it be predicted?"

He nodded agreement. "That's a good area of study. Don't neglect your mathematics and higher sciences when you get to them. They often explain just such things. Meanwhile, young scholar, if you get stuck, come ask me. You should not worry so much about something that it makes you cry."

"I shall. Thank you, uh?" Alex paused and angled her head at him inquisitively.

"Just call me Rabbi. It's what all the students do."

"Thank you, Rabbi."

He went back over to his table and Alex wondered when every dialog would stop being a minefield. Should she have had earth sciences in school by this age? How many of the possible science subjects should she know? And how much depth in those? And what was a Rabbi? Should she have known what that was? By context, a yeshiva would be a school.

Her fingers resumed tapping the Italian-English dictionary and she bit her lower lip. Should she stay? How much of a threat was the Marino family to her? She'd apparently passed their test. If she moved on, would she just find another test that she might not live through? This was an excellent library with so many books she still wanted to go through. Would Sal still want her help at his store? The income had certainly been very nice. Their concern was with other Italian families and the police, but would they punish her for lying or try to exploit her?

As she walked the books back to their shelf, she whispered every curse word that had been in the dictionaries, in Italian, trying out the phonetics, and feeling the shapes of the different sounds. As she put the books on the shelf, she looked at the other language books, and with a determined frown, took them all back to the table and started through them. Never again would she make that mistake. She'd save the pages for winter to actually wade through and learn them. She also wanted to go through a few comprehensive dictionaries and find out more about this Rabbi. That sent her on a foray into religious texts and she was forced to stop as the library was closing. She found a flyer for the local yeshiva, which was also part university, and a major contributor to the library.

All night, she stared up at the stars, unable to sleep, unable to shake the terror. The huge round hole of the gun barrel in front of her face replayed in her memory with unfortunate absolute clarity.

Alex debated leaving as the predawn light replaced the stars. She raided more dumpsters to make sure her decision wouldn't be made based on hunger and then returned to the library's stairwell. She leaned against the building. There was so much knowledge on the other side of these bricks and none of it would tell her if it was safe to stay. There would be other libraries she could visit, but this one was the best she'd seen due to the additional funding from the yeshiva. Could she deal with Sal? She supposed she ought to at least go speak with him. The potential for food and money throughout the summer was too great to pass up. She had to be practical.

Instead of waiting until noon, Alex returned to Sal's store about an hour after it opened. She stepped in and the bell jingled quietly. Sal was sitting at the counter looking at another of the catalogs - as if nothing at all were different.

"Hi," she said softly, standing just inside the door, on the oriental carpet she'd dripped water on just about a year ago.

Looking up and seeing her enlightened and determined expression, Sal inquired, "Have you forgiven me?"

Alex inhaled and made herself speak. "No. Never again, Sal. You don't ever get to do that to me ever again. Not any of your family or hirelings either. If you ever don't trust me or think I'm working for someone else or are bored of me or just want me gone, just say so, and you will never see me again. But don't ever threaten me."

"I understand that." Sal nodded. "It was necessary; I have a responsibility to my family. I'm glad to see you back though. I really thought you'd probably run."

Alex set her backpack down and walked toward him, hands clearly open, clearly empty. "I probably should. It makes sense to do that, but I like the library, and I like the money you pay me, and I like that the street thugs leave me alone."

Sal stood and got a couple teacups and filled them with hot water, and took them over to the table and chairs. He'd already had the teapot warmed and cups out. Alex sat down across from him and took a tea bag and put it in the water. Sal prompted, "How about we start over?" At her shrug, he continued, "Hi, I'm Salvatore Marino. My family owns this community. My younger brother runs the family business for me so I can dabble with these antiques. We're wealthy and defend what's ours. The F.B.I. and police take an, ah, irritating interest in our affairs. We also have some competition with other Italian families."

"Hah." She snorted at the 'irritating interest'. "Hi, Mr. Marino, I go by Alex Smith, even though that's not my name. I'm a homeless kid, with no family, and no living friends. I've been on the streets for just about 5 years now. I come into the city during the summer so I can memorize books, and I spend winters underground so I don't get picked up for truancy. I have perfect recall. I can glance at something and I will remember it forever. Yesterday, I memorized an Italian-English translation dictionary and I now comprehend everything that I've heard spoken in Italian. That's why I go to the library - to memorize things."

He didn't blink at this list, but what he said was, "I've known you're homeless."

Alex nodded once. "I figured. Was it you that had me followed when I left your store that first day?"

"Yes." His tone held no apology.

43

She drank her tea even though it was borderline too hot and refilled her cup. "I'm glad you didn't have me shot for lying then."

He waved his hand dismissively. "It's a lie, but not one that will hurt our family. Would you do me a favor, though?"

"Depends." Her newfound caution made her hesitate. Was this where the deal would include something she was unwilling to do? Homeless children were so easily exploited.

He ran his finger along his teacup's handle and looked into the liquid as he explained, "If someone asks you about me or the family, will you tell me who and what they asked for?"

"Oh, that!" She exhaled the breath she hadn't realized she was holding. "Sure. I won't ever forget you giving me a towel and shelter. I owe you and I pay my debts. That hasn't changed." She hesitated then. Full honesty. "I stayed in the shop that night last fall when that horrible storm came through. The night you gave me the combination."

His mouth twitched as he looked up at her. "I know - silent security alarm and security cameras. It's why I gave you the shop key. I saw the weather forecast. I also don't have mice. I had someone search your backpack."

She almost laughed. "Thank you, Sal. As for the 'irritating interest' the police have in your affairs, be assured, I will not rat you out. Not everything I've done is legal either."

Sal countered, "That's merely a side-effect of living on the street. You're a good kid."

She didn't comment; instead she pushed her memory away with vicious firmness. "If I get picked up, I will say I lied to you and that you employed me with no knowledge or complicity. You are merely a dupe."

Sal chuckled. "That'll be good for my reputation."

Alex shrugged. "Have we an understanding?" She watched him closely. Would he call the cops on her? Would he have her picked up? Surely he would have already; he'd known she was a street kid. He would have already tried to exploit her if he was going to.

"I think so." He held out his hand for her to shake.

Alex shook his hand once, firmly. "Good. Can I keep calling you Sal or do you have some mafia title I should be using?"

"We are not mafia. We're just a rich family with interests. Keep calling me Sal. It's annoying Mario."

Alex squinted at him. "Who's Mario?"

Sal calmly sipped his tea. "My brother - the man you met last night."

"I'm not sure I want to annoy someone who so casually ordered me to be terrorized." Alex made sure her tone indicated a hint of censure.

Sal rubbed his chin. "Alex, Mario only recommended last night's interrogation because he was worried you were a spy leaking information to one of the other families. We've been having some business issues. When you disappeared without a trace anywhere, we figured one of the other families was hiding you. You're young enough that it makes sense that you'd have to go back to school. When you magically reappeared, we were sure the other family must have dropped you off." He inhaled and then confessed, "I ordered that interrogation."

Alex digested this. "Would they have shot me?"

"If there were any indication at all that you worked for our enemies, yes. We couldn't figure out how you were getting information, but we knew you were making the information drops in the library somehow." At Alex's frown, Sal continued, "Alex, kids don't go to libraries voluntarily every day and they certainly don't look at the types of things you do."

"Shit, Sal. If I was somehow getting information and leaving it for someone, wouldn't that someone have to come pick it up?"

"Language, young lady." He shook his finger at her teasingly. "We couldn't find anything and we didn't see anyone come by after you. Your backpack isn't bugged. You aren't wearing any electronics that we can detect. You don't search through my office. You don't ask any questions."

"I ask a lot of questions!" Alex said indignantly.

"Not about the family or the business," said Sal calmly.

"If there's no indication that I'm spying, then why?" Her voice sounded whinier than intended.

"Because a street kid doesn't just walk into a neighborhood and accidentally choose to ingratiate herself to the local godfather," Sal explained.

Alex pondered this. She weighed in with, "Shit."

"Don't swear." Sal frowned. "It's unbecoming and won't help you in the long run. You should learn better ways to express yourself."

"Does it annoy you?" Alex tilted her head and grinned at him defiantly.

"Yes," he growled.

"Good!" she said cheerily, "Then I'm not ingratiating myself to you. Shit, I'm deliberately provoking you." She smirked.

He refused to rise to the bait. "Have you eaten today?"

"I had a muffin earlier." Her stomach growled traitorously with its more honest answer. The dumpsters had been very sparse.

He nodded and stood up. "Let's go get you a proper breakfast then. Scavenging from trash cans has to stop. You're going to make yourself sick. You have to let me feed you if you're going to stay."

It took several days for them to adjust to the new friendship. Alex was able to forgive Sal's betrayal by reminding herself that he was loyal to his family and she might benefit from that integrity, and by reminding herself that she herself had done things that were necessary, if distasteful. Sal had been obliged to test her, not enthusiastic about doing it. That was the difference.

Now that neither one of them actually had to be careful of what they said to each other, they both felt better and an underlying tension that neither had been particularly aware of dissolved. The week passed pleasantly. Sal started stocking extra food in the store refrigerator and Alex would swing by and eat before going to the library. The afternoons were spent in the store, helping Sal with inventory and cleaning or playing chess.

When the weekend arrived, Sal took Alex to another museum. Sal let her set the walking pace as he'd been there many times before. Alex stopped for a long time in front of a still life painting of a dinner table by Willem Claesz Heda. "Two years ago, I'd've laughed if someone said they painted food instead of eating it." She could feel herself changing, becoming less instinctive animal and more self-aware human.

"All that book-learning isn't a real education," Sal noted on the ride home. "You have to see it and experience it for yourself."

"The pictures in the books don't look anything like those paintings at all," Alex agreed.

"A lot of things are like that. Books will give you a basic knowledge, but understanding requires more." A few minutes later, he asked, "So what's the deal with your memory?"

For a moment, Alex was paralyzed with fear. It took her by surprise, because she certainly trusted Sal now. To comprehend it, she took the fear and turned it around in her mind, studying it. At the core was her piano playing - the last time she'd truly let anyone see her real self - and the subsequent events. Sal asking about her memory was different; would be different.

Alex took a deep breath, fortifying herself, and explained as best she could. "I like to think of myself as having three kinds of memory. I can look at something or hear it, and it's like taking a video. I can go back and see it again later, but I don't actually know it." She unconsciously crossed her arms in front of herself, noticed the trepidatious action, and deliberately uncrossed them and set her hands in her lap again. "So if you were to ask me about it, I'd have to find the right reference and remember it. That's too slow to be useful, mostly. I have to go back and study it to learn it and build all the connections between information that I know and the new information, so I can recall it quickly." Her right foot started tapping, and she stilled it with a mental frown. There was nothing to be anxious about. "Then, if I really want to understand it and apply it, I have to rebuild the information in a way that makes sense to me. Once I have that, I'm done and can move on to the next thing. It takes a lot of time and focus. I mostly save that step for winter."

"That's quite a gift."

Alex winced at the word gift; she never wanted to be gifted again. Her heart rate picked up and she could feel herself stiffening.

Sal quickly continued, "So what do you plan to do with all that knowledge?"

She took three deep breaths before she could calm herself enough to answer. "Earn enough money to buy safety, I think."

"Safety?" He leaned forward and took two bottles of water from the small refrigerator. He handed one to her.

"I want to be able to go in a room, lock the door, and sleep, knowing for sure no one could possibly come in and hurt me. Maybe some body armor, so even if you put a gun to my head, the bullet would ricochet off." Alex opened the water and drank.

Sal nodded agreeably. "That seems... narrow? Understandable, but narrow. So what type of job would you want to do?"

Alex glanced out of the limousine window at the passing concrete buildings. "Park ranger, maybe. I really like the forest and I'd get to carry a gun, have authority, but most of the people I'd have to deal with would be happy on vacation, and my boss would be a long way away."

That made Sal laugh.

"It's not enough money, though," Alex said. Back on a neutral topic, she was much calmer again. "I'll need a lot more eventually."

Sal sipped his water. "I can't imagine you'd spend too much as a park ranger."

"I need money to build something," Alex replied.

Sal raised an eyebrow. "Oh?"

Alex hesitated. How much could she really trust this man? Wouldn't it be nice to actually talk with someone about her ideas? Someone to bounce ideas off of and help her fine-tune her plans. She inhaled and answered, "A perpetual energy battery. It's that physics I was working on last year. The initial creation is going to be really expensive." Interestingly, this confession didn't have any anxiety or fear reaction. Alex thought that was very odd and seemed backwards. She felt no concern at all telling Sal about her memory, and her whole body reacted with signs of stress. Telling him her plans for the future and about her battery made her very wary because he could steal the idea from her and she wouldn't be able to use the money to buy safety and food, and yet her autonomic responses were no more than if she'd been discussing his antiques.

"Ah." Sal didn't seem to notice Alex's internal conflict and stated, "I thought a battery stored power, not created power. Like capacitors. How can it be perpetual energy?"

"Technically, it's more of a gatherer of energy than a storage unit, but for all practical purposes, it's going to look like and work like a battery. Might as well call it a battery. Besides, if people think it's storing a lot of energy, their efforts to reproduce it will fail." Alex still wondered why she felt so calm discussing a secret that, once known by anyone else, could destroy her future.

"Ah, good point. How much money do you have saved up?" Sal asked.

"I only have the cash you gave me this week," Alex said lightly.

Sal took a sip of his water before answering. "Nothing? A girl as determined as you?"

"Until I'm 18, it all belongs to the State. No point even in having it and hiding it somewhere. You never know when someone would just come along and take it, and if I carried it with me, it'd be gone if I got picked up." Alex recited this fact without sadness.

Sal rubbed at his chin. "This memory of yours is quite impressive. Are you sure you don't want to use your natural ability for the common good or something?"

Alex scoffed and repeated one of her old street gang's thoughts, "The common good ain't never done nothing worthy of my time. Let humanity burn; it's choosing its own fate."

"Hmm." Sal shifted on his seat to a more comfortably position. "I think your experience thus far in life is too narrow to make a statement like that. There are good people out there that are worth helping and people worth being loyal to."

"Like you are loyal to the Marino family?" countered Alex, "These the good people you speak of?"

"Not all Marino's are good people. You could even make a case that I'm not a good person." Sal shrugged. "But they are my family and I'm loyal to my genes. You might consider choosing something or someone to be loyal to. Take, for example, your experience on the streets. Should kids be treated like that? Should they be scared and digging in trash cans for food?"

"It's just the way it is." Alex replied. Then she shook her head at his arched eyebrow. "No, I suppose not."

"Maybe you find a way to make children safe so no one else ever has to go through what you did."

Alex scoffed at him. "That's impossible."

"Is it?" Sal argued, "You just said you can create a perpetual energy battery. If you actually can, you could sell it for a lot of money and then use that money to influence society."

Alex conceded, "I suppose I have a few years to decide exactly what I want to do when I'm 18."

"I could help you work out a potential business plan. I may not know physics, but I do know business. You'd have to figure out what such a society would look like, and then figure out the steps to create it. Just like a chess game. Plan how to get to the win."

In yet another leap of unprecedented trust, Alex found herself saying, "I'd like your help, Sal." She drank a large gulp of water. "I dream about it sometimes - what I might do."

Sal rubbed his chin. "What do you dream?" He asked gently.

Alex recognized the speech tactic and muttered, "Going to psychoanalyze me, Sal? I've been through all the psychology texts. I already know what's been done to me ain't my fault. Ain't nobody's fault but them that did it and I'm still here. I'm not going to let them win. I also accept what I've done. No point in dwelling on any of it. There's just now and forward." She silently observed that when she thought too much on her street years, her language devolved.

Then it occurred to Sal, or maybe to Alex, or maybe just even at the same time, that she could use her memory to try and identify actual antiques at auctions, and they planned out a course through the next month to visit auctions and estate sales. He promised her a fair share of any profits, which he'd save for her, to negate any potential exploitation. He'd provide money; she'd provide talent, and together they'd get rich. They both cackled at that, and spent the next day ordering detailed references, magazines, and books. When they weren't discussing antiques, they discussed business possibilities and began working on a solid business plan.

The day Sal and Alex planned to go to her first auction, Alex arrived at the antiques shop to find Sal pacing behind the counter. His brow had small beads of sweat. When he saw her, he said, "Have I apologized for scaring you with that interrogation yet?"

"Eh? It's ok. You were just protecting your family." Then Alex joked, "I'll have nightmares for years..." She laughed to make sure he understood she wasn't upset anymore. As he still appeared tense, she said seriously, "Look, Sal, I understand it. Are you ok?"

"I'm sorry for putting you through that." His eyes held a sadness she couldn't fathom.

Not knowing what to do about his melancholy mood, Alex shrugged and said lightly, "Don't we have an auction to go to?"

"Yeah, we do." Sal called his driver to bring the car and grabbed a couple small paper bags that were on the counter. Holding them up, he explained, "Breakfast. We can eat on the way."

"My stomach loves you, Sal." Alex had skipped scavenging in dumpsters that morning, because she'd known Sal would get her lunch, but breakfast was an unexpected boon.

"Nah, your stomach loves Irene. She put these together for us." Sal set the store's alarm system and they stepped out into the summer heat. Luckily, the driver had already cooled the air in the limousine.

Once they were seated inside, Sal handed her one of the bags. Inside of hers, Alex found a freshly baked, homemade cornetto, a pear, an orange, and a small container with a mixed assortment of homemade cookies. Alex took out the croissant-like pastry; it was filled with marmalade.

Sal set his bag aside and reached instead for the already-prepared steaming

49

coffee. He poured some into a small cup, offered it to Alex, who shook her head. He leaned back to drink it in one quick swallow and then set the cup aside. Coffee seemed to be an odd choice as Alex had only ever seen him drink tea. He was certainly in a strange, sad mood, and whoever had made the coffee had known.

Alex found that when he hurt, she hurt. It was a weird, foreign feeling. Her brain helpfully provided the word 'empathy', and she finally understood what it truly meant beyond its dictionary definition. She had no idea how to address the pain though; no one had ever taught her compassion.

Thinking that maybe she could take his mind off whatever was bothering him, Alex asked, "Did you ever have a wife, Sal?" She nibbled at the pastry and decided she'd never tasted anything so fabulous before. She was immediately torn between savoring each bite and swallowing the pastry whole.

Sal moved the cup back by the coffee pot. "No, but I loved a lady once enough to want to marry her." He closed his eyes briefly.

"What happened?" Alex licked the edge of the cornetto where the marmalade threatened to drip.

"I loved her too much to risk her in family warfare. Things were a lot less stable when I was younger. Mario's lost two wives. He's on his third now." Sal reached for a napkin and handed it to her.

Alex nodded soberly and tried to shift the conversation to something less morose. "I didn't think people who had money and families had that kind of problem."

"It depends on where you are and what family, I suppose. Most people go through their lives blissfully unaware of the harsh reality perpetrated on others." He eyes glazed over as he stared at something she couldn't see in his own memory.

Alex changed the subject yet again, hoping to find a cheerful topic. "Do you suppose we'll see anything good at the auction?"

The corners of Sal's mouth lifted into an almost-smile and Alex knew she'd finally hit a good subject. Sal answered, "You never really know for sure. If you do see something valuable, don't point it out. That'll just drive up the price. Instead, pick something else on the pallet and say it will go nice in your bedroom. That'll be our secret message that I should buy the pallet." For the rest of the ride, they talked about their plans for covert communication, and whatever was bothering Sal was forgotten by both of them.

Over the next month, they made quite a team, Alex with near-instant recognition of potential things of value, and Sal with the money and wisdom to know what was really worthwhile. Sal had one of his appraisers give Alex a crash course, ostensibly to help her appreciate antiques more, but in reality to help her properly evaluate the things she found that matched the desired items in the antiques wanted-to-buy ads.

Almost all of their sales were direct to the customer. An item would be purchased and they'd call the person who had posted a note wanting that particular thing. If the customer was a regular, they got the item for the price Sal paid for it, appraisal costs, plus a small store markup. If not, they went for value-of-item plus appraisal costs plus the full store markup. Sal diligently deposited a share of the profits into an account with his name, but that he said was hers. He told her that if she ever needed any money, she only needed to ask and he'd do a withdrawal without a question. She never asked. Her stomach was full. She got sleep most nights. The balance of her account steadily grew, but was not nearly enough to build her first battery.

A couple weeks later, while they were riding home in Sal's limousine from another particularly profitable auction, Sal stated, "If you are going to hang out with me, you need to know how to use a gun."

Alex shook her head. "I know how to use a gun." The memory wasn't particularly pleasant. In fact, an unfamiliar guilt-feeling seemed to creep in when she thought of those girls in that house.

Sal grinned, eyes twinkling, and announced, "Good. We'll get some practice. I've rented a space for the afternoon."

Just then, the car pulled up in front of a large, low building. The sign over the door said, "Guns and Range". There was another limousine parked outside. Three men in business suits stood outside. Alex recognized them from the Marino restaurant. Two were bodyguards, while she didn't know the function of the third.

Before they got out of the car, Sal pointed at the third man. "That's Milo Paul. He's my man of affairs, also a lawyer. You can trust him."

"Ok?" she replied doubtfully.

"If he says he has a message from me, it'll be true. He works for me, not my brother. If it comes from anyone else, you're going to have to evaluate motivation and who is choreographing them," Sal explained.

"Ah. I understand." Alex wondered at what point she would ever have a reason to interact with any Marino other than Sal. From her perspective, the farther away she stayed from his mafia family, the better. Her plans for the future didn't involve rotting in some prison somewhere or being found dead on a beach.

Nodding firmly, Sal said, "Good. Let's go in."

They got out of the car. Milo Paul studied Alex intently and it made her a little uncomfortable. What had Sal told him? The two bodyguards stayed outside while Milo followed them in.

The store was filled with a large variety of guns in glass display cases, ammunition, assorted attachments, and the usual hobbyist hats, shirts, and signs. The clerk immediately rushed over. "Mr. Marino, the range is all set up.

Is there anything else I can get for you?"

"No, thank you. My man here will watch the store. You take the afternoon off." Sal smiled at the man.

With practiced ease, Milo handed the clerk some money and escorted him out, turning the store's sign from open to closed, while remaining inside. The clerk glanced back once, but left. The two bodyguards outside went to their limousine and retrieved three large cases from the trunk and brought them in.

"Rented a space for the afternoon, eh?" Alex quirked an eyebrow at Sal.

Sal shrugged unrepentantly.

The bodyguards took the cases into the back and Sal and Alex followed them in. Milo took up position at the store's counter, and pulled a book from his pocket and settled in to wait.

The gun range itself was a long hall with targets at the end that could be adjusted with switches. The bodyguards set the cases on the counters and silently departed. Sal withdrew a key from his pocket and opened the cases. "This is part of the family gun collection. Pretty much every type we have." Inside the case, guns, both legal and illegal, and their ammunition were neatly packed in grey foam.

Alex whistled. "I retract my comment about knowing how to use a gun. Teach me."

For the rest of the afternoon, Sal did. Disassembly, assembly, cleaning, checking, loading, shooting. Historical use, strengths, weaknesses, comparisons. Everything he knew about each gun, he shared. Alex's prior hunting ability to stand perfectly still gave her a steady hand and excellent aim. Muscles developed from processing game gave her strength to lift even the larger guns, although some were unwieldy.

The afternoon went really fast. When they were done and everything was put away and the cases relocked, Sal paused and put his hands on her shoulders, facing her. With absolute seriousness, he said, "Don't ever let my brother know you can shoot like that. I've seen many people shoot, but none who started with your accuracy and ability." He let go of her shoulders. "You know any martial arts?"

"Read a bit, but no. That needs a teacher." Alex was pretty certain the fighting skills Mason had taught her were incorrect.

"I'll get you one," Sal declared. "If anyone ever tries to hurt you, I want you to be able to defend yourself."

Alex blinked, startled. How had she gotten this lucky? "I'd like that. I've been thinking on my business. How am I going to make enough money fast enough to keep my business afloat? That's a huge failure point in every scenario. There's no job I could do that would cover it."

"Well, that's definitely a challenge," Sal answered, speaking slowly, studying her. "The Marino's have been working on ways to gain money for generations. You've got several advantages other people don't have. I'll help you work it out. With your memory and knowledge of people, you won't have an issue." He grinned.

The next month and a half was filled with Alex's real education. Sal not only hired people to teach her things, he himself gave her an unparalleled view into the Italian Mafia business; describing individuals, groups, and families, their motivations, their purposes, and their use. He detailed what his family did to make money. He showed her pictures of everyone on his phone. In return, Alex described her perpetual energy battery and how it would work. He didn't understand the physics at all, but he had a lot to say on how she could market it, as well as what would be necessary for her business to survive.

Toward the end of this education, Alex found herself following Sal at yet another auction. This one was massive. People could place bids, but only things with multiple bidders would actually go into the voice auction. Bidders were encouraged to negotiate the final prices before the voice auction to speed up the proceedings.

"I want that lamp for my bed table. Buy it for me?" Alex murmured plaintively as well as loudly enough for their absurd audience to clearly hear. The other antiques collectors thought they were being discreet in their observation of what attracted Sal's attention. Luckily, they still hadn't twigged to her yet. Sal's recent profits had not gone unnoticed by the community.

"That lamp? Really? But it's worthless." That, sadly, was true.

"Oh yes, please! It matches my room perfectly." Alex closed her eyes a moment, pretending to look all dreamy, when in fact, she was studying the hilt on the sword she'd spotted toward the back of the pile of junk. She was almost completely sure that was THE sword. It would have to be dated, but if it was the right one... it was the find of a lifetime. The fake plastic gems glued on the handle were criminal. "Birthday present? Please?"

Sal shrugged and sighed. "Ok. I spoil you too much. Your mother is going to lecture me again." He opened his book and jotted down the number. He obviously remembered that secret phrase he'd mentioned for the first auction too.

Alex had a hard time even walking away from the pallet that held the sword, but they moved on leisurely, and she noted things of interest, comparing them to her memorized references. Occasionally, she would rub her nose, as if it were slightly stuffy, and several pallets later, he'd write down the correct one in his book. Their audience diligently scribbled away too, hopefully writing down the wrong pallets. That was a problem with the really big auctions - too many knowledgeable collectors. Sal wrote down a few numbers himself and Alex scrambled to figure out why.

During the actual auction, if Alex didn't know the value, she linked her hands together, if the bid was under the value, she opened her right hand, if it was approaching or over, she closed her hand. Sal considered these movements and made the actual purchasing decisions based on his experience and wisdom for selling and profit margins.

When her "lamp" pallet came up for bid, only one other person kept bidding. Alex did not recognize him, so he must have wanted something else in the pile. She hoped it wasn't the sword. If the price crept into the millions, Sal would surely veto it. The price jumped to $16,000 and Sal glanced at her and asked if she still wanted that lamp, and in an appallingly loud plead, she said she simply must have it, with a kid's long semi-whining "please". He sighed, shook his head, and kept bidding. Several people chuckled. The opponent caved at $45,000. She did a kid-bounce and planted a thank you kiss on his cheek. The rest of the auction continued uneventfully.

Afterwards, Alex and Sal went to the pickup point to arrange shipping. The other buyer was there and approached them. His eyes were silver, jewel-like, with faint eyebrows. His wispy salt and pepper hair was long and neatly pulled back into a hair tie.

The man stood confidently sure of himself and his larger-sized sleeves hid muscle, not fat. "How'd you like to sell that sword? I'm a collector."

Before Sal could answer, Alex said, "My dad would like that. He does those SCA events and needs a better weapon."

Sal sighed, opened his hand in apology, and replied sadly, "I'm sorry, Sir. I just can't say no to those baby blues."

That the man nodded sadly and moved away meant he didn't know what the sword was, or at least he wasn't sure enough to take the risk.

Alex bounced excitedly, "Can we take the sword now and give it to him tonight? Can we? Please?"

Sal shrugged an apology at the attendant who was waiting to take their shipping information, and said to Alex, "Sure, sweetheart."

They had the lamp wrapped extremely carefully, as Alex diligently watched to make sure her "treasure" wouldn't get hurt, and then they left, with Sal carrying the sword under his arm.

In the car, Alex about melted into the seat as the tension and stress of escaping with the sword finally released.

Sal climbed into the limousine across from her and handed her the sword. "Well? Is it worth $45,000?"

Alex unwrapped the sword very carefully. "Can we get it dated on the way home? If it's what I think it is, it's priceless."

"It's got plastic on the handle. Can't be too valuable." Sal reached over to the limousine's bar and withdrew two bottles of fruit juice.

"Criminal what they did to you," Alex said to the sword, stroking the blade gently, whispering to it. Then she looked up at Sal and grinned. "Here, under the dirt." She took her shirt and wiped at the blade near the hilt. The partial indentation of the watermark became more visible. "It's going to need substantial restoration, but we won't have to do that."

"We won't?" Sal handed her one of the juices.

Alex grinned. "Oh no. Not our job. We, being the honest and caring people that we are, are simply going to return it to its proper owner for what we paid for it."

Sal lifted his left eyebrow. "You do recall that the point of these purchases is to make money, right?"

Alex opened her juice and explained, "Yeah, but this belongs to the Hamasaki family. Fifteen years ago, they posted a reward notice for one million Euros."

He whistled. "That's a profit."

"Yeah, but you don't want it. I researched them back when I saw the listing to see if it had been found yet. Your family is rich and powerful. You have a lot of business through the southeast United States and Italy." Alex drank some of her juice and continued, "The Hamasaki family is the same, but worldwide. They're a lot more subtle and control a lot of things not in their name. I expect the reward amount was merely them fishing for the thief. Obviously, we didn't steal it or vandalize it like this. We have receipts."

"Ah," said Sal with enlightenment. "They'll be grateful to have a family heirloom back." He took out his phone and scheduled a stop at his usual appraiser.

"They're here," Sal announced as the rented limousine pulled up in front of Sal's store.

Alex went to make sure the tea water was hot. It was and she hurried back. She carried the sword tied to her waist, in an early traditional style. It looked a little strange with the t-shirt and jeans, but at least the clothes were new and not street-dirty.

Both Sal and Alex waited patiently while two bodyguards swept through the store. When they finished, they took up position at the shop entrance and an immaculately dressed middle-aged Japanese woman came in, followed by scholastic-looking older Japanese gentleman. Sal and Alex bowed to them in greeting.

In Japanese that Alex hoped she wasn't mangling too badly, Alex said, "Please come in. This is Sal Marino, owner of this shop. I am Alex Smith, his assistant. I would be happy to translate."

"I speak English," the woman replied suavely and introduced herself as Kaiya Hamasaki. To Sal, she said, "Your email was quite a surprise. The sword has been missing for a long time."

Sal led them back into the shop and gestured to the armchairs by the table and Ms. Hamasaki and Sal both sat. Alex untied the sword and carefully set it on the table before sitting. The extra lights were on so that the sword's details could be clearly seen. The scholastic man frowned at the plastic gems. He picked up the sword and studied it, checking balance. He took a cloth from his pocket and rubbed at the watermark.

"It's exactly as we found it. We did not do any restoration because we thought you'd prefer to," Sal explained while Alex poured tea.

Ms. Hamasaki nodded. "I appreciate that. If it is ours, we will have it done."

The scholastic man took a loupe from his pocket and began studying the sword while the rest of them sipped tea and waited. After a few minutes, he announced in Japanese, "It's the sword."

"How certain are you?" Ms. Hamasaki asked, also in Japanese.

"Entirely certain, Ms. Hamasaki." He placed the sword back on the table and bowed to her. He then retreated to stand outside the shop. He did not get into the limousine.

The woman smiled and ran her finger down the blade. "Your email said you saw one of our reward notices?"

"Yes." Alex cited the issue name and date. "But this is what we paid for it." Alex removed the receipts from her pocket and set them on the table in front of Ms. Hamasaki. "If you would cover our costs, that would be enough."

Sal added, "I usually include 10-20% to cover store expenses, but consider this a gift from my family to your family. I'm happy to be able to return something that was stolen from you."

Ms. Hamasaki nodded coolly. Alex was impressed at how little emotion the woman showed. She couldn't have expected anything less than the full reward value. "May I take it with me now?" She withdrew a checkbook from her small purse.

"Please!" said Alex enthusiastically.

Startled, Ms. Hamasaki looked at her quizzically.

Sal chuckled. "My assistant has not let it out of her sight since we picked it up."

Alex agreed, "I didn't want anything to happen to it."

Ms. Hamasaki smiled at Alex. "Very kind of you." She wrote a check that covered the auction and appraisal fees plus 20% and handed it to Sal, who passed it to Alex.

They all stood and Alex went to put the check in the register. It was a subtle thing, saying that Sal was too rich to handle money. Alex was certain the nuance was not lost on Ms. Hamasaki.

Ms. Hamasaki bowed and said, "Mr. Marino, I'm sure my father would like to thank you personally. I'm sorry to inconvenience you, but would you come to the car to speak to him? He is not as spry as he used to be and is waiting there."

"Of course." Sal also bowed and subsequently followed Ms. Hamasaki out to the limousine. Ms. Hamasaki passed the sword into the car and then took up position outside the car along with her appraiser.

Alex stayed inside the store and wished she could have been accompanied Sal. She cleaned up the used teacups, wiped down the table, and moved behind the counter. She sipped at her own tea, trying to admire the antique cup. Anything to keep from pacing. She took a cloth and polished the already pristine counter. She glanced at the clock, an expensive wooden cuckoo clock with actual hands pointing to numbers that were supposed to be moving around much faster. Alex made more hot water. She thought about taking drinks out to Ms. Hamasaki, but the woman was in deep conversation with her appraiser, and likely bringing hot tea to someone standing in the Georgian summer sun wasn't the best activity.

A very long two hours later, Sal climbed out of the limousine. He shook the hand of someone Alex couldn't see, then shook hands with Ms. Hamasaki, and bowed. Mr. Hamasaki's daughter and staff got in the car. Sal watched the car go and then came into the shop.

"Well?" Alex pounced. "What did he say? Was it worth it? Did you make a deal? Will it be good for the family?"

"You and I are going to dinner," Sal answered calmly.

Alex felt like throttling the information out of him.

"At the Marino restaurant," Sal proclaimed. Gente Di Mare. Where she'd almost been shot.

Alex paled and stepped back. "It couldn't have been that bad."

Sal reached inside his blazer and withdrew a business card. He handed it to her. Hand-written on the back was elegant Japanese kanji. It took Alex a full minute to decipher it to "Full courtesy to bearer." and Kuro Hamasaki's personal signature. There was also a handwritten phone number that was different from the one on the front of the card. "That one is yours. I have mine in my wallet."

She blinked and whistled.

"That was what you wanted, wasn't it?" Sal poked her on the shoulder so she'd look up from the card.

"Oh yeah," Alex breathed. "My chance for survival just went way up."

"Let's go get dinner. You can give Mario his card." They closed down the shop and Sal's driver showed up to take them to the family restaurant.

Sal delivered Mario's card while Alex waited at their dinner table, trying to ignore the stares of the people she now recognized by name from Sal's lessons.

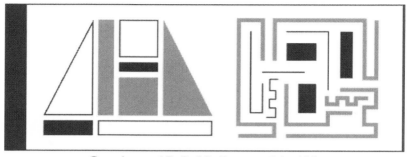

Alex arrived at the antiques store wondering how to tell Sal it was just about time for her to head away for the upcoming winter. She definitely wasn't looking forward to the long days stuck in her cave, even though she could use the time to hone her martial arts skills. She pushed open the door, listening to the welcoming ring of the bell. Sal was not reading a catalog today. He was sitting there with a cup of tea, watching the door, waiting for her.

As she set down her backpack, Alex said, "Hey, Sal, we need to talk."

Sal held up his hand. "Me first. We do have to talk." He handed her a warm cup of tea as she arrived at the counter. He inhaled deeply and said, "I have a gift for you and an offer."

She raised her eyebrow at him and took a sip of her tea.

"Yes, and I hope I'm giving them to you in the right order." Sal handed her a key and led her to the back room. There was a trunk-size metal box that hadn't been there before.

Alex kneeled and using the key, opened it to find two black and white cardboard boxes of the kind that people used for filing.

"Police evidence regarding a certain missing person case," he said unnecessarily. The boxes were stamped and labelled. "There's a lot of ugly stuff in there. You don't have to look. We can just destroy it, if you want."

Alex hesitated only fractionally before taking the lid off the first box. News clippings of her piano performances, pictures of her (and others), stills taken from video feeds, a few dvds, reports buried in reports. Too many images from her blood-covered escape, all viciously recorded by hidden cameras she hadn't known existed. She inhaled deeply, trying to still her panicked heart. "You saw these?" her voice was breathy, wavering.

Sal nodded. "Yes, my private investigator dug them up. All digital copies are gone, including the ones on backup disks. Even the group home records and digital copies of related news articles. You destroy these boxes and there's no trace at all. Your origin disappears."

Alex swallowed. "Sal... Oh, Sal. I never wanted you to know. How long have you had these?"

"I received it the morning of the first auction we went to together. It took awhile for my investigator to locate and assemble everything," Sal replied softly. "Tracing back from your arrival here was challenging."

Alex opened the other box. Instead of more gruesome clippings about her captivity and escape, there were reports and random security camera images from her time with the gang, not all of it, but enough to accurately place her at the location and time. She'd left fingerprints in the house with those girls. These were labelled with "probable shooter" and were linked to the young pianist. "Did your brother see these?"

"No, but I did tell him about it," Sal answered. "No one should ever see this kind of stuff."

Alex's hands shook as she lifted and looked at the pages. "No copies anywhere?"

"None. No future blackmail copies. Nothing at all." Sal put his hand on her shoulder, a gesture meant to offer support.

Alex finished glancing at the last page and declared, "I want to burn it."

Sal nodded again. "I have a metal barrel out back just for that."

As promised, the metal barrel was in the alley behind the store, far enough from the buildings to be safe. Several cans of lighter fluid, some wood and charcoal were all set up. Sal lit the fire. Alex glanced at each thing before tossing it in. She didn't need to see the dvds to know what was on them. These were also crushed and tossed in. When the last of it was in, they added more wood, and watched in silence until it burned away completely. A few locals came by to investigate the smoke, but seeing who stood there, they immediately departed without approaching.

When they went back in and each had a cup of tea, they sat on the armchairs by the table. Alex bit her lip, knowing what was coming next, and hating the idea of a criminal life. "So you want me to come work for the family?"

Sal swirled his tea, staring at it a moment before answering, "No, I don't. I set up an apartment for you in one of our residences. We can fake an airline stewardess mother and you go to school. I'll pay for everything, unless you want to tap your savings from the antiques. You'll be safely off the streets, able to close and lock your door, and sleep safely without fear that someone will come in and hurt you. The front desk has a security guard that won't let anyone in without permission. When you turn 18, do whatever you want."

Alex blinked. "Really?" She wondered if just helping him make a profit at the antiques shows was useful enough.

Sal set his cup down and tented his fingers in front of himself. "You have nothing to fear from me. I'll never step into that apartment. I'll never even be in the building when you are there for propriety's sake."

"But what do you get?" Alex persisted.

"A daughter I never had?" Sal opened his hands, palms up. "Look, I'm an old man, and you'd be wasted dead in some ditch somewhere. I have more wealth than I can ever possibly use. Why not?"

"Your brother agrees with this?" Alex still remembered the gun's deadly opening pointed at her.

"Not particularly, but he'll indulge me." Sal sounded certain when he said this.

Alex snorted at that.

"What was it you wanted to discuss?" he asked.

The room seemed to be spinning. Could Alex really stay here? Would she be safe? Feeling like she was leaping off of a cliff, she answered the only logical way, "Apparently nothing."

"Good. You'll stay in here tonight," Sal declared. "You sleeping out in that lean-to makes my skin crawl even if I do have guards posted."

Alex set her half-empty teacup back on the table. "You have someone watching me?"

"For a while now. Let's play chess." Sal went to get the chessboard.

They ignored the auction crates that were waiting and played chess as if they had all the time in the world. Alex won again even though he tried a new tactic.

Later that night, as she drifted to sleep on the cardboard stack in the back of Sal's antiques shop, she whispered, "Goodbye, Mary."

Milo Paul took Alex to the apartment building. On the short ride over in Sal's limousine, Milo gave Alex his business card. "If you need anything, Miss, or get in any trouble, you call me and I'll take care of it."

"Thank you, Mr. Paul." Alex nudged the travel luggage at her feet that was part of the move-in show. It was odd to think of that hard purple case with wheels as hers. She didn't even know what was inside it. Sal had given it to her just before turning her over to his man of affairs.

"Please call me Milo. All the family does." He smiled at her warmly.

Dutifully, Alex corrected, "Thank you, Milo."

He inclined his head as if to say, "No problem."

Milo went with her into the apartment building and introduced her to the security guard. "This is Alex Smith. Her mother is a good friend of the family. No one goes up to their apartment without permission."

"Of course, Sir," the guard said, making a note. He reached into his desk drawer and handed Alex a key. "Miss, you are in apartment 608 and the elevator is just down that way. Movers already brought your things. If you are going to have guests or get something delivered, just let myself or whoever is on shift here know, so we can pass them through."

Alex acknowledged, "I will, thank you."

Milo shifted his weight to his other foot and said, "I can't go up. I have other business to attend. Call if you need anything."

"Ok." Alex grinned at the two men and portraying a confidence she didn't feel, headed toward the elevator, dragging the purple suitcase with wheels along behind her, as if she'd done it all of her life.

On the sixth floor, she unlocked... her?... door. It was a dizzying thought. She stepped in. The front door opened into a living room combined with a kitchen. Everything was already unpacked and set up. Eclectic, mostly used furniture was part of the deception. The kitchen table, offset into a windowed alcove with a balcony, had a stack of school things on it and a small card. She pushed the front door closed, locked it, and walked through the apartment, trying to feel like the space belonged to her.

The small corner apartment had two bedrooms with one adjoining bathroom. One room was decorated in the fashion of a well-travelled adult, with a mix of decors, and the other room was set up in the style of a "teenager who liked art" with posters and random half-used art supplies. Both rooms had equivalent clothes, all neatly hung or folded and put away. The bathroom had a full-size tub as well as a stacked washer and dryer unit. Two sets of new toiletries had been set out.

Alex returned to the kitchen table, where she found school supplies, notebooks, pens, pencils, books, a mobile phone, and a laptop. She opened the card. "I thought the new year and the new place needed a new laptop. Love, Mom." The refrigerator was already stocked with fruits, vegetables, nuts, meats, and some home-cooked frozen meals. The cabinets were also stocked. Sal must have been planning this for a while to have everything so well-prepared.

She took an apple, rinsed it, and took a bite, while pondering. "Ah!" she muttered and went back to her purple suitcase. She opened that and underneath some travel clothes, found a folder with money, credit card, account statements, and passwords. She went back to the phone, tapped the password, and called Sal. When he answered, she said, "It's perfect. Thank you!" He told her he'd see her tomorrow and to have a good night.

Alex spent the evening setting up her phone and the laptop. Someone had already done the bulk of the work, having installed a large assortment of software and necessary updates and connecting it to the wifi. She changed passwords on all of the accounts and swapped the picture in the background to solid black. She searched through the apartment and found the wifi router in the "mom" bedroom, under the dresser. After some digging on the internet, she changed her router password as well, and made sure both it and the laptop were as secure as she could make them. Whoever had set it up originally had done an excellent job.

Alex then went out on the balcony and listened to the night sounds of the city. It hardly seemed possible. In a week, she'd be going to high school as a freshman. As Alex was 14 years old, she and Sal had decided that was a good place to join in. There would be enough new kids that her sudden appearance wouldn't be too jarring. She hadn't been in a classroom since second grade. She had no idea what to expect. The textbooks on the kitchen table were way below her self-taught education level. Sal suggested she maintain a strict low-B average - nothing to stand out and draw attention to herself. She was in complete agreement.

As Alex lay in the bed that night, in clean, new pajamas, in a bed with clean, new sheets, and a clean, new pillow, behind safely locked doors, in a building with a security guard, she couldn't help feeling disoriented and confused. Wouldn't the apartment's owner arrive home unexpectedly and have her arrested? Where was the threat of another street denizen determined to take everything from her? Even in her cave, the threat of wild animals or a random park ranger loomed. The sounds of the street outside were muted and the apartment itself was quiet, even with the low hum of the air conditioning and refrigerator.

It was hard to accept that she might be safe. Alex was too used to sleeping lightly and immediately waking if anything around her changed. Her sharpened environmental awareness refused to let her sleep, refused to accept that the quiet stillness was safe, not a warning sign of impending disaster. She crawled out of bed and went to stand outside on the balcony, where she could hear the night sounds clearly. Occasional cars passed, but very few people were out walking.

Alex went back inside and poured herself a glass of orange juice and sat at the table. Staring at the glass, Alex decided she needed to do something to thank Sal. For the first time in her life since being on the street, she was able to think of life beyond her next meal and her next day. The concept of being this overwhelmingly grateful was completely foreign to her. This certainly demanded some sort of repayment. The only thing she really had of any value that was truly hers was her perpetual energy battery and that was just a concept and he wouldn't be able to do anything with it.

Between one breath and the next, she knew. She would take her concept and paint it. If she were slow and careful, and tried every step on another canvas, she could do it. She certainly knew the foundational design principles, and she had memorized a lot of books on how to do oil paintings. She could figure it out. The end result might not be art and couldn't be truly in the baroque style, but maybe, just maybe, he might like it.

The very next day she asked Sal for $2500 cash from her account and no questions. Milo Paul brought it over before the end of the day. She left the antiques store early, took the subway out to a large art supply store, and went shopping. She chose only professional, light-fast paints, professional grade brushes, and high-grade, large canvases. She also got cleaning supplies and a sturdy easel that was big enough for the canvases. She then arranged to have everything delivered within the week to her apartment.

Alex spent that evening sitting in her apartment, with her eyes closed, designing her painting. It would be worthy and Sal would know its true value even if no one else ever understood it.

The week passed really quickly. Alex got a haircut at a real salon (much to Sal's delight), and watched seven of the latest hit teen-friendly movies so she'd have something to discuss with the other students. She helped Sal sort the latest auction crates, and spent every spare minute in her apartment working on her painting skills. She ended up having to buy a pair of really large fans to cycle the apartment air off of the balcony. Oil paint and cleaning supply fumes were toxic. Her hand, arm, and shoulder muscles hurt in ways she'd never even thought possible, but her test attempts were going well.

For all of the anxiety she put into worrying about what school was going to be like, the actual attending of it was eventless. The kids, all new to high school, accepted her inclusion in without pause. Most were glued to their phones whenever they could be anyway. Alex couldn't fathom the lure, but periodically pretended to play with her phone also. The usual cliques formed and Alex attached herself to the artsy group and took up drawing in her notebook so she'd fit in.

Alex spoke as seldom as possible, because she recognized that her conversation style and topics wouldn't match theirs at all. They merely labelled her shy and let her hang out with them anyway. The classes themselves were great for giving Alex time to think through her business plans as well as her physics to manipulate matter. When she needed to listen in case she might get asked a question, she just drew another picture in her notebook.

After school, she would visit Sal for a while and help sort antiques or play chess, and then head back to the apartment to paint until her shoulder screamed, then homework, then more painting. She'd be in bed by 10 p.m. and up again at 4 a.m. She still couldn't believe she was sleeping in a safe place. She told this to Sal a month later.

"It's really weird, Sal," Alex said as she sipped her tea and pretended to think of her next chess move. "Sometimes it feels too safe. I'm afraid to let go completely."

Sal frowned at the chessboard. "That's understandable. You can't change life habits overnight."

Alex moved a pawn toward its inevitable capture. "I know. This particular life is just so completely alien to me. The kids at school have no idea how good they have it. You should hear the things they complain about."

He chuckled. "I'm sure. You can always find something to complain about even if your life is perfect."

"I don't have any complaints, Sal, thanks to you." Alex watched him move the wrong piece again - short term gain for long term loss.

Sal smiled happily. "Oh, that reminds me. My birthday is coming up next month. I want you to come to the family birthday party. It's a huge deal. Family members fly in from all over. You can finally put actual faces to all the names I gave you."

Alex moved her knight so it could be captured. It wouldn't prevent her from winning, but it would give Sal a bit of joy. "I'd be honored to attend your birthday party, Sal. Do I need to bring a present?"

His eyes narrowed at the suspicious knight. "Yes, but don't put too much into it. You'll also need a formal gown. I'll take you shopping when the time gets closer. I think you'd look rather pretty in green or blue." Instead of taking the knight, he moved his bishop.

"Good grief. You get me a nice haircut and now you want to change my clothes? What are you trying to do to me?" Alex moved another piece, still leaving the knight unguarded.

Sal took the knight. "Hey, I put up with your hacked hair and two outfits plenty long enough. It's time for you to change those habits too."

Alex giggled and moved her piece. Checkmate in 16 moves. While Sal figured out his moves, she worked out a schedule that would get her painting done in time to give it to Sal on his birthday. It would probably still be wet, but it could be done. She'd have to cut back some of her sleep, but it was a worthy cause.

Sal's birthday party was overwhelming. There were easily a couple hundred people. Alex's new green dress made her feel more self-conscious, rather than more confident as Sal had promised. Most of the family was already there. People ambled about the beautiful park enjoying the cool November day. Children ran around, chasing each other, or playing with their kickball. At the center, a huge temporary pavilion had been erected and its white roof was decorated with colorful flags. Underneath, tables had been set with real china. Several additional tables held presents in different sizes and shapes, all beautifully wrapped.

The three men behind her that were carefully carrying her meticulously crated and packed painting waited for her direction. A fourth carried a stand for the crate. Her crate wasn't wrapped at all though. It would look terribly out of place next to the other presents. Alex wasn't sure what she should do. She looked about her in dismay. It took her a full minute to find Sal in the sea of people. He was with Mario and several others. She wasn't going to go over and interrupt that discussion to ask him.

Luckily, Milo Paul saw her standing there and waved and came over. "Hi," he greeted her with a slight bow, "Sal will be delighted you're finally here." He looked quizzically at the large flat crate and three men. "Is that...?"

Alex was incredibly relieved to have someone familiar nearby. "His present, yes. Maybe we should have it delivered to his store or house instead of here?"

"No, it'll be fine, Miss. Right this way, gentlemen," Milo beckoned the men to follow toward the nearest present table. They carefully propped the crate up on its stand and departed, under the family security's watchful gaze. Milo turned to her and said, "A painting, eh?"

"He likes them." Alex tried not to sound defensive.

"No kidding. It's a good gift choice." Milo smiled at her. "How about if I take you around and introduce you to people?"

"Sure." Desperate not to be left alone in this crowd of strangers, Alex quickly tacked the card she'd brought with her to the crate. The card read, "It's still wet; don't touch it. No photographs. Happy birthday, Sal. - Alex". She followed Milo, who introduced her to the adults in their path as "Alex Smith, the person who is working in Mr. Marino's antiques shop". They expressed varying degrees of curiosity. The women were generally more welcoming. All were polite, but whether they were naturally gracious or conscious of Milo Paul's close relationship to Sal, Alex was unsure. The people did not exactly reflect their photographs on Sal's phone; some of the photographs had been quite old.

"Irene, this is Alex Smith," Milo said, introducing her to a tall, beautiful woman with gorgeous wavy brown hair.

"Ah! Mr. Marino's young assistant. It's a pleasure to finally meet you." Irene's voice was filled with sincere welcome.

"You must be the chef responsible for all those divine meals," Alex guessed, shaking the woman's hand.

Irene flushed happily. "That's me."

Alex smoothed her dress down, wondering if it was sitting right. She felt so awkward, like she was wearing a costume, and wasn't herself at all. Could this person she was pretending to be actually manage small talk? Alex tried with, "You're amazing. I've wanted to meet you so I could tell you that myself. I always look forward to your lunches and that cornetto you made was divine."

"Thank you," Irene said, obviously pleased. "I studied for a while in Tuscany in a private cooking class. It's always been my passion."

Alex asked several questions about Italian cooking and shortly had Irene enthusiastically explaining things. Milo didn't seem to be in a hurry to move on at all, as if this had been his destination the entire time. The three of them watched the children play and discussed the differences between red sauces and their paired pastas until it was time for the meal and the opening of the presents.

Alex and Milo joined the table with Irene and her husband and two bubbly young girls that Alex thought might be 8 and 10 years old. Sal was seated at a table on a platform, near the present tables, along with Mario and select others that Alex recognized as the core business men of the family and their wives. Waiters and waitresses brought plates of Italian food and giant serving bowls to each table.

As people ate and talked, the younger children took turns opening Sal's presents and taking them over for him to admire before returning them to the gift table. Sal knew all the children by name and made each one feel appreciated and proud of their moment in the spotlight. Milo suggested that Irene's girls might open Alex's gift with Alex's help, and Alex shot him a thankful nod. When it was their turn, Alex followed the girls up, and had them take the card over to Sal first. Sal read it aloud and stood to come over and watch the opening of the box, which Alex was directing. Alex herself didn't help the girls, but told them how to undo the latches and a couple men from a nearby table came over to help them lift the lid away. Sal murmured a "well done!" to the girls and turned to look at the painting.

At first glance, it looked like a painting of a glowing galaxy overlaying randomly placed mathematical symbols on a background of misty blue so dark it was almost black. Fine line golden orbits were perfect ellipses that turned the flat galaxy into a sphere. Careful observation showed that the galaxy was actually two separate planes of stars embracing each other and there was a flow to the symbols. At the bottom of the painting, hidden in the shadow, were slightly brighter forest trees reaching toward the heavens. The bottom right had her barely visible signature. Not visible with the painting still in the crate was the rest of the formula for her perpetual energy battery painted onto the sides of the canvas.

Sal turned to Alex. "Is that what I think it is?"

"Yeah," she answered solemnly.

"Truly amazing, Alex," he whispered, leaning forward to kiss her cheeks. "Thank you. We'll talk about this later."

Alex nodded and returned to her chair by Irene, as Sal returned to his table. Alex heard one of the nearby kids say to their father, "But Daddy, I thought Mr. Marino liked those people paintings? That's not a person." He was shushed. The party resumed. When the presents were all opened, and everyone had finished eating, and Sal's "thank you" speech was concluded, people were free to mill around and socialize again. Children squealed and ran back to their games.

Milo turned to Alex and said, "That's an odd painting to have commissioned for Mr. Marino. What's it mean?"

Alex laughed. "I didn't commission it. I painted it." Without pausing, she added, "It's a thank you for the art education he's been giving me." Milo looked back at the painting with more respect.

As the party continued, people went by to admire the presents and stare curiously at her painting. They honored the "no photographs" directive. Milo and Alex continued to socialize with Irene, whom Alex inspired to talk about

66

her daughters for the remainder of the party. When the crate to her painting was closed again and men carried it away, Alex felt like part of her was being ripped away with it. She hadn't expected to feel so attached. Sal had been more right than he knew; paintings held the soul of their artist.

The next day, while drinking tea at the store, Alex answered Sal's question about her painting, "All the particles, the white, gold, and orange dots, are precisely positioned. If we could pry them off the canvas and make them 3D and small enough, it would work. That's the formula, too, if you follow it from the center out, it finishes on the sides of the canvas."

Sal shook his head in wonder. "The family thinks you had that commissioned. Mario wanted to know why you would get me a modern style painting when everything I own is baroque or renaissance." He chuckled.

Alex took their empty cups over to the sink to wash them. "You didn't tell him, did you?"

Sal got the dish towel for drying. "No. Well, I did tell him you painted it. To which he said he finally understood my interest in your welfare. He thinks you are a budding artist."

Alex snickered. "Maybe the next one should be in the baroque style."

He grinned. "No more park ranger?"

"Naw, a ranger is a good fantasy, but I'd rather make that painting a reality. I'm sorry I couldn't make it baroque for you. I just didn't have time to learn how to paint the lighting correctly. My attempts were poor," Alex confessed.

"It's perfect the way it is." Seizing on the crucial part of her words, Sal asked, "You have copies of this in different styles laying around your apartment?"

"Not anymore. They're destroyed. I can't let the information out, you know." By how sad Sal looked at the pronouncement, Alex suspected he would have immediately gone to raid her apartment for all of the cast-offs. Alex commented, "I thought you knew what I was doing?"

"I had no idea. At least the mystery of the $2500 is solved. Art supplies are expensive. I wondered if maybe you got furniture or were decorating, but I didn't think you'd be interested in that."

Alex ran her fingers through her hair, confused. "You didn't have people watching me or the apartment guards reporting back to you?"

He shook his head. "You have a couple bodyguards following you, but they're not reporting to me. Or to Mario either. I've been feeling guilty about having you interrogated. I wanted you to have privacy."

"Sal, you have nothing to feel guilty about. You were just protecting your family."

He paused closing the cabinet on the teacups and asked seriously, "Would you protect my family?"

"Of course. I'd do anything for you," she answered without hesitation. "That is, if they'd let me. I can certainly dump money back into the family when I get my business going strong. I don't think your brother likes me very much."

Sal nodded, content. He closed the cabinet. "How about we skip that auction this weekend and go to another museum instead?"

"Whatever you'd like." Alex would be equally happy at either one. She loved spending time with Sal. He made her feel like she could do anything.

On Tuesday, she noticed, but did not worry about, the different car in the school's parking lot. It was just an unremarkable, standard grey four door sedan and could have belonged to anyone. No one was sitting inside it so the owner must have gone inside the school.

During the math test, Alex forgot to pay attention because she was thinking about how to manipulate matter and answered all the test problems correctly. She realized it just as the teacher was collecting the pages. Maybe she'd get marked down for not showing her work? She'd need to do worse on the next test to balance her grade.

Although in a different parking spot, the sedan was still there on Wednesday and then Thursday. Maybe one of the teachers bought a new car? Alex mentioned it to Sal that night when she got to the store.

"I wouldn't worry about it if you didn't see anyone inside." Sal was sorting mail and pulling out the latest magazines. "Probably one of the faculty's."

Alex brought out the small vacuum for the carpet by the door. Maybe because she was already hyper-observant from the sedan, she saw the dark blue, rough car with four people inside go by the store. The second time it passed the store, it was going the same direction, so it must have circled somewhere, it seemed to slow down just the tiniest bit in front of the store. One of the guys in the back was looking directly at the store. The car continued on.

Alex quickly turned off the vacuum. "Sal, that car just passed the store a second time. There are four men inside. One was looking directly in the window."

Sal immediately stood, "Get back here!" He kicked the wooden panel under the glass display case and it snapped free. Alex arrived to see him pulling out a semi-automatic gun. "Don't go out the back door. It'll be covered. Go get my phone from the office and call Mario."

Alex turned to run to the office, but it was too late. The car squealed as it backed up. Machine gun fire tore through the front of the store. Both Sal and Alex instinctively crouched down, and Alex noted, to her complete surprise, that the display case was made of bulletproof glass. The four men exited their vehicle, coming in. Sal lurched upward and shot at them. One went down. The others ducked behind the antique sofa and dressers. They simultaneously returned fire. Sal gasped and fell backward.

Instinctively and operating on sheer adrenaline, Alex pulled the gun from his hands, trying not to look at the spreading patch of red on his suit coat, and dove around the display case, between the shelves. She did a blind fire underneath the shelves toward where she'd seen the men go, hoping to hit their feet or ankles.

Alex didn't stay in the same position. They were shooting at her. She dodged forward, glancing at the security mirrors, and then in a moment of inspiration, dove between the shelf boards, knocking a $25,000 vase to its death as she went. That gave her a good angle to shoot two of the three remaining men. The last opened fire at her as she ran toward the front of the store to draw him away from Sal. She tried to return fire, but her weapon jammed.

Alex dropped the gun and sought out the man Sal had shot, an action which probably saved her life. He wasn't dead and was pointing his gun at her. She lunged toward him, tackling him, landing her fist, thumb on the outside, thanks to her new martial arts training, directly in his wound. He screamed and she twisted the gun from him. She pulled the gun up just in time to shoot the fourth man who was about to kill her. She put a bullet into the head of the man she'd taken the gun from, and scurried to do the same to the other three, just to be sure they stayed dead.

Certain of their deaths, Alex ran back to Sal, heart pounding. There was so much blood. Sal's eyes were glazed over when she knelt next to him, but he saw her and blinked to focus. She let the gun fall from her hand and ripped open his shirt. The wound in his pectoral muscle might have gotten his lung. She couldn't tell. She grabbed his opposite hand and pressed it to the opening. "Hold that! Do not let go!" she commanded him. She ran to his office and got his phone. Her hands were slippery with blood and it took her way too long to get her finger clean enough to unlock the phone. She called Sal's brother while rushing back to Sal.

When Mario answered, Alex screamed, "Sal's been shot! He's alive, but we need an ambulance. We're at the store. I need you." She didn't wait for the answer. She dropped the phone next to Sal and pressed her hand to the wound to hold in the blood. She pulled him up to see if the bullet went through. There was no exit wound. "Sal, don't you let go. Your brother is on his way. I know that gunshot hurts, but you're going to be ok. It didn't hit anything critical." She hoped. She lowered him back down.

Sal wheezed, but she saw comprehension in his eyes. Alex rushed to comfort him, "I know anatomy, Sal. Just focus on breathing." He tried to say something. "Don't talk. Save your energy."

"Back door," Sal gasped. "I'll keep pressure on the wound." He reached up and she helped him get his hand to the right position.

Alex grabbed the gun and checked the ammunition and went to the back. She slid behind one of the shipping crates just as the back door opened. They had the door combination.

Alex leaned around the crate, made sure she didn't recognize the men who entered, and shot the first. The second ran forward with his semi-automatic firing. She rolled away from the crate as it exploded and fired a shot at his legs. She got the gun up barely in time to shoot him in the chest. She put a bullet in both of their heads too, wedged one of the crates in front of the door and hurried back to Sal. He was so pale, eyes completely glazed over, but he was still breathing. She moved his hand and put pressure on the wound herself.

Tires screeched outside and Marino family men poured in, followed by Mario Marino. One was carrying a portable medical kit. "Over here!" Alex called. The one with the medical kit took over, cleaning and taping the wound while Alex watched in a panic. "Where's the ambulance?"

"We'll get him to the hospital faster," Mario said succinctly. Four men lifted and carried Sal away. Alex moved to follow them and Mario stopped her with a hand on her upper arm. He was way too calm when he commanded, "Tell me what happened before the police get here."

Midway through her explanation, Mario turned to one of his men and said, "Get the security footage." He finished listening to her, and then asked if she was hurt.

Alex shook her head.

Mario released her arm. "All right. Go home, get cleaned up, and get changed. You weren't here. I'll send someone for you later."

Alex argued, "No. I have to go to the hospital to be with Sal. When he wakes up, he's gonna be scared."

"You do exactly as I say," Mario growled. "Or you will be a casualty here." Mario pulled out his gun and pointed it at her. "Now, get out."

Alex snagged her backpack and staggered back toward her apartment. As the adrenaline wore off, she began to shake. She steadied herself and stepped into the apartment building's lobby.

"Miss, do you need a doctor?" the guard asked, rising.

In her best street-kid-can-lie calm voice, she answered, "Naw, naw, I'm fine. It's paint. Damn if I didn't drop a whole can of the stuff. It was a horrible mess." She added some frustration to her voice, "And now we have to buy more paint tomorrow, 'cause we didn't have enough to finish. I'll try not to get it on anything."

The guard sat down again, but watched her walk back to the elevator. Alex got to her apartment and stripped just inside the door. She got in the shower and washed down, and then she washed the shower out, and then went back and cleaned up everything by the door. She made sure there was not a single drop of blood anywhere. She bagged her clothes and shoes in a black plastic trash bag, but decided she didn't want it anywhere in the apartment with her. That was Sal's blood on those. Her whole body shook in a massive tremor. She took the trash bag out and dropped it in the community trash can at the end of the hallway. She checked the hallway for blood and returned to her apartment, willing Mario to send someone.

The knock at the door surprised her. The desk guard was supposed to call her if anyone was coming up. She supposed Mario's men might walk through that stop-point without question. She hurried to the door and opened it to find not Mario's men, but two police officers.

"Miss Smith," the first officer said, "We need you to come with us." He showed her his obviously legitimate badge.

Alex froze with the exact stillness of a hunted animal. Her heart stopped. With a calmness she didn't feel at all, she inquired, "Is there a problem, Officer?"

"We'll discuss things down at the station." The police officer turned to his partner and said, "Go get her some shoes."

"They're in the closet of my bedroom," Alex offered helpfully. Inside she was screaming. "Second door on the right."

The man returned with her spare shoes and a jacket. It was hard for her to acknowledge that she had spare shoes - she'd only gotten them because Sal had insisted in case the others got wet. Kids shouldn't go to school in wet shoes, he'd explained. She'd never even worn them and now she was overwhelmingly grateful to have them.

"May I call my mom?" Alex asked.

"You can call her from the station," the first officer said.

As they passed the front desk, she noticed the guard was gone. Outside, they put her in the back of the grey four door sedan she'd seen at the school. She spent the ride to the station trying to make her heart slow down. They could have picked her up for any number of reasons. She had to wait to see which one they had before saying anything incriminating. It could be as simple as missing school records. She hoped it was as simple as missing school records. Had Mario turned her in? Was Sal ok? What was going on?

They escorted her through the busy station and into a back interrogation room with a one-way mirror and told her to have a seat. "Can I make a phone call?"

"You aren't under arrest, Miss. The officer in charge of your case will be in shortly to discuss things with you." They left, closing the door.

Alex sat and waited. She wanted to pace. She wanted to scream and beat her fists against the mirrored window. The room smelled like rusty metal and day-old coffee. Alex recalled a book on meditation she'd scanned and never bothered processing, and quickly worked through the pages. It was bloody useless given her current stress level. She tried anyway. She reviewed the telltale signs of lying and knew she'd have to answer promptly, with unchanging details, and maintain a relaxed, easy body language.

After way too long, a woman officer came in and sat opposite Alex, setting a closed manilla folder on the table. "Alex Smith. Is that your name?" She had brown eyes, a broad forehead, aquiline nose, and glossy lips.

"Yes, Ma'am." Alex was sure to make steady eye contact and did not fidget. She tried to limit her visible tension to what might be expected of an innocent teenager picked up by the police.

The woman rested her hand on the table near the folder. "Do you have a phone number for your mom? We'll call her for you."

"Am I in trouble?" Alex let her voice quaver just a little.

The woman's eyes narrowed and she said, "No, of course not. We just want to talk, Miss Smith."

Alex gave the woman the phone number Sal had given her that would go to a voicemail account for an airline stewardess that would say she was in flight and to leave a message and she'd return the call when she landed. "She sometimes doesn't answer."

"Are you home alone a lot?" the woman queried.

"Mom's single, so yes, but the woman in the next apartment over checks in on me all the time, and the building's guard won't let anyone in. I'm old enough to be left alone. Mom calls every day whenever she's not home." Alex quickly fabricated reasonable phone call times for the last week as well as what they might have discussed, in case the details were needed.

Instead of pursuing that topic, the officer said, "Tell us about your relationship with Salvatore Marino."

The officer mispronounced his name. Alex corrected her and then said, "He owns an antiques shop not too far from my apartment. I help out after school sometimes with sweeping and dusting. He's a nice man, but he's getting too old to do physical tasks."

The officer tilted her head slightly. "Does he pay you?"

"Naw. Sometimes he buys me lunch or dinner, though." That wasn't illegal.

"I see." The woman touched the folder but didn't open it. "Why would you choose to hang out with an old man?"

"He's not that old," Alex muttered, frowning. "He's teaching me chess. I'm getting pretty good, too." She crossed her arms, sitting up straighter, in what she hoped would perceived as pride, not insolence.

"Has he ever touched you?"

"Huh?" Alex choked, feigning bewilderment. She uncrossed her arms and opened her hands upwards, aiming for body language that would indicate confusion.

The officer clarified, "Stroked your hand? Run his fingers through your hair? Perhaps more than that?"

Alex leaned back a shade, indignant. "No! He's not like that. He's never been anything but a complete gentleman."

"You're safe here, you know," the officer stated. Her voice echoed flatly in the small room. "We can protect you. It's ok to be honest with us."

"I am being honest with you." Alex snapped, angry. "Sal's a good and decent man."

"He's a crime lord." The officer countered sharply.

"No," Alex managed to act completely surprised. "He's not. He can't be." She pitched her denial carefully to match her bewildered expression.

Alex must have been convincing, because the officer responded by trying to correct Alex's ignorance, "Do you think all store owners own limousines?"

"He said he had family money he inherited," Alex mewled.

"Didn't he take you shopping recently?" The woman opened her folder and withdrew a picture of her and Sal coming out of the department store where they'd bought her party dress for his birthday party.

"Sure. He paid for a dress for his birthday party." At least Alex didn't have to act outraged.

"A seductive evening gown?" The officer pulled a picture from the folder and pushed it toward Alex. It was a picture of Alex outside Sal's party.

"It's just a dress. The event was formal," Alex asserted.

"And you don't think that's odd? A man his age buying a teenager who is not a relative a dress like that?" The officer exhaled tiredly.

"I didn't have enough money. Mom's paycheck hasn't come in yet. I'm going to pay him back in parts." Alex thought that would sound reasonably convincing.

"I'm going to be more frank with you here, Alex. Did Salvatore Marino ever have sex with you?"

"No!" Alex was really indignant. She didn't have to act.

"Miss Smith, we know you've been visiting him every single day," the officer said.

"Chess," Alex interrupted stonily. "And art."

As if Alex hadn't spoken, the officer continued, "Weekdays and weekends. You go places with him in his private limousine. You live in an apartment building he owns. You do not have adequate adult supervision. Do you see where this is going?"

"Salvatore Marino is a kind and generous man. He puts up with me asking him questions all the time. Mom even suggested I've been pestering him too much, but he said he didn't mind." Alex couldn't keep the irritation from her voice and stopped trying.

The officer growled in frustration. "Miss Smith," she started, and then there was a knock on the door, and an officer leaned in and beckoned Alex's interrogator out. Unfortunately, the woman took the manilla folder and pictures with her.

Alex swallowed, worried and scared. That would be news of the shooting at the antiques store catching up to them. Was Sal ok? Had they gotten him to the hospital safely?

When the officer came back in, her expression gave nothing away. "Miss Smith, why didn't you go to Mr. Marino's store today?"

"I wanted to paint. I've been learning oil painting." Her apartment definitely had paint supplies spread everywhere, but they weren't open or set up. "I got stuck working on a design in my notebook instead."

"I see." The officer nodded. "We're waiting on a call back from your mother. In the meantime, we have a psychologist here who specializes in women who have been traumatized. She's going to come talk with you for a while. Just remember, you are completely safe here. You can tell us anything."

"There is nothing to tell," Alex repeated.

"We'll see," the officer said ominously and left Alex.

After a few minutes, a motherly-looking middle-aged woman came into the small room. She introduced herself and spent the next three hours grilling Alex on things Sal or any of his family might have said or done to her. Alex was exhausted, still somewhat in shock from earlier, and going crazy needing news about Sal. She tried to correctly moderate her responses, but she was sure her underlying tension and anger were slipping through to the woman's way too observant eyes.

When the first female officer came back, the psychologist said, "I'm recommending a full, immediate physical. This girl is clearly showing signs of trauma and stress, even though she won't admit it."

"We're still waiting on a call back from her mom," was the reply.

The psychologist nodded. "I'll write the authorization. I feel she's in immediate danger and we'll need the hospital exam to put her into protective custody."

"I don't need an exam!" Alex gasped. "I'm not in any danger. Sal never did anything to me. Not once. Not ever."

The officers ignored Alex and left. Alex did get up and pace like a caged tiger then. She'd missed dinner and recognized that her energy level was dropping off. How late was it, anyway? She sat down again. Where was Sal's brother? Surely he had contacts in the police that would tell him she'd been picked up. What was going on with Sal?

The original two officers that picked her up from her apartment arrived to escort her to the hospital. When they demanded she strip for the exam, she went wild, kicking and fighting. They sedated her and did the exam anyway. In the morning, she was handcuffed and transferred to a psychiatric hospital across state lines into Alabama, well away "from the potential danger of the Marino family".

○ ● ❭ ❭ ● ❬ ❬ ●

Alex arrived at the psychiatric facility mid-afternoon. The sedation had mostly worn off by then; she'd been given another dose just prior to leaving the hospital. The heavy duty metal locked doors with tiny windows were intimidating enough. The place looked like a prison. The doors buzzed loudly when opened and staff at every step of the way did not leave much hope for escape. Inside, they were passed through yet another two layers of security, and they eventually arrived at a psychiatrist's office.

The psychiatrist, a lanky man with stiffly combed-back amber hair, squinted at Alex's handcuffs and said to the officers, "Is she dangerous?"

"Calm as a mouse since last night," the one officer said. "This is only because she did a bit of kicking and hitting prior to her medical exam last night."

"Drugs?" the psychiatrist asked.

"Bloodwork came up clean." The officer handed the doctor Alex's paperwork.

The doctor looked at Alex and said, "If we remove the handcuffs, are you going to behave?"

Alex nodded.

"Use words," the doctor ordered.

"Yes," Alex ground out, and at the doctor's glare, she added, "I'll behave." Truly she felt like she might pass out or throw up. It was a close call for which action would win.

The doctor nodded at the officers who removed the handcuffs. The doctor waited a moment, told Alex to have a seat, which she did. The doctor signed some papers and handed them back to the officers who then left.

"Ok," the doctor said, glancing through her papers. "We're admitting you for a 30 day evaluation, during which time you will attend daily group therapy and individual therapy 4 times a week. The rules are simple. No physical contact with anyone, not the orderlies, not the other patients. You will not hurt yourself nor anyone else. We do not allow unprescribed drugs."

"May I make a phone call?" Alex inclined her head toward the phone on his desk.

"We do not allow any outside communication without prior approval from your treating psychiatrist. No phone, no email, no internet. No visitors without authorization and no unobserved visits." The man recited this as if he'd said it a million times.

Alex inquired, "Who is my treating psychiatrist?"

"Me. And I'm not allowing it until you prove you are ready for it." The doctor continued his litany. "You will eat your meals. You will not damage the facilities. You will be respectful and you will not interfere with the treatment of any other patient."

Alex really thought she might pass out at any moment. "What do I need to do to prove I'm ready for outside communication?"

"We'll see. I need to review your case file." He pushed a button on his desk. "Do you understand the rules I've just stated?"

Alex nodded.

"Use words," the psychiatrist demanded.

"Yes, I understand," Alex ground out.

"Good." The door opened and two male orderlies came in. "Take Miss Smith and get her washed, changed, and settled into her room."

They took Alex's arms and practically carried her out. They took her through another set of locked doors that did not buzz when opened and into the common room of the psychiatric ward that was to be her new residence. The place smelled equally of antiseptic, urine, and vomit. The caged TV was loud and tuned to some home improvement show. The windows had bars on them. Easily cleaned vinyl furniture looked uncomfortable. Several tables held board games. One had coloring books and crayons. The residents, all also female, stared at her as she was brought through. The orderlies stopped at a barred off door, where Alex was issued a hospital gown, approved hospital underwear, and some small toiletries by a bored, bitter-sounding woman from her shelves of supplies.

The orderlies took Alex down a hallway past a dozen rooms with open, but lockable, doors to a large multi-person bathroom. There were no doors or stalls. Showers were toward the back and had no dividers or curtains. A loud buzzing bell rang making Alex jump from its sudden near-deafening noise.

"Activity bells," the one orderly informed her gently. "Every 2 hours during the day. Checks occur once per time block randomly. Approved activities will get you points toward privileges. Breaking rules removes points." He indicated one of the showers. "You'll need to shower now, Miss. We have to check your hair for lice and make sure you aren't smuggling anything inside the ward."

Alex winced. She could kill them easily. She knew that. She was wearing street shoes with hard soles and she knew deadly martial arts. They were just a couple of beefy guys who probably had light training in subduing crazy women. But they were just doing their job and not unkindly. At least with two of them, the chance of abuse was lessened. She submitted to the shower, inspection, and put on her new uniform without protest. She cried the entire time.

They brought Alex back down the hallway to room 8 and informed her that it was hers for the duration of her stay. The door was to remain open during the day and would be locked at night. There was a night pot in the corner if she needed to use the bathroom during the night. A simple institution spring bed with thin mattress on top was the only other thing in the room and it had a thin pillow and an equally thin blanket.

Alex went in and sat on the bed and the orderlies left her. As soon as they were gone, she relocated to the floor in the back corner. The spring bed was too uncomfortable to sit on. She pulled her knees in to her chest and rocked. She was dozing off just as the loud activity buzzer sounded again, making her jump. It took a full minute for her heart rate to return to normal.

A few minutes later, one of the other patients was standing in her doorway. "Gotta love those alarms, huh?" the woman said. She looked to be in her mid-20's. Her hair probably hadn't been brushed in a week. "You drugs?"

Alex shook her head.

"Oh, an actual crazy," the woman sung and came in and sat down on Alex's bed, facing her. "Self-admitted or involuntarily visiting?"

"Involuntary. You?"

"D.I. Drugs. Involuntary," she explained. She tried rearranging the flat pillow against the bed's bar so she could lean back. She swung her feet up on the bed. "Don't suppose you brought any in with you?"

"Sorry," Alex apologized.

"Well, if you can get your hands on any or manage to save any of your prescribed ones, I'll pay for 'em." The woman tried rearranging the pillow by folding it in half, but even that didn't help. She shrugged and sat up straight.

"Good deal," Alex felt herself sliding back into her street personality, the animal that thinks moment to moment and offends no one and evaluates everyone based on what they could do for or to her. "So what are the approved activities?"

"Pretty much anything social. We'll get a point for sitting in the same room talking to each other." She peered at Alex closely. "We'd lose them all if we were found kissing."

"Sorry, not gay," Alex replied.

"Too bad." The woman shrugged. "Oh well. I'm saving up for a room radio anyway."

Alex's stomach rumbled. "When's dinner?"

"Next activity bell," was the woman's disheartening answer.

A nurse came by with a clipboard, looked in at them, wrote on her papers, and moved on. Alex's visitor grinned and stood up, "Ta-ta, C.I.!" She headed for the doorway.

"Wait, what's your name?" Alex asked.

"Doesn't matter." The woman skipped away.

Someone screamed down the hall toward the common room and there was a loud crashing noise, followed by wailing. When the wailing didn't stop, Alex covered her ears and tried to imagine herself anywhere else.

The psychiatric hospital was going to make her insane. Between the activity buzzer, the TV, the other patients, and the pointless therapy sessions,

Alex was sure of it, even without the stress of not knowing what was going on with Sal. The psychiatrist kept asking her about her relationship with Sal and Alex kept reiterating the same things she'd told the police.

Group therapy was even more entertaining. "Jan, how do you feel about Marsha taking your pillow?" "Alex, what do you think about this TV station discussion?" Alex had lost a point for suggesting they smash the TV and throw it out with the garbage. "Violence cannot be condoned," the moderator had said, removing a point from her record. Alex's psychiatrist continued to refuse to let her make a phone call, even though she asked (politely!) every session.

Twenty-four days into her incarceration, two F.B.I. agents arrived to speak with her while her doctor sat in to take notes. No unobserved visits, indeed.

The F.B.I. agents introduced themselves and showed her their credentials. They were both trim men, with close-cropped hair, serious eyes, dressed in clean, but slightly wrinkled grey suits. They could have been brothers "Miss Smith, is that your real name?"

"Yes." Alex wondered how she could get them to tell her Sal's status without asking them. Maybe if she mentioned his name often enough?

"What is your home address?" the lead agent asked.

Alex gave them her apartment address in Sal's building.

"We know that's the apartment Salvatore Marino set up for you, complete with a fabricated mother. What's your real address?" At least he pronounced Sal's name correctly.

"That's it. The only address I have," Alex answered calmly, her insides twisting around into spasms. Her lies couldn't last forever. She'd known that. Just tracking down her fake stewardess mother would lead them... Lead them where? Sal would not have tied anything back to the Marino's. The family was too smart for that. The agent was fishing for answers.

"Was it your idea or Salvatore Marino's that he set up the apartment for you?" The lead agent posed the question while the other agent leaned forward slightly, watching Alex's responses.

Alex noted how adroitly the agent worded the question to incriminate Sal either way. "Sal didn't set up the apartment for me." She was too tired to play the body language game, yet she knew she had to. She tried for slightly befuddled eyebrows.

The lead agent didn't seem very happy by her response. "Then how did you get the apartment in Salvatore Marino's building?"

"I arranged it. I faked a call from my mom, transferred rent, and moved in. Sal never knew anything. I didn't even know he owned the apartment building until you said just now." Alex was reminded of the conversation she'd had with Sal where she'd told him she would say she deceived him and that he was merely a dupe. In her memory, Sal chuckled and commented, "That'll be good for my reputation." Forgive me, Sal, Alex thought.

The lead agent twitched. He knew she was lying. "Where'd you get your money?"

Alex shrugged. Maybe she could pull off a "matter-of-fact" attitude? "I'm a courier. I take messages people want delivered and I deliver them. Sometimes people give me gifts. It's not illegal. It's not tax evasion." Alex hoped they'd overlook the potential hazards of a courier job.

That reply startled the agent and Alex could see the greedy hope light up in the lead agent's eyes. "Messages? Like what?"

"I don't ever read them," Alex said with horror in her voice. "That's a good way to get shot." Alex could feel the psychiatrist's glare even though she didn't look in the man's direction. Nothing like a bit of misdirection to confuse the interrogation. Let them think of her as her own operator, outside of the Marino family.

The lead agent cleared his throat. "Did you carry messages for the Marino's?"

"No, but I would have. Sal didn't need a courier; I don't think he ever had anything he wanted to send discreetly. The antiques business isn't all that secretive, you know. Have you asked Sal?" Alex really needed to get control of this conversation. The lack of sleep was really making it difficult for her to think clearly.

Neither agent answered her question, either by words or body language. Instead, the second agent spoke up. "Would you say you are very observant?"

"Not particularly," answered the girl with the photographic memory and perfect recall.

Again, the second agent spoke and Alex wondered which of the two of them was really the lead agent. "When you were working for Salvatore Marino, did you ever see or hear anything that would suggest criminal activity? From him, or Mario Marino, or anyone related to them?"

They certainly were good at wording questions to incriminate based on any answer. Mario Marino was Sal's brother. Alex dodged, "I wasn't ever working for Sal. Sal was teaching me chess and art. If he was doing anything illegal, I never saw it."

The second agent continued, unperturbed by her evasion, "Miss Smith, we didn't find anything about you on your laptop. We didn't find anything about you in our database. No fingerprints. No missing person record. Nothing at all. No school records even. Do you know what that says to us?" The first F.B.I. agent's hand was clenched and he was rubbing his fingers together, the first real body language tell either of them had made; he was frustrated.

Alex gazed at the second agent blankly. Her laptop had a search history of oil painting techniques and business human resources documents. She bet that delighted them. She rarely turned the laptop on. Oh, and there were a couple "B-grade" school papers, she remembered. As she thought about her laptop contents, she realized she'd cited a couple periodicals from the Charlotte library, not the local library, on those papers. If they were digging, that might stand out, but maybe they'd think she found those magazines somewhere else? It was really too obscure to mean anything, but she should have been more careful.

The second agent concluded, "That you are deeply involved with the mafia. So much so that they are willing to erase your history for you."

Thank you, Sal, Alex thought earnestly. This interview would have been much worse if her history had been discovered. Alex countered, with concern in her voice, "People have that much access to your databases? You shouldn't be worrying about me. You should be worried about that. As far as I know, I should be in your system. I'm actually surprised you haven't turned up my school records yet." She'd be happy to have them spending more resources looking for something that didn't exist.

The first agent resumed, "Where did you come from, Miss Smith?"

Alex rolled her shoulders and stretched her neck. "It really doesn't matter, does it? I've been living on the street pretty much my whole life. I don't have parents. I don't have relatives. I've been taking care of myself and doing a fine job of it until the police forcibly removed me from my apartment. My SAFE apartment, incidentally. And then subjected me to an illegal, invasive physical exam, and incarcerated me here without cause."

With a glance at the first agent, the second agent offered, "Miss Smith, we could get you out of here. Put you in protective custody. Give you a new name, a new life, parents even. You'd be completely safe."

"And for that, I'd only have to perjure myself and say I saw Salvatore Marino doing things I've never seen him do?" Alex stood up. "This interview is over, gentlemen. Sal is a good and kind man and he taught me chess and about art and antiques. I never saw or heard him do anything illegal. I don't have anything for you."

The second agent also stood. He handed Alex his card. "If you think of anything you'd like to say differently, give me a call."

You let me near a phone and I sure as hell ain't callin' you, Alex thought, aggravated. She nodded politely to the men and let herself out to the indifferent care of the waiting orderlies. The second agent prevented the doctor from calling her back.

In the common room, Alex fidgeted, spinning the card between her fingers. There was no way that psychiatrist was going to let her out now; he knew that she had lied on earlier interviews. She'd accrued enough points for a room radio, but she'd been saving them to spend on a walk outside with a potential opportunity for escape. She went over to the supply window and asked the woman in charge for a radio and earphones. She carried them back to her room, reflecting that it seemed odd to reward her for being social by giving her an item that would help her be antisocial.

She unscrewed the back with her fingernails and noted what parts and supplies it had on the inside, and tucked the F.B.I. agent's card inside. It would be useful eventually. That night, she discovered the psychiatrist had ordered she be placed on antipsychotic medicine. She tried to decline, but they forced her to take the pill after dinner anyway. She broke out in massively itchy hives and threw up the entire night. The night shift orderlies ignored her pleas for help. The other patients screamed at her to shut up so they could sleep.

The nurse forced her to take the pill again in the morning, despite Alex showing her the rash and pointing out her obvious allergy. The nurse merely told her to take it up with the psychiatrist when he came in. He was too busy to see her for 2 days. She couldn't keep any food down at all, her thoughts were fuzzy, and she was dehydrated. The orderlies had gotten tired of cleaning up her vomit, accused her of doing it deliberately, and often let it sit longer than reasonable. Her fellow inmates started calling her V.Q. (vomit queen) and admired her determination from afar.

Desperate, Alex offered to brush her teeth really well and kiss the woman who'd first approached her, in exchange for a really good distraction during the medicine distribution. Alex kept her eyes open during the kiss to prevent any flashbacks. D.I. pulled away after a minute and said, "Yeah, you're not a lesbian."

That evening, D.I. quietly taunted one of the other women into attacking her during the medicine distribution. Careful to not be seen on the security cameras, Alex grabbed 2 needles from the lower drawer and a single harmless sedative pill. Alex was fast and she was not caught. She stashed the needles in a tear in one of the couch's seams, and then the pill on top of one of the shower heads. Naturally, the missing inventory was discovered and the place searched. The orderlies didn't find anything and everyone was locked in their rooms for the night.

Alex again spent most of the night dry-heaving and itching. The next afternoon, she took apart her radio again and withdrew the F.B.I. agent's business card, and removed some of the radio's parts. She closed the radio back up, and went to her bed and chewed the card into a thick pulp, which she then jammed into the door's strike plate hole so the latch assembly wouldn't be able to catch. She moved her bed around and then tried to get an hour's sleep before the loud buzzer jarred her awake again.

The evening buzzer sounded and Alex helpfully pulled her door closed as many of the patients routinely did for privacy. She quickly tore her blanket down the middle to make a long rope and tied one end to the doorknob and put the other under the corner of the bed, out of view from the door's window. She lay down on the bed and curled up facing away from the door. The evening orderly came by, peered in the window, locked the door, pulled on it (and it didn't give because it was tied), and moved on.

Alex waited until the ward settled into their normal night sounds (crying, thrashing, and snoring). Alex slid out of the uncomfortable spring institution bed as quietly as possible. The tile floor was so cold under her bare feet that it felt like it was burning. She tiptoed over to the door and listened intently. The midnight patrol had gone by and wasn't looping back. She untied the doorknob and pulled on her door. The thick wadded paper had indeed done its job and prevented the lock from catching.

Alex slipped from the room, pushed her door closed again, and went silently down the hall, ducking below room windows. In the common room, she retrieved the needles she'd hidden away in the couch's stitching. She attached these to a couple pencils by jamming the sharp end into the erasers and into the wood far enough to be secure. As lock picks went, they were really rough, but they could be made to work with the parts from the radio. She hoped whoever was monitoring the security cameras was asleep on the job.

Alex hurried over to the main door and with the needles and the radio's stiff wire, she picked the lock. She quickly went through the door and secured it again. She ran down to her psychiatrist's office and picked that lock also and went in. She grabbed the phone and dialed. Sal's phone rang but he did not answer. She hung up and dialed Mario's phone. That rang a few times and then a gruff voice said, "Hello?"

In Italian, Alex said, "This is Alex. Is Sal ok?"

There was a sharp inhale, the sound of a light clicking on, and movement. "Where are you?" Sal's brother demanded, also in Italian.

She continued in Italian, "I'm in the Rosewood Meadows Psychiatric facility in Alabama. I was picked up by the police the day that Sal got shot. Is he ok?" Alex heard a door open and footsteps coming down the hall outside. Clearly, she'd been spotted on the security cameras and they'd managed to organize a posse to come get her.

"Sal's dead," Mario reported emotionlessly.

The ground disappeared beneath Alex and she dropped into the abyss. Every cell in her body screamed. When she managed to remember to breathe again, she begged, "I need help. Please get me out of here. I'll do anything. I'll come work for the family. Whatever you need."

The office door crashed open and four orderlies came in. One was wielding an ominously large hypodermic. Alex dropped the phone as they rushed her. She didn't even bother fighting them, until they touched her, and then she kicked and screamed. Somewhere in the back of her mind, she knew not to use deadly martial arts on them. It wasn't their fault. She broke bones before they subdued her anyway.

This was followed by two days in a straight jacket, chained to a bed. Heavily drugged, Alex alternated between horrible memory-nightmares and babbling complex equations. At moments when she was coherent enough to really be awake, she found herself laying in vomit and wished she were dead too. They'd killed Sal and she hadn't been there for him. He must have been worried and frightened and she wasn't there to comfort him. The doctor came by several times and Alex thought that her mumbling would just confirm her crazy diagnosis, but she was unable to stop herself.

Eventually, they reduced her medication and thankfully stopped the antipsychotic medicine and let her rejoin the patient population. An hour later, she was escorted to her psychiatrist's office where she refused to discuss things she'd said while drugged. She asked to make a phone call and the psychiatrist refused. She was escorted back to the patients' common room. She saw D.I. and sat across from her at the checkers board.

"So I hear you lost all your points, V.Q.," D.I. observed, randomly moving a checkers piece illegally.

Alex also moved different piece of the same color. She whispered, "Third shower head from the left. Be careful it doesn't fall down the drain." Alex stood up and went over to the room's corner and threw up.

Part 2

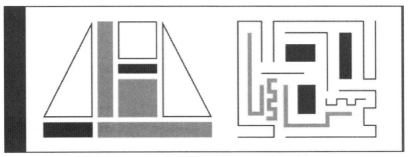

L minus 9:20:16:25   ~29π/20

Alex took a seat near the barred window, looking out. How long would it take Sal's brother, Mario Marino, to send someone for her? Would he, even? Her still mostly drug-fogged brain refused to focus and her hands trembled. Despite the blaring activity bells marking time, Alex couldn't be sure how many days passed as they blended into a nightmare of nausea and sameness. One of the other patients came up to her and asked about checkers, but Alex merely shook her head and the woman wandered off again.

She was still sitting at the window when the limousine pulled up. Her hand touched the glass, willing the mirage to stay and be real, yet terrified it would be. She remembered the gun barrel to her head all too clearly. What deal, what future-destroying job would Mario come up with? By now, he would have reviewed the security camera footage. Would he want her to be a bodyguard? An assassin? A spy? Whatever it was, Alex was certain it wouldn't be legal.

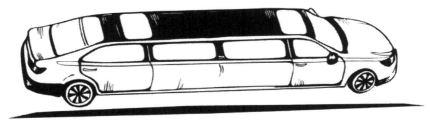

"This isn't the future I want," Alex muttered to herself. "I need to tell him to go away. That I've changed my mind. I'll talk with the damn psychiatrist and make shit up and get myself out." She saw Milo Paul and one of the other Marino family lawyers get out of the limousine. They were both carrying

85

briefcases. "What have I got myself into?"

One of the patients, walking by, giggled, and whispered conspiratorially, "Talking to yourself is bad... bad... bad... crazy cuckoo... crazy cuckoo..." The patient stumbled away.

Alex swore and stood up, running her fingers through her hair. She glanced down at the hospital gown and slippers. Not the most confidence-inspiring attire for the upcoming interview. She went to wait by the door, trying to calm her nerves. They were unlikely to shoot her in the hospital with witnesses, weren't they? Would they at least listen to her first?

After what seemed like an especially long time, a pair of orderlies came to escort her to the psychiatrist's office. All three were seated when Alex entered with the orderlies, but both lawyers stood. The doctor did not. The orderlies continued to hold her arms.

"Miss Smith," said Milo. He nodded at her deferentially.

"Mr. Paul, Mr. Dioli." Alex greeted them, "Grazie per essere venuti." Thank you for coming.

Milo turned to the psychiatrist. "I need to speak to my client alone, please."

The doctor shook his head. "It's against hospital policy and I don't recommend it. She's unstable and dangerous. She seriously injured two of our orderlies. I can't guarantee your safety." His hand moved under his desk.

"We accept the risk," Milo said.

Luciano Dioli added, "Get out," with a significant sharp tilt of his head toward the door.

The psychiatrist said caustically, "It's your life," and left, taking the orderlies with him. The ease with which he relinquished his office more than adequately described the conversation they'd had prior to her arrival. Mafia lawyers had a blessed knack for intimidation.

Milo, seeing Alex's shaking hands, asked, "Are you ok? Here, have a seat." He helped her to his chair.

"Kill the recorder behind the desk," Luciano said to Milo, turning his chair so he could more comfortably talk with Alex. He switched the conversation back to Italian. "Miss Smith, are you under the influence of drugs?"

"No," she lied. She was clear enough. Her heart pounded. She felt like she was facing a loaded gun already.

"Good. I have papers for you to sign." Luciano reached for his briefcase.

"Lu," Milo cut in, shaking his head in censure. "Miss Smith, I represent you and Lu here represents the Marino family. Sal left me to you in his will."

Alex blinked in confusion and yelped, "He what?"

"He set up a trust fund for my employment. Before you sign anything, we should go over it in detail." Milo quirked a smile at Luciano.

Luciano, having retrieved a stack of papers from his briefcase, handed these to Alex. "These authorize a transfer of funds to Mario Marino and the family trust."

Alex went through the pages, slower than usual, due to her foggy brain. She was having a hard time comprehending what she was seeing. It didn't help that the papers were unsteady in her hand and the letters jiggled and refused to focus. "Why am I giving money to Mr. Marino? He's got my accounts. There's nothing in them, except a few hundred dollars for groceries, and well, there's the one for rent, I suppose." Then she got to the pages on asset transfers. "I mean, he can have it all, of course, it's Sal's, but this doesn't make any sense."

Milo quirked an eyebrow. "Seriously?" Both Milo and Luciano gazed at her closely, reminding her a little of the F.B.I. agents' intense scrutiny. "Sal left you everything."

"He what?!" Alex's heart stopped beating. When it restarted, she demanded, "Give me a pen."

"Don't do anything hasty," Milo said quickly, "I have some alternatives to that document and you can't possibly know exactly how much there actually is until you review it. The Marino family will not be..."

Alex interrupted him. "The Marino family is going to kill me." She wondered why she wasn't dead already.

Milo shook his head. "If you die of anything other than old age and natural causes, all of this goes to donations. There's absolutely nothing the Marino family can do. It's all legally sound and above board."

"It's not mine. I don't want any of it." Alex finished going through the pages.

Luciano handed her a pen, shrugging at Milo without apology, "It's in my best interest that she signs it."

"Miss Smith, as your lawyer, I'm telling you we need to go over that." Milo sat down in the psychiatrist's chair on the other side of the desk.

Alex was already scribbling in her signature on each page. "No, no delays. How many things have become defunct or overdue with this money sitting in legal limbo? It's been months. I have no idea what Sal was thinking when he did this, but it's not right." To Luciano, Alex said, "You tell him that. You tell Mr. Marino I didn't know anything about this and that I'm deeply sorry for any trouble it's caused the family. If I had known, I would have talked Sal out of it. I swear." She handed the papers to him. Luciano had already signed the witness lines. "Take this to him. Right now. I don't want any doubt in his mind that I had anything to do with this."

Luciano put the papers back in his briefcase and stood. He glanced once at Milo and then left. Milo did not get up.

"Milo, what was Sal thinking?" Alex put her head in her hands and covered her eyes, near tears.

"That's not everything, Miss," Milo said gently.

Alex wiped at her nose with the back of her hand. "I'm afraid to ask what else."

"Pass me my briefcase. I have a copy of the will for you to look at."

Her hands were shaking so badly she nearly dropped the briefcase handing it to him. The briefcase bumped and knocked over a jar of pens and pencils the psychiatrist had on his desk. "What did Sal tell you about me?" Alex asked Milo. Neither of them reached to pick up the spilled writing utensils.

"That you would sign over the money and assets immediately. That you didn't need me to go over any legal documents." Milo opened the case and passed her another stack of papers. He waited while she went through those. "He also left you nontransferable things. Me, for example. Also his house, his store, and everything in those. His own personal bank account. It's all in trusts so the State can't touch it either."

Alex thought she might vomit and would have if she hadn't already completely emptied her stomach just after breakfast. Her stomach was still busy trying to leave her body through her elbow. She blew her nose into her hospital gown sleeve instead. "Mario Marino is going to have me assassinated."

"No he's not." Milo paused. "At least not immediately. He can't."

"Why not?" Alex couldn't get the blurred text on the page to come into focus.

"Sal named you his heir," Milo explained.

She was obviously missing something. "What does that mean?" Alex flipped the stack of papers back to the beginning and handed them back to Milo. Maybe she could decipher the blurred text later?

Milo put the papers back in his briefcase. "It makes you the head of the family. Until you name your own heir, Mario can't be guaranteed to take over. There are several other men equally qualified who would jump at the chance. Mario is stuck with you."

Alex bit her lower lip. "When did Sal do all this?"

"The day after his birthday. Mario was livid, in case you are wondering. Sal told him about naming you the next head of family, but not about the money and assets. We drew that up separately."

Alex winced.

"Then two days later, he's shot and you're the only witness. Then you go missing. You should have called sooner," Milo admonished. "The coincidence is incriminating."

"I called as soon as I was able." Alex sincerely hoped Milo would believe that. Her life depended on Milo and Sal's brother believing that.

"If it helps any, Miss, Sal told me that you are a gift to the family, even if we don't know it yet. Sal said that he was leaving you all the money and assets so Mario would know he could trust you. He said he was leaving the family to you because he knew you'd be good for them." Milo paused and then continued, "Don't name Mario your heir yet. Take the same deal Sal had; a small stipend from the family while letting Mario continue to run everything.

It's all smoke and mirrors. Everyone knows no one in the family would follow your orders anyway. You aren't family and, forgive me, aren't a man."

Alex recalled he'd been the one to destroy the video surveillance at the gun range. He'd surely viewed at least some of them to get the right ones. He was probably also responsible for the police evidence she and Sal had destroyed. She had no choice but to trust him. "Can you get me out of here?"

Milo's eyes twitched the slightest bit and Alex hoped she hadn't offended him. Milo's voice was unchanged as he responded, "Yes, I have three choices for you as foster homes. All family, of course. Whoever you stay with, though, gains some degree of power within the family. Sal didn't expect to die before you were legally an adult, so he didn't make any arrangements."

"Put me in whichever home Mario wants me in." Alex had no idea how she was going to survive this. "Sal told me I could trust you. Are you going to be ok? Will there be backlash on you for this?"

"My stepmother was a Marino. I'll be fine." Milo took out his cell phone and hit one of the speed-dials. "Mr. Marino, Miss Smith says she will stay with whichever family you'd prefer. Yes. I understand. I'll take care of it." He disconnected. "Rico Marino it is. Sal said he's told you who's who in the family?"

Alex wiped at her nose again. "Yeah, he did."

"Do you have any more questions for me? I can go get the paperwork for the foster family in place so we can get you out of here later today." Milo seemed very calm and certain and his attitude helped soothe Alex's panic although it didn't alleviate it.

Alex rubbed her stomach and willed it to settle. "Thank you, Milo," she said, more from terror than politeness. She couldn't offend him or any Marino in the slightest way.

Switching back to English, Milo said, "It'll be ok, Miss." He stood.

Nothing would ever be ok again, Alex thought. Her only friend was gone and he'd dropped her into a pit of deadly vipers. Why had Sal done that to her? Did he really think his family would tolerate her? Alex had a moment of inspiration. Could she test her status in a non-deadly manner? Alex whispered, "I do have one other thing, Milo."

"Yes?" Milo stopped picking up his briefcase, giving her his complete attention.

Alex swallowed and made herself say, "The painting I gave Sal for his birthday. Do you know where it is?"

Milo raised an eyebrow. "Yes, Mario has it at the restaurant."

Alex frowned. Sal could have least taken it home. Her voice was barely audible as she stated, "I want it destroyed."

"I'll see what I can do," was Milo's steady response. As that was neither a yes nor a no, Alex could place her status as ambiguous at least, which was better than a reply of "You don't get to ask for things."

The psychiatrist and orderlies were waiting outside. To the psychiatrist, Milo said, "I'll be back later this afternoon with a court order to have my client released. She's not to be given more drugs. None. Get her clothes and have her ready."

The psychiatrist frowned unhappily. "I'm going to file a formal protest. This patient is not safe to release. Not to herself or others. She has serious psychological issues that need to be addressed."

Milo did not rise to the bait. "That will be our problem, not yours. Thank you for the use of your office. We took the liberty of turning off your recording device to save your batteries for patient sessions."

The orderlies escorted Alex back to the common room and Alex immediately went over to the window. The limousine was still there. Was Sal's brother in it or had he just sent Milo and Luciano? Did Mario Marino believe she didn't know about this? What had Sal done to her? She saw Milo come out of the building and get into the limousine. She was unable to see who else was inside.

Milo returned that afternoon as promised. The staff hadn't returned her clothes yet so there was some scramble while they did that. They'd also forced her to take yet another mind-dulling, "calming", sedative so she was particularly brain-fogged and uncoordinated. Her hands hadn't stopped shaking and the orderlies had to help her dress. The actual checkout went very quickly and Alex found herself outside in the bright Alabama afternoon sun.

Milo helped her to the limousine, not commenting on her inability to walk steadily. He assisted her into the back and climbed in himself. They were the only two passengers. This limousine was obviously rented with a somewhat gaudy interior that was entirely seats and without a food or drink counter.

"Take me to Sal's grave, please," Alex mumbled in Italian. She leaned back, closed her eyes, and fell asleep.

"We're at a gas station, Miss. Do you need to use the restroom?" It took her a moment to comprehend the sentences. Milo was speaking to her and waving his hand in front of her eyes.

Alex whimpered and nodded and Milo assisted her out of the limousine. The sun had set, but the heat hit her like she had just stepped into an oven.

"Are you ok enough to go by yourself or do you need help?" Milo's voice sounded unnaturally loud.

Alex leaned against the limousine. The brightly glittering lights of the gas station made her head hurt. "I'll be fine. Just give me a minute. What time is it?"

Milo glanced at his watch. "Just after 9 pm, Miss. We're still in Alabama though, so it's really 10 pm our time."

It took Alex a lot longer than a minute to use the facilities, but she felt better once she'd splashed her face with cold water.

When she came out finally, Milo offered, "Can I get you a drink or anything to eat? You slept through dinner."

Alex wasn't sure she'd be able to eat. "Um. Any kind of fresh fruit and water, please. If I can afford it?"

Milo gave her an odd look. "You have just over half a million dollars, not including any physical assets, or any cash Sal has stored inside his house. I think we can find you some fruit."

It was his use of "we" that made Alex actually focus. Near the front of the car, she saw both a driver and a bodyguard. She felt like she should know their names, but she was too groggy to think about it. Milo sent the driver inside for food. The driver was also wearing guns under his coat so he was also likely a bodyguard.

Once they were seated inside the limousine again, Alex felt like she should say something, anything to break the awkward silence. "You handle all my finances?"

"I took care of everything for Sal. It's up to you whether you want me to continue doing so for you. I have all your records ready for whenever you'd like to go over them." Milo politely did not point out that she was clearly not coherent enough to review them at that moment.

Alex wondered when she would wake up. She and Sal could have a hearty laugh over this nightmarish dream. "So what is it that you do exactly? Sal told me you were his man of affairs."

Milo replied, "Whatever you need me to, actually. In addition to handling finances and legal issues, I'm a capable bodyguard. I can take care of anything that annoys you. I can procure things, legal or otherwise. I'm family."

She digested this. She wondered if he could get what she needed for the first battery. She weighed in with, "I wish you could get Sal back for me."

Milo sighed. "I miss him, too. He was a good man."

The driver returned with a bag of assorted fruit (likely every fresh fruit they had in the convenience market) and a bag of different types of bottled water. "We'll be underway shortly. Would you be interested in stopping at a hotel for the evening or shall we drive straight through?"

Milo looked to Alex, who then asked, "When is Mario expecting us?"

Milo answered, "Whenever we get there will be soon enough."

Alex looked back at the driver. "If you get tired, stop, otherwise, go on through."

"Yes, Miss." He closed the door. A moment later they heard him open the front and get in. The car began to move.

"This is going to be very strange," Alex commented. "Thank you for helping me navigate it. I still feel like I'm walking on a tightrope above a deadly pit."

"Every day that passes, the less close to death you'll get, I think. Give Mario a chance to get used to you," Milo advised.

Alex lifted her hand and wiggled her fingers, noticing how uncoordinated they were. Then she realized what she was doing and lowered her hand back onto her knee. "Do we know which family killed Sal yet?"

Milo pretended not to notice her hand. "Yes, I think so. Mario will know for sure. I don't think whoever did it realized exactly how much damage they'd do. No one expected the financial glitch."

Alex winced. "How badly was the family hurt by that?"

"We'll recover," Milo reported. "There were some penalties and overdue bills, but no property was lost. Another month and we'd've had to start selling things."

Alex was going to have to pay the family back before she could even think about her business. "I should be able to recoup the losses selling antiques."

"The store was pretty well destroyed," Milo informed her.

"I know. I was there." Alex pushed the memory that tried to resurface out of her mind. "I was actually thinking I could go to some of the auctions and resell things." She yawned and continued tiredly, "I know what to get and who to sell to. Sal trained me. It shouldn't take too long. Just give me an amount and I'll get it. If I can pay back the family, maybe they won't hate me as much."

"It's an interesting idea, but while Sal's inheritance is fully protected, anything you earn would go straight to the State." Milo spoke gently. "Foster care doesn't grant financial autonomy. You should avoid being adopted due to family politics. Hmmm... Although given your unknown past, that would get tied up in a search for your parents until it was too late to matter."

"Are you responsible for my unknown past?" Alex needed to know who else knew about her and this was the best opportunity she was likely to get.

"It was Sal's wish, yes." Milo's eyes shifted away from her briefly. He'd definitely seen the police records Alex and Sal had burned.

"Thank you." Alex leaned back and closed her eyes.

Milo added, "I'm it, though. It was just me and Sal. No one else saw anything. You'd have to have an eye-witness step forward who recognizes you and you look a lot different now than you did when you were eight. The hackers that were hired to delete the data don't have any link back to the family, and I personally made sure they kept no records."

Alex nodded and forced herself to sit up again, realizing she hadn't tried eating anything despite asking for food. She didn't want to insult Milo or the driver and so she dutifully dug through the bag with the fruit and selected the best looking apple. Then she took out some water. She unscrewed the lid and sipped at it. Her stomach swirled threateningly. She took a bite of the apple and chewed it really well before swallowing. It also landed in her stomach like a tornado. She set them aside.

Milo frowned. "What did they give you today?"

92

Alex hoped he would understand. She didn't want to throw up again. "I don't know. Whatever they've had me on since I called Mario has been giving me the shakes really bad. I can't think clearly."

"You were incoherent when Lu and I stopped by a few days ago," Milo said.

Alex blinked, confused. "You came by?"

"Yes," Milo confirmed. "The doctor gave us a tour of you chained to that bed in a straight jacket. You were mumbling to yourself and didn't answer us when we tried to talk to you. I've never wanted to voluntarily kill someone before. That doctor, though. Lu stopped me."

"I have no recollection of you coming by." That scared her. "What was I saying?"

"I don't know. It sounded like math, maybe." Milo helped himself to one of the water bottles from her bag.

Alex groaned. There was only one math formula she was likely to recite. The last person she wanted to know her new physics formula was that awful psychiatrist. Why couldn't she have been given into the care of someone who would actually listen to her? "Was there surveillance?"

Milo rubbed at his chin. "I'm not sure."

"Shit." Alex needed to believe that Milo was telling the truth about being in her employ now. "Ok, your priority once you drop me off is to go find out. Destroy any video of me, any recordings that psychiatrist might have. All of it."

"Can do." After a few minutes, Milo prompted, "So... math?"

Alex reached over to the limousine's control panel and dimmed the lights a bit. Then she put her feet up on the opposite seat and leaned back. "I've been working on a few things I don't want anyone to know."

Milo turned in his seat to get more comfortable. "You don't want anyone to know you can do math?"

"Something like that," Alex glossed over. The last thing she need was her perpetual energy formula getting out. "Sal and I had an agreement that I'd not draw any attention to myself." She dozed off for a while until the car went over a bump and woke her up. Then it hit her - she thought she'd been tied down two days. "What day is it today?"

When Milo told her, Alex closed her eyes again in disturbed silence. A week. She'd been out for a week.

As requested, the limousine brought Alex and Milo directly to the cemetery. It was raining with thick dark clouds obscuring the midday early spring sun. Alex asked Milo which grave and asked him to wait when he pointed. She didn't take the umbrella Milo offered.

Leaving Milo behind, Alex walked over to the tall stone plaque in front of the family crypt. The plaque was a beautiful orange-hued marble engraved simply with his name and the dates. Although wet, the flowers were recently changed and were barely wilting at all.

"Sal, I remember everything," Alex whispered. "As long as I'm alive, you aren't gone."

Alex sat down next to the stone and rested her head on the plaque. She didn't care that she was sitting in mud or that the rain was going to soak her completely. That was fitting. She was drenched when she met him. She'd be drenched when she said goodbye. The thought made her cry and once she started crying, she couldn't stop.

Eventually, Milo came over with the umbrella. He helped her stand and walked her back to the car.

"I'm too wet to get in," Alex said at last, wiping at her face, unknowingly smearing more mud on her face from her hand.

"Don't worry about it. Here, you can sit on my coat." Milo took off his suit coat and laid it out on the seat. "I called Mario and told him we'd be going by Rico's house before coming to see him. We moved all your clothes from the apartment over there and you can get changed."

Alex turned the compartment's heat up to maximum and sat there, shivering. After a few minutes, she warmed up enough to think and asked, "Isn't your suit coat more expensive than this limo seat?"

Milo grinned. "It is, but I didn't want you standing outside any longer and you looked like you might argue. That rain is cold. My coat will clean or it will be replaced. You, on the other hand, can't be replaced."

Rico Marino met them at the door of a narrow, two-story row house in desperate need of renovation. Rico was a comfortably-sized businessman whose facial wrinkles looked like he spent most of his time being cheerful and laughing. He had a pronounced widows peak hairline that didn't look at all like Sal or Mario. "Welcome to our home, Miss."

Alex stepped up and shook his hand. She needed to make these people like her. She just wished she didn't feel like vomiting at the man's feet. "Thank you for taking me in, Mr. Marino. I won't be any trouble. You'll hardly know I'm here."

"It's no trouble. I'm glad to be helpful to the family." He called over his shoulder, "Emma, they're here."

His wife appeared in the small hallway to greet them. Alex saw Rico wipe his hand unobtrusively on his pants in her peripheral vision. Whatever Emma had planned to say, she cut off when she saw Alex's clothes and face. "You're soaking! Let's get you some dry clothes. Your room is this way." Emma led

Alex up the narrow staircase which became an equally narrow hallway. Milo stayed to talk with Rico and the two of them moved farther into the house out of earshot.

Alex repeated her thank you to Mrs. Marino.

"Nothing to worry about, Miss. We have the extra room."

"Please call me Alex and tell your husband to do the same. I don't want to be a burden."

Emma pointed out the bathroom a few doors down from the room she identified as Alex's. The bedroom was small, but they'd brought in her desk and drawing supplies. It only had a twin-size bed and tiny window, but it was clean. Alex thanked her again and Emma retreated back downstairs.

Alex crossed to the closet and saw the clothes Sal had given her and she bit her lip to keep from crying again. She picked out a pair of jeans and a black t-shirt. From the dresser, she retrieved undergarments and a towel. She then went down the hall to the bathroom.

Her reflection in the mirror was terrifying. Her face was gaunt and bony and her eye sockets were sunken and dark. Her skin was a pasty grey, liberally smeared with mud. She stripped and put her wet clothes in the sink and turned on the shower. While she waited for the water to get warm, Alex rinsed out her clothes and wrung them out. She was quick in the shower, despite the lure of heat, and she used the shampoo and soap that were already in the shower and hoped that would be ok.

Alex wished she had her toothbrush. She used the comb on the sink. When she was done dressing again, her color wasn't quite as grey, but she still looked cadaverous. She took her damp clothes back to her room and draped them on the desk's chair to dry. She grabbed her light jacket and headed downstairs. She couldn't afford to irritate anyone by taking too long.

Alex found Milo and Rico in the small kitchen toward the back of the house, seated at a small worn wood table. The formica countertops were clear of everything except an expresso machine, breadbox, and bowl of fresh fruit. Alex pulled at her shirt, straightening it. She saw the table itself merely had a small flat dish with a variety of vitamins and prescriptions medications on it.

Milo immediately stood and with a simple parting nod to Rico, escorted her out. In the limousine, Alex tried to drink more water, but it just made her nauseous. She wasn't sure if she should blame nerves or post-medication.

"Would something else be better? I can get you anything," Milo observed quietly.

"Maybe later." Alex's insides swirled threateningly.

The restaurant was almost exactly as Alex remembered it - low light, white and red tablecloths, real china. Scattered bodyguards. Sal's brother, Mario, was at one of the back tables, surrounded by family in an informal meeting. There was something about one of the men standing there that troubled her, but Alex was too light-headed and brain-fogged to recognize what. She would have to figure out who he was later.

Everyone seemed to stare at them as Alex and Milo entered. Mario excused himself from his group and said something to one of the men, who then approached them. Mario himself disappeared into the back of the restaurant. The man nodded deferentially to Milo. To Alex, he said, "Come. He wants to talk to you."

Milo gave her a reassuring pat on the shoulder and Alex followed the man into the back. Sal describing this particular family member snapped into focus in her memory. She knew the man's name, his wife and kids, his tendencies, his trustworthiness, and his weapons of choice. Alex wished she also had time to remember Sal describing everyone else in the restaurant. She inhaled deeply and continued along.

In the back of the restaurant, her escort knocked twice on a wooden door, waited for the gruff "Enter," and opened it, standing aside and letting Alex pass into the room. He closed the door again after her, staying on the outside. This room had a beautiful table, surrounded by six brown leather chairs. There were photographs of Italy on the windowless walls. It could have been a private dining room, except for the safe and lockable filing cabinets. Sal's brother was standing. Alex went over to one of the chairs and steadied herself by holding onto it. They stared at each other in silence.

Alex could see Sal's features on Mario's face. His eyes, the shape of his mouth and ears. Even Mario's stance reminded her of Sal's, except there was no warmth in Mario's gaze. He looked at her as if she were a particularly distasteful problem he had to solve, one that he'd prefer to put a bullet in and toss in the ocean somewhere. Dark circles under his eyes reflected his recent lack of sleep.

Alex began in Italian, "I would have saved him if I could have. I tried."

Mario's hard gaze didn't soften. "I have the security footage. For a while I thought you were quite the actress."

"I would have given my life for him, Mario," Alex said softly. "He was my only friend."

Mario sighed tiredly. "Sit down. It would be easier if I didn't believe you."

Alex carefully lowered herself into the chair she was holding on to and Mario sat across from her.

Mario frowned at her. "We have things that need to be taken care of for the family."

Alex nodded. "I'll do whatever you need me to. You have my full cooperation and support. Sal never should have done what he did and if I had known his intentions, I would have talked him out of it. I swear."

"You'll name me heir at the next family meeting and pass the title back to me," Mario instructed coldly.

Alex didn't hesitate. "Absolutely." Her survival depended on him believing he could trust her and that she was valuable to keep alive. "As soon as I am able, I have every intention of repaying the family for all of the monetary losses incurred from this debacle."

Mario scoffed at that. Angrily, he growled, "You are a child and a girl. You cannot possibly begin to comprehend what this has done."

Alex, realizing she needed his respect, too, answered with an equally angry tone, "If Sal wanted me to look after his family, he only needed to ask. He didn't have to go through all this nonsense to tie me to you and the family."

"You? Look after us?" Mario scoffed.

"I'm going to be the richest person alive," she declared.

"Artists don't make that much, kid," Mario said derisively.

"Artist?" Alex was confused for a moment. "Oh. That painting. That wasn't art. Sal knew that. Didn't he tell you what it was?" She was trying to find out if he knew about the perpetual energy. Probably not, or he would already know her value, unless he didn't believe it, which was also possible.

"No. We didn't discuss it. I wondered why you gave him something that wasn't his type of thing at all." Mario looked like he wondered why they were talking about the painting at all.

Relieved, Alex lied, "It was a game, an eclectic mix of styles. A tribute of sorts to all the museums he kept taking me to. But that's irrelevant. As soon as I'm legally able, I'm going into business." Yes, let that painting be unimportant. Let it be destroyed.

"What kind of business?" Mario's voice held more than a little bit of contempt and condescension. He was already a formidable businessman.

Alex really needed this man to see her as an equal. She paced her reply to sound confident and determined. "I trusted Sal. I don't trust you. He worked with me on the business details. You, on the other hand... I know you want me dead and out of your life forever."

The corner of Mario's mouth lifted up in amusement in a way that so reminded Alex of Sal that she could have wept. "By all means, let us be honest with each other."

Alex continued, because amusement was a lot better than hatred. "It would be bad for the family if I died, but you don't know me well enough to realize that yet. All I ask is that you give me a chance." She breathed in deeply and pushed on. "Don't have me killed. I promise you my full support in anything you need from me. I'll stay out of your way. I won't ask for anything. I won't do or say anything to ever harm the family. As my wealth grows, I'll see the family gets its share. For Sal."

Mario stared at her in disbelief. "That's not what I expected you to say today."

"Yeah, well, when I called you, I expected you to put me to work being a maid or a courier or something to pay for the rescue from the hospital." Alex very carefully avoided including bodyguard or assassin on that list.

Sal's brother rubbed his chin. "I'll see you tomorrow. We have a family meeting. Come beforehand and I will tell you what to say," he directed stonily.

Alex nodded and rose from the chair, clearly dismissed. She stumbled out and went in search of Milo. He was reading at a table. When she approached, he pointed at the chair opposite him, indicated that she should sit down, and waved at one of the waitresses. The waitress immediately brought a full plate of fine Italian food and set it in front of the empty chair. Alex sat down tiredly and stared at the mountain of food in dismay. No doubt the veal parmesan and spaghetti were worthy of a five-star restaurant. She took one of the slices of toasted garlic bread and tried a bite. It went into her stomach like a lump of clay, but at least it didn't spin and twist and make her feel like heaving. She nibbled a bit more.

Milo's finger remained in the book, marking the page, and he said quietly, "Luciano is taking care of that task you asked for. You need me here for tomorrow."

Alex inclined her head in acknowledgement. "Could you take me back to Rico's? I need sleep."

"After you eat," Milo said firmly.

"I can't eat this much, Milo."

"More than two bites of bread, at least. And drink some of this water." Milo pushed Alex's water glass toward her, and went back to reading his book. It wasn't rudeness, but a kind way not to demand more of her than she currently had to give.

Alex set the bread down and took the glass with both hands to keep it steady and drank. It helped the dissolve the clay-feeling of the bread. She ate more bread. Then she sipped more water. After a few more repeats of this, so very slowly, she tried a small bite of the veal. Indeed, it was exquisitely prepared and magnificent. With just a little bit at a time, and a lot of pauses, Alex managed to eat until she felt full although the plate was still mostly uneaten when she was finished. She ignored people staring at her curiously and noted people who looked at her with malice. The latter unfortunately outnumbered the previous.

Alex awoke around three in the morning, hungry again, but finally clearing up mentally. She rolled out of bed, changed into fresh clothes, grabbed her jacket, and tip-toed downstairs. She hit a single squeaky stair, went through her memory which was finally starting to function again, recalled where the other squeaks were, and avoided the rest of them. She went to the kitchen and took some fruit from the refrigerator. As an afterthought, she also tore off some bread from the loaf on the counter and pocketed that also.

By the door, Alex put on her shoes and slipped out into the pre-morning darkness. The night sounds still promised danger, yet were so comfortingly familiar. She followed the shadows to the antiques shop.

The shop's broken windows were boarded up and police tape was generously applied across the whole storefront, including the door. There was still glass in the street. Alex went around to the back, entered the combination to the lock, and went in. The storage area was a mess, with chalk outlines and blood where the men who'd come in the back died, but everywhere Alex looked, she could see Sal with perfect clarity as he moved around, unpacking, repacking, setting things aside for sale.

Alex moved farther into the store, turning up the heat in passing. She stopped in the bathroom to use it. There was dried blood on the hand towel where someone had washed their hands, but not well enough. She took a clean towel from under the sink and hung it up neatly after using it to dry her hands. The other towel she left draped on the sink.

Sal's office was ransacked. Papers were everywhere. The safe was cut open and any contents were long-gone. The file cabinet drawers were dumped on the floor. Alex left that mess and went out to the main store. That also was as she remembered it on that horrible day. Broken pottery, bullet-shredded furniture. More footprints in blood than she recalled. The large, dried puddle of red-brown that was all that remained of Sal was still there. The cash register was open and empty. Alex went back to the kitchen and started filling one of the large spaghetti pots with warm water. While she waited, she remembered her card from the Hamasaki family. To her delight, she found it still wedged in one of the box-storage shelves' frame. She pocketed it and went back to the sink where the pot was just finished filling.

The back door security box beeped and when the door opened, Alex called out, "It's ok, guys, it's just me." That proved the silent security alarm was still functioning. The two men came up to the kitchen with their guns drawn anyway. She recognized them.

Alex made no sudden moves and kept her hands in the air next to her head. "False alarm," she offered tentatively. "I'm just here to clean up." She saw recognition in their eyes, but they didn't lower their guns. "It's about time it gets done, don't you think?" She waited, counting silently in her head, preparing to defend herself.

After a full minute, one of them lowered his gun and said, "You need to call security before coming in here so we can cancel the alarm."

"Thank you. I'll remember that in the future." She didn't have her phone. She didn't have their number. Was the shop's phone still connected?

The other man lowered his gun and put it away. Alex escorted them out and closed the door again. She went back, took the stained towel from the bathroom and the pot of water, and went to clean up.

Around mid morning, Alex heard the back door keypad again and the door open. She was unsurprised when Milo appeared. The floor was almost finished.

Milo frowned as he saw her on her hands and knees. "You don't have to clean up. Now that the money isn't frozen, we can get a cleaning crew."

"No one comes in here but me. They wouldn't know what's salvageable and it would risk breaking even more." Alex stood up, stretching. It was time to swap the water again anyway.

"You need to tell Rico or Emma where you are at all times," Milo instructed. "In case the social workers come by. That psychiatrist filed another complaint this morning. He wasn't too pleased about his office getting broken into last night. As Luciano only destroyed your files, the guy must have been specifically looking for your case."

Alex took the pan of dirty water back to the kitchen, letting Milo follow. "I'm glad it's taken care of. Tell Luciano thank you for me."

Milo watched her empty the pot with disapproving eyes. "I will. Why don't you wash up and I'll take you to get something to eat."

Alex ignored this. "Bring something here. What time do I need to meet Mario?"

Milo didn't argue, although Alex could tell from his stance that he wanted to. "6 p.m. What would you like me to bring?"

"Anything fresh. Fruits, vegetables, unsalted and oil-free nuts. A clean protein if you can find it." Alex began refilling the pot.

"Ok," Milo conceded, but added, "If you leave here, let me know?"

Alex tilted her head at him. "How?"

Milo hmmm'd. "Good point. You didn't get your things back. I'll see if I can find your phone."

"And my laptop," Alex added. "The F.B.I. apparently has it. Speaking of which, how come you guys couldn't find me? I'm guessing you were looking. With the money frozen, it had to be pretty important to find me." She tried not to sound like she was reprimanding him, but it was difficult. Why hadn't they come for her sooner?

"We were looking," Milo declared. "Desperately so. We even talked with our contacts at the police station. You just vanished."

"That shouldn't have been possible. I was at the station for quite a while," explained Alex. "I kept expecting you guys to bail me out. The whole time I knew Sal was probably dying. It about drove me crazy."

"Apparently did drive you crazy," Milo stated. "What were you doing at the psychiatric hospital?"

Alex didn't try to hide her disgust and frustration as she replied, "They were trying to make me confess to Sal's corrupt sexual relations with a minor. They didn't find any condemning evidence on my laptop so they needed my testimony. They were going to arrest him and throw Mario in for complicity."

"Oh." Milo's frown deepened and his eyebrows pulled together in thought.

"Apparently they can't get them for something real and need to fabricate evidence." Alex exhaled and picked up the pot of water. She walked back toward the front of the shop. Milo followed. "Which is good, I suppose. I wouldn't give them anything to work with and it pissed them off so they sent me for psychiatric evaluation, convinced that it was my fear of the family that prevented me from talking. They recorded everything. I thought you guys had all of it and that's why Mario didn't have me killed."

Alex set down the water near the next section of floor and turned to Milo, "Look, I really just want to be alone for a while. I won't leave the shop."

"I'll go get you some food." He still looked deeply troubled.

Alex nodded and lowered herself back to her knees. Milo let himself out. Alex stopped and buried her face in her hands and rubbed at her temples. She could leave, she supposed. She could disappear. Head west and south. Relocate into Mexico, maybe. Rico wouldn't be able to foster or adopt, but she doubted he ever desired that to begin with. Sal's assets would just sit in legal limbo, but they were really insignificant compared to the family holdings which were already released.

Alas, there was the not-so-minor issue of Sal making her head of the family, making her responsible for his family. Just because the family didn't want her involved didn't mean she wasn't. She sighed. She couldn't leave. Sal had glued her feet to this path and he'd known she would see it through for him.

After she finished cleaning up the bulk of the gore, she cleaned out the refrigerator. Several month old food was pretty rank. She took one of the larger packing boxes out behind the shop and started using that as the waste bin.

Milo arrived after a short time with several filled grocery bags. "Do you want help unpacking this?"

Alex shook her head. "No thank you, Milo. I've got it."

Milo contemplated her as she began unpacking the groceries, and then said, "I'll come by to pick you up at 4:30."

Alex put the last of the fruit into the now-clean refrigerator bin. "I thought I wasn't needed until 6?"

"You'll want time to go home and change. You should dress up for the meeting," Milo explained.

"Ah, ok." Alex turned to the other grocery bag. She was getting hungry and the medication-shakes had mostly worn off.

Milo nodded to her and left.

While Alex was eating a carrot, it occurred to her that she might be able to restore the broken things once she had her inventions working. She was planning on doing a lot of molecular rearranging anyway, so how hard would it be to reassemble antiques? It would be a good exercise at the very least.

Alex started at the top shelves and worked her way down. Everything broken got carefully wrapped and put in a big box in the back labelled "NFS - Not For Sale". Tiny pieces and sandy grit were collected into a large ziplock bag and saved. At each item, she paused and remembered Sal's lecture on it - where it was from, what made it valuable, how much it was worth. She barely got two shelves done before Milo was back.

As commanded, Alex waited at the back of the large, very private room in the restaurant, leaning against the soundproofed, wood-paneled wall. The room was still empty, but it was exactly as Sal had described it. She even knew which chair was his. When Sal had been telling her about these family meetings and its attendees, she'd thought he was just being chatty and reminiscing. Alex was going to have to go back through all of their conversations and consider them with this new insight.

Alex had changed into a black dress that she knew only made her look more pale and gaunt, and perhaps a touch sinister. She wore the simple gold chain necklace that Sal had given her and her hair was newly trimmed - Milo had slipped in a hair salon visit, too.

Milo was going to be mad. He recommended not naming a heir, but Alex thought giving Mario her full support was the better option. It was also part of what Sal's brother had dictated she say. "Screw this," Alex whispered to herself and went and sat in Sal's old chair to the right of the chair Mario would take. It was going to be her chair now and if she didn't claim it, someone else would. Sal had been very clear about chair seats indicating pecking order.

The men of the family entered as a group, with Mario coming in last. Each and every one of them saw her and frowned disapprovingly, except for Milo, who saw where Alex was sitting and closed his eyes a moment, looking like he was saying a quick prayer. As Sal's brother approached her, Alex stood up and nodded to him deferentially. Everyone sat down and Alex remained standing.

Alex cleared her throat. Off script, she said in Italian, "Before we get started, I'd like to apologize to everyone here for the recent problem with the family money and offer my condolences on the loss of Mr. Marino."

The uproar settled when Mario waved his hand. "Go on," Sal's brother commanded her. The underlying harshness promised severe violence if Alex failed to perform as directed.

Once again, Alex did not go from the script, which was ignored in her hand. The message, however, would be exactly the same, but wouldn't make her sound like a whimpering fool. "The family cannot continue in its current state of political unrest. Many of you have claim to run the family and would do an excellent job. However, there can only be one, and I trust Sal's choice before he named me. For the good of the family, I will do as Sal did, and step aside and let the right man do the job. Mario will continue to run the family and is henceforth formally my heir in all things." She half-bowed to Mario and sat down. Mario looked like he wanted to throttle her.

"Pretty speech," one of the men growled, "But you do not dictate to us what we do."

Alex said nothing. It was Mario's job to defend himself and seize control.

Mario cut in, "The formality is done. We have business to discuss."

"She can't be here," another of the men snarled.

"She stays," Mario declared firmly, putting his hands on the table and staring down the speaker. That was the one concession Alex had demanded. She had promised not to interrupt, but pointed out she could hardly do the job Sal asked her to if she weren't present to offer input. She'd also given him a frightening taste of how much she knew about the family's business affairs already. If she were going to incriminate them, she would have done it a long time ago.

Mario overruled the objections by setting his gun on the table. The discussions began, with many looking in her direction trying to judge if she'd be a witness to the police. The men talked as much with their hands as with words, and Alex avidly absorbed this body language in case she needed to use it someday.

There was only one topic that concerned Alex and when Sal's brother asked, "Do we know for certain that the Caro family ordered Sal's death?", Alex's attention snapped to sharp focus.

The man at the far side of the table answered, "It's confirmed. Straight from the top. Caro ordered it himself."

There were all sorts of reprisal suggestions. Most were either too risky or too expensive or too mild. Mario listened without comment and when the brainstorming slowed, he announced, "I will think about it and make a decision." The conversation went on to other things and eventually the meeting ended.

A few days later, Milo escorted Alex to Sal's house which was another part of her unsolicited inheritance. The house was a custom built two-story Italian-style Neo-Renaissance building with a flat roof and symmetrical round-arched windows and arched front door. A balustrade railing enclosed the roof. Due to the compressed nature of the city, the surrounding garden was small, if generous when compared to the neighboring houses. Alex had seen it before when exploring, but hadn't known it was Sal's.

Milo punched in the door's security code, opened the door, and stood aside to let Alex pass. The front entranceway was a grand space, with a curving staircase off to the left and an archway off to the right. The large room off the staircase had meticulous antique chairs and a magnificent grand piano. White columns toward the back separated the area from the main house. She recognized some of the famous paintings on the walls and the interior reminded her of an art gallery. Every nuance screamed Sal's name, as if he'd chosen every detail himself.

Alex walked through with Milo following silently. They arrived at a medium-sized, ransacked office. Papers were everywhere. The desk drawers were overturned and both file cabinets emptied.

"I can't imagine Sal leaving the room like this," Alex stated dryly.

"Mario has been through here looking for account information as well as the combination to the family vault," Milo explained. "Technically, the vault is on the premises and now belongs to you, but it's got a lot of the family heirlooms in it. You should consider giving them to Mario."

Milo kept speaking, but Alex didn't hear him. Instead, she saw Sal, clear as a sunny day, bent over a piece of paper in his shop.

"Whatcha doing?" Alex had asked, dropping her book bag behind the counter. She'd just arrived from school.

"I changed all of my accounts, passwords, and combinations. I do that once a year. I'm trying to memorize them. Can't leave these things written down anywhere." Sal grinned at her. "Hey, do me a favor and quiz me."

He handed the paper to Alex and she glanced at it before she realized she shouldn't. "Sal! You shouldn't be giving this to me."

"Why? Are you going to rob me?" Sal had said teasingly.

"No." She'd made a face at him.

"Then be a friend and help me learn them." They'd burned the paper afterwards.

Alex felt like she was spinning in a full circle. Sal must have known even then that he was going to leave everything to her. She tried to focus on Milo. "Hmmm, what did you say?"

"Did he happen to give you anything, Alex? Any paper? Did he tell you the combinations?"

"Not that I recall. I'll have to think about it," Alex lied automatically.

Milo shook his head sadly. "Yeah, I didn't think so. He must have written it down somewhere. That combination hadn't been changed since the vault got put in."

She bet a lot of the other 'annually changed' stuff hadn't ever been changed before either. "Where is the vault?"

"In the basement," answered Milo.

They went through the house, starting upstairs. Every room showcased beautiful original paintings and exquisite antiques. Several had famous statues and vases. One of the sculptures even looked like an original by Gian Lorenzo Bernini. With each room, the Marino family wealth shrunk in comparison to

Sal's personal wealth. Upstairs, Sal's bed was still unmade and some of his clothes were still piled on a nearby chair. His bedroom smelled like him. Alex didn't linger.

Alex and Milo eventually got to the basement. The vault could have come from a bank, given its high end electronics and impenetrable metal. Alex stared at the door, but didn't approach it.

Milo sighed. "Mario has tried every combination he could think of already. If the family money hadn't been frozen, he would have hired someone to come in and cut it open."

"Well, give me some time to think about it. If we have to cut it open, then we have to cut it open. I'll search through the house and store first. Maybe I can find something you guys missed." Alex shrugged. "Let's go get a drink."

When Milo was finally gone and Alex had the house to herself, she went back down to the vault and opened it. Inside, a small mountain of cash and mixed jewelry boxes took up the shelves on one wall while the opposite held crates that she recognized from the gun range and assorted other weapons and gear. The far shelves held several safes and filing boxes. In the center of the otherwise meticulously clean floor was a folded piece of paper with her name on it. She picked it up and read the ornate Italian script.

Alex,

If you are reading this, I'm gone and you are probably terrified. It is my wish that you and my brother become friends and this was the only way I could think of to make that happen. If I can't be there to protect you, he has the resources to do so as well as enough to help you start your business. I made him promise to take care of you, but it will take him time to adjust. Go easy on him. He has a lot of responsibilities. I imagine you've already signed over everything you could, but I cannot leave this house and the store to him. He won't know the value of things and someone will take advantage of that. Sell it, use the money for your business, whatever you want. It's yours. I wish I could have been there to see your new world. I would have liked it very much.

All my love and all my faith,

Salvatore

Alex sat down and leaned against one of the gun crates and thought. What could she do to make Mario trust her? An hour later, she knew. It would risk her whole future on one night, but if successful, she could stop being afraid and actually focus on her plans. She could trust Mario to leave her alone and with any luck, she could leave behind all the garbage in her life that was holding her back, and never have to do anything illegal again for a very long time. And it was justice, if not legal. She set the note back where she'd found it, closed and locked the vault. Then she went to the office in search of some blank paper and a pen. She needed supplies.

Four days later, Alex finished up the last of the arrangements. The audio recordings were ready. The cardboard shadow controllers were set up and tested. The cash was out for the pizza. Climbing rope, weapons, grapples, gloves, new clothes, new shoes, wigs, all set and stashed in an also new backpack. She called Milo and met him at Sal's front door. She was just finishing her note to Mario.

She'd written, "Mario, tell everyone to have an alibi tonight. Everyone with a gun. An undeniable, non-family alibi, until at least 2 a.m. At 7:30, I will call you and ask you to come to Sal's house. Arrive at exactly 8 p.m., not a moment earlier or later. Bring your Fed surveillance with you, but leave them (and everyone else) outside, and let yourself in. They're our alibi. Do not deviate from instructions. Destroy this note."

Alex signed the paper and handed it to Milo. "Give this to Mario directly. Don't let anyone else see it."

Milo scanned the note. "May I ask what you are doing?"

"I'm having a private meeting with Mario. That's all. I mentioned the Caro family's involvement in Sal's murder to some of my old street friends. They suggested tonight would be a good night for a family party." She shrugged. "You get an alibi for tonight, too. Don't come by Sal's house. I'm going to have a very private and frank conversation with Mario and it does not need your witness."

"You aren't planning to kill Mario?" Milo asked trepidatiously.

"Good grief, no. Mario's family." Yes, Milo had definitely viewed the video at the gun range that one time and he surely knew Sal's gun collection was in the house. Milo had probably even arranged some of the other lessons Sal had provided. "As much as Mario hates me, he's still Sal's brother and I won't dishonor my best friend's apparent last wish. It's just a conversation. Please make sure Mario does as that says. It won't matter to the family if he doesn't, but it will matter to me."

Milo looked like he wanted to say something else, but instead, he nodded, half-bowed and left. As soon as she made sure he'd driven off and wasn't coming back, she took her cell phone back to her laptop and connected it. The timer would call Mario and play the recording. She grabbed the backpack she'd prepared and slipped out through the back door of the house.

Alex was a different person by time she crossed the first public surveillance cameras, but she still did not allow her face to be seen. Three hours later, approximately 7:30 p.m., sturdy hiking got her to a subway station about 15 miles from Sal's house. She blended with the crowd. She changed costumes again. Shortly thereafter, she was at the Caro residence, where she watched and waited. She timed the security guard patrols. Her targets arrived home and settled in. The kids were put to bed. The sun set.

Eventually, the lights in the house went out. The parents' bedroom light came on. The bathroom light came on. The lights went out again. The evening security patrol went by. Alex cut the phone and internet connection to the house by triggering the tiny remote bomb on the electrical box down the street. The whole neighborhood would be without landlines, but it would kill the remote security warnings, showing up as a temporary outage. She was inside the house a few minutes later, glass panel cut on the window with the tiniest of holes, security alarm connection bypassed, window opened, her inside, window closed, all before the patrol went by again. She was quiet, despite the added bulk of profile-changing padding. Any accidentally missed video would show someone taller, bulkier, male, in a ski mask. Even her head shape was different with padding. The house was silent.

Upstairs, the first room she looked in had two sleeping children. Pity that. She left them sleeping. Both parents were sound asleep when she entered their room. They were silently dead within seconds, knife across the throat, through their vocal cords, through their carotid arteries. She left the knife buried to the hilt in the patriarch of the Caro family.

Alex didn't pause. She was out of the house again in under five minutes. Next, a half hour of waiting in a bush before she could get by the evening patrol, with her heart traitorously pounding. Through the streets, in the shadows, a clothing change. Back through the subway. Clothing change again. Just in case.

The unmarked police car outside Sal's house as well as the limousine waiting on the street suggested Mario had indeed arrived on time. Alex went around the back and made sure there were no other observers before sneaking in the back door.

"So you agree these papers should be burned?" Alex's recorded voice came from the front study, where the outside officers and their listening devices could clearly hear it.

"Yes," Mario answered, reading from the script, yet at a fine, natural pace. "Is that wine barrel still in the kitchen?"

"I think so," her prerecorded voice answered.

"Let's use that."

Alex was busy stripping down and throwing her clothes into the barrel. Mario entered just as she was tossing in her underwear. She was naked. She bared her teeth crazily at him at him and reached over to the table where she'd left some of her own clothes. She put those on and took a clean washcloth, wiped her hands and then any dirt on the floor. She tossed the washcloth into the barrel, too.

"You know what? Let me toss these old newspapers in too. It'll beat dumping them in a landfill somewhere," Alex said, as if she'd been conversing

107

with him all evening.

"Good idea." The script had run out on "bring that cardboard cutout of me into the kitchen; I'll meet you there."

Together, they rolled the barrel out through the front door, in plain view of the unmarked police car, and added lighter fluid. When the fire was high enough, they made a show of tossing in the script Mario had been reading from.

For the sake of the surveillance car's audio pickup, Alex said, "There. No more nasty love letters to smear Sal's reputation."

"I appreciate you bringing these to my attention. Some of the family would have been very hurt reading those." Mario was not slow.

"Let me just reiterate to you: I am loyal to the family," Alex said. "Sal was my very best and only friend. I will never, ever let any harm come to the family if I can prevent it."

"I'm beginning to believe you." Mario's eyes were calculating. "It's late. How about if I drop you off at Rico's?"

"Sure, let me get my books and lock up and I'll meet you in the limo." Alex went back to the house, securely deleted the recordings from her laptop, disassembled the robotics that had been used to move the cardboard cutout of her in front of the light with such pristine animation for a shadow on the window curtain for the police surveillance, grabbed her backpack and laptop and left, locking the door behind her.

In the limousine on the drive over to Rico's, they didn't say a word. Mario dropped her off at Rico's house where Rico and his wife were entertaining a couple from Rico's office - non-family. Alex greeted them politely and went up to her room. Her adrenaline suddenly dropped off and she began shaking. She crawled into bed, fully dressed, and curled up. For a long time, she stared straight ahead, unseeing.

Early the next day, Milo arrived at Rico's house to tell Alex she was summoned to speak with Mario. Alex was picking at, but not eating, some strawberries for breakfast. Her stomach was still clenched in knots from the night before. Rico had already left for work and Emma was upstairs doing laundry.

"What's up?" Alex asked, feigning ignorance.

"The head of the Caro family was murdered last night along with his wife. Police are going to be all over the place, interviewing everyone, checking alibis," Milo informed her dryly.

"Really?" Alex sighed. "That's certainly going to cause some trouble."
Milo squinted at her.

Alex added, "The other families aren't going to be very happy. That's two patriarchs. I hope it isn't a trend. I'd be in the running." Alex called upstairs,

"Emma, I'm going with Milo over to the restaurant." Alex put the uneaten fruit in the refrigerator and her plate in the sink.

As they got into the limousine, Alex commented, "I think she's happier when I'm not there. I make her uncomfortable."

They rode over in silence. Milo studied her the whole time. Alex looked out of the window and ignored his gaze.

Mario was already in his office when they arrived and Alex was immediately escorted back. Mario dismissed the two men with him and after they left, Alex went over to a chair and sat down without being invited to do so.

Mario began to say something, but Alex cut him off with a gesture. "Before the police get here, did anything go off script?"

"No." Mario also sat down. "Did you do it?"

"Sal told me never to tell you he had me trained. It was for self-defense. To protect me, you understand, not to become an assassin." Alex nodded, just once, but that wouldn't show up on any voice recorder. "I can use all of his guns."

"Caro was killed with a knife." Mario pinched his lips together in a frown.

"Messy," Alex replied.

"Rumors are saying it would have required a highly skilled assassin. No one saw or heard anything until one of the kids went to wake their mom up for a drink of water around 2 a.m." Mario rested one hand on the table, but his other hand remained suspiciously close to his gun.

"Isn't that type thing expensive?" Alex inquired brightly.

Mario's eyebrows scrunched together, reminding Alex so much of Sal that she flinched.

"The police can follow the money trail to who's responsible," Alex explained. "I mean, we didn't pay for it, did we?"

"No." Mario looked thoughtful.

"I can't say I'm particularly sorry they got killed," Alex went on. "Caro had Sal murdered. You might even say I'm glad."

"I didn't order this," Mario admonished.

"We'll send flowers to the funeral," Alex offered.

After a moment, Mario admitted, "I underestimated you."

"I know." Alex said this with a calm assurance she really didn't feel. She needed to convince Mario that she was family.

With a quietly low, deliberately menacing voice, Mario asked, "So was last night's demonstration you threatening me?"

Alex shook her head firmly. Setting her tone to a frank authority, she stated, "Sal left the family to me. I won't dishonor him. He was my best and only friend. I'm going to keep repeating that until the family understands. He. Was. My. Best. And. Only. Friend." With a harsh grit in her voice, she growled, "It was my BLOOD RIGHT. I'm not your blood, but Sal was mine." Then, more gently, she said, "Besides, you have his eyes. The worst I could ever do to you or any of the family is abandon you. I asked you there because I have to trust you. I can't go on not sleeping, thinking you are going to come after me at any moment. I need you to see my value so you'll stop hating me, stop trying to cut me out."

Mario nodded at this. There wasn't complete trust in his eyes yet, but there was finally respect. He inquired, "Do you want to claim the kill?"

"We send flowers to the funeral," she repeated. "We'll buy them on a 2 for 1 sale. You can do that if they're equivalent flowers. Just leave the receipt with them. The message will get across."

Mario hesitated, pondering, and then decided, "Welcome to the family, Alex Smith."

"Thank you, Mario Marino." Interview over, she stood. She reached in her pocket and withdrew a small slip of paper and set it on his table. On her way out, she said softly, "That's the combination to the vault. Everything inside is as he left it, including his note to me. Also, all of the account passwords."

When Alex went back out into the restaurant's main room, she saw the man who'd troubled her that first night when she arrived back from the hospital. He was married to one of the Marino women. They had no children. Sal had barely mentioned him beside naming him employed as a bodyguard. Alex walked backward through her memory and tried to figure out why he stood out. She went through every time she'd been in the restaurant and then every time she'd been with Sal. Nothing. Nothing... And then she saw it. The day she'd been arrested, the day Sal was shot, he was at the police station across the busy room in a distant hallway. When he'd seen her, he had quickly ducked into a room. She hadn't noticed him at all at the time. He was wearing a badge. The family had been desperately looking for her, tumbling into financial ruin, and he'd known where she was and had said nothing.

Alex walked over to him. "A moment of your time, Mr. Furlren?" Because she'd just come out of Mario's office, those nearby assumed she was inexplicably tasked by Mario. She moved out of earshot of anyone else. Alex smiled thinly and spoke so quietly no one else could overhear. "I saw you at the police station. You're an undercover cop and you have betrayed the family." He paled and Alex continued, "Leave now and don't come back. Tomorrow morning, I'm telling Mario. You'll be shunned from the family activities anyway so your job is finished." She didn't need to point out the other downside of betraying an Italian Mafia family. He scurried out. She'd tell Milo later so he could pass along the information that their police contacts were compromised.

She went over to Milo who asked, "What was that about?"

Alex shrugged. "Just some family business. Tell you about it later."

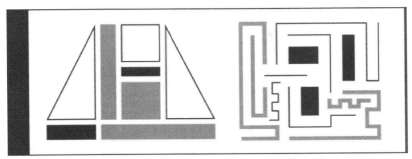

A month later, Alex and Milo sat at Rico's kitchen table while Emma moved around putting dishes away. Alex finished cutting an apple and put the tiny slivers in her oatmeal.

Milo informed Alex, "You've been transferred to Kingsport Academy for the upcoming school year." Milo smiled at Emma as she set a traditional Italian caffè in front of him. "A couple of the kids in the family go there and they've been told to help you. You'll travel by limo with bodyguards at all times. No more running around the streets by yourself. It's too dangerous."

Alex picked up her spoon and poked at the apple bits, pushing them in. "Won't that seem odd for just going to school? Isn't there a school bus?"

Emma silently retreated from the room to go somewhere upstairs.

Milo drank his coffee in three quick swallows and set the cup back down. "It's a private school. A lot of the students are from affluent families and get dropped off. It's got on-site security guards and is generally considered the top school in the state. Besides, it's a solid one hour drive one way. You might as well ride in comfort."

Alex ate some of her oatmeal while Milo popped open his briefcase. He pushed a set of papers at her. "Your class schedule and syllabi. I was unable to get you out of the required music class. I put you in choir as it was either that or piano."

Her heart skipped several beats and Alex was afraid she paled considerably. When she could speak again, she said, "Ah, good. I need something to fail to keep my GPA down."

"Your textbooks should arrive tomorrow so you'll be all set when school starts. Do you need any more supplies or do you have enough notebooks, pens, pencils and such?"

"I have plenty. I still have all the things Sal bought me."

"I noticed their lack of use." Milo's mouth quirked. "You might try actually doing some of the assignments. You might learn something."

"I'll consider it." Alex set her spoon aside and glanced through the papers.

Music class was going to be a problem.

Kingsport Academy was an imposing brick building inside a tall brick-walled compound. As Milo had promised, most students were being dropped off in private cars and hers wasn't the only limousine. Alex got out and stared around. Students peered at her curiously and Alex tugged at her white uniform blouse self-consciously.

A girl with long auburn hair pried herself from the railing by the steps and came over to her. She was carrying her backpack in her hand rather than wearing it. "I'm Karen Marino. You must be Alex Smith. May I call you Alex?"

Alex nodded. Alex's own heavy backpack was pulling at her shoulders. "Of course."

"I'll take you in and show you around. I'm a junior so I'm not in any of your classes, but I'll try to meet you after classes if you want." Karen started walking toward the school and Alex followed.

Alex replied, "I should be fine if you just show me where things are. Unless you want to spend time with me."

Karen held the door for Alex. "Well, I'm naturally curious. Did you really hang out with Salvatore Marino?" At Alex's nod, Karen continued, "I would have been too scared to. What did you guys talk about?"

"Mostly antiques and art." Alex wondered if Karen found the conversation as awkward as she did. It was likely considering that Karen sounded like she was babbling more from nervousness than genuine curiosity.

"Huh. I only ever saw him at family gatherings, you know. Dad warned me not to bug him." Karen shifted her backpack to her other hand.

Alex remembered seeing Karen at Sal's birthday party. She had indeed steered clear of approaching Sal. Her father had dropped off the gift from his family - a very expensive high-end laptop. Alex briefly wondered where that had gone. Many of Sal's birthday presents had been redistributed. Sal had said it was all part of the tradition. He certainly hadn't needed a new laptop. "What did your dad say about me?"

Karen winced and a guilty flush warmed her face. "Just that I should help you get settled in."

He'd said a lot more than that. Alex shifted her book bag on her shoulders. "I'm glad you are. I'd be lost in this mausoleum. Why aren't there any numbers on these doors?"

"Oh, those are in the door jams. See?" Karen pointed to small, barely perceptible numbers near the top inside edge of the door frame. "The administration didn't want ugly signs interfering with the gloomy ambience."

"Ah." Alex rolled back through her memory and captured the room numbers. It was an absurd policy. How were emergency workers and guests supposed to find things?

"This is the sophomore locker room here," Karen announced. "Did they give you a locker and combination?"

"Yes." Alex hoped she could leave her books in the locker permanently. They were heavy.

"Do you want to drop off any of your books? I can wait. Different grades are not allowed in each other's locker rooms. I think it's supposed to prevent couples from making out." Karen smirked as she explained this.

Alex peered in. It was a standard size school room, lined with lockers, with two sets of lockers forming low rows in the center. The entire room was completely visible. Directly across from the door, a couple was doing a lip dance. "Maybe later." Alex bet her locker was behind those two kids.

Moving farther along the hallway, Karen lectured, "Here's the history study hall. You'll get two half-hour breaks, one in the morning and one in the afternoon. You have to sign in at one of the study halls or the cafeteria." Karen continued her tour and eventually pointed out all of Alex's classrooms as well as the rest of the study halls, cafeteria, and gym. The choir room contained a piano, a bunch of music stands with music books, and nothing else.

Karen left Alex at her first classroom and ran off to her own class. The school was small enough that each grade only had 25-30 students and the entire grade moved from class to class together. Her new classmates sized her up curiously, but cliques had been formed in their first year, and with the school uniform, there was no way to tell where she belonged. Alex expected she belonged nowhere.

The teacher cleared her throat. "Everyone, we have a new student joining us this year. Please welcome Miss Smith to our school. Miss Smith, please stand and tell us about yourself."

"I'd prefer not to," Alex said clearly. Many of the students smirked and laughed under their hands.

The teacher was unfazed. "Nevertheless, introductions and speeches are a part of life and a skill worth practicing. Do it anyway."

Hah. That was certainly true, particularly if she was going to run a business. Alex tilted her head in royal acquiescence and stood. She paused briefly, recalling some talking tips for self-introduction speeches from books she'd read: state your name clearly, give some context for yourself, add some of your background, talk about a hobby or goal, share personal details, show something in common with the group. Alex would add the standard speech trick of complimenting the audience for good measure. "Thank you, Mrs. Kinsey. I would like to start by saying what an honor it is to have been

113

accepted into this elite school. It has an impressive academic record which speaks well of both the teachers and the students here." Being accepted meant throwing a large wad of cash at the school; no academic merit required, but that was just incidental.

Someone snickered. Alex continued, making eye contact around the room. "I certainly hope to live up to your standards. As Mrs. Kinsey said, I'm Alex Smith. I recently transferred from a public school. My hobbies include antiques and art, mostly traditional fine art oil paintings of the Baroque period. I find the rendering of material - silks and brocades - particularly fascinating. I'm looking forward to the more exacting standards of a rigorous education and I hope we can find many things in common as we continue our scholastic pursuits." She sat down.

Mrs. Kinsey shushed the giggles and comments that followed. "That was nicely done, Miss Smith. Now if everyone would please get out your books, we'll go over this semester's syllabus."

Alex pondered the things she could have said - recently escaped from an insane asylum, nominal head of a mafia family that she wasn't actually a part of, and zero desire to actually attend school. She supposed rumors would catch up to her soon enough. None of it was being kept secret as far as she knew. As for the real secrets, well, those belonged to her and she wasn't likely to share them until they no longer mattered, if ever.

While pretending to listen to the teacher's lecture, Alex looked back in her memory from when she was making eye contact with her classmates and studied them. Milo could get her a report on each of them. Each and every one looked like a privileged kid. They'd never known desperation, hunger, or true fear. The world would give them whatever they dreamed of having. They could focus on their education and excel in their chosen field, and yet, they were likely sacrificing their lives on video games and social media.

Alex turned her attention to her next biggest problem. Money. She was going to need a mountain of it. She wouldn't be able to just borrow enough either, even if she got all of Mario's and a good bit from the Hamasaki family. She'd need a lot of different sources and diversified assets so she'd appear small, inconsequential, and not a threat. She should also avoid tapping the Hamasaki family until things got desperate. If that alliance got out too soon, the oil cartels would end her venture. Assuming the Hamasaki family could be convinced to join the battle on her side. How valuable was that business card? She thought she could make the alliance work if she could talk with the right person.

After class, Alex ignored the whispers and comments about her. No one approached her. During the next class, she designed her tax shelters to be entirely legal if pushing loopholes in the laws. She'd have to check that some of the laws hadn't been changed, but overall, she was happy with the plan. A lot of the money could be moved offshore. She could certainly write some books based on what she knew from her extensive reading and gain some income that way.

In study hall, Alex started thinking about implementing her business. She'd have to be certain of all the moves and countermoves. It would be chess, not checkers, and her opponents needed to remain ignorant of the game for as long as possible. There were so many details she'd have to take care of. Sal had helped her with a lot of the strategy, but there were so many variables and contingencies to plan for.

Unfortunately, midway through her third class, Alex remembered that she'd have music class directly after lunch. The sudden, overwhelming fear made her chest hurt. Her heart began racing, her hands trembled, and she felt like she couldn't breathe. She recognized the anxiety attack for what it was, but that didn't make it go away. She managed to avoid horrific flashbacks, but only just barely.

Alex might have been able to tolerate a violin, maybe; she'd never played one of those. But singing? A piano? She'd joked with Milo about having a class to fail, but she wasn't sure she could force herself into any kind of performance ever again. Not that she couldn't logically tell herself there was nothing to fear anymore, that it was completely different, but her autonomic response had music performance hardwired to terror and pain.

The girl at the next desk looked at her oddly so Alex steadied her hands by grabbing onto the sides of the desk. Inhale. Exhale. Try to think about anything else.

After class, Alex went straight to the bathroom and splashed her face with cold water. This made her late getting to the cafeteria. She glanced around the large room. Only a brief look, but in that moment she'd memorized the layout, marking the exits in particular. The large windows overlooking the garden both thrilled and terrified her. She reminded herself again that she was on the guarded terrain of an exclusive private school; no gang members would be driving past, emptying their weapons into the room.

Alex allowed herself to relax just a fraction and got swept up in the last remnants of the queue. She was the last to get her tray of food and the tables all had people at them. Not that it would have mattered very much, although she supposed the chance of having someone friendly to talk with would have been increased if they joined her rather than her having to pick someone. If she could navigate a conversation with a mafia boss, surely she could manage a simple high school dialog.

Alex picked a table with four girls by the large windows overlooking the gardens, a spot long since reserved as theirs. "Can I join you?"

"It's 'may I'," a girl with short curly hair corrected sunnily, "Don't let the teachers catch you using it incorrectly."

"Sure, have a seat," another girl said at the same time.

Alex set her tray down and lowered herself into a chair. They were supposed to set the table properly, but it was easier to eat from the trays. The food didn't seem to merit the effort anyway. Dainty steamed carrots, cauliflower florets, and a grilled lump of pale protein, probably chicken.

"That was a rad introduction you gave this morning," the girl with the short curly hair said.

Alex didn't know what "rad" meant, but hoped it was a compliment. "If you have to do it anyway, you might as well overdo it?" Alex replied. Her stomach was busy doing flips and her pulse was refusing to slow. She swallowed, hoping not to vomit right there and then.

"We were almost certain you weren't serious," giggled the same girl. "I'm Sophy."

"Oh, I was serious all right." Alex worried that she looked sickly grey, but made herself grin and wink anyway, letting her tone shift to teasing lightheartedness, with an exaggerated southern-belle accent. "I just adore silks and brocades. I could study them for hours and still never see it all." She rolled her eyes up in mock despair. "And no one ever stands and looks at a painting long enough with me. It's such a terrible burden I must bear."

They laughed. The others introduced themselves as Lucy, Carina, and Pamela.

Alex pretended to take a sip of her orange juice. There was no way she was going to put anything in her stomach. To her left, Lucy threw her fork down, pushed her tray away, and peeled open the dessert offering. The lone strawberry atop the chocolate mousse looked suspiciously fresh, likely sculpted from sugar with the barest trace of what may originally have been organic.

"So what are you really interested in?" Pamela pushed a soggy carrot around on the dull perspex plate.

"Business, actually." Alex took her fork and poked at her food. "I'm going to start one."

Pamela wrinkled her nose and offered, "Oh, you should talk to Ethan. His father owns Cartwright-Jaxon Engineering. I think business is in his blood." She pointed. The kid in question was surrounded by a table of boys who seemed to hang on his every word.

Cartwright-Jaxon Engineering was in Alex's list of competitors. Her batteries wouldn't put them out of business, but it would certainly steal from their bottom line. The conversation shifted to the latest virtual reality video games, and Alex continued to push her food around with her fork and pretended to eat. When they asked what game she liked to play the most, she simply joked that she didn't have much time for games, "what, with all the silks and brocades, you know", and then asked which they thought she should try first, which turned into a lively discussion of the merits of various games.

Lunch was over far too soon and the group dropped off their trays and headed toward the music classroom. Ten students broke off to go to piano class, and the rest filed into the choir room. Alex stood outside the room a moment, heart pounding, and feeling like she might throw up. "I can't do this," she whispered to herself.

Alex went directly to the teacher. "I'm not feeling very well. May I go to the infirmary?" Alex certainly looked ill.

The teacher peered at Alex. "Of course. Miss Dewinter, please escort Miss Smith to the infirmary and come right back."

Alex smiled greenly at the red headed girl who stepped forward and followed her out of the room. Behind her, someone started playing the piano - a nice loud 'concert A' for pitch and tuning. The 440 Hz frequency sounded spot-on to her trained ear and she knew it was a well-maintained piano. Alex put her hand over her mouth and walked quicker, putting as much distance as she could between herself and that echoing note. Her legs felt like jelly.

"I'm Jessica," the red-headed girl said, looking at Alex in concern, "Hey, are you going to throw up?"

Alex shook her head and walked faster.

"There's a bathroom over here." Jessica turned Alex down a hallway, slightly away from the infirmary. "It's for the juniors, but we can use it."

As soon as the bathroom door was in sight, Alex ran. She barely made it to the toilet before she was heaving up breakfast and then dry-heaving. Jessica waited outside. The piano note echoed in Alex's head. There were some good memories she could call up, but she focused instead on the current moment and getting her body to calm down. It took a few minutes, but she was finally able to relax a little. She cleaned up, splashed her face with water, and dried off with a paper towel.

She left the bathroom, thanked Jessica, and followed her to the infirmary. Alex explained to the nurse, "I'm just a little nauseous. I think if I lay down for a short bit, I'll be fine."

"She threw up in the bathroom," Jessica offered helpfully.

"Probably something I ate at lunch," Alex countered with a glare at Jessica.

The nurse dismissed Jessica and proceeded to take Alex's temperature (which was fine), and let her sit on the couch. "So you threw up in the bathroom?" the nurse prompted.

"Only a little. I'm fine, really," Alex said, adding her best "I'm healthy and ok" smile.

"I have to call your parents." The nurse waved her hand as Alex was about to object. "It's policy."

The nurse went to her computer and pulled up Alex's record. She took her phone from her pocket and dialed. "Mr. Marino? Sir, this is the nurse at the Kingsport Academy. No, sir, she's fine. She was throwing up though. I can keep her here... Yes, sir. I'll do that. Uh huh. Yes. Ok." She hung up and turned to Alex, "You're to call your driver and have him take you to the nearest hospital. Mr. Marino will meet you there."

Alex frowned, picked up her backpack and dug inside. She retrieved her cell phone and made the call under the watchful eye of the nurse. A few minutes later, the nurse escorted Alex out to the limousine and gave the driver explicit instructions.

As soon as the limousine was off campus, Alex activated the intercom to the driver. "To Sal's house, please."

"Certainly, Miss," came the snappy response.

Alex raised the window again and called Rico. She assured Rico that she was fine and not poisoned or sick or anything and that she would talk with him later that evening, and that she was not going to any hospital. Less than three minutes after she hung up, Mario called.

"I'm ok," Alex assured him. "Really."

"You can't be ok if you are throwing up," Mario argued. "What did you eat?"

"It was just a couple dry heaves. I only wanted to get out of class. I'm on my way to Sal's."

"What's wrong with class? Didn't Karen meet you? She was supposed to take care of you. If she didn't..." Mario's voice promised punishment.

Alex rushed to correct that misunderstanding before it could take hold. "Karen showed me around! She's great. I just... had a hard time getting used to being in classes again. That's all. They're very serious about education here." Alex tap danced around the real issue. She wasn't going to discuss it with him.

"Well, ok, but you can't ditch school again." Mario didn't sound happy at all. "The foster care system will relocate you."

"I know. Thank you for being worried." Alex bet he wanted to reach through the phone and throttle her at that. She disconnected and powered down the phone, not wanting to take any more calls. She leaned back and closed her eyes, trying not to think of or remember anything.

When Alex arrived at Sal's house, she dismissed the driver, and let herself in. Alex closed the front door behind her and stood at the door, staring across the room at the piano. She let her backpack slide to the floor. Maybe by herself, with no one here, she could work past the issue?

Tentatively, she tried a step toward the piano. The room felt incredibly warm and her heart started spasming. Alex bent forward, put her hands on her knees, and hyperventilated. It didn't seem to help. Maybe she'd try a glass of water first? After all, she hadn't eaten any lunch.

Alex quickly skirted around the far side of the room, as far from the piano as she could, and went to the kitchen. She got some water and sat at the table, gripping the glass with both hands. Her hands were trembling so much that the water bounced in the glass as if it were in an earthquake. An anxiety attack is not deadly, Alex told herself. She took a sip and then it occurred to her that if she was going to throw up again, maybe she should do so on an already empty stomach.

"Don't think about doing it; just do it," Alex told herself firmly. Her voice echoed hollowly off the kitchen walls. She stood, grabbed a plastic trash bag to throw up into, took a deep breath, and forced herself to walk steadily back to the piano. She knew if she hesitated at all, she'd fail. She touched the wood of the piano and found it incongruously warm and glass-smooth. She could see her pallid reflection on its shiny black surface.

Alex lifted the fallboard and sat down. Her hands shook and the keys seemed slightly smaller than she remembered. She tapped the middle A key and the sound resonated out through the hall, also perfect in pitch, with the more resonant timbre of an expensive concert hall piano. She swallowed.

She swore repeatedly to prevent the flashbacks. Her stomach was rolling and twisting and sweat rolled down her face and neck. She dry-heaved into the plastic bag and hyperventilated. Her heart beat wildly. Do. Don't think. She set the bag aside and played a simple chromatic scale. The movements came back to her so easily - thumb crossing under, middle finger crossing over, dancing on the keyboard, wrists high, hands floating. Magnificent notes echoed through the hall.

Alex allowed her heart to pound and her abdomen to cramp. She did not perceive the front door opening and closing softly behind her, although she'd notice it later in recollection. She played the introduction to Claude Debussy's Deux Arabesques No. 1. The arpeggios glided flawlessly through the hall, notes building with the melody, flowing through the air like a butterfly across a spring field of flowers. She got through half of the piece before the flashback overwhelmed her and she was heaving stomach bile into the plastic bag, kneeling on the hard marble floor next to the piano, unable to stop the memory.

119

Milo came over and gently closed the piano fallboard to protect the keys and squatted down next to her and waited. When she finally tilted her tear streaked face up to him, he said, "You make me want to kill all of your enemies. Command me."

"Not a word to anyone." Alex wiped at her face. "That's not me anymore. That girl is dead."

"What can I do to help?" The concern in Milo's eyes made her want to weep more.

Alex steeled herself with analytical logic. "I don't think anti-anxiety meds are the right option. That'll just make it harder for me to keep the flashbacks away."

"Ok?" Milo sounded doubtful. He started to reach out to pat her shoulder, but pulled his hand back, closing it into a frustrated fist, and then reached up to run his hand through his hair instead.

Alex was thankful he didn't touch her. She tried swallowing, but her mouth tasted vile. "I think that's the worst it's going to get. I should be able to mitigate some of the physical side effects now that I can fully recognize them."

Alex pulled herself up, using the piano bench for support because her legs felt weak. She did not look in the direction of the piano. Milo again did not offer to help, although his hands twitched.

Alex tied off the bag and they went to the kitchen. She rinsed her mouth and face and sat by the glass of water. "I'm glad you weren't Mario. I wouldn't have explained."

Milo lowered himself into a chair opposite her. "You can't turn off your phone anymore."

"You guys worry too much." Alex rubbed the bridge of her nose. "I'm used to taking care of myself. I mean, really, what was the point of having Karen meet me at the school? Did you guys really think I couldn't be trusted to get to classes on time?"

"Ah, that. That's a family thing. We take care of each other," Milo explained. "If you go somewhere new and we have someone already there, they meet you and make you feel welcome and tell you what you need to know. Everyone does it for each other. If you go to a new town and we have family there, they'll give you a room to stay in. It's actually an insult if you stay in a hotel, although in your case, it might be necessary because you will also have bodyguards. The flip side of that coin is that you have to do the same if one of the family needs you."

"Oh," Alex said, comprehending finally. "I thought Mario wanted someone to keep an eye on me."

The way Milo's lip pinched suggested Mario did want someone watching her, but he said, "We have it ingrained in us pretty much since birth. Family takes care of family."

"So how are you related to the family?" Alex shifted the conversation away from herself. "Sal never did say."

"My stepmother," Milo answered after a brief hesitation. "If Mario had to choose between anyone with Marino blood and me, he'd choose them. I think Sal felt a little sorry about that, and took care of all my schooling. He said I was family even without the blood."

"So there was precedence for me," Alex observed.

They stared at each other with a shared understanding.

Alex's plan the following day included skipping breakfast as well as lunch and focusing on steady breathing, with recall as needed of different times in the forest, listening to the birds or streams, watching wild animals play - times of complete calm with as many of her senses as she could manifest while still being aware of what was going on around her.

That took her through the 'concert A'.

"Miss Smith, I want you to sing something for me so I can place you," the teacher directed.

"I'm an alto, Ma'am," Alex replied promptly. Her heart rate skyrocketed and she could feel sweat forming across her forehead.

"I'll judge that. Please sing something," the teacher requested politely.

"No, thank you. I don't sing solo." Alex swallowed. Her legs barely supported her.

"It's nothing to be ashamed of. Sing something." The teacher's voice carried a distinct edge this time.

"I'm not comfortable doing that," Alex countered, hoping that the woman would have pity. "I told you - I'm an alto."

"You don't have to be comfortable. You have to sing." The teacher's firm voice was distinctly louder.

Alex could feel the room darkening around her, threatening to suck her into a permanent memory. "No, I don't. I'm not singing." Even the argument taunted her perfect recall.

"Don't use that tone with me," the teacher commanded. "Two demerits. You can wait outside in the hallway until you are ready to participate."

Alex skirted around the teacher and wobbled into the hall. Pulling the music room door closed, she leaned on the wall briefly before sliding to the floor. She leaned her arm on her backpack, closed her eyes, and spent the time finishing off the last of the books she'd scanned and needed to integrate. She tried very hard not to pay attention to the piano coming from inside the room. When class finally let out, Alex wondered how the school's demerit system worked.

Saturday detention. That's how the demerits worked. Accrue ten, get detention. Two per music class times five days a week equaled detention every Saturday. Three hours of cleaning, grounds work, essay writing, or whatever torture the teacher on duty might dream up plus two hours in the car to get there and back. The teacher on duty always, without fail, tried to talk with Alex and help her. Alex was mildly satisfied that the teachers probably found this session equally torturous.

A few weeks later found Alex assigned to the science teacher, Mr. Frier. He was waiting for her when the limousine pulled up. Alex finished off the next sentence in a novel on her laptop, shut it, and climbed out of the car, leaving the laptop inside.

"Ah, Miss Smith!" Mr. Frier said cheerfully, "I'm growing quite fond of our Saturdays together."

"Mr. Frier," Alex greeted him, mirroring his tone, although truthfully she would rather have been in the car finishing off that novel. She'd need the revenue to help fund her business. She already had three waiting for her emancipated minor petition to get approved so she could publish. "Do you get overtime for Saturdays? You were here last Saturday."

"I volunteered for Mrs. Kenwood today. See the weather? It's beautiful out. I thought we'd go for a walk instead of the usual detention."

Alex sighed with resignation. Another one of those motivational 'you can do it' speeches incoming. She had a plan today though - Milo's suggestion which she'd subsequently researched. Mr. Frier was right about the weather; it was pretty out - a little chilly, but not too cold. Alex put on the lightweight jacket that was draped over her arm. Maybe she could get him to talk about science?

Mr. Frier started walking on a path that would take them around the building toward the garden outside the lunch hall. The pace was casual. "So I understand you like Baroque art?" Mr. Frier asked encouragingly.

"I needed something to say as part of an introduction speech," Alex hedged.

"I see, but what made you choose that?" Mr. Frier persisted.

"I'd just been to an art museum." Despite the well-manicured, still-green lawn, Alex spotted a small patch of chickweed, a nutritious if calorie-deficient green that remained edible throughout the year. She knew that bit would be inedible due to the fertilizers and weedkiller likely applied to the lawn, but it was still a comforting old friend to spot.

"You like museums?" inquired Mr. Frier, smiling at her.

Alex recognized his attempt to find common ground and create a personal connection so he could get to the real point. She wondered if she should make him work for it or if she should have mercy. They had three hours. She shrugged.

Mr. Frier continued, "I find they can be very peaceful."

He'd never visited sculptures from Auguste Rodin's Gates of Hell, she thought. "I s'pose," she said.

"Suppose," he corrected automatically. At least he didn't give her any more demerits for it.

Alex wondered how many grammatical corrections she could get him to make. She toyed with the idea, but then realized that Sal wouldn't have approved. The thought was sobering. "Museums are nice," she conceded, as if Sal were also standing there, listening. "Sal took me to a few."

"Salvatore Marino?" Mr. Frier didn't pronounce the name right.

"Mmmm hmmm." Alex watched a hawk circling off in the distance.

"You must have been very upset when he died," murmured Mr. Frier.

Not the direction Alex wanted the conversation to go. "I had more than enough counseling in the psychiatric hospital, Mr. Frier. Why don't we talk about science?"

"Why don't we talk about choir?" he countered.

Alex stopped to watch the hawk dive for a kill and then used Milo's suggestion, "Chocolate War, Mr. Frier."

Mr. Frier inhaled sharply. He masked this by also stopping to watch the bird's flight. After a full minute he quoted, "Do I dare disturb the universe?"

Alex responded, quoting more of the poem, "In a minute there is time for decisions and revisions which a minute will reverse. For I have known them all already, known them all: Have known the evenings, mornings, afternoons, I have measured out my life with coffee spoons; I know the voices dying with a dying fall, Beneath the music from a farther room. So how should I presume?"

He chose not to comment on her recall. "Who asked you not to sing?"

"No one," Alex answered honestly. "It is, however, an interesting social experiment."

Mr. Frier turned to face her directly. "You're not doing yourself any favors by failing to attend music class. It's part of a well-rounded education. You'll regret it later."

Alex genuinely laughed then. "Of all the things I have potential to regret, not singing in music class isn't ever going to be one of them." This was definitely a problem with small, private schools; the teachers had too much time to focus on individual students, too much energy to allocate to personal attention.

Indeed giving Alex too much attention, Mr. Frier inquired, "Miss Smith, what on earth could you possibly have to regret?"

It suddenly surprised Alex how many things she did have. She never used to regret anything. It was always just stuff that got done or needed to be done. Those two Caro kids, for example; they'd had parents who loved them and took care of them, and now they were orphans, just like her. Well, not exactly like her. They still had family that would protect and take care of them; they'd be all right, but Alex regretted making them orphans.

"I regret necessity, Mr. Frier." After a moment, Alex added, "I regret some forms of kindness, too." Alex was thinking about the girls she'd shot in the house. Had it been mercy and kindness to put them out of their misery? Had that even been what she was thinking? Unfortunately, now that she could see her younger self more clearly, she knew she'd been shooting herself, not those girls, to try and make the pain go away. Selfishness, masquerading as merciful kindness.

"Kindness, Miss Smith?" Mr. Frier's puzzled expression was almost comical in its intensity.

Rather than the truth, Alex chose something less incriminating because it was too late to change her words. "There was a drug addict in the psychiatric ward, Mr. Frier. I gave her a drug I'd stolen. At the time, I'd thought it was kind." She'd actually not thought anything of the sort. It was merely payment, a tip, like you tip the waiter at a restaurant for particularly fine service. A standard street-smart action in case she ever needed another service done. "Come work for me," that payment said, "I will make it worth your while."

Mr. Frier hesitated and then said, "Well, you're young. You're going to make mistakes and can learn from them. You have to figure out how to forgive yourself and move on. Was the girl all right?"

"Yeah. She's fine." Alex pulled her jacket closed and zipped it.

"Then no harm done," Mr. Frier proclaimed. "I wouldn't worry too much about it."

They moved on to the garden which was winter-sparse. Alex, unwilling to continue the melancholy philosophical thread, inquired, "What got you into science, Mr. Frier?" For the remainder of the conversation, Alex asked pointed science questions and didn't let the conversation turn back to herself. She'd already said more than she'd planned.

125

Alex's fingers silently tapped the beautiful dark wood desk of the Kingsport Academy. The teacher, Mrs. Kenwood, continued describing some simple Geometry problem with enthusiastic animation, but Alex was barely listening enough to be able to answer if called on. In her thoughts, she was outlining yet another novel.

As soon as Milo got her emancipated minor court order pushed through, Alex would start publishing, buying and selling antiques, and accruing money for her business. She already knew which overseas publishing houses she would use and where to set up accounts so the money could be neatly and legally distributed to hide her total wealth. The business papers were already prepared. She could have a working prototype of her battery within three months of getting the supplies and maybe have a functioning bioshield by the end of the year. She would finally be able to sleep soundly again.

Milo had flinched at her shopping list, but everything was all legal if wrapped under the pretext of the business, even the extremely expensive and rare hazmat items. It would burn through the cash in her account and more, but she would never sell any of Sal's things. A trip through some of the antiques shows should recover costs. She hoped. Money, money, money. It was going to be a problem for a long time.

"Miss Smith! Perhaps you'd care to enlighten us?" the teacher's sharp voice suggested at least two repetitions.

"Hrm?" Alex looked up at the board, swearing at herself silently. She'd forgotten to half-listen. Again.

"Miss Smith, stay after class," Mrs. Kenwood instructed. "In the meantime, please come explain problem 34 on the whiteboard."

Alex was halfway to the front of the classroom before she realized she'd left her book on her desk. She went back for it, ignoring the snickering of her fellow students. She pretended to study the problem, think about it, and then wrote the solution up on the board. The teacher frowned, but let her return to her seat, and went on to explain the solution in great detail. Alex stopped listening again.

After class, the teacher half-sat on her desk and crossed her arms at Alex. "You have so much potential. Is it that hard to pay attention?"

"No, Ma'am." Alex stood perfectly still and waited, afraid to see how many demerits she was going to be given. She'd soon have Saturday detention well after the school year ended.

The teacher rubbed at her thigh. "What is it you think about so intently? Clearly it isn't Geometry."

"Just stuff." Her Sal-directed movie-research suggested that was a typical teenager answer.

The teacher sighed. "Do you have your homework?"

"No, Ma'am." Alex decided she really hated school. How much trouble would she be in if she called her driver and left? Unfortunately, social services would probably just find another psychiatric ward to terrorize her in.

"Why not?" The teacher sat on the edge of her desk, apparently settling in for an extended interrogation.

Alex suppressed a groan. "I was busy doing other things."

"What things?"

"Just stuff." Alex watched as the teacher ground her teeth together, looked up at the ceiling, maybe counting to ten in her head? "Look, Mrs. Kenwood, you're a fine teacher, but you don't have to worry about me. Focus on the other kids. I'm covered."

"You aren't covered," Mrs. Kenwood asserted. "You're failing and I know you know the material. You don't put in any effort. You haven't turned in a single homework assignment."

Giving up on the sullen teenager ruse, Alex tried logic, "My lawyer is working on getting me declared an emancipated minor and I'm leaving school as soon as that happens."

"That's a mistake," Mrs. Kenwood opined. "You should never skip education."

"You're a good person, Mrs. Kenwood, but really, you don't need to worry about me." Alex wondered if there was anything at all she could say to make the woman leave her alone. Alex couldn't be angry with her. The woman was just doing her job and doing it well. In fact, all of the Kingsport Academy teachers were excellent. They just weren't what Alex needed.

"It's my job to worry about you," the woman insisted. "You're young and inexperienced. Right now everything seems like an emergency, that life will pass you by if you don't rush forward. It won't. Take your time."

Perhaps the teacher was right? What difference would a few more years make? Alex walked over to the window and peered out. "Mrs. Kenwood, I noticed you are reading Silverman's Arithmetic of Elliptic Curves. What page are you on?"

"What's that got to do with anything?"

"Humor me. What page are you on?"

"Fine." Ms. Kenwood reached behind her and yanked the book out of her bag. She opened to her bookmark. "202."

Alex stepped over to the whiteboard. "Exercise 7.3, the Weierstrass equations, uh, on page 203." Alex wrote the given equation up on the board and then explained the answer. She set the whiteboard marker back in its tray. "Mrs. Kenwood, please, I'll be ok." Alex erased the whiteboard and left.

At least that's what Alex wanted to do. Instead she touched the glass window pane. Outside, it was a sunny, wintery cold, with scattered clouds - the type of day that she used to hope for when she was living in the woods - perfect hunting weather. "I'll consider it, Mrs. Kenwood, honest. Can I go? Mr. Stratdeer will be starting English soon."

Mrs. Kenwood sighed and dismissed her, with "It's 'honestly' and 'may I', and yes, you may go. Bring your homework tomorrow."

Alex fervently hoped Milo would come back with the approved paperwork before she did do something irreparably stupid. Part of her necessary business strategy involved hiding her intelligence. She had to let people believe she was stupid and foolish.

The next day Alex actually turned in her geometry homework. It was a pointless waste of her time, but Milo had informed her that the social worker was coming by later that day and Alex wanted to be able to honestly say, "I turn in homework." Mrs. Kenwood rewarded her by calling on her three times during class, interrupting her thought process and making her unable to work out the details of her next novel.

"Miss Smith, perhaps you can shed some light on Mr. Jaxon's dilemma. Miss Smith!" the teacher's voice was loud and somewhat grumpy.

A fourth time calling on her? The equations for her battery cascaded out of Alex's focus. She'd almost completed another full variation, too. She clamped her teeth together to avoid swearing and glanced up at the equation on the board that Ethan Jaxon had written. She didn't even bother checking the triangle's labels in her book.

"He's comparing parts of the side instead of the whole side." It was a simple geometry mistake. As soon as Alex said it, Ethan saw the error and quickly corrected it.

"Perhaps a little more attention to detail next time, Mr. Jaxon," the teacher reprimanded, nodding at him to return to his seat.

Someone chortled. Ethan Jaxon flushed and went to sit down. His glare at Alex promised retribution, but she barely noticed, already refocusing on her own formulas.

That evening, the social worker arrived, with her clipboard and a dour expression. She walked through the house while Emma trailed behind, clearly upset at having a stranger going through her personal space. Rico and Alex waited in the small living room, each pretending not to notice how upset Emma was. After the home inspection, the social worker and Emma joined them.

The social worker glanced at her clipboard, "Are you doing ok here, Alex?"

"Yes, Ma'am." Alex had at least gained a significant grasp of polite responses between the psychiatric hospital and the private school.

"Do you get enough to eat?"

"Yes, Ma'am. Mrs. Marino is an excellent cook." An exaggeration, but Alex thought it might help. Maybe Emma would even be a little pleased?

"What did you have for breakfast this morning?"

"Oatmeal and fruit, Ma'am." Alex hadn't eaten it because of the upcoming choir class.

"No protein?" The woman tapped her finger on the clipboard.

"Oatmeal is 15% protein, Ma'am. I'm not nutritionally deficient. Mrs. Marino made a fine meat lasagne for dinner tonight." Which Alex also hadn't eaten, because she found the extra acid from the tomato sauce made her empty stomach nauseous from skipping breakfast and lunch. Alex did not glance at either Emma or Rico, who were both perfectly aware of her erratic abstinence.

The social worker added some notes on her clipboard. "Are you sleeping?"

"Yes, Ma'am."

"What time do you go to bed?"

"9 p.m., Ma'am." Alex really had no idea. She just picked a time at random. She knew she was often up until early morning working on her novels or battery equations. Emma and Rico also knew this. Emma frequently came by her room to tell her to turn off the light and go to sleep, and Alex usually just nodded and waved her away, ignoring her.

"What time do you get up?" the social worker continued.

"6 a.m., Ma'am."

"Does Mrs. Marino come in and wake you up?"

"No, Ma'am. I have an alarm clock." Alex never set that alarm clock. Emma had come by to wake her up on more than one occasion, but Alex bet there was some checkmark on that form that said, "adult enters child's bedroom without permission".

The social worker put a checkmark on her form. "I received a report from your school. Want to tell me what is happening there?"

"It's an ok school, Ma'am, but it's a private school. I'm getting some demerits and detention because I'm not used to the rules. They have a lot more than public school, Ma'am." There, that should be sufficient.

"Is there a reason you can't get your homework done?" the social worker inquired. She didn't sound the least bit curious; she was just following some required procedure.

"I turn in homework," Alex replied. "Just not all of it." With that, Alex slipped a truth into her lies, even if grossly misrepresenting a single assignment.

"Is it too hard?" the social worker asked.

"No, Ma'am. It just takes me a long time."

The social worker made a note on her clipboard. "Your teachers say you are frequently distracted. Is there anything bothering you?"

"The teachers are a lot different than my last school, which was public. They're very intense. It's just hard to concentrate all the time, and I swear the second I look out the window, the teacher yells at me for not paying attention, and gives me a demerit. I'm sure I'll start adjusting soon." Alex hoped that account wouldn't reflect poorly on Kingsport Academy's fine educators.

The social worker frowned and wrote some notes. The interview

129

continued for some time, with Alex diligently stretching the truth or outright lying. Both Rico and Emma listened but did not contribute or contradict anything. After the social worker had left, Rico turned to Alex, "Do you ever plan to do your homework?"

Alex answered honestly, "No."

Rico cleared his throat. "Going to participate in choir class?"

"No." Alex wanted to go crawl into bed. She felt a little light-headed, probably from not having eaten all day. Maybe she'd eat a bit of bread first.

Rico frowned. "I know Milo is working on your emancipated minor application, but until then, you are still our responsibility. If there's anything at all we can do to help you..."

"I'm doing just fine, Rico. There's nothing to worry about." Alex gave him a winning smile, which felt false on her face, and went toward the kitchen. She could hear Emma, still in the living room with Rico, angrily whispering her concern and his attempted calming reply; the house was simply too small for anyone to have a truly private conversation. Alex ignored this. Hopefully they'd be free of her soon.

Alex expected the emancipated minor petition to get approved any day. She had everything lined up and ready to go just as soon as it was signed. It was time for her to find a CEO for her company that could handle the day-to-day business while she worked on money, strategy, and battery production.

Alex stared at the brick building of the Kingsport Academy and thought, "Why not? The point of these private schools is to build future business contacts. Might as well see if such a thing has any merit." She walked over to Ethan, who would one day inherit Cartwright-Jaxon Engineering. Maybe she could merge with them for startup cash and not have them as a competitor? Ethan was standing with his usual following of classmates.

"Ethan, may I have a moment of your time?" 'May I' still sounded pretentious to her. In her old street gang, Mason would have boxed her for condescension if she'd spoken like that. Communication had to be completely designed for the recipient's expectations or the immediate negative impact would prevent any hope for success. Ethan, on the other hand, would surely berate her for 'can I'.

Ethan shrugged. "I guess." His tone suggested she was bothering him despite the 'may I'.

"Privately?" Alex indicated his classmate-followers.

"Ok." He rolled his eyes at the young men standing with him who moved off. "What is it?"

Alex asked, "Going to work for your dad when you graduate?"

"When I graduate from college, yes," Ethan answered patronizingly.

130

"I am starting a business," Alex chirped happily, despite his dour attitude. "I don't suppose you'd be interested in blowing off the rest of your school and being CEO of a startup company, would you?"

"Of course not." He rolled his eyes.

Alex pressed on, "Could you recommend some people who might be interested in the position? Perhaps get me an interview with them?"

Ethan thought a moment and then said, "No."

Alex blinked at this curtness. "Why not?"

"First, I don't want any connection with the mafia." Ethan ticked this off on his finger.

"This business is entirely legal and above-board." But, sadly, connected with the mafia, which was unavoidable considering Alex was the head of the family if only in concept.

"Second, startup businesses are everywhere and they collapse within five years generally. They're a poor risk." He held up his hand to keep her from interrupting. "And last, if you are going to take a risk, you have to evaluate all aspects. You, oh mafia lord, are a poor risk. Not once since coming to this school have you shown anything that vaguely resembles talent - not in any subject. You can't even bother yourself to sing a couple notes in music class. You don't have what it takes to be a success. You're not a good risk and I won't contaminate my reputation by recommending you. Get your degree. Get a job if you have to, but leave business to professionals."

Alex bit her lower lip and then conceded with as much grace as she could muster, "Ok, well, thank you for your time as well as your honesty, Ethan."

Ethan half-bowed to her and strode back over to his friends.

Alex had known he wouldn't agree to be her CEO, but he didn't need to be so mean about it. He could have at least given her a couple names. She rubbed at her temple and went to get a drink from the nearest water fountain. So much for private school business contacts. She'd have to start looking for random resumes online. Alex decided she wouldn't share any of her business with another company; her business model wouldn't fit any modern company anyway.

Later that day, as Alex was grabbing books from her locker, Alan Pickering came over to her. He was one of the young men who routinely followed Ethan around. "Um. Excuse me," he glanced over his shoulder toward the room's doorway. Ethan and the others had already gone out.

"Yes?" Alex finished shoving the remainder of her books into her locker and closed it. She certainly didn't need to bring any of them home. She turned to Alan who held out a piece of paper to her.

"Ethan said you were looking for someone to CEO a startup business.

131

These are some people who will see you if you give them my name." Alan cleared his throat and shifted his weight uncomfortably. "They won't take the job, but they might know someone."

Alex raised an eyebrow at him and took the offered paper, glancing at it. Six names, addresses, and phone numbers were written in painfully neat block letters.

Alan shifted his weight and looked at his toes. "Ethan can be a jerk sometimes, but the rest of us aren't that bad."

"Thank you, Alan. This is unexpected." His deep red blush suggested he was surprised that Alex knew his name.

Alan raised his eyes to hers. "I wish..." his voice trailed off and his hand pulled at his jacket, and then he whispered, "Please don't tell anyone I gave you those." He turned to leave.

Alex reached out and touched his arm. "I won't say anything, but I will remember." She let her hand fall back to her side.

Alan half-nodded and strode quickly away, blush still strong on his face. Alex stared after him thoughtfully. Whatever prompted him to do that? How likely was it those names were a standard high school joke? Milo would find out for her.

The names checked out. Not only were they CEOs of startups, but when Alex called the first, he told her he'd been expecting her call. Unfortunately, he was not interested in a new venture at this time; he was still getting his current project stabilized, and no, he didn't really know anyone who was looking for a new job, but he wished her luck. From the six names, she got three more. Alex scheduled two interviews from that and Milo reminded her that she couldn't actually do anything legally binding until the emancipated minor paperwork got approved, which hopefully would happen any day.

When Milo met her after school in her limousine two days later, Alex was thrilled. "Did it get approved? YES!"

"Er. No. We have some things we need to discuss." Milo's mouth was set in a grim line.

When the limousine was underway, Alex asked hesitantly, "What's the bad news?"

"First, there's the matter of your current school record. The judge is screaming about your demerits and Saturday detentions. Your grades are also not helping your case." Milo didn't need to say which judge. Alex's petition for the emancipated minor was apparently stalled.

Alex clenched and unclenched her fist, but kept the frustration out of her voice. "It will help future cases though. What concession does he want?"

"All B's and no more demerits at all." Milo reached over to the refrigerator and withdrew some water and an apple. He handed these to Alex.

"Transfer me to a school without a mandatory music class." Alex set the apple aside, but opened the water and drank some.

Milo frowned at the apple, but continued with his standard factual tone, "We can't. It's not safe. Your outer perimeter has picked up two teams in the last month. They can't get to you in the school, and outside the school, you've already got a dozen people protecting you."

Alex felt her heart skip several beats. "I thought it was just this car, driver, and bodyguard."

Milo's lip twitched guiltily. "Mario didn't want to worry you."

Alex swore. "Ok, those supplies I said I needed? I want them immediately." Some of them, without the shelter of the company, would be illegal.

"The money in your trust is still locked until you are legally an adult and can't be spent," Milo informed her. "We might be able to get some of it from the family, but it'll be close and will definitely limit the family's ability to do business. You could potentially get a business partner to front some of the cost."

Alex winced at the suggestion, recalling Ethan's disdain. "No. It's my company. No partners, no stockholders, no investors, no non-family loans." Ethan had certainly cemented that decision.

"That's not normally how businesses work." Milo got himself some water.

As it looked like Milo was about to go into a long, if knowledgeable dissertation on how to operate a business, Alex cut him off with a gesture. "I know."

Milo sighed at this and cleared his throat. "That's not everything we need to discuss."

Alex groaned. What else could there be? When was she going to have some good luck to balance all her recent bad luck?

Milo pulled some papers from his briefcase. "Have a look at these." While she scanned through them, he explained, "That's a court order saying that Sal's estate, now yours, is liable for all your medical and psychiatric bills, and because you had no insurance and were not covered by the state at the time, the estate is required to pay the full amount immediately."

"Unbelievable." Alex shook her head. "They kidnap me and lock me up against my will, torture me with drugs and buzzers, and then they want me to pay for it?"

"Yes." Milo opened his hand, palm up. "If you'd like, I can take care of this. I can issue a countersuit for mistreatment, but again, your grades and demerits are going to get brought up, and as you still aren't legally an adult, any resulting funds will go to the state."

"Hmmm. That sounds good. Oh, wait. Demand a full itemized listing of everything first - all services, medications, incidentals."

133

Milo rubbed his chin and then his eyes opened in enlightenment. "Medications, I see. We can finally find out what that doctor gave you. That could certainly be useful information for the countersuit, particularly if we can prove you were allergic to them and they were aware of that."

"That's if they can produce a list in a reasonable time and don't lie about it. Luciano destroyed all the records, yes?" At Milo's nod, Alex continued, "They'll have to make stuff up. It'll be a strange balance between greed and not wanting to incriminate themselves, if they think about it."

Milo rubbed his chin "Timewise, you entered the hospital after Sal died but before the reading of the will, so inheritance is going to be blurry. They can say the trust was yours already and we can say it wasn't until the reading of the will."

Alex closed her eyes and leaned back. "Take care of it, Milo," she sighed. She needed that emancipated minor status.

"Very well." He pulled the papers from her hand, which she readily released, and put them back in his briefcase.

Still with her eyes closed, she said, "On my laptop back at Sal's house, I have 3 finished books. Publish them with you as the pseudo-named author and account holder and use the money from those toward the shopping list. I'll give you all the publishers' information. It won't be very quick money, but should make a lot of it. Also get a million or so from Mario and we'll hit the antique show in Lithia Springs Saturday morning."

"Aren't you due in detention on Saturday?" Milo knew perfectly well that she was.

"Yes, send Rico and Luciano to tell whoever is administrating it that I'm going to be late and if that is unacceptable, I can certainly make it up next week." Alex opened her eyes and looked out the window. "I'll also need the latest listing of the antique show's inventory. The annual Lithia Springs auction usually returns a high profit."

"Skipping detention is not going to help your application for emancipated minor," Milo noted without amusement. "The judge is watching your activities very closely."

"Can't we just break his legs?" she muttered.

"I thought you didn't want to do that?" Milo responded in all seriousness.

"I'm joking!" Alex shot up, eyes wide open. "Milo, I'm joking! Don't hurt the guy, intimidate him, bribe him, or do anything at all to him. He's just doing his job responsibly. Can't fault him for that."

"Bribe? Heh." Milo snorted. "That's not how the family operates. You have so much to learn, young neophyte," he teased.

"Speaking of learning..." Alex pushed the intercom to the driver. "Take us to the library, please." She needed more books to absorb while waiting on music class.

○ ●)) ● ((●

It took five weeks to get all the items she needed for the prototype, mostly purchased with money from antiques, although her books were starting to gain popularity due to some enthusiastic advertising. The judge was still sitting on her emancipated minor paperwork. All three of the interviews for the CEO for her company went badly. They only took one look at her - a young girl still in high school - and politely declined while giving her hollow words of encouragement.

The music teacher continued to give Alex demerits for failing to participate. With Saturday detentions to clear out her demerits, six days out of every week were spent in a frustrating state of wasted time and book-writing meditation. She tried doing homework for class during class and got two more demerits for failing to pay attention, so she started doing it while she was supposed to be sleeping. On the limousine rides to and from school, she dictated her books into her laptop.

Every minute that she could, Alex spent at Sal's house, in the vault, working on her battery. It was painfully slow going, with each step meticulously microscopically and mathematically checked and rechecked. At one point, her sample became contaminated and she had to wait while Milo acquired equipment to turn the vault into a clean room before she could start over.

Alex would later describe the process as harvesting balloons on a variable Gaussian surface using two new particles. Charges moving at a constant speed but changing direction on their circular orbits bounced on a Gaussian surface twisted to make two segments. The balloon surrounding the charge then expanded and shrunk, changing the balloon's shape quickly which resulted in a minuscule net flux in the field lines per unit area.

That net flux was then converted to energy. The individual amounts of energy gained were insignificant, but together they were used to feed a new symmetrical particle that mutated the large number of electron neutrinos attempting to pass through it into an electron. The process was so incredibly fast and the number of electron neutrinos so great that a massive amount of stored energy resulted. As the energy drained off, it was replenished almost immediately. So long as the new particles stayed inside a vacuum, they didn't suicide by being absorbed into the nearest matter and neutralizing and becoming a scatter of redistributed original particles.

Sleep deprived, frustrated, starving, and angry, Alex felt like she might scream. She was also a little terrified she might make a mistake on her battery construction. If the slightest thing were off, the loop wouldn't stabilize and the spinoff radiation would be deadly. All she needed was the first one and then it could be grown and harvested to make more. It wasn't organic, but that was the best way to think about it. She ran through all of the equations for the thousandth time, checking that everything was within parameters. Every test she could think of, she'd done. All she had to do was flip a simple mechanical light switch.

It only took one more Saturday detention to convince Alex to do it. She went straight to Sal's house afterwards, and strode down into the basement, glancing at the piano as she passed it. That was nothing, compared to the fear of a possible excruciating death. Again, don't think, do. She changed into her clean suit and punched in the vault password and went in and flipped the switch before she could hesitate. The light bulb she had attached popped and the resistor panel in front of it burst into flame.

Alex shouted profanity and scrambled back out of the vault and shut the door. The lack of oxygen would put the flames out. She stripped off the clean suit and dropped it on the floor next to the vault. She taped a note on the door above the combination that said, "Radioactive waste inside. Do not open door. Dispose of vault intact underground per hazardous waste laws and regulations of the Resource Conservation and Recovery Act (RCRA)."

Alex rubbed at her arms and wondered if she had power or radiation poisoning. She was a bit wobbly as she went upstairs to the kitchen and made herself a simple sandwich to eat. She had a Geiger counter, but it was now locked in the vault where it wouldn't do her any immediate good at all. If she were exposed to a deadly dose of radiation, she'd start seeing signs any time within the next three days.

Sunday, Alex spent doing homework for the upcoming weeks and discreetly checking her temperature with Emma's thermometer. Her nerves were too frayed to focus enough to process the few remaining antiques or dictate her books. On Monday, she accrued enough demerits from lack of attention to require Saturday detention again. Tuesday, she had Emma call the school and excuse her due to being ill.

Aside from a case of terrified nerves, Alex seemed fine. She stayed in bed anyway and tried to catch up on her sleep. She assured Rico, then Mario, and then Milo that she was just tired when they called. She wished she could power off her cell phone without incurring their wrath.

By late afternoon, she'd had enough. Alex had to know. She called her limousine driver to take her to Sal's. In the basement, she stared at the vault door and then willed herself to open it. She didn't bother putting on the clean-suit that still lay in a pile on the floor. The intact empty glass container with two electrical leads attached was promising. The resistor board was melted into an obscure black and brown lump and glass from the lightbulb crunched under her shoes.

Alex switched on the Geiger counter and measured everything, starting with herself. Everything was normal with no residual traces of anything abnormal. She took her industrial strength multimeter and checked the glass tube's leads. The multimeter popped with a brilliant spark between the leads. The hairs on her arms stood on end.

"Well, that's power." Alex's voice sounded flat inside the vault confines. She leaned against the wall and pondered the seemingly empty glass tube with a sealed tray-slot in its side. It was new physics. Her formula, sorted out on many long cold winter nights in the tiny cave in the forest, was accurate. Even now, the particles would be multiplying to fill the vacuum, if they hadn't already finished.

Alex took two halves of round flat metal dishes about the size of the smallest hearing aid batteries and set them inside a clamp inside the glass tube's tray. She pushed the tray in, waited a moment, and activated the clamp. She withdrew the tray, extracted the tiny sealed battery and took it over to one of the shelves, where she installed it in a flat rectangle the size of her laptop battery that contained not a battery, but a circuit board that would moderate and convert power as needed. She wished she hadn't fried the multimeter. She took her new "laptop battery" with her, closing and locking the vault behind her. She grabbed her backpack with her laptop in it and left.

Outside, Alex instructed her driver to take her to the nearest hardware store that might sell multimeters. Milo called her and lectured her about random unplanned destinations, particularly when she'd been "too sick to go to school", and she pondered the nature of her cage. She might pretend these people would help her, but ultimately, they, even Milo, reported to Mario. She supposed she should try a little gratitude for having the extra protection and the ability to make her battery years before she'd originally thought would be possible due to funding, but instead, she felt trapped. At what point would she be free?

Using the credit card Milo had given her, she bought not only the best multimeter, but a laptop repair kit for her model. She'd forgotten the other one at Sal's in her rush. Back inside the limousine, she tested her battery. It was exactly as she expected and within specification. She ripped open her laptop and installed the new battery, hoping the lack of a decent grounding system wouldn't fry her computer. Alex powered the computer on. The operating system showed the battery at 100%.

The driver activated the speaker system and asked where Alex wanted to go. It was all she could do not to say "The moon and then the stars. Take me off this crazy planet." Instead she had him take her back to Rico's, where she spent the evening in her room, looking up potential CEOs on the internet. Her computer never dropped below 100% battery and she knew it never would within her lifetime. She felt like flying.

Unexpectedly, the bravery it took to actualize her battery completely neutralized her response to music class. She didn't enjoy it and still had a negative feeling toward it, but the constant gut-wrenching twist in her stomach was gone, as was the annoyingly rapid heartbeat. Apparently nearly dying in excruciating pain from radiation poisoning was more terrifying than mere brutal memories.

"Two demerits and wait in the hall, Miss Smith," the teacher sighed with resignation upon seeing Alex.

Alex shrugged, "I'd like to participate today, if possible?" Her announcement riveted everyone's attention.

"Certainly." The teacher nodded at the pianist who played the 'concert A'.

Alex tentatively tried to repeat it. Her voice had changed since she was a child and was deeper and not as pleasant as it used to be and she had a hard time matching the note. The pianist walked up a few notes and then down a few notes.

"Ok, go stand with the altos over there. Miss Kensington, please share your sheet music with Miss Smith."

Alex moved to the indicated spot and lip-synced the rest of the class. No demerits and she had a working battery. It was time to start working on her picobot fleet so she could build her bioshield. Compared to the math underlying the battery, the picobots were super simple. The hardest part would be getting the initial programming onto them.

The picobots would be impossibly small robots that would operate with a hive-style neural network and would be able to manipulate matter and relay environmental data. They would work in layered units, each with specific functions. She could flood a space with them and know everything about the space at a microscopic level. High speed projectiles (bullets) could be decelerated and caught safely in a net of picobots. A final layer around her would prevent anything from piercing her skin, even if moving slowly. She could be completely safe with a working bioshield.

Alex began designing the picobot programming, taking huge blocks of code from artificial intelligence programs and proven networking and recognition algorithms, specializing the picobot units while allowing them to communicate and share instructions. This kept her busy while attending classes although she acquired a few demerits for lack of attention.

Alex walked into the government office where the judge who wouldn't approve her emancipated minor petition sat. The desk was standard-issue, as was the chair. The items on the desk - a tiffany style lamp that had a pretty stained glass lamp shade with a round brass bottom, a matching brass picture frame (facing the judge), and a very nice leather desk blotter and pen set -

looked like gifts more than personal choice.

Behind him, three bookshelves were filled with thick tomes with creases in their bindings - more for use than show. The judge himself was a round, grandfatherly-looking older man, wearing reading glasses. He set down the papers he'd been reading, took off his glasses, and looked up at her.

"Thank you for agreeing to see me, Judge Newton. I'm Alex Smith." She walked over to the right-most guest chair confidently, set her backpack down, and lowered herself into the standard issue metal padded chair.

"Your lawyer was very persistent." The judge emphasized "very" with negative censure.

Alex replied pleasantly, with a comfortable smile. "At my request."

"I have been curious about that. Why would someone leave you a lawyer in their will, completely separate from the rest of the estate?" The judge leaned slightly to his right, and rested his elbow on his armchair.

"Sal Marino knew my business plans." Alex explained, "I think he knew a lawyer would come in handy for getting that up and operating."

"Milo Paul is not a business lawyer," Judge Newton remarked.

"No, Judge Newton, he isn't. He's a criminal defense lawyer, but he does have a minor in tax accounting and it's only a small jump to becoming a full tax lawyer. He's already signed up for another class." That morning. "I'm pretty sure it was handling taxes that Sal had in mind. The company I want to start is potentially going to be dealing with a massive cash flow."

"That sounds overly naive and optimistic," said Judge Newton, sounding almost exactly like Mrs. Kenwood, telling Alex not to leave school - that "I am old and wise and you should pay attention to my words" attitude. Their experience and wisdom couldn't actually help her because they didn't have all of the information about her plans, and secrecy was critical. Sal, who knew the details and who was also experienced and wise, had approved Alex's plan and helped her work out the schedule and strategy. Alex had to choose which words to listen to and apply and she trusted Sal.

Alex acknowledged the judge's wisdom, "I did say potentially. It's also possible I'll lose the entire estate Sal left me as well as any funds I manage to borrow, but I do have high hopes and will be putting all of my energy into it." Just after she said it, Alex realized how apt 'putting energy into it' was and told herself to never use that word again until her battery was public.

"I don't see it working. Miss Smith, as I told Mr. Paul, I don't believe you have the maturity necessary to act responsibly as an adult." Judge Newton was definitely in lecture-mode. "You should finish high school and perhaps go to college. You'll be 18 soon enough."

Alex wondered what she could say that would help him realize she wasn't just a petulant, unthinking child. "Respectfully, Judge Newton, that's three years. That's three years of lost potential income, and perhaps all potential income if someone else comes up with my idea before then. The time when my

139

product will be most useful is now. Every day that passes cuts my profits. My company needs to be in the market first."

Judge Newton reached for a folder off to his right. "I have here a psychiatric evaluation that says you should be under observation and attending routine counseling sessions."

Alex countered, "From a doctor that gave me drugs that I had an allergic reaction to, and then made his judgement based on my drug-induced incoherence."

"I've seen the countersuit Mr. Paul has submitted." He opened the folder and flipped the page. "I also have a report from your school with a steady history of demerits and detentions."

"I know, Judge," Alex confirmed. "I had a problem with music class. I didn't want to sing in front of anyone."

"Shy?" His tone indicated complete disbelief.

Alex grinned. "A bit of anxiety. I've worked that out now."

"Sing something then," Judge Newton ordered.

The instant, ghastly flashback whipped through Alex like lightning and she was suddenly chained in a windowless room with an old upright piano and a dark, ugly man demanding she sing with those exact words as she played. She shook free of the memory.

Alex's voice wavered unsteadily, but she managed a barely audible rendition of the chorus to "It's a Small World". This was a kind of subtle revenge: let that song get stuck in his head for the afternoon. That song was also aptly fitting.

"Are you ok?" The judge looked at her with concern. "Do you need a glass of water?"

Alex swallowed. "I'm fine. Bit of anxiety is all."

"That's quite a performance." Judge Newton clearly thought she was acting anxious, not truly anxious.

Alex wished she was acting with all her soul. "Judge Newton, my ability to sing or not has nothing to do with my suitability to handle adult transactions. There are many adults who don't sing."

The judge turned the page in the folder. "I also have here letters from three of your teachers. They describe you as," he put his glasses on and read, "remarkably intelligent, yet socially challenged, distracted, irresponsible, unconcerned with education, and disdainful. You don't turn in homework or participate in any activities voluntarily."

Alex ground her teeth together. This man was not going to sign her petition. What could she possibly say to convince him? She needed to decide between three years of torture and a serious risk to her business' survival. Alex knew she should wait out the three years rather than risk her business strategy, but she had a working battery; it wasn't a dream or a hypothesis or a potential failure. She could adjust her strategy if she needed to. Alex heard herself say,

"May I share a secret with you, Judge Newton?"

Clearly frustrated with her stubborn unwillingness to listen to reason, he exhaled in resignation and gestured at her to go ahead.

"The classes are boring and a waste of my time," Alex stated honestly. "I find sitting in them torturous, considering I could be getting my company underway, and your admittedly honorable and noble concern for my best interests is frustrating and would be demoralizing if I weren't so determined to succeed."

"If you are so bored," Judge Newton articulated precisely, "You should ask for harder classes and prove that you belong in them."

Alex retorted, "That school does not offer classes that would challenge me at any level."

"Bull."

"I'll prove it. Pick a book from behind you." At his glare, Alex gestured at him encouragingly.

When Alex kept nodding at him to do it, Judge Newton randomly picked the nearest thick tome. He went to hand it to her and she shook her head.

"Which one is it?" Alex asked brightly. He told her and Alex demanded he pick a page and read the first sentence from one of the paragraphs. Different editions would have different page numbers. She then closed her eyes and finished the paragraph for him. She opened her eyes and turned her palm face up toward him. "You could choose any one of those books and any page."

Judge Newton reached behind himself to the shelf and took another book, thicker with small dense text and Alex repeated her demonstration.

Midway through her recitation of the appallingly boring paragraph, she stopped and inquired, "Do you really think hours writing out material in high school textbooks is a good use of my time? I have not neglected my education, Judge Newton. I just don't advertise it. Only two other people know. Please sign the emancipated minor papers," she pleaded.

After a moment, Judge Newton declared, "No. Deception is also not a qualifying trait."

Milo had known how this interview was going to go, Alex realized. Milo had filled her backpack with bribe-money, but Judge Newton wouldn't take a bribe; he was painfully honest and forthright. Maybe she could use the money in another way? Alex reached in her backpack and withdrew a bundle of one hundred dollar bills. She set it on his desk, but close to her.

"Is that a bribe?" his voice had an acid edge. No way would this judge ever take a bribe.

"No, Judge Newton," Alex answered caustically, deliberately pitching her voice to reflect sour anger. "It's my pocket change." She withdrew another one. "Do you know why the Marino family is interested in me?" She paused, adding another stack of bills. "I accompanied Sal to auctions for just about 10 months total." She put two more bundles of bills next to the previous three.

"During that time, I made Sal approximately two million dollars on antiques trading. All legally. We have receipts." She put the final bundle next to the others. "Four times the amount of money sitting on your desk in fact. Milo Paul isn't an asset. He's a leash." She swiped the stack of bills back into her book bag and stood up. "And you can set me free, but you're looking at a folder of documented nonsense and trying to do the right thing by it."

The judge's eyes had gotten bigger with each stack of bills. "I'll have you moved to a new foster home immediately."

"No! Don't do that!" Alex yelped and then explained, "They're going to fund my business startup expenses. All legally of course," she added quickly. "We're all going to make a mountain of money. That is, if I can get started and don't miss this window of opportunity. Please consider it, Judge Newton. I know exactly what I'm doing and what my goals are. Thank you for hearing me." She left.

Outside in the hallway, Alex went to the nearest water fountain and got a drink. The tremble in her hand wasn't an act. Curse him for bringing up that memory. She was sure to have nightmares again that night. Maybe if she focused on the picobot programming she could get it out of her head enough to get some sleep.

The Founder of Colony One wishes everyone to know that she is human. She made mistakes. She did things inefficiently. On many occasions, she could not see the trees for she was too focused on the forest. Without the people paying attention to such things, Colony One would not exist.

When you spot her errors, forgive her. The answers are obvious sometimes, especially when you are not head down, rushing from task to task, often not even able to sleep, so bent on doing and getting done, that evaluating and improving the process is beyond comprehension.

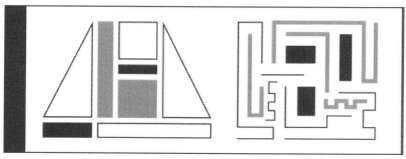

L minus 7:268:20:55   **~61π/45**

Alex climbed into the limousine where Milo waited, reading a book. As soon as the door closed, she let out a string of profanity that would have impressed her old street gang. They were on the fifth month since Alex had been granted the emancipated minor status and were now in Alabama on yet another CEO interview.

Milo closed his book. "Went well, did it?"

"This one was the rudest yet," Alex growled. "You would not believe some of the things he said to me." Alex's hands curled into fists and she knocked them together. "I keep wondering if you should be doing these interviews, but ultimately, he or she has to be able to work with me. I am the age I am and I am a girl. This was supposed to be the easy part."

Milo hmmm'd sympathetically.

"You don't want to be a CEO, do you?" she asked plaintively.

"I have a job, thank you. A very nice one with a brilliant employer who gives me eclectic and interesting tasks," Milo replied calmly.

Alex exhaled tiredly, letting her anger fizzle. It was wasted energy.

Milo set his book aside. "Might I suggest an alternative? A little bit of a break?"

"Sure. Why not?" Alex sighed deeply and rubbed at her thighs. The black business skirt, pantyhose, and low heels weren't very comfortable. "I need to come up with more interviewees anyway." The idea of wading through even more resume-search websites made her feel ill.

Milo smiled. "The Hoover Auction house is having its annual bash tomorrow and I couldn't help noticing how close we are."

"I don't deserve you, Milo. That is an excellent idea." The tension in Alex's shoulders released. Yes, she could take a break and do something she knew she'd succeed at. It would certainly help her battered ego.

"We can stop at a bank, grab some cashier's checks, and be there in time for the opening." Milo handed her his open laptop which was suspiciously conveniently located on the seat next to him. It also contained one of her new batteries. "I already pulled the public catalog. I also purchased tickets to the private auction and the very nice woman on the phone has promised to send that inventory list later this evening." He leaned over and hit the intercom to the driver. "The bank, Jef."

The limousine pulled into the bank's parking lot and Alex stretched. "I'll go make the withdrawal. It'll be a good exercise in trying out my new ID, don't you think?"

"You do like to get beat up." Milo followed her out of the car. "I have to go in and use the facilities anyway. Just wave if you need me."

Alex nodded. She joined the queue and Milo went past her toward the restrooms. She looked around avidly. This would be her first time doing anything in a real bank. It made her oddly nervous. Her eye caught an animated conversation going on inside one of the glass-windowed rooms and she decided to practice her lip reading. The skill might come in handy one day.

"And I'm telling you, Sir," the young man facing her was saying, "You can't do this. It's illegal. I have a degree in business and I'm telling you it's illegal. It puts everyone's money at risk."

The man whose back was to Alex said something, gesturing wildly.

The young man shook his head. "I won't support you on this."

The other man leaned forward, probably speaking.

The young man shook his head angrily. "No, you aren't firing me. I quit!" He came out into the bank's lobby, looked around somewhat wildly, went to another office, jammed some items from the desk into his briefcase, and stormed out of the bank.

Alex's head spun. A degree in business. Newly jobless. Honest. Outspoken. Young enough to maybe take a chance. She quickly stepped out of the line and followed the man out of the bank. She ran as fast as she could in the low heels and skirt across the parking lot to catch up to him at his economy sedan, fumbling with his keys. "Excuse me, Sir?" The young man turned to face her and she asked rather desperately, "May I have a moment of your time?"

"I'm really not interested in whatever you are selling," he grumbled.

"Oh! I'm not a peddler." But she was selling something. "I couldn't help but notice your conversation in the bank. I lip read."

"I'm not going to discuss the bank's business with you. Go inside and ask if you want," the young man grumbled.

Alex smiled as if she were the sun. He would keep things confidential, too! She waved her hand in dismissal, shaking her head. "I... um... Would you like a job?"

"What?" He dropped his keys in genuine surprise.

"You said you had a degree in business and you're obviously concerned with what's legal and can speak your mind. Those are the top three requirements for this position." Well, in the top ten, maybe, but was that relevant?

The man groaned. "Kid, what are you going on about?"

Alex grit her teeth. "Please don't call me kid. I have had a miserable day just like you. The last thing I need is yet another person discriminating against me because of age."

He rubbed at his temple with his left hand. He obviously wanted her to go away.

Alex pressed on, "I'm an emancipated minor which means I'm legally an adult. I'm super smart, super rich, and my new company needs a CEO."

"I'm not a CEO. I'm a bank accountant," the man stated.

"But you could learn to be a CEO. Wouldn't you like to have a try at running a company? Do it right. Not have to deal with that..." she pointed back at the bank, "kind of idiocy?" She saw Milo come out of the bank, looking around frantically. He spotted her and headed in their direction. "Look, why don't I treat you to lunch and we can discuss it. At worst, you get a free lunch and an interesting story to tell your friends."

Milo arrived with an exasperated, "Alex, what are you doing!"

The young man looked at Milo hopefully, "Is this your daughter, Sir?"

Alex introduced Milo with, "This is Milo Paul, my lawyer. He's here to sort out any problems with people not believing I'm an emancipated minor, and to make any necessary adjustments to legal documents for the job I was telling you about."

"Alex, you cannot hire some random person," Milo looked over at the young man apologetically, "In the parking lot!"

"He's got a business degree," Alex countered. "I've done 38 interviews in offices. It's about time for some variety." Milo looked like he wanted to throttle her, so she continued cheerfully, "I didn't get a chance to make the withdrawal. Could you do that and then meet us for lunch?" Rather than give the young man a way to say no, she phrased her question so that acceptance was inherent, "Where's a good place to eat around here?"

"There's a sandwich shop not too far that has good food," the man said. He was obviously still in a daze from having quit his job.

"Great!" said Alex, pretending he'd just agreed to lunch. "Meet us there, Milo?"

Milo looked like he wanted to say something else entirely, but instead asked, "How much money do you want?"

"Um. 400,000, and maybe a thousand in cash?" Alex answered. "Oh, and tell Mario to audit this bank. There might be problem with our money in the near future."

"Ok, boss." He left in the direction of their limousine where he knocked on the window and then pointed over at Alex.

The young man's eyes went wide. Alex offered brightly, "I did say I was rich. Come on, we'll give you a ride if you want or we can follow."

"It's only two blocks that way." The man pointed farther down the street.

"Let's walk then." Alex raised her eyebrows at him enthusiastically. The weather was warm enough if a bit overcast for a November day. She didn't think it would rain any time soon. "I would love to stretch my legs. That barge is roomy, but it's still sedentary. What's the name of the restaurant?"

The young man told her and she took her cell from her pocket and texted the name to Milo and her driver with the comment, "We're walking." She ignored the following beeps indicating incoming messages. "Shall we? By the way, I'm Alex Smith. You are?"

"Brian Kimberly."

"Nice to meet you, Brian. I hope both our days improve." They started walking and then had to go back for Brian's keys, which gave her bodyguard/driver a chance to catch up. Alex introduced him to Brian and the bodyguard/driver said Milo would bring the car and then proceeded to follow a short distance behind them.

Brian shot an uneasy glance at her bodyguard and Alex shrugged it away with, "Unfortunate side effect of wealth."

"So what is your company?" Brian asked. His darting eyes suggested he was rethinking coming with her.

"Manufacturer at its foundation," Alex answered without actually answering. "Although it'll have some community scope so we can support employees with services, much like the companies in the early 1900s did."

He seemed to finally settle into the idea that he was going to lunch with a stranger because his shoulders relaxed. "What's the product?"

Again, Alex didn't actually answer. "I have a working prototype that violates no patents and no laws and will sell to a large number of people. You'll need to sign a non-disclosure agreement before I tell you, and even then, not out in the open where anyone might overhear."

"That sounds extreme for a simple job interview," Brian remarked.

Alex could tell he still didn't believe he was on a job interview. She nodded agreeably. "Yeah, but secrecy is absolutely essential to the initial success of the company. Do you have any idea how thrilled I was that you refused to discuss the bank's business with me? Particularly after just getting fired. It shows great self-control."

"Well, I'm probably going to have to go and ask for my job back tomorrow," Brian grumbled. "I have bills that need to be paid."

Alex glanced at his hand, which was wedding-ring free. "Are you married?" He seemed too young to be married. It wouldn't matter either way.

"No. I have a mountain of tuition bills." He seemed resigned to the fact.

Alex planned to pay tuition for her employees and knew it would eat a significant amount of her money. Education and self-development could not be compromised though, not if she wanted to create a society where individuals would truly care about each other. "Recently graduated?"

"Last year. You'd think that a degree would guarantee a job, but it doesn't. It took me eight months to find this one," Brian complained.

They arrived at the restaurant - a small, busy delicatessen. Alex's bodyguard waited outside and Alex promised to get him take-out. The person at the check-in table greeted Brian by name and peered at Alex curiously. They were given a table along the middle of the wall.

Brian's phone buzzed and he ignored it. "How much does the job pay?"

"It's less than normal for a CEO." Alex started and Brian rolled his eyes. "Everyone, including myself is on the same pay scale. You start at the base salary of $30,000 and each year, we'll have a cost of living increase, as well as potential for an exemplary service bonus increase. We balance the low salary with amazing benefits."

"I make more than that entry level at the bank," Brian pointed out.

"Not once you add in benefits." Alex knew the base salary was going to leave many of their positions unfilled for a while. "Medical, dental, eye care, insurance, tuition. All covered entirely by the company for the employee and for direct family members and dependents."

Brian snorted. "Your company is going to fail."

At least he thought her company would fail because of its policies, not because of her gender and age. Hopefully he didn't think her gender and age created those policies, although that could be useful for her competitors to believe. Alex declared, "I certainly hope that's what our competitors think. The company will also cover rent and utilities on an apartment with size adjusted for family members. We're going to operate at a significant loss for a while, but I have our finances covered and we can go over it in detail once you are hired." His phone buzzed again and Alex asked, "Do you need to take that?"

Brian shook his head. "They'll call back. I've always thought it was rude to play with my phone when I'm with someone."

Alex wondered guiltily if he was referring to her texting Milo and her driver earlier. Luckily, the waitress came and took their order, interrupting that topic. Brian ordered 'his usual' and Alex ordered food for Milo as well as two to-go lunches and told the waitress not to wait for their third person but to go ahead and bring the food when it was ready.

"So where is this company of yours located?" Brian prompted.

"Atlanta. Our initial building is under construction already." Her money was dissolving quickly under "unexpected building costs". Sal had forewarned her of this phenomenon, though, so she was prepared.

"You're building? It's almost like you want to fail." Brian pulled on his ear in bafflement.

"Mmmm hmmm," Alex said cheerily, with her eyes sparkling. "I have a community interest there. I'm dumping a lot of money into the area to fix up local buildings and the environment for the residents. Besides, our company building has a few unique needs for security and I wanted to make sure there aren't any unanticipated loopholes. For example, the building will be a faraday cage except on certain floors where we'll have extra boosted antennas to compensate."

"What are you producing?" Brian emphasized 'are' in concern.

Alex returned her menu to the little metal clip designed for that purpose on the table. "Your office space will take up an entire floor in the building which can be the top floor if you like. I thought it was a nice design, with space for your secretary, a couple different size meeting rooms, and your own private office, but as we're still building, you can change it if you like. You'll also have

147

nearly complete autonomy with respect to the daily operation of the company. You'll have control of anything that doesn't interfere with the company's long term goals."

Brian listened to this list with his head slightly tilted to the left. The way his eyes looked up every so often meant he was actually listening and thinking. "Why are you interviewing me? It sounds like you need a real CEO."

"No one else will hear me out," Alex grumbled. "I mentioned I've had a really awful day. This morning's interview, hmmm, let's just say it was not pleasant." She unwrapped her napkin-covered silverware and set it aside. "Think of it this way: You come work for me, stay long enough to get some decent resume fodder, and then jump to a much higher paid job. Blame any failures on the company owner's impossible and crazy demands. For example, you know that building a space and offering amazing benefits are a recipe for financial disaster, and you warned the owner that this was so, but the owner wouldn't budge on it, so you are simply executing your job as directed."

Brian coughed. "Why would you say that? That's not what you should say in a job interview."

Alex grinned. "Because once you have signed on, seen the product, and heard the long term plan, you aren't going to leave. This is a life-long career that will be the most amazing and fulfilling adventure that you could possibly imagine."

"I think you're looney," Brian commented.

"I think there are 38 people I've interviewed that are going to be kicking themselves in 10 years." Alex's toes wiggled inside her shoe anxiously. She wouldn't show any outward sign, but she really wanted him to say yes. She liked him. More specifically, she liked that he spoke to her as if she were an adult. She liked his honesty. Alex had a very strong gut feeling that Brian was who she needed. Maybe she couldn't hire the CEO she desired, but she could grow one, and she could tell that sales pitch was convincing him. "Give me three months to prove I'm not."

Brian's phone buzzed yet again and he continued to ignore it. "You don't know anything about me. You have no clue if I'm even capable of doing the job."

"You seem bright. Learn anything you don't know on the job. Take whatever classes you want. I'll help and support you in any way that you need." Alex wondered how desperate she sounded. Probably too desperate. "I'm putting everything I have and everything I ever will have into this."

"Why aren't you taking CEO for yourself then?" Brian returned swiftly.

"I'm research and development and money acquisition. I won't have time to take care of company operations." Alex saw Milo arrive outside with her briefcase and stop to talk with her bodyguard before coming in.

Their food arrived just before Milo who handed her the briefcase and sat down. "I thought you might need this. Sorry it took so long. Apparently, the bank's accounts manager walked off the job this morning and they had to call corporate for authorization."

Brian asked Milo, "So have you seen this product prototype she's talking about?"

Milo was busy rearranging his plate, silverware, and food. He was a little bit on the obsessive compulsive side about the arrangement of certain things. "I have."

"Will it sell?" Brian apparently wanted someone else to verify that the job even existed.

Milo looked at Alex, who nodded permission at him. Milo answered, "It'll sell. Every bit of crazy paranoid secrecy she exhibits is valid. Don't let her age or insane business plan worry you. I've reviewed it. It'll work." Milo finished orienting all his food. "What do you do for fun, Brian? What's your hobby?"

"Huh?" Brian set his sandwich back down, without having taken a bite.

With a sideways glance at Alex, Milo said, "Alex is all business and has no clue how to conduct an interview. I'd say it's inexperience, but it's more a complete disregard for the traditional way of doing anything."

Alex set the water she'd been sipping back down and shot Milo a teasing glare.

Brian sipped his soda and answered, "I like astronomy. I don't get to do much here - too much light pollution, but I go out west once a year with my telescope."

Alex bit her lower lip. "I've always liked the stars myself," she agreed. "I've thought about being an astronaut on more than one occasion."

Milo contributed, "Atlanta has worse light pollution than here. She did tell you that's where the job is?" Milo bit into his sandwich.

Brian nodded. "She did." He ate some of his own sandwich.

Milo finished chewing and swallowed and said, "Why don't you tell us a little about your qualifications?" Milo requested, with an encouraging tone.

Brian drank some of his lemonade before answering. "I have a Bachelor of Science in Business Administration with a minor in Energy and Resources from the University of California Berkeley. I have a few minimum wage retail jobs and eight months at a bank that is probably going to record me as being fired." He hesitated and then added, "And I have three summers being a dinosaur performer at The Living Desert in California."

Milo pushed his now used but carefully refolded napkin back into place. "What would you say your greatest strength is?"

"Honesty, maybe. I speak up about how things might improve. Might also be my greatest weakness," Brian amended ruefully.

Milo looked over at Alex briefly and then continued his questions, "What are your goals for the future?"

Brian thought for a moment, and then answered. "I've always wanted to run an environmental cleanup company. See things get done right. There are too many shortcuts that leave the underlying contamination in place."

Alex inhaled sharply. Brian was perfect. She picked up the briefcase Milo had brought and withdrew a folder. "The job's yours if you want it." She pushed her plate with its uneaten hummus wrap aside and opened the folder. "Here's information about the company, including our federal Employer Identification Number, so you can check us out. The website isn't up yet, but you can arrange that if you take the job. Here's a cashier's check to cover moving expenses as well as an airline ticket out. Employee forms, non-disclosure agreement, yada yada. Eventually, we'll want a resume to stuff in the HR files. If you give me copies of your university tuition bills, the company will pay that off too. Think it over, discuss it with your family and friends, and some time in the next seven days, let me know. Cash the check if you might take the job; tear it up if you won't. My contact information is also in here." She gave Brian the folder. He looked daunted. "Oh, and please don't post to social media. It's not time for any kind of publicity yet."

Milo casually reached over and pushed Alex's hummus wrap back at her. "Eat. You're always in such a rush."

Brian set the folder next to his dish and then said, "If it sounds too good to be true, it is. What's the bad side of taking this job."

Milo snorted. "Hah. You have to work with her."

"Oh, thanks, Milo," Alex grimaced at Milo. Then seriously, she said, "For a while, people are going to call you a fool and an idiot because the company will have some absurd policies, like paying benefits and such. The business community is going to blame you and call you inexperienced and naive. Now, to counter that, I'm perfectly happy if you respond that you are only obeying the eccentric company owner, because you will be, but they're likely going to think you are a weak fool for not being able to convince me to run a business correctly."

Milo pointed at her hummus wrap and Alex ignored this, saying, "Also, you are not allowed to name me by name or gender so it'll be a little challenging. Just refer to me as 'the owner'. I'm also going to be working within the company as a custodian. It lets me go everywhere and identify any problems, and gives me some nice blocks of time to sneak off to do other work. Mostly though, it's going to be your reputation. You'll have to put on your dinosaur suit skills and pretend not to be perturbed. You can gnash your teeth on my shoulders as much as you need to, but only mine and only in private. Even the other employees aren't to know I own the business, at least for a while."

Milo cut her off with a gesture, and a stern finger toward her food. He said, "You'll be the public face of the company, but you are not a fall-guy; Alex just doesn't want to spend all her time arguing with employees about the business policies. The business is going to succeed. It just isn't going to look like it."

Alex picked up the wrap and nibbled at it, trying very hard not to stand and jump up and down screaming, "Please take the job! Please take the job!"

"That sounds really nuts." Brian's hand touched the folder where the really large check resided.

Milo drank some of his water. "Another downside is that you are really inexperienced. You will make mistakes. It's going to be a high pressure job for you and probably very stressful."

Alex put her fingers together in a tent. "That's true, but all you have to do is discuss things with me. We can figure out solutions together. We'd be a collaborating team. I'm not a micromanaging boss who is going to flog you over mistakes. I'm absolutely certain you'll do great in the position once you settle in and get used to being at the top of the food chain."

Milo reached over and turned Alex's plate so the wrap was closer to her hand. "Eat." When Alex opened her mouth to say something else, Milo shook his finger at her and pointed at her food. Then he turned to Brian. "I know this interview is bizarre. Take the folder. Read through the material. Come see the work site. The product is worthy and will sell. It really is a once in a lifetime opportunity."

Alex rewarded this with a reasonably sized mouthful of her wrap.

Alex was sorting antiques in Sal's shop when Brian's phone call came in six days later. She scrambled to retrieve her phone from her pocket and put it on speaker mode. "Hello?"

"Alex Smith, please." The audio had a little bit of static but was clear.

"Ah, Brian! Hello! Have you made a decision?" Alex glanced up to the ceiling and mouthed 'please please please!!!!'.

"I've been through the paperwork and I have a question," Brian stated.

"Yes?" Alex fidgeted nervously.

"That fitness requirement," Brian said. "Are you really planning to only get 25 hours per week from full-time employees?"

"Health, education, family, community, and loyalty. Our core values," Alex explained. "Our building's second floor is split between a gym and the cafeteria. 1 hour per work day to be spent in the company gym, with enough time on either side for changing and showering. So that's 10 hours on fitness. 30 minutes for lunch, plus two 15 minute breaks, one in the morning and one in the afternoon. That drops to 25. We get a standard 40 hour paycheck with a more European style time-commitment."

There was a pause before Brian continued, "That's crazy. You can't possibly make a profit like that."

"Most companies don't really get that many actual productive hours per week," Alex asserted. "People checking personal email, surfing the internet, talking over the water cooler, sitting around in a post-lunch brain fog. I actually think the fitness and healthy food will let people operate twice as efficiently during those work hours and we'll actually get an equivalent 50 hours per week."

"Would it be ok if I came to see the workplace and apartment before saying yes?" Brian inquired.

"Of course." Alex's hand drummed rapidly on her thigh and she bounced on her toes.

"Good, because I'm outside the building." Was that a hint of humor in Brian's voice?

Alex didn't hesitate. "Awesome!!!! I'm not there just now, but I can be there in 10 minutes."

"Does it matter where I park?"

"Not at all. I'm putting in a parking garage but I haven't started on it yet. See you shortly. I'm so glad you're here!" Alex disconnected and called her family security to let them know she was relocating. Brian was HERE!!!!! Alex ran, thankful she'd chosen a comfortable t-shirt and khaki pants with sneakers that day.

Brian was leaning against his car, talking on his phone, when she jogged up. He spotted her approaching and hung up. "I expected to see your limousine," he said in greeting. He was dressed in a nice business suit.

"Nah, I was just a few blocks down. Our buildings are close enough for walking. Fitness, you know." Alex hoped her building looked sufficiently impressive, even though it was simply a plain rectangle with few windows. It was taller than its neighboring buildings but obviously newer. The clear company logo stood out against an elegant frosted glass door, but no larger logo hung on the building. "I'm so glad you're here. How about we start over at the apartments? Give the construction supervisor a chance to clear out his crews."

Brian tilted his head in confusion.

Alex explained, "They don't know I'm paying for it. They're contracted. It's part of my attempt at staying incognito for as long as possible."

"Ah. I have to say that's the part that concerns my family the most and makes me wonder why I'm even here."

"Understandable. Really, it's just a schedule thing. Discussing the company goals and policies is a huge time sink if I have to explain it to each individual that works for the company. You can at least end arguments with 'I'm just doing what the owner has unreasonably demanded.' I know that's not a great answer, but maybe it'll make sense after the tour?"

Alex led the way down the street. Along the way, she pointed out the commercial laundry. "All employees and their families will have a laundry card. The company will have a standing account and will pay for services. The apartments are somewhat on the small side, so I didn't want people have to use the space for a washer and dryer. It also limits the laundry detergent contamination in the local water supply. The laundry has promised to only use allergen free, non-toxic, biodegradable soaps."

Brian walked over and looked in the window. The pristine laundry facility hadn't actually opened yet, but the equipment gleamed modern and new and could be operated with minimum staff. "You really want me to stay, don't you?"

"Yeah, but truthfully, the laundry's been part of the company plan from the beginning. It's a demonstration of our community core value. When you said you wanted to run an environmental cleanup company, I knew you belonged here. Eventually, we should be able to do pick up and drop off service." They passed several small, family owned shops. "That's the daycare. Employee costs are heavily subsidized. We can't outright pay it, because that would give unfair benefits to employees with children and I already expect some griping about family tuition being covered."

"How much money do you have?" Brian yelped.

"I'm going to invest so much money that it will drive the business community crazy." After a couple more steps, Alex said, "We're going to make back more and I'm going to sink it directly back into the company. I'm not in this venture to make money. I'm in it to make an ecosystem. I'm planning to change how humanity lives."

"You see? Everything sounds almost reasonable, viable, and then you say stuff like that."

"It scares me how badly I want you to join the company. I actually did a bunch more cost analysis charts to see if I could get you a higher salary. I can't and still make salaries equal for everyone. The funding line at the crossover to profit is just too close. Ah, here we are. This is the apartment building for company housing." The new, wide low-rise had replaced the most derelict apartment building in the area and the residents had been relocated to another nearby building, where rent had been reduced for everyone to minimize relocation pain.

The security guard at the reception desk glanced up from his video game and greeted them. "Hey, Alex, another resident finally?" His eyes snapped back to his computer screen.

"I hope. How's it going?" She stepped around his desk and peered at his screen.

"Not quite as good as yesterday, but I'll beat level 49 by the end of the week." The guard's rapid tapping of keystrokes didn't slow.

"Cool." Alex helped herself to several apartment keys from his drawer. They left him to his game.

Brian glanced back at the security guard playing video games with concern.

"Not much else to do right now." Alex shrugged. While she wished the guard were taking an online course or taking the opportunity to learn some useful skill, she wouldn't push the issue. People needed to find their own motivation. "These first two floors are common areas. We have the pool, gym, and library on this floor. Local residents can also use the facilities with a pass."

Alex and Brian peeked in at the pool which had a large size shallow end and a smaller deep end. The usual chlorine odor was vented outside and the fresh air from outside went through a temperature stabilizer, so the room was comfortably warm.

The library wasn't particularly big or impressive - computer terminals, printers, some empty tables with built-in power outlets, and a cabinet of relevant office and grade school supplies. A small shelf labelled "book swap" already contained an odd assortment of genres. The gym also wasn't much, with a weight-lifting home gym setup and a pair of ellipticals; employees and their families could use the much better gym over at the office building.

The door to the stairs was next to two elevators, one of which was over-sized so furniture could be brought in. Everything was clearly labelled; no subtle numbers in the door jams, thank you very much. Alex asked, "Are you ok with stairs or would you prefer to take the elevator?"

"Stairs are fine," Brian said, earning an approving smile from Alex. The stairwell's bright lighting and windows illuminated the wide, comfortable height stairs. Low pile carpet muted their steps and kept echoing down to a minimum.

Alex continued her tour on the next level. "This is the recreation hall." Inside, pool and ping pong tables dominated the left half of the room. The right half contained several large tables with a couple bookcases filled with both traditional and exotic new board games and puzzles. On the room's sides, there were a dozen glass-windowed, but soundproof rooms, including a couple with shiny black upright pianos. Several mini-theater areas were set up for group computer games. "For musical instrument practice and games where this room is just too noisy," Alex explained as she pointed to the security cameras.

The next room over had a children's playground that was divided into a miniature realm for age 3 and under and a beautiful climbing, slide, and swing fort for the older kids. The ground was safely squishy and strong lights brightened the already lively colors. Nearby benches and tables offered respite for parents. A large cabinet off to one side was clearly marked to contain first aid supplies with a nearby set of water fountains. Windows along one side looked out over the city street.

There were also two multi-stall restrooms, which were odd in that the walls between the restrooms and the play area were glass, allowing parents to see the hand washing area and stalls clearly. The stalls themselves had low, opaque doors where a child's shoes would be visible. Child-friendly cartoon people stenciled on the stall doors indicated whether the inside toilet was adult-sized or child-sized. Baby changing areas in both restrooms had raised privacy shields with adjacent sinks and trash bins.

"It's not as nice as being outside," Alex said at this luxury, "But this is a dense area of the city. Getting enough space just for this building, our company building, and a parking garage was challenging. Several of these lights are full-spectrum to help with the lack of sun."

Childless Brian nodded and probably didn't grasp exactly how much protection was built in for the children. Alex, however, sticking with her original company goal, would keep the children safe. This was only the start.

The last room on that floor had a computer lab. There were already several community-use computers, but most of the room was divided into varying size kiosks with tables and power outlets. Brian's eyes lit at the comfortable sofa-lounge area with its two large screens for group games.

"I feel like I'm back in my college dorm," Brian commented, amused. "I'm really beginning to worry about the size of the apartments." His voice held a hint of real concern.

Alex laughed. "As a proper real estate agent, I should describe them as cozy? Come on. Let me show you the one for a single person. It's small, but I think it's livable."

Alex took Brian up three floors by elevator this time. "This is one of the furnished ones. We have several floor plans, but they all have the same cubic footage."

The single-occupant apartment had a kitchen separated from the living room area by a counter with stools that would seat four, as would the sofa and chairs in the living room. Across from the low coffee table in front of the sofa, a fairly large wood entertainment center had space for a TV as well as a fold-out computer desk. The bedroom was large enough for a king-size bed, dresser, and had a small closet. The bathroom had both a rectangular jacuzzi tub and shower.

Brian peered around somewhat in dismay, perhaps wondering where he would put all his things.

"You can reclaim quite a bit of space just by ditching the jacuzzi tub and dropping to a queen size bed," Alex said. "The lights out in the living room are full-spectrum and the walls are soundproof. The air filtration system is state-of-the-art, so even if you were allergic to dogs, and the next person over had one, it wouldn't contaminate your air. All utilities are paid and each floor has its own dedicated wifi, as well as its own common room with TV."

Brian ran his fingers along the bed's comforter and then rubbed his chin. "What's your apartment look like?"

"You can come see it if you like," Alex said. "I won't come here except to sleep - going to be much too busy for the next ten years to spend much time here. I also own a house about a mile away, but I won't live there; I inherited it. I need to make sure this much space will actually work as a personal habitat. It's somewhat experimental to reduce humanity's footprint on the environment." And it was the only way to fit the number of employees she needed into the immediate area. She relocked that apartment and took Brian down the hall, where she opened another door. "Mine."

Inside, Alex's space reflected a tiny jungle, reduced to merely two rooms - a spacious main room and a bathroom. The unmade twin-sized adjustable bed disappeared into foliage. Large, beautiful ferns, orchids, and assorted houseplants grew under specialized lighting. Two magnificent Areca palms framed an empty computer desk with a lamp opposite the door. The desk shared an easily rotated chair with an art table. Nearby a shelf of painting supplies were ready for convenient use.

Alex nervously wondered if the room made her seem eccentric or just more insane. She adored the way the room smelled of earth and oxygen and made her feel like she was outside, but what would Brian think? "The bathroom has my closet with clothes. I don't need much."

"Um. Where's your kitchen?" Brian asked after a moment.

The room definitely made her seem more insane. Alex replied, "Don't need it. I'm going to be eating at the company cafeteria all the time. Food for employees is free there and someone else will make it and clean up the dishes. It's a time-thing. I might even hire someone to come and maintain these plants and take care of my laundry."

"Not going to adhere to the 40 hours per week maximum?" Brian said with an arched eyebrow.

"I have to maintain my cover and I have some family obligations in addition to acquiring money for the company. Also, I want to spend some time in the common areas socializing and getting to know everyone. If someone has a complaint, I want to hear about it so we can fix it. I need to cut away as many time sinks as I can."

"It sounds like you'll burn yourself out and this whole enterprise will collapse into a huge pile of bills." Brian reached out and touched one of the ferns.

As Alex routinely ran her fingers across the soft ferns herself, maybe he wasn't too appalled by her choice of decors. "Yeah, that's why I need you. You have to take care of everything I can't. Someone has to run the business infrastructure and delegate critical tasks." Her phone beeped and she glanced at it. "Milo says the building is clear. Shall I show you our facilities? Reception is done, as is my lab, security, and the manufacturing floor. The main offices should be complete today. I had them hold off on your floor in case you wanted to design it."

Brian's eyes went very wide.

"Did you bring the non-disclosure agreement?"

"It's signed and in my car."

"Great!" Alex beamed at him.

As they walked back, Brian asked, "So how much additional room does each family get per person?"

"It's equivalent to the bedroom in that first apartment I showed you. It's not much, but triple if the person is wheelchair bound. The system works on multiple levels. It reduces environmental impact and builds community - gets people out of their isolation to create strong friendships with their neighbors. If we care about each other, we'll help each other. I might say to my CEO, hey, help me cart out this trash today; there's a lot of it, and my CEO would help, rather than say, 'It's your job. You do it.' Even better, my CEO might see me struggling and just help without being asked. There are people who naturally do this, but most are too self-absorbed to even notice someone else struggling."

Brian snorted. "Sounds too idealistic to be actualized. Are you building a company or a cult?"

Alex chose her words carefully. "An ecosystem that will be funded by my product under the umbrella of a business."

"So, cult."

"Nah. A cult needs a crazy leader to worship. I decline that honor; it's got the wrong connotation. I expect the employees to grump about the strictly vegetarian cafeteria and hate the owner for it. This should unite everyone and give them something harmless to complain about. We can expand to allow eggs and fish eventually, and maybe meat one day, but not for a long time. We're aiming for environmentally sustainable." At Brian's unsettled look, Alex wondered if maybe she shouldn't be so candid about social dynamics. "People can still eat at the local restaurants and one of the local businesses is going to be an open 'cook-it-yourself' kitchen. We're not enforcing the lifestyle. Everything in our building will be organic, non-GMO, antibiotic free, and pesticide free. Easier as vegetarian."

They arrived back at the office building where Milo was waiting. Brian retrieved his non-disclosure form from his car and gave it to Alex who glanced at it and handed it off to Milo.

Milo filed the paper in his briefcase without reading it. "Do you need anything before I head home for the day, Alex?"

"Nope, I'm good. I'll need another set of mid-size packing boxes at the store tomorrow though."

Milo half-bowed and left in his car.

Alex turned to Brian and smiled. "Shall we?" She unlocked the door and let them in, locking it again behind them. She flipped on the lights. The reception area wasn't much - just an information counter near the entrance and a long counter off to the left in front of a huge open space. An archway behind it was clearly labelled "Shipping and Receiving". Alex pointed at the long counter. "Recycling drop-off. I have this absurd plan to ship off our product to customers wrapped in random sterilized, clean trash from employees and community families. It'll save us a fortune in shipping supplies and help sell our 'environmentally friendly and looney business'. Imagine paying gobs of money and receiving a cereal box with some newspaper stuffed inside, and our product. We save on the local landfill that way too."

Brain guffawed. "That would certainly stir up some publicity."

"I imagine a fan website with pictures of 'stuff that came with our purchase'. Mine came wrapped in this old t-shirt!" Alex grinned mischievously. "Would you like to start at the top and work down or in my lab and then go through the building?"

Brian shrugged.

"To the top then. I'll show you the beast you'll inherit before the product." They took the elevator to its top floor - the third floor, which was split between security and two massive locker rooms.

They passed through one of the locker rooms, and then through the security tunnel, and switched to a different elevator that actually went to the 20th floor. Alex pointed out the medical office as they passed it. "Most of the building is going to be storage while we build up inventory. We won't actually sell anything for... a while." The top floor was still completely unfinished, with construction debris everywhere. "Your penthouse," she announced with a flourish.

Brian peered in. "Why was the light on already?"

The more time she spent with him, the more Alex wanted Brian to take the job. That had been one astute observation. "The one light switch at the entrance turns on the whole building."

"That seems wasteful." Brian's tone indicated censure and Alex was glad he felt free to speak what he thought.

Alex contained her giggle, if just barely. As soon as construction was done and the building was entirely hers, she'd put her own power source in to cut their electric bill when they went operational. They'd still need some drain power for the electric company to bill for appearances, but the bulk of their use would be completely covered. "It does seem wasteful, but we'll fill the building and it'll be easier than going around and turning things on every day. Our electric bill will eventually balance out and tip in our favor."

Changing the subject, Alex said, "The next 12 floors all look just like this one. I'm going to use them for storage. We won't even bother finishing them. I'm just going to stack pallets in them."

The elevator took them down to level 7. The elevator opened to a short hallway with a door that would have been secure if there weren't a gaping hole where the door's keypad unit should be. "I'll put labels on all the elevator buttons. This is manufacturing. In order to get in, you have to have a badge that is encoded to let you in. Yours and mine will open anything, well, technically, yours will open anything but my lab, for safety reasons," she explained. She led him into the manufacturing area, which was split between a huge open space, and a glassed-off slightly smaller space. "This will be a hard-hat zone, and we'll mark off the floor for designated walk paths and store the hats here. That area behind the glass is for electronics and quality control. Everything feels so empty, but as soon as construction is done, I'll start bringing in equipment and furniture."

Floor 6 was parsed into multiple, differently sized soundproof meeting rooms. Alex pointed out the one room with a security-box door. "That's for spare parts and maintenance for manufacturing and electronics. We'll need a couple people who are really good at repairing equipment, because I don't want to bring in outsiders to do it."

They descended another level to a floor that was split into decently spacious offices. "For human resources and legal, with a few extra spare offices."

"Legal?" Brian choked.

"Yeah, for employees who need wills, tax help, or whatever. If we can find a lawyer who will come work for us for 30k and live in a closet. I'm going to handle the business' legal for a while with Milo's help. Believe me, we will be entirely legal. I can't risk our future on stupidity."

Brian relaxed again. "Glad to hear it. I don't want to end up in jail."

"Yeah, so if you see anything that seems out of place, bring it to my attention immediately so we can get it fixed. None of that bank manager nonsense." Alex was fully apprised on that bank's issues from Milo's report. Mario had already shifted the family money. "Floor 4 looks just like this one, mostly. It's for information technology and production. We're going to produce a lot of labels to stick on that recycled trash." She winked. "Next, my lab. Note, this elevator doesn't go below third floor. Push 7, 8, and 10 at the same time. That'll take us to the basement which is research and development."

Brian's eyebrows scrunched together. "Doesn't the construction crew know about this?"

Alex shook her head. "I cut the opening in the basement and reprogrammed the elevator myself." With the help of several discreet, strong Marino men, she thought ruefully. "The lab is on the opposite side of shipping and receiving's storage area. I'll put in a one-way emergency exit into the storage area once the construction crew is done and on their way."

The elevator opened to another short, if pallet-wide security tunnel. This time, the door's control pad was in place and lit. Alex took a card out of her pocket and ran the card over the panel. Her picobots silently verified her DNA against the badge and triggered the open-code.

Alex was incredibly pleased with how well her picobots were working out. They operated even better than expected. The almost impossibly small robots operated in mini-hives of neural networks with each hive performing a unique function and able to dynamically pull from or add to neighboring hives for different task requirements. They could even pass along information in a binary matrix.

Alex could leave the picobots in place or send them off on specialized tasks. Alex even had many layers of them around herself working as a bioshield and able to stop and track bullets, knives, and pathogens. The picobots in front of the door's security panel hovered, identified a security card, then the DNA of the person holding the card. If both didn't match, they wouldn't let the security panel shift to allow entrance.

Alex had left the original equipment that created the first molecule over in Sal's vault, but she'd relocated the glass container and the gear necessary to extract more power cells. The floor had some yellow taped walk-paths, but nothing was in the empty places. Eventually, wheeled pallets of batteries would build and she could take the batteries upstairs for storage. There was a cot with a pillow and a thin, crumpled blanket in the corner.

Alex went over to the wooden lab-desk where the seemingly empty glass container with two electrical leads and small sliding tray was pushed off to the side, and her laptop was taking the space of importance. The laptop was open, turned on, and obviously running some data calculations. She picked up the laptop battery she'd saved just for Brian and turned to give it to him. "This is our first product."

"What is it?" Brian turned the flat metal box in his hand.

"Laptop battery," Alex announced proudly.

"A LAPTOP battery!!!" Brian said incredulously. "You're cracked. You can't do all this for something already stable through the market. Why did you even bother?"

Alex shrugged, practically bouncing on her toes. "See my laptop over there?"

"Yeah? It's a laptop." He sounded disgusted.

Alex grinned mischievously. "See any power cords? Any power outlets in this room anywhere?"

Brian looked around, pausing in his anger.

She gesture for him to come over to her laptop. "This has been running calculations for about a month now, but it's definitely been on through our entire tour. See the battery level in the taskbar?" Alex pointed. It still read 100%. She minimized the app, and brought up a few other things and closed them again, to show it wasn't a screen saver. "This, my new CEO, is a power source created using new physics, that will not need recharging or any kind of maintenance for the next thousand years. It will outlive you and me and our children and our children's children. It can be scaled up to run small appliances, cars, boats, airplanes, and then houses, buildings, factories, and cities. It safely and cleanly replaces all power sources on the planet."

"Impossible," Brian said scornfully.

Alex remained calm, absolutely sure of herself. "It never needs a power outlet. It never fails."

Brian thought a moment, teeth grinding. "Even if what you say is true, the second you get the patent, another group will pick it up and make clones."

Alex nodded agreement. "That's why I'm not going to get it patented and our security has to be so obnoxious."

"But someone will crack it open and figure it out."

Alex rubbed her hands together gleefully. "It's self-terminating. If they open it, there will be nothing for them to study," she boasted.

Brian stared at the ugly plain rectangle in his hand. "The oil companies will never let you succeed."

"And that's why the owner is a crazy loon," Alex whispered, imitating a madwoman. "We're going to self-destruct without requiring any effort on their part whatsoever. They only need to sit back and laugh and watch us implode in a mountain of bills."

In a normal voice, Alex continued, "They can crunch numbers just as easily as we can. At least that's what I'm going to let them believe. I have some financial resources they don't know about. But they'll be waiting for us to sink to a point where they simply buy us out to save us from financial ruin. Except one day, we're going to flip a switch and go from barely making a profit to being unstoppable. The world isn't going to know what hit it."

Brian's eyes narrowed thoughtfully. "What about the lawsuits and the government requesting full technical specifications, in the interest of safety?"

"We'll have a large number of independent safety checks by then. I'm the only one who knows what's inside and I'm not going to tell anyone. They might throw me in jail for a bit, but I have lawyers who will get me out again. We aren't breaking any laws. I'm prepared for this." She smiled manically, "You said you want to clean up the environment? How does getting rid of oil drilling, coal plants, fracking, nuclear power plants, and fuel exhaust sound as a cleanup exercise?"

He turned the battery over in his hand.

"Tell you what, you brought your laptop with you, didn't you?" At Brian's nod, Alex continued, "Let's install that and you can try it out over the next day or two and see that I'm not lying to you, and when you decide to be my CEO, and we have all the legalities in place, I'll show you my long term projections and give you hard data on finances and strategy. It's going to work, but it's going to be an incredible and not always pleasant journey."

Two days later, Brian became Green World's second full-time employee. Alex turned over the company projection data for the next ten years and they worked out the initial hiring plan. Brian pointed out their need for an extensive IT department as well as detailed patent documentation for the laptop battery adapters.

Green World grew chaotically, wildly unpredictable, without any apparent plan. Brian got a secretary with the simple expediency of calling one of his old college friends. They got an IT department by hiring one of the Marino boys who was still in high school. After a brief delay while the Marino boy built their website to basically be a job application page with current postings, they collected random employees. No senior positions filled because the pay was too low, but the support positions filled in. A vegan husband and wife couple were hired to run the cafeteria. The stereotypic multicolor dreadlocks and piercings in no way impaired their ability to produce excellent food. Alex made sure they had any equipment they wanted.

It was an odd time in the company. If someone needed something done and the position hadn't been filled yet, they did it themselves or found someone to help, and fired off another point toward "we need this position filled". When enough points were acquired, the position got upgraded on the website as "hiring with priority; signing bonus". Within the company, every four months, if someone wanted to change positions to something open and they were qualified, they could, without any negative impact on their reputation. Tired of doing computer support? Take a break and wash dishes for four months. The paycheck and benefits remained the same.

The recycling team was actually the first one to be complete. Employees were finding the apartments much too small for their furniture and randomly acquired items. Some things employees sold directly, but much of it was dropped off at the company for recycling. These were sorted into piles - distribute, refurbish, reclaimable trash, or trash. The last category was by far the smallest. If employees wanted something that had been turned in, they could just take it. If multiple people wanted the same thing, they simply rolled dice to see who would get it. Non-employees paid a minimal processing fee for things and a number of thrift shops around Atlanta sent employees on "raids" to fill in their own stock. Alex was glad to see the excess go.

Alex herself took away the trash to molecularly rearrange into batteries, and started on producing pallets of batteries which she then stored on the upper floors that no one had access to. Some of her time was spent zipping around the building making sure things stayed moderately clean while talking with and listening to employees. Because everyone changed into khaki jumpsuits to go anywhere past the 3rd floor security, and they were not allowed to bring anything in with them, the upper floors remained mostly clean.

Alex cheated a bit on the bathrooms, letting her picobots clean and sanitize the facilities, and thus stealing herself a chunk of time to work on batteries, novels, and antiques trading. She really liked having her picobots, but recognized that the technology was really much too powerful and could be easily abused if anyone ever found out about them.

Most of Green World's hires came as friends and family of employees. The people who began work for her company suddenly discovered an oasis in the desert. Instead of being treated like cogs in a machine and being driven by unreasonable demands and deadlines, they were allowed to excel, solve problems that needed to be solved, able to pursue any educational dream they had, whether or not it was job related. Their concern over monthly bills lessened, and they found time for family and community activities. The exercise and health food began having its anticipated effect on people's mood and energy levels.

Green World finally got a manufacturing floor manager because of the tuition benefits. She was a widow with three kids just starting college and her old job just wasn't covering bills. As soon as manufacturing was functioning, Brian sent down specifications for things for them to build. Alex checked products in the evening and sent back anything that failed inspection with a simple "out of spec" sticker and added another point to the job announcement for "manufacturing quality control personnel". There was never any demoralizing lecture or embarrassing blame. The manufacturing team was doing their best; a fact which Alex knew because she'd go through cleaning and talking with people. It was just taking time to get the machines calibrated and personnel trained. Safety was the priority, then quality. Eventually, she knew they'd be a fine manufacturing team.

There was some speculation and concern that the company wasn't actually producing a product or selling anything for a profit yet, but Brian assured everyone that they were on schedule according to the company owner's directives. Alex, meanwhile, chose one of the annual largest technical conventions out of Las Vegas as their deployment location and began planning.

Manufacturing, under a dictate of absolute secrecy, finally started producing laptop battery adapters and storing those on the other empty building floors. They'd still need a full year's inventory in order to keep up with sales when the full impact of her battery became apparent. As far as the employees in manufacturing knew, they were going to be selling laptop battery adapter cases with some odd interior specifications. Some of the cases were designed to replace laptop batteries while others were external to be used as chargers for laptops whose batteries could not be replaced.

Alex happily found Brian at his desk when she rolled her cleaning cart into his office and pushed it against the wall. She threw herself into one of his leather chairs and leaned back, kicking her feet out. She waited for him to look up from his computer monitor and then said, "I want to hire some mediators."

"Oh?" he pushed his computer keyboard off to the side.

Alex explained, "We had one of the developers yelling at an order clerk for accidentally purchasing the wrong hardware. Typo'd model number. It sets him back and he'll miss his deadline, and he has to come explain that to you.

But honestly, it wasn't at all about the hardware. His girlfriend broke up with him yesterday. He's in a viciously foul mood. The clerk was nearly in tears."

Brian hmm'd.

"I had a talk with both of them individually and it'll be ok. Our dev is totally embarrassed at having lost his temper now and is going to apologize." Alex rubbed her kneecap and then said, "But we're going to have to mitigate this sort of thing if we're going to build a cohesive team. The person in the wrong is embarrassed and upset about having made a mistake, and generally wishes they hadn't done it. The person who has been wronged, disappointed, or hurt, can have overwhelming anger and frustration." Alex concluded, "We need counselors, people with both psychiatric and medical training."

Brian cleared his throat. "Normal companies hold training and the company president and management give motivational speeches."

"Good point. Do that, too." Alex stretched tiredly. "I still want to hire some mediators and a behavioral biologist. I want people who can step between the ones who are upset and help them master forgiveness and understanding and learn to care about each other. People make mistakes out of ignorance or distraction or physical or mental challenges. But we need them to stop screaming at each other and being upset."

Brian squinted at her skeptically. "Many religions have been trying to teach this since the beginning of time. Are you going to solve it overnight?" Alex merely smiled at him and he sighed, reminding her of Milo when she asked for something particularly challenging. Brian conceded, "Ok, then. We also need an employee handbook and signed company policy statements, in case we have to fire anyone. Legal protection."

It was Alex's turn to sigh. She lamented, "I don't want a legal system. That whole litigation, compensation, justification, and validation system is abused and pointless. Our security can view the video feeds of any incident, and we can determine if a crime has been committed. If a crime, the person can be fired. Otherwise, it needs to be a matter of 'it happened; get over it; do what needs to be done now that it's happened'."

"Yeah, but we still need the paperwork trail."

Alex sighed. "You're in charge. If we need it, we need it." After a moment, she added, "The mediators can hang out in the cafeteria, gym, and rec hall and talk with people. Don't give them offices."

Brian shook his head slightly. "This is a strange company."

Alex straightened and stood up. "You're doing a great job with it, too. I trust you. I want the best company environment my mountain of money can buy."

Six months later, Alex, Brian, and a small crew of Green World employees stood in front of their company's booth at the Las Vegas technical conference. The company wouldn't sell any batteries until the next year, but the booth's purpose was to announce their presence and set the idea that their company owner was crazy.

Alex studied her company's setup. Muted soft, light brown carpet was gentle on the feet with special anti-fatigue padding underneath. Three lighter-toned walls and a temporary ceiling with high-tech noise dampeners built in lined the back sides and overhead to reduce the vendor hall noise level. Alex's picobots would provide complete noise-cancelling when told to do so, but not many were likely to actually step into their space and notice it. Their booth had the feel of a spacious, deluxe lean-to.

Gentle, warm-toned lights reflected off the booth ceiling from hidden light fixtures along the ceiling edge, replacing the harsh lights of the conference hall with a natural color, but still bright enough to comfortably see. Their company logo hung in the upper left back corner of the enclosure, large enough to read clearly at seven meters, but not garishly prominent in any way. The only item in the space was a one meter square glass display case on top of an even lighter tan-toned box pedestal in the center of the carpet. It only came up to about mid-chest height and wasn't very impressive to look at. Inside was a slightly brighter spotlighted folded tent-card with the following year printed on it. There were no pamphlets, no tables, no chairs, no company spiffs, and this year only, no booth attendants. It was exactly what she'd imagined. Everything was powered by a completely hidden battery in the back wall.

Alex made a show of checking her clipboard and said to Brian, "I think that's it, Sir." The other six employees agreed. All eight of them were wearing the owner-specified company convention "uniform" - an extremely comfortably muted earth-tone green one piece jumpsuit that could have additional layers added underneath for warmth. These had two large zippered thigh-pockets for phones, money, and such. Their first names and the company logo were stitched on at the left shoulder. Even their comfortable walking shoes matched in a slightly darker green.

Brian announced, "I think so too. We've done exactly as the owner specified. Anyone want lunch?" His jumpsuit also had CEO stitched on underneath the company logo.

Around them, other companies were setting up their own booths with brightly flashing, somewhat garish signs and videos, some with music and sound effects, and cloth-draped tables with cases of additional handouts hidden underneath. The bigger, more affluent companies had additional temporary walls, while most companies just had high back-signs. The noise level outside their booth was echoing and loud and the conference attendees hadn't even filled the space yet.

Other vendors who happened to look up from their rushed setup tasks stared at them curiously but dove back into their own preparations. The eight matching outfits were impressive as a unit but wouldn't be that remarkable once everyone had split up. Alex definitely wanted functional comfort as the primary feature for everything.

Brian treated everyone (with the company's credit card) to a fantastic lunch at a local Japanese steak house. They laughed and joked, discussing the bus ride out with its mini-vacation stops, and peered through their conference attendee bags, talked about things they wanted to see at the convention. Alex was incredibly pleased with the casual family feeling of the group. No one treated Brian any differently by this point and he seemed less stressed.

The entire company, except for these eight people, were on paid holiday for two weeks. Their office building was secured, outside security consultants (Marino family bodyguards) had been hired to guard their building, and everything was on hold. These employees had volunteered to give up their vacation and "work" the convention in exchange for the rented luxury bus trip out and back, where they'd stop at several tourist attractions, and be able to attend the huge annual technical convention. Expenses were being covered by the company in exchange for their loss of "vacation".

This first year was going to be the easiest: each employee had to work four hours per day of the convention - sit somewhere in plain view, playing on a laptop that was not plugged in. They were told to charge any devices in their hotel rooms and to never be seen with a power adapter. That was it - a simple, subtle advertisement. Most of the employees themselves didn't know what the product was yet. The manufacturing team knew they were making laptop battery adapters, but they were still sworn to secrecy.

The employees split up after lunch to go to their hotel rooms and get settled. They were all free to be on their own schedule until it was time to pack up the booth.

Alex threw her duffle bag on the bed and looked around her hotel room. By hotel standards, the room was simple, if tastefully decorated, with two queen-size beds, an entertainment center, dresser, and balcony. Compared to her bed and bathroom apartment, this looked quite grand. She wondered if she should spend a little more time at Sal's beautiful house for equilibrium because even the generic, reproduction artwork in the hotel room looked nice.

Brian came by Alex's hotel room late Friday night after the convention activities had closed down for the evening. She was busy typing in another novel to publish. "What's up?" she asked, opening the door, and standing aside so he could come in.

When the door closed again, Brian strode farther into the room and kicked one of the still-made beds before throwing himself on it. His voice was laced with acid when he said, "The senior chairman of the convention would like the owner to call him at the owner's earliest convenience tomorrow morning. Our vendor display is unacceptable and they would like it removed. Additionally, even though I'm a CEO, my clothing is inappropriate for the executive lounge and my company, lacking any actual product, is not enough of a company to allow my inclusion in the any of the executive activities. I've been specifically uninvited."

"Ah. Want a drink?" Alex said softly. "There's some appallingly awful overpriced liquor stocked in the cabinet here."

Brian shook his head. "Aren't you listening? How are we supposed to launch our product here next year if they're going to kick us out?"

"It'll be fine." Alex moved her open laptop and sat on the opposite bed.

"It's not going to be fine! They want our display removed and they aren't going to let us have the booth again next year."

Alex spoke calmly, "In the morning, I'll completely activate the soundproofing on our display walls. At 10 a.m., I'll go inform the chairman that our owner is currently visiting Russia and is in business meetings. With the time zone differences, a phone call is impossible, but you would personally like to speak with him at our booth in the vendor hall. By then, the Saturday crowd will be swarming the hall and the ambient sound will be deafening."

Alex pushed her laptop lid closed. Alex briefly wished Milo were there; Milo would have stomped this nonsense before it could manifest. Brian, however, was not Milo, and needed some reassurance and direction. "When you see the chairman, invite him into our space to stand on the carpet. If the sudden noise difference doesn't impress him technically enough, remind him that we signed a five-year contract for our space in the vendor room that is binding for both him and us, and we would still like to launch our product here next year."

Alex searched her memory and found a useful note about the chairman in the conference's event booklet - they were having a small fundraiser mid-afternoon. "If that doesn't persuade him, tell him that the owner has agreed to privately donate $500,000 to St. Jude Children's Research Hospital in his sister's name if he would be so kind as to honor our contract. If he would still like our booth removed, tell him it will take some time to track down your employees to arrange for it, and then come find me."

"Good grief. How much money do you have?" Brian stood then and went over to the cabinet with the hotel liquors, chose a double-serving bottle of bourbon, removed the cost-will-be-added-to-your-bill paper and opened it. He drank it all in one motion.

"Enough. Don't panic. I think the sudden quiet will be enough for him to let us keep our display. We're going to be fine." Alex would keep any fears and doubts to herself and maybe Milo.

Brian returned to his seat on the bed, shoulders slumped forward. "I really wanted to attend the executive seminars."

"I'm sorry." Down the hall, an ice maker filled someone's bucket. It was barely audible.

"I've been too busy to take time to go to any classes and I feel like I'm

167

drowning most days." Brian rubbed at his neck. "They laughed when I said I our HR department was completely handling our recruitment. I looked that up today. It's in the top mistakes executives make. They laughed harder when someone pointed out we're all on the same salary scale." He bent forward and crossed his arms across his chest. "At least when I was a dinosaur performer, they were supposed to laugh and it wasn't mean laughter."

Alex rubbed her thigh, trying to think of something to say to console him. Words weren't enough. She went over and put her hand on his shoulder. "Brian, it's my fault. That laughter is vital to our company success."

"I know. I feel like giving up sometimes. I'm not the person you need here. You needed someone with experience. I never know what to do. I'm guessing 90% of the time. The company is getting too big, too fast. I can't keep up."

"Brian, you're doing an excellent job." Alex sat next to him, keeping her hand on his shoulder. "You chose Mark for HR and he's doing just fine at recruitment. I'm paying attention to all the departments. We have no major problems."

"These people are counting on me for their jobs. They're worried about the company folding. Now this conference is going to throw us out."

"Nah. Just the conference chairman. I have a contingency plan if he refuses to let us continue." Alex held onto her visible confidence. A different product rollout venue wouldn't be nearly as effective.

"How can you be so calm?" Brian pulled away from her hand, stood and went back to the bar, but instead of more alcohol, he took one of the equally overpriced waters and opened that. He leaned against the hotel dresser, crossing his arms and staring at her.

"Because we're going to succeed." Alex leaned back against the hotel bed's wooden headboard that was glued to the wall. The top edge stuck out and poked into her back and she pulled one of the pillows out and put it behind her. What idiot designed a bed headboard that couldn't comfortably support a person's back? Particularly in a hotel where sitting on the bed was an expected activity. "Look, when we get back, I'll come by your office and see what I can do to help out."

"You don't have time. I see you working. You never stop. Not even this late at night on a vacation trip."

True enough, Alex thought ruefully. "I have time."

"The head of manufacturing came to me before we left and wanted to know how the hell we're going to keep the company afloat selling laptop battery adapters," Brian said.

"It's a fair question." Alex knew from talking with employees that they were worried.

"I know! I couldn't answer her, Alex. I just sat there stuttering like an idiot. She stormed out."

"Practice saying, 'We are doing what the owner directs. I'll pass along your concerns,'" she advised.

"They aren't satisfied by that, Alex. They're worried about their livelihoods, their families. They've finally had a chance to work for a company that puts them first. They know what a good thing they've got. They're scared of losing it."

"Ok." Alex ran her fingers through her hair. "I'll write a forum post for you along the lines of 'having a firm belief that the owner is prepared for the long-term continuation of the company and that you have discussed this at length with the owner'. It won't solve the problem, but will let everyone know that you are aware of the precarious nature of our enterprise. I'll see if I can't redirect everyone's energy toward our vegetarian menu. Maybe we can distract them for a year with that?"

Brian groaned, rubbed at his neck again, standing upright.

Alex stood to walk with him to the door and offered, "When we get back, I'll come by and we'll see what I can do to lighten your workload. I need you. I'm not going to let you fail. We'll work it out."

Brian nodded once, sharply, and left.

After Alex closed the hotel room door and locked it, she stood there a moment thinking and then went back to her computer and fired off a message to HR from Brian to add a chiropractor and massage therapist to the job announcements and another message to maintenance to prepare rooms for them. She then sent Brian a note telling him that when they got hired, he ought to visit them until his neck pain went away.

Brian replied almost immediately that his pain wasn't going to go away until he retired and didn't have to deal with this company anymore. Alex chuckled at that and fired back a note that he should get off his computer and get sleep. He sent back a message that he'd sleep when she did. Alex didn't reply to that one, but went back to punching in the next novel. She might need another $500,000 in the morning. She finally crawled into bed at 4 a.m. for a couple hours of much needed sleep.

Alex got good news from Milo when her alarm went off at 7 a.m. Being in an earlier time zone, he'd been awake for a few hours already and had closed a movie deal with a major studio for one of her novels, and voila, there was the $500,000 she didn't have and she didn't have to spend the day trying to figure out where she was going to get it. She was still in a chipper mood when she got over to the convention center a couple hours later, and her step was light, practically skipping.

On her way to the vendor room to adjust the sound acoustics of their booth, she saw Ethan Jaxon who was surrounded by a group of older business men. All were in fancy suits. Alex recognized two as CEOs for direct competitors. Her product was going to put them out of business unless they adapted and did something else. She didn't alter her walking trajectory and passed close enough to them to politely nod to Ethan.

Ethan nodded back and asked with the tiniest hint of derision in his voice, "Alex, how's your startup going?"

"You were right. It was a bad risk. I'm working with Karen now," Alex answered pleasantly.

Ethan did not bother to introduce her to the men he was standing with. No doubt he'd tell them later about how he went to school with her until she dropped out to start a company. She smiled politely and said, "Enjoy the convention, gentlemen," and continued past them.

As Alex approached their booth, she noticed that it did look absurdly out of place in the middle of the amazingly chaotic market. A pair of attendees were looking at her booth when she walked up.

"Who pays this much money to show off a card with a year in it?" the one asked.

"There's not even any spiffs," the other answered somewhat grouchily. They moved off.

Alex went into the enclosure and the noise level from the room dropped considerably, but was still loud. She went to a discreet panel in the back left corner and pushed it open. She entered the combination to the small security box there, and turned a small dial inside all the way to maximum. The small temporary three-walled room went completely silent. She closed and relocked the security box and pushed the panel closed. If you didn't know the panel was there, you wouldn't see it. The dial itself hadn't actually done anything at all; her picobots were filtering out incoming sound waves entirely. Anyone dissecting the walls and carpet weren't going to find anything.

"Well, that's better," Alex said to the empty space. Her voice absorbed into the fabric on the walls and did not bounce back. It sounded like a high-end recording studio.

When Alex stepped back out into the noisy aisle, she saw a young man watching her. He was maybe a year older than her. "So what did you just do?" he asked curiously.

"Not much. Adjusted the sound a little," Alex replied, aiming for as bored as possible.

"I'm Noah." He held out his hand.

"Alex." She took his hand and shook firmly.

"So what's the deal?" Noah indicated the booth with an incline of his head.

"We're launching our product next year. This is the press release."

Noah's eyebrows pulled together and the one lifted slightly. "What's the product?"

"Still a secret, apparently." Alex winked. "We've been directed not to discuss it."

Noah reached in his pocket and handed her a business card. "I do a tech vlog. When you decide to go public, message me, eh?"

"We'll be here next year. Come by and I'll show it to you," Alex said.

Noah grinned and moved off.

Alex was really glad he hadn't stepped into their booth. She went in search of the convention's chairperson.

Some time late Saturday evening, their booth's odd acoustics became public and they had a steady stream of people going through to hear the silence for themselves. Alex did not need the additional $500,000 to keep their booth for the next year.

Several months later, Brian was still keeping everyone's fears tolerably well controlled. Alex didn't need to direct the employees' attention to their vegetarian cafeteria because one of the outspoken high protein diet people decided to organize a rally to demand meat be served in the kitchen, even if employees had to pay for it. Alex joined the employees in the street outside their company building. It was warm for a midwinter day, but most people still wore light jackets or sweaters.

"Isn't it rather wrong for you to be out here with us protesting?" Karen Marino asked Alex, walking up. Karen knew who owned the company.

Alex shrugged. "I want an omnivorous diet just like everyone else. I just also happen to know that it's not sustainable and can't be done."

Karen shook her head in wry amusement. "But it's a protest to get the owner's attention!"

"Well, the owner is certainly noticing," Alex grinned, proudly holding up her sign on which was painted with large, friendly letters: "We Want Meat!"

"They might lynch you when they find out." Karen waved her own sign which read, "Employees Vote Meat!"

They moved into the crowd. People milled around, blocking the street, and commenting to each other that the owner would definitely have to pay attention to this. After an hour, Alex texted Brian that it was time to deliver her message. He arrived 10 minutes later.

"Excuse me, could I have everyone's attention, please?" Brian shouted.

People settled down to listen. They really were good people.

"I've consulted with the owner about both this protest and the possibility of changing the vegetarian menu," Brian announced.

There were cheers. Alex tried not to wince.

"The owner recognizes that the majority of employees would like to have meat selections added to the company cafeteria. The owner is impressed that you have joined together as a community to make your wishes known, even those of you who really don't care either way are supporting each other, and the owner says that's awesome and deserves a reward."

More cheers. "Everyone will be given the day off with full pay and there will be no penalties incurred for the protest. All production schedules will be adjusted accordingly so there will be no rush to 'make up' work." An odd silence fell over the group as they anticipated the next sentence. "The owner says that unfortunately, adding meat selections to the company cafeteria is not environmentally sustainable and cannot be done at this time." There were shouts of "No!" and "That's not fair!" before Brian continued, "Everyone is free to stand out here and continue the protest or head home, at your choice. Work resumes tomorrow. I'm sorry, everyone. Truly, I tried."

Alex was one of the last people to leave. She set her sign aside and moved among the people, quietly offering anger-diffusing comments, consolations, and generally listening to complaints.

Alex was in her lab working on another program for her picobots when her phone buzzed, startling her. She reached over and picked up her phone, noting with annoyance that she needed to take the next pallet of batteries up to storage so the next set could be built. In her concentration, she'd apparently missed the quiet beep indicating it was done.

She saw Milo's identifier and answered, "Hey, Milo, what's up?"

"Mario would like to meet with you," Milo's voice said without emotion.

"Ok," Alex closed her eyes and studied her schedule. "Tomorrow at 4 p.m.?"

"Right now."

Alex rolled her head, stretching her neck. "I'm in the middle of a dozen things that all need to be done right now. Can it wait?"

"I'm on my way in the car to take you directly to his house," Milo's voice informed her blandly.

Alex rubbed at the bridge of her nose. She could feel a headache starting. "Is everything ok?"

"As far as I know. He did not tell me what he wants."

Right. "I guess I'll meet you out front then." Alex disconnected. She stood and stretched fully, frustrated. She hated stopping in the middle of a block of code. It was always so tedious to recapture her pace. At least she'd be able to finally give Sal's brother his bioshield ring; she hadn't had time to drop it off yet.

Alex took the pallet to storage before exiting the building. Getting enough of those batteries ready was near the top of her priority list, almost overtaking "do whatever the acting head of an Italian Mafia family requests".

Outside, she walked the two blocks to the antiques store where the limousine was waiting. As a general rule, she didn't want to be seen getting in or out of a limousine in front of Green World. That would defeat the whole "custodian" cover she had going.

She climbed into the limousine, letting the driver close the door for her. Milo was immaculately dressed. Considering that it was after his normal work hours and he usually liked to relax in comfortable clothes and read a book in the evening, he'd obviously deliberately changed for this duty.

"Am I in trouble, Milo?" At least Alex didn't have that overwhelming fear that used to accompany a meeting with Mario. Her picobot bioshield would protect her and she was confident she'd be able to handle any repercussions from that. Milo was wearing his ring, as directed, even though he didn't know what it was for. He presumed it was a tracking device of some sort. She'd simply told him to wear it at all times as part of his job.

The limousine began moving and Milo shrugged. "He sounded annoyed."

Alex yawned exhaustedly. "At least we'll be in the same mood."

Milo cringed.

The car arrived at Sal's brother's house soon thereafter and both of them went to the front door, under the watchful eyes of the outer perimeter of bodyguards. The door opened as if by magic and the inside bodyguards stepped aside to let them pass. "In the study, Miss Smith," one of them said. "Mr. Marino is expecting you," he added unnecessarily.

Milo led the way through several hallways as Alex had never been inside Mario's house before. The house was big, but not a mansion like Sal's. His walls were covered with pictures of family members, not expensive original oil paintings. These included pictures of his current wife as well as his deceased ones. Milo opened a door and gestured for Alex to enter before him.

The first thing Alex saw when she entered was her painting hanging on his wall - the one she'd done for Sal that had the secret formula to her battery embedded in its design. Mario was standing across the room, looking at it, with his arms crossed and a frown on his face.

"I requested that be destroyed," Alex said after a heartbeat.

"I. Don't. Understand. This. Painting." Mario growled with sharp, punctuated emphasis.

"Do you normally understand art?" she countered.

"You," and Mario emphasized the word, "Said it wasn't art."

"Well, it isn't. It was a private message from me to Sal. There better not be any photographs of it anywhere," Alex added ominously.

Mario paced. "He comes into the restaurant after his birthday party with that painting and sets it up in my office and says, 'I'm naming her my heir. She needs our family and she'll be good for us." He went over to his desk. "Good for us!" he shouted, taking a stack of papers from his desk and throwing them at her.

Alex caught one of the pages out of the air and glanced at it, as the rest drifted into chaos around her feet. The real family financial ledgers; the ones the F.B.I. would have loved to get copies of. The balance on the page she'd seen showed their wealth going steadily down. She expected the rest of the pages floating to the floor did the same. She walked over to his desk, careful not to step on any of the pages, and set the paper in her hand on the desk and took the ring from her pocket and set it on top of the page.

Sal's brother peered at the ring, frowned and glared at her, shaking his head disapprovingly.

Alex turned to Milo who was trying very hard to be invisible. "Do you have your gun, Milo?"

Milo glanced at the door before nodding trepidatiously. Bravely, he whispered, "I'm not giving it to you."

Alex grinned psychotically. "I want you to shoot me. Head or chest. It doesn't matter."

"No," Milo replied firmly, although quietly. His foot turned suspiciously toward the exit.

"Just make sure it's a kill shot." Alex moved to stand in front of her painting. "I want you to splatter my blood across this reminder that my best friend is gone. And when I'm dead, sell off the business, everything I own, and give all the money back to the family."

Mario took a gun from his desk and fired it at her.

Alex frowned, staring down at the bullet hovering next to her arm. Plucking it out of the invisible picobot net, she walked over to Sal's brother and handed it back to him so it could be recycled. "That wasn't a kill shot." She pointed at the ring on the page. "That ring is for you. It's a bioshield. As long as you are wearing it, no bullet or knife will ever reach you. You can die comfortably of old age." As Mario was still staring at her in disbelief, she added teasingly, "I can't believe you shot me. What were you thinking?"

"Cathartic release," Mario said without shame, blinking, and reaching for the ring. "I wanted you to feel as angry as me."

Alex snorted. "Put that on and don't ever take it off. These things are nearly impossible to make," Alex lied. "Just me, you, and Milo have them. Don't abuse it, though. We need to keep what it does a family secret. Do I need to say why?"

Sal's brother shook his head and put the ring on his finger. It fit him perfectly. Milo glanced at his own ring with wide eyes.

"I have other tech coming." Alex bent to pick up ledger pages, taking the opportunity to glance at each one under the guise of putting them back in order. "This money will be restored and increased within three years. You don't need to worry, Mario. I'll take care of this."

Mario was still staring at the ring now on his finger. "When is your birthday?"

The topic shift was so sudden, it took Alex a moment to grasp the question. "It doesn't matter." She wasn't going to give any information that might tie her back to who she used to be.

"Rico asked me the other day when it was." Sal's brother took the ledger pages and put them in his desk. He'd return them to their hidden location later. "The family has an obligation to throw you a party."

"I don't need a party," Alex informed him.

Milo spoke up, "It's for the family, Alex. It's how we redistribute certain items of value to specific people without causing undue F.B.I. interest."

"Oh." Enlightened, Alex answered, "Then give me Sal's birthday. I'll adopt his." That's how Alex acquired March 12th as her birthday.

Back in the limousine, Alex said to Milo, "I need another source of money. The family can't afford to give me any more." She thought for a long while and then whispered, "I'll sell some of Sal's art. I'll just have to buy it back if I can."

Milo shrugged. "Go talk with your CEO. I know appearing crazy is part of your strategy, but you've got an in-house expert. Use him."

Once again at the technical conference in Las Vegas, Alex studied her clipboard with their vendor booth specifications. It looked almost exactly like it had the previous year, with a few additions. The muted soft, light brown carpet still had anti-fatigue padding underneath, and the walls were still bare except for the company's logo. The centered glass display case now had a small square in it just about the size of a compact flash card. It's folded tent card said, "Long life laptop battery or charger. $1200."

There was a matching display case off to the left with another folded tent card in it with a date three years out. The right front and left front now had pretty green counters just wide enough for a pair of laptops with padded stools behind them, but someone would have to approach the counters to talk to whoever sat there. The noise reduction acoustics were already maximized.

"I think that's it," Alex said to Brian, handing him the clipboard.

"Nice job setting everything up, everyone," Brian said to the crew. Again, they'd brought 6 other people. Everyone would get two hours in the booth, and two hours "being seen using a laptop that wasn't plugged in". They'd all been trained in battery installation and sales processing, although Alex didn't expect them to need it for a while. The group went to lunch, with one lonely soul left guarding the battery display case (and the inventory underneath the counters).

Alex took the first shift when the vendor room opened, along with one of the more nerdy employees whose nickname was Tank for the type of video games he liked to play, one of which he sat at his counter playing. Alex set her laptop to play some quiet ambient forest sounds and worked on yet another novel. Their booth sounded odd with ambient birdsong accompanied by

175

gunfire and explosions.

Alex saw Ethan come by, but he merely looked at the sign next to the battery, rolled his eyes, and walked on, without approaching. This seemed to be the same thing everyone did. Their booth just didn't have enough flash to draw anyone in.

Tank's vehicle exploded and he swore and leaned back, stretching. "Alex, I think our company marketing is screwed up. No one is even coming in."

Alex rotated her own arms, standing to pace and get some circulation back in her legs. "The owner must have some plan."

"I think our owner is bonkers. This battery rocks." All of the employees had been given one of the laptop batteries as a company bonus just before the crew departed for the convention. The implications were only now being noticed and only by the super-nerds like Tank. "I've been burning up the processor and this thing is still showing 100% power."

"Really?" she walked over to peer diligently at his laptop. "Maybe the display is broken? Have you tried refreshing it?"

"Hrm. Good point. I'll try a reboot."

The reboot was just finishing when Noah stepped into their booth's "room". "Whoa!" Noah exclaimed, and then stepped back out, and then back in again. "How'd you do that?" He repeated his step out and then back in.

"Soundproofing in the walls, I think," Alex said cheerily. "Hi, Noah, how's the vlog going?"

"You remember me!" His eyes lit up.

"Of course. And I know you remember my name is Alex." She grinned.

"I do indeed, Alex," Noah said, walking over to the center display case. "A laptop battery?" he asked with some confusion.

Tank was muttering to himself and trying different diagnostic applications.

"Yup," said Alex, moving to stand next to him to stare at the lonely little unimpressive flat square in the case.

"How long does it last?" Noah turned to her.

Alex answered, "R&D is still working on the duration. Our directive is to just say 'long life battery'."

"I think you'd do better selling your soundproofing mechanism to convention booth people," Noah said. "That room is deafening out there."

"It's been suggested to our company owner, I think," Alex replied.

"Maybe I'll mention it in my vlog." Noah gave her a winning smile.

"How's that going?" Alex asked.

"Really well. I just crossed 1.5 million subscribers last month."

Alex, who didn't follow that type of thing at all and had no idea if that was truly good or not, said enthusiastically, "Rad."

"Would you mind if I brought my good camera gear tomorrow and did a clip of the noise reduction?" Noah inquired.

Alex shrugged. "Fine by me. I'll be on shift at 4 p.m."

176

"Great, I'll see you then. I've got to finish scoping out the wares right now." Noah smiled at her again, bowed, and left.

"I think he likes you," Tank commented, not looking up from the diagnostic application he was running. "Bet you a dollar he asks you out tomorrow."

"Hah." Alex went back to her novel writing. She was now up to three major movies and two of her books were on the New York Times best sellers list. She was regularly using six pseudonyms by genre: Ray (romance), Rei (mystery), Rayy (western), Rey (sci-fi), Rae (fantasy), and Rai (self-help and textbooks). Inside each, there was a blurb about the R-writers - a small group who'd met online and were amused at having the same name with different spellings and decided to form a club to take turns inspiring and proof-reading each other's works. They cross-pollinated their audiences by giving website urls to all the R's in each of their publications.

By 4 p.m. the next day, the company had not sold a single battery and they were being mocked as the "biggest disappointment in the history of the technical convention". The green jumpsuits attracted snickers as employees moved about the convention using their power-cord free laptops. Employees had been specifically told not to take offense or try to defend their product, or engage in any way. Alex and Tank took over from the previous two workers and settled in for their respective activities.

Shortly thereafter, Noah appeared with his camera and mic on a stick to record their audio, or rather, lack thereof. "Hi, Alex, is it still ok to do a recording of your soundproofing?"

"Sure," Alex answered, smiling up at him. "Do you want our ambient computer sounds or should we mute them?"

"Leave them going, I think. It'll make it obvious that I didn't just mute the sound on the video. May I interview you when I come in?"

Behind Noah, Tank grinned and made a kissy-kissy face at Alex. In revenge, Alex said, "Interview Tank over there instead. He can talk for hours about his video games."

Noah nodded amicably and stepped out of their booth. They could tell he was recording, but couldn't hear what he was saying. He stepped onto their carpet, and spoke into his microphone with his camera pointed at himself. "And it instantly goes quiet. All that noise in the vendor hall is gone completely. Here, I'll do it again." His camera panned across both Tank and Alex. He moved out and back in. "Isn't that awesome? So, you might ask, what are they selling this technology for? Nothing, you guys, they're not selling it. Instead, they are selling what they are advertising as a 'long life laptop battery or charger'."

"Which you should totally buy, dude," Tank contributed, not looking up from his video game that was clearly audible with gunfire.

Noah brought his camera to focus on their pathetic little battery display. "And that, everyone, is a lot of money to dish out for something you already have. We'll have to see what their specs are when they get published to decide if it's worth it." He turned off his camera and went over to Alex. "Say, what are the chances of my getting one for review? It would go well with the video."

"You'd have to buy it," Alex answered, palm up, begging forgiveness. "The company isn't passing out samples, even to reviewers."

"Too bad." Noah wrinkled his nose. "That's more money than I can part with."

"Yeah, it's a lot." Alex pretended to think for a moment. "You know what? You could buy it tonight, run your analysis overnight, and return it in the morning."

Noah raise an eyebrow and smiled warmly, "If I did, would you come to dinner with me tonight?"

Alex glanced over at Tank who rubbed his fingers together in the universal sign of "gimme my money" without looking up. Alex ignored this. Why not? She needed a break. Noah was attractive, lighthearted, and would keep her entertained with stories about his vlog. She answered, "Only if you absolutely promise you'll return the battery in the morning. I don't want anyone ever saying I bribed you to buy the thing."

"Awesome," said Noah happily. He set his camera on the floor next to the counter and reached in his pocket and withdrew his wallet.

"Our purchase agreement is rather detailed - covers the services that come with the battery and the usage restrictions protecting it," Alex informed him, "But you don't need to worry about that as you are returning it tomorrow anyway. Although technically, you can return it at any time for a full refund with no questions asked." Alex pulled up the legal document on her computer and turned the screen toward him. "The company is only selling to individuals and each person is only allowed to purchase one. It has a full lifetime warranty provided the battery itself isn't tampered with. If you change laptops, the new battery adapter will be shipped to you free of charge. Uh, what kind of laptop do you have?"

Noah told her.

Alex smiled. "Nice! Your battery is removable, but would you prefer an internal or a charger? I recommend the internal one."

"Internal, then," he answered.

Alex started entering in his information. "Oh, hey, do you want to type this stuff in rather than dictating to me?" It was the usual name, address, phone number type of data entry form.

Noah nodded and typed in his data. He typed faster than Alex and she wasn't slow.

Alex instructed, "Click that continue button. That next page has the legal agreements, just click on them. You agree not to tamper with or alter the battery, or try to reverse engineer it, and so on."

Noah went through the page. "That's an awful lot of legal notices. You've even got one in case I die." And then he got to the one about understanding that each battery had a remote locator in it in case of theft. "What? It's got a built-in tracking device? No way. That's crazy. No one's ever going to agree to that."

"You're only keeping it for a night. Don't sweat it," Alex grinned. "If you hit the disclosure icon there, you'll see that the location is kept encrypted on our servers to a password only you know. Should your device get lost or stolen, you give us the password, and we will retrieve the battery for you and if we are unable to do so, we'll remotely disable it and issue you a new battery free of charge. Oh, and don't bother plugging in your laptop to recharge it until your laptop reports the battery at 20% or less remaining."

He punched in a hopefully secure password for the remote location.

Alex got the credit card machine from under the counter as well as a compatible battery adapter and battery and ran his credit card. She scanned the battery's serial number with her laptop's camera and then popped open the adapter and pushed the battery until it snapped into place. She tested it with a multimeter from the counter's cabinet and nodded when it showed in spec. She put the credit card machine and multimeter away. "I can help you install it if you want to bring your laptop back, or I can bring the installation tools with me when I come to dinner?"

"I can install it," Noah winked. "I'm a tech-type."

Alex beamed at him.

"What time do you get off shift?" Noah asked.

"6, but you need to give me time to change into some jeans and a t-shirt." Alex figured she better say what she was wearing so he wouldn't plan somewhere formal. She didn't have any formal or even date-appropriate clothing with her. "How about I meet you at 7 in the convention lobby by the fountain?"

"Agreed." Noah retrieved his camera, took his new battery and the legally required pamphlet of device information, and departed.

The entire time Alex showered and dressed, she wondered if going on a date was a good idea. Not only didn't she have time for dates, let alone relationships, she knew at her core, she had trauma that would probably resurface. She'd said yes because she desperately needed a break in her routine and Noah seemed like a genuinely nice guy.

Why shouldn't she have a single evening like other girls her age? Every moment of Alex's life was so serious, so regimented, so deliberately planned, from the very moment she opened her eyes in the morning until she fell exhausted into bed, she had to be either making money, taking care of the company, or meeting some family obligation. She was tired, no, she was exhausted, burned out. She needed a happy, low-stress evening. Wasn't Milo always telling her to take a break?

She chose her favorite t-shirt - a comfortable cotton dark blue shirt with a space nebula on the front and the nine planets on back. It was sufficiently geeky without endorsing any franchise. She thought Noah might like it, but it needed to be washed. She'd worn it a couple times on the way out to the convention center. With a sigh, she had her picobots take care of cleaning it. Technically, that was a risk if someone happened to notice and calculate that she'd not had time to do laundry, but it was her favorite shirt and she wanted something that made her feel less anxious.

The simple earrings she'd brought to wear during the day seemed too plain and woefully boring for a date. She thought briefly on trying to locate some makeup. Wasn't that something girls were supposed to do? Apply makeup? Her fingernails were functionally short and unpainted, although neatly trimmed. Asking Milo to research and acquire some dating attire for her seemed like overkill.

Alex shook herself. How much of a date was this anyway? She only had tonight. Her company would pack up the next day and head back. As employees figured out just how long that battery would last, sales would start rolling in, and she'd be hard-pressed to keep up with the company growth. Money was going to become absurdly critical at an unknown rate and she was going to have to maintain the near-zero balance without going under.

Noah was waiting for her in the lobby. He'd also showered and changed into a nice pair of jeans and a relaxed Dr. Who t-shirt. His hair was still slightly damp and neatly combed. He did not have his camera.

Alex smiled in greeting as she walked up. "Did you get your battery installed?"

"I did," Noah said. "It's running the battery burn-in test now, complete with my camera running to record the exact moment it runs out. I'm not sure why your development team hasn't run test software yet. I can get you the name of mine if you'd like to pass it on. It's really good. It'll give a full report you can publish."

"I can certainly pass it on." That was another company her battery would put out of business if they didn't adapt. Alex tried not to feel guilty. "You didn't write it?"

"Oh, no. I just bought it. I have a lot of evaluation tools." Noah grinned and added, "Mostly donated, too. Reviewers can get a lot of things for free if they promise to do a review."

"Aren't there a lot of things at this convention to review? Why our battery?" Alex might be tempted to think he was only reviewing it because he wanted to take her on a date, but he seemed too smart to compromise his vlog for a girl.

"Eh, things from this convention will keep me busy for the next few months," Noah explained. "I roll out one review a week. I can't really say which week I'll get to your battery, or if I get a chance to."

Alex nodded, glad he was honest.

Noah adjusted his shirt, an indication of a bit of nervousness his voice didn't show. "So what kind of food would you like?"

"Anything marginally healthy. I have a strong love of vegetables." At his disbelieving eyebrow lift, Alex declared, "Really. I really do." She saw Brian arrive across the lobby and waved to him. He'd obviously hoped to catch her before she left. Tank hadn't wasted any time celebrating his newly won dollar with the Green World team. Brian waved back and then turned to go back into the convention.

"Your CEO?" Noah asked.

"Yup. I'll catch up with him later."

Noah turned to lead Alex to the door. "How about Thai?"

"Sounds great!"

They walked the short distance to the restaurant. Over dinner, Alex plied Noah with questions about his vlog which she'd never seen to his dismay. He was very enthusiastic and easy to listen to. His life was so completely foreign to hers that she had a hard time comprehending how such a lifestyle could even exist.

Alex was thoroughly enjoying herself when she saw Ethan enter with a group of other businessmen. Unfortunately, Ethan spotted them. He strode over while his colleagues were being taken to their table. "Noah, my man, don't tell me you wasted your money on one of those batteries?"

"Hello, Ethan," Alex said dismissively.

Noah shrugged. "I'm running the burn-in on it right now," he replied, nonplussed. "It's what I do."

Ethan leaned over and put his arm around Alex's shoulder. "Alex, did you tell him you're a high school dropout with a failed business?" His breath smelled like vodka.

Alex pulled free of his arm and gave him a bit of shove. "Ethan, go away."

Ethan frowned at her. "You shouldn't be mean to me, Alex. You're going to need another job pretty soon." He grinned maliciously and added, "Although you might want to go back and get your GED. Our custodial staff is already full. We might be able to put you in the mailroom."

Alex pointed. "Your business partners are waiting for you." She wondered how he knew she worked as a custodian.

"So they are. So they are," Ethan said. He turned to Noah, "She's not a good person for you to hang out with. You should reconsider your choice." He stumbled off.

Noah took a drink of his tea and appeared to be deep in thought.

Alex explained, "Ethan and I went to high school together for a short time." She wanted to say that Ethan was even more obnoxious drunk than he was sober and that one day he'd regret every cruel word he'd ever said to her - the imagined slight in geometry class had certainly been unintentional. Instead, she asked Noah another question about his vlog.

Their conversation continued, but it was stilted and soured. Noah requested the check, paid, and they walked back. Ethan was rich as well as powerful enough in the technical community to kill Noah's vlog if he took a mind to. Alex could tell Noah didn't think she was worth the risk and she wouldn't say otherwise. They wished each other a good evening and did not linger.

Alex went back to her hotel room, and hugged her pillow for a while, and then got up and dumped words into a brand new book - this one for young adults about the angst of dating while cruel classmates interfered. She was still typing when her wake-up alarm went off.

Alex washed her face, brushed her hair, and changed into the next day's jumpsuit and went in search of her coworkers and breakfast with her laptop tucked under her arm. The hotel restaurant was busy, but her coworkers had already secured a corner table. She took a tray and went through the buffet and then joined them.

"Good morning!" Brian said brightly.

Alex suppressed a sleep-deprived groan. "Hi, guys," she said sliding into the chair they'd saved for her.

"How'd it go?" Tank asked, and then seeing her expression, dropped his voice sadly, "Oh, I know that look. So sorry, babe. He seemed like a nice enough guy. You want me to go beat him up?"

Alex's eyes snapped to Tank, but then she realized he was just being friendly, not actually offering. This wasn't a Marino making that offer. "Naw, he's ok. We're just not that compatible."

"Did anyone get a chance to check their email this morning? I had some internet issues in my room." Brian wondered aloud to no one in particular. He was not directing his gaze at Alex, but he was surely speaking to her as if he were grabbing her shoulders and shaking them and shouting directly at her nose.

Alex wondered what she was missing. She'd deliberately left email off, ostensibly to focus on writing, but really because she hadn't wanted to answer any date-related queries. She'd check as soon as she was able. "I didn't get a chance to. Woke up late."

Others reported not having any internet issues at all, cementing Alex's conclusion. The conversation turned to some of the convention events. The discussion was merrily underway with a lively debate over some technical concept when Noah came into the restaurant, looking around somewhat wildly. He spotted her and came directly over.

"I can't return it," Noah said to Alex, setting both hands on the table and leaning toward her. "And you knew it."

"No," Alex pointed at Tank, "He knew it. I still think you should get your money back. You promised after all."

"You're not going to hold me to that," Noah gasped.

"Of course not," Alex replied. "I look forward to seeing your vlog, Noah."

Later when Alex opened her email, she saw their company forum had been flooded with requests by employees to open online sales before Monday. They wanted their family and friends to be able to get a battery before orders got backlogged. Alex fired off a note directing that employees were to be given a code that if entered along with an online order within the next 48 hours, would push the order to the front of the queue.

Sales began rolling in as soon as the online store opened. The backlog was nearly instantaneous.

Six months later, Brian summoned Alex, via text, to his office. When she entered, she saw yet another huge stack of papers on his desk. "Another one?" Alex asked, walking around his desk to look at them.

"That makes five this week alone," Brian informed her.

"Five?" Alex cringed.

Brian nodded. "Two others arrived this morning. I already sent those down to your Mr. Dioli, but out of curiosity, I read some of this one."

Luciano Dioli was set up in their new legal murder room one floor down, despite not being a direct Green World employee. Alex felt the room name was appropriate, but it was just the floor, converted into a massive legal library with large, magnetic white-boards in its common area and eight hopeful private offices. Alex picked up the stack, which contained at least 500 pages and went around his desk to one of his tables. "Go ahead and attach the increased signing bonus to the lawyer job postings."

"Already done. Look at page 4." Brian gestured at the papers.

Alex, who had randomly split the stack and was squinting at the tiny print on the page, reached back to the top half of the stack. She swore softly, peering at the court summons. "I guess you won't have to worry about having an anonymous owner anymore. Who sent this?" She dug through the pages until she saw it at the top of a list of five of their competitors including Cartwright-

Jaxon Engineering, Ethan's dad's company. "Ok, I'll take care of this."

"I've already issued you a team of research assistants and dedicated IT personnel. Anything else you need?"

"Thanks, I appreciate that. I'll let you know if I think of anything." Alex collected her pages. "Don't worry over this. I'm prepared." She went downstairs, taking the stairwell instead of the elevator to burn off some frustration in physical exercise.

When she entered, Lu saw Alex's stack of pages, and growled, "No. I can't do another one. There's too much here already. I have got to have some help, Alex. Real, competent, corporate law attorneys." He added, "And not Milo. This stuff is out of his area of expertise."

"Don't panic. This stack's for me, Lu. It's got a court summons for the company's owner attached to it."

Lu winced sympathetically.

"We're getting research assistants and dedicated IT support," Alex said.

"I've already got a team. Your CEO allocated personnel for me last week. They're one floor down."

"Ah, good." Alex set the pages on one of the desks, claiming the workspace. She fired off a message to Milo that simply said, "204. ASAP." He had a massive folder of detailed instructions for every contingency Alex had been able to dream up. That one said to arrange her GED and bar exam.

Alex started back at the top of the mountain of papers, and went through each page, first the glance-memory, then closing her eyes, and really digging into the text. By page 25, she decided it was finally time to issue the counter-attack. She stood up and went over to Lu's desk. "Those the two new ones?"

Lu nodded and without even taking his eyes off the page he was reading, he pushed those relatively smaller stacks toward her. Alex flipped through those quickly, only looking for the responsible parties. She left to retrieve her laptop from her lab.

Alex paused in her lab to send off a note from Brian, to both the website team and the sales department. The website was to say: "The following companies have chosen to submit lawsuits against us. A company is made of its individuals who are accountable for their actions. The employees of these companies and their employees' direct family members and dependents are no longer eligible to purchase our batteries. When the companies withdraw these lawsuits or they are successfully resolved, purchases can be resumed after a 5 year penalty period. All pending orders from these individuals will be moved to a waiting list until the penalty period is completed or the individuals have moved to companies not trying to put us out of business. Only then will their orders be added back onto the end of the order queue."

Alex included the list of the names of the companies, in the order which the lawsuits had been received. That would cut down their order queue by a significant amount, and cause screaming by people who'd been waiting a few months, and cheering by people whose estimated delivery time got pushed forward. Technically, she ought to add the representing law firms to the list but this would create enough trouble.

Alex set her laptop on top of the latest pallet of batteries her picobots had finished, and took the pallet to its storage location, and then her laptop to the murder room where she spent the rest of the day going through her case and planning her response. She sent off a note from Brian to the custodial staff manager and human resources saying that Alex had been reassigned and to fill the position.

Two afternoons later, while Alex was sitting in the murder room eating the lunch she'd brought in against company rules, she received a text from Milo. Judge Newton, the man who'd finally signed her emancipated minor petition, wanted to see her and would not discuss with Milo why. Alex told Milo to arrange it for the following morning, thinking that she might as well go find out what new legal nightmare awaited sooner rather than later. Alex went back to preparing her defense.

The next day, Alex was escorted to Judge Newton's office by one of the court clerks. She was carrying her briefcase with her laptop in it just in case she had to wait and could use the time to work on her case or the latest novel that was now overdue. Judge Newton nodded in greeting as she entered. Alex set her briefcase on the floor and sat in one of his chairs.

"Thank you for coming," the judge said, clearing his throat. He had years of practice not showing what he was thinking and his lack of body language gestures offered no clues for what he might want. The office was unchanged from the last time she'd been there. The same tiffany lamp with its patterned glass shade and brass bottom lit his desk where a matching brass picture frame set next to the leather desk blotter and pen set. The books on his shelves had been rearranged slightly with a few new additions.

Rather than waste time on small talk, Alex asked directly, "What can I do for you, Judge Newton?"

The judge lifted his hand from his armchair and let it rest on the edge of his desk. "Not too many years ago, a gangly teenager sat here and put a mountain of money on my desk equivalent to a year of my salary and called it pocket change."

"I recall." That day with the backpack full of cash seemed like a lifetime ago. Alex felt like she went through that sum almost daily now.

The judge shifted in his chair. "I've had a lot of time to think about that lately."

"Do you need money, Judge Newton?" Alex tilted her head quizzically. Of all the people that might ask her for money, he was at the bottom of the list.

185

He'd proven himself painfully honest and forthright in everything, a fact which had frustrated her when he'd been refusing to sign her petition.

The judge made a tiny shake of his head. "What's your relationship with Green World?"

Alex wouldn't lie, but she wouldn't answer either. "Need a battery?"

"I have one, thank you," Judge Newton replied. "No, I was wondering if you were in a position to slide some resumes to Green World's human resources department. Discreetly."

"Oh!" Alex couldn't hide her relief. "That, I can certainly do. I thought you were going to give me another court order to deliver."

"That type of thing is sent by courier." Judge Newton rested his fingers on the folder on his desk and said after a moment, "The legal community isn't that large, not at the top levels. Lawyers get together and talk. For example, I know the owner of Green World was recently subpoenaed and cannot get out of appearing in court." His gaze was penetrating.

Alex maintained a neutral expression and waited for him to continue.

"I've also seen what Green World has done for the local community. The salary your company offers is incredibly low, even with benefits, yet Green World has a 100% employee retention rate. Once an employee, a person never leaves, not because they are being forced to stay but because they enjoy working there. Even when people have been offered six times their salary to change companies, they stay."

Alex wondered who'd been offered that much. Money was really going to have to start cycling pretty fast to keep her company afloat.

Judge Newton continued, "I would personally be very sad if Green World were to fail." He slid the folder over to her. "Resumes for my son and three of his best friends. All completely trustworthy and willing to come work for you. They believe in the future, too."

Alex opened the folder and read. Four ivy league lawyers, all specializing in corporate law. Alex whistled in a long, deep inhale.

Judge Newton put his hand back in his lap. "You see why they couldn't go through any computer system to apply?"

"Yes, Judge," Alex answered. If they weren't hired and word got out, they'd be blackballed. "I will certainly see these get to the right person."

The judge stood. "It was a pleasure seeing you again, Miss Smith. I wish you the best of luck in your upcoming legal battles."

Alex also stood and shook his hand and left, thunderstruck. Outside in her limousine, she set her picobots to spy on the Judge. She had to know if they could be trusted. She couldn't risk a betrayal and they weren't family. But if... if only... she really needed the help.

Later that night, Alex waited in her windowless basement lab for the picobots to finish the next pallet and watched the picobot-relayed video feed of the dinner conversation going on at Judge Newton's house.

"Do you think she'll call us?" Randy Newton, the judge's son asked. This came after a long conversation with several other unimportant (to Alex) topics.

Alex's attention snapped to focus.

"I don't know," Judge Newton replied. "She didn't give any indication positive or negative. She didn't even acknowledge owning the company, but she has to. It's the only thing that makes sense. There's too much money involved. It has to come from the Marino family."

"Those bastards are going to tear that company apart until there aren't even scraps left for anyone to purchase. It's vile. I haven't plugged in my computer in three months. You know what those batteries could mean for the world if they scale up?" Randy pounded his fist on the table, shaking the flatware.

"She did boast that she was going to make a mountain of money. I can't see the Marino family risking this much for just laptop batteries." There was a pause and then the judge continued, "That girl sat in my office and showed off a photographic memory that would make any law student blind with jealousy. She may not need you boys."

"She needs us. Did you tell her about the legal war that's coming?" Randy said.

"It didn't seem appropriate." The judge refilled his wineglass from the open bottle on the table.

"Did you tell her about Fred's daughter?" Randy persisted.

"No," Judge Newton said firmly. "Again, it wasn't appropriate. She's part of an Italian Mafia family. I can't just announce, 'Hey, my kid and his schoolmates want to join your cause' and have it be believed at face value. 'Let me give you a bunch of reasons why you should trust them' is going to look even more suspicious. You know she can't just let anyone walk in and see all her legal plans."

Too true, Alex thought. It appeared at least Randy wanted Green World to succeed. She turned the picobot feed off. She moved over to her computer on the public internet and searched until she found Fred's daughter. There was one of those please-fund-me websites to get help for medical costs. She read. Even an ivy league lawyer wouldn't have enough for those absolutely imperative surgeries that the medical insurance was refusing to cover based on it being a 'pre-existing condition'. The website showed the surgeries were only 25% funded.

Green World itself couldn't cover another large expense; Alex's company was just about bankrupt and strategically had to remain so for a while longer. Alex deliberately imposed the artificial maximum amount of daily sales due to shipping personnel limitations. She would not let more than one shift work on it, and she would not let her people work overtime, nor skip exercise, breaks, or lunch. Another shipping shift would not be added that forced people to work late hours without the support from other areas of the company (namely, the gym and cafeteria).

Alex's ghost-written forum posts from Brian explained that the core values of the company (health, education, family, community, and loyalty) were not to be compromised for profit. The company sales were almost enough to support the business, but Alex was still sinking in money to keep the company afloat. Public records of the company's finances showed that the company would collapse any day, as soon as the idiot owner ran out of money. Despite the influx of court cases, this kept the major players - the oil cartels and power companies - from investing too much effort into destroying her. Money for Fred's daughter would have to come from somewhere else.

A week later, Alex had confirmed that all four lawyers actually did want to help her company survive, honestly and truly, with no hidden agendas and no espionage intent. Alex didn't deserve to be this lucky. The four of them had put every bit of their own money that they could into Fred's daughter's account, but it wasn't enough. His daughter's medical treatments needed to be started during the next few months or it would be too late. Green World's full medical coverage was needed and Alex had to find enough money to throw at Green World to support its medical coverage. She wondered if she could overhaul the medical industry after she got done with the energy industry. Medical only for the rich was criminal.

Mario wasn't likely to give her even more money directly. Alex went to talk with Mario at the restaurant that night anyway.

"No. Absolutely not," Sal's brother growled, not even waiting for her to ask for more funding.

"Actually, I had an idea. I need lawyers and they should be paid standard wages, but I can't hire them at Green World. How would you feel about setting up a company that I can contract for their labor? You give me some money and I'll turn around and pay the company, which pays them and takes its cut. At least some of the money comes back to you, all legitimately. They can work directly out of Green World so the business would have minimal overhead. Ultimately, the family gains because Green World still has to pay the family back for the loan." Alex conveniently left off the rather large amount that would go out to medical. That was just an incidental detail that Mario didn't need to be troubled with.

Mario rubbed his chin. He sighed. "Ok. Have Milo set it up."

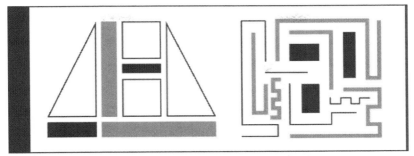

Milo was waiting for her in the limousine when Alex came out of the building with her GED certificate in hand. "One down, one to go," she announced as she got into the back of the car.

"Congratulations." Milo handed her a small wrapped jewelry box and explained, "It's tradition to receive a graduation present from family."

"Tradition?" Alex carefully peeled the tape back and removed the paper. Inside was an exquisite gold necklace with a small sea turtle pendant decorated with a diamond. "It's beautiful."

Milo helped her put it on. "I thought it might go nicely with your court clothes."

"I'm sure it will. Thank you, Milo." Alex was touched. Kindness almost felt harder to deal with than problems. She blinked away wet eyes and reached for her laptop to continue preparing her case. There were so many things to get typed in for all of the contingencies.

Milo rolled his eyes. "Maybe you should sleep instead of work? The bar exam isn't going to be easy."

Alex sighed, pulling down the table in the limousine. "I'm not done yet despite the help from you and Green World's staff." She realized if she hadn't gotten those four lawyers, she wouldn't stand a chance at surviving this. They were taking care of the 'easier' cases. Alex continued working through the afternoon and evening as the car took them toward her mandatory court appearance in Washington D.C. At the midway point tomorrow, she'd take the bar exam in the most rigorous state that most of the other states would honor and then the following day, she'd be in court.

The next day, Milo accompanied Alex into the bar exam's check-in. He presented her credentials to the serious looking woman at the table. The woman's eyebrows went up. "This child is going to take the bar exam?"

I'm not that young, Alex thought, frustrated. But that's what she brought Milo along for - to mitigate these roadblocks.

"Yes, she's signed up," Milo said smoothly. "The fee is already paid. You'll see here, she has her GED as well as both honorary bachelor's and master's degrees. I'm her sponsoring lawyer. Here's my credentials." The two

189

college degrees were something Milo had worked out by calling in a family favor at a standard degree-mill university. They were barely worth the paper they were printed on, but they had the dean's legally binding signature on them.

The woman described the testing procedure, which was entirely computerized with a much more extensive multiple choice exam replacing the traditional essays. At the end, she'd get a printout of her score sheet and a temporary certificate if she met the 75% passing score. This new testing system mimicked the latest trend in certification tests that reduced cost while still maintaining the same fee structure. Milo settled into the waiting area with his latest book and Alex went to the larger room to take the exam.

The test took longer than Alex expected it would, simply because the computer interface forced her to process one question at a time with a delay as it called up the next random question. It was tedious, but three hours into the eight hour exam time-slot, Alex hit the "Finish - you will no longer be able to go back and change your answers" button. Her score, a solid 98%, flashed on the screen, with instructions to go pick up her certificate. The 2% bothered her, but she knew experimental questions had been mixed in along with real questions and it was likely her interpretation of something was probably different than the answer-author's. The score would certainly satisfy her needs.

Alex stood up, stretched, and went in search of her printouts. The woman who had checked her in was looking at Alex with wide, amazed eyes as she handed Alex the certificate and score sheet. "Congratulations, counselor," the woman said. "That's an impressive score."

Alex smiled, "Thank you. I'm going to be in court tomorrow. Could I get you to put your name and cell phone number on the back of the certificate in case the judge wants to verify this? I'm dying my hair brown tonight, but you might note my blue eyes and appallingly young age."

The woman acquiesced. "I suspect you have a very promising career ahead of you, Miss Smith. I look forward to reading about it."

"I fear you just might." Alex gave her a slightly tilted smile and bid her goodbye.

Alex collected Milo, who upon seeing her score sheet said, "For crying out loud, Alex. You couldn't get those last 2 points? I'm extremely disappointed in you. Lost all faith. May I retire now? You're clearly unworthy."

Alex laughed. They rode onward to the courthouse. On the way, Milo gave her a matching set of "congratulations on passing your bar exam" sea turtle earrings.

A mob-scene of reporters and enthusiasts waited outside of the courthouse in downtown Washington D.C. for the arrival of Green World's owner. Alex bet more than a few competitors were also in that crowd.

"You sure you want to hang out here?" the hired driver asked, pulling into the pick-up/drop-off only zone. "It looks like it's going to rain and I heard the crazy owner isn't even going to show up."

Enjoying her last few minutes of anonymity, Alex grinned at the woman. "The owner isn't going to risk getting arrested. I'll be fine. Besides, I hope it downpours. Maybe it'll cut this heat and drive away some of the people."

"Well, if it does, there's a cafe four blocks that way, around the corner to the left, where you can get shelter for the cost of a cup of coffee. I doubt too many of these people know it's there so you should be able to get a table."

"Thanks! I've really enjoyed your company." Alex handed the pre-paid woman a reasonable cash tip. She grabbed her satchel-style briefcase that could be mistaken for a really large purse and climbed out of the car.

As she walked toward the building, Alex took a badge that looked vaguely like a press badge from her pocket and slid the lanyard over her head. Alex's hair was newly brown and tied back in a neat braid with a few stray curls off on either side of her face. She was also wearing makeup that helped her appear older, but was not overdone. The beautician Milo had hired for the early morning had done an excellent job.

Alex worked her way through the people and went into the courthouse. She presented her I.D. and the attendee ticket Milo had acquired for her. She was an hour early and had no problem getting into the courtroom despite the crowd. She took an unobtrusive seat in the middle of the audience area, off to the right, and settled in to wait, watching people arrive, and listening to conversations.

People were talking and worrying that the owner wasn't going to show up at all. A no-show would definitely mean an arrest warrant would be issued, just after the disclosure warrant demanding her name. Alex waited, wondering if she should have brought Milo along, both for the company and a less vulnerable appearance. There was no reason for both of them to be tied up in court; she was prepared.

Ethan arrived with three older, obviously high-power lawyers and they stood talking quietly for a while near the front. Ethan took a seat in the front row, directly behind their table, and the lawyers moved into position.

At precisely 2 minutes until the hour, Alex stood up, followed the side aisle to the front, crossed to the center, and went through the courtroom gate. She set her briefcase flat on her table and took a seat. The room erupted into conversation. Alex then opened her briefcase and withdrew a small stack of papers. She did not look behind her. Several cameras flashed anyway, illegal in the courtroom, but unpreventable.

The judge entered, heralded with the loud, "All rise!"

When everything settled down, the judge peered over his reading glasses. "Who are you, young lady?"

"I'm Alex Smith, your honor, the owner of Green World, as well as the

191

inventor of the long life laptop battery." Alex strained her ears for Ethan's gasp, but didn't hear it over the roar of conversations that followed in the audience. Nuts. She wanted to surprise him and she certainly wasn't going to give him the satisfaction of seeing her look back at him.

"Where is your counsel, Miss Smith?"

"I'll be representing myself, your honor. I'm a fully qualified lawyer."

He took his glasses off and raised his eyebrow.

"I have my bar exam certificate with me if you would like to see it, your honor," Alex said.

The judge gestured. "Approach."

Alex took the papers she'd removed from her briefcase with her. Once at the judge's desk, she spoke softly. Let the opposition stew. "My GED, diplomas, and certificate, your honor. Here on the back of the certificate is the name and phone number of the person who administered the bar exam yesterday, if you need this authenticated."

The judge went through the pages, slowly. "Yesterday?" he asked incredulously. His eyes flicked over to the three grey-haired lawyers representing her opposition.

"Yes, your honor," Alex kept her facial expression neutral. "Ah, that's a page with Judge Newton's information on it. He can verify my identity as well as my ownership of Green World."

"Very well, counselor, go take your seat." The judge kept the papers. Alex wasn't worried. She could retrieve them or get copies again later.

What followed was a nauseatingly long recitation by Alex's opponents describing every law and patent that required investigation and a formal cease and desist directive. They shuffled their papers and went through things in great detail. Alex listened carefully, planning her opening speech to counter all points they'd brought up in the same order.

"Miss Smith, your opening statement?" the judge said.

"Thank you, your honor." Alex stood up, and choosing her words very carefully, cited opposing laws, case rulings, and dismissed patent claims for open technology. Each item directly matched and countered something the other lawyer had said, in the order that had been presented. She did not once check any paper, and in fact, had none on the desk in front of her. Her opponents scribbled away furiously.

When Alex concluded this longer and equally nauseating list, the judge proclaimed, "Court will resume tomorrow at 8 a.m."

Alex turned to face her opponents and spoke clearly, "See you in the morning, gentlemen." She took her briefcase and left. She did not look in Ethan's direction. Some of her picobots attached themselves to her opponents, the judge, and the attendees. Inside the courtroom, people parted like she were Moses and they were the Red Sea. Alex kept the corners of her lips upturned in a slight smile and stepped along briskly. Outside, Milo had eight bodyguards and the limousine waiting. Alex took up position in the center of their sturdy buffer zone and ignored the shouts of reporters and flashes of cameras.

Alex arrived the next morning in the limousine with her bodyguards. No point in trying to be anonymous anymore; Milo assured her that her face was plastered all over both news and social media. The judge opened the day by requesting all counselors attend him in a private office. He made them all sit and then started with, "Miss Smith, I took the opportunity last night to verify your credentials."

"Did you have any questions, your honor?" Alex asked. She held her back straight and tried to radiate both energy and confidence.

"Why did you wait so long to make your identity known?" The judge had dark sleep-deprivation circles under his otherwise bright and penetrating gaze.

Alex, who had spoken with Judge Newton that morning and knew exactly how detailed that conversation had been, replied, "My employees at Green World have a problem with our vegetarian cafeteria. I'm too busy to spend every moment arguing the point."

The judge coughed, obviously surprised by that answer. "Why don't you just allow meat?"

"It's not environmentally sustainable, your honor."

The judge turned to the three lawyers. "I don't suppose your clients would like to withdraw their case?"

"No, your honor," the senior lawyer among her opposition answered.

The judge sighed. "Very well. We'll resume in two weeks to give both parties a chance to review the opposition's opening statements."

The senior lawyer said, "May we ask for a temporary cease and desist order while the case is pending, your honor?"

The judge paused, thinking it over, and then declared, "No. All of you presented valid legal support for your sides yesterday. I'd prefer to hear discussion on these points before making any ruling. You're dismissed."

As Alex stood to leave, the judge held up a finger. Alex waited while the others stepped out. She pulled the door closed again and turned back to the judge.

The judge studied her a moment and then said, "Your credentials." He handed her documents back to her, eyes narrowing at her thoughtfully. "They have no idea what they're getting into, do they?"

Rather than answer that, Alex said, "Thank you for not issuing the cease and desist order, your honor."

The judge's fingers tapped his armchair. "How does your battery work?"

A court order to reveal how her battery worked would be challenging, but Milo, fully prepared, would take care of that. "Respectfully, your honor, the simple answer is magic. The complex answer would take you years of study to even understand the language necessary to begin to discuss the technology."

The judge rubbed his chin. "Hmmm. Go ahead and go. I didn't think you'd tell me."

Alex counted her blessings and departed. She had two weeks to sort out her employees who were going to feel she deceived them. Then she was going to have to justify the vegetarian kitchen. After that, she was going to have to go help her lawyers with the other cases. Then she'd have to work with Brian on business growth. She also needed to empty her lab so the picobots could make more batteries. And she was going to have to arrange the sale of yet another one of Sal's paintings - royalties from her latest novel weren't quite high enough this quarter. She could get twenty million dollars from that painting upstairs. After that... maybe after that, she'd be able to get some sleep.

Brian sweetly scheduled an all hands meeting for when Alex arrived back, with the agenda "Owner answers questions". They didn't have a meeting room big enough so they ended up in the cafeteria with most people standing. At least Brian had the decency to forewarn her: as Alex came into the building, he sent her a text message. She wasn't actually surprised; he'd been telling her that was his plan since the court session began.

Alex entered the cafeteria and Brian announced, "Everyone, the inventor of the long life battery and our owner, Alex Smith." There was applause.

"Thanks, Brian." Those that knew her well enough to catch the amused tone laughed. "First, I want to assure everyone that I'm the exact same person that's been taking out the trash, scouring the toilets, and hanging out with you in the gym and cafeteria." Technically, her picobots scoured the bathrooms, but that was a minor detail.

"What's with the vegetarian cafeteria?" someone asked loudly. "You were out at the protest even."

"Get right to the point, eh, Jon?" Alex grinned.

"You bet!" he replied.

The light tone and joking was actually very promising. They weren't angry. They weren't intimidated. They weren't upset. Brian had obviously interceded and laid the groundwork well.

Alex explained, loudly enough to be heard, "I'm omnivorous just like most of you. The fact is, it's just not environmentally sustainable. We can import meat, but it would be extremely expensive. I've been very careful to keep our food organic, non-GMO, pesticide, hormone, artificial ingredient, and drug free. You've noticed the health benefits of an improved diet and exercise, surely? Meat that falls into that category is very hard to acquire and is expensive to produce. We're relocating for more space and we'll be able to harvest our own greenhouses to cut some of our food costs, but we can't do a cattle farm to generate enough meat to serve everyone."

"Relocating?" someone asked.

"Yeah," Alex smiled at the change in topic. "I'm still working out the details of where, but our campus is too small. We've got to prepare for the next product rollout and we're going to need more space. If you have any ideas, pass them to Brian. And for the record, everyone, I'm still just an employee like you. Brian is in charge. I'm making super-long-term business decisions, but he's responsible for the near future and day-to-day activities. Your jobs are secure."

"What if the court shuts us down?" This came from someone in the back.

"It will not last. The law is in our favor." For the moment. "Paychecks will continue. Benefits will continue. We operated almost two years without any income at all and we can go more if necessary. Our products are going to change how people view energy."

For the next two hours, people asked questions, and Alex answered them, careful not to say too much about the long term plans, and never giving away the next product, or the secret to the battery. Afterwards, she was exhausted, but went to her lab to move the next batch of batteries.

Milo arranged the purchase of a securable property in Waldorf, Maryland which was south of Washington D.C. The daily commute would take an hour or two depending on traffic, but Alex could use the time to do work on her laptop and she would be able to hear crickets at night. It was far enough away from the courthouse and obscure enough that only the most persistent reporters would follow and those would be stopped by the gate and guards. They would simply sell the property again after the court case.

Alex had thought school was tedious, but court proved multitudes times worse. Endless droning and unrelieved reiteration of absurd minutia filled her days and unlike school, she couldn't drift off and think about important things. Instead she had to intensely focus and plan her counterarguments. Then she herself had to stand and present for hours. How judges and lawyers did this every day Alex couldn't fathom.

Alex seized the opportunity to spread her picobots around key locations and people in Washington D.C. Information gathering was critical. Eavesdropping on the government and her competitors was illegal, but she couldn't afford to get blindsided. Alex had triggers for when her name, company, batteries, or energy were mentioned. That's how she discovered that congress was working on a law to prevent energy device exports (i.e. her batteries). Congress was busy pushing it through in secret, buried as an appendix to some other bill. Alex sent notice to Brian, who could pass the information to her lawyers.

Meanwhile, Alex's court case dragged on. They were up to five weeks of endless rehashing of laws and rulings and jurisdiction issues. Alex had managed to dodge the safety issues by presenting 75 independent safety evaluations, including 3 by subsidiaries of Cartwright-Jaxon Engineering. They moved on to patent infringement possibilities and Alex was prepared for this too.

All morning, the lead lawyer for her opponents presented patents. Alex listened, mentally organizing her rebuttal. The session had an intermission for lunch and Alex sorted through her patent evidence and put it back into her briefcase.

"All rise!"

Alex was starting to hear "All rise!" in her dreams when she got a chance to sleep. During the week, she was researching new facility locations, catching up on the other law cases, consulting with Brian about their expansion, checking the reports from her picobots, and still trying to add to the novels that were bringing in a reasonably large cash flow. As soon as court let out on Friday, she'd take the family's private jet back to Atlanta, where she'd work non-stop on moving batteries her picobots were creating up to storage. On weekends, she only got sleep while the picobots were building, in 45 minute increments. 40 minutes of snoozing. 15 minutes to relocate the pallet up to storage, repeat. She flew back in time to go directly from the airport to the courthouse.

The judge cleared his throat. "Miss Smith, please present your counter-arguments."

"Thank you, your honor. The battery itself does not violate any patents." Alex stood. "I will take one apart and let you see it for yourself in a moment. The patents my colleagues presented reflect things on our battery adapters." Alex had noticed that the other lawyers really got annoyed when she called them her colleagues, so she'd been doing it ever since.

Alex opened her briefcase and pulled out a large stack of papers. "I have documents here for every sale we've ever made, and the adapter that was provided to the customer. I have here full design specifications and a list of the patents that were used for each adapter, and who holds that patent. I've also included the patent holders' requested payment and copies of our company checks to these companies per those agreements. I'd like to submit these for review. I'll be happy to go through each one in detail if you'd like."

The judge waved his hand for her to bring them over. He looked through the first few pages which were accompanied by a small USB thumb drive with complete information. "This is sufficient, Miss Smith. I'm sure we can read them ourselves later." He handed these off to a clerk to enter into the case as well as make copies for her opposition.

Alex, relieved at not having to go through that stack over the next four days, went back over to her table, opened the wheeled suitcase she'd brought in that day and removed a microscope, a multimeter, a couple of her batteries, a tiny flat screwdriver, a miniaturized electric cutter/welder, some gloves, and a small electronic device about the size of a square coffee coaster with a battery-sized red square printed on the surface. She said what each thing was as she withdrew it and set it on her table. The coffee coaster she labeled "Activation pad" although it did precisely nothing at all. Her picobots would do all of the work.

"The battery itself, your honor," Alex said, "Is just two metal squares pressed together and sealed. There's nothing special about how they lock together. There's nothing special about the design. No patents exist. As for the part that makes the battery work, your honor, if a patent existed for that technology, mine wouldn't be the only battery of its kind."

Alex held up one of the batteries. "If my colleagues and I may approach the bench, I will demonstrate, although I point out that the demonstration will not offer any insight into how my battery works." The judge nodded and Alex brought all of her items up to the front.

Alex made a show of testing her sample batteries with the multimeter and showing that all of them were in range for a laptop. She carefully set one on the electronic coffee coaster in the red outline, and pushed the small red button on the coaster. "Deactivates the battery." She used the multimeter to show that the battery was now dead.

Alex then put on her utterly pointless safety gloves and ran the cutter along the sides of the battery. The tiny blue flame was smaller than the tip of a fine point multi-liner pen. It looked impressive but didn't do anything. Alex's picobots diligently split the battery sides. Once she'd gone all the way around, she used the tiny screwdriver to pop the plates of the battery apart. She was left with two metal squares. There was nothing else at all.

Alex handed the metal squares to the judge. "As you see, your honor, two metal squares simply welded together." The exact same thing that everyone who'd taken one of her batteries apart had found.

Alex was certain this was infuriating to the poor sods who were paying $1200 at the very least to make someone to give up their only battery. A molecular cross-section of the metal only showed three layers - a non-conductive casing, a metal shield that prevented x-rays and other diagnostics, and a decorative satin plastic exterior. Small positive/negative conductive strips went through the layers from the microscopic dent in the center where her own molecule lived in its tiny vacuum. Other small dents merely made that dent seem like part of the metal's surface, and when the vacuum was broken, it was exactly like all the other dents and utterly useless.

The judge and opposing lawyers diligently looked through the microscope at the battery's plates.

Alex continued, "Your honor, the materials used are not patented, a square of metal is not patented, and melting two bits of metal together is not patented." She spoke softly enough that Ethan, still watching from his place in the front row, would not be able to hear. Let him think she was explaining how it worked.

The judge inspected the small squares and then passed them around. When they arrived back to Alex, she reversed the process, resealing the metal plates, setting them on the activation pad, pushing the tiny green button, and then showing that the battery worked again with the multimeter. Her picobots inserted the rescued molecule.

"Miss Smith," said the judge, "How does that work?"

"I can explain underlying physics, if you'd like, your honor, but it's complicated and won't satisfy you or anyone else," Alex responded, pitching her voice to be neither encouraging nor discouraging.

The judge rubbed his chin. "Yes, I want you to do that." Then louder, he said, "Court is dismissed until tomorrow."

For the three weeks, Alex gave a confusing, post-doctorate level explanation of forces, magnetic fields, and particle physics, complete with complex physics equations, which she diligently read aloud for the court recorder while writing them on the whiteboard with multicolored dry erase markers. Not a soul in the courtroom understood what she was saying. She included the equations that made the splitting of particles at CERN work. She made an offhand comment that it was the scientific research done at CERN that helped her figure out her battery so they could get more funding. Throughout she made note of everything that had associated patents and explained those and pointed out that her battery did not violate the patent. Never once did she touch on her new physics or her new molecule. She also never made eye contact with Ethan, a point which she hoped angered or annoyed him at the very least.

Her competitors were going to have to hire expensive top-level physicists to dissect her lecture, and when they were through, they were going to report that there was nothing new here, and then some bright soul was going to point out that she said she'd explain underlying physics, but not how her battery worked. It made a nice, distracting detour through smoke and mirrors.

On the day of the judge's ruling, Alex already knew what the judge was going to say from her picobot spies. She still got a lot of pleasure out of it.

The judge spoke loudly and clearly, "I find no case against Green World or its owner for copyright or patent infringement, safety violations, or any other discrepancy that would prevent Green World from continuing the production and sale of its batteries. Miss Smith, how many hours did you spend preparing for this case?"

"It's hard to say, your honor, I was working on other things at the same time. I've been very busy. I'm also salaried so I don't have to track which specific projects I'm working on or for how long."

"I see. What about you gentlemen?" the judge asked her opposing lawyers who glanced at each other and indicated that all three of them had been working for half a year on this case alone. "Miss Smith, what's your salary?"

"I'm on the same pay scale as everyone else in my company, your honor. With my annual increases, I'm at $35,000 plus benefits." Someone behind her made a choking sound.

"What about you three?" The judge peered at the other three lawyers. They named salaries in excess of $400,000. The judge wrote on a piece of paper, commented off-hand, "Plus benefits. Um." He wrote another minute. "Ok, Green World is to be compensated $1.5 million for time spent on this case."

"Thank you, your honor," said Alex with the same calm and clear intonation she'd used throughout the rest of the case.

"This case is closed." the judge announced. "Court is dismissed."

Alex took her briefcase and left. The people again parted like the Red Sea. Outside, she was surrounded by her buffer of bodyguards and she made her way over and climbed into the limousine where Milo waited.

"Do you want to know what the press is saying?" Milo asked Alex, just like he did at least once a week.

"Nope. I have enough to worry about without conjecture and rumors." Her standard answer. "We won. It's time to go to Hamasaki Corporation," Alex said, reaching for her laptop.

"How about a vacation and celebration instead?" Milo suggested dryly.

"I can sleep on the flight out. We go directly. Have someone at the other end buy us some clothes." She started tapping away on her laptop, sending directives to her law team, going through the company forums, and responding to Brian's emails.

Milo sighed and pulled out his phone.

On the private jet, Alex sat working on another novel while a woman re-dyed Alex's hair "just fixing the roots". Some of the dye splattered down on her keyboard as the stylist picked through her hair to make sure everywhere was covered. Alex wiped at the dye with the apron designed to protect clothing, but that thin, shiny material just smeared the chemical into a dark brown streak. The stylist, having missed the original splat, saw this, and rushed to apologize. Alex, bone-weary and headachy from the toxic odor in the confined space, snapped, "Just get me a wet paper towel."

Milo, across the cabin from her, shook his head at her in censure causing his oxygen mask tube running up to the jet's ceiling to twist around wildly giving him an alien antennae appearance. Lucky man over there with the untainted air. He went back to the book he was reading.

The woman scurried to comply, and Alex apologized, "Sorry, I'm just tired. I didn't mean to yell at you." Alex shifted on the padded chair again and bumped her laptop causing it to slide on the table. Alex pushed it back into place, frustrated. She supposed she ought to try for some sleep when her hair was finished.

For an exquisite moment, Alex daydreamed about ordering the jet to take her to a lovely Caribbean beach somewhere. She could build a nice grass hut and never go back. If the company dissolved, it would be enough to repay the Marino's. Did she really need this life? She never had a moment's rest. If only she could time travel so she could give herself more time to get everything done like that girl in that movie... what was that movie Sal had suggested before she went to high school? She was beyond tired if her memory was failing.

Sal had warned Alex that this would take years of constant, grinding work and that she'd likely give up. "Sustained effort is impossible," he'd said. "You work. You toil. You have the best intentions. But multi-year, sometimes even multi-month goals, are too hard. You're going to have to forgive yourself for not being perfect, and then you're going to have to pick yourself up the next day and start all over again. You'll have to find the drive, the motivation, every single day, and most days, you're going to have to carry on without that. You'll have to set aside thinking about doing it and just do it."

Even with masterful delegation, too many things needed Alex's direct attention. If she failed to get money from Hamasaki Corporation, she was going to have to cut a deal with one of the oil cartels or one of the governments. The former would hurt the environment, because the larger batteries would then need to be hybrids. The latter would cost individuals astronomic amounts due to regulations that required them to pay for energy monthly again, and would also tip the world's political balance in chaotic directions. At this point, even a merger with Cartwright-Jaxon Engineering wouldn't save them. She needed Hamasaki's deep pockets; her carefully cultivated community would be the first casualty in any other scenario.

Break things into steps, Alex told herself. She could only work on one thing at a time anyway, and first, she needed her hair to be finished and she needed her laptop to quit sliding around. Once again, she hoped with all her heart that the woman dyeing her hair wouldn't be paying attention to the novel Alex was typing. Alex didn't need anyone finding out all those R-authors were her. If only she could have some privacy and an input device that wouldn't move around! She adjusted the laptop to a comfortable typing position yet again.

Then Alex saw it - the computer that she wanted. Private, always available, comfortable to type on. Could she get her picobots to bend light? She closed down her laptop and spent the remainder of her hair service designing an interactive heads-up display. She could program her picobots to respond to touches on the "screen", or via a super comfortable keyboard forming under her fingertips. Her picobots could even give her tactile feedback.

App windows could move with her head, with an uncovered space in the center to let her see what was directly in front of her. The picobots could track her eyes and expand things she was trying to see. Her picobots could emit light directly toward her retina so only she would be able to see the "screen". The picobots could even collect stray light waves that might bounce off her eyelids should she blink.

Alex inhaled and exhaled deeply, giving her body extra oxygen beyond the chemical odor of hair dye. She could tie the input and output to a computer that she could literally leave anywhere and she could make the HUD easily control her picobots and she could ditch her bioshield ring. It was a lot of programming, but she could have a rudimentary setup by the end of the flight if she skipped sleep. She yawned.

Hermione. That's who she needed to be. Alex decided she'd take a couple extra days in Tokyo at the hotel to get some sleep before going over to Hamasaki Corporation. She couldn't risk being exhausted at that meeting.

Alex studied Kuro Hamasaki's business card. The elegant handwritten Japanese kanji on the back that said "Full courtesy to bearer." with his personal signature still clearly legible, even though the card had somehow gotten bent and a tiny bit rumpled. She hoped that wouldn't be construed as a horrible insult. All things considered, it was in remarkably good condition. She slid it carefully into her meishi case, a hand-stitched exquisite leather business card holder that Milo had somehow managed to acquire for her.

She tucked the meishi case into her jacket pocket, located safely above the waist because below the waist would be an insult. Despite the tutor Milo had arranged, she wondered how she'd manage to conform to all of the cultural expectations if Kuro Hamasaki would even see her.

Alex inhaled deeply and gazed up at the massive skyscraper blocking the morning sun. Somewhere inside, Kuro Hamasaki was going about his business, unaware of her standing outside. Should she have gotten an appointment first? No, she couldn't risk the cartels finding out about this move. She was not carrying any trackable electronic phone or laptop, although her new picobot HUD was marginally functional. With the private rented jet, Alex had barely made a blip on customs. The elegantly wrapped dagger that was her offering gift had been purchased after their arrival.

Alex checked her outfit - a trim navy blue skirt with a matching jacket and flat shoes with a pristine white shirt. She wore no jewelry, except for her bioshield ring. She could have been any of the business people striding in and out of the building if it weren't for her too-light brown-dyed hair. She'd reviewed her Japanese pronunciation. She carried a matching elegant briefcase. It was time. She needed a small mountain of money and another distribution point for her business to survive.

Alex stepped into the lobby - a cavern of marble and simplified beauty with a living wall of ferns, orchids, and other jungle plants muting the area with a quiet waterfall off to one side. Alex walked up to the desk confidently, knowing that Hamasaki security teams were already trying to identify her. Security cameras covered every part of the lobby, while an actual security booth with guards was farther back, beyond the reception desk; a person would have to pass that security to get to anywhere else inside the building.

The woman behind the desk stood. On the counter in front of her was a standard guest sign-in page and a fountain pen. Alex bowed, precisely at a 30 degree angle, and in flawless Japanese with absolute courtesy, she said, "My name is Alex Smith. I'm an associate of the late Salvatore Marino. I do not have an appointment. I would like to speak with Kuro Hamasaki." She carefully withdrew Kuro Hamasaki's business card and held it out in both her hands, with the handwritten side facing up and oriented so the woman could clearly read it, and waited with a neutral expression on her face.

The woman reached out and took the card with both hands. She read it, then turned it over and read the back. If she was surprised, she did not show it. "If you would please have a seat over there, I will see if he is available." The woman gestured toward a circle of comfortable looking sofas and chairs with end tables and magazines.

"Arigato gozaimasu." Alex went over and sat in one of the chairs. She watched the receptionist disappear into the depths of the building with the business card. Alex resisted the urge to run after it screaming, "No, wait! I need that!" Alex settled in and watched people come and go. Hamasaki corporate headquarters was a busy place.

About 10 minutes later, a woman dressed similarly to Alex approached and bowed, speaking English. "Miss Smith, Mr. Hamasaki is in a business meeting right now, but he requests you wait. It should be no more than a half hour. May I check you in? I regret that we must go through your briefcase and take you through an X-ray for security purposes."

"Thank you. Yes, I'd like to be checked in." Alex stood and followed. Alex signed her name on the check-in as requested and was given a visitor badge.

Along the way to the security check-in room, Alex counted no less than eight discreet, but heavily armed guards. Their weapons would not penetrate her bioshield, yet she still couldn't help feeling more than a little bit of trepidation. The security check-in room was spacious with an airport style millimeter wave scanner for personnel and an X-ray belt for items.

Alex set her briefcase on the counter under the watchful eyes of the guards, unlocked it and opened it. The only items inside were the gift-wrapped dagger, a battery stamped with her company logo and a small, plain ring in a small, plain box. They X-rayed all four items separately and then had her stand in the gate for people. Using her new HUD interface visible only to her, Alex toggled her picobots to allow the scans and passed their security. She reactivated her bioshield and they returned her briefcase and items.

"If you would please come this way, we have a private waiting room." Her escort said, ever so politely.

"Thank you," Alex replied, and followed to a large, tastefully decorated waiting room where there were more sofas, chairs, and tables with magazines. Another beautiful living wall decorated one side.

"There is a restroom through that panel," the woman gestured. "Please do not go wandering around the building. An escort is required at all times."

The woman bowed and left.

Alex set her briefcase in a basket apparently set there for that purpose and went over to admire the living wall. The woman returned almost immediately with a tray and tea, and poured Alex a cup. Then she departed again.

After Alex had admired each plant, she selected a magazine and flipped through it to give security something to observe. She did not sit down. Almost exactly 30 minutes from the original estimate, her escort arrived again.

The woman bowed and said, "Mr. Hamasaki is ready to see you now, if you would please follow me."

Alex nodded, returned the magazine to its original position, collected her briefcase, and followed. The woman flashed her badge at one of the elevators, which then opened. Alex had a moment of vertigo as the high speed elevator shot up to the 84th floor much faster than any elevator she'd ever been in. They were the only passengers. They passed more security guards as they went through several hallways. Two guards stood in front of a double door which one guard opened without comment.

They stepped into a very large, private office. A massive L-shaped desk with two leather chairs facing it barely took up an eighth of the room. A separate table would comfortably seat ten people. The far wall was entirely glass, looking out over the city, and along the right-hand wall was yet another living wall of ferns and orchids, while the remaining walls had glass display cases that showcased a magnificent collection of Japanese swords. Alex happily recognized one of the swords.

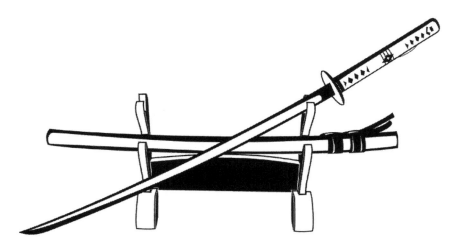

A bodyguard stood inside by the door, but Alex ignored him, focusing instead on Mr. Hamasaki who was standing by the window looking out. He was wearing an impeccable grey suit, and his grey hair had been trimmed very short. He turned when she entered.

Alex's escort announced, "Alex Smith-sama." She bowed and then left. The doors closed behind her.

Mr. Hamasaki walked over to her and offered his hand, which Alex shook gently, telling herself to relax and follow his cues. In formal Japanese, Alex began, "Mr. Hamasaki, thank you for seeing me without an appointment. I know you are a busy person and this could not have been convenient to arrange." She conscientiously gazed toward his chin, not directly into his eyes.

Alex bowed at a precise 45 degree angle, exhaling as she leaned forward and inhaling as she straightened - 'saikeirei' she reminded herself, for respect to people with very high rank or social status. Mr. Hamasaki returned the bow at a smooth 30 degree angle.

Alex then set her briefcase down and withdrew the carefully wrapped dagger and using both hands, offered it to him. She didn't turn to look, but suspected the bodyguard twitched. "Please accept this token of appreciation."

Mr. Hamasaki accepted the gift and replied, "Domo arigato gozaimasu."

Alex opened her meishi case and withdrew one of her cards. Bowing again, she offered Mr. Hamasaki the special business card that Milo had prepared. Just like she had practiced on the flight over, she held both her card and the meishi case with both hands, using her thumbs on the corners not covering any of the Japanese text or Green World's logo that were oriented facing him. She tried to appear as if she'd been doing this formal ritual all her life and hoped she was doing ok. Then she remembered her feet and realized they weren't at the correct angle, but she refused to adjust them and draw attention to this faux pas. She said her company, and her position as owner, and finally her name.

Kuro Hamasaki took the card, using both his hands, bowing again. He read the card and then also read the English printed side. "Hajimemashite, Smith-san." Smoothly, he offered his business card with both hands.

Alex took this with both hands, and reverently holding it on top of her meishi case, examined the English print, noting that some of the contact details were different from his previous card. Computer-printed Japanese kanji on the back simply translated the front. She did not show any sign of disappointment at this and she did not ask for the other card back.

Mr. Hamasaki offered, "My condolences on the passing of Salvatore Marino, Miss Smith. I always wondered when one of those cards would show up again. I was beginning to doubt they ever would."

"It was very kind of you to give them to us." Alex gestured toward the sword case. "I'm happy to see the sword restored and in your collection."

"Yes, our family is grateful to have it returned to us. What may I do for you?"

Alex thought that more small talk would have been in order before getting down to business, but maybe he was in a hurry? "The U.S. government is about to pass a law forbidding the sale of my batteries outside of the country."

He waited for her to continue.

"Mr. Hamasaki, this is a ploy to try to make me recant on my rule to sell only to individuals, as well as to unbalance political power in favor of the United States. While I'm not disloyal to my country, I am a businesswoman."

"What is it you want me to do? I do not control your government." Mr. Hamasaki gave her no clues to what he was thinking either in tone or body language.

Alex pressed on. Technically, he could influence her government and had in the past, but that wasn't what she was there for. She didn't have a use for his dark organization. "I would like Hamasaki Corporation to buy our entire stock within the next 36 hours before the law goes into effect." That got his attention; his eyes widened the slightest amount. "More specifically, to buy and resell to as many individuals as you can arrange. We have just about 856,000 units. I will sell them to you, for ¥111,000 each." This would be ¥22,000 less than Green World was selling them for. "You resell them, using our company's original individual ownership agreement, at a price of your choosing. That will make your company a reseller, not a purchaser, and my company's integrity to only sell to individuals remains intact."

"You have an eight month backlog on orders. How do you have that many units?" Mr. Hamasaki asked directly.

Kuro Hamasaki was certainly paying close attention to her company, or maybe some staff member had just handed him a full dossier before the meeting. Alex supposed the recent court nonsense riveted eyes on her company in any case. She could work this in her favor.

Alex walked over to the glass case with the sword. It was excellently restored, beautiful with that glowing watermark. "Foresight, Mr. Hamasaki. I'm prepared for a number of possibilities. By time you have sold your inventory, I should be able to get the law repealed because it is illegal. Should the law be repealed before that, I will not sell outside the United States until you give me permission to do so, and even then, we can continue to split the sales across the world."

Mr. Hamasaki came over to stand next to her, also gazing at the priceless sword that Alex and Sal had returned to his family. In the glass reflection, Alex saw the bodyguard tense slightly, wired for immediate action, should any threat be made.

Alex continued, "I know ¥19 billion minus labor expenses isn't a very high profit for you, but my company needs the influx of money."

"Until just now, I thought your company was going to fail. The community has underestimated you."

Alex merely looked at him and gave him a knowing nod. While she felt like smiling, she didn't. Smiles could be interpreted as not understanding, embarrassment, or disagreeing.

Mr. Hamasaki observed, "The sheiks will not be amused."

Alex responded, "Yes, that's why this meeting was unannounced. Hamasaki Corporation is more powerful than the sheiks. I would very much like you to be my partner. The laptop battery is not the only battery Green World is going to produce. Profit margins will grow higher, but our expenses will match."

"Did you bring legal documents for this?"

Alex was rather surprised at this directness. She'd been told decisions took time in a Japanese company. "I thought you'd prefer to have your own lawyers finalize it to make sure Hamasaki Corporation's interests are secure. The website listed on my business card will take your people to my draft, which you can modify if you'd like. I am an honorable person, Mr. Hamasaki. This is an honest offer. I have other contingencies, but this would make me the happiest."

"Do you know," Mr. Hamasaki paused, "That day when I came to your little store, Salvatore Marino said the only thing he wanted from me was a promise to listen to you should you ever come to me to ask for something? He didn't want anything for himself or his family. He said that only once in every ten generations there might be someone as worthy of support and protection."

Although Alex was shaken to her core, she chuckled and said lightly, "Mr. Marino was biased. I was keeping his store clean."

"Was he? What is the secret to how your battery works?"

"A secret, Mr. Hamasaki. I'm the only one that knows it and I'm not sharing. There is no point in taking them apart; the energy source cannot be discovered."

He nodded. He'd surely taken apart more than a few trying to get that answer, as had every other government and group with the means to do so. "Miss Smith, perhaps you would allow me to take you to dinner this evening with some of my family and associates?"

Alex nodded, trying very hard not to jump up and down gleefully. The dinner invitation meant a business relationship could be built. All she needed to do was not insult anyone, never pour her own drink, but pour his occasionally, enjoy some odd food, and maybe sing karaoke, or whatever Mr. Hamasaki had in mind, without making a complete fool of herself. "I would be honored. I'm staying at Palace Hotel Tokyo as is my personal assistant whom I'd like you to meet."

Alex went back to her briefcase. "I also brought two other things for you, Mr. Hamasaki," Alex said, opening it. "First, a battery. It's not in the system anywhere. Give it to whomever you like." He came over to see and she gave the battery to him using both hands, bowing at the 30 degree angle. Alex explained, "There are only four others that are in circulation that aren't tracked."

Alex then opened the box with the ring and took out his ring, identical to the one she wore, that would masquerade as a bioshield generator. "Second, this." She set the ring back in the box and held the small box out, again with both hands. Her picobots had fixed the ring size for him as she'd entered the room. The ring itself had microscopic electronics that if tracked very carefully, merely looped confusingly back on themselves pointlessly in a pretty, if super-complex multilayered Celtic knot. The actual bioshield was made of her picobots that would stay with the ring.

Mr. Hamasaki removed the ring from the box and stared at it. It wasn't very impressive. He at least understood enough to not take it at face value like Sal's brother had. "What is this?"

Alex glanced at the bodyguard, not really wanting to explain in front of him, but had to accept Mr. Hamasaki's trust in him. She could set her picobots to spy on him later. "As you said, the sheiks are not going to be happy. This is protection. It's a bioshield ring; bullets and knives won't reach you while you wear it. It would be easiest to demonstrate."

Alex held up her hand to show she was wearing a matching ring. "To show you its value, you will need a gun. I will stand over here by your window, well away from you and the gun so as to not be a threat."

Mr. Hamasaki peered at her curiously as she walked over toward the window. He turned and opened his office door. The guard outside gave him his weapon without question. Mr. Hamasaki closed the door again and turned toward Alex, wielding a MAC-10.

Out of the window, Alex could see a train gliding by below. Off in the distance, huge ships decorated shipyards and several moved about a busy port. The Tokyo Gate Bridge was visible and she wished she had time to visit the city's magnificent properties. Although the day was clear, haze still blocked any view of the Chiba shoreline across Tokyo Bay. Everything looked so tiny from this height.

Alex reluctantly turned from the incredible view and positioned herself so a stray bullet would go into the wall, not the window. "Shoot me, Mr. Hamasaki. You can't hurt me. Go ahead." She stood there, unafraid, confident, nodding to him.

After a brief hesitation, he raised the gun and shot at her. Alex didn't even flinch. His guards immediately rushed in at the sound of gunfire. Despite the suppressor, the shot was quite loud. Mr. Hamasaki looked at her still standing there even though he knew he just shot her in the shoulder. He handed the gun to his guards and dismissed them.

Alex walked over to Mr. Hamasaki, reached up to just in front of her shoulder, where the armor piercing bullet was seemingly hovering in the air a centimeter from her suit jacket, and pulled the bullet free and handed it to him, again with both hands as an offering and with a precise bow. The bullet was in pristine condition and could be easily recycled. The bodyguard's eyes were wide, but Mr. Hamasaki merely nodded and put his ring on. Alex continued, "There are only four other rings. Once you have power, you'd be surprised what you can do."

Several months later, Alex stood outside an Indian cultural center north of Las Vegas. Corbin May, the tribe's leader, had turned down Milo, so Alex was there to try and change that no to a yes. Just off the reservation was the perfect land for her new complex - open, beautiful, undeveloped, flat, environmentally dead desert, far enough away from Las Vegas to make competitors and spies more obvious. There was even enough space to expand to the size complex she wanted. It was neighboring the reservation, which had a community that desperately needed an influx of money and resources. It was perfect. And it was owned by Corbin May who'd told Milo, politely, but unwaveringly, to look elsewhere.

Alex sighed. She turned around and tossed her sunglasses into the rental car. She'd left her entourage back at the hotel, much to Milo's annoyance. How many crowds of people were likely to be at a remote Indian cultural center anyway? Probably not too many assassins. With her bioshield, she was in no danger anyway and she honestly wanted a chance to stand alone in the open desert and stare at the sky. She wanted to see if she could shake off the sense of crisis that was hovering constantly in the back (and sometimes front) of her mind since her lucrative deal with Kuro Hamasaki.

Alex adjusted the purse Milo had thrown at her angrily while yelling "take this, you fool!" just as she was getting into the rental car to leave the hotel. Alex greeted the somewhat bored person at the ticket counter politely. This was a small community. Everyone would know everyone else. "Just me," Alex said, opening the purse to look inside. She hadn't realized until just now that she was going to need money. Good grief. Even when he was livid at her, Milo still thought to take care of her. And to think she'd thought he'd thrown a purse at her so she could use it as a costume accessory to better blend in. Alex handed the woman one of the 20 dollar bills from the purse and got change.

Alex ambled through the center, carefully looking at each display and reading, absorbing the text on the little plaques and watching every multimedia presentation. Who knew what might help her convince Corbin May. The center only had a few other visitors and they outpaced her. One of the displays described how Soaring Eagle created the cultural center to educate and bring in funds to help the community. The center was responsible for the new waterline from Las Vegas 20 years prior. A little bit later, there was a small plaque with the caption "In honor of Corbin May in thanks for the waterline."

Alex arrived at the gift shop and diligently picked up books that she'd not seen when she was researching this tribe. She also picked out a beautiful handmade vase that she thought Sal's brother might like and two rugs, one for herself, and one for Milo that she expected Milo wouldn't like at all. She paid, again silently thanking Milo for the large sum of cash he'd put in the purse. She took everything out to the car and stood there in the painfully sweltering heat and went through every book.

Then Alex hiked back into the cultural center and went to the ticket counter. She took her ticket receipt and borrowed the guest pen and wrote her phone number on its back while the woman watched her silently. Alex handed the receipt to the woman and said, "Please give this to Soaring Eagle. Tell him," and she switched to their native tongue, "The desert rock weeps for the future."

Alex turned to leave and saw a couple of local teenagers coming in. One of them instantly recognized her and squealed, "Oh my God!" He immediately rushed over, leaving his friends to catch up. "Ma'am, I love your battery! It's amazing!"

Alex blinked, caught off-guard. Here? "Uh, I'm glad it's working for you."

His other friends gathered around and he asked, "Please can I have my picture taken with you?"

Alex could hear the Kingsport Academy teachers screaming "It's 'may I'! One demerit!" It jarred her sense of the present. "Uh, sure," she answered wishing she didn't sound so stupid. Then after a moment's panic, she added, "But please don't post it to social media until tomorrow? I'm on vacation. Kind of incognito." She pushed aside her thoughts on the future Green World complex and focused on the teenagers.

The boy nodded enthusiastically, "Of course!" He handed his phone to one of his friends. "I can't believe you're actually here. Of all places you could go, our reservation wouldn't seem to be at the top of the list."

Alex smiled for the photo and then repeated the same with each of them. "Oh, I don't know about that. Your desert is amazingly beautiful."

"Have you been through our cultural center already? We can take you." His eyes sparkled with enthusiastic excitement.

Alex pondered the time. She supposed she could postpone the novel writing that she had planned for later that afternoon. "I have, but I'd be honored to go again and see it through your eyes."

He beamed at her and for the next hour and a half, he and his friends gave her a tour of the cultural center with detailed commentary about all sorts of things. Alex asked questions and kept them going with a focus on tradition and their community and what interested them. The education she received was far superior to just going through and reading the plaques. They confirmed that Corbin May was indeed Soaring Eagle.

Afterward, Alex thanked them and got a group photo for herself of all of them which seemed to be the expected thing to do, and bade them farewell. She got into her rental car for the long drive back to her hotel in Las Vegas. It was several hours later than she'd intended and the sun was setting.

After an hour on the black dull night road where there were no lights at all and no cars, Alex sorely missed having a driver. She was exhausted and noticed her car drifting across the road lines several times. She stopped the car on the side of the road but not off the road so far that the hot engine would ignite the dry, flammable desert shrubs. She got out to stretch her legs.

The night air was chilly and Alex shivered. She supposed she should have brought a jacket, but it hadn't even occurred to her. She wasn't supposed to be out after dark. Then she looked up. Stars, more than she'd ever seen in her life, gazed back at her. "Wow," she breathed. "Oh, Brian, why didn't you tell me?" She wondered if she could eventually build a spaceship and see them even more clearly. She bet Brian would approve.

When Alex got too cold to stand there looking anymore, she got back into the car and drove on. She knew immediately when she got back into cell phone range because her phone started beeping and then ringing. She ignored it; they could track her location by her phone's GPS. When she got back to the hotel, Milo was waiting, along with her bodyguards. They escorted her in.

Alex slept through noon in the ornate Bellagio suite with a rare abandon. She yawned, stretched, and rolled out of bed. Over at the window, she saw the sun was high and checked the clock. Silently groaning, she rubbed her eyes and padded out into the common area. Milo sat at the table working on his computer. One of her off-duty bodyguards sat on the sofa, watching a movie on his tablet with earphones plugged in. "Good morning, gentlemen," she said quietly.

"Afternoon is more accurate," Milo replied. "Did you enjoy your outing yesterday?"

The previous night, Alex had ignored all inquiries, tossed her phone on the counter, and stumbled directly to bed. Alex retrieved her phone from the counter. "Please order room service. I think I need to hear what's in the news about me." She unlocked her phone and pulled up her picture with the kids. She handed the phone to Milo and went back to her room to shower and dress.

Alex stood in the hot water for a long time contemplating her next moves. The alternate building sites weren't nearly as good, but at least she could count on the owners taking a pile of cash and stepping aside without hesitation. She'd send Milo to do those negotiations. Too much time had already been wasted here. She heard the hotel room's front door, then trays rattling and soft voices. She got out of the shower and dressed. Her stomach rumbled.

Midway through the meal, the hotel room phone rang. Milo answered it. "Yes, thank you. We'll be down in a moment." He hung the phone up and turned to Alex. "You must have done something right. There's an Indian named Soaring Eagle down at reception waiting for you."

Alex immediately left Milo and the off-duty bodyguard to clean up the lunch mess while she took her eight on-duty bodyguards and went to greet Soaring Eagle and escort him up to their suite. After Milo's description and examples of the current news coverage over lunch, she realized she wouldn't be going anywhere without a buffer of bodyguards for a very long time. It wasn't just masses of reporters she had to worry about. Her pictures up at the reservation with the boys were already flooding social media. Luckily, her hair was still brown, and she'd been wearing her makeup which had only slightly wilted in the desert heat.

In the chaotic lobby, Corbin May was still easy to spot. He was the one in full, magnificent, formal Indian garb being escorted by two younger men who were equally decked out. He was possibly the oldest person Alex had ever seen. Wrinkles covered his face and hands. White braided hair was barely visible under his headdress. He stood proudly, his bearing holding him apart from the mass of people.

Alex walked over to him. People were taking pictures of them, both Alex and Soaring Eagle, and she would have been hard-pressed to decide which of them people found more fascinating. Perhaps they thought he was a performer.

Alex's bodyguards, keeping the crowd back really well, parted enough for her to approach Soaring Eagle. In his language, she said, "Thank you for coming."

Soaring Eagle stared at her, studying her for a long time, and then replied in the same tongue, "Wind Walker told me where to find you."

Name for one of the young men she met the day before, maybe? Alex hoped he wasn't there to tell her to go away. "Would you accompany me to my room so we can have a private meeting?"

211

"Come to my house this evening before sunset. I will hear your proposition." Without another word, Soaring Eagle and his escorts turned and left.

Alex watched him go and then took her entourage back to their room. Milo was waiting, pacing anxiously. Not seeing any Indian following her, he asked, "Did he turn you down?"

Alex shook her head. "He wants to talk with me this evening up at his house." She smiled at her bodyguards. "You guys are going to have to take me. That drive was awful. I have no idea how you do it."

One of them smirked and joked, "About time we got appreciated. Can we get a raise?"

Milo answered lightly, "Ask Mario. If you dare." They all laughed at the ongoing joke.

Later in the afternoon, the stretch limousine pulled up on the dirt road next to a single story flat-roofed box house. Neighbors peered out of their windows and then relocated to stand on their doorsteps and stare. Alex climbed out, waved to them, and went to the door and knocked.

Soaring Eagle was no longer wearing his full Indian formal dress and was now just in jeans and a t-shirt. From his bearing, however, he could still have been formally dressed. He stood aside to let her pass and then took her to the kitchen which was quite likely the only common room given the size of the house.

"Soda?" he asked in English.

"Just water, please," Alex answered.

He nodded and got two glasses which he filled from the tap and brought over. Alex took a sip and noted the water had a slightly sulfuric odor, not toxic, but not particularly pleasant. She drank anyway and waited.

Soaring Eagle sat and after a moment, he continued in English, "Ever since your man came to inquire about buying my land, I have been plagued with disturbing dreams. I have consulted our ancestors many times since and each time, they say the same thing. The desert rock weeps for the future. How did you know to say that?"

Alex blinked in surprise. "I... didn't. I just wanted to give you a message that might make you curious enough to speak with me. I want to purchase your land for a while and build my community here, respectfully, honoring the desert and your traditions. I want to coexist with and build up your community and people. When it's time, we'll pack up and leave, returning the desert to its natural state and ownership back to you." She was planning a full island settlement out in the Pacific Ocean, but she needed the intermediary step to grow large enough to protect an island from pirates or an invading government.

"Hmmm." Soaring Eagle closed his eyes, not speaking for so long that Alex wondered if he might have fallen asleep on her. Just as she was about to gently prod him, Soaring Eagle opened his eyes again, and said quietly, "Do you know mother earth is dying?"

Alex answered slowly, wondering what his desired response was. "The human race has certainly done a lot of damage. I'm hoping my batteries will stop some of that. We are dumping a lot of our profits into environmental cleanup." As Soaring Eagle frowned, Alex wondered what she'd said wrong. She waited.

Soaring Eagle cleared his throat and looking even older and incredibly worn out, he said, "Our ancestors tell me that it is already too late - that mother earth cannot support us any longer. The desert rock weeps for the future because our generations are the last on this planet for many moons."

Alex's eyebrows scrunched in concentration. He was trying to tell her something else, too, from his expectant gaze. Finally she just asked, "What else do your ancestors say?"

Soaring Eagle inhaled and in a tone that made Alex's skin prickle with goosebumps, replied, "That the one who sees the weeping desert rock can save our people. They show me a great city in the sky, close enough to touch the stars, where our people will be safe. They direct me to tell you to build it with secrets. That time is short." He remained perfectly still, avidly watching her response. "Does that make any sense to you at all?"

What in the world? He wasn't joking. Alex swallowed. She felt compelled to answer honestly, "I'm not a mystic. I believe in science. It's true that I have thought about traveling to space and I might even have a way to do it eventually." She'd only just considered it the night before actually.

Soaring Eagle put his hand flat on the table as if stabilizing himself. "I'm going to give you my land even though every bone in my body screams not to trust white people ever again." His eyes were wet but did not drip. "You will build a city in the sky and when you go, promise me that you will take my people."

Alex couldn't imagine how she might build a space station in the near future that might be sustainable. She could barely get the people in her company to accept her vegetarian menu. A space station would be even more restrictive. She'd have to rethink her entire plan for the future. "I promise that if I can, I will. Is that good enough?"

Soaring Eagle nodded, just once. "Will you stay and do a pipe ceremony with me, despite your science deity?"

In his language, Alex replied, "I'd be honored, Soaring Eagle."

The ceremony was beautiful, with several locals as well as Milo and her bodyguards attending, but Alex did not experience anything mystical or particularly enlightening. When Alex finally arrived back in Atlanta, she started going through every scientific paper she could find on earth-related issues. She built formulas, crunched numbers, and studied the results. Her conclusion scared her to death. Everything she was doing had to be accelerated and she was going to need a space station as soon as possible. All of her plans had to be reprioritized to put the space station first, above everything else, including her business. She went to speak with Brian.

Several months later, Alex surveyed the beginning of their Pacific Ocean island. Right now, it was just a small, functional habitat for the ocean cleanup crew. Under the pretense of reducing the Pacific Ocean trash island, Alex was creating their third location in international waters to eventually be a beautiful resort and safe habitat - an Earth-side residence when her desert habitat launched into space.

The island would eventually lift into space to become part of the space habitat too, but that didn't need to be done for some years yet. Right now, it was just an inconsequential floating barge that would collect and sort trash that she could recycle into the next battery casings and island mass. With luck, no one would notice the size of the facility growing into an island. Alex didn't want the United States government getting the idea that she was forming her own country. She'd need to come up with a good excuse for the expansion.

The living quarters would still be as small as those in Atlanta. It was the only way she'd be able to enforce the rules necessary to have a sustainable habitat. She'd only told Brian about her plans because the employees were positively livid that the new facilities weren't going to have larger living quarters. In Atlanta, they could understand the cramped apartments; there really wasn't anywhere to expand to, but out in the desert and here in the Pacific, they had space, and yet she was still building a cramped high-rise in the desert, and demanding their ocean facility match.

Despite the leaps forward and the money she was dumping into both new locations, she was very unpopular. Out at the reservation, the locals were screaming about her high-rise buildings ruining the environment and taking over their horizon. Soaring Eagle was supporting her, but at what cost within his community, Alex did not know. Her original plan to keep everything low and spread out had to be scrapped in favor of creating a habitat that could be lifted into space. She needed the extra land for oxygen producing plants and the illusion of a larger environment.

She didn't expect her unpopularity to change even when she announced SEL the following month. That's what she'd decided to call her solid electricity, that was neither a solid nor electricity, but a wall of picobots and mutated molecules that could be dynamically reconfigured into any shape or size. It was stronger than steel, could be made impermeable or permeable, hard or flexible, solid or transparent. She was going to use it to enclose their desert habitat to moderate the temperature and keep out unwanted guests, and then to create the new buildings as she hired even more people. Over time, she'd also use it to create ground, air, and water vehicles and get people used to safer traveling as well as heights.

SEL required a large amount of matter and energy initially to provide the correct particles for the picobots and she was currently staring at an island of trash that was just what she needed. The environmentalists she'd hired were busy setting up and working out the best way to harvest the trash while not harming any sea life.

The island facility also had a gym and cafeteria, but would be missing other support staff for a while. They could still cross over to California if they needed to or travel to either of her other locations. Alex had added facility-to-facility travel expenses to the company-covered costs. Money was evaporating while the world and her competitors went crazy trying to figure out how she was still in business with such insane practices. Even the influx of Hamasaki Corporation's money wasn't going to last forever at her current spending rate.

Alex personally shook hands with every employee on the ocean cleanup barge and thanked them for their dedication and sacrifice living in such a remote location. She assured them that their labor was worthy and necessary and would help the planet. She called them noble heroes and promised them her continued support and funding. She made sure they knew to report any problems or needs to Green World's direct environmental efforts manager so they could be addressed as quickly as possible. Alex wanted this project to be an environmentalist's dream job that would attract the exact type of future citizens she wanted.

Alex departed by helicopter and reflected that travel was consuming far too much of her time. She needed to get back to the Atlanta facility and get the next set of batteries ready and figure out exactly what the desert facility needed to look like in order to become a space station. Instead of working, Alex slept, bone-weary, and knowing that 24 hours in a day weren't enough to get everything done that needed to be done. The bumpy helicopter ride wasn't nearly as comfortable as transportation Milo would have arranged.

In her Atlanta lab, Alex was buried making more batteries when the text from Milo arrived on her HUD inviting her to lunch. Alex wondered what new demand Milo would relay on behalf of Sal's brother. She wasn't as up-to-date on family business as she should have been; there were just too many other things pulling at her attention and time.

With the new desert facility creation and the Pacific "island" growth and keeping the Atlanta facility steadily producing batteries, while trying to get more novels written for the income, all of her time was taken. As soon as the desert facility was set up, Brian would relocate there along with the bulk of their employees who were providing support services that helped create a community. Atlanta would remain mostly a shipping and distribution office.

Alex sent back an acceptance text; after all, family had to come first. She owed the Marino family fund a significant amount of money. Although she assured Mario every time she spoke with him that he only had to wait another few years at most, their family balance was barely enough to maintain business. Alex had reallocated some of Hamasaki's money back to the family as part of the loan repayment, but the debt was still huge.

Every time Alex sold one of Sal's paintings, she felt like wailing, but Sal had told her to in his letter so he'd realized it would be necessary. The art vultures were having a good year because Alex simply didn't have enough time in the day for everything and random influxes of several million kept Green World's balance sheet positive at moments when her other money sources weren't quite enough.

Brian, who assumed most of the company growth planning and work, had suggested they increase the price of their battery - a proven business strategy to compensate for high demand and low budget - but when they were finally able to sell overseas again, the price had to be low enough for the less wealthy. Alex was still trying to maintain the appearance of a business about to fail so her competitors wouldn't invest as much effort into destroying her company.

Alex stretched in her chair, yawning. The cracking sounds from her bones were ominously loud. Maybe she could get a workout in before lunch? Alex was spending entirely too much time sedentary and her muscles felt stiff when she stood up. She also needed to work on another book, but she knew her physical health was more important.

Alex changed out of her normal Green World fatigues and into a typical young business woman's skirt-suit. She added a some sunglasses, a hat, and exercise shoes, so she would look like someone taking a work-break. Employees who recognized her would realize she was "off-duty" and wouldn't bother her. She thought briefly about calling her bodyguards, but Sal's brother had security patrolling the streets already. She left through her lab's back door so no one would see her leave except Mario's security patrol.

The heat hit Alex like a crashing tsunami when she stepped into the sunlight on the hot Atlanta street. Combined with the humidity, it was so hot that the air was hard to breathe. Alex immediately changed her mind about a brisk outside stroll for exercise. No one out walking lingered and cars crept by, adding their exhaust fumes to the heat. It was hard to imagine that the heat never bothered her when she lived on the street, but now her body had fully adjusted to climate-controlled interiors and couldn't adapt or cope.

Realizing it would take longer for her limousine to arrive and then drive her to Gente Di Mare than it would take her to actually walk the distance, Alex set out at a reasonable pace. After a few minutes, she directed some of her picobots to cooling the air around her so she wouldn't arrive at the restaurant as a puddle of sweat. It was a subtle thing but nearby people were so intent on getting out of the heat that they didn't pay any attention to her.

As Alex approached Sal's shop, something thudded into her chest's bioshield, causing her HUD alarms to trigger and she skipped a step. She rebalanced and looked down. A bullet was lodged in her picobot net, just over her heart. A second bullet immediately landed a mere inch from the first - a controlled pair, not a double tap.

Preprogrammed, her picobots were already tracking the bullet trajectories back to their source and relaying visuals to her HUD. Alex grabbed both bullets and stuffed them into her pocket as unobtrusively as she could, noting as she did that these were standard hollow point rounds designed to do maximum damage to an unprotected body.

The nearest person was plodding along staring at his cell phone and didn't look up, and no one else was at an angle to notice.

Alex started walking again, keeping her steps normal, so she wouldn't attract any attention. Her heart beat wildly and she felt her palms flush with adrenaline. She hoped the assassin wouldn't swap to a higher velocity round that would break the sound barrier. Any chance of her bioshield remaining unknown would be gone. She was already insanely lucky she didn't have her bodyguards with her because they would not have been paying attention to their phones.

Her picobots found the assassin with his gun secured in a backpack trying to depart a low-rise building's rooftop a good distance down the street. The picobots instantly surrounded and immobilized him. He was fast to have packed out that quickly. Alex directed her picobots to give her a view of the roof and then had her picobots walk him back to the space between a tall air conditioning unit and a raised utility shed, where he'd been hiding from the view of adjacent taller buildings.

Alex detoured to the other side of the street to investigate. The street-denizen movements returned to her and actually felt more natural than walking down the street had. She slid along the street, angling and setting her pace for the target alley next to the assassin's building, so that when she arrived, she could duck in without anyone seeing her. She'd be in the street and then suddenly not in the street, actions timed perfectly to avoid notice.

Setting her picobots to bend light around her and hide her from view, Alex climbed the fire escape, wishing she weren't in a skirt, and pulled herself up the last bit to the rooftop by a drainpipe. Her arms complained at the now unaccustomed exercise. She was definitely going to have to move around more and stop skipping the company's required gym-time. She strode over to the man.

Alex tried not to look at his eyes which were rapidly darting around trying to figure out an escape, but the memory seared into her brain anyway. He was dressed as a homeless man and given the pile of detritus nearby, he'd been living on the roof for some time. She dug through his supplies, looking to see if there was anything that would indicate who had hired him, knowing without a doubt that he wouldn't be carrying such a thing.

He did have a meticulously maintained FN SCAR converted to fire 5.56mm instead of its original 7.62. The Special Operations Forces Combat Assault Rifle was a much higher quality than the one in the Marino family vault. He also had a high end scope, a satin-black full tang combat knife, sharpening stone, and three close-up pictures of her from outside the courthouse in Washington D.C.

She moved her picobots enough to look through his pockets. Unsurprisingly, he had no personal identifying items. He would have gotten the hit from a database with no direct contact with his employer.

Search complete, Alex sat back and rubbed at her neck. In addition to trying to kill her, he knew about her bioshield. She couldn't let him live. She instructed her picobots to block light and incinerated him, and then after a moment, did the same with the rest of his gear and all of his trash. Within a minute, all that remained were small piles of ash that would blow away with the wind. She didn't need his gear and maybe his employer would think he took the first half of his payment and ran, disappearing into anonymity.

By time Alex arrived at the restaurant, residual fear and panic had replaced her adrenaline. Which organization had spent that kind of money to kill her? Should she look to mafia families or oil cartels or governments or any one of the businesses hers was destroying? She could task Mario with finding the responsible group and taking care of them. How long could she keep her bioshield secret?

Milo had already arrived and was seated in a private alcove toward the back. Alex joined him. He stood when she arrived, and she shook her head when it looked like he might come around and pull out the chair for her. His eyes sparkled and he was practically bouncing with energy. Good news, then, she thought, pushing aside the assassination attempt. She'd have to deal with that unpleasantness later and certainly not in a public restaurant in any case.

As they sat down, Alex observed, "Is that a new suit?" His meticulously tailored grey suit was untouched by the sweltering heat outside; apparently he had the sense to take a car.

Milo grinned proudly, eyes twinkling. "Brioni. It's Italian. I'm not going to let you sit on this suit coat, no matter how cold and wet you are."

Alex laughed, remembering the limousine seat he'd protected from mud with a suit coat easily five times more expensive than the seat. "Right now I could go for being cold."

A waitress and a waiter brought them drinks, salads, and bread with olive oil for dipping. They would not be given menus and Alex bet the chef was scrambling in the kitchen for just the right meal to serve. When the staff had departed, Alex noted, "You look like you just won a Nobel prize. What's up?"

Milo sat up even straighter, full of enthusiasm, and reached in his pocket and passed her a small decorative envelope with her name on it.

Alex peered at it quizzically and opened it. It was a wedding invitation for Milo and a woman named Kelly Sue Marino. "You're getting married?" Alex gasped. She hadn't even known he was seeing anyone.

"I am!" Milo's broad smile made it clear how happy he was. "Mario sent me to help her about nine months ago. She was recently widowed and was having some legal problems. Her husband was a Marino. We've been seeing each other for a few months now. I'm still in a bit of a daze myself that she accepted."

"Congratulations! Tell me about her?" Alex didn't use her HUD to pull up the relevant information, preferring to hear it from Milo instead.

"Kelly's a chemical engineer. She has two young sons, ages 1 and 3, who are adorable and super energetic, respectively. And she's fantastic. Amazing. Hard to believe I'm this lucky."

"I think she's the lucky one. I'm so happy for you, Milo. You deserve a fine woman to love you."

"She asked if you wanted to be one of her bridesmaids?" Milo continued smiling, but didn't add any pressure to the question.

"I really don't have the time, Milo. I'm sorry. I have too many things I'm trying to take care of to add any more activities."

"I told Kelly that's what you'd say, actually, but I promised her I'd ask anyway."

Their food arrived - classic ragu alla Bolognese sauce over tagliatelle pasta - which was perfectly prepared. While seemingly mundane, Alex knew it was the national dish of Italy and very apropos. They set to eating and Alex continued to ask Milo questions about Kelly and her two sons throughout the meal.

Afterwards, Alex had Milo drop her off back at Green World; no more walking in the heat and being a potential target for assassins. She didn't bring up the attempt because she didn't want to disturb Milo's joy and because she didn't want to hear his lecture about taking her bodyguards with her everywhere. She disappeared into her lab to study the problem of security.

Her conclusion: Mario needed to hire more people and he would need more money to do that. This meant she was going to have to cut him another check from Green World toward what she owed him. Given how closely she was balancing Green World's funds and the expenses of building both in the desert and in the Pacific, that would push her company negative and into bankruptcy. There simply wasn't enough money at this compressed timeline schedule.

The only way Alex could do it would be to roll out the second product a year early, and that would make more enemies to potentially hire assassins.

She groaned and launched their second product anyway - an appliance battery (for televisions, refrigerators, stoves, and desktop computers) a year ahead of schedule, without fanfare, with the simple expediency of just having the programming team add it to the company webpage as a purchase option.

This battery was the size of a coffee cup with a power outlet on it and sold for $2200. Orders rolled in as soon as someone noticed and word got out. Again, only 1 per customer and only for individuals, with the exact same absurd legally binding contract. A reasonable backlog of orders was nearly instantaneous. Each employee was again gifted one as a bonus and there was a 48-hour code for family and friends of employees to be expedited.

Then some bright idiot on the internet pointed out that the battery was strong enough for cars and boats and published some instructions for adapters and converters, and overnight, the backlog quadrupled.

Lawsuits from the oil cartels rolled in along with violent threats. Even with Mario's increased security measures, Alex was losing at least three hours a day to analyzing potential attacks her picobots noted and dealing with them. Her violence intending enemies experienced equipment malfunctions, gas leaks, car accidents, heart attacks and strokes, unexplained gang shootings with ammunition that couldn't be tracked back to any specific weapon. Her picobots quietly did as directed and dispersed. Alex regretted necessity and felt some of her soul slipping beyond recovery. She rarely left the direct security of her facilities, not wanting to endanger her bodyguards.

Due to the data analysis workload, Alex announced SEL three months later than she wanted. She began with transparent, shimmery domes over the desert and ocean facilities. People were nervous about it at first, but it gave them single entry points to secure, and as business and life continued as usual and employee movement was unrestricted, they adjusted. The desert facility enjoyed a more stable temperature, and a dome inside the dome was made into lush forest habitat that matched the Chattahoochee National Forest. The reservation's residents staged a protest but Soaring Eagle dispersed it.

Alex added a SEL-only enclosed high-air climbing fort, with slides, rope courses, and semitransparent platforms. Each day, the maze rearranged to become a new puzzle. This was ostensibly another exercise area, but in actuality, it was designed to get people used to both SEL and heights. Molecular scans of SEL items only showed the expected matter particles; the picobot security prevented their detection.

Alex's picobot fleet reported Hamasaki's dark organization finally entered the combat on the side of her lobbyists and got the law forbidding overseas sales repealed. She felt a little sorry that the government officials hadn't caved sooner because they surely hadn't deserved the consequences.

Shortly thereafter, a courier from Kuro Hamasaki arrived at her desert facility to deliver the message that Mr. Hamasaki would personally ensure her supply and distribution chains if she would consider allowing him to continue with overseas sales in select Asian and other countries. Alex instantly agreed, arranged the first shipment of both styles of batteries to Hamasaki Corporation, and the war truly began.

As violence escalated, Green World, the Marino family, and Alex remained as white and innocent as newly washed angels according to the local and foreign law enforcers, who searched desperately but couldn't find any connection back to the violence clearly being waged around her batteries. Alex didn't mind at all that a large chunk of her profits went to Hamasaki Corporation. While everyone was focused on her batteries and money, the real task could be addressed. All her energy went to creating a sustainable environment and community that could survive living on a space habitat.

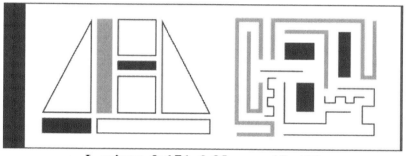

L minus 3:171:6:38   ~19π/18

Alex picked up her shoe and dropped it again, watching it fall to the floor with a thud. She was in her Atlanta lab, waiting on the picobots to finish off the next pallet of batteries, and trying to figure out what to do about gravity. Gravity was a weak force when compared to the others, so weak that in order to see gravitational waves, neutron stars or black holes had to collide.

Her space station, while as large as she could make it, would still be minuscule compared to other celestial objects, and just like the International Space Station and the moon, would be in free fall around the Earth, flying in a curve to never hit the Earth. People and things would appear to be weightless unless she could find a way to locally create gravity. Human muscle mass and bone density would deteriorate without gravity to push against long-term.

In Alex's research, science fiction solved this problem easily with spinning constructions, miracle orbits taking advantage of centrifugal force, or tidal forces created from collapsed matter. Alex had to deal with reality, not fiction. She needed the mass of the Earth, proportionate and localized to something the size of a space station that wouldn't affect the gravitational fields already in

221

place around the Earth and moon.

The space station also had to be close enough to Earth to allow routine transport between the station and the Pacific island and whichever airports politics allowed. At least SEL could provide better shielding than current technology and easily protect the habitat and transports from radiation and temperature issues.

The soft chime sounded indicating the batteries were ready, and just for variety, Alex took it upstairs to storage with just one shoe on. The odd limp was depressingly comforting. Her life seemed to be stuck in some horrible daily time-loop and there were never enough hours to get everything done. Sometimes she felt like collapsing into a puddle of tears, and sometimes, she did sit in the corner of her lab with her knees pulled in and her head down, waiting while the picobots worked. This never actually helped, though, because in her mind, she still splattered formulas across the horizon trying to find solutions.

When Alex returned from dropping off the pallet, she decided to do something she knew she could succeed at - making a vehicle she was happy with. She'd take it out to the ocean and test it against the depths. She wanted to see that ecosystem while she was able.

Alex phoned Milo and as soon as he answered she said, "I need you to buy me a large, ocean-worthy yacht to take from here, through the Panama Canal, and over to our Pacific installation. It needs to be operable by a minimum crew, all family, and we'll need a helicopter transport back to the mainland afterwards."

"How big and how soon do you want it?" was the yawning reply.

"Doesn't matter how big. I'm going to add it to our Pacific installation. Just something nice and by tomorrow morning." Alex glanced at the time on her HUD. It was already 11 p.m. She had no real concept of time in her windowless lab and monotonous routine.

Milo yawned again before answering. Alex could hear his steady, unhurried inhale and exhale. He finally said, "The family will need more time than that to pack."

Alex sighed. "Yeah, I know. Just give me a call when it's ready."

It was almost five months later by time both the yacht and latest high tech equipment were assembled and Alex and six family members took the brand new custom yacht through the Panama Canal. Milo did not come along, citing his own family obligations.

As they waited for their turn through the canal, Alex deployed a massive amount of picobots for South America. At some point soon, she'd have to visit South Africa and do the same to that continent. The fresh air and sunlight helped shake off some of her stress, although she continued to work on her novels.

Halfway between the Panama Canal and her Pacific installation, their ship made a quiet, unscheduled stop and Alex tested the first personal SEL vehicle, which was just big enough for herself and propulsion and atmosphere units. She made sure the inside atmosphere had stable pressure, composition, and temperature, and took it down into the Aphotic zone where no light reached. At one point, a giant squid came to investigate her light which scared her in its size but thankfully left her alone. New vehicle designs would have a SEL reserve to convert to repellants and weapons if needed, but the SEL shielding didn't bend or buckle.

Using an invisible column of SEL anchored on the ocean floor, she lifted an equally invisible basketball-sized sphere with diagnostic units skyward. Alex planned to lift her space station the same way. No splashy fast fuel expenditure, just a nice elevator column skyward until they were high enough to gently launch into a stable orbit. Then they could maintain orbit with minimal fuel use. She adjusted the base of her column for better support and her sphere achieved orbit with a subtle push. Picobots relayed back information from the diagnostic units and she ordered them to destroy the sphere, diagnostic units, and column. SEL would easily be able to provide the necessary shielding and the launching system would work.

When the yacht reached her Pacific installation, Alex was pleased to see the facility was growing nicely. The shimmering dome enclosed the facility along with a one mile buffer in every direction. The dome dynamically reconfigured to only be solid if an unidentified vehicle or violent storm approached. The ocean and its denizens were unimpeded.

As trash was carefully extracted, with absolute concern for marine life, it was dumped into a bin that "melted" it (picobots molecularly rearranged the matter) into huge blocks that were then tacked onto a platform on one side of the barge. When the blocks were eight-deep, they used the new space for buildings. Inconspicuous SEL columns secured the island's location.

Common areas were built: the gym expanded, a really nice recreational facility was added, a library appeared with a wide variety of books, and a large, protected pier became home to a small collection of company owned leisure yachts that trained personnel were free to use. The workers were pleased to have another fine yacht added, but more delighted with the new testing and reclamation equipment.

On the private jet flight back to Green World's Atlanta facility, Alex took the opportunity to scan through the reports from her newest picobots. She squinted at her HUD. That wasn't right. She was missing a large block of data. Some of the picobots weren't sending their reports. She dug deeper. No, they weren't just failing to send their reports, they were completely gone.

That shouldn't have been possible. No one else had Alex's picobot technology or was even aware of it. Alex felt her stomach drop. Apparently, someone else did have her technology; someone who could actively destroy it. Alex was no longer playing a simple game to create a country in the Pacific Ocean where children would always be safe. She needed a space station to survive the Earth's inevitable upheaval. She couldn't allow herself to fail.

Trying to subdue her panic, Alex fired off requests for diagnostics from all of the South American picobots. While she watched the message spreading out from her local picobots, she dug her fingers into her thighs, rubbing at them nervously. She wouldn't get a full analysis until she was back in Atlanta. Unable to think about anything else, Alex stood and paced, ignoring the curious gazes of the Marino's returning with her.

The rest of the flight, Alex considered contingencies. Could she recruit whoever it was? Could she convince them of the greater good? Could they be bought? What would she do if they destroyed all of her picobots? Her entire space station design relied on having those available to create the necessary habitat. Would it be necessary to kill them?

Alex tried briefly to work on gravity equations, but simply could not focus. She tried working on her novels, but the words refused to assemble. She couldn't even comprehend the posts on Green World's internal forums. She paced more, desperately brainstorming every solution that she might need, hoping that the necessary one would be peaceful.

When the jet arrived in Atlanta, Alex went straight to her lab, ignoring a summons from Mario and subsequent texts from Milo. The diagnostics began rolling in. They were active in all of the northern countries of South America. The picobots went the full length of Chile and were in Uruguay, but not a single picobot reported from Argentina. That certainly suggested a nation-state threat which might be harder to convince of her noble intentions than a small corporate board or stockholders.

Alex called Milo.

Milo answered on the first ring. "Mario's been trying to reach you."

"I need a flight to Buenos Aires as soon as you can arrange it," Alex said, already thinking about what diagnostic and collection equipment she was going to need. There might already be an opposing picobot fleet.

"Alex, you need to meet with Mario. There's family business that needs your attention."

"I want double the number of bodyguards I normally have and I want some of the family arsenal with me." Alex listed several of the guns that would be most useful for defense.

"Alex! What are you talking about?"

"Just take care of it, Milo." Alex ground her teeth together, and then added, "Tell Mario I'm going on vacation." She disconnected the call and began building specialized equipment. Then she built herself a high end standard bulletproof vest. It would be heavy and awkward, but it was better than dying. She supposed showing up in bulletproof full plate armor like a medieval knight was too impractical. She'd really become dependent on the security her picobot bioshield provided. Alex vacuum-packed some picobots so they couldn't be affected by whatever was there until she could monitor the interaction with her equipment.

As soon as her airplane door opened, all of her picobots, including her bioshield and HUD, dissipated. Not leaving the Marino private jet, Alex turned on her diagnostic equipment and ran some tests. As soon as she released the vacuum-sealed picobots, they were modified by rogue code. There was another picobot fleet made of her own picobots but with someone else's programming.

It took her four trips back to Atlanta and two months to reverse-engineer the foreign code and write counter-code, and three months to alter the code on her already-deployed picobots to increase security, evade detection, and prevent altered picobots from infiltrating. Overall, the picobots' efficiency dropped way down, but they were more robust. Alex wondered if it would be enough to repel direct attacks.

Alex ignored messages from everyone, telling Milo to take care of family business and Brian to take care of Green World business. Alex spent another month creating seek-and-destroy picobots to hunt down modified picobots, which she didn't deploy. Instead, she vacuum-packed them and hauled them back to Buenos Aires for ground-zero deployment.

Finally, after way too long, Alex sat in a hotel room in Buenos Aires, watching the super-fast pattern of picobot conversions and deployment of her original picobots on a geographic overlay of Argentina. An hour later, she found the epicenter where her original picobots changed into the altered ones in a laboratory at Instituto Balseiro on the western border of Argentina. Maybe her opposition wasn't the government of Argentina after all. Could she be that lucky?

Instituto Balseiro was an extremely prestigious technical school. Alex packed up her entourage and left immediately for San Carlos de Bariloche, the school's home. Rather than fly, which would have been much faster but would have announced her arrival with a huge red flag, she chose to drive in a three-car parade. They used standard rental cars instead of limousines and she had bodyguards in the lead and trailing cars, as well as in her own car. They took the toll road and arrived 24 hours later.

After the flat, open roads of central Argentina, Bariloche itself was a lovely, green town with the school next to a beautiful lake across which could be seen magnificent mountains. Now that Alex was closer to the epicenter, she could get a more specific reading. The epicenter wasn't in one of the laboratories, as Alex expected, but in the student housing, which was odd.

Leaving behind everyone but one bodyguard, Alex took one of the rental cars and went to the campus. At the guard entrance, her "father" asked to tour the university. The guard gave them passes and let them enter.

Alex went directly to the dorm where the picobots were being modified. The student wasn't home, so she sat down in the hallway to wait, while her bodyguard leaned on the wall across the hallway. The young man in his mid-20's who arrived two hours later, saw her, hesitated mid-step, but approached anyway. Alex stood up, shoving her laptop back into her backpack. She missed her HUD, but with the rogue picobots dueling her new picobots, she couldn't rely on her HUD.

"Hola, ¿sabés quién soy?" Alex said in Spanish, asking if he knew who she was. She was still keeping her hair brown, so that one day when she went back to her natural color, she might be more anonymous.

He nodded once, nervously, and glanced back down the hallway where some of his classmates were headed toward their own rooms. He stepped around her, unlocked his door, and invited her inside with a silent gesture. Due to the room's small size, she left her bodyguard in the hallway.

The culprit for the picobot alterations was an odd, hollow rectangular tube made from a recycled desktop computer case with a small fan blowing through it and some unique electronics. It wouldn't have been able to create picobots, but could obviously hack them.

When the door closed, he answered in strongly accented English, "I was hoping it was you. Those robots show an understanding of physics that is not being taught at any university. " He set his backpack on his desk, took out his own laptop and plugged it into the wall for recharging.

Alex watched him try to assuage his nerves by routine actions. She supposed if their roles were reversed, she'd be a quivering mass of panic just now. Alex explained calmly, matching his chosen language, "A sad necessity due to people trying to steal my batteries on their way to customers. That's what the picobots are doing - helping my batteries reach customers." She continued in English. "Just keeping our delivery people safe. I'm sure you've seen the news?"

The young man nodded again. His eyes were wide with a hint of underlying anxiety. He proceeded to unpack his books and stack them neatly on his desk. After a moment, he started putting them back in his backpack again.

Alex took one of the several laptop batteries she'd brought along from her own backpack and set it on his desk next to his laptop. "Want one of the batteries? Consider it a thank you gift for pointing out some serious security flaws in my picobots." As of that morning's research, only two of the professors here had her batteries and she suspected they'd pooled their money for it. Overseas shipping, the US dollar unadjusted-for-geography prices, and import taxes made them harder to acquire. Alex added, "A flaw which I've now corrected, incidentally."

His curiosity doused his anxiety instantaneously like a bucket of water poured on a lit match. "How does it work?" he asked, reaching for the battery and picking it up.

Alex's mouth quirked into a sideways grin. "Don't bother taking it apart. It'll stop working."

"So the Internet says." He inspected the small wafer from all angles.

"I'm Alex," she said with the amused smile still on her face. Her own stomach was still swirling about. So many things depended on this conversation.

"Lucas." He was turning the battery over in his fingers, measuring its dimensions by touch.

"What's your major, Lucas?" Alex didn't think she'd ever met anyone quite so intensely focused before.

"Estoy estudiando para una licenciatura en física." Lucas was getting a bachelor's degree in physics. That he answered in Spanish showed his distraction by that small metal wafer.

Alex waited patiently for him to stop fondling her battery.

When Lucas finally looked up again, he bit his lower lip. In English again, he said, "Tell me how it works or I will tell the world about the robots." He set the battery on the desk near his laptop, with only the slightest hesitation before pulling his hand back away from it.

She quirked an eyebrow at him. Did he really have the nerve to threaten her? Alex replied calmly, "All that will do is create panic and elevate the violence to the subatomic level as other people figure out how to abuse the technology. You know from the programming on mine that all they do is catch sound and light waves." The specialized ones, like SEL and her bioshield... well, she had no intention of letting him near those. "I think you know that or you would have already told your fellow classmates and professors." She shifted her weight to her other foot but managed to stop her unconscious attempt to cross her arms in front of her. She needed to maintain nonthreatening body language. "Why do you want to know, anyway? Want to make your own to sell?"

Lucas continued to chew on his lip. "It's new physics. You've done something impossible under the current models. How? We've been taking apart formulas and we have not found any errors. I just want to know." He unpacked his backpack again. "Green World is turning out new physics almost annually so we're missing something critical. Do you have any idea how frustrating it is to know that there's knowledge being deliberately withheld? You might as well show a dying man in the desert a picture of water." He sorted his books so that the biggest was on the bottom of the pile. "You create perpetual energy. You cancel sound waves on an impossible scale. What is SEL? It can't really be solid electricity. What else could be done if more people were able to study the formulas?" The frustration was clear in his voice.

Alex might have been concerned about his threat, except she was having a hard time not laughing. The poor young man was putting his books back into his backpack again without even realizing he was doing it. Alex took out her laptop and ordered her picobots to build the correct adapter for his computer next to the battery.

Lucas gaped as the adapter built up out of nothing, as if being printed by a 3D-printer, but without the printer. A book was forgotten in his hand.

Alex set her laptop repair kit on the desk and took his laptop, unplugged it, and flipped it over. When the adapter was finished a mere minute later, she took the battery and snapped it into the adapter. While she was installing it, she commented casually, "I'm building a space station. You don't happen to have any ideas on artificial gravity?"

"It can't be done." He glanced at the backpack and book in his hands, frowned, and firmly set them both on the floor next to his desk.

Alex felt her soul wailing, but then realized that sometimes technical people needed question variations because they always answered so literally and specifically. She tried again, "How about real gravity on a space-station scale?"

"Your picobots create that adapter?" Lucas asked astutely, watching her reseal his laptop again.

"Yes." She opened his laptop and pressed the button to power it on.

"Should be able to make gravity easily, then," Lucas stated.

His offhand, distracted confidence nearly made Alex scream in frustration.

She'd been working on the problem far too long and she needed the solution desperately. "How?"

Lucas bit his lower lip again and then exhaled. "Trade." He crossed his arms in front of his chest.

"I can't. Lives depend on my success. Mankind has proven too many times that they tear up the environment for greed and abuse technology." Alex turned his laptop so it better faced him as the login screen appeared.

"You don't think your robots spying on people is abuse?" Lucas tapped in his password.

"No," Alex explained, "It's keeping the violence down and protecting innocent bystanders. Today alone, our couriers have avoided 11 ambushes, one of which would have blown up a busy street corner. Dozens of people would have died. We use the picobots' information to reroute our couriers. Those intent on hurting people seek out another opportunity." She sighed. "Only a couple people might actually be able to grasp the underlying theories anyway."

"But I might be one of them. Hire me." Lucas launched his battery status widget. It was showing the full 100%.

"You might have started with that instead of threatening me," remarked Alex. She hoped he wouldn't realize just how desperate she was for both his silence and the solution to her gravity problem. The need for the space station outweighed everything, even the need to keep her battery design secret.

"I'll give you gravity. You give me what the community is missing. I want in. I promise not to tell anyone or discuss what I learn with anyone - I'll keep your secrets. I swear it." He looked so earnest that it was almost painful to see.

Just then, as if whispered on the wind, Alex heard Soaring Eagle say, "Build it with secrets. Time is short." Goosebumps spread across her arms and she rubbed at them to smooth the hair back down. She couldn't trust him, or could she? Feeling like she was jumping off a cliff, Alex heard herself ask, "How soon can you be packed?"

Lucas blinked, almost as surprised as she was. "I have to get a work visa for the U.S."

Alex shrugged. "I can get that done before we reach the airport. We'll start you on a student visa and transfer it over to a work visa." And then it wouldn't matter at all if his visas expired, because she'd have her new country.

"But I'm mid-semester." Lucas glanced around his room, obviously considering the possibilities.

Alex shrugged. "You said yourself that my picobots show an understanding of physics that is not being taught at any university. Apprentice to me."

He pushed his laptop closed, not bothering to turn it off. "Will you teach me how the battery works?"

Alex nodded, but what she said was, "I'll help you figure it out on your own."

Lucas' lower lip again bore the brunt of his daring, "May I ask you to give everyone here at the school one of your laptop batteries and give the school a couple of your appliance batteries?"

Somehow that question suddenly made Alex's spontaneous decision seem all right. Lucas wanted to apologize to his peers for leaving them behind. Alex put her own laptop back into her backpack. "Everyone has to sign the company purchase agreement. I'll also give them an appliance battery. I can't give any to the school. Our batteries only go to individuals."

Lucas nodded, flushed and somewhat dazed at the sudden restructuring of his life, but he stopped chewing on his lip.

On the flight back to the United States, Alex taught Lucas how to use the picobots to build things so he'd be able to set up his own lab at the desert facility with whatever testing equipment he might want. She gave him the formula for her new physics and then left him to dissect it. She pretended to sleep, but secretly, she used her picobots to observe him. Lucas truly seemed more interested in the physics than in disclosing her secrets. She certainly hoped Soaring Eagle was correct. Before they landed, she gave him a crash course in environmental hazards and Earth science that made him pale and quiet, and she shared the urgent timeline for her space station.

L minus 2:166:17:0   ~59π/60

Milo met them at the airport with two limousines. "Welcome to Las Vegas, Lucas. Take the second car so you can relax from your trip on the drive to the facility," he instructed and then turned to Alex. "I have some things to go over with you."

Alex nodded and followed to their limousine. Milo took a paper from his briefcase when they were settled in. "At the top of the list, your editors are demanding the next set of books. There are three movie contracts sitting in your email for you to review. The family needs your personal birthday shopping list so things can be purchased before your birthday. You are invited to a dinner party at one of your lawyer's houses in Illinois on the 14th - a celebration of a full recovery of his daughter, apparently. Also, your house's air conditioning system has reached its end-of-life timeframe and needs to be replaced. Mario wants you to assassinate Rico. Corbin May has requested you go see him as soon as possible."

Alex's picobots still reported Lucas going over yet another attempt at rearranging her formula to understand it. "Milo, these are all things you could have just called me about. No need to fly all the way out here."

"I want you to sit up and pay attention."

There was something in Milo's tone that seemed off. Alex stopped watching Lucas and thought back to what he'd said. "Nice crack about Mario there. I'm sure he'd appreciate it."

"That took you way too long to notice," Milo reprimanded. "You've been distracted like this for several months."

"With good reason," Alex said without apology. Truthfully, she was still reeling, both from not having a massive picobot war to mitigate and from sharing her most dearly kept secret with a veritable stranger.

"Alex, even Brian has voiced his concern to me."

"He shouldn't be talking with you about me," Alex said, reaching for a bottle of water.

"He's worried. I'm worried. What's going on?" Milo asked, concern obvious in his voice.

"I've just been working on another physics problem," Alex answered honestly, if incompletely. "Lucas should be able to help me with that and I can get back to other things."

Milo sighed and looked back at the paper in his hand. "You are also due for your annual gynecological exam."

"No way am I doing that." Alex opened the water bottle and took a long drink.

"Also, the Caro family has invited both you and Mario to their family head's birthday party."

The son of the couple Alex had assassinated. Alex sighed.

Milo added, "Mario has politely declined and sent the boy a Corvette."

Alex rolled her eyes up and searched her memory. "He's only 14."

"Yeah. Mario commented that it would be a good torture-present and the kid might off himself driving illegally and dangerously. His family advisors will stop him though. They've been remarkably sensible."

Just then Alex became aware that the limousine still hadn't started moving from the tarmac yet and there were sirens in the distance that were getting louder.

"One other thing," Milo continued blandly, pausing for emphasis. "You are being arrested for tax evasion."

"I'm what?!" Alex yelped.

"Tax evasion. If you had answered any one of the urgent phone calls or

231

emails or returned any of the urgent messages I left with your bodyguards, you'd have known not to come back to the States until Lu and I can get the case dismissed." Milo's unemotional recitation didn't change. "It's spearheaded by Cartwright-Jaxon Engineering under the table. You are entirely legal. I even offered to pay their bogus tax fines, but the judge they picked isn't going to do that. We'd get the money back anyway. The case will get thrown out, but I think Cartwright-Jaxon Engineering is going to take the opportunity to launch a smear campaign and a new legal assault on Green World."

Alex pulled out her phone and called Brian who answered immediately. "Hey, sorry I haven't been in touch. Milo tells me I'm about to be arrested."

Brian's deep voice answered, "Yes, we've discussed it at length. Our law team is ready for the fallout."

Alex frowned. "Launch our third product tomorrow. Switch all of our facilities to our own power and take them off-grid." The sirens were growing deafening. "I'll still be able to send emails. Assure Lucas that everything is ok and give him anything he needs."

"Who's Lucas?" Brian asked.

"Our new research and development recruit," Alex answered. "He's on his way to our desert facility right now."

"Milo thinks it won't take too long to get you out. I've got everything under control here. Take care of yourself, eh?" Brian said.

Alex hung up.

As if he'd never been interrupted, Milo said, "Cartwright-Jaxon Engineering was trying to get you thrown into general population, but Lu and I had you transferred to a white-collar location while you await trial."

Six police cars pulled up next to the limousine. How many vehicles did they need to arrest her, anyway? Alex nodded to Milo and pushed the limousine door open. She climbed out with both her hands in the air completely visible. At least she didn't have to wear the bulletproof vest anymore.

Some bright soul over at Cartwright-Jaxon Engineering pointed out her history of violence at a certain psychiatric institution and got her incarceration changed from Milo's chosen destination at the last moment. Because Alex was over 21 (22 by her declared birthday), a possible flight-risk with her own personal private jet, with the history of violence, the judge ruled that no bail would be allowed and she be put in a facility equipped to handle potential violence. Alex refused to unleash mafia terror on the judge and directed Milo to just present his case logically. The obviously bribed and corrupt judge ignored all of Milo's arguments and declared she'd wait for trial in prison.

After a whirlwind of processing, Alex found herself locked in the mandatory two day segregated drug-check cell before her incarceration in general population with the violent criminals. She'd been issued her orange pajamas, had the humiliating shower and contraband check, and her cellmate was obviously hallucinating. Luckily, the woman's psychotic manifestation was limited to talking to herself and screaming as opposed to anything dangerous. Alex merely set her picobots to filter out sound completely and lay in her bunk catching up on two months of emails and phone messages using her HUD that only she could see and hear and using her thighs as a keyboard.

In addition to the topics Milo had cited, Alex had three days of hourly emails from Milo that were accompanied by half-hour phone messages warning her to stay out of the country for a while. Messages from the Green World law team with urgent 'please help' attachments that were no longer valid. Messages from Brian needing feedback on company policy and expansion, as well as defunct time-critical funding requests. She prepared replies to things, but couldn't actually send them out until she supposedly had internet access again.

After the invasive check-in process, Alex didn't dare sleep for fear the nightmares would catch up to her. At least she felt completely safe with her bioshield. If she could avoid anyone discovering it, that would be good, but she wouldn't compromise her safety for the secret. She rearranged herself on the thin mattress on the awful solid-metal plate bed and kept scanning messages throughout the night and most of the next day. When she was finally caught up, she began punching in the next novel that was overdue. Eventually, she was too tired to stay awake and slept without dreaming.

She was woken up by a female guard shaking her. Alex turned off her sound-suppressors.

"Come on, Smith," the female guard ordered. "Time to go to your new home."

Alex rolled out of the bunk, allowed chains to be added, and followed the woman. Alex was handed bedding and taken to wait with another prisoner.

The guard shook her head at the other prisoner waiting. "Trisha, what the hell are you doin' back here again? Thought you were gone for good?"

"Broke parole. Didn't show up for work," the woman answered. She had ash brown hair that was slicked back and framed a sculpted face, with a thin nose and brown eyes under sparse eyebrows.

"Well, you two wait here." The guard went back over to the glass-windowed office slightly down the hall.

Trisha turned to Alex, "Luciano Marino sent me to show you the ropes and keep you out of trouble. You listen to me and do what I say and you'll be fine."

"Who are you?"

"Trisha Decanter. My mother was a Marino."

The name wasn't familiar to Alex. As she set her HUD to search out relevant information, Alex asked, "Did you violate your parole for me?"

"Yeah. It's no big deal. This is my turf. They're going to walk us through

233

the cellblock, and people are going to catcall and spit, but don't flinch, and don't run. I've bribed the warden to throw us into the same cell. Keep your eyes straight ahead and don't stare at anyone."

Trisha's information was scrolling across Alex's vision. Trisha was indeed a Marino even though she wasn't close to the family. She'd been incarcerated for drug dealing and had been out on parole for almost nine months after serving 8 of her 10 year sentence. "Thank you, Trisha."

"Call me Dec and don't ever thank me again."

The guard came back, removed Alex's chains, and ushered them into the cellblock. The individual cells were open-barred, closet-size rooms with metal-plate bunk beds, a lidless metal toilet, and small sink. Prisoners stood at the bars, shouting at them. The walk was every bit as awful as Alex anticipated, but she did as Dec had instructed. No one dared spit on Dec, but several well aimed globs splattered Alex. Alex twitched and felt queasy, but didn't block them with her picobots. She and Dec were put into the same cell and the door lock clicked into place with an appalling finality.

Dec turned to her. "Top or bottom bunk? For prison seniority, I get top, but for family, whatever you want."

"You take the top."

Dec threw her stuff up on the bunk and swung herself up with practiced ease and proceeded to make her bed. Alex went over to the small sink and rinsed the spit off and had her picobots do a microscopic clean to get rid of any residual germs. She went over and made her bed too. "Now what?" she asked Dec.

"Eh? Now we do time. We have lunch in a few hours."

Alex went back to her novel typing, stopping every now and then to listen to the prison sounds. From some of the things she heard, she knew she was very lucky in her cell mate. This would not be a good place to be alone.

After a long time, Dec leaned over the side of the side of the bunk. "Where you sit at lunch today is critical. You can't come sit with my group until I have a chance to talk with them. Don't sit with anyone not white. That will get you beat up. I'll point out the safest person to sit with. Are you a lesbian?"

"No."

"Don't sit with them either then. After today, won't matter much, but this first choice will define you within the population and there is attention you don't want. Come on. It's time. After lunch is yard. Stay with the group from the lunch table until I come get you." A loud buzzer sounded and the cell door swung open. Alex wondered how Dec had known what time it was. Dec jumped off the bunk.

Prisoners were falling into a line outside their cells and moving toward the cafeteria. Alex blended into the ocean of orange. When they reached the cafeteria, Dec got into line behind Alex. Several people greeted Dec, who seemed to be respected and well-liked. About halfway to the food counter, Dec leaned forward and whispered, "Brunette getting corn, sit with her."

Alex nodded inconspicuously.

Alex got her food and walked toward the table where the indicated woman sat, but about halfway there, a tall black woman stepped into her way and blocked her path. The woman could easily have been a professional basketball player.

"Oh, creampuff, ain't you just som'in special. You come sit over next t'me. I'll protect ya."

A shorter, broader white girl came over. "You just leave her be, Shwanda. She ain't for you. This is Alex Smith, the one that did that battery. She's famous. She wants to sit with..." her eyes flicked up to something behind Alex.

Alex adjusted her HUD to give her a full view behind her. Dec had arrived.

The woman finished her sentence, "Whoever she wants to." Both women in her path moved away.

Alex didn't even turn around, but she definitely kept the rear-view on her HUD. She went onward to the table Dec had recommended, populated by white women. Dec went to her own table of apparent mixed race and sexual orientation. "May I join you?" Alex asked.

"Shit, bitch, you talk like that in here, you gonna get tore up," the woman with the brown hair said. She tilted her head toward the empty seat.

Alex set her tray down and took a seat. The mushy institution food looked pretty scary and she had a moment of time-vertigo realizing that at one point in her life, she would have considered this a feast. She set her picobots to converting the pesticides and harmful man-made compounds and sipped at the sugar-water masquerading as fruit juice.

"Ain't you the battery lady?" the woman with the brown hair asked.

"Yeah." Alex set her glass back on the table, vowing to only drink water for the duration of her incarceration.

"I seen you on TV, comin' ou' o' court," one of the other women confirmed.

The brunette pushed her food, separating the different kinds that were touching. Alex had seen Milo do the same on occasion. The brunette asked, "Ain't you rich?"

Alex pondered the huge mountain of bills that were waiting on her payment authorization that would drop her personal cash to practically nothing until her new books starting bringing in income. She was going to have to borrow from Sal's brother again to take care of the current bills for Green World unless the latest battery suddenly brought in a massive cash influx.

Reminded, she called up Green World's latest financial records. Even though it was very expensive, they had a steady backlog of orders for the third battery, which would provide enough power for a 4-bedroom house. Green

World's finances were covered, at least until she could get out and spend it on habitat building. She saw Brian was already approving the backlog of funding requests. She realized the brunette was still waiting for an answer, and said, "Yeah, I'm rich."

The brunette tore off part of her bread that had touched the gravy and set it aside. "Whatcha doing in here then? They put rich people in deluxe resort prisons."

"I thought this was the deluxe-est resort prison?" Alex countered.

Her table-mates laughed.

"Rachelle," the brunette offered. "What are you in for?"

Alex introduced herself and pondered her replies. Rumors and conjecture? Revenge? Corporate sabotage? Failing to read email and listen to phone messages? "Taxes," she said finally.

"So you steal from us?" Rachelle's voice reflected humor, but had an underlying disgust.

Alex shook her head. "Naw. All my taxes are paid and everything is entirely legal."

"Ain't we all innocent?" one of the other women cackled.

There was more laughter.

"Cupcake, you better adjust. You're just like the rest of us," Rachelle advised.

"Oh, I am. I'm just not guilty of tax evasion." Alex didn't want them thinking she was an easy target. "I only look like a princess." Comparatively, she was sure she did, too. She had an expensive haircut, if overdue for a cut, manicured, nail-polish free nails that were also overdue, clear, healthy skin from a vitamin and mineral rich diet and exercise. All of these were things only people with money and leisure time could afford. Not that she had much leisure time, but she had the appearance of it.

Overall, they looked like they didn't believe her, but she couldn't expect them to. Alex poked at her food and tried it. She'd surely been spoiled. The child that dug through trash cans for anything vaguely edible was also apparently long gone. She ate anyway.

"You smart?" the woman across from Alex asked.

"Sometimes," Alex answered. Pointing out that she was degreed as well as a lawyer was probably not the best idea. The news stating the owner of Green World represented herself in court did not necessarily mean she was a lawyer. She could see her entire day being spent answering legal questions.

"So you read a lot?" The brunette chewed on the uncontaminated-by-other-food bread.

"I used to hang out in libraries sometimes." Alex reflected that the understatements might catch up to her eventually.

"We just got a bunch of new books added to our library. They'll bring a rack by your cell and let you check them out." The conversation turned to the latest library additions and when that was exhausted, Alex asked them pointed questions about how things operated. They were pleased to be experts and expanded nicely.

After lunch, Alex followed her table-mates to the prison yard - a cement, plant-less, walled courtyard with basketball courts, tables, gym equipment, and a single unused faded hopscotch board. As they entered into the yard, the prisoners bunched up slightly as they entered the open area. Alex didn't even realize what was happening until it was too late to make a difference. She was surrounded, cut off from Dec's recommended protection with the efficiency of a wolf pack picking off its prey. She dodged the only direction available and into a waiting ambush.

Alex was shoved, toppled to the ground, and violently kicked. The bioshield prevented her from actually being hurt, but she curled up anyway, reflexively. Hard-toed shoes kicked and stamped. Just as Alex was realizing she needed to get up and fight back, her bioshield stopped a knife blade embedded in someone's shoe. The weapon would have instantly killed her and been easily discarded or hidden away before any response could have been initiated by the prison guards. Instead of dying, Alex found and grabbed the foot and pulled, twisting, ripping the shoe off its owner's foot.

The animal in Alex that hunted in the forest and defended her on the streets took over, combined with the training she'd gotten under Sal's guidance. Alex grabbed the other foot and severed the woman's Achilles tendon. Three of Alex's assailants were down before they even knew she was moving. Alex dropped the shoe and launched herself up. She kicked another woman backwards into the pack of women hard enough to knock several over. Ribs cracked under her foot.

Dec and her crew arrived, elbowing in, clearing out around Alex, as the prison alarm sounded and the guards fired warning shots. Prisoners dropped to the ground, hands over their heads. Dec pulled Alex down and lay over top of her chest and head, protecting her from any possible stray gunfire.

Alex lay there, gasping heavily, trying to will her adrenaline to back off. Her enemies weren't going after her company. They were going for something more direct. She should have seen it coming. Predicted it. Not too far away, the four women Alex had cut were screaming. Alex blocked the sound with her picobots.

Guards flooded the courtyard. Finally regaining control of herself, Alex set her picobots to destroying her fingerprints on the bladed shoe and then to erasing the security footage inside the prison for the last hour with a simple computer virus. Hopefully no camera had captured her bioshield's protection, but she couldn't take the time to find out for sure.

Dec was pulled up by one of the guards and then Alex was too. The guard asked if they were injured and they said no. They were escorted along with the other now mild-mannered prisoners back to their cells and locked in.

As soon as the guards were out of earshot, Dec grabbed Alex's shoulders with both her hands. "Are you ok?"

"A few bruises. Nothing major damaged." Alex thought about creating bruises on herself, but decided to postpone it until group shower time, when she could decide if she wanted bruises or the illusion of bruises.

"Lu said there was a hit out on you," Dec informed her. "I didn't expect it so soon."

Alex grit her teeth in frustration. "It had to be fast. I'm certain Milo and Lu are working on getting me transferred. You should have told me. This is the first time I haven't been surrounded by bodyguards in a really long time. I forgot to be careful."

"I'm so sorry." Dec let go of Alex's shoulders and slumped back against the bunk.

Alex winced. This woman had just thrown herself across Alex to protect her. Dec didn't need to be lectured; she needed praise. "No, no, no. My fault. Not yours. I should have known it was coming and taken more precautions. I should have dodged through the first group of people instead of going the direction they were herding me. It would have been much worse if you hadn't come to my rescue."

Dec shook her head. "What happened?"

Alex quickly scanned back through her memory. She'd been on her feet again before Dec and her crew arrived. "Just a simple attempt at beating me up. I have some martial arts training." She was really good at down-playing her abilities. "I'm not going to be that easy to take out."

"There was a blade in the mix. People were cut. You could have easily been killed."

Too true. She'd definitely be dead if she didn't have her bioshield. So reminded, Alex spawned one off and attached it to Dec. It was the least she could do for someone willing to die for her. "Will the inmates talk to the guards?"

"No way. And you shouldn't either. Not a word. If they ask about the bruises, you say you fell out of your bunk. That's the standard code for 'not going to tell you anything'. The yard security cameras will have been blocked not to show anything. Everyone knows where the blind spots are. They won't find the blade, even, but there are a lot of blades in circulation so even if that one got confiscated, it still wouldn't be enough to protect you."

"It's ok. Now that I'm aware of the threat, I'll take precautions. Thank you for protecting me, Dec."

"You're family. Don't thank me. I'm worthless, low-life scum. I hurt people. I use 'em. I'm the kind of person hell was made for. You, though."

Dec inhaled. "You are a precious innocent, a treasure to humanity. If there's anyone on this planet worth saving, it's you. Maybe if I die saving you, maybe God will forgive me and let me into heaven."

"I'm not an innocent, Dec. I'm family. Salvatore Marino would never have given the family over to an innocent. And you are not worthless, low-life scum. I've met those kind of people. They don't feel guilt. You and I are the same. We do what's necessary."

Alex continued to speak with Dec, listening and building Dec's self-confidence and self-esteem. It was the most intense therapy session Alex had ever performed. They both sat on Alex's lower bunk, whispering to keep their voices from carrying. Alex told Dec that outside of the prison, Dec would have a position at Green World where no one would ever treat her like scum and no one ever need know she'd done prison time. Alex built a vision of a normal life for Dec and gave her hope.

Several hours later, when Alex judged that she'd done as much as she could possibly do for a while, Alex changed the topic. "How did you know when it was lunch time earlier?"

"S'easy. When you spend 7 years, 9 months in here, you just know these things."

"Well, that's certainly not a skill I want then!" Alex grinned at her. "I'm going to lay down for a little bit, I think. I'm tired."

"Oh! I'm sorry! I should have realized you'd need some rest. Are you sure you are all right?"

"I'm sure. If I can't thank you, you can't apologize to me." Alex stuck her tongue out at Dec, who had jumped up from Alex's bunk as if burned.

Dec rolled her eyes and shook her head in relieved amusement and climbed into her own bunk.

Alex opened her email, determined never to miss anything again. The newest email from Milo made her blood run cold. She wanted to scream, demanding to be let out. The attack on her was only one quarter of the plan. Without the SEL, Green World wouldn't exist anymore.

The full SEL enclosure with a gated security checkpoint prevented the kamikaze bomb from getting inside the desert facility. The experienced security guard on duty with amazing observation and reflexes sensed something wrong with the man in the vehicle, and ran back inside his office and punched the button to close down the SEL door. The explosion ricocheted off the SEL wall away from the Indian preserve, leaving a black scorch mark seared across the uninhabited desert.

The other two facilities weren't so lucky. About a third of her Pacific island was blown up by the ship that routinely brought in supplies with the

239

simple expediency of slipping the bomb into the stack of supply packages and remote detonating it. Ten people died and it would have been worse if the ship hadn't docked at their newest pier. None of the boats at the pier could be salvaged. The island, held in place by SEL pylons reaching to the ocean floor, didn't destabilize and capsize, although it certainly would have if it weren't attached. Competitors and governments were now aware their "clean-up barge" was a full, stable island.

The worst attack was in Atlanta. Realizing they couldn't attack the facility directly, they put the bomb in the restaurant building adjacent to Green World's headquarters. The SEL enclosing her building's wall reflected the explosion through the city block. Emergency workers were still on site.

Alex rolled over on her side, facing the wall, and set her picobots to create a full sound-shield around her and called Lucas. When he answered his new cell phone, she spoke briskly in Spanish, "Hey, Lucas, it's Alex."

"Did you get arrested? There were rumors when I went to lunch." Lucas' heavily accented voice sounded surprisingly chipper.

"You haven't left your lab lately, I guess?" Alex shifted on the uncomfortable mattress.

Lucas continued excitedly, "I've been setting up. Your CEO has given me unlimited funding. He told me to send the shopping list to purchasing. I'm just about done getting the list together. Most everything basic I've had the picobots building." He switched his phone to video mode and panned the camera around the underground space. It was unnervingly similar to Alex's lab.

"Um, Lucas." Alex had a hard time interrupting his enthusiastic description. "I'm glad you're settling in nicely, but I need you to do something."

"Hmmm?" He turned his cell phone around so his face was in the video and then switched off the video feed.

"Take your laptop and whatever you need and go explain to Brian, er, the CEO, about picobots and how they work. Only him though. There's been some explosions. I want you on a plane out to Atlanta with him. Program those picobots to find people in the wreckage and help the rescue workers. Don't tell anyone about the picobots. Pretend to use some high-tech scanning equipment."

Alex heard Lucas inhale sharply. She continued, "I'm altering the security to let you go directly up to Brian in the executive elevator. I need you to go immediately. He's likely to be headed to Atlanta any minute. If he's already left, just follow. Um. I'll dump some money into your bank account to cover expenses. I'm also going to surround you with a picobot shield. Don't mess with it. It'll keep any random bullets from hurting you. I can't be there so I need you to be me." When he didn't say anything, Alex asked, "Lucas, are you still there?"

"Yes, I'm here. I'm not a fast programmer." He sounded distressed.

Probably biting his lower lip, Alex thought.

Alex needed his confidence. "You can do it. You got into Instituto Balseiro. Only the best can do that." She heard his inhale, so she added, "Keep the altered picobots localized to Atlanta. You won't be able to call me back. I'll have to call you when I can. Oh, and tell Brian to tell Milo I do not want to be transferred. Lucas, I need you to go right now. People's lives depend on it."

"I'm already in the elevator." Lucas had either crossed the campus to the main building fairly fast or Lucas had built his lab too close to the main building.

"Thank you, Lucas." Alex hung up, transferred enough money into Lucas's account for first class plane tickets, hotel expenses, and food. She killed her soundproofing. She thought she might go crazy. "Hey, Dec? When can we get internet access?"

"They rotate us through, once a week. We'll get a chance in six days if we don't get any penalty points."

Alex would be a raving lunatic by then. She avidly watched the news feeds on her HUD, growing more upset and distressed as the hours ticked away. She opted for strategically placed real bruises that looked ghastly, but didn't hurt at all or impair her movement, merely because then she wouldn't have to pay attention and slowly heal simulated bruises.

Dinner was luckily uneventful. Alex, feeling extremely wired and tense, joined Dec at her table. Rachelle noted this position change with narrowed eyes, but didn't dare comment. Alex was glad because given her mood, Alex would have been happy to thrash someone.

The next day, the guards monitoring the showers noted her bruises. The interview with the investigation team went as expected, with a lot of "You need to tell us what happened in the yard." accompanied by bribes, threats, and emotional pleas. Alex repeated that she saw nothing at all in the yard as there were too many prisoners in the way and she got the bruises falling out of her bunk trying to get to the toilet in the night.

Alex spent all of the time in her bunk alternating between obsessively watching news coverage of Atlanta on her HUD and trying to find out how she missed the incoming attacks. The responsible parties must have met somewhere out in the ocean where her picobots didn't reach, with no indication at all on land that something was going to happen. She set her picobots to reproducing and spreading. In another four months, she could have them covering the Earth, although distribution would be incredibly sparse.

Any discussions related to the bombings were automatically flagged by Alex's picobots. That's how she caught the meeting between Mario and Kuro Hamasaki. Alex was powerless to do anything about their decisions. The

241

resulting violence and devastation made her want to weep. Casualties, both guilty and innocent, piled up. She felt herself sliding into an unrelenting depression. How could her planned country survive with this much violence so casual in society?

Hopelessness infiltrated Alex's every waking thought. Watching the news and following the escalating warfare only made it worse. She decided that she didn't want to know what was being done on her behalf anymore. She couldn't change it and all it did was upset her. Milo's provided summaries would have to be enough, for her own sanity. Alex went back to typing out novels, although the plots turned bleak and scary, reflecting her sour mood. Maybe one day, historians would refer to this as her artistic 'dark period'?

On the 6th day of her incarceration, Alex got one hour of computer time in the heavily monitored lab. She opened her email, encrypted to the screen, and "approved" all of the pending messages waiting for her "review", without even bothering to open them so prying eyes wouldn't have anything to read. Maybe the watching guards and F.B.I. would think someone else was actually running Green World and she was just a decoy. Her publishers would be very happy.

On the 13th day, Milo came to visit her as her lawyer. They met in a sterile metal room that had an ugly flat metal table with equally ugly flat, metal chairs that proved even more uncomfortable than they looked. A shiny black security camera in the upper corner would record the entire room.

"How are you holding out?" Milo asked, setting his stack of papers on the cold metal table and taking the chair opposite Alex.

Alex tried for flippantly light, despite her foul mood. "I was due for a vacation."

Milo squinted at her. "The guards tell me you have bruises."

Alex lifted the side of her shirt and showed him the mottled purple on her ribcage. "I fell out of my bunk on the way to the toilet one night. No big deal. Dec helped me stand back up."

Milo's hand, resting on the table, clenched and unclenched again and he looked vaguely like he wanted to throttle her. He knew the bioshield would have protected her from anything. Instead, he said, "I like your Lucas. He's been very helpful. He's so very earnest, though, and I don't understand half of what he says." Milo frowned. "He told me about your first conversation. You hired him anyway?"

Alex quirked a half-smile and shrugged. Given his reproachful tone, Milo was definitely referring to Lucas threatening her. "I thought he would fit in really well with the family," Alex said.

"Well, he's certainly been informative." The "more informative than you" was clearly stated in Milo's tightened eyebrows and penetrating stare.

"He tells you things?" Alex was going to have to speak with Lucas about who he talked to.

"He tells Brian. Brian tells me." Milo seemed somewhat cheered at

242

having vexed Alex as much as she did him. "And I have a message for you. Lucas says that thing you wanted him to create is finished and just needs to be tested on a more accurate scale."

Gravity! YES! Alex did smile then, feeling as if a horrible weight had been sudden lifted from her chest. Maybe, just maybe, humanity had a chance. "Excellent!"

"Now, to business." Milo tapped the stack of staple-free papers he'd brought in with him. "Read." He slid them over to her, spinning them until the words faced her.

The United States government was offering her a transfer to a lower security prison in exchange for the secret to the battery. She scoffed and turned the page. That had only been the first offer. She went through the next ten pages, all offers with increasing benefits. There was an exemption from owed taxes which she didn't owe. There was lawsuit case dismissal. There was a relocation into the witness protection program. The last page made her grin. It was a paper menu for a nearby deli, printed on standard printer paper without pictures, but with an informative ketchup smear and grease stain. "I might accept this last one," Alex said with a smirk.

"Huh?" Milo got his glasses out of his pocket and looked at the page she handed back to him. "Oh!" He laughed. "I must have accidentally taken it when I was going through these."

She grinned. "Not a subliminal hint that I should consider one of these so I can get a real meal again?" Alex bet even now the Federal cryptographers were busy trying to decipher it. It's the ketchup smear, guys! The message is embedded in the angles and thickness.

"Sadly, no." Milo glanced up toward the glass-windowed door as someone passed by and then said, "The judge is stalling. He's moved your trial to December. I expect it will get postponed again due to people going on vacation; it's a coordinated delay tactic. You're looking at a full year before you can even get the start of a trial."

"You need to get Dec out then. Doesn't need to be here. I want her given a job over at Green World, whatever she wants that she's qualified for. Make sure she has enough startup cash for a wardrobe and household supplies. Take the money from my personal accounts," Alex instructed.

"The Feds have frozen your assets while the case is pending," Milo replied without inflection.

Alex cringed. "Get it from Mario then." Sal's brother had justifiably cut Alex off from the Marino family funds, which were still depleted from Green World's use, but Milo would know to tap her overseas accounts that were sheltered under token foreign companies.

Milo nodded. "I funded your prison commissary for the next year on my way in."

Alex certainly hoped it wouldn't take a full year for Milo and Lu to sort out her case. "Thank you. How is Green World doing?"

Milo took the scattered papers from in front of Alex and neatly stacked them again as he answered. "Brian is delighted that the company balance sheet is showing growth now that you aren't around to spend the profit. The company is taking care of all expenses for the victims of the bombings and their families. It's also rebuilding and repairing damage."

"Good." Money certainly wouldn't replace the people lost, but at least the financial burdens would be less.

Milo added blandly, but with a sparkle in his eyes, "Brian says that the company will be stable if you would be so kind as to stay incarcerated at least another four months."

Alex laughed so hard her eyes watered. Milo joined her. When they stopped laughing, they looked at each other without saying anything for a few minutes. Finally, Alex nodded. "It's good to see you, Milo."

"Same. Do you need anything other than the obvious?"

"Naw." Anything Alex really wanted to say was not for the prison security footage and F.B.I. analysis teams. Besides, she could email or call him when she got back to her cell if she had any urgent requirement.

"Be safe." Milo stood and departed with his stack of papers. Alex was escorted back to her cell, where she resumed typing out the latest novel. Gravity. She had gravity!

Over the next month, Alex ignored the prison dynamics. She was always escorted by Dec or one of Dec's minions. Dec's crew kept people away from her. Rachelle's group stayed neutral while the rest of Dec's group engaged in petty retaliations. Alex paid for this support with commissary items.

Alex also had an odd buffer from people who had been at ground-zero of her attack and knew how much of a beating she'd actually taken. Alex was unnervingly spry for someone who'd been so viciously attacked. They'd seen her resulting bruises and knew these couldn't possibly match, but lacking any way of knowing how it could possibly be otherwise, they had to assume they'd failed. They were giving her a wide berth while waiting for their leader to return. That woman was undergoing operations for her severed Achilles tendon and wouldn't be back for a long while.

Alex lacked any hint of fear or intimidation and her attitude was noticed. Sometimes her distraction as she thought out new novels came across as boredom and rude detachment. The prison population seemed to be falling into two hostile camps, either against Alex or for her. Alex refused to engage, but she wondered how long that was going to be possible. Alex needed to avoid anything that would aggravate her sentence, but the cost of that innocence was paid by the other inmates who were defending her. She decided that when she got out, she would fund commissaries for those who helped her. It was the best she could do.

○ ● ◗) ● (◖ ●

"Smith, come with me. The warden wants to see you." The guard might have ordered dinner in a loud restaurant with the same volume and tone.

"Yes, ma'am." Alex allowed the barbell she'd been lifting to lower back into place under Dec's watchful eye. Alex stood and followed the guard, while Dec's crew escorted them to the yard's exit. Alex nodded to Dec and continued into the prison interior where they could not follow. Two weeks had passed since Milo's visit and Dec was scheduled to be released on parole in couple days. The tension among the inmates was volatile; it only needed a match to set off a full scale riot. Alex hoped it would hold off at least until Dec was safely out.

Alex instructed her picobots to show around corners and into adjacent rooms as they moved through the hallways, but she arrived at the warden's office without incident. The guard led Alex in and closed the door, waiting outside.

The warden's office was fairly large, but simply furnished with a desk with three chairs in front of it, a small round table with four chairs, a bookshelf, and a double window overlooking the prison yard. The warden herself was older, nearly retirement age, and almost as gruff and hardened as the prisoners themselves. She pointed at the chairs in front of the desk. "Miss Smith, please have a seat."

Alex did as asked, waiting curiously for the warden to speak. The "Miss" was unexpected.

The warden tapped her fingers on her desk and leaned back in her chair. "What happened to you the first day you were here? In the yard."

"Nothing, ma'am. I fell out of my bunk later that night." Alex kept her voice neutral, waiting to see what direction the warden would take the conversation.

The warden's eyes narrowed but she didn't press for answers. "I work very hard to keep this prison safe for our inmates, but we are perpetually underfunded and understaffed. I argued against your placement here, but I was overruled. I then argued for solitary confinement, but that was also overruled." The warden stood up and went to her window to look out. "Decanter seems to have stepped up to provide the additional security I could not. I'm glad I bunked you with her."

Alex waited silently; she didn't envy the warden's position. Prisoner-law outweighed prison-law due to the increased consequences both for herself as well as those around her. Alex couldn't help the warden.

The warden sighed in resignation and returned to her desk. "I'm moving Decanter into protective custody until her release on Tuesday. She's being transferred as we speak. Honestly, I was surprised when she broke parole. I really thought she might make it." The warden inhaled and continued, "I know she's going to work for you at Green World, but don't just cut her free. She needs the support network our parole system is equipped to provide. It's tough for long-time inmates to adjust to being outside."

Why was the warden telling her this? Alex commanded herself not to fidget. "We have a counselor on staff that she can meet with. He doesn't specialize in criminal rehabilitation, but he's a good guy."

The warden nodded and then announced, "You're being released. The case against you has been dropped." She pushed a button on her desk and the guard came back in. "Your lawyers are waiting for you in Processing."

Alex blinked. "Really?" she choked in surprise.

"Good luck, Miss Smith. Don't come back."

Stunned at the suddenness of change, Alex followed the guard through the hallways in a daze, again setting her picobots to check corners and adjacent rooms. The guard took her to a side room, gave Alex a box with the clothes she'd been wearing on her flight back from Argentina, and waited outside for her to change. When Alex peeked out, the guard handed her a clear plastic bag with toiletries from her cell, and took her to a waiting room where both Milo and Luciano sat.

The Marino lawyers stood when Alex entered and without a word, Alex followed them outside where a limousine was waiting with two of her bodyguards.

When all of them were safely inside the limousine, Luciano said, "Next time, you let us handle it our way to begin with."

"Take me to the desert facility," Alex said, leaning back in the limousine. It was a toss-up for which she wanted more - a private shower or edible vegetables.

"No," Milo replied.

Luciano added, "Mario wants to speak with you directly. No overnight stops. We're to go straight to him."

Alex sighed in resignation. "Ok. How'd the case get dropped?"

Milo looked out the window and Lu answered her. "Cartwright-Jaxon Engineering has declared bankruptcy and has closed down. The Cartwright's have been exiled to Brazil while the Jaxon's have relocated to Russia. They will not be leaving their respective countries for a while. There were a few unexplained deaths."

Milo, still not meeting her eyes, clarified, "Your classmate was not touched. He's fine."

Lu didn't wait for Milo to finish talking. "The Jaxons now have standing arrest warrants for tax evasion themselves, which is why they chose Russia - no extradition treaty there. The other companies that were backing them have also been dissolved. The judge who ordered you into general population was in a freak car accident and is dead. He was riding with the lead lawyer against your case, who remains in a coma. A certain psychiatric doctor has been arrested for forging medical records that declared you violent. He'll do prison time."

Alex tried not to wince and failed.

Lu rolled his eyes at her. "It's a family matter. They can't attack our matriarch and expect to get away with it."

Alex inclined her head in acquiescence to this. "What about the bombings?"

Milo seemed content to let Luciano do all the talking. "The oil cartels were responsible. The Hamasaki family is taking care of it."

Alex nodded. "What's the cost on that?"

Lu said, "You will provide 50 of your bioshield rings to Kuro Hamasaki at your earliest convenience."

"Is he waiting on payment or is he already taking care of things?" Alex supposed this was destined to happen eventually anyway.

"He did not wait, but your CEO has not given him any of the newest batteries to sell yet." Lu's reply still indicated that he felt Green World was separate from the Marino family.

Alex didn't even try to hide her wince. "Phone?"

Milo took his from his pocket and tossed it to her and went back to watching the landscape go by.

Alex dialed Brian. "Hey, I'm out," she said cheerfully into the phone.

Hearing Brian's voice was a welcome thing. "Great! I have a huge backlog of changes I want to discuss with you. We can go over it when you get here."

"I'm on my way to Atlanta first," Alex informed him. "Look, I need you to put all local orders for the household battery on hold and send the remaining stock to Hamasaki Corporation with a very politely worded formal apology. Assure Mr. Hamasaki that more will be en route as soon as they are available."

"We couldn't send him anything while you were unavailable to make more. We're almost completely out already. You need to delegate that production. Our entire business has a single point of failure."

"Right. I'll see what I can do." Alex disconnected. As Milo was still sturdily gazing out his window, Alex looked back over to Luciano. "What else do I need to know?"

Milo replied softly, "Corbin May died. Passed away in his sleep just over a week ago. No foul play."

Alex closed her eyes for a moment, trying to calm the sudden whirlwind in her heart. The Indian had to have been over a hundred years old. What was it he had wanted to talk with her about? "Did he leave any message for me?"

"Not with any of us." Milo still wasn't making eye contact.

Alex pondered getting an alcoholic drink from the limousine's stash. "Please tell me Brian at least went to the funeral."

247

Milo answered, "He did. I also went on your behalf."

"Thank you, Milo." At least they hadn't managed to completely insult their Indian hosts. What impact would Soaring Eagle's death have on their desert complex?

"I extended your condolences, but the general attitude is very much against Green World and yourself. You might want to do some damage control there," Milo elaborated.

Alex took a fruit juice from the limousine's small refrigerator and drank it. "We're a city next to their once peaceful town. Short of packing up and leaving, I don't think there's too much damage control I can do."

Milo rubbed at his neck and commented indifferently, "Lucas seems to think you are building a space station."

"Lucas needs to stop telling people things," growled Alex. She really needed to have a talk with that young man.

"Are you?" Milo stared right at her then.

Alex answered truthfully, "Yes. I'm going to lift the entire desert complex into space as soon as I'm sure the technology works."

Luciano's eyes got wide and his mouth dropped open.

Milo elbowed Luciano and said, "Told you. You owe me $100."

"Ah, it's good to be out," Alex said. She leaned back and closed her eyes. "Wake me when we get to a bathroom."

Sal's brother's office at the restaurant was exactly as Alex remembered it, except it felt smaller. It was hard to remember that she once felt afraid entering this room. Mario himself was seated behind his desk, writing on some papers. He glared at her as he raised his eyes.

Mario waited for her to sit down before starting. "Your CEO has not sent me or anyone else in the family one of the new batteries. Family first. He turned down employment of Gil Marino, whom I personally sent over. He has also insulted Mr. Hamasaki."

Alex normally handled all of these things without Brian even being aware of them. "Sorry, Mario, I'll take care of it." She bet Brian hadn't even known Gil Marino applied. HR handled that sort of thing and she always flagged any applicant that needed to be an automatic hire.

"It should never have happened in the first place." Mario leaned back in his chair and rested his hands on his hips.

Given how often Mario spoke with added hand gestures, Alex could tell he was really pissed by that simple non-gesture. Brian was lucky Mario hadn't sent a physical reminder of his duties to the family. "He didn't know."

"Make it clear this is not to happen again," Mario directed.

Alex nodded. "Of course." The farther apart she could keep Mario and

248

Brian, the better.

Mario sat up again. "I have promised Kuro Hamasaki more of your bioshield rings."

Again, Alex nodded. "Luciano told me on the way here. I will personally deliver them before the end of the week." Her requirement at this meeting was to simply say, "Yes, Mario." to anything he demanded. Brian had insulted both the family and Hamasaki Corporation. One simply does not insult fund-providers, not to mention the small detail of how those two families also do business.

"The other families have been laughing at us. In the future, you will allow Luciano and Milo to do their jobs." Mario emphasized this by pointing at her sternly with his index finger.

"Sorry, Mario. I thought it would resolve better," Alex answered. "The law is on my side. I'm entirely legal."

Mario grunted. "Naive. Not at our level." He rubbed his eyebrow as if pushing away a headache. "So what's this I hear about a space station?"

"Good grief. Is it published on a billboard somewhere?" Alex had to remind herself to keep her voice subservient. Mario did not need to be any more aggravated than he already was.

"So it's true?"

"Yes, but it has to remain secret," Alex said, somewhat desperately. "How many people know?"

"Just Milo, Luciano, and me. And anyone else you've told."

Alex exhaled in relief. "Keep it that way."

For the next hour, Mario caught her up on the family business; she had missed almost a full ten months of family meetings. When they were through, Alex went straight to her lab and spent the evening creating more batteries. Brian was correct; she was going to need this process automated.

While waiting on the picobots to build pallets, she worked on creating a robot to cart filled pallets up to storage, and wondered why she hadn't done so previously. She hoped her long term strategies didn't have equally glaring mistakes. She issued her robot an employee badge to operate the elevator, programmed it to avoid personnel, had it locate and fill empty storage spots, and generally instructed it to keep inventory at fifty to seventy-five percent capacity. She also set up a way to check on it and control it remotely. When that was done, she created the 50 bioshield rings for Hamasaki as well as another 50 for Mario to distribute.

After that, Alex called Milo who answered with, "Do you know what time it is? For crying out loud, Alex." He sounded particularly tired and grumpy.

"I need a flight to Tokyo in the morning," Alex said brightly. "Hamasaki Corporation."

"I should have left you in prison," Milo muttered and hung up.

Alex grinned. She saw her robot was trying to take the pallet too soon and spent some time debugging the program. It took two full cycles through to make sure it was working correctly. Her brain was foggy from lack of sleep and she was suddenly aware of a gnawing hunger and a lack of food.

Alex let herself into the company kitchen, noting that the first employees wouldn't arrive for another half an hour, and made herself a plate of real food. The cafeteria tables were too "institutional" for her peace of mind so she took the plate back down to her lab to eat. Just as she was finishing off another novel, Milo called back to tell her they had flight clearance for 8 a.m. and he was on his way over with the limousine to pick her up.

When Alex climbed into the limousine, Milo peered at her and observed, "Aren't those the same clothes you came back from Argentina in?"

Alex yawned. "Yeah, better have someone at the other end have a wardrobe ready for me."

"Hah. You think I'm an amateur?" Milo's carry-on was sitting on the seat next to him.

"Of course not." Alex rearranged her HUD and started working through emails, trusting Milo had taken care of everything. Her trust was not unfounded. Not only had he prepared a suitcase for her, he'd arranged full bathing and sleeping facilities on a specially rented airplane. He had also hired two beauticians, a massage therapist, a dental hygienist, dentist, and a vegan chef for the flight over.

With family duties handled and Mr. Hamasaki appeased with everything promised as well as a personal apology in the form of a "prototype" battery that would power his entire corporate headquarters building, Alex could finally turn her attention toward Green World. When Alex arrived at the desert facility, the first thing she noticed, and it would have been impossible to miss, was the new huge building taking up a very large part of her precious real estate. Alex asked the gate guard what it was.

The guard continued diligently sweeping through her limousine for threats as he answered, "That's the new stadium, Miss. We have our own soccer and football teams now. There's job postings up for rugby and field hockey. My wife and I went to a game last night." He proceeded to tell her how fantastic the game was while Alex tried to figure out how she was going to make her carefully planned ecosystem to survive using less space.

The guard cleared the limousine and Alex's driver entered the dome and proceeded toward Brian's office. Some things were as she remembered. The original buildings had lovely Earth-clay SEL stonework with rounded corners and modern angled edges while residential buildings were painted white with bright, decorative patterns. Rocks and cacti provided natural landscaping. The complex was supposed to fit into the desert as if it had grown up from the

Earth.

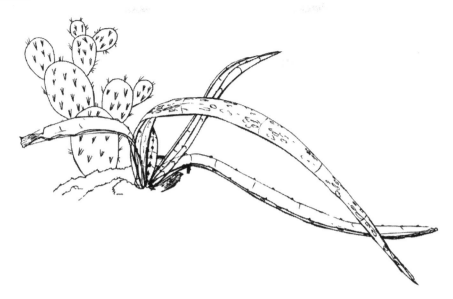

Now, however, walking paths had white covers to provide shade and the enclosed stadium, while architecturally interesting, was modern in design. The residential buildings had expanded upward according to plan and were now too tall to be natural. The first massive greenhouse was already in place and Alex's additional ecosystems would also detract from the native ambience. Almost everything had been converted to easily reconfigurable SEL.

Brian's secretary announced her and Alex went in. His office here was much less showy than the one she'd set up in Atlanta. It was smaller, more functional, with several large computer screens. His window overlooked the large garden that flourished in the campus' SEL enclosure. He had his window open so fresh air could come in. The last time she'd been in his office, the window wasn't even openable.

Alex went over to the window and peered out. The main residential building across from the cacti garden dominated the view, reaching up its full twenty-five floors. The aerial play area was only partially visible, but people were out in the visible part of the fort-maze. She was pleased the slides and rope courses drew people in despite the height.

Brian got up and moved to stand next to her. He said, "Lucas changed the window for me. I really like that young man. I don't understand what he's talking about when he gets going about math, but he's been wonderful. You should have seen him in Atlanta. He saved people we never would have found in time."

"I'm glad," Alex went over to his drink counter and poured herself some water from the specially installed fountain. "How are you holding up?"

251

"Well, your arrest and the bombings have everyone worked up, but I've added more counselors and keep assuring people that you are innocent and we've heightened security substantially. The company itself is doing great financially. I have reports for you." They went back over to his desk and Brian went through everything she'd missed over the last few months.

"I notice how carefully these reports avoid using the word 'stadium'," Alex commented dryly.

Brian grinned. "Lucas wanted it and you did say to give him everything he asked for."

"I said everything he needs, Brian. We needed that space for ecosystems."

"It's been great for morale," Brian informed her. "Corporate culture and morale are an ecosystem as much as your plants and animals and dirt."

"Well, I can't argue that." Alex drank some of her water. "I shipped you specs for another three greenhouses." Greenhouses were an understatement. They were fully sustainable SEL-enclosed environments - a tall-grass prairie matching central Argentina, a tropical rainforest like that of the Amazon basin, and a montane rainforest mimicking Reserva Biológica Bosque Nuboso Monteverde in Costa Rica. The cost to import plants and species with the required permits, authorizations, and donations would be astronomical. These would match the already installed habitat that mimicked the Chattahoochee National Forest.

"I didn't get them?" Brian pulled up his email and they were there, unread. "You sent these as you came into the building!"

"And you haven't approved them yet?" Alex teased.

Brian was scanning down the plans. "Alex, this drains off all of our money," he complained. "It drops us back to nothing again."

"Yup. Money is pretty pointless. Our habitat is critical."

"Where are we supposed to put these?" Brian rubbed at his neck.

"Well, I was planning on using that space where that stadium is. We were going to have to stack them anyway, I suppose." Alex moved back over to his window. The slight breeze coming in was artificially generated, but the temperature was being maintained by the dome and was only slightly on the warm side. The cooler temperature in the room was maintained by an unobtrusive, silent cooling plate near the ceiling.

"Your Indians are going to love that."

They weren't HER Indians. "Yeah. I don't suppose Soaring Eagle gave you a message for me?" Alex went and sat down in one of his comfortable leather chairs.

"No. His son has sent several messages demanding you meet with him, though. He wants you to put a limit on the height of our buildings. If you put these on top of our forest, which people like hiking in, by the way, the height is going to be appalling."

"World's largest indoor ecosystems. With the world's most enthusiastic and knowledgeable biologists." Alex smiled and opened her hands as if she were conducting a magical orchestra on a single beat.

Brian tapped his fingers on his desk, thinking. "I suppose we can offset some of the cost with tourism..."

"They aren't going to be ready for tourists for a bit. The trees take time to grow, even if we do bring in ones that are fairly large." Alex watched him reading the documents for a moment and then added, "Oh, we also need to double the size of our farm fields and it's time to increase the size of our ocean island."

"Couldn't you have stayed in prison for a while longer?" Brian rolled his eyes.

Alex laughed. "I'm hearing that a lot lately. I'm going to go harass Lucas. Carry on. Call if you have any questions."

"Mmmm hmmm," he was already crunching the new numbers into the company's budget.

Alex found Lucas' lab installed as an underground bunker with equipment and machines scattered around in a layout only he understood. Three of the walls were covered with dry erase boards with equations covering them, while the fourth wall was a monster digital display, showing a beautiful high-resolution photo of the mountains by his university in Argentina. He was currently sleeping in a bed pushed off to one side.

Alex wandered around, looking at his formulas. He was close to solving the battery physics, but he was missing a critical part. One of the boards had the formula for gravity. She recognized it instantly and knew it would work. The solution was elegant in its simplicity, although she supposed people might find the formula itself less than simple.

The picobots would create super-dense matter, calculated at an intensity to create the gravity fields. So long as the station stayed an adequate distance from Earth, the gravitational field strength falloff at a $1/r^2$ relationship would be too minuscule to impact tides.

The last board contained yet another version of a possible solution to her battery. It was closer than the other board. Alex picked up a green dry erase marker and started adjusting the formula until it was correct. When she finished, she set the marker back down, and stepped back to survey the formula and bumped into Lucas. He'd woken up without her noticing.

"I don't understand how that works," Lucas said, "I've looked at it that way."

"You're missing particles and another energy field." Alex fiddled with her HUD and created a 3D zoomed model for Lucas of the twisted Gaussian surface showing the two new particles and circular orbits of the charges. She

253

then threw the formula into the 3D space and merged text onto their appropriate parts.

"How'd you do that?"

"I just visualized the physics in my head?" Alex answered, shrugging.

"No, I mean the 3D model with the formula like that." Lucas reached out and ran his fingers through the hologram.

"Oh. That." She set her picobots to building him an equivalent HUD to hers. "Virtual interface."

"I wondered how you made a phone call from the prison. Having my new employer immediately arrested was disturbing, but Brian assured me you would be out again soon."

"Yeah. Sorry about that. The lesson's to not avoid emails and messages." Alex adjusted her commands and made a HUD appear for Lucas. "There you go. Virtual interface. No one can see yours but you. The light waves go only to your eyes and are then filtered to prevent bouncing."

Alex then spent some time explaining how the display could be used with the strange thigh-interface. She didn't hold anything back. 'Build it with secrets,' Soaring Eagle had said. Alex was definitely obeying that directive. When she was sure Lucas had a good understanding of how to operate his HUD, Alex said, "Do I need to tell you that this isn't something anyone else has and you shouldn't mention it to anyone, not even Brian, yet?"

"No. I didn't realize you hadn't told Milo about the space station. I'm very sorry. Brian knew and he and Milo seemed to know everything. They really weren't too surprised about the picobots." Lucas bit his lower lip and released it.

Alex shrugged. "Well, they know about it now, but in the future, don't discuss our technology without checking with me first."

Lucas nodded solemnly. "Speaking of technology, let me show you the gravity formula." He walked briskly over to the other whiteboard.

Alex understood the formula, but she let him explain it anyway to get a feel for how he thought and communicated. She asked directed questions and helped him adapt to not having to explain foundational principles.

Midway through his explanation, Lucas said, "You know, usually at this point, people's eyes are glazed over and I've lost them completely."

"I heard you explained physics to Brian and Milo." Alex smiled at him.

"They asked how the picobots worked," Lucas said defensively.

"Then it's their fault. Carry on." She gestured toward his whiteboard for him to continue.

When he finished, Lucas asked, "Does it make sense? I can explain it more."

"Makes perfect sense. We need to test it."

"Oh! Let me show you!" Lucas was practically bouncing. He went over to his bed and tucked the sheets in, and then put away a glass that was out on one of his tables. He did a quick run to each piece of equipment to stare at it inexplicably and then he went over to a low cabinet. He reached for the cabinet door and then said, "Oh, wait. Here, come hold this."

Alex went over next to the cabinet, and saw there were odd holes in the side of the cabinet, just about the right size for her hand. She raised her eyebrow at him, but did as he instructed, holding onto the cabinet. He opened the cabinet door and flipped a switch inside.

Gravity disappeared. Alex's legs floated upwards and she quickly readjusted her grip to be more secure. Prepared, Lucas didn't float as much. He grabbed the cabinet with both hands and swung himself so his feet stayed on the floor. Alex's inner ears were confusing her. She then noticed all of his equipment, and even his bed were secured to the floor. How had she overlooked that earlier?

"That just counteracts Earth's gravity." Lucas was grinning. "Localized to this room. The people above us just feel a bit heavier than usual. No one's noticed it yet." He reached and flipped the switch again, and Alex slid back to the floor as gravity slowly normalized. "I set it to go slow so I wouldn't smack into something if I accidentally floated away. It's also on a timer, so no more than 5 minutes. Just a precaution. I didn't want to be stuck floating in the middle of the room indefinitely if I screwed up."

Alex bent to look inside the box at the complex circuitry there. "Lucas, this is incredible!"

"The picobots make it possible. They can make things that are impossible to make by any traditional means. The actual matter is condensed up at the ceiling. Because we're on such small scale, if you go over to the corner of the room, you'll actually slowly fall toward the ceiling directly above us at an angle."

Alex set her picobots to giving her a full systematic specification for his device.

"We need to test it in space." Lucas peered at her quizzically. "You do have a way to get to space, right?"

"Not without attracting attention." Alex ran her fingers through her hair, wondering when she'd be able to do a test or if she'd have to wait until the launch to find out for certain.

Lucas looked over at the 3D model of her battery particles that was still hovering where they'd left the picobot display. His gaze turned inward and he said, "Give me a little bit of time. I might have a way."

"Ok. So you're a big sports fan?" Alex asked, changing the subject.

"Not particularly." Lucas walked over to her model and used his HUD to rotate it. After a few minutes, he said, "Oh, you mean the stadium. Brian wanted one. I told him to use me as an excuse if he wanted, because I'd just solved gravity and you wouldn't deny me anything after that."

Alex laughed. "Too true. Call if you have any questions." Alex let herself out of his lab. Lucas was too busy studying her energy model to even say goodbye.

Dec finally arrived, having gotten tied up in legal jurisdiction limbo until Luciano could correct it. Alex gave her the full Marino family welcome and got her set up in the company housing, with complete supplies and clothing. Alex took Dec around, introducing her to people as her cousin. Dec was warmly welcomed. Only Brian, one HR person, and the counselor knew anything about Dec's past. She was given a completely clean start without anyone judging her. Alex was vaguely reminded of Sal helping her burn her own police records.

Alex attended yet another torturous family birthday party honoring herself. Her gifts were great and she didn't get to keep a single one of them. Not that she had any use for anything. The event itself seemed kind of pointless; she could have been replaced with a cardboard picture of herself except the guests would have been insulted. She had too much to do to spend time at parties.

Eight months passed. The locals held protests over the newest "building" - a vast four-story enclosure that covered several square miles. The habitats were really too small to be completely sustainable, but once they got to space, they could expand them out. In the meantime, Alex made each "floor" tall enough that the tallest full-grown tree wouldn't reach the ceiling. Equipment at the ceilings created full-spectrum seasonal lights and atmospheric weather and maintained pressure. Money vaporized into soil, rocks, water, plants, animals, food, and knowledgeable staff.

Employees were issued flying cars for inside the desert complex so they could fly directly to the floor of their choice, which created a whole program to train employees and family members on how to navigate within a 3D space. Alex even created an "air bumper car" amusement park for all ages to serve as both fun and learning and to get everyone used to the idea that the vehicles were safe. Only employees and direct family members who'd attended training were allowed to fly the vehicles, although guests were allowed to ride along as passengers. There was no age limit placed on drivers for the air vehicles, but young children needed parental permission. Parents (or security) could remotely direct the cars to come back and land.

Employees at the now expanding Pacific facility were given both SEL air cars and submarines to play with, along with the same training, so they could explore the ocean floor and wildlife. The facility was expanded downward, underwater, to hide the true scale of the expansion. Marine animals came by frequently to investigate the humans behind the SEL windows and the humans got excellent photos and video of the visitors.

Alex got tied up yet again in another patent-infringement law case, but as the "vehicles" used invisible SEL stilts to simulate flying or diving, no patents were violated and the judge was forced to throw the case out. Safety inspectors couldn't find any fault with the vehicles. Alex overlooked the necessary Marino "legal" support that helped expedite the case. Alex gave Brian his own HUD and taught him how to use it.

Many groups were trying to figure out or steal the secret of SEL, but no SEL objects were allowed outside of Green World facilities. Green World acquired a few spies in the employee roster, but Alex's picobot fleet kept her apprised of people running experiments and snooping around. Alex was unconcerned. She was outpacing them and she made sure the picobots were unobservable and that their measuring devices reported what she wanted reported.

Most of her energy was devoted to making sure her employees and neighboring communities were safe. The governments and corporations that wanted her technology were getting more determined. Alex could feel the danger level reaching critical mass. The United States government, in complete secrecy, was preparing to seize her technology.

Alex went to visit Lucas at their desert facility again. He now had several aisles of whiteboards that expanded downward to a maze-like cavern the height of three full floors. He'd created walking shoes that let him materialize floor and stairs just by moving his foot as if he were stepping upward or downward. "Hey, Lucas!" Alex called out into the cavern, waiting for an answer that would say where he was hiding.

"Don't move!" Lucas shouted up at her from an aisle three over from the lab door. "Let me get you the updated shoe software or you might fall. The old version is buggy."

That inspired confidence, Alex thought. "You could always adjust the gravity so a fall wouldn't hurt!" she hollered back, but waited anyway. Shortly thereafter her HUD showed a software update message from him. She installed it and carefully stepped into the direction his voice had come from. She had a hard time getting her brain to overcome the concept of walking on air whenever she came in here. She always felt like she was about to fall even though she completely understood the technology. "The floor will be solidly there. Just walk naturally," Lucas kept reminding her when she visited. It was easier said than done.

Alex closed her eyes and walked, imagining a room. Every so often she stopped, peeked below her, and then continued, until she saw him below. She again closed her eyes and imagined a staircase going down and stepped toward him.

"You know you don't have to close your eyes," Lucas said.

"Yeah, I know. It's easier," Alex replied, gazing at the massive whiteboard. It was covered in tiny text, all part of some prodigious equation. To see the whole thing, she'd have to walk the length of the room from top to bottom.

"To what do I owe the honor of this visit?" Lucas asked enthusiastically.

Alex stared at the part of the formula on the whiteboard that Lucas had been changing. It looked like gibberish, even to her educated mind. Lucas seemed so excited to have someone visiting and someone with whom he could speak about his passion that Alex felt bad that she didn't have more time to give him.

Alex said, "I have some numbers for launching into space that I want you to review."

"Sure." Lucas rubbed his chin, thinking, and then tapped at his HUD, and the room dynamically reconfigured to make the aisle wider. A new digital display shot up in front of them and her HUD showed a hook to the screen.

Alex connected and sent her calculations over and waited while Lucas studied the equation and numbers. "Um. Hmm." He again tapped at his HUD and the whiteboard behind them moved back to make more space, and a simulation of the desert facility lifting off the planet appeared in the air next to them. He adjusted things a little and reran it, and did that a few more times. "Yes, it'll work just fine as you had it, but you're going to need more mass to fill in the hole we're leaving behind. The air differential if we move too fast is going to cause a massive wind-storm if we aren't careful." Lucas punched in an equation, and said, "That's max speed." After a moment, he added, "And my lab is going to have to come above ground."

Alex nodded. "How soon do you think we could do it?"

"We could launch tomorrow if we had the extra mass." Lucas' eyes slid back to his own astronomically more complex equation.

"Ok, thank you." She smiled. "So how's your equation going?"

"I think it might work." Lucas nodded firmly at his equation, not at her.

"Going to tell me what it is yet?"

"Not until it works." Lucas tweaked one of his numbers.

Alex shrugged, content to let him tinker. She pondered his lab jealously and wished she had time to gain his obvious mastery of her technology. Instead, she knew it was time to start making arrangements. She left for her own desert office which was just a token closet-sized room where she could sit quietly and think without being disturbed. Time. She needed more time and Alex knew she didn't have any left at all if they were going to space.

Part 3

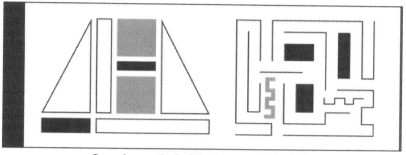

L minus 0:8:23:0   **~73π/90**

Alex couldn't delay any longer. The United States government was planning to seize their facility in the interest of national security. Alex expected troops to arrive by August 9th. The officials making the decisions hadn't passed word to the military yet because they didn't want Alex to find out about it until it was too late, lest she manage another maneuver like her battery sale to Hamasaki Corporation.

Alex reviewed the message about to be sent to all the employees:

"We will have an all hands meeting starting next week on August 3rd. Attendance is mandatory. I realize this interferes with several people's vacations, but we chose the date based on the least number of people that would be impacted. The meeting will last through the week. Family members living with employees should also attend as the last day will be a party. If scheduling conflicts impact you financially, pass receipts and explanations to the finance department and you will be reimbursed. We will be reviewing things like the vegetarian menu and employee residence size, as well as discussing our future products and deployment schedule. We will also announce some new technology that everyone will have the opportunity to try. During the meeting, no outside communication will be allowed to prevent any accidental propagation of company secrets prior to the August 5th launch. Both the Pacific and Atlanta facilities and residences will be closed down on July 29th. Please either bring your pets or make sure they have enough food and water to live unattended for a week - we're going to secure facilities with a full SEL shield so security personnel can also attend the meeting."

Alex hit send. The announcement went out to employees, signed by both Alex and Brian. If people chose to read that "launch" as "product launch", she wouldn't correct them.

Over the next week, Alex and Brian, with the help of human resources, planned out meal schedules and who would be working when. Alex arranged continued shipment of products on schedule through the week; Sal's brother, Mario, would take care of that. Alex and Brian planned several special security teams and announced that a random selection of people would be chosen to help present the new technology deployment and those chosen would be notified on the morning of their meeting.

Alex sent Milo to invite Soaring Eagle's son and two guests of his choice to attend the entire meeting and provide their input on the future of the land. Alex then gave Lucas several possible desert designs for the empty space that was going to replace their facility. Lucas would work with the Indians because he could wield the picobots to create whatever they wanted if it was possible.

The chess move, the strategy, the end game. The time was now. Every cell in Alex's body screamed, checkmate, do it now!

On July 30th, employees and their families starting arriving from Atlanta and the Pacific facility and settled into the temporary SEL housing. Everyone had been told to report to the stadium at 9 a.m. on the morning of the 3rd. No one noticed the subtle extra weight they seemed to be carrying - a side effect of the slightly dense matter underneath the entire complex, except for a few people who liked to stand on their scale each morning, and they'd just wonder how they'd managed to gain ten pounds overnight.

While waiting for the meeting day, sports games and movies alternated in the stadium, and people toured the habitats, socialized, and speculated. Spirits were high. Employees had a schedule that gave them a time-slot for minimum necessary duties. People with first aid and medical experience were 'on call'. Security personnel had shifts. Food and farm workers got allocated random people to help from the rest of the labor pool. No one except Alex, Brian, and Lucas had extended duties that would require more than six hours per day.

On the evening of August 2nd, just after sunset, Alex left the complex. It was time to start. Her heart continued to beat anxiously. So much depended on the next couple of days. This step was the easiest. She drove the little sedan the short distance to the small town just opposite the reservation from her own complex. The street address was easy to find, even without the help of the GPS unit one of the security guards had programmed for her.

Alex climbed out of the vehicle and looked around. The house was small, probably only two bedrooms, kitchen, living room, and family room. No garage. It was simple, but well-maintained. No extravagances. A tricycle, a wagon, and two bicycles were parked by the car. The cactus garden contained transplanted local plants.

Alex peered down at her outfit, smoothing out the wrinkles in the light earth-tone jumpsuit, although she knew no one would notice any wrinkles. The owner of this house, Bill Stateman, wouldn't care. He may have been a reporter, but he was a fair one - a down-to-earth, solid, no-frills reporter (which was likely why he was still just a small-town news man; not enough scare-mongering). Nor would his family care. Alex supposed she could have her picobots fix her outfit to pristine condition. She wasn't wearing any makeup. She was done with that, although her hair was still brown. She would let it grow out blond.

Alex glanced back at her legacy car. The technology felt so repulsive now - spewing pollutants both in power source and emission, hazardous by its lack of automation and picobot protection. This would be the last time Alex would be in a car like this for a long time. Even if the government tolerated their departure, they wouldn't overlook Alex's part in it.

Alex realized she was stalling. Don't think. Just do. She strode over to the doorbell and rang it.

"Honey, are we expecting anyone?" Bill's wife's voice carried, but not the answer.

After a moment, Bill Stateman answered. He'd obviously just pulled his shirt on. The TV in the background was playing a children's cartoon. Water from a kitchen sink in the adjacent room shut off and silverware rattled briefly. He looked at Alex's jumpsuit and made the connection to Green World.

"Sir," Alex began, "I wonder if I might have a few moments of your time this evening?" Her voice triggered his recognition.

Bill nodded and gestured Alex in, holding the door for her, only slightly wide-eyed.

Alex waited for him to find his words again. She'd been wrong about the house. The wall between the living room and family room had been knocked out to make one large family room. It was a comfortable room, messy with some toys, books, and newspapers, but it was clean. The older computer in the corner was off. His young daughter was seated on the sofa.

"Honey, who is it?" His wife, Tara, came in from the archway to the kitchen.

Bill introduced Alex, and after a heartbeat, Tara welcomed Alex to her house. Then she moved to the TV and shut it off, saying, "I'll bring some tea in a moment. Come on, Sweet Pea, time to get ready for bed. Your daddy has a visitor he needs to talk to." It spoke well of their parenting that the girl didn't cry or whine.

"Please, have a seat." Bill gestured at the sofa. He pulled the chair over from the little computer desk so he could sit facing Alex. "I thought you avoided the press. To what do I owe this honor?"

"Thank you." Alex sat, leaning back, her body language carefully relaxed. "Our company all-hands meeting is taking place over the next three days." His eyebrow went up. Alex wasn't sure how closely he followed their company

261

activities. After his initial coverage of the company when they'd first arrived, he'd not done any stories on Green World or Alex. "I think," Alex paused for dramatic emphasis, "That it would be criminal if the result of that meeting were not covered."

"Aren't you supposed to be in a courtroom tomorrow?" Bill asked.

So he did follow the company news. Failure to show would result in another arrest warrant. Criminal indeed. "Yes, but I'm sending lawyers instead. I'm sure the judge will be greatly entertained." Alex's directive to Luciano Marino's law team was explicit: tie up the case for 4 days. Shuffle paperwork, file countersuits, pontificate, cite obscure cases. Threaten to break the judge's knees only if absolutely necessary.

"You know I report things as I see them?" Bill said.

"I do. I particularly liked your coverage of the cactus contest at this year's county fair." His eyes squinted as he tried to decide if Alex was serious. "The puns made me laugh."

"Ah."

"I can't tell you what we are meeting about. Company confidential. Besides, our CEO does press releases, not me." Alex was cheered by that thought. How much of the aftermath from this could she foist off on Brian? She silently reprimanded herself for such an unworthy, mean thought.

Luckily, Bill couldn't read her mind and replied to her comment about not doing press releases. "So I've noticed. Is Green World announcing another product?"

"My employees are going to discuss it and make a decision. Just observe. Report if you think it's newsworthy. Report whatever you choose to. Good. Bad. It won't matter, although I'd personally prefer a positive angle obviously."

Bill's daughter came running in, giggling, wearing sparkly pink pajamas. "Kiss goodnight, Daddy?" She leapt into his arms for a hug. A sharp wave of sadness and jealousy startled Alex, a vision of a family she'd never had, wouldn't ever have. It was a little disorienting and unexpected.

The girl giggled again and squirmed down, stood a moment looking at Alex, as if unsure to include her. "Good night," Alex said to her.

The girl tilted her head and said, "You're the lady on TV. You make the batteries."

"Yes, that's me."

"Daddy says you're going out of biz-ness 'cause people don't like you."

Tara arrived just in time to hear this. She winced. "I'm so sorry."

Alex shrugged and laughed. "It's ok. Your daddy is a very smart man. I've certainly made some people very unhappy because my stuff is better than their stuff." Alex reached into her pocket and took out a SEL card. It was semitransparent, about the size of a credit card, with a finger sized white circle on it. "Here. I'll give you something for your honesty."

The girl glanced at her parents, who nodded permission. "What is it?"

"A park pass. Hold the card on the circle and say your full name." She did. "That will let you and your Mommy and Daddy and two other people visit the new park we are building."

"Will there be a playground there?" the girl bubbled.

Alex smiled at her. "I'm not sure yet. It depends on what the Indians decide."

The girl stared dubiously at the card that now displayed her name.

Alex said, "Your Mommy and Daddy can help you use it."

"Say thank you and go to bed," Tara directed and took the card and set it on their computer desk. "We'll put this here so it doesn't get lost, ok?"

The girl gave her dad another giggling hug, kiss, and mock-tickle, and was escorted off to bed by her mom.

"So you're building a park out at the reservation?" Bill asked.

"Yes. A thank you of sorts to the Indians for letting us use some of their land. If she loses the card, she can just go get another one at the park office. Her name will be on the list."

"Ah. You realize that bribing my daughter, however appreciated, is not going to make me report favorably if I think your company or you is doing something wrong?"

Alex nodded. "I know. I've always liked the honesty in your articles." Alex took an envelope from the same pocket. "I know it's late, so I won't take up more of your evening. This has locations and times on it, as well as some suggested camera gear." Alex stood and handed him the envelope. Inside were detailed instructions for locations that would give the best angles and views of her complex lifting off into space. "I implore you, get the footage. Decide later what you want to do with it. There's only going to be this one chance."

Standing also, Bill inquired, "You aren't going to kill everyone in some demented cult move?"

Alex recalled Brian asking if she was building a company or a cult when he'd first come to Atlanta. She'd created a lifestyle and community, not a religious following. "Good grief, no. It's just another potential product launch."

"I don't do business advertising," Bill said firmly.

Alex grinned at him. "I know. Thank you for your time, Mr. Stateman. I really did enjoy your cactus article."

Alex left and drove back toward the facility. Halfway around the reservation, she stopped her car and got out to look at the stars. She inhaled the chilly air and wondered what her world would look like at the end of the week. She crouched down and put her palm flat on the hard sand, trying to feel the Earth in its entirety.

The next morning, Alex sent out the list of people needed to help present the new technology. She had them gather in one of the conference rooms. When she entered the room, they looked eager and particularly delighted to have been selected. She deployed her invisible SEL cages and sat down at the table, setting down a stack of folders.

"Ladies and gentlemen," Alex greeted them somberly, "I appreciate your coming so promptly today. I have a lot that I need to get done before the general meeting in a couple hours." She began passing out the folders. "These are your severance packages. Your families and your belongings will be waiting for you at security. I leave it to you to decide what to tell them." Inside each personalized folder was undeniable proof that they were working for other organizations, governments, or corporations, along with a check for three months' salary.

Alex stood again and left, not waiting to hear what they might say. The special security force, who'd been shown how to operate the SEL cages would float them to a SEL enclosed opaque structure adjacent to the park, where they would be kept with their families until the launch and then they would be released.

Alex took a few minutes and went through her emails and found Milo had signed yet another movie deal for her. She peered at her finances and transferred the rest of the money Green World owed her. She sent Milo a note that read, "It's time to settle accounts. Disperse all of my money. 51% to Mario for the family fund. 6% to Luciano, 5% to Irene, 2% to Rico and Emma, 1% to Alan Pickering, my high school classmate, 35% to yourself as an employee bonus. After those last couple tasks, take a vacation. I owe you, Milo. Thank you." As 2% was still $16 million, Rico and Emma weren't getting cheated. Her books and movies would still bring in a substantial income, dumping to private offshore accounts, and Alex wouldn't have any personal expenses for a long time.

Alex and Lucas met the son of Soaring Eagle and his two friends at the security gate. "Thank you for coming, Running Fox," Alex said in their native language to the son of Soaring Eagle.

All three were clad in standard American clothes - jeans and collared shirts. Only one of his friends kept his hair long, and it was pulled back into a neat ponytail. In English, Running Fox said, "Soaring Eagle told us to trust you. He was an old fool. What do you want?"

Very softly and still in his native language, Alex answered, "Soaring Eagle was my friend. I've missed his wise counsel." She was sad they didn't have a message for her. It seemed whatever Soaring Eagle had wanted to tell her was forever lost. "I would like you to attend our first meeting today to hear our plans for the future. Afterward, I would like you to work with Lucas," she nodded toward Lucas, "To decide what you want on this land when we're gone."

Running Fox snorted derisively. "You've already torn up the land and covered it with your tall buildings and pavement. You've destroyed it." English still.

Again speaking in his native tongue, Alex answered, "My buildings have been in your sunset too long. Our part of the land will be turned into a natural park and given back to your people as agreed. Your land that is part of this complex can become part of the park or whatever you'd like. This is the first half of my promise to Soaring Eagle. I will honor that promise and leave." Alex pointed to Lucas. "Lucas will help you with some possible park layouts, building designs, and trail maps."

"What is this going to cost us?" Running Fox asked caustically in English.

"Nothing more. The price was use of your land. That price has been paid. The son of Soaring Eagle and his friends are always welcome at my fire." Alex bowed her head respectfully toward them, turned, and walked away.

Behind her, Lucas said, "If you will come with me, I have rooms ready where you can store your belongings. The meeting will start soon. Have you eaten breakfast? Can I get you anything?" He was making a special effort to talk as clearly as possible given his thick accent.

Alex toggled the facility's SEL enclosure to opaque from the outside and blocked all incoming and outgoing communication, except her own, and went to finalize the next step.

Alex and Brian sat in comfortable SEL chairs in the center of the stadium, waiting for everyone to gather.

"This stadium sure is useful right now, isn't it?" Brian remarked.

Alex agreed with an amused grin and nod. "I'm certain Lucas is delighted, although he hasn't gotten to a single game, I've noticed."

"You work him too hard."

"You seem to get to most of the games," Alex observed.

"Someone has to make sure Lucas' investment is worthwhile. You let him do whatever he wants."

"You aren't going to give in on this, are you, Brian?" Alex was still trying to get him to confess to wanting the stadium himself.

"Nope." Brian was perfectly aware that she knew the truth, having heard it directly from Lucas, with whom he had dinner frequently. They'd become friends, mainly because Lucas had no interest in how the company was run and Brian had no interest in physics, and the two of them could leave work in their respective offices and discuss more important things like how they were going

265

to find wives. Brian adjusted himself in his chair and changed the topic. "Somehow you failed to mention this job morphing into running a country when you were interviewing me."

"I couldn't; you already thought I was crazy and starting a cult. You were so jumpy and insecure back then, I was afraid you'd skip out." She also hadn't planned on it morphing into a space station; her original idea was a really luxurious Pacific island. She winked at him and then more seriously said, "Hiring you was the best decision I ever made. You did good." Alex's HUD, as well as Brian's, displayed the count of people arriving and sitting in chairs. "That's everyone," Alex said. "You ready?"

"I'm never going to be ready." Brian switched on the projector, using his own HUD. The image of the two of them appeared in four huge, perfectly clear 3D holograms above them so that their faces could be easily seen by every person in the stadium. Their voices would be amplified so they could speak normally and be heard clearly.

"Welcome, everyone," Alex said, "I appreciate you taking time out of your schedules to attend the meeting this week. As of right now, we are on an information blackout and no outside communication is allowed until the meeting is over. We have a lot to discuss and not much time to do it and we have some decisions to make as a community. Be assured, your questions will be answered as thoroughly as possible so we can make the best decisions by popular vote."

Alex waited for people to absorb that and then continued, "At the top of the announcement list, we are rolling out artificial gravity and relocating this facility into orbit around Earth, giving the locals back their horizon as well as their land."

Alex projected the 3D hologram of their facility lifting into space and waited for the din to quiet. The launch would merely be SEL pushing their habitat away from the planet, slowly, until it floated free. The lie that their gravity would be artificial was just more deception for those that were going to try to duplicate it.

Alex said, "This is perfectly safe and we'll use the SEL vehicles to commute between the space station and our Pacific island. Everyone will have the opportunity to choose which facility you want to live at and we'll adapt our business activities accordingly. Your day-to-day life won't change much at all."

That announcement took much longer for people to finish talking. Alex and Brian waited patiently.

"In addition to choosing which facility you want to live at, we have a more important decision to make as a community." Alex inhaled, fortifying herself mentally, and said, "The United States government is preparing to seize our facility and technology which will require us to disclose full specifications and will require us to become a common carrier. This will subject us to laws applying to monopolies and force us to share our technology and business with the power companies."

Alex continued, "We will no longer be able to sell our batteries overseas. The U.S. government is doing this under the pretense of using it to rebuild the country's infrastructure, but what they will be doing is using it for the military, and to force individuals to pay utility companies and taxes on electricity and vehicle power again."

Alex practiced deep breathing until the uproar died down. "We have two options to deal with this. First, we can comply. We will become just another company." She paused. "Or. We can declare our independence from the United States and become our own country." Again she waited for the noise level to reduce and then continued, "I am a patriot, but even our ancestors looked at England and said, 'The price to be part of your nation is too high.'"

"Should the majority of people choose to form a country, we will continue to operate as our company while we define our new nation. This means we will keep the U.S. dollar as our currency. Everyone who chooses to join the new nation will work for the country and continue on the same pay and work schedule. We will continue to sell our batteries worldwide and reinvest the profits into our own people. This means that everyone living at our facilities must become citizens and work for the country. We will not require anyone to renounce other citizenships."

Alex continued, still at a slow pace to give people time to adjust and absorb what she was saying. "If you choose to join the new nation, and this is entirely optional, you will not be trapped and will be able to leave any time after the initial three months. I predict it will take approximately three months to get our space station and island configured and get other countries to recognize our new nation. You will have full internet access and communication; any travel restrictions will be set by other countries, not us."

Alex exhaled and inhaled again. "In either case, I already sold our Atlanta buildings this morning and we will expand our Pacific facility into a full-size island to be our Earth-side location." Milo was also off transferring ownership of their entire desert complex land to the son of Corbin May at that very moment. It would be done before the new law got passed, throwing yet another legal wrench in the "we're here to take over your company by military action" should anything go wrong with their launch.

Brian took over, "I know this is a lot to absorb and you have many questions. We're going to adjourn until 11 a.m. so you can review the information on the internal corporate website and post your questions. Come back here at 11 and we'll start working through answers."

By the end of the very long day, the employees had voted to create their own country and about 75% of them had made the decision for which facility they wanted to live at. Several families, for personal reasons, were taking the four year pay severance package with the understanding that they could reapply for citizenship with priority in four years.

Alex began the process of sorting living quarters into "undecided, staying, relocating, or leaving" across all three facilities and planning out how the living quarters could be most efficiently rearranged the next day. Everyone from Atlanta that was staying would be relocated to new apartments. Without exception, everyone needed to be decided by the time of the launch.

People were generally in good spirits, if slightly dazed. Many would have preferred a lot more time to make the decision, but the imminent invasion didn't allow that luxury. Alex provided proof that it was coming. The carefully nurtured community and team spirit pulled people together and allowed them to think of each other as family and pioneers. Alex published a short documentary simply titled "The Reasons I Seemed Crazy" that explained some of the strategic decisions that had kept their company alive.

On the following day, everyone was issued a bracelet that activated a HUD and was trained on how to use it for communication, company server access, and "locating living quarters". Alex set her picobots to morphing and rearranging housing at all three locations. The opaque SEL enclosures hid all activity from outside observers, but many personal photos and video were taken of the apartments floating around that they would be able to share later. Alex and Brian held more answer sessions, and people planning to become citizens were grouped into teams for layout design and local rules.

If people were already trained on vehicle use, their HUD let them create and destroy a vehicle for their personal use, although no one was permitted to do that while buildings were floating around rearranging themselves. They started the first course in space-travel, where the number one rule was "never ever trust your eyes to get to a destination". Everyone was kept busy, and even the children were given a reduced gravity playground to bounce in, courtesy of Lucas.

Lucas reported that the Indians had decided on a park plan and that it was under their budget for matter use. He had completed the program necessary to create the park when they departed. Alex had Lucas take over the housing rearrangement.

Milo informed Alex that the government had indeed passed the law regarding energy and energy technology, and the government had issued orders for troops to assemble. Luciano sent a note saying she had to be at court on August 6th or the delayed arrest warrant would be issued. Alex was unconcerned.

Everyone and their housing were sorted based on their decisions, and everything inside was raised up to create two stacked massive rooms underneath the entire complex. The lower one began its conversion into a beautiful desert park, minus the plants and animals. The waiting area outside of the main complex contained moving trucks for people who had decided to leave as well as the corporate spies and their families.

The second level was made into a huge party room, half with an opaque floor and half with a gridded but mostly transparent floor so people could watch the Earth as they lifted off. On their main level, above their soil, the new building created for the space station residential units was located on the eastern side of the facility so it could catch the morning light. This had been configured into a beautiful golden castle for showmanship. They wouldn't keep it like that once they reached their destination, but everyone voted that it would make some awesome historical pictures.

Long before dawn, Alex sent the FAA a no-fly order for the space above all three facilities and the enclosures began to slowly expand upward. Alex's picobots indicated Bill Stateman had followed her instructions and had sent teams to the specified locations with cameras and video gear. Alex sent a note to Luciano to tell him where to find Bill to deliver the chilled wine and hors d'oeuvres she'd gift-wrapped so Bill could participate in the launch party.

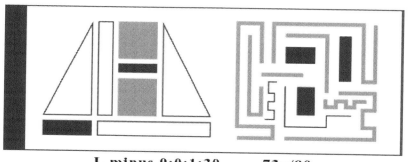

L minus 0:0:1:30   ~73π/90

Just before dawn, Alex dropped the opacity of their desert facility so the morning sun could glint off the castle and other buildings. Those electing to stay as well as Running Fox and his friends were allowed to depart. The distance slowly grew between the desert park and the party room, careful not to move so fast that air would pull in disruptively fast. The movement was barely noticeable.

As the morning progressed, everyone who had opted to belong to the new nation made a video and signed a document that said they were doing so voluntarily without coercion. People chose times for "departure photos" at specific altitudes, where they would be able to lay down in a specially designed "sunken" area and get their photo taken with the Earth below. Videos and photos were encouraged, although the outside communication was still blocked.

A balloon with a viewport room split off from their rising space station headed toward the Pacific island with the people who'd chosen to live there.

269

Residences from the other two facilities were also rising in bubbles at the same time as the desert facility, although they remained an opaque pearlescent white, looking like large balloons floating away. These continued on to their final destinations.

Alex expected Bill Stateman could actually perceive their height difference. Alex went over to the side of the party room where he might be able to see her with binoculars or his long-lens camera. She waved and toasted him with a champagne glass that only had apple juice in it; she and Lucas needed to remain sober and awake just in case there was some adjustment that needed to be made to their calculations. Bill could take all of the pictures and video he wanted of the party going on. Citizens had been warned not to wear skirts or other revealing clothing.

People who visited the party room were told that if they got dizzy or scared walking on the transparent gridded floor to simply close their eyes and raise their hands. If someone saw someone doing that, they were to escort them over to the solid floor and make sure they were ok.

Kids ran around playing. Adults could drink if they wanted to. Plenty of food was set out, buffet style, but sadly to the consternation of the majority of new citizens, still vegetarian. They would add fish and chickens for eggs as soon as the space station was able to allocate enough space. Music, games, and dancing kept the party going. People were free to go anywhere inside the facility, and could even go take a nap in their apartment if they wanted.

Motion sickness, nausea, anti-anxiety, and sleeping medications were freely dispensed by any of the first aid or medical personnel if people requested them. Counselors were on hand to relieve people's fears and any panic. Overall, people were unconcerned and unafraid, and they could always head back to the comfort of their rooms and rest if they felt overwhelmed.

At any time, people could look on their HUD to see how high up they were, what the estimated time for their arrival in stable orbit was, or an overlay of a map below them. People who had pets arriving in one of the balloons could check and see how their animals were faring. The lift was so steady that unless one stayed perfectly still and studied the Earth below, they couldn't tell they were moving.

Alex and Lucas could actually increase the speed of the SEL columns pushing their new home skyward. Lucas adjusted their gravity to compensate for the acceleration. When they reached an altitude above where most planes flew, Alex issued the release order for the spies, who'd been in a complete information blackout with their families. They found moving trucks with their personal effects ready to take them back to Las Vegas.

Alex published the videos and statements of their new citizens to the company's, no, now country's, website, along with a list of assigned telephone and internet time slots for contacting family and friends. Everyone would eventually be able to use the network freely, but this temporary restriction was necessary to prevent the network from getting overloaded all at once.

Lucas started compensating for gravity and Alex published the predetermined terms for the new park that belonged to the Indians. Any Indian could get a free lifetime park pass at the new Indian-owned office in Las Vegas. The pass would be genetically matched to the owner, and they were allowed to bring in four visitors. Local residents could also purchase annual passes with the tribal leader's approval. Other people could purchase single day-only passes.

The genetically-bound passes were SEL and would show a map of the area, informational overlays, a "this way out" arrow, and would create temporary small bathrooms with running water and trash disposal anywhere inside the park. The park itself had beautiful rock sculptures, a natural amphitheater, hiking trails, and a pretty lake for swimming. The SEL enclosure around the park maintained the temperature, weather, and atmosphere as well as security. It would let desert animals and plants in, but not people without a park pass, and no vehicles at all. In another five years, with some care, the land would be restored to pristine natural desert beauty.

Alex published Brian's pre-recorded message for the government of the United States and the rest of the world. Their long-life batteries were for the individuals of the world, not for any one country. Orders would be on hold until shipping routes were identified, and then orders would be sold to individuals in countries who formally recognized the existence of their new country and its citizens, temporarily named Colony One.

Colony One's space station would operate in the same time zone as their Pacific island. Phone numbers, with a new international calling code, were published for Colony One offices, although these would only become available as support was added internationally. Citizen communication channels were reestablished and the temporary restriction lifted, although the network was understandably overloaded.

The United States government issued arrest warrants for the terrorists and kidnappers named Alex Smith and Brian Kimberly. Alex and Brian responded by posting a picture of themselves in the specially designed sunken-photo room toasting the world with champagne with the magnificent vista of the Earth below. Lucas even temporarily adjusted the alcove's gravity so they could hold their glasses in an orientation aligned with them, not the party-room.

By 1 a.m., they were in a stable orbit, slightly farther from the Earth than the International Space Station. Majority vote declared August 5th their first national holiday - Launch Day. By early morning, the other apartments arrived in their balloons and Alex moved them inside so people could get to their pets and homes. She accomplished this by sending SEL rope to grab and reel them in and then having the station's SEL hull expand over them and absorb them. Sal's house and antiques shop arrived, but Alex didn't have time to do anything but bring them inside.

After checking everything, both Alex and Lucas were certain the orbit, gravity, SEL enclosure, atmosphere, oxygen, temperature, and environment were stable. Alex sent Lucas off to sleep and went to answer questions and help organize the groups designing their new habitat's layout. When that was done and Colony One's citizens felt empowered to make decisions and could be trusted with their future, Alex stumbled toward Sal's house in a post-adrenaline zombie haze. They'd done it. The rush was over and she could finally rest.

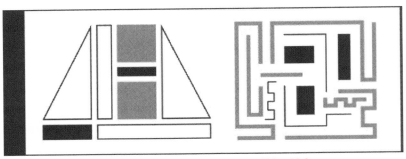

T plus 0:1:20:15   ~73π/90

Alex's HUD blinked and beeped with an incoming message. She peered at the time. She'd been in bed in Sal's house precisely twenty minutes and at least half of that she'd spent trying to decompress enough to sleep.

"What is it, Brian?" Alex tried not to sound grumpy, but she hadn't slept since Monday night, and they were already at early Sunday morning. Getting everyone situated and people divided into groups to organize their new home was proving more challenging than Alex had anticipated. Now that people could claim complete ownership of their home and work environment, opinions were running strong.

Brian's panicked voice choked out, "We have a plumbing crisis. We need you."

Alex groaned. "Have Lucas handle it."

Brian growled, "We can't reach Lucas. He's not answering his messages and we can't get into his lab. He's sealed it off somehow. No one else has the ability to manipulate SEL well enough."

Alex whimpered and made herself roll out of bed. "Ok. Send me a location. What's the problem?"

"We have sewage all over the residential quad," said Brian.

"Ok, where's the quad right now?" Alex wasn't even sure where she herself was at that moment. Buildings were still being rearranged.

"Um." There was a pause and then a dot appeared on an updated map on her HUD.

When Alex arrived a few minutes later, she knew exactly what had happened. The program to rearrange the housing hadn't been updated to also include plumbing connections. The people designing the new residence building moved everything around until they were happy with it, keeping it temporary until they were sure they liked the layout. When they were ready, they added the final mark for "permanent location".

While temporarily situated, the pipes were closed over in each unit in small septic systems, but when they got the final mark, the pipes reconfigured and unsealed. Two days of temporarily contained sewage, expecting to be connected to main pipes before being opened, well, opened. The smell was overwhelming. Alex immediately gave herself a picobot air filter.

Alex saw Brian standing with a large group of people off to one side, on an elevated land mass. People trapped inside the residence island peered out of their windows. Alex overrode the "no flying vehicles while things are moving" ban and made a vehicle and flew over to Brian, and the people who had been trapped began abandoning their apartments.

Alex climbed out of her seat and said to Brian, "Let's not put this in the Colony One history books."

Brian nodded somberly. "Good luck with that. It's already all over Earth's social media, complete with pictures and video. It's creating the most appalling jokes and commentary."

Alex winced. "Ok, first, evacuate everyone to one of the environmental habitats. Have them take their pets, except for fish and lizards and stuff that needs to live in a container. Then I'll clean this up. Assure everyone it will be fine and that one day we'll laugh about this." She started creating a SEL wall to keep the mess from continuing its horrible outward seep.

Alex began the tedious process of designing a cleanup program for her picobots. The sewage was everywhere, even inside some of the residences and down the hallways. Some of the citizens in non-SEL units had broken their windows to leave apartments which hadn't been configured to have balconies yet, and shards of glass mixed with the sludge.

Alex already had technology she was using for the temporary bathrooms in both the Indian reservation and the environmental habitats. These used the molecules in the immediate atmosphere reconfigured with picobots to create the temporary room. When the room was disbanded, the picobots simply reversed the process back to atmosphere, converting the waste into dust after a quick scan to make sure it wasn't going to destroy non-bacterial/non-viral organisms or jewelry.

The dust was then scattered back across the ground and recycled into part of the environment. It wasn't ideal, but it was certainly better than this mess. She supposed she could ditch plumbing entirely and just give everyone a bag of dirt to dispose of periodically. Water could be directly purified and recycled.

Alex wished her brain would function. She was too tired. She recognized that every task seemed to be taking four times longer to accomplish, but it had to be done. Everything in the immediate area had to be molecularly scanned. The atmosphere had to be purified to remove the odor. Anything the sewage had soaked into had to be rebuilt. She started at the top and worked her way down. Residence by residence. Lifting them up, cleaning them out, moving them into an air bubble that was filtered and clean.

Alex got through four residences and requested several of the more detail-oriented scientists with molecular knowledge come join her. She trained them and put them to work. If they had any question about something at all, they asked. Eventually, after too many grueling hours, the area was clean. Using air, the pipes would carry waste dirt to a central location for proper redistribution. Any waste could be thrown into the toilet, lid closed, and flushed away. A menu option was added to everyone's HUD that would let them create a temporary bathroom that resulted in a small bag of dust to recycle in a permanent toilet.

Alex sent off a note to Brian with instructions that nothing was to be finalized until she'd approved it and went in search of her bed again. She slept like the dead.

Alex awoke a satisfying eleven hours later, starving. She briefly scanned her email and saw Brian had published a statement that no one was going to be blamed for the plumbing incident. "People make mistakes," he wrote, "We learn, we evolve, and we move on." The people she'd taught how to manipulate things at the molecular level with her "SEL matter adjusters" (privately also known as picobots) were busy teaching their peers.

Alex studied the latest station map which was again completely different. Sal's house had been moved while Alex slept inside. It was scheduled to become a museum as was the antiques shop, and they'd moved both to the outer edge of their new tourist zone. Alex would have to see if she could get them moved to the school zone. She'd much rather visit there than risk being accosted by tourists... one day when they had tourists.

Alex stepped outside of Sal's house. Overhead, the high dome ceiling faced space and full-spectrum artificial lights gave the appearance of daytime and blue sky. The air was comfortably warm, matching the ambient "outdoor" temperature of their desert installation. Alex smelled the heady perfume from Sal's late-season azaleas, and looked over his small garden that had accompanied the house. Some of the plants needed water and Alex directed her picobots to convert some of the nearby soil and she added a temporary moisture-dome over the whole garden. Desert atmosphere was too dry for Georgian autumn plants. Eventually, groundskeepers would be around to maintain everything, but Alex bet everyone was too busy to settle into a normal routine just yet.

The tourist zone was mostly just paths and scattered desert plants at the moment between open lots for future buildings. Edges of the rearranged land masses kept their odd gaps, creating a really odd patchwork quilt made of packed desert sand. As Alex crossed the nearly desolate area, she tried to imagine what it would look like complete and filled with people. They'd need to put up street signs along the roads; the paths curved along a grid very much like a spider web, logical but not boring. Alex wondered what they planned for the center.

Separating the tourist zone from the shopping zone was a new gently winding stream bed, also waiting on water. A wide, golden bridge connected the two zones. The shopping zone followed the same general road layout. Here, some buildings were already in place and open. People who noticed Alex waved at her and she waved back but continued her quest for food.

Lunch was fully underway by time Alex reached the buffet. The space currently reminded her of a mall food court, but she knew they planned to turn it into a delightful food-town with the atmosphere of a renaissance fair with kiosks and buildings.

People saw Alex and stepped out of her way deferentially. They did not let her wait in line but instead sent her straight to the food. She was hungry enough that she let it happen, setting a terrible future-precedent that she would later regret. Alex picked a table at random and joined the citizens there, adroitly asking questions so that they spent the meal telling her about things they'd done so far and Alex didn't have to talk hardly at all.

Noise dampeners, both obvious in ceiling decorations, and subtle, in the form of picobots between tables, kept the conversations localized to small groups of tables, and set the sound falloff such that you could easily hear the people at your own table without shouting.

As Alex was finishing, Brian arrived carrying two cups of tea. He nodded politely to Alex's table-mates, and sat down, putting one of the cups in front of Alex. Brian's HUD contained Alex's extended programming that allowed him to locate people without having to go through dispatch - their newest solution to inter-team coordination and people-finding with built-in privacy. After a few minutes of general small talk, the others got up and moved to another table so Alex and Brian could talk.

Brian pressed the privacy button on the table that cut sound to their table only and prevented their voices from carrying. Overhead a subtle red holographic ball appeared to indicate to others that they wanted no interruptions. "How are you doing?" Brian asked. "You've been under a lot of pressure this week."

"I'm good. I got sleep finally. I knew we'd have some unexpected challenges. More importantly, how are you doing? You've been under the same pressure," Alex said.

Brian rubbed at his stubbly chin. "I'm still in a bit of a shock. Despite that sewage spill, people are in a good mood. They're trusting us to hold everything together. They think we're miracle workers. Feels like my responsibility just expanded to infinite. I'm not ready for this."

Alex could certainly sympathize. The plumbing incident really highlighted how incredibly unprepared they were for this evolution. "No real way to be ready. I guess we just solve one problem at a time?"

"Ah, good. I'm glad you brought that up." Brian said with a fake casual tone, picking up his teacup.

Alex winced.

Brian continued, "There's a specific forum for issues that got started last night. Usually, I'd just pass things along to Milo."

"But Milo isn't here," Alex finished for him. "It's ok. What's up?"

"Tell me you have a stockpile of disposable items? Toilet paper, diapers, feminine hygiene products, soaps..." Having set his teacup down again without drinking, Brian pressed his hands together hopefully.

The blood drained from her face and Alex stopped breathing a moment. "Oh. We forgot that. How'd we forget that?"

"Yeah. We have food and water; we have oxygen. We even now have miracle plumbing. But diapers, no. We've got a group of people who are now compiling a list of urgently needed products. Not a single country has acknowledged ours yet, so we can't buy anything. There are a few people sharing what they have, or selling it." Brian frowned at the thought of the opportunists.

"It's not a problem," Alex said, hoping that it wasn't. "Lucas can take care of this sort of thing."

"Lucas hasn't come out of his lab," Brian informed her.

Alex blinked. "He hasn't? When was the last time you saw him?"

"I think you saw him last," Brian shrugged.

The last time Alex had seen Lucas was when she had told him to go off and get sleep after their orbit stabilized. "Ok, I'll go find him next."

Brian shook his head. "Diapers have to be next. We've already run out and it's making people panic. And you know what panic will do to us."

Alex inhaled and told herself to calm down. Their population was not going to panic and demand to go back to Earth. "Tell everyone I have this covered and we'll have some supplies in a few hours." She could set the picobots to making supplies instead of batteries.

Brian nodded.

Alex peered at her HUD map again, muttering to herself, "Now where did my lab go?"

Alex found her lab buried underneath the recycling building near the residential zone - nowhere near the top half of the factory building, which had been pushed over into the new industrial zone. The citizens thought the basement-lab was storage for excess recycling materials and kept the basement and her lab together. Her picobots had stopped building batteries because they couldn't move the batteries to storage and a bug in her pallet code caused her error notification to fail.

Alex sent off a message to the zoning committee via the dispatch team to have her lab moved, with priority, and turned her attention to designing the molecular structure for diapers. With a cheerful grin, she realized she was no longer bound by patent regulations.

Creating diapers, however, proved more challenging than Alex expected. She could synthesize a diaper's sodium polyacrylate without an issue and she could the sprinkle the dust in cotton fibers, but getting randomly sized leg-holes that wouldn't leak on a suitably baby-soft fabric was nearly impossible. Ideally, parents should have a dispenser that would recycle the matter used for the diaper itself. The dispenser could then give them a small tray of dirt to throw in the toilet. They shouldn't need more than two diapers per child. One for wearing and one for changing when it was needed.

After studying the problem for a while, and looking online for solutions, Alex decided to just ask the experts. She put out a notice for all parents who needed diapers to meet her in one of the larger company conference rooms to discuss diaper design. She could tackle feminine hygiene products next. That would be a similar task. At least they wouldn't ever have a landfill problem; she needed all the matter she could acquire so the particles that made up the atoms could be rearranged into what they needed.

On the way, she went by Lucas' lab to enlist his help. Unfortunately, his whole lab was still sealed off with custom picobots that shifted in a protective grid which her own picobots were unable to penetrate. The door itself had a weird shield configuration, but was also solid and unopenable.

Alex didn't have time to decode their programming and override it. Hopefully he wasn't stuck free floating in the center of his lab and in need of rescue. She thought he was probably just hyper-focused on that equation he was working on and didn't want to be disturbed. She'd have to come back by later and see if she could sort the rogue programming out.

After 12 hours of nonstop design meetings followed by training sessions for the few qualified people on the production of the various items, Alex was tired, hungry, and more than ready for a break. She was a little peeved at Lucas for being unavailable to help. Surely he recognized that the new space station would have problems that needed to be solved? It was selfish to hide out in his lab. She supposed it was her project, not his, but still she wished he were helping.

Alex followed her HUD to the new food court cafeteria and wished for the first time since creating Green World that she had her own private kitchen.

Every tenth step toward her destination seemed punctuated with a random citizen who needed something. She kept the irritation from her voice and added the things people asked for to her list and assured them that she would get to it as soon as possible. She corrected one woman's broken hearing aid on the spot, giving both devices permanent tiny batteries.

Alex was almost done eating her highly interrupted lunch-dinner when she saw Lucas enter the area. Giving her head a slight shake in annoyance, she stood up and headed toward him with the intent of giving him a discreet lecture on his responsibility to the community. As she crossed toward him, she saw him stumble.

Alex reached for Lucas to keep him from falling. "Lucas! What happened?"

"Why didn't you come for me?" his voice was raw and scratchy. "I left you a note."

"A note? What? Where?" She rolled back through her memory and didn't see anything. "Never mind that. Sit here. Let me get you some water."

"And food," Lucas croaked. "Carajo, Alex! I could have died." His hands were shaking.

Alex ran off to get him a drink and something to eat. She brought back the closest things she could reach - some apple juice and a bowl of cereal. She jogged these back to him.

Lucas took the glass of apple juice with both hands. When it looked like he might drop it, Alex helped him, sliding in next to him on the bench. He gulped, and then took a second drink, letting that liquid sit in his mouth a moment before swallowing. They set the glass down and he grasped the spoon and ate some cereal.

Alex waited, her toes twitching impatiently inside her shoe. She wouldn't show any outward sign of her anxiety for people surreptitiously watching them. She checked her email on her HUD. There was no message from him. Had it been lost? She needed her communication system to function correctly. She sent off a message to their tech team to check that all messages were being delivered promptly.

After a few minutes of eating, with his pace picking up as the sugar in the apple juice reached his bloodstream, Lucas announced, "We can't be here. It's too dangerous."

"Here... in the cafeteria?" Alex asked, carefully keeping her voice low.

"Space. There's just too many variables."

Alex glanced around. Luckily no one was within earshot. She activated the table's privacy button. The last thing she needed was people hearing their resident physicist saying they had a problem. Several tables had the subtle red

278

holographic ball overhead so at least their table didn't stand out. Alex would deploy HUD-created personal privacy shields as soon as she got a chance. Looking back at Lucas, Alex asked, "How about we take some food and discuss this in a more private location?" She didn't want lip readers following what they were saying either.

Lucas paled and his eyes shot around wildly. "Uh. Yeah. Sorry."

Alex went and collected more food and brought it back. "Your lab?"

Lucas winced. "Definitely not my lab."

She leaned forward and peered at Lucas in worried concern and decided, "Mine then. It's not too far just now. Can you walk?"

"Yeah, now that I'm not about to die from dehydration." He pushed himself to his feet. He was still unsteady but better than he had been. "I thought I might, though, after I managed the heat issue."

"What did you do?" Alex's eyebrows scrunched together. She couldn't imagine any scenario where heat would be an issue inside her space station. It had full SEL shielding with specialized reflective shielding to block harmful radiation. Some areas were designed as heat exchangers to stabilize the inside temperatures while some crossover points for transportation and communication weren't equally protected, but overall, the station was designed to prevent radiation from the sun cooking everyone and the coldness of space from freezing them. Additionally, each of their ecosystems had its own internal temperature stabilizers.

Alex asked, "Do we have radiation shield failure?" Did she need to evacuate the station? Her heart skipped several beats. She pulled up the latest sensor reports on her HUD. The sensors remained stable-green.

"No, no," Lucas rushed to reassure her. "The station is fine." This would have been somewhat comforting if he hadn't added, "For now."

Alex wanted to run toward her lab, but paced herself for Lucas and the trays she was carrying against the station rules to keep food in the food zones. When she finally closed her lab door, she made a soft SEL chair for him and a table for the trays and sat across from him on her cot. Her picobots were diligently building boxes of nose tissues. Lucas' chair was a SEL hack, whereas the tissues would be actual items. SEL could be quickly formed and solid or flexible as needed. Actual items had to be somewhat slowly built at the molecular level. "Let's start with what note and go from there."

"I left it in the picobot shield around my lab. Surely you came to check on me? I was gone almost two full days!" Lucas ignored the trays of food.

"Yes, but I didn't have time to dissect your code. We had a few crises that I could have used your help with." Alex set her picobots to locating some of the altered picobots around his lab and retrieving his programming.

"What crises can you possibly have? This place is in a stable orbit. Everyone is fine. People here are safe. I needed you!" Lucas' hand opened and closed into a tight fist and his eyes shifted from angry to more a more shell-

279

shocked, traumatized glaze. He pulled his knees up, feet on the chair and leaned forward, hugging them.

Speaking softly in Spanish, Alex asked, "What happened, Lucas?" On her HUD, she was frantically trying to figure out what was in his custom code that was in any way a note to her. At least her picobots reported his lab was still secured.

Lucas answered in Spanish. "My formula worked, but it only worked one way. It wasn't stable."

"The big formula you've been working on for a while?" Alex asked.

"Yes." His eyes darted around her lab, but didn't focus on anything.

"What is it?" Alex prompted quietly. Maybe she should have insisted he tell her when he first started working on it?

Lucas' eyes finally settled on the pile of tissue boxes that was growing slowly, but steadily. "It's a door to anywhere so long as you know the address."

Alex stiffened and shut down her HUD. She focused solely on Lucas. His breathing was erratic. His legs trembled, but he simply tightened his arms around them. "Where did you go?" Alex kept her voice soft and calm.

"Saturn. Well, technically near Saturn. I almost crashed into Titan. More accurately, Titan almost crashed into me."

Alex had to remember to breathe. She weighed in with, "That must have been terrifying."

"Why didn't you come for me?" Lucas' voice was angry, accusing.

Alex answered gently, not accusingly, "I didn't know I needed to. I didn't see any note."

Lucas fiddled with his HUD and hers snapped on, showing the picobots by his lab. He color-coded them. He made the picobots with the pointy side toward the station ceiling blue and the ones with the pointy side toward the station bottom a faded yellow. Clear as day there were words built into the mesh overlaying his lab. It was obvious to anyone who really looked. It read, "Alex, I've built a teleporter and I've taken all precautions, but if something goes wrong and you don't see me by 7 p.m., reactivate it by pushing the blue button. It's configured to open to where I am. Entry passcode is 3684."

Next time send an email, Alex thought bitterly, frustrated with herself for having missed the message, but she didn't speak this though. "Good grief. I missed that? I'm very sorry." Then, trying not to panic, Alex inquired gently, "Is this door to Saturn still open?" The station didn't need another heat loss.

"No, it's closed now. Unstable as I said. Can't reopen on its own." Lucas' shaking got worse. He wasn't cold; he was experiencing traumatic shock. He needed medical attention, not a lecture. Alex created a soft moderately heavy SEL blanket and went and wrapped it around him. "It's ok now. You're safe here. Just breathe and try to relax. I've got you now. Everything on the station is completely stable. I'm monitoring everything. All our sensors are reporting normally. You are going to be fine. You're safe now."

Alex adjusted her HUD and requested a doctor and some anti-anxiety and calming medicine, and proceeded to rearrange her lab so an extra wall hid most of her things, including the building of the tissue boxes. She created and arranged some suitably large computers and screens and shifted Lucas' chair into a daybed and got rid of her own sleeping area. The room transformed into the stereotypic expectation of a science lab.

The doctor on duty arrived in a few minutes with a comfortingly recognizable "doctor bag" and Alex opened her lab door to let him inside. Dr. Kgomotso Jakande was an average height African-American who'd joined the company to both pay off his mountainous tuition bills and to work for a smaller community practice outside of the mainstream stress of hospitals. Alex had only spoken with him in passing and she didn't know him very well, but he received good reviews from all of his patients and had earned an annual bonus for all three years he'd been with the company.

"What's going on?" the doctor asked, striding in, and studying Lucas sitting on the daybed.

"Delayed traumatic shock," Alex responded. "Lab experiment gone bad. It was pretty scary. Lucas got to see space up close and personal." Lucas snorted at that but didn't focus on either Alex or the doctor.

"Are you physically hurt anywhere, Lucas?" Kgomotso asked, opening his bag and setting it near Lucas.

Lucas answered with sudden violent, uncontrollable shivering, but managed to shake his head.

Kgomotso proceeded to examine Lucas, testing his pupils, taking his pulse, listening to his heart, and checking his limbs, fingers, and toes. "You have a bit of a racing heart there, Lucas, but you're going to be fine. Let me give you a little something to calm you down." He pulled out a needle and small jar. He pulled Lucas' sleeve up, swabbed a spot, and gave Lucas an injection. "I think rest and sleep will see you back in top form by tomorrow. So what happened?"

Alex put her hand on Lucas' shoulder, silently encouraging him not to mention Saturn. She explained, "He got trapped for a bit in one of our experimental space vehicles. That problem is corrected now."

"Ah. Well, Lucas, you might want to visit one of the counselors for stress management techniques if you have flashbacks or nightmares, but you're going to be just fine. I can always give you some anti-anxiety medicine later if you think you need it, but I'm pretty sure once you have some sleep and rest, you'll be ok."

Lucas nodded. The medicine was already showing its effect because Lucas was noticeably relaxing and he'd stopped shaking. "I'll just stay here for a bit," Lucas leaned over onto his side and snuggled into the blanket. He closed his eyes and was asleep.

The doctor turned to Alex and instead of lecturing her on safety procedures as she thought he would, he said, "I can't tell you how much of a joy it is to be able to give people what they need without having to deal with forms and reports, insurance claims, and justifications. You'll have to watch medical staff for drug addiction abuse eventually, but right now the team is small enough that it's not going to be a problem. You do have a way to purchase more pharmaceuticals?" He twisted a ring on his finger anxiously while watching her response.

"Oh. Um." Alex hadn't thought about it at all. "It shouldn't be a problem once we have other countries acknowledging ours. In the meantime, I can see about synthesizing what we need if you give me samples."

The doctor nodded, accepting that with terrifying faith. "We have some people on regular medicines for blood pressure and cholesterol and such, and, of course, insulin. The mandatory diet and exercise seems to be wiping out a lot of the need for routine pills, although the way people complain about it, you'd think we were killing them."

"Too true." Alex shook his hand. "Thank you for coming, Dr. Jakande. Just let me know what you need and I'll take care of it." She seemed to be promising a lot of people that, she reflected ruefully.

"My name is Kgomotso, but call me David. It's easier to pronounce."

"Thank you, Kgomotso," she grinned at him. "Call me Alex."

"I hear we're officially calling you 'Founder' from now on." Kgomotso winked.

Alex sighed. This was inevitable, she supposed. "I guess it's too late to get that changed to 'Supreme Goddess of the Universe' or something?"

Kgomotso laughed. "I won't take up any more of your time, Founder. Call if you need anything."

After the doctor was gone, Alex created a few more pillows and arranged Lucas into a more comfortable position, and then put her lab back in order. Then she alternated between reading, manufacturing, and responding to forum posts while watching Lucas sleep.

Alex swapped production of tissue boxes to production of shampoo. She would need to delegate all of this at some point. She already had select individuals from the sewage spill cleanup team secretly working on other items, although after repairing the hearing aid, news of new matter-rearranging technology was inevitable. She found a post by Kgomotso during the all-hands meeting before their launch asking if pharmaceuticals were covered and Brian's response that it was handled.

Alex sighed and sent Brian a note to ask what his plans were and got an almost immediate reply that said she had told him she had the consumable items planned and asking if there was a problem. She rolled back through her memory, and sure enough, way back when she'd first sold him the idea of a space station, she had mentioned it in a long list of other things that she was going to take care of. She sent back a message that it wasn't a problem and that she was just trying to make sure they weren't duplicating effort. Alex didn't want to worry him with the truth.

A little over six hours later, Lucas woke up. Alex could see his location confusion as he slowly became alert as well as the moment he remembered because he bit his lower lip.

"I'm sorry I yelled at you," Lucas said.

Alex stood and walked over toward him. "I'm sorry I yelled at you, too."

"Did you?" Lucas pushed the blanket off and dissolved it into a small solid cube of osmium. Osmium, the densest metal, was the most efficient way to store matter they needed. The pillows went to the same fate as he sat up. Changing between the different types of matter was carefully moderated and controlled by the picobots to prevent problems with nuclear fission and fusion. Excess energy was absorbed or provided using the same physics as Alex's batteries.

Alex carried the cubes to the pile that was feeding her manufacturing unit. They were heavy, despite their tiny size. "Yeah, I just wasn't quite as direct as you. No worries. Are you ok?"

"I think so. Hard to believe I'm the first human to ever see Saturn up close. I thought the rings would be pretty." Lucas stretched.

"Were they?"

"Unimaginably beautiful. Heart-stoppingly beautiful," he murmured.

Alex tempered her sudden jealousy with a strong dose of near-death reality. "I'm glad it didn't actually stop your heart. Tell me what happened?"

"I was sure my formula was correct. I tried calling you to have you come confirm it, but you had that 'sleeping, do not disturb unless urgent' thing so I modified the picobots around my lab for you."

Lucas went on to explain that he chose Saturn because it was a reasonable distance to test. He opened the door a good distance from Saturn so he wouldn't have to deal with as much gravity, and was very careful to put the full shielding over it so space couldn't interact with the station.

Then he created one of their space vehicles and drove it through the door. He spent a couple minutes gazing at Saturn, unable to believe he was actually there and then he noticed that he was getting cold. The shielding heat exchange wasn't correct because there wasn't as much solar radiation for heat and so he fixed that. When he finished, he discovered that the door had closed. He then spent an unknown duration of time hyperventilating and panicking.

"I told myself you would see my note and come for me. All I had to do was wait. I made sure I was stable and would stay where the door would open when you did it."

Alex winced.

"So I got some nice pictures of Saturn and Titan and I waited." Lucas sent some of the photos to her HUD. His photos of Saturn rivaled ones taken by Cassini while the images of Titan looked like a large blurry orangish sphere due to its hydrocarbon atmosphere.

Alex could barely imagine what scientists would do with the ability to deploy probes across the solar system and retrieve reports instantly. No more seven year delays. They could even recover the frozen corpse of the Huygens Probe if it was still there. They would still have to design equipment that could withstand hostile environments, but they could afford a more trial and error approach. Alex wished Lucas had had more advanced imaging and measurement tools.

Lucas continued, "After a while, I had to set up some additional oxygen-generators, and going to the bathroom was a smelly, unpreventable necessity. Then I had to create a bunch more picobots to work on that, except I didn't have enough matter to create picobots, so I had to use my clothes and shoes. Fingernails, toenails. I may never cut my hair again."

Alex saw his fingernails had been chewed off to the quick and she'd thought his unusually short hair was just a recent haircut.

Lucas ran his fingers through his hair and then said, "You missed the 7 p.m. deadline according to my HUD and I started wondering what I was going to do if you didn't come. Four plus years of travel back to the station with no food wasn't promising and I didn't have enough picobots and condensed matter to create a door back, and I needed a heavy duty computer to do the calculations to get the right address from my location. Then about 12 hours later I realized I didn't choose far enough from Saturn and Titan was going to run right over me, and if you happened to open the door while Titan was there..."

Alex shuddered. Space station, meet Titan. What would cross this portal Lucas created? Her carefully modulated habitat didn't need Titan's gravity, or its -179 degrees Celsius methane, or the possibly radioactive elements from Titan's core.

"I expended some of my matter to create enough propellant to move out of the way, but then realized even if you opened the door after Titan had passed, you wouldn't be able to find me. I needed a lot of matter to build a computer and then a door."

Alex tilted her head, thinking, and then said, "You took it from the ship's gravity module."

Lucas clenched his jaw and pointed his index finger at her. "It took me a while to realize that and here you sit and casually mention it as obvious."

Alex held up her hand, gesturing negatively. "I'm not in a state of panic right now. You did good."

"I couldn't even spare the matter to make something to hold onto, so I just floated there, waiting on the computer. At least Titan passed by the address without any apparent incident. It took way too long to get the calculation for the address of my lab, which would only be correct if you hadn't changed the course or rotation of the station."

Or the location of his lab on the station; the station was still undergoing dramatic dynamic changes. They'd gotten inconceivably lucky on a number of points. "Wow, Lucas, I'm so sorry. I can't imagine how terrifying that must have been."

"We humans do not belong in space. It's too big, too massive, and we are way too vulnerable." Lucas stood and began to pace.

"Technically, even if we're on Earth, we're still in space," Alex offered, aiming for a bit of levity.

"You know what I mean."

"I do." Alex crossed over to the trays of food and handed him an apple, which he took and hungrily bit into.

"I really should have waited for you before making the door. It was reckless and stupid, but I was just so excited. If we could have instant travel, getting from Earth to our station and exploring our solar system would be easy. Imagine the implications for our knowledge of the universe."

Alex nodded. "I know some scientists who would kill for those pictures you took. Why don't we go get something warm to eat and visit your lab and you can explain your formula to me and maybe we can figure out why it closed on you?"

"So it's time travel." Alex reiterated. She and Lucas had been in his lab for over three hours, staring at the massive whiteboard that spanned three levels and about six classroom-lengths. They were standing midway up the wall, using Lucas' techno-magic boots. "You got there faster than light and traveling faster than light is time travel."

"No, it's changing locations, not traveling. You were here." He closed his fingers together on his left hand. "And now you're here." He closed his fingers on his right hand.

"But it's going faster than light. That's time travel, by definition," Alex argued.

"Maybe we should redefine time travel, because time stayed the same." Lucas began pacing, making Alex cringe as he seemingly walked on air without any hesitation at all. "I just jumped points. Light took the long path. Distance doesn't exist. You think it does because it does in 3D space and everything we have defined is within those parameters, but the whole universe is a single point and you just need to know where inside that point you are and where you want to be."

"I don't get it." Alex glared at the massive wall displaying his formula.

They'd been through his formula twice already. "I don't understand how that can possibly work."

"The closest thing to explain it is the infinite improbability drive in *The Hitchhiker's Guide to the Galaxy*," Lucas said.

"Huh?" Alex rubbed at her eyes and the bridge of her nose, shaking her head.

"Alex, you built a freakin' space station. How can you not have read *The Hitchhiker's Guide to the Galaxy*?"

"I've been busy!" she griped, carefully enunciating each word with emphasis. Yet another message for urgently needed supplies appeared on her HUD. She ran her fingers through her hair and swore. "We're going to have to come back to this later or the station is going to fall apart around us." At Lucas' sudden panicked expression, she quickly amended, "Not literally. We just have urgent requests for consumable items, like bath soap, deodorant, toilet paper, and so on. I've got to go make items. I sure could use your help. I'm drowning in requests."

"So long as we eat first," Lucas said as his stomach growled.

As they made their way out of Lucas' lab, Alex said, "Oh, before I forget, don't mention this technology to anyone. We need to be sure it is completely ready and stable before it gets announced."

"No kidding." Lucas snorted.

Brian caught up with them in the cafeteria and pulled Alex away to other duties. Lucas promised to whittle down the pending list of needed consumables without her. They needed to start training people.

To Alex, this felt like too soon. Was mankind ready for the power of picobots? Did she have any choice? Getting into space was only a step; they still needed to be able to live sustainably without supplies from the Earth if humanity was going to survive. Soaring Eagle's prediction and a mountain of scientific evidence could not be forgotten or ignored. Alex could even imagine the face of an old-school stopwatch with the time hand relentlessly ticking down toward zero. She had no control at all over this deadline.

Everyone lived or died depending on how ready she could make them, and yet, she couldn't demand and control how things progressed. She had to allow her people to make decisions and humanity's ark would grow however it wanted, despite her guidance. She didn't have enough time to micromanage everything and she needed to reserve her own authority for truly critical decisions.

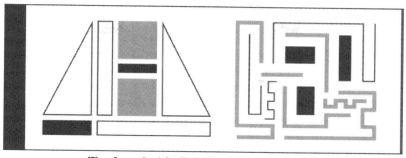

Alex arrived at Brian's newly located office at his summons. Some humorous soul had tacked a sign to his door that read: CEO, President, Emperor, King, Sultan, Czar, Overlord, Scapegoat, followed by "Mr. Brian Kimberly". Everything but Scapegoat was crossed out, but each was still clearly legible. Alex knocked.

"Cute sign," Alex said, entering without waiting on the response.

Brian snorted. "Yeah. I refuse to check security vids to see who is responsible. I may just leave it there until my replacement gets stuck with the title."

Alex laughed. "CEO isn't valid anymore anyway."

"Yup." Brian pointed to one of his large monitors. "At the top of the list: the United States has vetoed our application to the United Nations in the Security Council."

"Well, that didn't take long," Alex said, shaking her head and sighing, reading through the formal response letter displayed there.

"Japan, Russia, and most of southeast Asia have formally recognized our nation status," Brian reported.

That would be Hamasaki Corporation's influence. Alex nodded.

"We also have a few scattered other countries - Iceland, Australia, Egypt, Norway, South Africa, and Argentina. Most of the countries seem to be following the United States which is claiming we are still part of the United States, with all taxes, penalties, and applicable laws. You and I now top the most wanted criminals list."

Alex stretched and then settled into one of his chairs, leaning back and kicking her feet out. "I already did my prison time. It wasn't so awful."

Brian grimaced, reminding Alex of Milo when she said something particularly exasperating. "The guys watching our satellite feeds say that the U.S. is moving its military around to take our island. Lucas updated the SEL dome to a semitransparent solid that will prevent them from entering our territory."

"We should probably go have a talk with their commanding officer. When is the fleet due?" Alex asked.

"Maybe tomorrow. Maybe tonight. We can't both leave the station at the same time. I know you're magically pushing out supplies as quickly as you can, but the idea of flying back to be arrested isn't my idea of a brilliant plan." Brian stood and walked the length of his office, rubbing at his neck.

"They can't arrest you. You aren't a U.S. citizen anymore." Alex watched him pace and pulled her feet in closer out of his way as he strode along a path in front of her.

"There's a fleet of ships and submarines coming that say they can."

Alex shrugged. "It would be really stupid of them to expend ordnance against our SEL shield," Alex said. "It can stand up to the vacuum of space; they must realize it can stand up to missiles and we can easily create ordnance. I don't think they're thinking this through too well."

"We aren't going to shoot at them," Brian said, stopping and crossing his arms to glare at her.

"Of course not. You know those bioshields we have? We're just going to upscale them. Go ahead and get underway to the island, and I'll go have a long talk with our programmers and Lucas to give you some options. We can handle this." As Brian was rolling his eyes, Alex added, "Also take the latest batch of batteries for Hamasaki Corporation. They can handle our downside distribution for a while." She grinned. "You take care of politics and I'll take care of technical."

Brian rolled his head, stretching his neck. "Think about what you want to do about the International Space Station and satellites while you're at it. People are asking. If we claim space as our territory, those are in our domain."

"We aren't going to do anything about them so long as they don't pose a threat to us. Space is big enough for us to coexist."

"Good. That's what I've been telling people. Let me know what you come up with to deal with that fleet." Brian offered her his hand to unnecessarily help her to her feet and they both departed for their respective destinations.

After a long meeting with the programming staff, Alex spent several hours training even more people on the use of picobots. She quietly verified that the picobot security was actively evading detection on the SEL cards for the Indian reservation's park. Then she went around to visit Colony One's habitat teams, checking for problems, and generally making herself available to answer the endless questions that plagued any appearance in public.

That night, Alex managed an almost-healthy three hours of sleep and pushed herself out of bed to repeat the day. Her main goal was to empower people to make decisions so their habitat and ecosystem could grow and survive and calmly assure everyone she met that they would be fine and happy. Change was unsettling and now that people had a chance to calm down from

288

the launch, they were beginning to realize just how different their new lives were.

Alex was eating breakfast when the news feed for their Pacific island arrived. It was put up on a big screen for everyone in the cafeteria. Their own satellite feed showed a fleet of United States Navy ships surrounding their island which looked remarkably small compared to the mass of ocean and number of ships. Colony One wouldn't filter its news to biased summaries, but would show live-feeds of events. Earth-side people wouldn't be so lucky unless they watched Colony One's website.

On the screen, Brian radioed requesting a meeting with the fleet's commander at Colony One's eastern pier and then reduced the side of their protective sphere to put part of the pier on the outside of the protective dome. The eastern pier, while not the largest, was wide and long. It was used for their supply ships and visitors. Given the bombings while Alex was in prison, non-local ships could no longer approach too near the actual island. No boats were currently docked at that pier.

Brian walked out to the end of the pier, alone, dashingly attired in an elegant island floral collared shirt, white shorts, and beach sandals. He carried a simple beach chair - no weapons, no papers, and nothing intimidating at all. He looked like he was on vacation, complete with sunglasses. Tiny, nearly invisible picobot cameras captured both video and sound from all angles, and Colony One's media team was busy splicing the best views together for their website's news feed and internal network.

Brian arrived at the end of the pier, unfolded the beach chair, and settled in to wait. His bioshield would protect him from both sunburn and drowning, as well as any man-made hazards. After a half hour of the world watching Brian sunbathe, which apparently everyone in the cafeteria found riveting, several small motorboats departed from one of the U.S. vessels, complete with fully armed Marines and a man in officer's whites. Three of the boats remained a good distance away while one pulled up alongside the pier and men deployed onto it, surrounding Brian.

Brian interlocked his fingers, stretched and yawned, and stood up.

"Welcome to Colony One's Pacific island, gentlemen," said Brian. The man in officer's whites climbed onto the pier.

"You're under arrest for terrorism," the officer announced bluntly.

Brian ignored this. "We realize that the United States is having a hard time recognizing our independence. We haven't made any threats and we have no intention of doing so. Our citizens are concerned that you might try to forcibly remove them from their homes and prevent them from visiting their family and friends still in your country. To alleviate their fears, I request you take your fleet, go home, and tell your Commander in Chief to recognize us as an independent country and reverse your veto in the United Nations Security Council."

"I represent the United States Navy. Those are our citizens you're holding hostage on that island."

"We don't have any hostages. Every one of our citizens has a video on our website stating their free will and choice to become citizens."

"We're going to cordon off your island to protect and rescue our citizens." The man turned to his men, "Arrest this terrorist."

Brian's arched eyebrow suggested amusement or maybe boredom. "Colony One does not recognize the right of the United States government to arrest any of its citizens," Brian proclaimed as the men discovered they could not come within arm's reach of Brian due to the invisible picobot shield around him. One of the men tried to use a taser, but it flared uselessly against the picobot shield and didn't reach Brian. "Truly, gentlemen, go home." Brian turned and walked back down the pier, whistling Dvorak's Humoresque, and passing through the SEL dome without even slowing down. Only the beach chair remained on the pier with the men who soon departed. The news coverage by her media team split to a prerecorded video of Brian telling the citizens they had nothing to be concerned about.

People in the cafeteria around Alex cheered, but she did not. Alex didn't want the "them vs. us" mentality. These people weren't their enemy. Time was. Colony One's community still needed a lot of work to survive. Humans needed to pull together.

One of Colony One citizens came over to her. "They're going to send everything they have at us, you know. Not just the United States, but also their allies."

Alex nodded. "They will. We have this covered. We got away in time to prevent our technology from being seized and they wont be able to penetrate our shields or disturb our habitats. We're safe. We even have other defensive abilities if we need them." Aggressive abilities which she wouldn't deploy. "You don't need to worry. We'll start political negotiations for technology to prevent military actions." Not that she would let anyone have the technology, but she and Brian could actively string them along until Colony One's nation-status was firmly established.

Alex retreated to her lab to work on the next item that the station critically needed, knowing that the shield around the Pacific island would stop any attempts by the United States military to enter or harm. Any deployed ordnance would be captured and collected and turned into more land mass. Colony One vehicles leaving or arriving would have the same shielding.

To prove the point, Brian sent one of their people to deliver Hamasaki's latest batteries. The small yacht motored right past the blockade (which the United States was calling a Naval Cordon to keep with their stance that Colony One was still part of the United States). The blockade fired a tentative shot at it, but the ordnance simply absorbed into the picobot shielding. Subsequent ships arriving or departing could be lifted and carried over the blockade with the same protection.

Alex stared at the angry forum posts with disgust. Her citizens were illogically and ignorantly riled up. They were not a population of slaves being exploited by a megalomaniac to gain a massive personal wealth. Yes, her personal finances had grown incredibly since the launch, but this was a result of the novels and movies royalties, not any abuse of Colony One's national budget. In fact, the budget and how every penny was earned and spent was publicly available on their internal website. Alex was not hoarding any future-necessary items, and their team creating consumables wasn't overcharging citizens.

In another set of posts, citizens demanded a formalized political structure, ignoring the fact that they had one that just didn't quite match any of Earth's nation-structures. Brian's position as "Scapegoat" (he'd kept the title) stayed until a majority of citizens voted him out or he wanted to change to another job. He'd be replaced by a random selection from qualified applicants, just like any other job around their nation. It was a position, with duties, not an all-powerful command.

Alex, while being called 'Founder', was given preferential respect on committees, but she was just a normal citizen, like the rest of them, and currently held the job title of 'General Labor Pool' and went around the station to help wherever needed. Currently, it appeared she was needed to sort out mass hysteria, craziness, and stupidity. They didn't have time for this kind of nonsense. She needed the community cohesive and caring toward each other. When the Earth finally failed, humanity was going to need to focus on humanity's survival, not individual goals. This misinformation seemed deliberate to divide Colony One's people and erode their faith in their country.

Alex peered through the other forums. Too many skewed-perspective topics were making people unreasonably angry or scared. Why was there a whole set of posts on the cancer citizens were going to get from space radiation? Where was this nonsense coming from?

Alex started digging through logs and building data-path maps. Several hours later, she had it. Behind many layers of obscure vectors, several nation states were deliberately engaging in misinformation warfare and sabotaging her country - actively trying to make people distrust Colony One's leadership and laws through Earth-side social media in the form of articles, posts, comics, and twisted news stories. The more emotional triggers they could push, the more likely the stories were to get shared.

Colony One, given its decisions by citizen votes, was highly vulnerable to misinformation campaigns. People who naturally tended toward extremist behavior and beliefs, both non-citizens and citizens, forwarded things along without research, and actively engaged in teaching others their 'facts'. This effectively polarized people on issues and created absurd flame wars in both public arenas and their country's private forums. Factual information was so dense, people didn't have the time or desire to dig through it. Even educated people fell into the emotional-trap on occasion.

Alex groaned and scheduled a meeting with the Colony One political structure committee and the information technology staff. Their solution, although labor intensive, was to create a department to preview and analyze every post before it appeared (either directly or edited) on the Colony One forums. Posts would not be modified or filtered, but would gain information analysis tags: Fact, Opinion, Hypothesis, Speculation, Inaccurate Correlation, Incomplete, Satire, Inaccurate, Advertisement, etc. These tags linked to supporting evidence.

If a citizen wasn't sure if something was real or valid, all they had to do was post it to the internal network. This wasn't a full solution, because the Earth-side networks were still inundated by certain nation-state generated propaganda, but it helped alleviate some of Colony One's citizen's ignorance. They also implemented mandatory flame war training, that while not enthusiastically embraced, at least sounded really fascinating and was made entertaining by applying copious levity.

Alex, with the help of several carefully selected people from Colony One's programming team, sent off a few server-crippling viruses to the two main groups producing the inflammatory content, and while it didn't stop them, it at least slowed them down long enough for Colony One's internal measures to take hold.

Specially created teams made sure Colony One's internal network was secure from external hackers. Not only was it completely separate from any external network, it was monitored and protected by both programs and humans actively dedicated to the task. Alex's picobots also invisibly watched for spies and internal threats and she dealt with these silently.

The United States and most of the other countries finally recognized Colony One's independence after a year and a half of absurd politics, and while Colony One wasn't accepted into the United Nations, at least they were allowed to trade, have limited tourism, and use travel passports. Both Alex and Brian were prohibited from traveling to the United States or any of its territories. Alex couldn't decide which brought more tourists - their location in space or the dynamic technology of SEL. Both citizen and tourist HUDs offered approved designs for vehicles and items, although tourists could only use a small subset and wouldn't be able to take anything created off the station.

Applications for citizenship rolled in and their population control team limited their growth to station-sustainable numbers. People applied and citizens could add bonus-points to their friends and family, recommending them for citizenship. Additional bonus-points were also given to people with necessary skills. Acceptance was then done by random selection of families, without regard to age, race, or education, weighted with the bonus-points. With this process, most people that were accepted were either skilled or known.

T plus 0:285:23:20   **~3π/4**

Having been requested from the general labor pool by Brian, Alex finished reviewing the security video and leaned forward and put her head down on her desk. The kid was clearly responsible for destruction of property - namely, one of the paintings in their local-art museum. He was completely out of control, temper-wise, and his heroin withdrawal symptoms were just starting. The tourist shuttle log showed his heroin stash getting quietly destroyed in transit as part of the security sweep. The kid's parents were overwhelmed.

Alex reviewed their current laws although she already knew the answer. The United States government had finally accepted Colony One as a country but diplomatic relationships were still strained. The teenager and his parents were United States citizens, but had signed the mandatory legal paperwork to obey and be bound to all Colony One laws, rules, and restrictions. They were already detained and awaiting sentencing.

The boy was barely 15 years old, but he'd reached his adult size and looked older. He was better dressed than the gang members that used to terrorize her when she lived on the street, but he had the same bearing, the same violent temper, and the same self-absorbed hatred. Statistically, his current path would either land him in jail or dead from gang activity or drugs. His parents were typical middle-class, caring people, and they'd certainly done their best and tried, but they couldn't control a heroin addict in a gang-controlled community.

Alex closed her eyes and recalled the painting the boy had destroyed. There had been a lifetime of skill and soul in that huge oil painting. Historically, it was important because it had been the painting that tipped the vote to create a paid, professional artist job within the community. The artist had donated it to their museum, so the painting hadn't been appraised, but Alex was certainly qualified to estimate it at half a million dollars.

293

Alex should have realized that with the influx of tourists, she needed to start staffing security personnel in the museum. The citizens understood value and wouldn't have considered destroying a community resource. But a tourist, having heroin withdrawal, combined with typical teenage angst...

Alex went to talk with the artist, Francis Wagner, a woman in her 40's who'd originally joined their company as part of the information technology team. Alex stepped into Fran's studio, noting that the air filtration system was working to keep the toxic fumes clear. Three of her walls were full-size digital displays currently showing the rolling hills of Ireland. The fourth had shelves with art supplies. The canvas in front of her was a full two meters with a landscape painting barely started.

"Hey, Fran," Alex said.

"Founder," Fran tilted her head in respectful greeting and set aside her brush and palette.

"I'm sorry about your painting," Alex said. "I should have protected it better. Now everything is encased in a SEL shield to prevent this from happening again."

Fran sighed. "Is the boy ok? I stopped reading the forums since realizing my fellow citizens want to space a kid." Fran's face stayed emotionlessly blank and she shifted her eyes back to her painting.

"He's fine," Alex replied. "He's just detained for the moment. We aren't going to execute him. Our laws aren't going to allow that. I can't say it was just a painting because I know better."

"Well, what's done is done. We have a digital image of it so it isn't gone completely, and truth be told, there were some things about it I didn't like." Fran finally made eye contact with Alex.

"The bane of being the artist. You see flaws no one else ever will and know which parts don't match your intentions." As far as Alex knew, Sal's brother still hadn't destroyed her own painting as requested. The people desperately trying to figure out her batteries would be shocked to know the answer was right there.

Fran smiled wryly. "So what can I do for you, Founder?"

"The law clearly says the boy has to pay for it. He's a minor, according to United States laws, so technically his parents are responsible, and there's no way they can pay what that painting was worth."

Fran nodded, listening intently, but the slight furrow in her eyebrows gave away her confusion.

"I don't think money matters anyway," Alex said.

"It doesn't anymore," Fran agreed, eyebrows still pulling together. She'd definitely benefited from having art supplies purchased by their country.

"The kid, though, he might be salvageable. He could be an adult if he were in our country," Alex continued, wondering what the best way to approach the subject was. She decided she might as well just say it. "We could put him on a work visa, keep him here until the debt is paid. Surround him with counselors and good examples. But he'd be on station and a constant reminder of the pain he caused you."

Fran frowned. "Wouldn't that have serious political repercussions?"

Alex was pleased the woman was thinking of Colony One more than herself and Alex half-smiled and shrugged. "His parents signed the waiver that they'd be bound by our laws and punishments while they were here. It could be made to work in our favor."

Fran nodded again. "I don't mind if he's here."

"I estimate your painting was worth around $500,000." Fran rolled her eyes at that so Alex continued, "He obviously can't pay that at our $40,000 per year wage. It would take him 12 years. I'm going to charge him $60,000 which will give him a year and a half sentence, and I'll cover the rest."

Fran's eyes narrowed. "But the money just goes back to the country anyway. I'm a professional artist."

"Actually, that painting was done before you were transferred to an artist job position so the money goes directly to you," Alex informed her.

Fran shook her head. "I don't need it."

Most citizens had discovered that they didn't have as much need for money - with housing, utilities, tuition, medical, and food expenses being fully covered by their six hour a day job, coupled with no real place to store a bunch of possessions, money wasn't as critical. Mostly, citizens used money to travel out of the country, to buy "real not SEL" things from Earth, or to pay bills for non-citizen relatives. Colony One's only export, long-life batteries in several sizes, not only covered any ambient loss of national wealth, but saw their balance increasing steadily.

The dynamics of this economy were only now beginning to become apparent. Distribution of limited goods was decided by random lot. The longer a person waited, the more times their name was added to the list. If a service wasn't available, people added a point to the job hiring priority and made do. Colony One was even gaining a subgroup of people who changed to priority jobs because they recognized that the station needed them. The general labor pool to which Alex was permanently assigned took care of the odds and ends as much as possible, but citizens were taking personal responsibility for the success of the society.

Alex agreed that Fran didn't need the money, but said, "Donate it if you like. You're the one who's been most harmed by the boy. Would you be ok with my solution?"

Fran glanced at her current painting project. "Yeah. It won't bother me. Might annoy other people though."

"Thank you, Fran. I'll see what I can come up with, but I wanted to check with you first." Alex realized from Fran's body language that the woman was a bit upset about her painting's destruction, but Fran seemed to be handling it well enough and would be all right. Alex left and went to discuss the punishment with Brian.

After a long talk with Brian about the potential repercussions, Alex set up the forum vote for the kid's punishment. She still had enough sway with the population that it would pass simply because she posted it. She rarely used that authority, saving it for when it was absolutely necessary. Brian added his clout. As Alex expected, the vote passed by majority before Alex arrived back at the security complex, despite not being a popular solution.

Alex spoke with the security guards, giving them explicit instructions, and went to the room where Cal and his parents were waiting. The room had a comfortable sofa, two soft chairs, as well as a door to a bathroom. One of the walls was a digital display set to the rainforest-style living wall in Hamasaki Corporation's lobby. Alex toggled it to a non-distracting neutral grey and said, "Mr. and Mrs. Park, I'm Alex Smith, Founder of Colony One."

Cal's parents stood and shook Alex's offered hand. They'd dealt with Cal being in trouble so many times before that they merely looked resigned, if slightly boggle-eyed at having the Founder's personal attention. Cal remained seated, bent forward slightly, with a surly expression on his face, but Alex noted he was also discreetly rubbing his side - that would be muscles cramps from his heroin withdrawal.

Alex didn't keep them in suspense. "Before coming onto our station, you agreed to be bound by our laws and rulings. The citizens of Colony One have ruled in accordance with our laws. Your son is an adult under our age-guidelines and is responsible for his own actions. He is being charged $60,000 for destruction of property." They cringed. Alex knew that wasn't in their budget. She continued indicating both parents, "And you are both being immediately deported for bringing a criminal into our country."

Cal's mother said, "We don't have that much money."

Cal's father took his wife's hand and said to her, "We can figure it out, dear."

Alex ran her fingers through her hair and said, "You aren't paying." She pointed at their son. "He is. He's to remain here on station and work at our standard citizen pay of $40,000 per year."

Cal's mother gasped and his father paled significantly.

"It comes to 390 work days, approximately a year and a half. Because we are not creating an indentured servant, his housing, food, and medical services will all be paid for." Out of Alex's own money. The 24-hour / 7 day per week social workers were going to be expensive, too. "You will not be permitted to pay any of the $60,000. That's his debt alone. He will also be required to personally apologize to the artist of the painting." That's when Cal finally seemed to recognize that he was actually in trouble and his parents weren't going to be his shield. His look of panic was almost enough payment.

Alex opened the room's door and the two security guards that were waiting there came in and asked Cal's parents to follow them.

"You can't keep our son," his mom cried.

"You signed the legally binding agreement before arriving on station," Alex said bluntly. "You're being taken to the shuttle port for immediate transfer back to Earth. All your belongings are waiting for you."

Cal's father, clearly intending on arguing the matter, said to his wife, "The United States government isn't going to allow this." He followed the security guards out, taking his wife with him. One of the security guards closed the door again.

Alex stared at Cal while he stared back sullenly; the look of panic was gone and was replaced by the promise of stubborn disobedience. Alex waited, giving the security guards enough time to take Cal's parents to another room where they could watch this conversation on a digital display until she had a chance to go talk with them. After a few minutes, the message from the security guard appeared on her HUD that his parents were watching.

Alex took a deep breath and said, "Cal, I want to be clear about your sentence. While you are here, you're required to follow the rules and regulations of our citizens, but without the benefits of being a citizen. You'll live in one of our permanent residences. You'll participate in the daily one hour exercise period. You will not be permitted to work more than 5 days per week, and to prevent any harm to yourself, our citizens, and our property, you will have a security escort at all times. While food and lodging are paid for, any non-essential incidentals are not covered, and you'll be responsible for any charges you incur. If you check your HUD, you'll see a list of current job openings for which you are qualified, as well as your current bank account balance." His account was set to -$60,000. He would not be able to remove either of those information boxes from his HUD. "Do you have any questions?"

Mutely, he shook his head and Alex didn't tell him to 'use words'. Instead she commented as if she didn't care at all, "That muscle cramping across your abdomen is standard heroin withdrawal."

"I don't use drugs," Cal denied vehemently.

"Certainly not anymore," Alex replied. "Surely you noticed that your private stash was confiscated during the flight up when we did the baggage scan. We don't have any heroin on the station and anything prescription is monitored. The withdrawal symptoms will get worse before they get better. We have medical technicians that can help with the pain. Medical is also covered and will not cost you anything. Would you prefer to visit them first or go directly to your new apartment?"

"I ain't gonna work for you guys. You can't make me." This was accompanied by pursed lips and a sneer.

Alex kept her voice coldly neutral. "True, but you're stuck here until the debt is paid. Medical or apartment, Cal?" Alex put her hand on her hip and raised her eyebrow at him.

Cal frowned sickly, like he might throw up, and doubled over as a massive cramp shook him. "Medical."

"Good choice." Alex opened the door again and a pair of security guards came to escort Cal to medical. Alex then went to join his parents. This conversation would determine how much political backlash Colony One was going to get.

The small office had a desk with two occupied guest chairs. The digital display on one wall showed Cal being taken to medical. Alex reduced the volume on the display, and said, without preamble, "Your son needs help."

"We'll get him help," Cal's father said. "Let him come home with us. We'll pay the $60,000. I have medical insurance. We can put him in a rehab hospital."

Alex moved around the desk and sat down and said, "I want you to seriously evaluate this opportunity I'm offering. Consider this a rehab hospital. The $60,000 was just a token amount to give him a goal. We'll have him with a fully trained social worker or counselor at all times and our medical staff is excellent. He won't be able to relapse because he won't be around his old drug-dealing gang-friends."

"But $60,000?" Cal's mother whispered, "That's too much."

"Not really," Alex said. "It creates enough time to get the heroin out of his system completely and for new habits to form. The painting was valued at $500,000. By time you add medical costs, psychological staff, and living expenses, the bill is substantial. I'm personally paying the difference."

"Why?" Cal's father asked.

"He's a kid in need. I lived on the streets when I was younger than him." They looked surprised. Alex's past was not published. "I can tell you right now that he's headed for drug overdose, gang death, or prison, and I've personally seen all three of those up close and intimately. If I can help him, maybe it will relieve some of my own ghosts?" And what ghosts had Sal appeased when he'd helped her? Alex shoved that thought aside for later reflection.

Alex shrugged. "Look, you can keep your HUDs and see and hear him whenever you want, so you'll know he's safe and not being mistreated. I'll give you my personal phone number so you can call me and talk about his rehab at any time. Let him think he's alone and has to take responsibility for himself. We'll make sure he can't hurt himself or anyone else. This is a safe, healthy environment. I'm simply offering you help for your son, not trying to inflict some horrible punishment." On the monitor, Cal doubled over, grabbing his stomach. His guards waited patiently until he could straighten again, and then helped him to their outpatient office.

Cal Park was a piece of work - stubborn, rude, insubordinate beyond belief. He'd been on the station for four months. Almost all of his heroin-addiction symptoms were gone after the first month. He celebrated not having to go to school (that was a citizen benefit) by buying himself a gaming console and then spent almost all of his time playing video games and ignoring his "escort". He refused to bathe and after his social workers complained about the smell, Alex had surrounded Cal with a SEL shield that filtered the odor, although Cal still thought he was torturing other people. He hadn't worked a single day and never went to the exercise areas. As he was not allowed to bring food back to his apartment, he had to go out at least a couple times a day to eat.

His social workers were told to just stay with him and listen if he wanted to talk. Cal had tried to cut his wrists at one point with a sharp knife, only to discover that the blade wouldn't go into his skin. He tried torturing the night-shift worker by going out to eat in the middle of the night, but that social worker had merely shrugged and pointed out that it was ok to go out at night if he wanted.

Cal's parents were understandably concerned. They were the ones who suggested taking away his gaming console and Alex agreed that it was time for more active intervention, but not a phone call from them. "I'll take care of it," Alex promised and signed up for a week-long day-shift as Cal's "security guard".

Alex arrived promptly at 7 a.m. on Monday morning. The social worker on duty passed her the bracelet with the invisible cage-leash that prevented Cal from simply running away. "No change," the man whispered. Cal was still asleep on his bed.

"Thank you," Alex replied quietly, switching on the light in Cal's one room apartment as the social worker departed. The room contained Cal's bed, desk, TV, gaming console, and a remote game controller in a comfortable reclining chair. Clothes from his suitcase were strewn about, unwashed. The room stank. Quite probably, the toilet in the bathroom with a half-height privacy door was not atomized and flushed. Alex activated a nose filter and pondered the room.

"Hey, turn off the light," Cal grumbled, not moving.

"Good morning, Cal," Alex said energetically and loudly. "Time to get up and get ready for the day. I have a lot of things I need to get done today and you're coming along."

"Am not," Cal grumbled, pulling the blanket over his head.

"30 minutes and we go for breakfast. You should probably get dressed. A shower is recommended."

"Where's my security guard?" came the mumbled voice from under the blanket.

"I'm it for the week," Alex answered cheerfully. "The regulars are all tired of watching you play video games all day."

299

"You can't force me to do anything. I'm going back to sleep." He rolled to face away from her and hid his head under his pillow.

"Technically, your other escorts have been instructed not to force you to do anything. I don't have that restriction. Today you're on my time." Alex sat down in the comfortable chair provided for the social workers and reviewed the country's forums until precisely 7:30.

Alex stood up, stretched, and announced, "Breakfast time." She had her picobots tilt his bed and roll him out onto the floor, carefully so he wouldn't be hurt, but fast enough to be jarring. When he stood up sputtering, Alex opened the apartment door and left. Her picobots pushed him along behind her. He was still in his underwear, so Alex adjusted the lightwaves around his invisible cage to give him clothing to prevent citizens and tourists from getting upset. Cal still thought he was in his underwear and said so, loudly. Not changing her brisk walking pace, she answered, "You had a half hour to get dressed. Maybe tomorrow will be different." She had her picobots give him SEL socks and sneakers.

Alex went directly to the local cafeteria and got in line. The cafeteria wasn't as nice as the fair-like atmosphere of the rest of the restaurant zone, but it was fast, with no custom orders slowing down the line. The individual restaurants in the zone were operating on a survival of the fittest method. To stay in business, they had to maintain a minimum monthly customer rate. Space and supplies were provided by Colony One and tourist-profit went back to the country. Food price included operation cost. People who really liked to prepare magnificent meals got to do so.

People saw who was following Alex and shook their heads in sympathy. She took a tray and offered it to Cal, "You want anything to eat?"

When he shook his head stubbornly, Alex shrugged and got herself some raw fruit and vegetables, letting the picobots steer Cal to stay with her. She found an empty table in the busy cafeteria and sat down. Cal refused to join her and stood over her, hovering with his arms crossed, trying to intimidate her. Alex used her HUD to fire off a reassuring note to Cal's parents, who were watching intently.

Midway through her breakfast, one of the chief architects came by. He glanced at Cal, but pressed on. "Hey, Founder, can I get you to review the plans for the new theater? The zoning people are trying to steal our location for another tourist shopping center."

"Ah," Alex said. "I saw that this morning. We didn't approve it yet because it needs to be bigger."

"We're within space budget," the architect said proudly, straightening his shoulders and grinning.

Alex nodded. "Yeah, we need to reallocate some things. I'll send off a note to zoning so they can't have your spot, but double the size of the theater. The resources planning committee wants a bigger theater."

The architect smiled, apologized for interrupting her breakfast, and wandered away, already adjusting things on his HUD.

Alex looked up at Cal. "You ever been to a real theater, Cal? Not one of those movie theaters, but one with a stage and live performers?" she asked conversationally.

Cal pursed his lips and deliberately, rudely, turned his head away from her.

When Alex was finished eating, she got up, returned her tray and dishes to the SEL recycling location, and went to make her rounds. Cal did not have a choice about following her, although at one point, he tried sitting down, and was pushed along behind Alex at no effort to her at all. Alex adapted and took the cobblestone paths designed to generate more exercise through subtle hills and less flat-walking. He acquired a few sore spots from the bumpy path, but he was in no danger. He stood up eventually and followed along sullenly.

Alex started at one of the food greenhouses. The kindergarten class was just arriving. "Good morning, everyone!" Alex greeted them happily.

They replied with an enthusiastic synchronized, "Good morning, Founder!"

"Field trip today?" Alex asked.

The teacher nodded. One of the less shy children announced, "We're going to plant tomatoes!"

Alex rubbed her hands together. "Excellent! I love tomatoes. I just had one for breakfast, in fact."

Several kids wrinkled their noses, adding their thoughts about that menu item.

Alex grinned. "True, it's not the breakfast of choice for everyone. Well, have fun, class. Learn a lot today."

The students followed their teacher back farther into the greenhouse, while Alex turned toward the greenhouse office. As they moved away, she heard one of the kids ask their teacher, "Isn't that the boy who destroyed the painting?"

"It is," the teacher answered, her tone trying to end the inquiry.

"But why would he do that?" the child persisted. "It belonged to everybody."

"He didn't understand what he was doing." The rest of the teacher's answer was lost as they moved out of range.

Alex didn't change her pace or look back, and she didn't smile, although she wanted to. Counseling by kindergartener was just right. She couldn't have done better if she had planned it. She went into the office, holding the door so Cal could enter too.

"Founder!" The woman at the desk smiled, looking up. "What can I do for you today?"

"I'm just coming by to see how things are going," Alex said. "Do you need anything?"

The woman glanced at Cal, but apparently decided if Alex didn't seem to

301

mind if he were there, she wouldn't either. "We're actually doing pretty well, although we could use more space."

Everyone wanted more space, Alex reflected. They simply didn't have enough mass to expand at a rate their population increase demanded, even with each shuttle bringing up at least double what it took down and her scavengers out collecting space debris. They needed a large asteroid to come close enough to capture and convert.

The woman pulled up statistics on her digital display, presenting atmospheric constituents, plant populations and needs, and soil chemical analyses. About 10 minutes into this riveting dissertation, Cal started opening and slamming the office door.

Alex stood up and said politely, "Excuse me a moment." She took Cal outside of the office and "secured" his invisible cage near the door. She soundproofed it such that he could hear anything outside, but no one could hear any noise he chose to make inside. She set her HUD to monitor him and she went back into the office. It only took him about three minutes to start screaming and punching the invisible wall. Alex modified the wall to be squishy so he couldn't hurt himself and focused on the woman's presentation.

Afterward, Alex went out and peered down at Cal. He had finally settled down and was sitting with his knees pulled up to his chest. He glared at her and stood up. Alex grinned at him and said, "I hear you've skipped a few exercise periods. I need to get mine done, so we'll do that next."

Just outside the greenhouse, Alex paused to create a double-size restroom in the designated area and went in. Cal got dragged in behind her. She raised a privacy shield for herself and used the facilities. Then she lowered the shield and told him, "Your turn. Go while you have a chance. We're not stopping mid-exercise. You should also drink some water from the sink. You're dehydrated."

"I'm not using the bathroom with you watching." Cal crossed his arms.

Alex raised the privacy shield half-way, pointed, and leaned against the wall, tenting her fingers, and waiting. He did actually use the bathroom, but he didn't use the cup at the sink to get a drink. She set her HUD to observe his vital signs, and sent off a note to his parents that she was monitoring him and wouldn't let him go beyond his capabilities. He did not wash his hands.

Alex led them to the deciduous forest and set out at a pace that would push him, although it wouldn't exert her at all. Cal panted behind her, dragging his feet. Although they were nowhere near their fully grown size, the mid-May, late spring trees were dropping pollen and showing early leaves. Leaves from the previous "winter" crunched underneath their feet on the dirt and rock path and only distant birdsong could be heard. An occasional newt could probably be found if they had stopped to pick up one of the larger rocks along the side of the path, but Alex chose to push onward. They were making too much noise to see any of the larger wild animals. Several groups of people passed them, walking both faster and quieter.

After a half mile, Alex judged Cal needed a break and slowed down a little. Then she turned to head back, picking up the pace again when his heart rate normalized. When they got back, she created a restroom again and this time, he did get a drink.

Alex went to the flat grassland habitat reminiscent of the Pampas in Argentina next and started on the high-walk, a semitransparent bridge that did a full loop over the habitat for animal watching. Matching its original habitat, the grassland reflected the comfortably cooler temperatures of late autumn, with golden and green tall grasses and scattered short red and brown-leaved trees and clumps of tall pampas grass with their white-topped plumes.

Again, Alex set a pace that would push Cal. He didn't make it as far before he again needed the pace slowed. This time, she didn't turn around, but instead kept going, just at a much slower walk. The entire time, joggers zipped past them.

Alex stopped briefly over a scrubby woodland area, created a pair of SEL binoculars, gave one set to Cal, and pointed out the beautiful spotted Geoffroy's cat. "That one's male. They're larger than the females. They eat lizards and rodents mainly." Cal didn't comment, but she could tell he was awed.

Alex noticed the time. "Lunch?"

He nodded mutely.

She created an air vehicle for two and flew out of the habitat. Again, she took him to the local cafeteria. This time he took his own tray. He turned to go to the cooked food line and Alex shook her head, "You're on my diet today. All the fresh fruit, nuts, and vegetables you want. Help yourself." She moved down the raw-food line at a pace that would let him select things, while getting her own food. He looked like he wanted to kill her, but he took a couple pieces of fruit. Alex smiled at him and suggested, "Might want to get a big salad also. I have a lot to do yet this afternoon before dinner."

Cal ignored her.

Alex picked another empty table and sat. He also sat and ate his fruit. She could tell that once he started eating, he discovered he was ravenous and the two pieces of fruit disappeared. She ate slowly, waiting for him to get the nerve to ask her if she'd take him to get more. His stubbornness won.

After lunch, Alex subjected him to a tour of Sal's house, offering additional insights to the tour-guides-in-training. Cal avoided looking at any of the paintings the same way Alex avoided looking at the grand piano. They navigated around the people studying unobtrusive signs explaining the art and sculptures.

Once they were done in Sal's house, Alex led him through the cloud forest habitat, again pushing him as much as she could. Here, the trail was a beautiful suspended walkway to keep feet safe from the mud below and keep the habitat safe from visitors. Invisible SEL shielding prevented snakes and other wildlife from interacting with the many visitors.

"Hard to believe we're at the tail end of the dry season, isn't it?" Alex commented, pointing out an adorable little frog on a nearby lush, green tree. "This place matches the Reserva Biológica Bosque Nuboso Monteverde in Costa Rica."

After they'd gone a short distance, she turned around and headed back out again. The poor kid was sweaty, hungry, and miserable, a condition exacerbated by the warm fog. The walkway was also more crowded than Alex preferred.

Alex announced, "Next up. Hair salon. You will get a wash and a cut, because I'm getting my hair done, and you're on my time this week."

Cal frowned but wisely chose not to argue or maybe he was just too exhausted to argue.

Alex instructed the stylist to cut his hair very short. Just having his hair less greasy was a huge improvement. No more gang-long hair. He might even look like a normal kid if he would lose the surly attitude.

"Aren't you supposed to be done working by now?" Cal asked grouchily, "You guys are only supposed to work six hours."

"Yeah, I'm only going to work six hours, but I've only clocked two so far. I'm not counting the exercise periods or the meal times, because I have to do those anyway." She planned to stretch it to a full two shifts. His counselors certainly needed the break.

His hopes dashed, Cal followed her morosely to the next activity. Alex then walked him through the shopping zone, checking in at each shop to see how the proprietors were doing and to ask if they needed anything. Everyone wanted more space. Alex reflected that with the number of people zipping around, the requests were certainly valid.

Three hours later, Alex judged Cal had had enough walking, and took him back to the cafeteria for an early dinner. This time, however, she had mercy and took him down the cooked food line. He didn't hesitate to take a large quantity of food. She picked yet another empty table and they sat.

"So what do you think of our shopping zone?" she asked, giving him yet another opportunity to converse like a normal person.

Cal glared at her.

Alex pretended he'd responded favorably. "See any stores you might want to work at?"

Cal didn't answer, but instead turned in his seat so he was facing away from her while he finished eating.

After dinner, Alex walked Cal slowly around the station until 6:45 p.m. and then returned him to his apartment. "I'll see you tomorrow morning at 7, Cal. You should probably be showered and dressed by 7:30. If you don't select a job to do, you can hang out with me again while I do mine."

His other social worker didn't comment as Alex passed along the bracelet.

"Have a great night you two!" Alex departed. When she got back to her apartment, Alex called his parents and had a long talk, reassuring them that their son was going to be fine.

The next day, Alex arrived promptly at 7 a.m. to find Cal still sound asleep. She took the bracelet from the social worker and sat down to review the forums in the dark until precisely 7:30 a.m. She then switched on the light and had his bed tip him out again.

"You didn't wake me up at 7," Cal grumped.

"Was I supposed to?" Alex asked calmly. He didn't answer and glared at her, so she again dragged him out into the hallway in his underwear, gave him socks and shoes and some clothing he couldn't see.

At breakfast, Cal took some fruits and ate them. Afterward, Alex slowly walked him around the station until she was sure his breakfast had digested suitably, and then she took him to one of the water parks. "Can you swim?" When he didn't immediately answer, she commented while studying her fingernails, "We can spend the morning walking laps in the baby pool or we can spend it on the adult side." She knew from talking with his parents that he could swim just fine.

"I can swim," Cal snarled.

"Excellent," Alex chirped enthusiastically. "We'll have more fun than we would in the baby pool." She created a double-size bathroom again. She went in, used the bathroom shielded from his view again, and swapped her SEL outfit to a one-piece swimsuit. She created some SEL swim trunks and held them out. "Put them on or swim in your underwear. Your choice."

He scowled but took the swim trunks behind the half-shield and put them on. He tossed his very nasty underwear at her. She caught them and set them on the sink counter, and made a show of washing her hands.

Alex turned and smiled at him. "Good choice. Now, you have to shower before you can get in the pool. There's shampoo and soap over there." She pointed at a newly added shower in their bathroom.

Cal crossed his arms stubbornly and didn't move.

"10 minutes. I'll wait." Alex leaned back against the wall and watched her clock while reading forums. He didn't move either.

Precisely 10 minutes later, Alex announced, "It's time. You still need a shower though." She pretended to think about this and then had the picobots push him into the shower and directed the shower to spray him with warm water. Then she had it douse him with warm, sudsy water, while he sputtered unhappily. When he was suitably bubbly, she stopped the water and advised cheerfully, "You should probably scrub under your armpits." This time he did as directed. She had the shower rinse him off again, making sure the soap was off both him and his SEL swimsuit.

"Great!" Alex said, surveying him. "Let's go swim!" For the rest of the morning, she took him up and down waterslides, careful to pace him so he didn't get over-exerted or exhausted, but certainly enough to make him a bit achy from a good workout. They had plenty of rest periods while waiting in lines to use the slides.

Afterwards, Alex took him to lunch, again going down the raw-food line. Cal gazed longingly at the warm foods, but didn't say anything. While they were eating, she asked, "Which park would you like to hike in this afternoon?"

"None of them."

Alex was privately pleased he actually answered at all. "Ah, good. My choice then. We didn't get very far in the cloud forest yesterday. That one is my favorite - so incredibly green."

Cal grimaced. "We did the one hour exercise period today."

"Aren't you four months behind on exercise periods?" Alex ate a wedge of tomato from her large salad. The perfectly ripe tomato delighted her. Colony One was quickly gaining a reputation for having the best food of any country.

Cal didn't reply this time and didn't respond to any of Alex's other attempts at engaging him in conversation either.

After lunch, Alex took him through the industrial zone, pointing out opportunities for employment that he was qualified for. Naturally, he showed no interest whatsoever and didn't even bother to acknowledge her speaking. When they finished that tour, Alex hiked him through the cloud forest until it was dinner time. Thankfully, there were less people on the suspended path than the previous day. The heat and humidity had both of them sweaty and wilted-looking, although only Cal was exhausted.

At precisely 6:45 p.m., Alex returned Cal to his apartment and repeated, "I'll see you tomorrow morning at 7, Cal. You should probably be showered and dressed by 7:30. If you don't select a job to do, you can hang out with me again while I do mine."

At 7 a.m. the next day, Cal was already at the cafeteria eating, hiding at a corner table with his social worker. Perhaps Cal didn't realize that his social worker had simply sent Alex a note about where to meet them and this relocation didn't inconvenience Alex at all.

Alex got her food and joined them at the table, noting Cal had a large meal of eggs, toast, and cereal. She took the bracelet from the social worker and let the tired man depart without comment.

Alex sipped at her tea and said conversationally, "Today, I thought we'd go through the farm fields to see if there are any jobs there that you might like to do."

Cal gave her a dirty look, but didn't respond.

Midway through their walking tour of the farm fields, Alex got a call from Brian. She answered it, not hiding the volume from Cal. Part of her plan was to let Cal experience someone else's day. "What's up, Brian?"

"We need you in Emergency Response immediately. Our people at our Pacific island reported a moderate, but extended, earthquake at 36 degrees north, 169 degrees west, which they said is in the ocean off Japan, and asked if it was enough for a tsunami. I got our Earth sciences staff to look at it, and they just registered a second 7.8 quake, which will definitely make one. We have confirmed the wave that will make landfall in the 2-3 hour range."

Alex inhaled sharply, trying to visualize the world map in her mind. The latitude and longitude text of the map in her memory was too small for her to make out. "I'm on my way. Put the information we have on our company website and let our employees know. Get word out on the social media networks."

"Already doing that. I'm also scrambling our pilots and medical personnel," Brian informed her. "The Pacific island is already sending what personnel and resources they can."

"I'll be there in about 10 minutes. Have the scientists ready to brief me." Alex cut off the call, selected a vehicle designed for two on her HUD, created it, and pushed Cal in as she got in herself. She flew as fast as safety would allow, muttering, "This station is too big."

Rather than navigate the inevitable traffic on its way to Emergency Response, Alex decided it would be faster to go outside the station and fly directly around to the space port and enter that way. She angled her vehicle, adjusted the shielding for space, and then sped through the station's sky-window. The picobots automatically adjusted the SEL window to create a temporary airlock to let her through.

Alex accelerated and the vehicle zipped over the edge of the massive disk-shaped station. The gravity in the vehicle stayed constant, negating any rollercoaster effect. The view of the Earth below was showing the beautiful hues of daylight over North America.

Only when they were almost at the docking bay did Alex notice that Cal was huddled into a ball, looking terrified. She immediately swapped the vehicle's transparent outer hull for an opaque one. "Sorry about that," she apologized, "I forget not everyone can handle being so close to the reality of space." She brought her vehicle to a sliding fast landing, and dissolved it, sprinting toward the Emergency Response's conference room with Cal floating behind her so he wouldn't have to run.

The conference room was configured as a moderately sized theater with huge floor-to-ceiling digital displays in a semi-circle with terraced desks and chairs facing it. People were still arriving and filling in the space. No one was sitting. People saw Alex and parted, clearing a path for her toward the front where Brian waited. He spotted her and flickered the lights so everyone would stop talking. To one of the scientists, Brian commanded, "You're up."

With his voice amplified so everyone could hear, the lead scientist began detailing both earthquakes and the aftershocks, complete with Earth-image overlays and wave-estimates on the center screen. Actual data was displayed to the right and graphs and predictions on the left. He talked fast and did not explain any of the underlying concepts.

When he stopped speaking and looked at Alex, she said, "Put line numbers on that data display." As she was now standing with Brian and the scientist on the dais, her voice was also amplified. There was a delay while that was done. When the line numbers appeared, Alex said, "Line 38 looks wrong. Where's Lucas? We need that math checked." Alex reflected that having Lucas handle all recent calculations had left her woefully out of practice. She ought to be able to sort this out.

"Visiting his family in Argentina," Brian replied. "We haven't been able to reach him."

"How many models do we have for this scenario?" Alex asked.

"Just the one up there that we just did," the lead scientist answered. "We've got some land-based earthquakes modeled, but we haven't had time..."

"Don't apologize," Alex said. "Let's see what we can do for the problem at hand."

Someone shouted from the back, "I've found the error; I'm sending the new data to the server now. It affects... um... everything after line 34."

The data refreshed and someone else shouted. "That can't be right. Line 58 is missing the tidal amplitude."

Alex bit her lip and said, "Ok, I want everyone calculating scientific data on that side of the room." She pointed to her left. "Medical personnel and supply people to the back center, and pilots, over here." People self-sorted. Brian nodded to Alex and went to the medical group. Alex set up sound barriers between the sections and joined the pilots. Cal floated along behind her, forgotten.

Alex lowered her arm like a hatchet through the center of the group. "Everyone this side and over, I want you in your vehicles and out right now. Head for Hawaii. We'll get you destinations as soon as our scientists have landfall calculations. Your task is to pick up and relocate people until the waves hit and then to help with rescue efforts." Those people departed. To the remaining people, she said, "The rest of you are going to do the same thing, but you're taking medical personnel and supplies as soon as they're ready. As soon as the other vehicles are out, get your own ready."

Alex left them and relocated to the scientists. They'd thrown a pair of formulas up on their display and were discussing adjustments while someone made the edits. Alex added her own comments. Fifteen precious minutes later, they were mostly in agreement. "Is that what we use, Everyone?" Alex asked.

Most nodded. The presenter replied, "It's as good as we can get without more data and statistical analysis."

Alex looked back at the screen and said, "Ok, then, let's see the data." The screen changed. They had an hour and twenty minutes before the first landfall. Their first pilots couldn't be there for another hour. Alex phoned Brian, even though he was just across the room, "Get those medical personnel out right now even if they don't have enough supplies. We'll send more down as soon as we can. They can also get some from locals."

"If we can get airspace restrictions lifted. We should already have requests in to the major governments." Brian disconnected.

Alex looked around at the eight scientists. "Good job, everyone. You saved lives today, recognizing the threat and getting the warning out. I need everyone to pick a location in the top eight by population and that's your domain. I'll issue you pilots based on your geography and urgency and I need you to coordinate rescue efforts. Spread out in this room. I'll give you people to help as soon as I can." They self-sorted while Alex used her HUD to pick a pilot to send to the Aleutians West Census Area at the northern side of the Pacific, and direct two pilots to start at the smaller islands south and west of Hawaii.

Alex's HUD lit with an incoming call and answered it. "Founder, the Prime Minister of Japan is on the line. Shall I patch him through?"

"Yeah." Alex created as small, private room around herself and Cal to cut the noise down. In Japanese, without preamble, Alex said, "Prime Minister, you have a tsunami that will reach Chiba in one hour and seven minutes."

"We're already evacuating coastline areas. We appreciate the warning. We'd like assistance from your flying vehicles."

"I'm already sending what I can to you along with medical personnel. May we enter your airspace?"

"Yes, of course."

"Do you have an English-speaking point of contact I can give to my coordination team?" He gave her the information and Alex thanked him. "Prime Minister, we will do everything we can to assist you, but I have other people I need to speak with." She hung up on him and looked over at her charge. "How are you doing, Cal?"

"I have to use the bathroom," he whispered.

Alex turned their little room into a bathroom, but with the smaller size, she merely faced away from him to give him privacy, and then made him do the same. She dropped the room when they were done, and scattered noise dampeners all over the room so people could hear others standing next to them without shouting.

For the next forty-five minutes, Alex fielded phone calls from different governments and redirected communications to the right people. Brian issued the scientists additional personnel and delegated the parsing of the pilots to his HR manager. The three screens showed updated data and one of the programmers had managed to tie the wave peak data to the map so they had a real-time indicator of the waves. The room braced for the first impact.

Even with an almost two hour warning, the 30 meter wave was devastating. They started receiving live video feeds from their pilots and someone began sorting through them and putting key ones up on the left-most screen. Someone came over to Alex and after pulling on her arm to get her attention, said, "I have a room full of medical supplies out there and no qualified pilots to take it to the surface." Alex nodded and said she'd take care of it, but she was immediately snagged to sort out a communication failure for the Philippines team.

Even with noise dampeners, the room volume was high as people tried to coordinate rescue efforts and medical personnel. Images of buildings being pushed over with people still on them appeared on the screen, with her solitary pilot at that location trying desperately to get people from the water with dangling rope ladders and baskets. Colony One personnel were doing their best, but they were unprepared for rescue response, and there simply weren't enough personnel at each location to make much difference. They were also reporting to and working with the local governments so there was some confusion in coordination. This was the biggest wave in a long time. The center screen split into news feeds with graphic images.

Cal touched Alex's arm and she glanced over at him. "Medical supplies," he whispered timidly, afraid to talk.

"Oh! Thank you, Cal. I forgot." She left the chaotic room and dashed into the abandoned adjacent spaceport with Cal trailing along behind her. She looked at the massive pile of supplies and felt like weeping, instead she swore. "I have twelve locations that critically need supplies in proportionate amounts and they give me one mound of supplies?" She swore again. "Cal, help me get this sorted into twelve piles. Make it as equal as you can. I'm going to go get some help." She cut his cage loose and left him.

Alex came back with a group of teenagers and a dozen adults. Cal had made some headway on creating individual piles. Alex generated location-destination signs above each of the twelve piles and sent everyone in the room a list of which location should get what and then she split the volunteers into twelve groups. The supply lists were based on information coming in from the local governments. She put Cal in the highest-need group because he was most familiar with where supplies were located in the mound.

Alex stepped off to the side and created a sound-bubble around herself and began programming drones that could carry supplies to their needed locations. It was faster than trying to explain to someone what was needed. She periodically glanced up to see how the sorting was going. When she thought she had the programming correct so the drones would avoid any collisions, she sent the code off to their lead programmer for review. He responded about ten minutes later with a few minor edits and the comment that the anti-collision code was now right but he had no idea if the location physics was. The piles had just been finished.

Alex instructed everyone to move off to one side and wrapped each bundle in its own drone-vehicle and sent it on its way. These would start reaching their destinations in about 30 minutes because the station had relocated above the epicenter and had its orbit adjusted to match. They would still need to wait until the wave subsided enough to let the rescuers in safely and the local governments directed distribution. She thanked and dismissed the adults and teenagers and reattached Cal to herself with another bathroom break. When that was done, she went back into the Emergency Response conference room.

The high school students returned and passed out bag lunches to everyone. Alex didn't get a chance to eat hers, because people kept needing her for something, and it was eventually forgotten on one of the desks. Cal ate his and got pulled along after Alex as she went from location team to location team helping however she was able. At each team, she made sure to say encouraging things and thank them for their effort. Colony One's programming team launched a database for people to register so they could find their families and translators were brought in to log people in rescue vehicles.

At one point, Alex paused to watch the graphic video displayed on the left-most monitor. Those were raw, unedited live-feeds of the massive destruction, rescue efforts, and medical services. She wondered briefly if she should be exposing Cal to that, but she didn't have the energy to try and find a suitable escort that could take him away. She resumed going from team to team.

Eventually, the same high school students came and distributed bag dinners. Alex managed to get a couple bites of the hearty vegetarian sandwich, before getting pulled away again. Around 3 a.m., teams started finishing up, having delivered those rescued to appropriate medical facilities in their native countries. Medical personnel and pilots were given the option to stay and help if they were invited to do so by the local government and the others were told to return home to sleep.

Alex created a cot for Cal off to one side of the room and continued assisting with translations and anything else that people had questions about. She started sending people off to sleep in shifts and worked with those who remained to keep their communications up. She noticed Cal didn't sleep either, but instead, lay on his cot watching her. She sent him a reassuring smile and a nod every so often, and went back to the task at hand.

This continued for another day and pilots and medical personnel started returning and local organizations took over disaster recovery. Alex kept Cal with her. She personally shook each person's hand and thanked them and told them they were heroes. Each and every one had that glazed war-trauma stare. Alex had counselors waiting to help. She often repeated, "Rescue swimmers and rescue teams have a lot more training. You did awesome. You saved a lot of people."

Later that night, Alex called the key people to one of the company conference rooms. "We did good, people," she began. "That was awesome teamwork. But we need to know what to do better for next time."

"He shouldn't be here," Brian said, indicating Cal.

Cal shrunk back into himself. Alex responded, "He stays. He was critical to getting our medical supplies out as quickly as we did."

Cal blinked at this and uncurled a little.

"So what can we do better?" Brian asked, returning to the topic without argument.

The brainstorming session lasted three hours. While Cal did not say anything, he was certainly listening.

After the meeting, Alex made her way back to Cal's apartment as he followed behind. She opened his door and said, "Sometimes one of my work days is pretty long," Alex smiled her thanks to the waiting social worker and then refocused on Cal. "Look, these escorts you have with you all the time are trained counselors." The man waiting nodded in cheerful affirmation of this and Alex continued without pausing, "You saw a lot of scary and disturbing things in the last two days. You might experience nightmares or waking daymares. If you need to, talk with them. They'll keep it confidential. It's not a weakness to be upset or disturbed. It's a normal human response to trauma." On that pleasant note, Alex went to find her own bed.

Alex was eating a late dinner the following Wednesday when Cal's morning counselor found her. He sat down with a token drink.

"What's up?" Alex asked, yawning. She'd had a busy five days since leaving Cal back at his room. Their emergency response was woefully inefficient and she and a team of people were working on plans to improve the system.

"He asked about you three times," the counselor said.

"Three, huh?" Alex set down her spoon.

The counselor grinned. "For him, that's loquacious. He asked if you were coming back to guard him again. About two hours later, he asked if you knew what the news is saying about you. Then, just as I was leaving my shift, he asked how often we counselors talked with you."

"Wow. That's practically a soliloquy," Alex said with a grin.

"Yeah." The counselor tilted his coffee and swirled it, but did not lift it to his mouth. "He hasn't turned on his video game console either. He watches the news and stares at the wall."

"I'll come by tomorrow during your shift," Alex said.

"Thanks, Founder." The man took his drink over to recycling and dropped it off, and then headed toward the residential area.

The next day, Alex chanced to arrive for her breakfast midway through Cal's lunch. She took her tray over to Cal and his counselor. "Hi, guys! Mind if I join you?"

"Please, Founder," the counselor said. "I need to use the restroom." He passed her the bracelet and left the food court to politely create his temporary room in the designated area.

Cal watched the man go with a look akin to desperation, as if he wanted to run after him, shouting, "Please don't leave me with her!"

"How are things going, Cal?" Alex asked, wondering how obvious the ploy was.

"Ok, I guess." Cal looked at his plate and pushed his sandwich over a little.

Alex waited. Compared to her last cafeteria meal with Cal, his reply was a miracle.

After a minute, Cal said, "Have you seen the news?"

"I have." She'd reviewed the latest that very morning in preparation for this conversation. The media was viciously attacking her and Colony One, saying that more lives could have been saved if Colony One hadn't been so stingy and uncaring. "They aren't very happy with Colony One this week. What do you think? You were there."

"They're lies," Cal pronounced. "Why don't you defend yourself?"

"I could argue all day long and never change their mind; they won't believe the truth. It's a battle I can't win." Alex shrugged in acceptance of this sad fact. "Besides, I've been too busy working on our emergency response. Got to overhaul it so we can do better next time."

Cal stared at his plate and said nothing.

Alex waited again, eating some of her oatmeal.

"I want to work in the emergency response center." Cal's voice was barely audible.

Alex set her spoon down. "Hmmm. What would you like to do there?"

"I dunno." Cal pushed his sandwich again. "It could be a lot better organized, is all."

"How so?" Alex was careful to set her tone curious, not the least bit derisive.

The response was a long time coming again. "Well, everyone's so busy looking at the details, no one sees the whole picture."

Alex and her team had been considering that very thing that morning. She and Brian couldn't run response in an emergency. They were needed in too many other places. She studied Cal. "You were in a unique position to observe everything. What do you recommend?" He didn't answer so Alex prompted, "You know, without critique, we can't improve. It's ok to speak up."

313

After almost a full minute, Cal said, "That one big room doesn't work."

"No, it doesn't. What do you think we need?"

"Well, a separate cafeteria. All those lunch bags got in the way at the computer stations. People were too burned out and made mistakes. They need to leave the room every so often to clear their head."

Alex nodded. "I agree. What else?"

"It also needs a viewing area. Lots of people kept coming through and getting in the way even though they weren't working. They kept interrupting people for updates." Cal spoke quickly, as if afraid to stop once he started.

Alex hadn't noticed the interruptions probably due to her own constant interruptions, but she looked back through her memory and saw Cal was correct.

"People didn't know what they were doing or where they were going." Cal stared at his food.

Alex said, "I have a team of people working on this problem."

Cal exhaled, slumping forward, obviously disheartened.

"You could join them, I suppose," Alex said quickly. "You don't have the background or experience necessary, but that doesn't make your observations invalid."

Cal finally made eye contact with her. "Really?"

"Sure. I'll create the job posting for you and you can start tomorrow. Your counselor can help you find it." His counselor, having received a message from Alex, arrived back in time to hear this.

"I can," Cal's counselor said, taking his seat again. Alex passed him the bracelet. "Thank you, Founder."

Alex smiled at the two of them, took the remainder of her meal to recycling, and went back to work. She had a detailed conversation with the team working on their new emergency response center and then set up the job posting with Cal flagged so others wouldn't apply.

○ ● ◗) ● (◖ ●

Lucas arrived back at the station two months after the tsunami, having spent a month at their Pacific island sorting out new earthquake measurement devices and another month back in Argentina finishing off his vacation. When his message arrived on Alex's HUD, she directed him to meet her in her office, which was currently a large open room with a small desk and chair pushed off to one side. She'd closed over the windows so she could focus on the huge 3D hologram in front of her showing the new, separate housing district where the Earth refugees would find temporary shelter when the time came. They could be integrated into Colony One after the initial rescue operation.

The refugee area, unfortunately compressed as much as possible, was a half circle, centered around a new medical complex and a massive cafeteria. Initially, the stacked skyscraper buildings would have the density of the long-gone Kowloon Walled City, yet would have clean water, food, medical, school, and law. It would still be miserable living, but safe, and the housing could be shifted into Colony One's better structure as the population became trained citizens and they increased the station mass.

Alex would have to get the new populace producing food and supplies almost immediately. At least the new toilets were correctly connected. Sanitation wouldn't be a problem if she could get people to clean up after their pets. While giving space and resources for pets seemed to be stealing from humans, they would need the long-term comfort these provided to help recover from the trauma. She also allocated space to religions, careful to separate incompatible ones, and added recreation and fitness zones.

Colony One's station was due for yet another reconfiguration. She had no idea what the station design committee was going to try next. SEL made it too easy to change. The zones themselves generally stayed in the same layout, but how the zones were arranged and the shape of the station's hull kept changing. They'd been through a few designs already. The committee kept swinging between functionality and structural beauty. Before they could drive her crazy with their antics, Alex had delegated technical support to Lucas.

Alex was trying yet another walking path layout on the separate refugee unit when she heard Lucas clear his throat behind her. She cancelled the image she was studying with a wave. "I'm really glad you're..." Alex turned and paused, eyebrows lifting slightly. "Here." She blinked. Snuggled next to Lucas was a petite woman with wavy, dark chestnut hair. She was pretty with large grey eyes, but Alex could see nervous tension in her uncertain expression.

Lucas himself positively glowed with pride and happiness. "Founder, I'd like you to meet my wife, Sara. We met while I was on vacation. We'll have a second wedding here on the station, but we wanted our families at a traditional wedding first."

Because Lucas spoke in Spanish, Alex did too. Sara must also be from Argentina. Was Lucas being kind to her because her English was lacking or had he merely forgotten which language he was speaking? "Congratulations! Sara, it's very nice to meet you. Welcome to Colony One. You've chosen yourself a good man."

Sara replied in perfect English with a soft, musical voice. "Thank you, Founder. I'm really looking forward to seeing the amazing things that Lucas has been telling me about."

"Most of the high-tech areas Lucas designed," Alex said, switching to English. "The amusement parks with dynamic gravity are some of the most popular."

Lucas gave Sara a happy squeeze and said, "Sara's a teacher."

"Physics?" Alex asked.

Sara laughed. "Third grade. Although I may try my hand at a few other professions. Lucas says I can do that?"

Alex nodded. "Certainly. Every few months if you want. It keeps people from getting burned out and lets them find somewhere they are happy. It causes some issues as people learn their new jobs, but most people are tolerant of mistakes and slowness."

"It's being called the changeover challenge," Lucas added.

"Changeover carnage, last I heard," Alex said.

Lucas hugged Sara and kissed her head. "On the plus side, you're going to get the best service ever from places where people have stayed, because you know they truly enjoy doing it."

"I like being a teacher so we'll see." Sara smiled up at Lucas and they gazed at each other.

Lucas said, "You can teach our kids when we have them." He sighed happily. "I can't believe I'm this lucky."

"I'm the lucky one," Sara said. "I saw you across the market first and knew you were the one."

"No, I definitely saw you before you saw me." Lucas shook his head. "Why do you think I was standing in front of the vegetables? I assure you, I wasn't that hard pressed to decide between eggplant and squash. I don't like either of them."

Sara giggled at Lucas. "It's a good thing you stayed put. I had friends posted at your exits to block you in until I could get brave enough to talk with you."

They'd forgotten Alex was still standing there, lost in their own two-person world. Lucas wouldn't be thinking about work for a while. Alex realized she would have to design the refugee camp's streets by herself. She'd gotten used to getting Lucas' opinion on things, but she certainly wouldn't begrudge him his happiness. "I'm glad you found each other," Alex said.

Lucas looked back over at Alex and bit his lip with chagrin. "Was there anything you needed? Sara and I want to go look at apartment locations."

"Nah, I just wanted to catch up. We can do that later. There's no rush." Alex shooed them off with a wave of her hand.

Lucas nodded. "I'm letting Sara pick our home. I can move my lab anywhere." Lucas and Sara exchanged another long, love-mushy gaze.

"Have fun, you two. Congratulations again!" Alex smiled at them.

Lucas half-bowed to her and they started back toward the main station.

"Nice meeting you, Founder!" Sara called back as Lucas dragged her off.

Alex watched them go and then turned back to her street network. She retrieved the last holographic projection. It was a tradeoff between convenience and available space. If she cut a few access streets, she could give more space to individual apartments, but that would create too much foot traffic at certain hubs. She added a simulation of people's expected walk-paths to find the worst congested locations to try and alleviate some of the bottlenecks.

Wheelchairs were going to be an issue until they could replace them. Alex sighed and set up one building to be handicap accessible. They wouldn't be able to get into the other housing units, but at least they could get to all the public areas. Elevators took less space than stairs, but wouldn't handle the sheer volume of people. They needed both because they wouldn't have time to sort out who couldn't physically do the stairs.

Alex supposed she could make each floor its own habitat. The cafeteria itself would have to be multilevel anyway. Alex shrunk the cafeteria length and width and stacked it. Colony One citizens could deliver food and supplies to each floor easily enough. That would minimize the need for elevators. It would still take someone walking at a normal speed about fifty minutes to get from the farthest apartment to the food court.

New arrival processing was going to be a nightmare. When the time came, she could create a huge open floor underneath the complex and create temporary elevators, but the influx of people would drown any amount of station personnel she could throw at the problem. The refugees would have to self-sort after the initial relocation.

Alex wanted additional help with this design, but she was unwilling to bring in anyone other than Lucas. While she knew with absolute certainty that the Earth was failing, she recognized that she herself wanted to pretend it wasn't for as long as possible. As soon as the information became public, she'd have to deal with it directly. Alex marked that design as a possibility and started on another simulation. She would at least be able to provide options to the necessary committees.

The emergency response center underwent a huge change over the next nine months. Colony One dumped resources and personnel into it as much as possible. Job positions for scientists and response personnel were given priority listings.

The center's new floor plan was designed almost entirely by Cal with a lot of assistance and feedback from both the team and the station's architects. Individual scientific departments got organized by likely shared needs. A dedicated technical team arranged system-wide support for information dispersal. Individual HUDs could request specialized updates. The programming team created skill databases to help locate personnel with the right abilities needed during an event. This would also prove useful for other projects. The emergency response center also included a recuperation area to give workers respite as well as nourishment.

Alex was pleased with the progress of both the center and Cal. While Cal had some expected issues dealing with people as an adult and had to adjust to working, he left behind the surly, angsty teenager and began recognizing that he made a difference, that his insights and help were useful and even sometimes vital to the project's success. The team of people working with him treated him like an intern, giving him help and gentle instruction and allowing him time to research and learn. The center and Cal matured together. Cal's parents were amazed although Alex knew they didn't yet comprehend the natural conclusion to his astonishing progress.

When Cal had only two months left to repay his debt, he began skipping work and his attitude dropped significantly. He refused to speak with his assigned social workers.

Alex again picked up a shift to accompany him. She arrived promptly at 7 a.m. Cal was up, playing a video game. Alex took the bracelet from Cal's escort, waited until the man departed, and went over to the TV and turned it off.

Cal frowned at her, but a guilty look crossed his face.

"So, Cal, what's the problem?" Alex sat down in the escort's chair.

He set aside his game controller and looked at his bed. "No problem. I just want a break, is all."

"They miss you in the center." Alex leaned back, preparing to stay as long as necessary.

"It doesn't matter," Cal said. "They should get used to me not being there. I'll be gone soon."

Alex studied his hunched over, unhappy expression. "Don't you want to go home? Your parents miss you."

"But there are things that need to be done at the center," Cal said.

Alex nodded. "You need an education to truly be an asset though."

"I can get an education here." Cal stood up and began to pace.

"Politically, you know I can't keep you here. You're a United States citizen." Alex scratched her forehead and then rubbed at her chin. She wished she could keep him on the station. They needed all emergency response workers they could get.

"I don't want to be. I want to stay." Cal crossed his arms.

Alex could see the remnants of the stubborn surly boy he'd been not so long ago. "So go home. Talk it over with your parents. Come back if they agree. If they don't, get an education and then come back when you're legally an adult. I'll personally sponsor your citizenship."

He stopped pacing and gaped at her. "You will?"

"Sure."

Cal hesitated a moment and then asked, "Even after what I did?"

"Everyone makes mistakes when they're young, Cal. Everyone does something they're not proud of. You were a different person when you came aboard this station. The people you work with now tell me that you're doing an excellent job; that they're pleased to have you on their team. Your input has been vital to the center's reorganization."

Cal blinked at this, apparently unaware that she'd been keeping track of his progress. "Then you'd let me come back?"

318

"Absolutely." Alex wondered if Cal's parents happened to be viewing this conversation. Their own jobs and obligations meant they couldn't watch all day, every day.

Cal turned to face her. "Which would be more useful? A degree in emergency response or earth science?"

Alex hmm'd. "You know more about the center than I do. What does it need most?"

"Oh." Cal's eyes moved to his hands which twitched.

Alex said, "You have to finish off high school first anyway. There's plenty of time to decide yet. That reminds me. I've been meaning to come talk with you about your return home anyway."

His eyes snapped back to hers. "What about?"

"Your parents love you, Cal. They aren't going to be a problem. They'll accept you, even if they'll struggle with realizing you're an adult now. Your friends, however, aren't going to understand who you've become. They're focused on themselves, their heroin, and their local gang. They've been brainwashed by the media to believe Colony One is evil and you will not be able to convince them otherwise. They're going to try to suck you back into their world."

Cal paled. "I hadn't considered that."

"You've personally saved not only the lives of people who got medical supplies before they would have if you hadn't reminded me, but you've saved the lives of people in the future who will benefit from your contributions to the center. You're important. You make a difference." Alex paused to let that sink in. "You're going to have to hold onto that and be gentle and understanding with your old friends."

"Gentle? With heroin addicts?" Cal snorted.

"Yeah. Don't engage in arguments you can't win," Alex said. "Show by example and stay on your path. You have two months to try to figure out a strategy to handle the culture shock of going home. You should talk it over with your counselors and practice responses so you don't get hurt."

"Practice?" He raised an eyebrow doubtfully.

"It's a skill just like any other skill." Alex opened her hand, palm up. "You don't think I was born this awesome, do you?"

That made him laugh. "Ok, ok. I surrender. I'll go home. You aren't going to run me around the station in my underwear again, are you?"

"You only thought you were in your underwear," Alex confessed. "I bent light so everyone else would see you wearing clothes."

"You're evil, Founder."

"You were the one refusing to take a shower." She grinned at him. "How about you show me around the new center instead?"

With stops for a mutually agreeable meal, Cal led Alex around their new Emergency Response complex and explained what had been done and why.

Prompted with questions, he shared the underlying data and statistics, showing a deeper understanding of the challenges and science than Alex had expected.

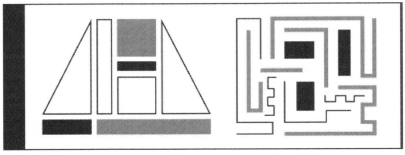

T plus 3:160:7:14   ~17π/30

"I hate this!" The woman's shrill voice carried across the stream from down the path leading to the forest's exit. Birds in the immediate area took flight and departed.

Alex rubbed her temple, trying to drive out her headache. Just what she needed. Downsiders. She'd hoped the oxygen-rich "outdoor" air would settle her nerves enough that she could eat lunch, but all it had done was give her excessive time to worry about tomorrow's defensive debate that she didn't want to do. Natural versus artificial environments. It would be a direct attack against her space station and Colony One, and would likely be based on ignorance, hype, and agendas.

It had been five months since Cal had returned home, and yet the political atmosphere between Colony One and the United States was still volatile. Brian had scheduled the debate to try and improve Colony One's image, optimistically thinking the press coverage would be helpful.

Instinctively, Alex pulled her feet up out of the water and scooted back against a leafy shrub. If she stayed still, there was a chance the noisy downsiders might not notice her. Maybe they'd be gone soon.

"I will never, ever like this. It's hot, buggy, sweaty! Sweaty! I tell you, I'm done with this. I'm done with you. We both know this isn't working out. We're done. Over. I'm going back to that hotel and getting a room of my own and then I'm going home. It's absurd to be forced to exercise for an hour every day. This place is a prison!"

Not long after this piercing tirade, a man walked into view. He looked about the same age as Alex, dressed in a pressed, lightweight fashionable, outdoor-style linen suit, with matching designer, new hiking shoes. His light brown hair was neatly trimmed and only moderately wind-blown. In a frustrated gesture, he ran his fingers through that hair, pulling at it. Gritting his teeth, he reached into his trouser pocket and withdrew something small in a white-knuckled grip. He threw it at the stream and turned to walk back, without watching it land with a quiet, anticlimactic splash near the stream's center.

Alex frowned. Bloody downsiders, always destroying the environment. Sure, he was having a bad day, but damn it, the Earth was being killed by this bullshit.

After about 20 steps, the man swore and turned back, dashing toward the stream and scrutinized the water with panic.

Alex exhaled with resignation and stood up. "I saw where it went. I'll get it." He blinked at her in confusion. She supposed she might have looked like she had just teleported in. With practiced grace, she stepped across the scattered stream rocks until she got near the center. Then she waded in and reached into the water for the object. It was a small, blue-green jewelry box. She took it to him.

Up close, she saw the man had classically handsome features - strong jaw, squared eyebrows, intense green eyes. These complemented his broad shoulders, surprisingly trim body, and general fitness level.

"Thank you." Opening the little box and letting the water pour out, he commented softly, "It was my grandmother's." He took out the elegant diamond ring, carefully dried it on his shirt and gently tucked it in his shirt pocket. He shook the excess water from the box and stuffed that in his pants pocket where the dampness immediately made a rather large dark wet spot which he didn't notice. "I hope we didn't disturb you. It's just I..."

"It's ok. I understand," Alex offered kindly.

"I'm not sure how much you heard just now."

Alex didn't say anything.

His cheeks reddened. "Sorry. I was going to take her to see Earth-rise and propose. I think... No, I'd hoped that it might fix things. She's a city girl, but we've been incompatible from the beginning." He shrugged, refocusing on Alex. "You aren't going to get in trouble for wading in the stream?" Colony One had many rules about how people could interact with the environment.

"Naw, it's a designated swim area."

His hand gestured in the air as he studied his personal HUD. He was obviously trying to find the map of the area.

Alex waited patiently, accustomed to the delay in responses people didn't even realize they inflicted on the person next to them when they were working with their display. When he seemed to have found what he was looking for and his eyes refocus on her, she commented, "You know, your friend might be happier in one of the dance clubs; those are designated exercise areas too. Lots of deafening music and flashing lights. Very city-like."

"Huh. I hadn't thought of that. I'll mention it to her if she'll speak to me again." His eyebrows pulled together thoughtfully as he studied her. "Are you here to see Earth-rise?"

No, I'm here hiding from my responsibilities, playing around in that useless cave project, and desperately trying to find some way out of tomorrow's debate. Alex settled for a simple nod instead of that thought. "The best view of Earth-rise is just up around the bend, at the top of the waterfall. We have about 30 minutes. It's enough time to get there."

"Been on the station long?"

The question made her pause. Alex hadn't realized he didn't recognize her. She'd stayed out of the press photos since departing Earth, but she didn't think she'd changed that much. She did have her hair pulled back out of her eyes with a rolled bandana and tied up in the back in a rough ponytail, and she was in a simple, design-free, comfortable SEL standard shorts and tee citizen's leisure outfit.

Most people spent their funds on specialty designs. Tomorrow's debate outfit, for example, was a one-off meticulous forest green and gold pants suit, a mere $40,000. Absurd, but expected. Alex pushed that out of her mind and realized the super-generic outfit probably made her look like a new arrival. After tomorrow, she'd probably never be anonymous again. Not that she was anonymous among the citizens anyway, but it had been nice not to be accosted by tourists everywhere.

Rather flippantly, Alex decided to seize the opportunity, even if she refused to lie outright. "I've been here for a while. Come on, I'll show you the way up. There's actually 4 different paths." They started along the stream edge. "There's easy, moderate, advanced, and extreme, just like most of the exercise tracks. There's also a handicap lift, but you have to be registered to use it. The easy path is just a long slope." She glanced over at him, trying to decide if he should be on the easy or moderate path. "You'd have to go pretty fast on the easy path though - it takes longer."

"Which one are you taking?"

"I'll go up the advanced track. I need to stretch and burn off some energy, but you shouldn't try to match me. There's crossover points for all four, so you can change if the one you're on gets to be too much." Alex wished burning off energy would burn off her anxiety, but she knew it wouldn't.

They came around the bend to see the base of the waterfall. The man's impressed inhale and wide eyes made Alex grin. She'd helped with the design. It was a full 31 meters, small by waterfall standards, but meticulously arranged for melodic sound, with scattered rocky outcrops covered mostly in beautiful green moss.

At the waterfall base, a large swimming area was exquisitely lit with dappled sunlight. When actual sunlight couldn't reach the station, the sunlight was artificially generated. Shielding collected and blocked sunlight as needed to create a normal 24-hour day/night schedule. Flat stones near the swimming area provided a sitting area for natural drying and lounging. The air smelled particularly fresh and clear. The entrance to the cave was hidden by the waterfall and plants.

"It's magnificent," he murmured.

"Swim after Earth-rise if you want. The center gets pretty deep." She pointed out the easy path start. "You just follow your map overlay on your HUD. It's pretty simple."

"So where's your path?"

Alex grinned and pointed at the rocky cliff face that went straight up beside the waterfall.

"That's the advanced? I've done some rock climbing. Wouldn't that be the extreme?" At her head shake, he asked, "Do I want to know where the extreme path is?"

"Oh, that goes up in the waterfall. It's a bit slippery, so you have to grip harder to stay on. Mostly the water just tries to push you down, so you have more resistance going up."

"Ah, well, I'll follow you."

Alex shrugged and did not comment about macho men. Most downsiders found the moderate tracks hard. She had daily workouts, no pollution, no toxins, healthy food (when she wasn't too stressed to eat), and a consistently active lifestyle. The advanced track would push her, although she did the extremes at least 3 times a week. There was a decently sized club of citizens that were "extremes only" and busily kept ranks and scored who was "the most extreme" based on time-to-complete and number of extremes done per day. They were a little obsessively crazy, but Alex was designing a couple "ultra tracks" just for them. The first was inside the cave.

As they climbed, he said, "I'm really glad you saw where that landed. I'd've been hours looking for it."

"Station personnel would have picked it up and returned it to you eventually." Specifically, Alex would have retrieved it and passed it along to station security, who would have reviewed the security footage, located him, and issued a warning about littering.

"I swear I don't ever do anything like that. I actually work a lot of cleanup initiatives. I was out on the Appalachian Trail two months ago, picking up trash and updating trail blazes."

"I spent some time in the Chattahoochee National Forest as a kid. This place has a lot of similar vegetation." That had been Alex's home for a couple years, she reflected. Some good memories, some horrible ones.

"Oh! Yes, I can see that. Now that you mention it, that's what this forest reminds me of. This waterfall is steeper than the ones there though."

"Less acreage. We're much more condensed." Alex grabbed the next outcropping and pulled herself up.

The man panted after her. Alex diligently pointed out the first crossover to the moderate track and he stubbornly shook his head. At the second crossover, he gasped defeat and switched paths. At the third crossover, she switched over to the moderate track too, more tired than normal. She'd not slept very well all week, worrying about the debate, and she hadn't eaten.

It was not that she was afraid of "losing" the debate but rather that she was afraid of what the press would do with whatever she might say. In her own country, Colony One reporters had been told they were only allowed to report what they witnessed directly, and were only allowed to state the truth as they saw it, with as little "bias" as possible. Violation of this would be banishment back to Earth, where they could join the Earth reporters who published whatever would incite people to the most fervor and rage. Tomorrow's debate would have a full set of "neutral" downsider reporters. As if they'd be neutral.

"I am not a villain," she growled to herself as she stumbled up the last step. She was still ahead of her visitor by a few minutes, so she spent some time stretching. She felt more spaghetti-armed than usual. Maybe tomorrow after the debate, she could take a few days off and get some real rest. She'd want to hide out from the conference attendees anyway.

Her guest arrived just as Alex was finishing her stretches. He was flushed, breathing hard, but not gasping like he was dying. That meant he was much more athletic than his expensive, sporty clothes suggested. Alex was impressed; no, she thought to herself, she was aroused. Damn, he was sexy. He bent forward a moment, hands on his knees, normalizing his breathing. When he straightened and gazed around, his eyes sparkled with impressed excitement.

Caught up in his wonder, Alex surveyed the area, trying to see the place as if for the first time. The stream that fed the waterfall came down from a steep mountainside slope. The trees were too dense to see the sky in that direction. Opposite that, a low wooden bridge crossed over the stream to a large grassy clearing. Chair-height rocks were arranged to look natural, but on closer inspection, were in a semi-circle facing an opening in the trees. This created an expansive, bold view where the sky was open to the clear SEL force shield and then to space. A slight slope curved downward toward the opening, creating a theater effect.

They crossed over the bridge. Alex expected citizens to start holding weddings here once the cave project got finished and there was more to see than a mere waterfall and occasional great view of the Earth. Whether the Earth was lit by the sun or showing off the nighttime lights of cities, it was magnificent to behold, particularly from one of the designated Earth-rise locations. The best time to experience Earth-rise was at station night, when the Earth below had day. The dark star-filled sky would slowly be overtaken by a brilliant blue, white, green, and brown sphere.

Earth-rise was possible because Colony One's station had been redesigned yet again and split into two double-sided plates. This created four "continents" that were split into districts and environmental habitats. Gravity and "ground" were shared between the plate sides with their "sky" facing space. Thankfully, the design committee seemed to have finally settled on this design.

The larger plate remained at a right-angle to the Earth so half always pointed toward the Earth and half to space. The other slowly spun allowing the Earth to rise and set. Going between them was as simple as either flying or taking one of Lucas' connecting shuttle tubes. The shuttle tubes had independent gravity so people wouldn't feel the spin and reorientation to the new gravity direction. Only the sky would be different when they stepped out of the shuttle tube.

Alex realized they'd each been lost in their own thoughts for a while. She said, "The best view is from the third row, center." She pointed. "It frames correctly if you want to take a picture."

"I don't take photographs. I prefer to experience the moment, not experience taking a picture of the moment."

In that moment, Alex fell in love. He understood how to live. Absurd, really, to fall in love over such a simple statement, but she recognized her feral animal attraction and admiration, and that warm tingle from the top of her head to the tips of her toes. She'd written enough of those silly romance novels to recognize it, even if she'd never felt it before.

Not that she could do anything about it. His relationship status was either taken or rebounding, and complicated, and hers was impossible; she couldn't unbalance Colony One's politics by introducing a random person as a spouse or even a boyfriend. Citizens already gave her priority, honor, and power as the Founder, but in order for this country to survive, in fact, in order for humanity to survive, no one could have power over anyone else. Yet, she held power and would keep it just to make sure no one else would take power and abuse it.

"I also like to experience the moment," she said, her voice coming out quieter than she wanted.

He studied his HUD a moment. "We have a few minutes yet." The clock on Alex's display was counting down from 3 minutes 16 seconds. He walked over to the waterfall edge and peered down. "The waterfall is pretty from up here too. Come see."

Alex diligently went over and looked, noting the changes from the last time she'd been up here. The forest trees were maturing nicely and getting that full spongy-carpet look to their tops. The artificial breeze looked sufficiently random-natural. Not too far away, Colony One's city buildings could be seen reaching upward in what looked like a scene painted on a science fiction novel, with odd shapes and a connecting maze of bridges between buildings. It changed and grew daily, a living organism by itself.

He squinted at it. "How can something look so big and so small at the same time?"

She laughed. "I've often wondered the same thing. We're microscopic compared to the Earth. The real trick is seeing the Earth the same way, as microscopic compared to the solar system." They watched several hawks circle and move off around the mountain and then they silently made their way over to the third row. Time ticked down in her display. He didn't spoil the magic silence with words and Alex was thankful.

Birds began to sing again and a gentle breeze pushed the warm air past them. The Earth rose over the forested horizon. Brilliant daylight below, clouds lit from the left in a golden sunrise hue, crossing over South Africa, to just a touch of shadowy grey night over on the right. Alex realized they were both holding their breath. The Earth continued rotating as it rose, showing the South Atlantic ocean in its blue-green glory and then South America, Brazil, and Venezuela. Colony One would eventually slow and hover a few hours over the Earth-side Colony One island in the Pacific Ocean so shuttles could go back and forth, before continuing its strange, ever changing orbit. The Earth rose above their clearing and when it got to a point where it was awkward to look at, they both relaxed.

Their eyes met in mutual awe and Alex felt like she was spinning away into the universe that was his soul. He looked just like she felt. Alex glanced away first. She was too important; her task too critical to allow personal desires to get in the way, and yet, she thought she might throw it all away for one real kiss. One moment of intimacy that would take away the horrors of her childhood. What was she? Some foolish teenager? This was absurd. She started back up the slope toward the bridge.

"Wait," he said quickly.

Alex stopped and turned. "Yes?"

He hesitated. Then obviously not saying what he'd meant to when he stopped her, he said, "That was incredible. Thank you."

Before she realized what she was about to say, Alex asked, "Would you like to see what I've been working on?" No one had been allowed to see her cave. Not yet. Not even Brian or Lucas. She couldn't believe she'd said that and there was no way to take the question back.

"Mmmm hmmm?" He nodded curiously, tilting his head. "I would."

"It's a pet project, really. I don't have much time for it, but Station Development approved it."

"Yes? Is it far?"

"Not far, I was actually on lunch break for Earth-rise." With sudden inspiration, Alex grinned. "Let's take the fast way down. How brave are you?"

He raised an eyebrow.

She winked saucily and ran toward the cliff edge. He shouted after her when he realized what she meant to do, but she'd already leapt off the cliff edge in a perfect swan dive. By time he'd reached the edge and peered over, the gravity cage had already caught her and she was drifting on her back toward the ground below. "Just jump!" she called up. "The farther out you go the faster you'll come down."

"I must be crazy!" he shouted back. He jumped. Not as far out as she'd gone, but far enough to make decent time. She also noted that he jumped in the direction of the deep water, just in case. It took a while to override one's own instincts.

As soon as she reached the bottom, she realized she needed to call security to get clearance for him to enter the cave. She quickly dialed, hoping to finish before he got within earshot. "Dispatch, I need you to tell Station Security to authorize... uh... the person with me... for a one time entrance to the cave. Duration until he leaves."

"Founder! Of course! Is there anything else you need?"

"Uh, no, thank you. That's all." She cut the call off and made sure her 'do not disturb unless dire' option was extended through the evening.

"Holy cow! That was awesome!" The gravity cage had oriented him into a standing position and set him down on the side of the stream near her.

"Yeah, jumping from any dangerous height anywhere on station will do the same thing, although doing it in an unauthorized area will get you a visit from Psyche and Station Security, in that order. This station is really appallingly safe."

"Hard to commit suicide, eh?"

"Where there's a will, there's a way, but the way ought to be a little challenging, don't you think?" Alex winked.

"I suppose so!" He was still grinning from the adrenaline rush from the jump. He obviously shared her passion for excitement.

"I need to tell you - this area is still unfinished. It's not open to the public and I've contacted Station Security to allow you to go in with me right now."

At his appalled look of concern, Alex hurried on to say, "It's not a problem. It's just an active construction zone so you need an escort."

"I thought Station Security is a draconian nightmare with zero tolerance and absolutely no exceptions?"

Alex was the key creator and most avid supporter for that policy. "Well, that old saying about asking forgiveness is easier than asking permission... not so true here. It's a safety thing. For all that this station looks like there's a lot of space, we're really a very compressed city with a lot of people. No room for hazardous behavior."

He nodded.

"Ok, so the bathroom designs are still being debated, as are the swimsuit designs. Um. Just a moment." Alex zipped through her HUD and published the prototype tourist-suite for the cave so it would show up on his display. "All right, you have a new icon set in the lower right of your display for proximity actions. Pick one of the bathrooms and go put on a swimsuit."

He gave her an odd look, but his gestures indicated he quickly shifted to studying the list of bathrooms. Egyptian, Japanese, Icelandic (her favorite), Wooded, or Geometrical. They all had sinks, showers, towels, toilets, and guest swimsuits but the differences were in the style and layout. Eventually, the committee would decide on one of them. Probably that ugly geometrical thing, Alex thought with resignation.

The man chose one and the door appeared in the air in front of him. He went in. The upgraded bathrooms were a strange thing - they created a box in front of the person, let them have privacy, and then converted waste to dust, and disappeared when the person exited. The waste-dust particles were then transported via the microtunnels to Colony One's soil distribution center so they could be properly distributed to the correct places in the station, rather than adding to the environment at the location the user was at. Water was created from locally available matter in the sub-soil and then returned afterwards to its original configuration. Lucas had set it up as an afterthought to one of his other projects.

Alex shifted her SEL into a custom designed green swimsuit. From the front, it looked like a bikini, but the back had a strategically solid panel that hid the scars on her back. She supposed one day she ought to repair the scars, but they were part of her, something of life before Sal that hadn't been burned away, expunged with mafia thoroughness. It felt weird to think of life without that history, without the drive necessary to create this place.

Her new companion, still nameless, because if she asked his name, he'd ask hers, and she wouldn't lie, stepped out of the chaotic Wooded bathroom, with his clothes neatly folded in his hands. He'd chosen comfortable boxer-style brown and green swim trunks. And he took her breath away. He looked like a Greek god - well defined muscles, reasonable, natural tan. He had a couple minor scars on his lower legs that were barely visible under his light brown leg hair.

When her eyes made it back up to his face, Alex saw she'd been caught appraising him. He was grinning; no false humility there. Blushing, she said gruffly, "Go ahead and leave your clothes here. No one will steal them." Trying to cover her embarrassment, she strode into the pool of water at the base of the waterfall. He followed. The water was neither cold nor warm, but a good temperature for the ambient atmosphere. "There's a dry entrance around by the easy route up, but the water entrance is much nicer. You can swim, right?"

"I can. I used to work at a marina. Don't know if you saw, but I've got some scars from tagging sharks on my legs. Scraped by fins." His voice held a teasing note.

"What is it you do now?"

He hesitated, his breathing momentarily pausing. Then he answered, "I'm an environmentalist of sorts. I'm here for that convention tomorrow. What about you?"

Shit. He'd be at the debate. Alex tried not to panic. Sal would not have approved of her stress-induced language this week, but it was appropriate. "I'm in the general labor pool. I mostly jump around to whatever is needed. That's why this project has such a low priority. There's always somewhere that is short staffed. Last week I was helping out at the hotel doing maid work." All true, but incomplete. Alex had been designing and testing the new automated room cleaning system and verifying that the rooms reconstructed correctly with random visitor belongings neatly sorted. "We go through the waterfall here."

Just above the hidden entrance, a rocky overhang slowed the water speed so the pelting water wouldn't hurt. Immediately past the cascading water, the cave entrance began - a tunnel into the mountainside with a stream running down its center. Ceiling and walls were natural grey stone, rough, but not sharp.

The stream's water flowed gently toward the exit although it wasn't challenging to move inward. The actual underwater lights weren't visible, but the water glowed an ambient teal color. The stream was about 5 meters across, with the deepest area being just over a meter deep in the very center. Smooth, flat and round rocks made up the stream bed so if a person walked or swam through the water they got exercise.

Alongside the stream, equivalent stony paths provided a walking area. The path was also designed for exercise and had both gentle and steep low hills. The cave opening had a calming effect that would naturally make people want to be quiet. The white noise from the waterfall made conversation impossible until they moved around the bend. Invisible noise dampeners immediately suppressed the waterfall sound.

Alex gestured at her guest to come over to the side. "If you look closely, the stones on the path have a triangular one every meter or so that points the way out. There's also some in the stream bed, but if you follow the current downstream, that leads out too."

"It looks hard for a wheelchair to navigate." At her quick glance, he added, "I have a cousin with spine issues from a car accident."

"Ah. You should suggest he relocate to Colony One. Wheelchairs work differently here." Alex gestured and they continued inward as she explained. "They get their own invisible track above the ground. It would be more accurately described as a hover-chair. It's why we have no special access ramps anywhere either. The person driving the chair can simply go anywhere a walking person can. Doors automatically open and hold open. The chair goes up and down stairs without slowing. The person can even set the height to match standing people so there's no looking down or up at the people nearby. If they want, the chair can be shifted for standing support." She went on to describe the specialty bathrooms and other independence-granting modifications.

"But everyone has to spend an hour each day in an exercise zone as well as 6 hours each day working. That can be impossible for people with medical issues."

Alex shrugged. "Unless a person is a quadriplegic with no voice, there are things they can do. Even then, we have enough assistive technology that getting up and moving isn't as energy-sapping. Getting showered and dressed, for example, is simple with SEL. A quick command will have your body clean head to toe, and your SEL outfit will change from pajamas to day wear. We also have plenty of jobs that don't require physical prowess, and some of the ones that do can be adapted." Alex found herself wanting to share her plans for medical advances also, but it just wasn't time yet. The medical complex was only beginning its expansion and it would be another six to nine months before they were ready for their first patient. If his cousin were a citizen, he'd get priority treatment after the initial tests.

"I don't know. It still seems harsh. You don't ever get to retire. You don't ever get a day off from the exercise requirement. It's pretty regimented."

"At least you didn't mention the lack of meat choices. That's the one everyone complains about most." Alex grinned. "But seriously, everyone contributes to the success of the society. We don't have the resources to support a welfare system. Even our babies, once they walk and talk, have to go to school as their job. Granted, those first few years of school are just play zones, but they get to interact and learn. Some of the elderly even enjoy telling stories and just being companions as their job. Mostly they're taking the advisor jobs though. They've got experience and knowledge that shouldn't be lost. It all works out."

They came around another bend and the path split. The left path changed lighting to a pretty light green. Alex pointed at the green one, but they continued on the teal path. "That path goes to another exercise loop with another climbing wall. I can show you later if you want. It's an impossible climb."

"How so?"

"There's a stone arch with the underside as the climbing wall and a bell in the center. The goal is to ring the bell, but you can't actually get to it. There's plenty of handholds and it looks possible, but as you get closer to the bell, gravity adjusts heavier and heavier. Even the strongest person will get pulled free just before they reach it. It's fun to see how far you can get and because you splash down into the water when you fall off, and you can just retry. It's a play area."

"But what's the point of it being impossible?"

"It's for the people who are bored with the extreme tracks." He gave Alex an incredulous look. Alex added, "Yeah, there are a few of them always complaining that we should make the extremes harder. This'll be the start of the new ultra tracks."

"I suppose. I've been to a few places where I wished the climbing walls were higher or more challenging. They tend to be indoors with a lot of safety ropes."

"So what's your favorite activity?"

"Sailing," he said. "I grew up around water. I think I spent more time on a sailboard than I did at school. My best friend and I raced a lot."

"I've never been sailing."

"Next time you're down on Earth, I'll be happy to take you."

Again, their eyes met and Alex thought she could feel sparks of electricity jumping between them. "I'd like that," she breathed. This time, he broke the gaze first. She forced herself to continue on. Absurd with her complications. Any government on Earth would be happy to toss her in a jail and throw away the key. The press would eat him alive, corporations would try to wield him against her, not to mention the criminal organizations that might take a pot shot at him just for entertainment.

"I have a..." He stopped speaking as they came around the next bend and the cave opened to the crystal cavern. Her pet project. Precious gems and stones from around the earth were carefully secured on the low cavern ceiling, each with its own specialized lighting to show off its beauty. A mere 2687 of them; one quarter of her wealth. Only 423 of them were currently placed. The rest were in individual boxes in several crates stacked off to the side.

"You have a what?" Alex asked teasingly.

"Hrm?" His eyes were riveted to the sparkling and seemingly glowing gems scattered on the ceiling.

"You were saying you have..." she prompted, grinning widely.

"Oh, a yacht," he answered distractedly. "Are those real?"

"Every one of them. I'm placing them and recording their history. There's a theater in the back where we'll have a constantly running documentary talking

331

about the different gems." Alex pointed toward a tunnel opposite the room's entrance, where the stream came in. "If you want to hear about a specific one, you have to come at a specific time to hear it. The whole presentation should run just about 15 days. What sort of yacht?"

"A gaff rigged schooner. That's the kind that has the extra bar at the top of the sails. It's got a big galley and a couple sleeping cabins." As he continued to talk about his boat, it was clear he loved it and knew every detail. Alex encouraged him with smiles, nods, and questions. He eventually forgot she might not know all the right nautical terms and spoke with confident authority, his baritone voice resonating through her soul. She thought she might be able to listen to him forever.

"It sounds really nice." Alex winced inwardly at this lame response.

He turned red as he realized he'd been talking about his boat for way longer than most acquaintances would want and changed the topic. Gesturing back at the gems, he asked, "How many more do you have to... are you gluing those up there?"

"Holding them at a molecular level." It was a bit more technical than that. The SEL holding each gem constantly reconfigured to prevent any constant pressure anywhere on the gems. Some of them would continue to grow over time. "Here, this is what it's supposed to look like when I'm done." She activated the projection overlay. She liked to look at it herself sometimes when she tired of placing gems. The whole room sparkled hypnotically with the image of dazzling gems. After a few minutes she turned off the projection. "Want to put one up?"

"May I?"

"Sure. Come pick one." She swam over to the crates. The individual boxes all had numbers on them.

He peered in a crate and randomly took out #987. Inside that box, an uncut red-purple hexagonal crystal attached to a rough glob of gritty almost cement-ish stone didn't look very impressive. The crystal was about two and a half centimeters long and thirteen millimeters wide.

"Red beryl. This one is from Utah." Alex reached over and took it from the box and ran her finger over it, turning it and looking at it from all directions. She triggered 987 on her display and the cave lights dimmed, leaving one bright spot with a semitransparent hologram of the gem in its expected orientation. Underneath, a white ladder appeared with a table near the top. She handed it back to him. "It's very easy to place." She fiddled around with her HUD a moment and a second ladder appeared next to the first. "When you get to the top, put the gem on the square on the table. I'll trigger the cleaning unit, which removes any dust, finger oil, and such, and coats it in a very thin layer of SEL. You pick it up, orient it to match the hologram, and push it into place. When you feel it grab, let go."

"How much is this one worth?" he asked, turning it in his hand and holding it up to the light.

"That was bought for just over 80,000 Euros at an auction. Overpaid, but the collection wouldn't have been complete without it. That's supply and demand for you." Many of the gems had been bought at a monetary loss, but it was for the future and a steal for that purpose. If only Alex could collect the great paintings, sculptures, and books as easily, but the museums and libraries held their assets too closely. The thought made her sad.

He held the crystal more carefully. "This project relies an awful lot on the zero crime rate. Someone could easily come in and take them all."

"Nah, it wouldn't be that easy. SEL is tenaciously hard to cut and security wouldn't even have to rush to get here, because the cave would lock down. You'd have to steal the whole mountainside, and even then, the cave itself would remain intact." Which would still meet her purpose - to save it for future generations.

He set the gem in the marked off square on the table and Alex triggered the cleaner. A soft chime indicated it was done and he picked it up and placed it. They both climbed down and she went and took another one, sticking the yellowish green crystal across the room from the red beryl. "Spodumene," Alex said, "Also known as Hiddenite or Green Kunzite. I think it's one of the prettier ones, but it's not as valuable."

"This seems like a terribly inefficient way to place these things. Wouldn't it make more sense to take the crate up the ladder and just have the ladder move around as needed?"

"It's not about finishing, it's about the adventure of doing it. Meditative when I get on a roll." With the pace and tune of a nursery rhyme, she chanted, "Take a box, enter the number, swim over to the ladder, up the ladder, clean the stone, place the stone, down the ladder. Splash splash, roll. Take a box..."

He chuckled. "With that kind of work ethic, how do you not get banished back to Earth?"

Alex giggled. "That's the punishment for an incorrigible deadbeat, certainly. As it happens, I work hard enough on my other jobs that no one cares about this one. It's my idea of a mini-vacation. Sometimes I even take a nap in the theater. Hey, let me show you that. Unfortunately, all the entries are me describing the origin, history, and molecular structure of the different stones."

"So long as you aren't singing each presentation..." he teased.

"Ah! What an idea! I should sneak in a singing entry and scare off the tourists who happen upon it." Alex led him through the tunnel away from the entrance. The water depth gradually decreased until they were walking on solid rocks. A fairly large chamber before the main theater created a space for bathrooms again. A rack of towels and robes along the right wall invited use. Nearby a bin existed for the used items, which were immediately recycled. As he dried and put on one of the robes, she changed her SEL to a robe too. The design was super soft and fluffy, in a monkish muted brown, accompanied by fluffy brown slippers. "The idea is to encourage a homey, family-room feeling, while keeping the voice echoes to a minimum," she explained.

The main theater was a circular dome, like a small planetarium. Several rings of reclining chairs and sofas with pillows invited people to stay. The presentation was currently showing the zebra rock, magnified so it nearly filled the ceiling, rotating slowly so each reddish brown and tan stripe could be appreciated.

From invisible speakers, her voice described how the stone came from the east Kimberley region of Western Australia. A map of Australia appeared showing the exact location. The map disappeared as the lecture went on to a short movie on how the sedimentary rock was formed during the Precambrian era when only the most primitive of life forms existed. Sedimentary rocks from that period were used to chronicle the development of the Earth's atmosphere and ocean.

"This is really cool!" He hopped on the sofa nearest the center, a 2-person love-seat, and raised the footrest, stretching out.

Alex joined him. "Best seat in the house." The lecture continued with a very technical description of how the rock analysis was actually done, and then went on to describe the molecular composition of the zebra rock. She could feel his body heat next to her. Maybe she should have sat on the next chair over?

"How much is it going to cost to come in here?"

"Nothing. It's public domain. It belongs to everyone."

"And you proposed this project?"

Alex nodded. Their eyes met again and this time neither of them looked away. He leaned toward her hesitantly, and she followed suit, shifting toward him. Neither dared to speak. He kissed her and damn the consequences, she kissed him back, turning off her bioshield.

Alex muted the presentation, but overhead a brilliant green emerald spun. When he moved on top of her, nothing bad happened. There was no pain and he treated her with respect and tenderness, attuned to her body language. They created a beautiful new experience, together.

Afterward, both of their faces mirrored befuddled confusion and awe. Feeling the weight of responsibility pressing in on her, Alex whispered the dreaded words, "We need to talk."

"So how would you feel about moving back to Earth? You could finish this project..." His finger traced her bare shoulder.

She cut him off with a hand-wave. "I need to tell you something."

At that moment, her incoming call lit up. Her 'don't disturb unless dire' flag was active and the call was from Station Security. Alex's stomach twisted and she swore. "Phone call I can't ignore. Excuse me," she explained, her voice gravelly with frustration and fear. She sat up, pulled the robe back around herself, ran her fingers through her now-damp-dry hair into some semblance of hopeful order, and activated a privacy shield.

"Founder, I'm so sorry for disturbing you. We have a situation. Some of the conference attendees are holding a protest in the restaurant zone. They brought signs and we've been monitoring the situation, but since more people are arriving for dinner, the tension level is volatile. We've got them and citizens shouting at each other now and making threats. We don't have any laws about public gatherings. We checked. What should we do? We can't arrest them without a stated law. Mr. Kimberly is in transit back from our Pacific island and he left you in charge."

Alex clenched her teeth and nodded. Brian could have chosen a better time to leave her in charge. She thought for a moment. "I understand. Thank you for calling me." Responsibility couldn't be ignored. The Station Security woman was chewing her lip nervously. Alex assured her, "You did the right thing in calling me. Please have all citizens evacuate the area until further notice. I will meet anyone who is interested in the event at the baseball stadium to answer questions in about 20 minutes."

"What about the non-citizens?"

"Well, if there's no one paying attention to their protest, it ought to dissolve."

"What about the restaurant staff?"

"Evacuate them too. Just keep tabs on anything anyone takes for billing. We're not going to space anyone. Not even going to confine them. Marching around with signs seems pretty harmless. If it turns into a destructive mob, then run up some individual SEL cages and hold them in place, and I'll sort it out when I get there. Alex out." She cut the connection and lowered the privacy shield.

Her new complication was stretched out on his robe, leaning up on one elbow gazing at her. Damn, he was handsome. "I have to go," she said without preamble and as kindly as she could. "Something's come up that I have to deal with."

"Is everything ok?" he asked, rising and pulling his own robe around himself.

"It will be. I'm just on call for Station Security backup." Alex didn't want to leave.

"Dinner tomorrow? I have a reservation at the Star Trek Memorial Restaurant at 7 p.m."

Those had to be made 6 months in advance. Alex would obviously be taking his ex's place.

"Yeah, I'll meet you there." Alex vowed she'd arrive early at the conference the next morning and talk with him then, before she had to go on stage. It wouldn't be the best solution, but would have to work.

Alex turned and hurried toward the exit. As soon as she cleared the theater seating, she began to run. If she scrambled, she might be able to get to the stadium in 20 minutes. She took the shortcut path out, running at full speed. She didn't hear him call after her, asking her name.

The gathering at the stadium was a nightmare. The local news reporter had been on scene at the restaurant zone, giving play-by-play live coverage to the public news feed and as soon as the evacuation announcement came, people speculated about what might get done to the protestors, and twice as many people as the stadium was able to hold showed up, all angry, most past-dinner-time hungry.

No matter how many ways Alex explained that people shouldn't be upset because the protestors had different life experiences and were making decisions based on that, the citizens claimed outrage. How dare these people show up and disrespect Colony One? Protesting anything on the station is something only citizens have the right to do, and there were already voting polls in place to address social, economic, AND environmental issues. Every visitor who participated should be thrown off the station immediately. It's bad enough that the Founder has to go defend environmental design at their conference tomorrow. How dare they come insult their hosts? They were here by invitation. They should be deported.

Alex's head throbbed and her hands shook badly enough that she had to hold on to the podium for stability. Irritated, she tried again. "We are more evolved than this petty arguing. The fact is - these people are on our side even if they don't think so. They want to defend and save the environment as much as we do. Tomorrow at the debate, we'll show them we are capable of a reasoned and civil discussion, without name-calling and childish tantrums."

Her HUD flashed with a message from Station Security. "We caged one person and the rest seem to be dispersing." Alex didn't want to know what the man had done. The law was quite clear and she really didn't want another international incident on the books, although she'd do whatever she had to.

Citizens voiced their opinions. Alex tried to insert reason. Citizens ranted and raved. Eventually, the decision was made to immediately create a forum to discuss the matter further and a committee to immediately make rules regarding "the incitement to riot" by station visitors, and to put these rules into effect by morning. Why, of course, Founder, we expect you to run the committee. Alex agreed to this merely to end the gathering. Three hours of this nonsense, just to be sure everyone who wanted to say something had a chance to speak and be heard.

That citizen meeting broke up. The committee members agreed to regroup in an hour and a half, so they could go eat dinner first, and Alex went to deal with their caged guest. Per her instructions, Station Security hadn't done anything except immobilize the man in SEL. They hadn't even relocated him to their office, which Alex discovered when she got to the Station Security office. Another 30 minutes for Security to go get him and march him back to their office.

Then time to review the security footage, where the guy enthusiastically yelled and screamed his views, tried to terrify people when citizens were ordered to evacuate by telling everyone they were about to get spaced, and ultimately ended up smashing his sign against a table, which is when Station Security caged him and he subsequently wet himself being scared that he was about to be spaced.

Alex then spent some time talking with the man and assuring him he'd broken no laws, wasn't about to be spaced or deported, and would, in fact, be released as soon as he calmed down enough to be reasonable and promise not to do anything remotely similar for the remainder of his stay.

In the middle of this meeting, Alex declined a phone call from Jay Ryko, who was the conference organizer as well as the man she was scheduled to debate in the morning. She delegated dealing with him to Station Security, who then summarized that he just wanted to put in a good word for their detainee. She didn't have time for more nonsense. It was already getting late and she was exhausted.

They released the man. Feeling too queasy to bother eating, Alex jogged off, stumbling twice because she was so tired, and arrived a mere half hour late for the committee meeting, where the consensus was that the 34 things they'd brainstormed as inappropriate behavior by a non-citizen should be dealt with by immediate deportation. Most of those things were absurd. Arguing with a citizen over the station's environment, political structure, or laws. Carrying a sign against any of these. Wearing a shirt that said anything against any one of these. And so on. They immediately pounced on Alex for details about the heinous crime the man had committed to get caged.

It was 4 a.m. before Alex managed to get them straightened out and the list trimmed down to things that incited violence or destruction. Punishments to range from fines to deportation, based on severity, as judged by forum vote like other station issues.

Rather than hike back to her apartment, Alex opted to hijack an office at Station Security to upload the new law for vote, catch up on the forums, respond to critical issues, and generally try to add reason to the crowd-insanity. The office was too hot and she pushed the air conditioning up until she got chilled and had to cut it back again.

Alex had a hard time focusing, but she had to get her posts in before people woke up and voted without having her opinion to sway them. Group democracy worked so long as people who thought things through managed to get their reasons into the discussion. Her position as Founder automatically elevated her vote and would sway those without a strong opinion. She enviously saw Brian had already gotten his posts done hours before.

Alex was midway through writing another critical post when her morning wake-up alarm went off. She finished off the post, barely had enough time to press through the full-body wash and change her SEL outfit to the green and gold pants suit, before rushing off to the conference center.

Consequently, by time Alex arrived at the conference, she was just over 15 minutes late. No time to look for her mystery man, to forewarn him, to convince him of the merits of discretion, to discuss the future. Her mouth was dry, her head throbbed, and she felt incredibly light-headed.

"Mr. Ryko is already on stage waiting for you, Founder," the conference's stage manager (not a citizen) informed her with censure when he found out who she was.

"Please bring me something to drink?" Alex asked as he ushered her toward the stage.

"I will. Get on stage."

Alex quickly stepped up the backstage stairs and stopped as the stage came into view. There on stage at the far podium was her mystery man. She stepped back behind the curtain, out of view, before he could see her. She felt the room begin to spin and bent forward to catch her breath and steady her nerves. She was sweating, yet felt cold.

Why hadn't she done her research? Why hadn't she bothered to look up the person she was debating? Why hadn't someone handed her a brief with all his details AND his picture in it? Why hadn't she accepted the phone call last night? Even better, why hadn't she kindly greeted him on his arrival at the station, instead of avoiding him the last two days?

All she'd heard of Jay Ryko was that he was a millionaire playboy who was currently spearheading environmental issues and demanding that natural environments be protected and unnatural environments (like her entire station) be minimized or destroyed. At least she understood why he never asked for her name. The same reason she hadn't asked for his. They both wanted to be seen as a normal person, not as their press-public profile.

Alex gave up trying to calm her fast heart rate. She stood up straight, pinned a neutral expression on her face, and strode out on to stage. She'd have to sort this out after the debate. She went directly to him, shook his hand, and apologized for being late. The color drained from his face.

To give him time to recover his composure, Alex went over to her own podium, apologized to everyone, offered the honest, if lame-sounding, excuse that she'd been handling some critical station affairs, and then generated some blank SEL papers that would look like notes. "I really appreciate everyone's patience," she added, as she shuffled the pages, pretending to put them in order. She glanced over at Jay Ryko. He was staring at his own notes as if they'd turned into a poisonous snake. "I believe the topic for the day is natural versus artificial environments and the merits of both?" she offered.

Someone in the front row, center, muttered loudly enough to be heard, "The merits of natural environments, at least."

Alex smiled thinly. Jay Ryko was still staring at his papers, so she began, "From the beginning of time, mankind has made use of artificial environments. A house is an artificial environment. Farm fields are an artificial environment. Even a chicken coop is an artificial environment. It would be more accurate to say 'controlled' environment, not artificial. It's a real environment, as subject to chaos theory as any environment mankind isn't actively changing."

Mr. Ryko... No, Jay. She was going to think of him as Jay at least in her own mind. Jay clearly skipped over a few pages and read, "What makes you think you can succeed where everyone else has failed? Every enclosed environment that's ever been created has collapsed in on itself, missing critical food chain species, imploding on confined environment psychology, or failing to provide enough supplies to sustain habitation. Your forest is barely 25 square miles, a fraction of a sustainable wild area. How will it succeed?" He cited several failed experiments including the Biosphere 2.

"We will succeed because we must. Psychologically, we have a significant population with the political structure to be safe, but enough input and freedom to allow individuals to be happy and form smaller communities within the whole. This is comparable to the large number of people on Earth that stay within a 2-3 hour travel distance from their homes."

The man in the front row interjected with a fake cough, "Freedom by censorship. Wouldn't let the people hear our views last night."

Alex ignored him. "Environmentally, we aren't imposing any contrived restrictions, rules, or challenges, and we're addressing problems as soon as we see them. We've done extreme analysis on microscopic and macro levels for each of the environments we have here. Each area has fully qualified staff who are dedicated to observing, analyzing, and growing that area by comparing it to and matching the same environment on Earth. We aren't limited by funds and we have very little overhead."

Jay asked some pointed questions about simulated randomness in the environments. Alex responded with detailed technical answers, showing the actual formulas used for the math and statistics, and how they applied on a functional level. She was really light-headed and desperately wanted a drink. At one point, she presented the wrong environmental analysis for what she was talking about, and when Jay pointed it out, she flushed, "Sorry, I grabbed the wrong one. That matches the Chattahoochee National Forest. Here's the correct one."

"All this data seems to indicate you're faking environments with technology," Jay stated.

Alex answered, "It's true that we manipulate light, temperature, wind, water, even the soil. We get as much natural sunlight as we can, but we maintain Earth's 24 hour day-night cycle with an elliptical orbit around the Earth that does not match." She posted a video diagram of Colony One's orbit with a sunlight intersection overlay as well as a Colony One day/night schedule overlay.

Jay reasoned, "Look at what you were able to do. If you focused your attention on the Earth, you could do great things toward cleanup and restoration."

The man in the front row added, "Instead you chose to abandon the Earth!"

Alex refused to engage in a verbal warfare with that man in the front row. Instead, she opted for proof that would support her position. "Our Pacific island has been working on cleaning up the trash being dumped there. We have been unable to turn the tide, so to speak, because other countries simply throw in more trash and act even less responsibly. The environment cannot be restored without the direct action and coordination of the political structures in power."

"No," Jay challenged, "You have the technology, yet refuse to use it."

"I have a finite amount of resources and time. It may appear that I have endless resources, but it is not nearly enough to save the Earth." As soon as the words left her mouth, she knew it was a mistake. She was so damned tired that it was hard to think clearly.

"There are things we can do to save the natural environments that you have the ability to do and are refusing!" the man in the front row shouted at her. The rest of the audience cheered him.

Goaded, Alex glared at the man and replied caustically, "The Earth as we know it is dead already. It was inevitable as far back as 1985. All the scientific data and information has been available, although much of it is suppressed. The environmental cleanups and programs are only postponing the inevitable conclusion of humanity's abuse."

"Right," the man in the front row scoffed sarcastically, "If you knew about it, why haven't you spoken up before now?"

Jay told him to stop interrupting.

"Spoken up?" Alex looked up at the ceiling and measured her breath. Her temper exploded. Without explanation, she started listing names of people, in order from the earliest ones who had 'spoken up' and were silenced, killed, threatened, hurt, thrown in jail, lost family, friends, jobs, finances. The ones who tried to defend the Earth, save threatened species, cut pollution, end fracking, end toxic pesticides, end artificial genetic manipulation of crops, end the carcinogenic chemicals in the food supplies, the ones who pointed out that global warming was true. Even with her lips and tongue going numb, she continued.

Jay tried to interrupt her, but Alex stared at her blank papers, pretending to be reading from them, and wouldn't be derailed. People from all around the world, ones who published articles, not just English ones, but all of them. She spoke faster and faster, wanting to name them all, wanting a testament to their anguish and their lives.

Alex concluded, "Why wouldn't I want to be one of them? The information is all there. It's been there, but people are too busy, too uneducated, too self-absorbed, too lazy to put it together and see the conclusion, or they are deluding themselves."

The auditorium erupted into a loud din and hissing. Alex continued anyway, "Colony One isn't about putting humans in space. It's an ark. I've been grabbing species from every environment, trying to save them for the future, trying to get them off our doomed planet. We have 8 to 13 years. 15 at the outside." The outside number was really 8 and her calculations put the end at 7 years; she wasn't sure why she lied. Maybe she wanted to give humanity a couple years of hope? "Your efforts are buying us time and for that, I thank you all, but it's already too late to actually save the planet."

"You're delusional," Jay gasped.

"Am I?" she shouted. "I'm so tired of the endless discussion that doesn't change the facts! Here, damn it." She reached into her database and retrieved the flagged articles, scientific data, lectures, both the public and classified ones. These she posted on the main screen of the conference in a crazy flicker that was too fast to read, but slow enough that the video recording frame rates would capture everything for later viewing. "That!" she pointed at the screen. "Go save the Earth if you can, but stop trying to hinder my efforts to save what I can!"

Leaving the stack of blank papers, she stormed off the stage. The backstage hallway spun threateningly. She shoved past people that tried to stop her and actually punched one of them who got in her way. Out in the daylight, she saw several people whom she recognized as medtechs coming toward her and she ran in the opposite direction.

Her world erupted into a splash of white confetti.

"Alex! Alex! Turn off your bioshield!"

She could hear shouting, but it sounded so far away. Everything was dark.

"Turn off your bioshield!"

She felt like she should recognize the voice. It sounded very demanding. Very urgent.

"Founder! We need to help you." A different person speaking this time.

"Don't call her Founder, call her Alex. Use her given name. Damn it, where's Lucas?"

It's not my given name, she remembered distantly. One time, long ago, she was someone else entirely. Who was she? They must be talking to someone else. Maybe it was dark because she was in her cave and her fire had gone out. Must be some hikers in the clearing. She should stay still and be very quiet so they wouldn't find her. Maybe it was a bear. She should get her shiv.

"Alex, you've had a seizure. You need to turn off your bioshield so we can help you."

The words held no meaning and she floated around contentedly. It felt so good to just lie there and rest. Her mouth felt dry. She licked her lips. That idiot had never brought her anything to drink. That annoyed her. Where was that drink? Who was it that was supposed to bring her a drink? That promised to bring her a drink? Why would someone bring her a drink in her cave?

"Alex. Turn. Off. Your. Bioshield."

She tried to say "drink", but it was too hard. It bothered her that she couldn't remember who said they'd bring her a drink. She always remembered everything. Maybe everything hadn't happened and that's why she couldn't remember?

"Alex, turn off your bioshield! Turn it off now!"

She felt someone shaking her. Then that same person pulled her right eyelid open. Too bright light and a blur of color assaulted her. The other eyelid was pulled open and that side was also too bright. Her head hurt. Why wasn't her bioshield protecting her from this torturous light? Bioshield. She had a bioshield. Nothing could penetrate it. No bullets, no poisons, no knives. She wanted to add bright light to the list. Where was that list. She tried to focus. Thinking hurt and she couldn't see her HUD clearly.

The voice continued demanding she turn off her bioshield. No, that would let someone kill her. She was too important to allow herself to be killed. She had important stuff to do. If only she could remember what it was, she thought as she floated around, wishing she could float away from that horrible bright light.

"Alex, you've had a seizure. Turn off your bioshield so we can help you. Your blood sugar is severely low."

"She's got the med alerts. I don't know why she didn't see them." Yet another voice.

"They're likely caught in her spam filter. Alex!"

She heard a loud clicking sound directly in front of her face. Damn reporters. She wanted to see which one it was, because she was going to kill him this time. She was going to kill all of the reporters. She forced herself to focus so she could make out who it was. No, not a reporter's camera. Someone's hand snapping their fingers right in front of her nose.

"Can't you override this thing?"

"I've tried."

"Don't we have any hackers that can get through?"

"Her blood sugar just dropped another point," another voice said.

"Through her security? It won't be fast enough, if it's even possible. Alex!!!!! Turn off your bioshield!"

She wanted to sleep. They were too loud. Too noisy. Too insistent. Why wouldn't they leave her alone? She turned off her bioshield just to shut them up. Then she closed her eyes and drifted away.

Alex blinked. She was in a medical bed of one of the pristine white rooms in the new medical complex. The medical monitoring equipment would be located just behind the head of the bed, out of her vision, while a sink and cabinets were off to her left. Missing were the typical whiteboard, clipboards, and information posters. Colony One's computer system replaced the need for any of that.

The room was deliberately plain to give patients a mental transition from their old life to the new one. Most patients wouldn't stay more than a few days and with HUDs providing entertainment, this white limbo wouldn't be that much of a problem.

"Alex?" whispered Brian from the guest chair to her right.

Alex tried to remember how she'd gotten there but the memory was missing. She panicked and struggled to remember the last thing she could. There was the debate. She winced as she recalled what she'd done. She also remembered storming out. Then nothing. "Shit," Alex muttered.

"Oh, thank God. I'll get the doctor." Brian's hand moved as he used his HUD. He had dark circles under his eyes and needed a shave. "Do you remember having a seizure?"

"No." She went to activate the security footage, but couldn't. "Where's my HUD?"

"We've disabled it. Your bioshield almost got you killed. It's hard to give you an injection when the needle bends away from your skin."

Alex narrowed her eyes at Brian. "You better not be giving me injections." Then she noticed the IV stuck in her arm. "Shit," she repeated, suppressing the horrible flashbacks that threatened.

Kgomotso came in at a run. He was the brilliant doctor who treated Lucas after Lucas' trip to Saturn and was recently helping her set up the huge medical complex. "Founder?" He skidded to a stop.

"What happened, Kgomotso?"

"Low blood sugar seizures. You should be fine in another day or so. You'd probably be dead right now if you weren't so healthy to begin with." Kgomotso walked beside her, but instead of looking at her, he studied the monitoring equipment that Alex knew was there. "When was the last time you ate?"

Alex winced. "It's been a while." She knew her last meal had been two days prior. She'd been too upset about the upcoming debate to eat.

"We're going to have to update our medical alert system. The routine notice went into the log which didn't get reviewed until morning 4 days ago." The doctor frowned as he continued his dispassionate explanation. "The reviewer noted it, but didn't make the connection to your I.D. and figured any diabetic would know to eat something so she just sent out a routine warning. She just pushed your I.D. into the alert system to keep sending you reminders until your numbers normalized. Except they didn't normalize. The reviewer the next day saw the critical alert, looked up your name and instead of sending a full medical staff, which is what he should have done, he called Mr. Kimberly, who decided not to panic everyone by pulling you out in the middle of the debate. Which is why I told him you were going to be a vegetable. Those seizures could have been prevented." Their obvious ongoing argument continued as Kgomotso and Brian Kimberly glared at each other.

Alex's mind did the numbers and latched onto the critical bit of information. "4 days?" She'd missed dinner with Jay.

"Yes, we've had you sedated for 2. Your body was showing serious signs of sleep deprivation on top of your low sugar. Didn't you notice the warning signs of low blood sugar, Founder? As you get older, your body changes. You need to adapt. You're on medical leave for the next two weeks." Kgomotso crossed his arms firmly as if he expected Alex to argue.

"Except we put it in as vacation to prevent any panic," Brian clarified.

"How many people know?" Alex asked. She dreaded the answer.

Kgomotso deferred to Brian who said, "Just the medtechs. And our friendly neighborhood reporter, who followed you out of the debate. He's agreed he's not reporting this; he knows it would cause mass panic. He says you owe him an interview though. Meanwhile, I've been ghost-writing entries on the forums under your account. Some of our citizens are a little annoyed that you can tell them they aren't allowed to have a temper tantrum but then you have one. There's also the matter of you punching one of our guests on the way out of the auditorium. We've convinced the man not to press charges, but he awaits your formal apology."

"Ok. I want this IV out. I want my HUD. And I want to make a private phone call. In that order, and right now."

Brian shook his head. "Alex, you can't tell anyone about the seizures. I think you need to review the forums before you speak with anyone."

Kgomotso frowned at Brian. "You should have some tests to see how you are functioning mentally too. It's possible you have some brain damage I've missed. You should also avoid stress and that means letting him continue to write your forum entries a few more days."

Brian waved his hand dismissing this. He knew Alex too well for that. "I also need you to authorize me to override your bioshield."

"And me," Kgomotso added, crossing his arms determinedly.

Alex shrugged and pulled her IV out and pressed the vein with her finger.
"Founder!" Kgomotso reprimanded sharply.
"Head's up display, Gentlemen. Don't make me ask a third time."
Brian didn't look happy about it, but his hand moved as he authorized it anyway.

The first thing Alex did was repair her vein. Then she ordered her picobots to clean up the blood that sprayed while she was doing that. Brian's eyes got wider, but Kgomotso knew what she'd been working on for the new medical complex. Then, she reactivated the bioshield, adding override authorization for both of them. Finally, she studied her medical report. This scared her and she inhaled sharply. She really could have died. She added immediate, constant monitoring of her blood sugar and blood pressure, setting very restrictive parameters, and obnoxious, impossible-to-ignore warnings.

"Ok, you two can stop panicking now." Alex tried for a 'I'm just fine' healthy smile, but thought it probably just made her seem more ill. "May I make that phone call now?"

Brian pulled Kgomotso out of the room as Kgomotso reminded her, "No stress."

Alex looked up Jay's schedule and her heart dropped as she saw he was already on his way back to Earth. She'd missed him on station by 3 hours. At least he'd still have his HUD so she could call him privately. She sat up, changed her SEL clothes to a standard stationer's jumpsuit, activated a privacy shield, and called.

Jay took longer to answer then expected. His face appeared with a standard white privacy shield behind it. "What?" His lips were tight and his eyebrows almost imperceptibly pinched with controlled anger.

"I'm sorry."

"Sorry for what? Sorry that you didn't have the decency to stay around after the debate and talk with me? Sorry you didn't show up for dinner? I thought you'd at least come to that, regardless of what happened at that debate. Sorry you didn't bother to send me a message saying you wouldn't be there? Sorry you ignored me for 2 days and didn't answer or return any of my calls? Or sorry that you needlessly frightened every person on Earth? People listen to you. They believe you. You aren't the person I thought you were. Did you enjoy making a fool of me? It was cruel. Don't ever call me again." He disconnected.

Alex wept. When she finally stopped, she went through all of the messages he'd left - begging her to call, telling her it didn't matter about the debate, asking her to make some retraction to the 'end of world' statement, but mostly just asking for a few minutes of her time. She went through the replies her station staff had given him. All were that generic 'The Founder is unavoidably busy; please leave a message' nonsense. How frustrated he must have been. She added his name to the list of people who would always be immediately forwarded to her, regardless of her call status.

Biting her lip, she realized she could access the station security feed and actually see him. She had the absolute trust of the citizens. No one would doubt her. No one would ever even know. But no crime had been committed. No crime reported. No valid reason to look at the security feeds at all. In fact, abuse of security feeds was one of the crimes likely to get a person sent back to their country of origin - a rule she'd added to prevent anyone abusing their privilege.

She barely even hesitated before pulling every security feed he was in and watching them all, from the time he first got his I.D. and HUD all the way through his departure from the London airport. He was indeed charming, witty, amazing, and flawed. He never should have been with his now-ex. It was apparent she treated him as an ornament and servant and only really liked the envious looks she got when he was on her arm, not to mention the obvious disconnect between his love of nature and her complete disregard for it. That woman would have never set foot on a sailboat. Maybe a cruise ship, but only if it didn't rock much.

Everywhere Jay went, if he noticed something that wasn't quite right, he fixed it. He picked up broken branches and moved them out of the walking paths, he straightened pictures, he helped people carry things and opened doors for them. He made kids giggle, showing them how to make whistles out of grass blades. Even as she hated herself for the invasion of privacy, she couldn't stop herself.

When Alex found herself watching him shower, she stopped, hating herself. She erased the logs of her accessing the system. Then she erased the footage of her time in the theater with Jay. She didn't want to risk that ever getting viewed. She left a note in the missing spot with her name on it.

"Power tends to corrupt and absolute power corrupts absolutely. Great men are almost always bad men." she recalled. Alex couldn't let herself do this, except she already had. How could she expect humanity to become better than itself when even she couldn't and she knew how important it was?

Resolutely, Alex shifted her mind away from Jay and looked up the warning signs of low blood sugar and made herself review them again, despite already knowing them. She could actually go back over the week before the debate and check them all off on the list.

Over the next month, Alex refused to retract her statement that the Earth was doomed. The Earth press had a field day and consequently, the majority of reasonable people refused to put their lives in the hands of a madwoman and mostly paranoid, slightly crazy people registered for citizenship. Hidden in this group, super smart people who actually dug through her data began to slip in. They were always quiet about it. They either recognized some of the names she'd listed during the debate (which someone had published on their website) or didn't want their peers to know they were going to trust a madwoman.

346

Citizens urged their Earth-side family and friends to relocate to Colony One as soon as possible and kept asking if there was anything at all that could be done. Ignoring Kgomotso's mandatory sick leave directive, Alex instead added more people to the Earth's geological monitoring and prediction team and began a task force to figure out how to handle a large influx of refugees "should something catastrophic happen to the Earth".

Then some movie star posted a video of herself nude surfing and people stopped thinking about the end of the planet. After all, people have been crying wolf since the beginning of time and bare breasts were contemporarily scandalous. Colony One's teams continued their research and planning.

Now that Alex was paying attention, she noticed her blood sugar had a tendency to stay low. She ate but some of the higher sugar fruits and heavier meals just didn't agree with her. She just couldn't quite get her body to normalize again. She was plagued with exhaustion and dizzy spells. Her lowered immune system allowed her to catch the flu and grinding her teeth with frustration, she went to see Kgomotso.

Alex found him in the center of the medical complex. His room's location reminded her of a perfect spider web with Kgomotso the resident owner. The office itself was a large square room with a huge collection of medical books and journals on shelves off to one side near a comfortable reading chair and a desk. The open area that took over the rest of the room was currently displaying a triple-sized three dimensional projected model of a woman with a leg split mid-thigh.

Kgomotso himself was standing in the woman's hip, studying the cross-section. With a practiced swipe of his hand, he zoomed in on the femur until the medullary cavity of the diaphysis was twice the size of his head. The nutrient arteries in the periosteum could be easily seen.

"Hey, Kgomotso."

"Founder." He stepped out of the projection. "I think we're ready for our first patient."

"Good. I'll start making arrangements tomorrow. I didn't come here about that though. I've been having some problems and I was wondering if you might help?" She described her symptoms to Kgomotso and concluded, "I've scanned myself and I can't find the virus. I haven't found any bacteria either. Is this post-seizure brain failure?"

"Well, we could scan your head and see. Most likely you're just tired. You never took any time off like I told you to," Kgomotso replied mercilessly.

"I threw up this morning," Alex confessed.

"Exhaustion can do that." He rubbed his chin and looked at her thoughtfully. "Hrm. How to put this delicately? You haven't been experimenting on yourself, have you?"

"No."

"I would understand," Kgomotso said. "I know we're getting ready to host the first patient and we have a lot of things to consider when doing repairs on such a microscopic scale."

"I haven't been experimenting. Just monitoring my sugar and blood pressure."

"Hormones?"

Alex knew the second he said the word. "I'm pregnant, aren't I?"

"Let's do a scan and find out."

Alex didn't need the body scan, but let him do it anyway, thoughtfully saying nothing until it was done.

His scan told him the same thing. "Congratulations."

"Kgomotso, you can't tell anyone. I have to talk to the father first. It's complicated."

"Most relationships are. You should go visit one of the gynecologists and get started on some vitamins and then come back and help me get this medical center operational."

Alex provided a wry smile, agreed to come work in the center soon, and went to stare at the stars. She massaged her belly and told her baby she was sorry she thought he/she was the flu. She hacked into the United States phone system and got Jay's unlisted phone number. She dialed it, but then hung up before it could ring. He'd want to know. He might not want anyone else to know he'd slept with "that madwoman", but he would certainly want to know. If it were possible, he'd probably even want to sue for custody to "protect" his baby.

Alex was emotionally drained to begin with. She didn't want to deal with him yelling at her again too. She hadn't recovered completely from his vicious denunciation a month ago, and she couldn't fix it without telling him why, and she couldn't let "Founder has medical issues" tip her citizens' already precarious faith in her. It wouldn't be a problem if she hadn't blundered so badly at the debate, and Earth-side social media hadn't declared her completely insane. Despite her information warriors, some of that sentiment had cascaded into her citizens also.

Colony One had to have priority over everything. It was humanity's future. She had just barely recovered from the debate debacle. In the back of her mind, where she didn't want to look too closely at it, was the guilt of having watched his security feed that was supposed to be absolutely secure and private.

So instead of calling Jay, Alex lay on her bed in her lab on the star-side of the station and stared at the universe until she fell asleep. The silence and endless stars were comforting. She was really looking forward to Lucas finally having his teleportation science working. She wanted to see space from Pluto.

The next morning, Alex read and watched everything she could find on

Jay Ryko. The press wasn't kind to him either. He had no privacy. Every date, every glance that lingered too long, a smile even, was torqued into a twisted mocking of a shallow nymphomaniac with too much money and too little to do. His volunteer work on behalf of the conservation organization was minimized and even noted as 'a way for the rich playboy to play with tanned svelte naive girls'. No wonder he didn't want to say who he was. Every interaction would have been tainted with people either thrill-seeking or trying to get money from him. She'd call him eventually.

Alex sat at a desk in a small, unused office near the middle of the medical center. Eventually, the offices would be given to doctors, but until the center had patients and staff, most of the rooms remained empty skeletons, without even furniture.

The phone rang. Alex waited somewhat impatiently for someone to answer it. This was her 23rd call trying to get someone to come partake of the new medical program. She reviewed the man's dossier while waiting. Physical therapist, himself an amputee, working with other amputees. An ex-marine, missing his right leg. By all accounts, honorable, brave. Someone who knew the right clientele to quietly spread the word until the program got enough staff to handle the inevitable influx of people.

When he answered, Alex said, "Hi, I'm looking for John White."

"Speaking."

His gruff tone suggested he got too many telemarketing calls. Alex supposed this qualified. "I'm calling on behalf of Colony One's new medical center. I was wondering if you'd be interested in participating in our first program." And here's where the other person either hung up, thought this was a joke, or called all Colony One people crazy for following a madwoman.

There was a pause and then some keyboard typing. "No new medical center is listed on the Colony One website. Good try."

Quickly, before he could hang up on her, Alex said, "Yeah, it's not announced yet. We're currently invitation only."

"I'll bet. Goodbye."

"Wait! If I put it on the website, will you at least hear me out?"

"Sure." His tone indicated his belief on that ever happening.

"I'll call you back in 10 minutes." Alex disconnected. She typed up a brief publicity announcement, called the website team, and sent it to them for immediate deployment. 'Colony One to open new Medical Center for the treatment of chronic conditions. Initially, the program will be invitation-only until the process is optimized. Then both citizens and non-citizens can apply through Colony One's standard random selection process, with priority to citizens. Applications to work at the new Medical Center are being accepted with precedence. Sit up and pay attention, Everyone(jw), this changes the medical industry forever.' She made the 'jw' a superscript to 'Everyone', so it would look like a typo'd 'tm'. John White should spot it, but no one else would understand it.

Alex waited for the website team to send her a reply, tapping her foot impatiently. Noticing her foot, she stilled it. Her fingers unconsciously took over with a fast drumming. The post only took a few minutes. A few incredibly long minutes.

Exactly 10 minutes later, she called John White back. Again, it took a long time for him to answer. "Hi, it's me again, calling from Colony One's new medical center."

"I honestly didn't expect you to call back. I thought you were playing a prank."

"I understand your doubt. I assure you, I'm entirely serious. If you'll look at Colony One's press release announcement page, the latest entry is about us."

Computer keystrokes, then silence. "Huh." More silence. "So what is it you think you can do for me?"

"I can't really discuss the details over the phone. We want to have our first few successes so we can get a good feel for psychological impact and rehab time before we openly announce what we are doing because people will demand details and answers which we don't have yet. You would be our first non-citizen client." She didn't say 'first client', which was also true. They needed a first patient. If they chose a citizen, word would spread like wildfire.

"I see." John White said, "You are looking for a lab rat to experiment on. I already have a state-of-the-art prosthetic leg. I can give you the names of some guys that need assistance though."

"And that's why we chose to call you. You think of others before yourself. You help people. You already know how rehab works. You're already aware of the psychological consequences of systemic trauma. You could give us invaluable feedback on our process and procedures and improve the experience for every future client." Alex pulled at her hair and wondered what it was going to take to get someone to agree to come. She supposed she could go with a citizen if she needed to.

"How much would this cost me?" John White asked.

"Time. While on Colony One, you'd be subject to all our laws and regulations as if you were a citizen. You can bring one person as a helper for the first week who will be allowed to stay in the room with you. After the first stage of your treatment, you'll be relocated to the standard visitor hotel for the duration of your rehab. The plan is to require clients to work the standard 30 hours per week at the job of their choice, through the duration of rehab as payment for services rendered. Travel, food, entertainment, and other purchases would not be covered. As you would be our first, we will also cover travel and food."

"How much time? I have people depending on me here."

"We estimate somewhere between 3 and 12 months. You will probably be closer to 3 months, given your rehab experience."

"What are you planning to do? Cut my stump off and give me a SEL leg?"

That was pretty accurate, except it wouldn't be SEL. It would be personal DNA-designed organic tissue, microscopically attached as if the leg had never been gone. Rehab involved training the brain to direct the muscles and process the nerve feedback again. Without directly answering, Alex said, "While the technology to do that is certainly possible, we think it would be a step in the wrong direction. Hrm. Um. You'd also have to sign a non-disclosure agreement. It wouldn't be forever, but just until we get enough staff on board to support opening the entire center."

There was a long silence. Alex held her breath. Then he said, "3 months is too long for me to be away from my men." He meant his rehab clients. "They're counting on me."

Negotiation. Alex exhaled. She had him. It was just a matter of price. "Bring your current clients along. I'll give them a visitor pass. They can stay in the hotel. We'll give you a rehab room to use and we'll count the time you spend with them toward your 30 hours per week."

Another pause. Then, "If you are looking for people to treat..."

Alex was impressed at how gutsy he was. The whole price was ridiculous and this verged on impossibly absurd. From his point of view. From her view, it would give her several clients all in a discrete social circle which would limit inevitable information leaks and would give them a social support group for the unavoidable frustration of retraining their brains. "Because we won't be able to hide what we're doing with you, if they want to participate too, we'll let them. I can't guarantee we'll be able to help them, but I'll add them to the list. We're only working with one person at a time for the actual procedure. The process is quite involved. They'd have to sign the non-disclosure agreement too."

"I'll talk with my men and see if they are interested. They really should get the same deal as me, and have travel, hotel, and food also covered, don't you think? We're all healthy, smart individuals with a proven record of working hard and serving others and we'd be doing you a favor..."

She laughed at that. "Shall I give you each a permanent mansion on the Pacific island too?"

"Come on, Founder - yeah, I recognize your voice - you've got money. These guys ain't got anything. They have astronomical medical bills. The military disability benefits take forever to process and most of them are living on donations. I have a girl whose boyfriend just dumped her because it was 'too much' for him. One of them is officially homeless as of last week. You want me, take them too."

Oh, yeah, Alex wanted this guy. He was going to beg to be part of the new medical complex once he figured out they were repairing people. Already trained rehab specialist and he'd make sure the people got a fair deal, and he'd be great at convincing people to come. Her goal wasn't actually healing people right now - it was about building a massive medical response team so when the Earth failed, her station would have the resources to help the refugees. Money, at this point, was pointless. It was going to be completely worthless soon enough. Alex waited as if she were debating it. "Ok, you've convinced me. Talk with your friends. I'll cover everything but incidentals, and they'd still have to work the 30 hours per week as well as do the 1 hour exercise period every day."

"How soon would we need to be there?"

"You could show up tomorrow if you wanted. We're ready. However, I understand it would take time to get everything organized. Sooner is better than later." Reminded, she tickled her baby's foot under her skin and got an obliging push back. "I'll give you a call Tuesday night." That would give him four days to speak with everyone he knew and get volunteers. Good. She could stop trying to find people. Kgomotso was going to be delighted. Incoming clients!

Alex was laying in her apartment's bed, checking nerve connections for their tenth patient when the call came in. Reclining was more comfortable than sitting sometimes. Figuring it was Kgomotso again, she didn't even look at the caller's name because she didn't want to lose her place in the 3D body maze. She answered in her best faux-Jamaican accent which was nothing like the real thing, "Yo, Mon, ya gotta let dings happ'n in der own dime. Mon, I'm'a gonna ship it in an hour. Chill out, Mon."

Silence. In her normal voice, she asked, "What is it, Kgomotso?"

"Is it mine?" Jay's voice halted her concentration completely. She shut down all her open projects with a single swipe, preparing to concentrate with all her energy. The caller's name flashed "Jay Ryko, transferred from Unlisted." followed by his actual phone number.

"Jay." Alex wasn't ready for this yet. It had only been 4 months.

"I'm not kuh-mot, mote-so, whoever that is. New lover? No - I don't want to know. Is the baby mine?"

There was an echo to Jay's voice. She was on speaker-phone, with an unknown audience. "Yours, yes."

"Were you going to tell me?" He sounded mildly drunk.

"I tried calling. I couldn't." Every day, trying to get the nerve to call him, replaying their time together in the theater in her mind. Alex loaded and flipped through the news media. There it was - a photo of her taken by one of the station visitors at just the right angle that the loose clothing designs didn't hide her stomach, with the caption, "Founder of Colony One Pregnant?

Medical Experiment or Lucky Man?"

Jay's voice was gravelly. "With all your resources, you couldn't get my phone number? Couldn't reach me through the conservation office?"

"I was afraid you'd yell at me again." Was honesty really the best option? Alex didn't want him to think she blamed him for the silence. She was at fault here, not him. "You're right to be angry. I should have called."

"I want a paternity test."

"Of course. I want you to come for the birth. She should get to meet her father on her first day. I'll pay for everything." Not that either of them cared about money; that was one of the benefits of having too much of it. Alex's books continued to bring in a large amount monthly, despite not having written any more since the launch. Jay had inherited family money.

Jay cleared his throat. "I want the test done by a doctor of my own choice. Not one of your lackeys who will say whatever you tell them to." His words were still slurred.

"If you give me a name, I'll add him and whoever else you want to come to a list of approved visitors."

"If it's mine..."

"She," Alex corrected. "She's a girl."

"If it's mine, you can't keep it from me."

"Her. She is yours and while I'm breastfeeding, you are welcome to come and stay here as many times and as long as you'd like. After that, she can spend up to a half a year, every year, with you, as long or as little as you want and are able. I have no intention of keeping her from you. When she's older, as much as she wants."

"If that baby is mine, I'm going to be its father. You can't keep it from me, no matter who you are. I have connections too." Maybe more than a little drunk. How much bolstering did he need to call her?

Another person spoke up, "I think she was just saying she doesn't plan to keep the baby away from you, Jay." The man's voice was higher pitched than most men, but still obviously male.

"Hello? You are?" Alex asked.

"Byron, Jay's best friend."

An intimate phone call, then. That was promising. Alex stood and paced the room, hand on her stomach.

Byron continued, "He was going to leave you a message. We didn't think he'd actually get through."

Alex massaged her baby. "He's on my automatic allow list now. I didn't get any of his messages while he was on the station until it was too late to matter. I've corrected that problem."

"She still could have called me," Jay mumbled. "Common decency."

"Yes." Byron's voice slightly muffled as he apparently turned away from the phone's speaker, "She could have called you. I think we've taken enough of the Founder's time, Jay."

"She should have called me!" Jay shouted. "Should have. Should have. Should have!" There was a shattering splash as a bottle hit a wall or something equally hard.

"Founder, I'll see he gets you a list of names when he sobers up," Byron said.

"Thank you. Take care of him, Byron."

"He's a decent man. You did one hell of a number on him. You'd better do what you said just now." The connection dropped.

Alex looked at her display's clock. It was 9 p.m. station time. She'd been working on the nerve connections since lunch. Her eyes snapped to her blood sugar display. At least that was stable. She grabbed a few walnuts and ate them anyway. She shouldn't skip meals anymore.

Alex sent Kgomotso a note that she wouldn't get to the review until the next day, and she retreated to her lab facing the stars again. She really liked looking out at the brilliant stars. Even with no artificially generated light, the sky was brilliantly lit.

"It's just a misunderstanding," she told her baby, running her hand across her belly. "I'll make it right when he gets here. You don't need to worry about having a drunkard for a father. If I had a choice between him and all the other men on Earth, I'd still choose him to be your father. Pheromones and basic animal attraction, kiddo. Don't underestimate them." And a compatibility of spirit and thoughts and goals. It shouldn't be possible to fall in love that fast; must be a standard crush. "He's going to teach you how to sail and how to fight for what you believe in even if it's not popular." She put on some classical music for her baby and tried to sleep. Her work could wait until morning. She was far too unsettled to focus on work anyway.

The young woman that the airport staff wheeled in was missing both arms and her left leg. She smelled like sewage that had been cooking in summer heat for three days. Alex did not cringe, but it was hard. Her baby objected with a few good thumps against her abdomen. The man pushing the wheelchair retreated with envy-inspiring speed. Other passengers moved away with their luggage. Alex strode over. "Patricia Madison?"

"Who else?" the young woman snarled.

Alex smiled warmly. "I'm Alex, your Medical Center tech. I'll have someone find your luggage. What are we looking for?"

"Nothing. I don't have any luggage. That bitch pretending to be my nurse refused to load anything in the cab."

"Sounds like you're having a terrible day. Want me to send someone to your house to retrieve it? It can come up on the next shuttle."

The young woman blinked suspiciously, then nodded. "There's a key in my front shirt pocket. My suitcase is in the back bedroom unless it got moved."

Alex retrieved the key and took it over to their terminal staff and gave instructions, taking the opportunity to inhale deeply. Then she immediately returned despite the lure of fresh air anywhere else. She initiated a full-body scan. The woman was miserable. A whole host of problems, with the most immediate being her need to use the restroom.

"You didn't register the name of your helper for the week?" Alex prodded gently.

"I don't have one. My ex was supposed to come but he backed out before I could get someone to fill out the form."

"Not a problem. We'll get you someone." Using her HUD, Alex immediately put in a request for round-the-clock social workers with home health aide experience. "Let's move you over here and run up a nice private room. The shuttle will build around us."

"In other words, you want to protect the other passengers from me?" The woman made a face, wrinkling her nose.

Alex gave a simple shrug and teased lightly, "Nah, that's to protect you from them for smelling so bad. 'Medical client lynched at airport' would be bad publicity, ya know." With the chair relocated, Alex created a large private room out of SEL. With an excellent air filtration system. "Let's start by getting rid of this antique chair. Useless thing."

"I have to use the bathroom."

"I know. Full body scan. Medtech," Alex explained as the woman flushed red. She created the SEL chair around the woman and had it lift the woman's body to the side. She created a door and shoved the chair out. Someone would return it to the local airport, if only to get rid of the smell. Then she created a toilet. "How would you feel about a bath, too, and swapping your clothes to a SEL suit?"

The woman's eyes were as big as saucers. "Uh, I guess so?"

"SEL. Solid electricity. It's not really electricity and not really a solid, but the name stuck. It dynamically reconfigures. Mind if I cut these off? Moving you around is going to be a bit difficult just now." Alex rubbed her abdomen tenderly. "SEL will be a much better choice for the near future anyway."

"Are you able to..." The woman seemed to focus on Alex for the first time, taking in Alex's nicely rounded abdomen.

Alex saw the instant that the woman recognized her as the Founder because the woman's eyebrows pulled together and her eyes squinted in appalled disbelief. Alex answered cheerfully, patting her baby, "Oh, sure. She's not done yet."

Alex made some scissors and proceeded to cut off the woman's clothes. So directed, the SEL chair moved her on to the toilet. Meanwhile, Alex created a bathtub and filled it with sudsy water. By time the tub was ready, the woman was done, and Alex did the necessary wiping, and had the chair lower her into the tub. She stuffed the clothes into the toilet and closed the lid, letting the unit burn everything into dust. Then she removed the toilet and added a chair for herself. Alex fully cycled the room's the air again too.

Alex directed the tub to rise until it was easy for her to reach the woman, and she proceeded to provide the necessary services as gently and thoroughly as possible. The poor woman had obviously been neglected. The SEL chair fully supported the woman, and everything rotated and tilted as needed.

"Do you prefer to be called Patricia? Pat? Some other nickname?" Alex asked.

"Pat."

Every time the conversation touched on something miserable, Alex listened intently, agreed it was awful, and shifted the subject. There would be time for counseling later. Now was a time for breaking the old routine.

"I can swap out the water. Would you like to soak for a bit? I could also trim up your hair if you want." Alex lifted the heavy, now clean, wet, tangled mass.

"You can do that?"

"Sure." She suspected Pat hadn't been properly groomed in the last year. "This is a full service Medical Center although haircuts aren't my specialty. You could visit a salon this afternoon if you want. In fact, you probably should if you are brave enough to let me cut some of these knots out."

Pat half-giggled, cutting herself short, not yet willing to admit she deserved to laugh. Alex smiled at her encouragingly. Yes, let the woman remember what it felt like to be a real, whole person, not a thing someone must take care of.

Pat nodded. "You don't mind taking me to a salon?"

"I'll go with you to one. You're going to take yourself, though."

"Right." Pat made a scoffing sound.

"I think you're going to like this. Let me show you how the HUD and chair work and are controlled by your verbal commands."

"I thought you were doing it."

"I am, but that's because I'm a medtech today. I have authorization. Proceed everything you want with 'Chair'. Try 'Chair, show display.'"

Pat did and gasped as the HUD appeared in front of her.

"You're the only one who can see your display. Now try, 'Chair, select directory and show hair salons.' You can display information about any that look interesting and call directly."

A few minutes later, Pat had a hair appointment for an hour after they would arrive at Colony One. Alex showed her how to control the actual chair and then how to select a SEL outfit.

As Alex picked through Pat's hair and detangled it, she described the other features of the chair and how it would help her eat and drink as if she had arms.

"While it's nice and social to have people help you, you really need your independence. We're going to give you that. I think you'll find Colony One a good home for the duration of your visit."

"Is the procedure painful?"

"I'm told the very end is shocking and disconcerting, but not painful. Recovery is frustrating. You remember how to move your limbs, but your brain doesn't remember how." Alex did a loose braid so the hair would still continue to dry. "How about you lay on your stomach a bit and rest, while I try to get some of the knots out of your neck and shoulders next?"

"Not much on privacy, eh?"

"Medtech. You can't hide shit from me. Literally."

Pat groaned, but there was the smile.

Alex created a massage table and told Pat how to get her chair to orient her into a face-down position. Alex lowered the lights, put on some peaceful music, and did her best to put Pat to sleep. While she worked, she did some minor tissue repair on bedsores and bruising from obviously negligent care.

"I feel like a new person, Founder. Thank you."

"You are a new person. We're going to ditch that old life of yours and you're going to make yourself all over again."

"I have to use the bathroom again."

"I know. How about I give you some privacy to do that? Think you know how to direct the chair well enough?"

"Really?"

"Really. If you get stuck, my number is at the top of your directory and you can call."

When Pat finally came out of the bathroom she'd created within their room, it was clear she'd been crying.

Alex nodded understandingly, "It's ok. Try 'Chair, wipe face' or 'Chair, clean face'."

She did and then asked plaintively, "Can I name this thing something other than Chair?"

"Nope. It's an incentive to lose dependency on it. We're pretty close to Colony One now, would you like to see Earth?" For the remainder of the flight, they watched Earth as it fell away from the shuttle.

On the way to the salon, Alex started to feel odd. Her blood pressure spiked, then dropped, and she started to feel contractions.

"Are you going into labor?" Pat followed Alex to a nearby bench.

"Naw." Alex massaged her forehead as the dizziness continued to rise. When the vertigo didn't dissipate, she fired off a medical alert to request assistance. "I just need to sit here a few minutes. Go ahead on to the salon. It's just up around the bend. Your HUD will direct you. I'll be along shortly." Alex sent off a request for someone to meet Pat at the salon.

○ ● ◗) ● (◖ ●

"Bed rest," the midwife pronounced dispassionately. "For the duration. No exercise periods. No work. No stress."

"I have a procedure tomorrow," Alex informed her.

"You have bed rest tomorrow, Founder."

Alex began designing her new bed that would operate very much like Pat's chair. "Thank you. I guess I'll catch up on my reading."

The midwife sighed and shook her head.

Two days later, Alex was reclined on her bed, next to and facing Pat, who was comfortably propped up on her own bed in the operation theater. In a happy role reversal, Alex would provide the distraction while Kgomotso would do the actual procedure. He was ready, even if this would be his first 'solo' job. Also present was John White, their patient zero, who was now the distracter-in-training and Pat's future physical therapist. In the neighboring room, on the other side of a one-way mirror, a half dozen doctors watched.

"We're going to start with some simple nerve tests that will take a bit of time. Mostly, it'll be us asking if you feel something and you saying, 'no, feel what?' It'll take us some time to get set up." Alex adjusted her bed height and pillows.

"Is the actual operation going to hurt?"

Alex deferred to John, who stood at the head of Alex's bed, on both of his completely functioning legs. The idea was to keep Pat focused on them and her HUD and not at all on Kgomotso.

"I got my new leg here." John lifted his knee and thumped it with his hand. "You don't feel anything at all until the nerve blockers are turned off. Then it's a bit like jumping into a cold pool. Lots of feedback that is overwhelming for a moment and then you get used to it."

"Do you swim?" Alex asked. Kgomotso was already seeing if Pat jumped when he poked her with a pin. She didn't notice at all. They'd grown/assembled her limbs earlier that morning from her DNA.

"Swim?" She shook her head disbelievingly. "I have a hard time wrapping my head around the idea of doing anything but laying in a bed or getting pushed around in a wheelchair."

"Yeah," agreed John, "The psychological repair is far harder than the surgery."

"It's not a surgery," Alex corrected. "It's a procedure."

"I keep forgetting that," John replied with a cheery smile and chuckle. Light, teasing, and joking - that was their cultivated atmosphere. "What was your favorite sport before the accident, Pat?"

When Pat looked a little distraught, Alex added, "I know it's painful to think about. You've got years of crying inside every time the subject came up, but you'll be able to do them again. Most of that sadness was from knowing you'd never be able to do them again. You've got a practiced reaction that you'll have to unlearn."

"I used to love swimming." Pat's eyebrows drew together and her voice was quiet.

"Great! We have excellent places to swim here. I'll add that to your rehab list." John nodded firmly, decision made.

Alex pulled up the list of swim locations on Pat's HUD and made it opaque so the image was perfectly clear for Pat and completely hid what Kgomotso was up to. "Let me give you a tour of them. My personal favorite is the reef tank. You get some snorkel gear and swim in a pool that is in the center of a huge aquarium. The fish can't actually get to you, nor you to the fish, but you can swim really close to them." Alex made the display do a full, slow sweep through the tank along the bottom so the coral reef could be clearly seen. Kgomotso was speedily making all the connections on Pat's new leg. "You can set your HUD to show information about each living organism too." Alex demonstrated.

"That's really amazing," Pat said. "Hey, is that a shark?"

"Mmmm hmmm. That one's a silvertip shark. They don't mind the proximity of humans too much." Alex let the image follow the shark. She was really proud of their aquarium that could keep the sharks alive. It was massive.

John coughed. "Aren't they the ones that attack swimmers?"

"Well, yeah," Alex said, "When we're in their habitat and making it hard for them to find other food. You can swim next to them here without fear. Once in a while one of them will bounce off the SEL divider trying to feed, but they learn the boundary pretty quick." She rubbed her chin. "We also have six other pool areas, including 4 water parks with slides, diving boards, sprayers, waterfalls, a volleyball court, and an olympic lap pool."

Alex brought up each one and showed off their assets. "Now, if those are a little too artificial for you, we have pretty beaches down at our Pacific island which you can visit." She changed the display to a beautiful flyover of the Pacific island and its beaches. Alex continued to talk steadily for another three hours, and between her and John, they completely distracted Pat.

Kgomotso worked steadily at the molecular connections both he and Alex had planned. It was an amazing sleight-of-hand, helped by the immobility inducers, nerve blockers, and a monster huge opaque screen in front of Pat's face so she couldn't see what they were doing. This was John's idea; they'd let him watch as they sliced off his stump, and he nearly had a heart attack.

When Kgomotso finished, he messaged Alex, and she said, "Hey, John, tell her about your rehab program." While he did that, Alex verified all of the vein, bone, muscle, and nerve connections. It was slow going, but Kgomotso's work was sound and John proved up to the distraction task.

"Ok," Kgomotso said, "I think I have everything set up. Close your eyes, Pat." She did. "Do you feel that?"

"Feel what?"

359

"That'll be the nerve blockers doing their job." Kgomotso was actually moving her new foot. He switched to her left hand and then right hand, with the same result. "Keep your eyes closed for a few more minutes. I'm going to remove the blockers on the count of 3. You'll feel a sudden rush of sensations, but it's all right. It's expected. 3. 2. 1..." He removed the blockers and Pat stiffened and cried out.

"That cold water splash," John told her. "Times three in your case. Go ahead and open your eyes. Don't try to move yet. It'll cause you to panic. Well, it caused ME to panic. You might be braver."

She lifted her right hand and looked at it with disbelief. "I'm dreaming, right? I'll wake up and this will all be gone."

"You're awake. This is real."

"Holy cow! You moved your arm! That's amazing!" John exclaimed.

Pat whispered, "Is it?"

"Definitely," Alex confirmed.

"I can't move the left one or my leg." Her eyes fluttered in panic and she was having a hard time breathing.

Kgomotso stepped up to her and put a hand on her cheek and held her left hand. "It's going to take a while for your brain to reconnect its commands. Deep breaths."

"Yup. Lots of deep breathing." John moved over by her feet and held onto both toes. "Any pain?" He was stronger than Kgomotso, so they normally had him holding the client's feet.

"No. It's just... weird." Pat closed her eyes and looked up at the ceiling. Her new leg pulled out of John's light grasp and nearly kicked him, but he'd been watching for it, and dodged out of the way. Pat flexed the foot. A moment later, she managed to twitch her left hand.

"Incredible," Kgomotso noted with a nod. "No one has ever responded that quickly before. Your recovery time looks very promising."

"Can I have a few minutes by myself, please?" Pat was staring at her right hand and her eyes were pooling with water.

"Of course." Alex navigated her own bed out of the room. Kgomotso and John followed, and Kgomotso toggled the viewing window to opaque, so their audience wouldn't see either. "Nice work, Kgomotso."

"Thank you." He tapped his fingers together. "Founder, that's the last work you're doing for a while. The excitement spiked your blood pressure."

"You're monitoring me?" She arched a disapproving eyebrow at him.

He shrugged unrepentantly. "We can play back the recording and I can point out every time you tried to sit up and strained your abdomen or gestured too enthusiastically."

"It doesn't take much at all to go through the procedure diagrams. I can still do that."

John and Kgomotso exchanged knowing glances and John added helpfully,

"I can arrange for a visit from the center's psychologist if the idea of leisure time is upsetting you so much, Founder."

Alex massaged her belly. "I am the center's psych."

Kgomotso laughed. Alex routinely did any job that needed to be done, although her focus was training other people to do those jobs so she could move on. "Well, Founder, this is MY medical center. I'm in charge. Don't make me ban you from the premises."

"Yeah, yeah." She waved her hand dismissively and drove her bed off in search of food. She knew they'd see Pat got all of the help she needed.

Over the next few days, she designed her baby's bioshield and monitoring unit that would not only protect her baby but let her see everything her baby did in a constantly running video feed in the upper right of her own HUD. Alex told herself this was necessary given the possibility of threats and political agendas her daughter would have to navigate, but realized she just wanted to make sure no one could ever do to her daughter what they'd done to her. She wondered how well she'd do at allowing her daughter grow independently and make mistakes that would ultimately let her be a stronger, smarter person.

She did not have a name for her baby and was hoping Jay would let her use his mother's name, but she needed to talk with him. Jay, along with his friend Byron, and a paternity test doctor would be arriving in two weeks. The 'list' had arrived by paper-mail, along with a date range that indicated that he was following the news which was annoyingly following her pregnancy. She and Jay had not spoken since the phone call. Alex had stayed busy enough that she didn't have time to worry about it, but now that she wasn't constantly working, she did nothing but think and fret.

Jay, Byron, and the paternity test doctor arrived as scheduled, but none of the 3 came to visit her and Jay was blocking her calls, and Alex refused to call Byron or the doctor. She was officially confined to her room, pending the birth, which would happen at any time. Medically, Kgomotso and the midwife felt everything would proceed normally, but politically, no one, especially Alex, wanted tourist or news coverage of the actual birth. Let them look on an appropriately adorable and clean little baby.

Alex tried not to let Jay's absence upset her. It would get sorted out. That she spent most of her time alone, with only a periodic checkup by the midwife, gnawed at the back of her mind. She knew every citizen by face, name, job proclivity, family, vote-tendency, and committee. None, however, could be counted as close friends, except Brian, who'd been with her since the beginning, but was too busy picking up her slack to come visit, and maybe Kgomotso, whom she only ever discussed medical center things with. Surrounded by this many people who all knew her by sight and name, how could she feel this lonely? Normally, she kept busy. Always so very busy.

The Marino family, including Milo whom she hadn't spoken with for almost a year, and Dec, the woman from her short prison stay, was still mostly Earth-side. They would be brought up as part of the main Earth evacuation. Alex didn't like to think about that at all. How much time did they have?

This enforced down-time might make her crazy. Odd as it seemed, the conversation with Jay in the gem cavern was the only extended non-work related conversation she'd had in a very long time. No best friend to do a baby shower. No gathering of lady-friends to come keep her company and discuss new-mom things. Just the HUD with endless forums, votes, news, television shows and movies which she did not watch, and mountains of scientific data on the decline of the Earth, and the ever-depressing prep for the rescue, rehabilitation, and processing of refugees. She'd run around naked through the buffet hall before she'd ever put in a request for a companion/social care worker. After a while, she just closed her eyes and let her mind replay her good memories with Sal and some of the better times alone in the forest.

Brian poked his head into the hospital room, not knocking. "Ah, good! You're awake!"

Alex smiled and adjusted her bed to a sitting position. She was really glad to have a visitor. She hated not being able to go out walking around the station. She hadn't realized how active she truly was until she had nothing better to do than sit in this room and ponder the fate of humanity. She could have flown her bed around, but that drew unwanted attention from both citizens and tourists alike. "I heard a rumor that there are people that can sit and watch TV for hours. This has got to be a complete fabrication. No one would ever be able to sit still that long for such mind-numbing hypnotic torture."

Brian laughed, stepping in. "Maybe you should play a video game."

Alex groaned. "I tried. They're worse!"

"Well, Milo and his family are on their way up in a shuttle right now to come see you. Milo told me to tell you not to have the baby until he gets here."

Alex grinned. "I'm letting her make this decision." She rubbed her baby. "And she doesn't know what a fearsome thing it is to disobey a mafia lawyer." Yes! Visitors!

Brian gave a mock gasp. "He's mafia? You said the Marino's are just a rich family with interests."

She laughed. "What do you think mafia is?"

"So where's this man of yours? I was hoping to get a chance to meet him in a less formal setting." Brian's last interaction with Jay had been to apologize for Colony One's Founder's sudden departure from the debate.

"He's waiting for our baby to arrive."

Brian studied her face a moment. "He hasn't been to see you? He's been on station for two weeks!"

"It's ok. He's here. He'll be along when our daughter arrives. So tell me what's going on in our country?"

"Just the usual. The Pacific island people are busy pushing through a geographic design that will make your hair stand on end. They're building a lot of redundant businesses so they don't have to make the long commute here for things. They're also building their own stadium."

Alex groaned. "Confess. You told them to do a stadium."

"Me? Certainly not! I don't interfere with community development committees. I'm strictly international politics and a bottom-line yes-man." He winked at her. "Now... Lucas, though, I'm absolutely sure he might have said something about putting in a stadium at all locations eventually and having each location create a team so they can have playoffs."

"Uh huh." Alex rolled her eyes. Brian knew Lucas was still working on his teleportation technology so his reference to multiple locations wasn't misplaced. Unfortunately, Lucas kept getting pulled away to handle other station physics inquiries, so he couldn't dedicate enough time to the problem. Eventually, they'd be able to put stations at each of their solar system's planets. "Has Lucas even been to a game yet?"

"Not that I'm aware of."

"You really need to find a better fall guy."

Brian chuckled. "Nah. You just need to accept that Lucas is a closet sports fanatic."

Brian glanced at the guest chair but did not sit. Apparently his visit was going to be short. Alex repressed a sigh. While she understood he was constantly busy, Alex wished he'd stay longer.

Brian said, "Oh, hey, did you see the citizens have vetoed the vote for mandatory genetic scans of all citizens?"

"I've been trying not to check the forums more than twice an hour." Alex shifted in the bed, trying to get comfortable. "I wish that had passed. We're going to need it eventually for the population bottleneck and it would be so much easier to get it through now than it will be in the future."

"Hey, you try to knock some sense into them. This system you have going of 'decisions by forum discussion and mass vote' is making our country do all sorts of crazy things. It sucks up a lot of my time too." Brian rolled his shoulders and stretched his neck with this complaint.

Alex could certainly sympathize with the time sink. No individual could possibly track and pay attention to every issue. While citizens could set alerts and warnings for topics they found interesting, even that was a lot to deal with. "It's the best I can do. Humanity has to evolve. Individuals have to take responsibility for our community and environment. We're about to get slammed with a massive influx of people. Our system has to be able to handle it."

"What if they vote to turn us back into Earth? Greed at the expense of the environment? Individual companies again. Actual paychecks and 60 hour work weeks?" Brian walked to the foot of her bed, nearer to the door.

Alex didn't demand he come back and sit down. Brian really had more important things to do. "Then me and the young lady," Alex pat her stomach, "And whoever else wants to come along, will move and start another colony."

"You are way too idealistic. By the way, we're creating a cattle farm. Lucas approved the mass and space." On that pleasant announcement, Brian ducked out.

Well, Alex thought with a sigh, if she had wanted to control everything, she wouldn't have invited anyone to join her and she'd still be stuck back on Earth because one person can't do everything. Individuals need other people to succeed - help, motivation, knowledge and ideas. That meant recognizing their value and allowing and empowering others to make decisions, even if she would not have done things that way.

But cattle? Alex ground her teeth together. Lucas should have known better. She pulled up her projected expansion data, studying the available matter and required space, atmosphere, plant farms, and then began the tedious work of adjusting her calculations. Lucas was more of a "now man" - they could certainly support enough cattle right now, but in a decade or two, with the added population, they wouldn't have enough meat to share equally. It would cause problems, but maybe by then, they might be able to solve them?

Alex dug through the forums and posted yet another scientific article on genetic variety in closed populations. Maybe it would help eventually. She'd just finished the final edit and post when a message from Brian appeared in the corner of her HUD. She activated it and a video link appeared. Alex's eyebrows scrunched together in confusion. She hit play.

"I want you to come with me," Brian said to Jay, who was eating lunch.

"Did she have the baby yet?" Jay set his sandwich back on his plate.

"No, but I want to talk with you."

"Nothing to talk about until the baby arrives and the paternity test is done." Jay pushed his tray over to Byron and stood to follow anyway. He was wearing tailored khaki's with a white button-down shirt and was just as handsome as Alex remembered.

The video skipped to Brian's office. Jay leaned against the wall by the door, with his arms crossed, looking extremely unhappy. Now that she could see his face better, Alex noted that he had dark circles under his eyes and his lighthearted demeanor was gone completely. She could have wept.

"I just came from visiting Alex," Brian said. Alex glanced at the video's timestamp. It was from 30 minutes ago, from Brian's point of view. Anything that had been said was forever locked in time and she couldn't affect it at all.

"Don't look at me like I'm a rapist. I didn't force her," Jay spit out.

Alex couldn't tell what expression Brian made because the video view was from his perspective. "Oh, I know that. It's physically impossible; she's wearing a full, invisible bioshield that nothing can get through unless she allows it. So what's the problem? I have no idea how the two of you managed to..." Brian didn't finish that thought, but instead said, "Why haven't you been to see her?"

"Why should I? She clearly just wanted someone to have sex with so she could have a child. You guys all treat her like a goddess, but she uses people and throws them away."

Alex winced and felt like she'd been stabbed through the heart. For whom did she dance if not for everyone else? How could Jay be so far from the truth?

"She what?" Brian asked, confusion evident in his voice.

"She deceived me; never told me who she was. Seduced me. Then she immediately runs off and reappears at that cursed debate to rub it in. Then refuses to take my calls or even see me. She's one twisted individual. She should be locked up."

"Oh, no." Brian's video feed went dark as he put his head in his hands. "I was afraid this was my fault. I'm sorry."

"She tell you to..."

"No." The video became active again as Brian looked back at Jay. "She couldn't take your calls and then I told her not to talk to anyone."

"Right." Sarcasm and disbelief dripped from Jay's voice.

Brian's HUD showed in the video. Alex winced at how cluttered it was. Didn't the man ever delete files on his main display? How did he focus on a task or even see around all that? She watched him access the security feeds and link them to the monitor in his office. Brian said, "This is seriously secret. Only a small handful of people know about it. We don't want a panic among the citizens, so please keep it to yourself."

The video of Alex storming out of the debate appeared. Brian scrubbed it forward, past her punching the man, and running from the medtechs, until she spasmed and fell to the ground. "Her blood sugar was so low she almost died." Brian fast-forwarded to them trying to get a needle in her arm and it bending away. "Her bioshield. We couldn't do anything to help her until she lowered it. I thought she was going to die."

Alex saw herself have two more seizures as she was carried to the hospital. Alex hadn't been told about those; it scared her. She kept watching.

Brian continued, "We sedated her at the hospital. Kept her under for days, trying to stabilize her." Brian cut off the security feed. "The first thing she did when she woke up was demand her HUD to make a phone call. I told her not to tell anyone. So you see, it's my fault. She's not the monster you think she is."

"I've got to go talk with her." Jay turned and strode out of the office.

Brian's voice said, "Alex, I'm sorry. I'm so very sorry. I would have fixed this sooner if I had known. He'll arrive at your room any minute now." The video ended. Alex looked at the timestamp. The walk from Brian's office to her hospital room would take another 15 minutes.

Alex summoned a comb and reached up to pull it through her hair. Outside in the hallway, she heard a medtech say, "That door there, Mr. Ryko." Good grief, he must have run.

Jay knocked and at Alex's immediate answer, came in.

Alex dissolved the comb and blushed, afraid she didn't look as neatly groomed as she would have liked. He was as attractive as she remembered him, classically handsome face under recently trimmed brown hair, muscled, broad shoulders. "Hi, Jay. Brian told me you were on your way here."

"Is it true?" Jay didn't need to specify what.

Alex chose to answer lightly, with humor, and maybe set the tone for this critical conversation. "Oh, it's true all right: Brian is definitely in trouble for inappropriate access of security video. I'm going to issue him a warning. Can't very well banish him back to Earth, I suppose." She'd have to banish herself, too.

"No, about your seizure." Jay took a step closer to the bed, green eyes inspecting her, studying her for signs of health problems.

Alex gave him a lopsided smile. "Yeah, that's also true. Moral: don't ignore medical warning signs or alerts."

"You should have told me," he admonished, but this time, his tone wasn't accusing and angry like it had been on the phone call. "Maybe we should start over? Hi, I'm Jay Ryko, environmental activist, and uh, notorious international playboy."

"Alex Smith, Founder of Colony One. I don't look like you expected because I dyed my hair and wore a lot of makeup while I was on Earth so when I got here, I'd be anonymous. The news media has my public image, not my real image. Or at least used to." Alex rubbed her chin thoughtfully and then pitched her voice deep and breathy, "Want to make a baby?"

He laughed. "Maybe the way we did it was the right way the first time."

Alex was absolutely certain they never would have connected had they exchanged names. She would have had to treat him like an honored guest (and one she didn't want to have to talk with because of the debate) and he would have handled her like a foreign dignitary. She said, "I'm sorry I didn't call you the minute I found out I was pregnant."

He looked up at the ceiling, exhaling, and then refocused on her and nodded once in acknowledgement.

"I nearly passed out when I saw you on stage," Alex confessed. "I thought you were just one of the conference attendees."

"Hah! You were completely calm when you walked out on stage. You even shook my hand!"

"It only looked that way. I wasn't. I had every intention of getting to that conference early, finding you, and telling you who I was."

"I had every intention of convincing you to come back to Earth with me over dinner. I spent the night planning my arguments and logic."

"I spent the entire night handling the fallout from that idiotic protest. I really hate those people for interrupting us. It still would have been awkward, but..."

"At least we could have talked," he finished. "So all that 'end of the world' stuff was just low blood sugar?"

Alex lowered her eyes. "I wish with every fiber of my being that it were." She met his eyes again, changing the subject before the conversation soured. "May we name our daughter after your mother? If we do, people will figure out you're the father. I wasn't sure if you'd want anyone to know or not."

"You don't think completely covering my expenses wasn't a dead giveaway? They wouldn't even let me override your funding."

Alex also bet her fellow citizens delighted in refusing to change it. Too many of them wrongfully blamed Jay for the debate debacle. "I pick up a lot of random expenses. The current theory is that it's an apology for walking out on you during the debate. Your name hasn't even made the 'potential fathers' list."

"There's a list?" Jay sighed, running his hand through his hair. "Never mind. I don't mind if people know she's mine. If she's going to spend time with me, people are going to notice anyway. Please use my mother's name."

Alex smiled brightly. "When do I get to meet Byron?"

"Um." Jay played with his HUD a moment. "I just sent him a note to come."

Just then, the door opened, and in trooped Milo, his wife, and his two kids. Milo looked substantially older, but healthy and happy. Kelly's long, wavy brown hair was still untouched by any grey. His two adopted boys, age 8 and 10, weren't acting timid, but had certainly been lectured to be on their best behavior. The room felt small. Alex shifted the wall, taking over space from an empty neighboring room.

"That's cool!" Milo's eldest said, watching the wall move.

"It is, isn't it? I have presents for the two of you," Alex said to Milo's sons. She reached into her pocket and pulled out two semitransparent SEL cards about the size of credit cards and handed them over. "Thumb and forefinger on the circles and state your name." They did. "Take them outside and play. I want to visit with your dad and mom." They thanked her and skipped out.

Milo raised his eyebrow, adding the familiar cringe that Alex knew so well. It warmed her heart, even as he asked, "Do I want to know what those were?" Milo went to the end of Alex's bed and straightened the light blanket that was draped over her.

Alex grinned. "Probably not." She wondered if Milo was even aware of his obsession with neat and orderly surroundings. How many times had she seen him arrange his plate and silverware? His action made her feel happy and content, not because he straightened the blanket; she didn't care about that, but because his familiar quirk reminded her of time they'd spent together over the years.

Milo sighed. "I haven't missed your daily surprises."

"Milo, Kelly, this is Jay Ryko, the father of my baby. Jay, this is my guardian angel, Milo Paul, and his wife, Kelly."

Milo sized up Jay. "Aren't you that environmentalist from the debate?"

Jay nodded warily, equally studying Milo. Jay definitely knew about Alex's mafia connections, at least everything that the Earth press embellished and reported. The Earth news media had proven itself unreliable on Jay so many times that Alex hoped Jay would apply some wariness to anything about Alex and her own connections.

"It's nice to meet you," Milo said, shaking Jay's hand, reminding Alex that she'd certainly given Milo enough surprises over his employment that nothing could really startle him. Milo glanced at Jay and then at Alex, taking in their expressions. "We'll come back by again tomorrow. We just wanted to stop in and say hi. We need to get settled in at the hotel."

Alex said quickly, "Milo, when are you moving up here?"

Kelly answered, "We've decided to wait as long as possible. I like my feet on solid ground. It's also good for the boys to know where they're from."

Alex nodded to her. "Visit Sal's house while you're here. It's set up as a museum, but you can get the family tour."

They thanked her and left.

Jay shuffled his feet. After a moment, he inquired, "What did you give the boys?"

Alex adjusted her bed so she was sitting up a little higher. "It's the latest SEL toy the kids have been playing with. It's not available to downsiders."

"Aren't they downsiders?"

"They're family. Special case."

"I notice yet again you didn't answer my question. What'ja give them?"

"Habit." She grinned. "It's an educational toy - it gives them a cubic meter of SEL that they can make into anything inorganic. They can design their own things and sell the design or use anyone else's. There's a contest once a month for the best new design. Children start with 60 kid money. Designs have a max price of 1 and can only make 50 before the design becomes 'public domain'. So basically, the first 50 kids buy the design for the community. If they run out of kid money, they can earn more doing age-appropriate community service."

"But they can make anything?"

"Yup. Younger kids can't make anything swallowable. Dangerous things like knives and guns are flagged for adult review and get safety-ized. You could point one of the guns at someone and shoot, point-blank, but it wouldn't actually hurt the person. Makes a temporary black and red tattoo." Alex tilted her head to the side, unapologetically. "One of the teens made a fortune creating a collection of historical guns. There was a rush of war games for a while, but then one of the brighter kids designed a dual-set laser tag system, so now they're all off doing that instead. We even built a special laser tag park for them so they'd stop tearing through the restaurant zone."

"You encourage violence?"

"No, I encourage exercise, social games, teamwork, community, education, and discipline. We have counselors that immediately stamp out truly malicious behavior. We pay attention to our kids. We have an occasional accident, but no one has been seriously hurt. The SEL building blocks seem to be more addictive than traditional video games and it encourages them to go out and visit with their friends to show off designs. The best designs are play-tested by friends. Here, check this out." Alex created a digital display by the bed and linked to it, pulling up a picture of a beautiful, white-marble sculpture of a puppy. "That was designed by a six year old using the 'clay to stone' option. She made clay, shaped it, then set it, and named it Flaffie. She's apparently working on a matching kitten. The Salvatore Marino Memorial Museum bought the design and has it on display in the modern sculpture gallery."

"How does that work?"

"She got 1 kid money from the museum, 49 from other kids, and now her puppy is available to anyone. There are a couple other kids trying to do designs that are 'good enough', but they're still building their art skills."

"But they can also create electronics?"

"Sure. There's a few fully automated robots in the public database as well as several vehicles. They take a lot more work. The kids that have the knowledge to do them have usually become teenagers and move on to other activities. The kids can dissect the designs and figure out how they work if they want."

"Culture shock. I can't fathom how that doesn't cause complete chaos. You have no control over who creates what."

"Our citizens are waking up. We're healthy. We're educated. We have time. We're evolving. It's bound to be chaotic." She dissolved the display again. "Hmm. Speaking of culture shock. You know that bioshield Brian mentioned to you?" He nodded once and Alex continued, "I'm giving you bioshield rings for you and Byron and anyone else you feel might be in danger due to your association with me. Earth is still dangerous. I don't want our baby to grow up without a Dad."

Byron arrived then, knocking boldly and waiting to be let in. "Hey," he said in a rush, "There's a couple boys out on the lawn with guns shooting at each other."

Alex laughed. "Yup. Milo's going to be pissed. Don't worry about it. They're toys."

"They looked pretty real to me," Byron said.

"Trust me. Toys. The red blood splatter is all hologram based for ambience. They'll eventually get bored and it'll self-clean, or their dad will catch them at it, and confiscate the cards that let them create the guns."

Byron looked between the two of them. "You two have reconciled I take it?"

Alex nodded and Jay answered, "Yeah. Misunderstanding."

Byron plopped down in the guest chair. "Ah, good. The Earth isn't ending. I knew it."

"Some things have to be explained in person," Alex replied and Jay's mouth twitched at the non-answer. At some point, she supposed she and Jay would have to discuss her dire predictions in more detail, but for now, it made no difference whatsoever. She'd see Jay, Byron, and their loved ones got to the station safely when the time came.

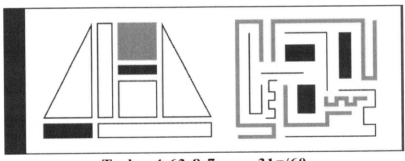

T plus 4:63:8:7   ~31π/60

Grace Ember arrived, kicking and screaming, two days later. Alex attached her baby's bioshield and monitor as soon as the umbilical cord was cut, which caused some consternation when the medical staff went to do a heel-stick to get a blood sample for medical condition screening and the tiny needle bent away. The nurse had to bring Grace to Alex so she could be carefully watched as she did the heel-stick.

Grace was washed, wrapped in a soft blanket and given back to Alex. Grace was healthy at 3.2 kg, 51 cm, with newborn blue eyes and a light fuzz of hair that could be either light brown or blond. She was passed around to Alex's visitors to be admired and held, starting with her father, and then Byron, and

Milo and Brian, their families, and Lucas. When Lucas was holding Grace, he leaned close to her ear and whispered in Spanish, "You come by my lab when you get older, Grace Ember, and I'll teach you physics and show you a world most people never see."

Alex tried not to smile, after all, that was a private comment between Lucas and her daughter. Alex would need some time to adapt to the constant video feed and filter out things she wasn't supposed to know, but no way would she let her daughter be hurt or manipulated or in any way used. When her daughter finally came back to her, Alex told her how loved she was and held her for a very long time. Eventually, people left, and only Alex, Jay, and Grace remained in the room.

"She's perfect," Alex whispered, pondering the schedule of ailments that would help her baby build a healthy, strong immune system.

Jay agreed, and then more quietly, he said, "I've been giving this a lot of thought. Should we get married?"

Alex tilted her head sideways. "Going to do the 'right thing'? Move to Colony One?"

"If you want."

"No. It's not what you want. Your work, your life, is on Earth." Alex also knew he'd be here permanently soon enough. "Do you think if we were married, you'd love Grace any more? You are going to be a good father whether or not we're married. I meant what I said during that phone call. I want her to spend equal time with you. She's half you." And Grace should see what Earth is like before it's gone.

"My father would have thrown a fit. He was always so adamant about family values and not having children out of wedlock."

Alex lightly touched Grace's perfect little nose. "Neither one of us is financially or emotionally dependent. We barely know each other. Our baby is ours, whether or not we are married."

Jay nodded. "If you're sure."

"I'm sure." Why did her heart felt like it was breaking?

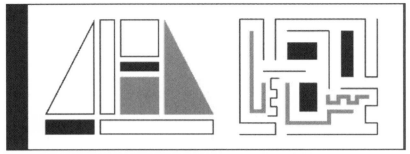

Alex and Lucas settled their children in the newly generated playroom and waited to make sure they could get along this time. Some playdates went better than others. Two year old Grace was sitting in the room's corner, playing quietly for once, chewing on a wooden block while building others into some sort of fort. Georgie, one year younger, squished his hands into a large lump of super soft SEL clay. Other toys were scattered around for when they got bored. Alex started some chipper children's songs playing and keeping the wall clear so they could keep an eye on the children, she sealed off the room so she and Lucas could get to work.

Alex poured tea and took a seat at the table across from Lucas, pushing his teacup toward him. While they could have hired a babysitter easily enough, this way they could easily steal a slice of quality time for their babies before and after. Nothing added perspective to their end-of-Earth discussions like having to stop and change a diaper. By mutual agreement neither of them would speak in front of the children about their dire circumstances. Children absorbed and learned, even when they didn't seem to be paying attention.

"Should we arrange Georgie and Grace's marriage?" Lucas asked, his eyes proudly glued to his son who was making an unrecognizable blob with the super-serious expression and concentration of a master artist.

Alex sputtered her tea across the table.

"Hah! Got ya!" Lucas cackled happily.

Alex thumped her closed hand into her forehead and shook her head. She ordered the picobots to clean up the tea. "Maybe we should at least wait for them to get out of the toddler stage?"

Lucas generated a semitransparent hologram of the Earth above their table. "You really going to send her off to live with her father for six months?"

"With Jay, yes. She's weaned and I want her to see what Earth is like. It'll also be good for her to not deal with the constant 'Founder's kid' aura she's got here. People just don't treat her like a normal baby." Alex added a date wheel under the globe and set it to current and adjusted the Earth to match its season and daylight.

"But she's your daughter. How can you give her away like that?"

372

"I'm not giving her away. Jay is her father. He can't keep coming here. His work is there." Alex knew Grace absolutely adored Jay and he was always the perfect image of an attentive and doting father. While unconcerned, Alex was a little curious how Jay would handle being a full-time dad. Babies needed constant care. She had hired round-the clock babysitters that spent most of their time on-call in case she suddenly got pulled away.

Alex's spying picobots had also let her know that Jay's current girlfriend, a woman named Avalon Dorsey, was safe. Ms. Dorsey was only slightly intimidated about having the Founder's daughter around for the next few months. Hoping that Grace could be bribed to like her, the woman had prepared and bought Grace some age-appropriate toys and had asked Jay questions about what Grace liked and didn't like. Alex wasn't plagued by a fear of the woman being around or even being left alone with Grace.

Instead, Alex was plagued by jealousy and daydreams of herself and Jay as a happy couple. They'd tried dating for a short time after Grace was born, but Alex's firm insistence that the Earth was headed for life-ending destruction drove them apart. He couldn't accept a relationship with someone so unreasonable and apparently crazy and she couldn't lie to him and tell him it wasn't going to happen. They were still amicable, particularly around Grace, but only if they didn't bring up the Earth in their conversation - an insurmountable hurdle as both of them were passionate about the environment.

Refocusing her thoughts on the present moment, Alex squinted at Lucas. Did he think she wouldn't be watching Grace? "Wait. You don't have full-time surveillance on Georgie?"

Lucas quickly looked down guiltily. "I didn't want to miss anything."

Alex shrugged at this confession. "I've had one on Grace since she was born. I know it seems wrong, but she's my baby. I have to protect her. I'm not going to let her get used or abused."

Lucas nodded at that. He exhaled. "So what do you want to tackle today? Carbon dioxide in the ocean, tectonic plates, or the trash dumps?"

"Your choice. We're just putting bandaids on things. Every step we take forward, two are taken backwards. Why can't they stop destroying our planet? Something will get us anyway. We don't need to rush it." Alex sighed. Despite Alex and Lucas trying everything they could think of, the inevitable end continued to draw closer. There was simply no way to get enough individuals to care and take immediate action, particularly as the local companies and governments were too focused on other goals.

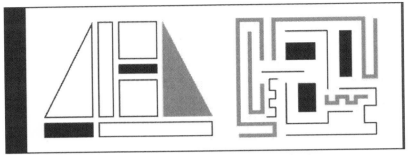

"Alex, would you come down here?" the Pacific island's governor asked when Alex answered the incoming message. "I have four... people here who would like to speak with you."

"Who?" Alex was busy digging through the forums and catching up on everything so she could take a couple days off when Grace arrived home again. Despite constantly watching Grace's activities on her HUD and having nightly video calls, Grace's third visit to Jay had been the hardest on Alex thus far. Alex's four year old was finally getting to a point where they could have conversations. These conversations weren't quite as disconcerting as the ones with Lucas' Georgie, who spouted random college-level science facts and ran off giggling, but definitely showed Grace had inherited Alex's photographic memory.

The Pacific island's governor shifted the video feed to show four extremely dirty, poorly dressed, and clearly starving street kids, two boys and two girls. "They haven't given us their names yet," the governor said. The eldest, a boy maybe 13 years old, was holding a knife. The youngest, a girl who was barely 7, if that old, cowered against the older girl and was clearly terrified. The older girl didn't seem aware of what was going on around her; possibly a drug-haze. The younger boy's attitude and hard body language reminded Alex so much of Mason, the street gang leader she'd lived with before meeting Sal, that Alex felt time-vertigo. The four street kids were in the supply ship's cargo hold, blocking the unloading of the supply shipment.

The governor turned his camera back toward himself. "What would you like me to do?" he asked.

Alex recalled that the governor had two young girls himself, which is likely why he hadn't just run up SEL cages and turned them over to security.

"Ah. Set up a digital display so they can see and hear me?" While he did that, Alex generated a sharp knife for herself and turned off her bioshield. She knew street negotiations, but which boy was actually in charge?

"You're on," the governor announced.

"Hello, I'm Alex Smith, Founder of Colony One. I understand you would like to talk with me?"

"In person," the younger boy whispered to the older boy in street-accent Spanish. The picobots creating the video feed picked up the audio clearly.

The older boy squared his shoulders determinedly and said, "We want political asylum."

Alex wondered if he even knew what that meant. "You're from the United States?"

The older boy nodded. "We don't want to be there anymore. We want to be citizens of Colony One."

"If I promise to seriously consider your request, will you put away your shiv and not threaten any more of our citizens?"

The younger boy leaned over to his friend again and whispered in Spanish, "No, make her say yes first. We can't go back."

Alex, in her best street-accent Spanish, said, "Blood oath. I promise if it is possible, I will make it so." She took her knife, held up her hand, and sliced her palm, vertically, from the "head line" below her middle finger straight down to her "life line", with a short, shallow cut. She spread her fingers, palm toward them, and let the blood drip.

Both of the boys' mouths dropped open and their eyes widened. Alex tilted her head at them in inquiry and waited. The older boy tucked his knife into his belt.

Alex said, "I want you to go with my friend there. He'll get you something to eat and I'll be there in two hours to talk with you in person." When the boys seemed to relax a little, she disconnected and made arrangements to ride on the next shuttle down. Just what she needed. Another political nightmare. The United States government was still trying to push through embargoes in the United Nations until Cal Park was "released" from his "slavery" even though he'd been back to Earth and been granted citizenship through the normal routes.

The governor had secured the four children in a private spaceport waiting room and had brought in the food Alex had recommended that wouldn't harm their empty stomachs. The room wasn't institutional, but a cozy meeting room, with pictures of sunny Caribbean beaches on the walls, and comfortable SEL-leather chairs.

Alex was privately glad the governor had kept them out of sight. She entered the room without pausing. When the boys went to stand, she shook her head and motioned them to stay seated. She sat across the table from them. The licked-clean bowls from the light vegetable soup were still on the table and the bread and crumbs were gone. The youngest girl still huddled next to the oldest girl who stared straight ahead vacantly.

Speaking in Spanish, Alex greeted them. "That was a brave crossing you did to get here."

The oldest, obviously the voted speaker, replied in Spanish. "What do we have to do?"

"Well, under United States law, all four of you are still minors. I have to do an official recorded interview during which you are going to have to tell me your names, and I'm going to have to publish those names, and send them to the U.S. government so your distraught parents or guardians can stop worrying about you." The boys and the youngest girl looked very upset by this. "Of course, if you were to lie to me, I'd still have to go with whatever you tell me, because I don't know differently. But those are the names you get for the rest of your lives. You can't change your mind, because that would be suspicious and I'd have to investigate to find the truth." Alex let that sink in.

The oldest boy was the first to comprehend, but he certainly didn't trust her. His gaze was calculating.

Alex tented her fingers. "I'll work with you so I can make you citizens, but you'll have to stay here as my guests for the near future. What that means is that you're going to be in a legal limbo for a while. I need you to ignore whatever you hear on the news and trust me to work it out."

The oldest frowned at her suspiciously. "But what do we have to do?"

"Go to school. Grow up and be productive members of our community, doing whatever it is that makes you happy. Generally, not cause any trouble and don't draw attention to yourself until you are 18."

"But what do we have to do for you?" the oldest persisted.

"I understand the question. That's still my answer. Neither myself, nor anyone else, will ever ask you for personal services again. Not ever. And if they dare, I'll kill them." She let that sink in. She found she was surprised that she meant it. "I was homeless when I was a kid and now nobody touches me without my permission. I can close my bedroom door and sleep without fear that someone will come in and hurt me."

The younger boy looked at the older boy and said, "See? I told you. She's one of us."

Alex tilted her head at this. "I am, but how did you know? Why did you come?"

"Jane saw that kid's parents doing an interview." The younger boy glanced at the oldest girl briefly, but she didn't react. "You know, that kid you locked up because he tore up a painting?"

"Yeah, I know that kid." Cal Park was currently running their Emergency Response department. He was working on his doctorate in emergency management. Alex waited patiently.

"Well, the parents mentioned you lived on the streets and recognized that their son was headed for overdose, gang death, or prison, and that you were just trying to help him, and they were ok with that." The younger boy spoke so fast, it was apparent that he'd said this same thing many times before while he was convincing their gang to come.

Alex recalled the video interview. It was an old one that people apparently had dredged up as part of a new documentary series on Colony One. The younger boy used the exact words from the interview.

Breaking away from the transcript, the younger boy added, "Dunno what kind of parents would just leave their kid like that. He's better off without them."

The older boy touched the younger boy's arm, silencing him. "We figured if you were trying to help him, you might help us too. And you got a kid now too."

"That's some really good thinking. Really brave." Alex nodded at this logic and quickly looked at her HUD's video feed of 'her kid'. Grace was subjecting Jay to every book store in the airport, in search of "a most special book" for the plane trip over to California, where they'd take one of the Colony One transports to the island. Jay hadn't quite grasped the implications of Grace's memory yet, although Alex had pointed it out. Grace had full access on her own HUD to any book she might want (subject to Mom's censorship). Grace's airport quest was to make Jay follow her around, paying attention to her every word, so he couldn't take any work phone calls.

The older boy drew her attention back. "If you turn us over, we have a plan so we can get back together again."

"It's smart to have a backup plan in place." Alex stood up. "Ok, I'm going to go get you an apartment. I'm guessing you want to stay together?"

The boys nodded.

"When I come back, and it'll be just a few minutes, we'll do the official recorded video. Can you remember your names by then?" She made air quotes around "remember".

"Yeah, we can do that," the oldest replied, obviously comprehending the real instruction.

Alex canceled her plans for the next three days and arranged to have her station apartment's contents transferred to the island. She could use video conferencing to the space station for a while, and maybe even take care of some things locally that needed to be done. Grace wouldn't care. She liked the beaches for the same reason Alex did - the water and sand kept changing. Alex chose two adjacent apartments. Technically, visitors should stay in the hotel, but there were some special allowances that could be made for extended guests, if they passed a forum vote. Alex's vote requesting an additional apartment for four guests was approved instantaneously. She paid extra for a "rush job" on interior decorating to get furniture and general supplies set up within the next hour. Guiltily, she bet Sal hadn't completely delegated the setup of her own apartment.

Alex spoke with the island's governor and Brian via a video conference call for a short while, making political arrangements, repeated the same call with Lucas for technical conferencing, and then picked up more food and a box of guest supplies. She hoped the children were ready.

Outside the waiting room door this time, Alex paused and let her picobots give her a full medical report on the four children. If she were a dragon, she

377

would have breathed fire. All four needed some sort of medical attention, but the worst was the younger boy. She was surprised he was moving at all. If only the medical complex weren't backlogged, and if only the boy wouldn't be terrorized to have people looking at his every trauma, she could fix him. Instead, he'd have to heal the old-fashioned way, with time, some medications, and some inconspicuous help by her picobots. At least he wasn't critically injured.

Alex knocked on the door and then went in. "Hi," she said in English this time, "I understand from our governor that you are looking for political asylum?" The interview went as expected, and Alex acquired four dependents, from oldest to youngest, Nick, Victoria (Tori), Brad, and Peggy. When they were through with the formalities, Alex announced, "And that's a wrap. No more recording."

She took guest bracelets from the box and passed them out. "These are your guest I.D.'s. You need to wear them all the time, even when you shower or swim. It works as a phone, camera, credit card, map, and computer terminal. It also acts as a locator and a safety shield should anything happen that requires additional protection. I'm even wearing mine."

Alex held up her wrist and showed hers. She made sure to tilt her hand so they could also see the place on her palm where she'd cut her skin. "Mine doesn't have the extra white stripe - that means you're a guest and will be given menus and lists with prices on them. All your food and drinks are going directly to my account, so don't worry about those prices. Let me show you how the HUD works." She additionally gave each child $500 in their own account for incidentals they might want. Alex showed them where their apartment was on the map, as well as key places, like the cafeteria and medical complex.

When Alex was sure they knew how to use the HUD well enough to get by, she gave them small disks, explaining, "These are SEL clothes, just the basic island set. It has pajamas, swimsuits, and a few casual outfits. When you get to your apartment, you can throw away what you are wearing, and just hold the disk between your palms and the clothes will fit themselves to you and you'll get another icon on your HUD that will let you pick what you want to be wearing." She demonstrated, changing her outfit through a couple of the standard island ones. "Mostly, guests don't get SEL clothes, because they can only use them while they are here. Non-citizens can't take SEL outside of the country, but ultimately, this will be better for you because I don't intend to let the United States take you back. They've surely failed you."

Three sets of wide-eyes stared at her. The older girl, Tori, still gazed straight ahead, but she was definitely listening as her mouth twitched.

Alex stood. "Ok, next up, we need to swing by medical." Brad cringed and Tori noticeably paled. "I need to pick up some things for myself. If you think of anything you want on the way there, just speak up. Anything you need that's medical is also going to be billed to my account."

"Isn't this stuff expensive?" Nick asked, his furrowed eyebrows indicating concern that they might be too much of a burden and cause her to deport them.

Alex echoed Sal, "I have more wealth than I can ever possibly use. Allow me to do something worthwhile with it."

Alex directed Nick, as the oldest, to use his HUD map to lead them to the medical complex. She wanted them to know where it was in case Brad had issues and she couldn't be found, but she didn't say so; she merely said it was a good exercise in learning how to use the display and map. At the medical office, Alex picked up a paper bag of things she'd privately requested during the interview. "Do you guys need anything?" she asked, not pressing.

They shook their heads; Brad most adamantly.

The nurse who'd assembled the order and knew precisely what those medications indicated, said, "Well, if you do need anything at all, you come back. We'll take care of you. Don't try to tough it out."

On that note, Alex let Brad navigate them to their apartment. She pointed out that their bracelets would unlock the door for them and stood aside. "I'm going over to my own apartment - that door right there - and rest for a bit. If you need anything, come get me."

As Brad was about to go inside, she touched his arm, and said softly, "Wait a moment." When the others were all inside and distracted by exploring, she handed him the paper bag. "I am a fully qualified medical technician and I did body scans on all of you." He turned bright red. Alex continued, "Can you read?" At his nod, she said, "There's first aid cream in there and pain meds, along with some other stuff. Everything has instructions, but if you don't understand something, just ask me. Also, Brad, and this is important - don't let Tori near those pain meds. Or Peggy for that matter."

The young boy nodded mutely and went into the apartment, clutching the bag close to his chest. His resemblance to Mason was gone. He just looked like a traumatized little boy who needed protection. Alex pushed the door closed, set her picobots to observe them, and went to her own room to lay down and watch so she could make sure they were going to be ok.

Nick was extremely observant. As soon as Brad was inside, he walked over, and asked in street-Spanish, "She didn't ask you to do anything, did she?"

Brad shook his head and held out the paper bag. "She gave me meds. She said she scanned all of us."

Nick looked inside the bag but didn't take it. "Sorry, man. Maybe they'll help though?"

Brad took the bag into the bathroom and dumped everything on the sink and carefully read through the instructions. He took two of the pain pills, which was the recommended first dose, and got into the shower. Afterwards, he applied the cream, and then activated the SEL clothes. From Alex's perspective, this wasn't the ideal way to treat him, but if he had to time-heal anyway, at least this didn't subject him to embarrassing, humiliating, if well-intentioned, medical inspections. It looked like he was going to be ok.

Meanwhile, Tori and Peggy, who'd barely managed to speak their names in front of Alex, had no problem at all with each other or Nick. Peggy, being the youngest and obviously most indulged, was told she could pick which bedroom the girls took, went between the rooms, trying out all the beds, which were SEL-generated identical, and eventually chose the bedroom farthest from the front door. Tori followed Peggy and watched, recommending pillow bunching and blanket crumpling for the ultimate bed-test.

Alex's first evaluation of Tori's lack of interaction was inaccurate. It was not a drug-haze. Maybe the girl had just been beaten by strangers and adults so many times that she shielded herself immediately? Tori had no hesitation talking when the kids were alone.

Nick, after his first look through the apartment, went out on the balcony which overlooked the beach and boardwalk, and stayed there watching a bit. The fact that the permanent residences had beach-view balconies if they wanted while tourists were farther in on the island sometimes caused grumbling among the tourists, but Alex had no regrets. Citizens were Colony One's first priority.

Nick came back into the apartment to find Peggy jumping on one of the beds while Tori stood in the doorway laughing. Nick pushed past Tori and scooped Peggy up on one of her bounces, tickling her. "Hey, don't jump on the beds. We need to be proper people now."

"How long are we staying here?" Peggy asked seriously, pulling free of him. Her earnest gaze said she completely trusted the wisdom of her protector. She was simply too young and malnourished to understand much of what was going on.

"Don't know how long," Nick answered, patting Peggy on the shoulder. He was a much different protector than Mason had been. Mason would have decked Alex for bothering him with 'stupid questions'.

"That lady seems nice," the young girl said.

"She ain't one of us, Katie. You can't trust her. Adults lie all the time." Nick told the young girl.

"She blooded the promise," Tori said.

Nick shrugged. "Could'a learned that anywhere. She just wanted her supplies from that ship and would'a said anything to get me to put away my shiv. Katie, you listen to me, you can't trust nobody but us." He saw Brad come out of the bathroom and said, "Jane, you're next."

Tori nodded, but corrected Nick, "Gotta start calling her Peggy, Troy." She went for her turn in the shower.

When all four children were bathed and in their new SEL outfits and had watched a short cartoon on the TV, Alex predicted they'd be ravenous again. They were a solid, tight-knit family. If she could win over either of the boys, the rest would follow. Alex left her apartment and knocked on their door. On her HUD, Alex watched all four start and look around like they were guilty of some terrible crime. Nick peered at the others. Tori shrugged. Brad mouthed "go ahead".

Nick answered the door.

Alex said, in a friendly, non-intimidating Spanish, "Hi, Nick! I'm headed down to the cafeteria to get something to eat. Any of you want to come along?" Maybe the Spanish would help them trust her more quickly?

Nick looked back at Brad, who nodded assent and carefully lifted himself off the sofa he hadn't moved from since coming out of the bathroom. "Yeah, we'll come," Nick replied.

As they walked down the hallway, Alex said, "I'll show you how to shop for and change your SEL clothes while we eat. You aren't limited to just those few designs. There's some pretty spiffy island-garb. Tori, want to try the map and getting us to the cafeteria?"

Brad answered quickly, "I'll do it." He fiddled with his HUD. As there was only one location with "cafeteria" in the name, he soon said, "We go out the front of the building and just follow the street. Why ain't there a kitchen in the apartment?"

"That's a great question, Brad," Alex replied. She wanted to use their new names as much as possible to help them adjust. "It's wasted space. We are promoting community by having everyone going out. We have some self-cook community kitchens for people that like to make things and clean up all the mess, but even those are community, so people can socialize while they cook. For special events and holidays, people can get a private kitchen and dining room. You can get something to eat any time you are hungry and it's a lot better than eating out of dumpsters." After a moment, she added, "Yeah, I've done that too."

As they exited their building, Brad inquired, "So how'd you get rich?"

"Someone helped me. Ain't no shame in that. Sal helped me. I help you. One day, you help someone else. It all works out." Alex turned and pointed at an archway next to their building. "That's the path to the boardwalk and beach. The water and volleyball pits count as exercise areas. Normally, everyone is required to exercise for an hour every day, but I've put all of you on a medical pass for a month so you can have time to adjust. The school is down that way. We have year-round school with a lot of teachers, so you can work at your own pace and level. It's not like United States schools at all. I think you'll like it."

Throughout dinner, Alex tried to help them with culture-shock, but without sounding condescending or asking them anything personal. She wondered how many of Sal's words had been so carefully chosen. She'd turned into Sal. The historical parallax made her dizzy. When they were midway through eating, she launched a group-display so they could look through SEL outfits together. Her purpose was to slow everyone down to give time for Brad to eat.

They started with stuff for Peggy, who instantly bonded with bunny-pajamas that had enclosed feet, a bunny-eared hoodie, and a large pouch for treasures. Peggy swapped into it.

Alex noted several disapproving glances from neighboring tables. Colony One's citizens were defining some crazy behavior restrictions. Alex sighed. Her table was already getting curious stares for speaking Spanish instead of Colony One's mandated English. "Generally, Peggy, we don't change our SEL outfits in public. It upsets the tourists. But wow! That looks great on you!"

Peggy was busy wiggling her toes in the floppy, soft pajama feet and ignored Alex. Nick looked like he was going to say something to her, but Alex shook her head at him, and said, "It's ok."

Tori finally spoke up timidly, "Can I get a matching one?"

"Sure. Just drag it down into your cart. Everything will resize for you," Alex answered, careful not to act surprised or make a big deal out of Tori speaking. Both Nick and Brad's eyes widened, but they didn't comment either.

Alex grabbed bunny pajamas for Grace too. They flipped through a few adorable kid-friendly shorts and t-shirts, and Tori picked a few for Peggy, who was now flopping her bunny ears around, trying to see them.

They moved on to clothes for Tori. She selected three shorts and t-shirt combinations, and then asked very quietly, "Can I get a dress?"

Alex nodded, "Absolutely. Whatever you want." As they were going through the dresses, Alex saw one she really liked and exclaimed, "Oh! That's new! I want it." She dragged the flowing, white mid-length halter-top dress into her own cart. It had a pretty lace criss-cross in the back and she thought maybe it might make her look attractive for when Jay was dropping off her daughter. Jay's current girlfriend had chosen not to come along and while Alex certainly didn't begrudge him the relationship, her pride made her want to look good. She usually just stuck to plain and functional stationer clothes so she wouldn't stand out. Unfortunately, here on the island, plain and functional would stand out. The residents here preferred bright Hawaiian-style clothes. She selected a few other things quietly on her own HUD.

Choosing t-shirts and shorts for the boys went really fast. They weren't excited by clothes; they went with whatever Tori decided.

Alex noted that Brad was still picking at his sandwich. Afraid to eat, but starving. She understood that. "Halloween's coming up. It's kind of a big deal. We don't pass out candy, but we do pass out unique figurines, er, I mean, toys. You should all pick costumes." She pulled up the costume shop. "I'm going to get some more juice. Anyone want anything?"

They shook their heads, distracted by the costumes. Alex brought back a clear, vitamin-rich vegetable broth for Brad anyway. It would be easy on his stomach and help replenish nutrients. When they finally found a costume for

Peggy and Nick was busy convincing Peggy that she'd look especially nice as a winged fairy, Alex leaned over to Brad and whispered, "Drink the broth. It'll help." Brad turned bright red, but did as she suggested.

Eventually, Alex returned four very tired, but satiated children to their apartment, and she turned in herself for an unexpectedly rare early evening. She watched all five of her children for a while. Her own baby was sound asleep and safe against her daddy's chest while he tried to get a few additional things done for work one-handed on his laptop in a first-class double airplane seat. Alex's four new children were huddled together on the floor in a corner of the girls' bedroom in a safe mountain of blankets and pillows, with a pair of soft floppy bunny feet sticking out.

As Alex drifted off to sleep, she pondered Peggy's fairy costume. What if she could make it really fly? She relaunched her HUD and sought out all the costumes where the kids might fly - dragons, butterflies, bats, bees, angels, birds, pegasi... Yes, she could do a simple controller for the kids, with up/down/left/right/hover/forward/follow. She could limit the height to around four meters. Costumes without wings could get shoe-wings, so anyone who wanted to could fly. It could be done safely...

The next couple weeks flew by in a whirlwind of commutes, political and technical meetings, and teacher and psychiatrist meetings. Alex wrapped up and delegated almost all of her station-side duties so that she could work exclusively on the island. She decided the island's oceanography lab might be a good place to settle for a few months. Quiet, set hours, definite schedule.

Alex could spend non-work hours with her five children. She hadn't quite realized the time-impact of four more children, particularly ones with trust and medical issues. She couldn't exactly hire a bunch of nannies and leave them to it, like she had for Grace. These four kids were tough and proud, used to taking care of themselves, but they needed someone who understood where they came from to help them adjust. They weren't able to trust counselors yet; they barely accepted Alex.

Grace had welcomed her four new siblings and lightly prompted by Alex, showed them the school and some of the local tourist attractions. Grace wasn't mean, condescending, or jealous, but it was apparent the children had nothing in common and didn't bond. Nick, Tori, Brad, and Peggy fell into a routine of going to school, then spending time on the beach, and returning to their apartment. All four were healing, both physically and psychologically, but the progress was slow.

Alex entered the door labeled "Oceanographic Lab - Employees Only". Technically, no one enforced the restriction and anyone could go in, but security video would catch anyone unauthorized if a complaint was raised.

Any non-citizen passing inside would immediately flag a security check. Citizens could go in and speak with employees if they wanted without restriction, but the sign meant it wasn't a typical place to visit without a specific related purpose. Restricted areas were listed as "Assigned Employees Only" and required the right bracelet to enter.

Alex rode the elevator down and crossed the hall to knock on the lead oceanographer's door. The plaque on the door read "Grand Sultan". Official offices around Colony One tended toward silly signs, reflecting Brian's Scapegoat title. This was one of Colony One's more amusing quirks. If the sign were plain, people knew to leave their humor outside. Karl James, the project's lead, apparently kept things informal.

"You may enter," came the super-serious, deep intonation from inside.

Alex opened the door and briskly stepped in.

The man leaning back with his bare feet on the cluttered desk reading a magazine looked up, paled considerably, snapped his feet off the table and set the magazine aside. He was wearing SEL as a bright island floral print. In a substantially more normal and humble voice, he squeaked, "Founder!"

"Hi, Karl! I'm registered as a floating scientist-at-large and I was wondering if you needed help with anything?" Alex gave him as non-threatening a smile as she could. The magazine was a marine-life scientific journal; he hadn't been goofing off, and even if he had been, policing work-ethics wasn't her domain or concern.

The man swallowed and his pronounced adam's apple shifted. He sat up straighter. "Have we done something wrong? Our last report was a little late, but not unduly so, and we had a good reason."

Alex slid into one of his guest chairs and leaned back, shaking her head and gesturing that he should relax. "Goodness, no. I'm just moving Earth-side for a while and thought I'd see if I could be of any use. You have a number of open job postings."

Karl looked mildly relieved. "Um. Well. Yes, we do. How about I give you a tour and you tell me what you want to do?"

"That sounds good," Alex answered. "Honestly, I wish I could have spent more time here already. You guys do great data gathering and analysis. We've learned more about the ocean in the last year than in the whole of human history. I always look forward to reading your publications." Always 'look forward to' was correct. She hadn't actually read any of them until that very morning, when she'd caught up. It just never seemed to reach priority with all of the other things she normally processed.

"Give me a moment to answer this one thing that just came in." He played with his HUD.

Alex could tell he was sending off a warning note to his staff. She was glad he cared enough not to let his people get equally blindsided by their esteemed guest.

In her own HUD, Alex watched Grace talking her teacher into letting her go for the day. Alex had the sound off, but she knew her daughter's body posture of supplication. Her daughter could be extremely manipulative when she set her mind to it. Sure enough, merely a few minutes into the school day, her daughter was skipping free.

Alex was unconcerned. She'd let her be a child as long as possible. Grace was already working on middle-school math problems with early high school reading comprehension and split time between tutors and school.

Grace's teachers had been told to allow her to leave if she wanted to. Alex's hired nanny would follow along and offer any needed assistance and Alex would be sure Grace had equivalent education-time.

The teachers didn't always agree with Alex's parenting choice, but they chose not to actively argue with 'The Founder'. Grace was an odd mixture of young child and young adult. Scholastically and conversationally, Grace was extremely advanced but she still liked to convert her SEL into stuffed animals and march them across the room in organized lines.

Karl stood, forcing Alex's attention back to the office. "Shall we start with the data lab?" he asked. He had snuck on a pair of open toed men's sandals, but Alex bet he normally walked around barefoot.

Alex expected that would give the underwater lab people plenty of time to clean up. "Sure. How's the new server working out for you?"

"Our network guy was over doing software updates and maintenance yesterday, so we lost a couple hours server time, but overall, it's much faster. We'll be more efficient with it." Karl glanced at her, apparently trying to ascertain if she was being honest about just looking for a job or was evaluating their program for cuts.

Alex suppressed a sigh. She didn't do budget allocations; that was thankfully delegated to a competent team. Alex smiled warmly at Karl and followed along on the guided tour through his domain, asking pertinent questions and slowly getting the man to relax and expand on his favorite topics. She hoped before the end of her Earth-time, she might get a casually intoned, "Kneel, supplicant," when she came into his office instead of that sudden terror. She'd give herself extra kudos if she could get him to keep his feet up and magazine open when he did it.

Just before they got to the underwater lab, Grace arrived. Grace's HUD always showed Alex's location on the map. "Hi, Mommy!" Grace jumped into Alex's arms giving her a hug. "Hiya, Grace. Aren't you supposed to be in school today?"

Grace wriggled down. "I told you. I'm going by Ember now."

"So you did, Ember. Sorry, I forgot."

"You don't forget anything."

"Habit then." Alex glanced over at Karl and asked, "Is it ok if my daughter comes along? I'm sure she'd love to see the underwater window."

"Of course. Ember, I'm Karl. It's nice to meet you." He dropped down to one knee to shake her hand at her height. He must have heard the rumors that the Founder's daughter was bright, because he spoke to her as an adult, not as a four year old.

The best way to impress a mom, Alex noted, was to adore her children. Karl either knew that or genuinely liked kids.

"You're really tall, Sultan James," Grace observed. She'd definitely seen the office sign on her quest to find Alex.

Alex sent Grace a private note that said, "Sultans are called 'Your Majesty'."

Karl laughed, the sound deep and full of joy, and Alex thought he probably really liked kids. He said, "I'm not tall when I'm kneeling. Have you seen any of the other ocean windows?" The island had a number of public underwater viewing rooms. This underwater lab was actually the deepest.

"I like the reef one the best," Grace answered proudly. The reef had been artificially created, but was now home to a large number of imported tropical fish. People weren't allowed to swim there, but several tube walkways let them go through and observe. The tubes themselves were sloped and angled to make the space qualify as an exercise area.

"Ours is much deeper. We don't have any of the small fish you see at the reef." Karl stood back up and escorted them down the hallway.

Grace took Alex's hand and moderated her normal running pace to match Alex. Alex smiled down at her with approval.

They entered the large underwater window lab. All the way around, a clear SEL floor-to-ceiling window showed the water outside. A dolphin circled on one side and an octopus hovered, staring inward on the other side. The center of the room had a ring of desks facing outward toward the windows. The three twenty-something residents were in pristine SEL white lab coats and Alex pretended not to notice the lingering smell of french fries.

Grace bounced and pointed at the octopus, squealing, "Look, Mommy!" She pulled her hand free and ran over to the window in front of the octopus, pressing her hands against the window, and leaning forward until her nose touched the window. The octopus moved closer and put a tentacle up. Grace giggled.

"The octopi are surprisingly friendly," Karl said. He turned to his colleagues and introduced them. They only goggled a little.

Alex shook their hands and repeated her praise for their work. They proceeded to tell her about their latest data, showing her on their screens. At one point, Karl looked over Alex's shoulder to where Grace was playing with the octopus and his eyes widened. Alex glanced at her HUD and spun around. "Grace Ember! What are you doing?!"

Her daughter was buck-naked, pirouetting in front of the window. "I'm showing him what I look like," she answered matter-of-factly. She lifted her foot toward the octopus and wiggled her toes. "You should show him what you look like, too, so he can see what an adult looks like compared to a kid."

Next to her, one of the techs choked, half laughing.

Alex was trying very hard not to laugh herself. "Grace, what have I told you about nudity in public?"

"This isn't public," she replied, showing the octopus her ears and then pointing at her mouth. "It's marked private on the map. I checked."

"Put your clothes on, Grace." Alex walked toward her. "New definition of public: anywhere where there are people who are not me or your daddy."

Grace shrugged and tapped her bracelet and her SEL clothes and shoes reappeared.

Alex went over to the window where the octopus was holding on and staring in at them with one of his large eyes. "He's certainly very flexible compared to us, isn't he?"

"They talk with colors on their skin," Grace said, quoting from some book.

"They also have multiple brains," Karl added, coming over to them.

Grace smiled at Karl and then indicating the octopus, said, "He seems really smart. I like him." Then Grace turned to Alex and asked, "Can you work in here so I can come too?"

Alex peered at Karl apologetically, "Need another data analyst and one future marine biologist?"

"I'd be delighted. We always have at least one cephalopod and one dolphin about. They chase away any sharks, but they don't seem to bother each other. Sometimes a whale comes by." Karl continued to tell them about the marine animals that visited them. Both Alex and Grace asked leading questions and soon had all four of the scientists happily telling them stories.

On the way back to the island's surface in the elevator and without any audience, Grace asked Alex, "Can I be nude in front of my husband?"

Alex peered at her precocious daughter, quirked an eyebrow at her, and teased, "Did you get married while you were visiting your daddy, Ember? Why didn't you invite me to your wedding?"

"No, of course not." Grace made a face at Alex. "Silly Mommy."

"Well, then. When you are old enough to get married, you can answer that question for yourself. Until then, my rules."

Alex settled comfortably into her new downside life. Spending time in the underwater lab turned into a nice break from her other duties and it made it harder for random people to seek her out with questions that could be answered by Colony One's regular staff. She still had to go to the station for certain meetings, but whenever she could, she either skipped the meeting entirely or attended remotely. This also let her spend time with her four new children.

For Halloween, Colony One would turn into a huge festival celebrated a full 24 hours from noon to noon so children could visit toy kiosks on both the island and the space station. While the day was considered a holiday, everyone still had to work their standard six hours to make it fair for support personnel (food services, medical, security) and those that chose not to celebrate the holiday. Exercise periods were waived for everyone to give people more time to wander around.

Grace opted to be an octopus and demanded the designer put a shimmering blue haze around her so she could pretend to be swimming through water when she was flying. The light bent around Grace's legs and arms, hiding them, and Grace could operate her eight costume legs with her fingers.

Alex had tried suggesting Grace create the costume herself, but Grace refused to focus on the project and said that learning the programming and design tools well enough to do what she wanted would take too long. Alex had simply hugged Grace and suggested maybe she might learn it in the future and transferred the money to their chosen designer. Then Alex spent the remainder of time until Halloween wondering if she should have pushed Grace and demanded her daughter figure it out. Her child could certainly have done it, but Grace was too busy being distracted by the octopi in the underwater lab. Grace frequently ditched school to visit the lab and Alex filled Grace's reading queue with marine biology books.

Alex studied her own costume in the mirror - Egyptian Queen Hatshepsut, who was known for trade, restoration and building, more than war. The SEL costume designer had opted for elegant and realistic, with matching hair, skin tone, and eye color. Alex ignored the historical pharaoh gender discussion and asked that the entire outfit be traditional for the time period for women. By time her appearance was fully modified by SEL, she wasn't actually recognizable. The illusion was complete and deliberate to prevent random people from trying to engage her in Colony One requests and discussions. People who knew her would recognize her children and Jay and know who she was by proximity, but presumably those people would know not to interrupt her family time.

Together, Alex and Grace marched over to the next apartment to collect Grace's foster siblings so they could go get lunch and then start visiting the Halloween kiosks. Flying wouldn't work until the celebratory bell rang at noon. They knocked and waited. Alex faded back the face part of her costume so the kids would recognize her.

Tori answered after a moment. Nick and Tori were assuming more parental roles every day and helped Brad and Peggy with their costumes. Both Tori and Peggy were in matching pink faerie costumes. Alex knew Tori had wanted to be a blue faerie, but Peggy had insisted they match and Tori had given in to the younger girl. Nick was sharply dressed in a dapper black and white tuxedo, complete with bow tie and top hat. He looked like any billionaire who might show up at a jet set fundraiser.

Brad had chosen a scary dragon skeleton. It was only mildly scary right now, but after the young-children curfew at 9 p.m., it would transform into a truly horrifying fire-breathing demon-dragon. The curfew wasn't Colony One enforced, but parental choice. Scary and racy costumes wouldn't come out until after the curfew and a number of late-night parties would pop up all over.

"You all look wonderful!" Alex declared and the rambunctious group made their way out of the apartment building. As they entered the outdoor luau-style cafeteria, Iron Man approached them in beautiful, shiny full metal armor. The circular battery on his chest glowed brightly.

Alex's HUD identified Jay. "Clever!"

Jay raised the face mask. "Yeah! No one will recognize me and I can fly around with Grace. Iron Man is still popular enough that the costume won't stick out." His eyes sparkled enthusiastically.

Alex felt a rush of warmth from the top of her head down to her toes. She swallowed. She wasn't sure if she should be upset or thankful that Jay's current girlfriend, Avalon Dorsey, hadn't wanted to come to Colony One.

The kids ran off to get their favorite foods. Jay's eyes followed Grace and then shifted to Alex. "You look stunning, Alex. That's a great costume."

Alex's mouth twitched up. He was just being friendly, not making an overture. "Thank you. Our designers are really shining this year. With tech taking over the mundane jobs, the creatives are flourishing. Why wear a shirt when you can wear a designer shirt?"

"Auntie Alex!" Georgie called out from the entrance, running over with his arms spread like he was flying.

Alex just barely managed to get a protective squishy buffer up as Georgie in his oversized Buzz Lightyear costume and head bubble bounced into her. She saw Lucas and his wife, Sara, trailing behind at a more reasonable pace. "Got some problems stopping, Georgie?" Alex helped Georgie right himself.

"Naw, simulated high engine airflow isn't configured for ground travel," Georgie muttered, his words slightly unintelligible from physically undeveloped vocal muscles. "The exit mass flow rate times the exit velocity minus the free stream mass flow rate times the free stream velocity is set up for flying." Georgie peered up at her mischievously, to see if she'd comment.

"Go get yourself some fuel, Buzz," Alex said. "I look forward to seeing you in the air."

Georgie giggled. "To infinity and beyond!" he shouted, quoting Buzz Lightyear's catchphrase and ran off toward the buffet line.

"Alex, Jay," Lucas greeted them with a friendly nod. Lucas and Sara were dressed in matching western outfits, with black and white cow pattern accents.

"I see you modified Georgie's flight mechanics," Alex said.

Lucas grinned. "I needed to do something to keep him occupied or we'd really be in trouble. He tried to launch himself out of the shuttle on the way down."

"Whatever Daddy can do..." Alex observed.

"Eventually, he's going to understand all those equations I'm teaching him," Lucas said proudly.

"He doesn't?" Jay asked.

"Naw, he just recites them right now," Lucas answered. "Gives him something to do while I'm working."

Sara rolled her eyes, squeezed Lucas' hand, and went to help Georgie at the buffet line.

After getting their food, the group rejoined at a table near the center of the area. Palm trees scattered between the tables provided shade from the midday sun.

While Jay regaled Lucas and Sara with an amusing account of his latest trail bridge restoration project, Alex sipped her tea and watched the children. Nick, being the oldest, avidly listened to Jay, trying to distance himself from the children and distinguish himself as an adult.

Peggy was more interested in her costume wings than eating. She kept turning her head to see them and Tori streamed a video from her own interface onto Peggy's so the young girl could see herself. Grace had forgotten her additional legs and was busy picking toppings off her pizza, and Brad was smearing mustard on Georgie's head bubble to create a face. Georgie simply stuck his tongue out at Brad and turned his SEL toy into a sticky-foot gecko robot to clean off the mustard.

Alex wondered if she should step in, but while Georgie was much younger than Brad, he was a native with their technology. Retribution would not be fair.

Before Alex could make a decision, Sara reached over and confiscated Georgie's SEL gecko. "I told you to leave this at home." Sara restored it to card-state and put it in her pocket. Sara raised an eyebrow at Alex.

Dutifully, Alex said, "Brad, keep your mustard on your sandwich please."

Brad didn't acknowledge Alex, but leaned over to Georgie and asked, "How'd you do that?"

Georgie wrinkled his nose. "S'SEL card. You don't have one yet?"

Brad shook his head.

Georgie opened his hip pocket to show Brad something. "Later," he whispered. "I got an extra."

Alex only heard this through her private surveillance so she couldn't comment. She saw Lucas' mouth twitch in amusement.

When the musical bell rang precisely at noon, followed by a loud, deep-voiced, "Wa Ha Ha Ha Ha! Happy Halloween!", Halloween officially started. Pandemonium ensued. Kids scattered around the luau launched into the air with gleeful shouts, forgetting their food. Alex's children were no exception. Nick gave up the pretense of being an adult and joined them.

The safety restrictions kept the children from bumping into each other although several tried. Natural and fantastical flying creatures and humanoids were joined by witches, wizards, and creative flying objects like kites and drones. A young girl waved from her flying blue British police box. The use of SEL for costumes made some startlingly realistic creatures.

Shaking his head at the chaos, Lucas said to Alex, "Did you really think this through?"

"We'll find out," Alex replied, eyes twinkling.

Sara started cleaning up their trays. "I guess lunch is over."

A palm leaf landed on their table but by the time Alex pulled up the flight-code to protect the trees, she saw Lucas had already taken care of it and he'd made sure other matter was equally protected. Both Lucas and Jay joined the kids in the air.

Grace drifted down and wrapped her tentacles around Alex. "Come on, Mommy! We want to see the first mystery clue!" The flight range was limited by the designated guardian so Alex adjusted the distance to let them go farther and took the remaining trays and followed Sara to the recycling bins. They followed their floating entourage to the mini-theater set up specifically for Halloween. A small sign listed showtimes although the information was available on the special Halloween map.

On stage, a man appeared at the railing of an octagonal lighthouse. The hologram was so realistic, having been previously recorded by real actors, that Alex had to check that it was indeed a hologram. The man said, "I began work in the lighthouse in 1934 when the Great Depression was in full swing and Adolf Hitler had just become Führer und Reichskanzler. While I didn't want to drag my dear wife and two children to such a remote location, it was work that came with a house and food..." The man continued with a brief history lesson on the Great Depression and took the audience on a quick tour of his lighthouse.

The man then returned to his railing. "Now we found this here logbook from the previous lighthouse keeper and we took to reading from it to pass the nights." A logbook icon appeared on the HUD for everyone in attendance. "We were shocked when we reached page 187 and he mentioned the shipwreck of the SS Malaine, a great metal cargo liner carrying treasures from the orient." A bookmark appeared on their logbooks. "My son built a model of the ship and I'm sure he would love to tell you about it. He was testing its buoyancy on the beach to the southwest. We would like your help finding the shipwreck and treasure. My wife wrote a letter to the ship's company and got the liner's route. She's around here somewhere and will show it to you. My daughter probably knows where and she's always avoiding chores by looking for shark teeth on the beach."

A mystery clue notebook appeared beside the logbook, listing the three tasks - speak to son, speak to daughter, speak to wife. These could be done in any order so the children could visit the toy kiosks and a large mob of children wouldn't travel from place to place together. The audience dispersed.

With Peggy dictating their direction, Alex's group headed toward the northern end of the island, flying up to travel and then down to land at the kiosks. Jay, Lucas, and Sara opted to fly along, skipping the downs, while Alex chose to walk for the added exercise.

The volunteers running kiosks got to design their booth and decide what type trade figurine they passed out. The SEL figurines disappeared into the children's "magic" bags, adding no weight at all. When the children got home, the bag converted into a book, and kids could just tap the page of the item they wanted to play with. The figurines could also be easily traded.

Non-citizen children were also encouraged to participate, and were given temporary SEL costumes for the day and would have their selected figurines converted to actual little hollow-wooden figurines as SEL only belonged to Colony One citizens.

Grace sloshed next to Alex for a while. "When do you think they'll figure out it's faster if we stay on the ground?"

Alex chuckled. "I think it's the adventure, Ember. The goal isn't the finish line, but the run along the track."

Grace shook her head and dashed off to a traditional Sioux tipi with an

Indian standing in front where she was given a beautiful feather. The feather disappeared into her bag and she shouted her thanks as she sped off to the next kiosk.

Alex got a message from Brian that Earth's social media was inundated by pictures and videos of the flying children and ignorant fools were screaming about the danger and how irresponsible Colony One's leadership was. Alex replied suggesting he publish a statement that Colony One would announce the casualty count after Halloween and that those concerned should take bets on the actual number. The invisible safety bubbles wouldn't let anyone get hurt, even on land.

Alex's group found the "daughter" for the mystery clue and after another history lesson, they received two more tasks. Alex cheated and pulled up the solution. The quest would take them all over the island, eventually ending in a specially designed underwater building, where the children could pick three mystery items from the treasure.

Georgie pulled on Alex's arm. "Auntie Alex, how come my landing time was off? I calculated it just right."

Alex pat his bubble-head. "Go ask your Daddy, Georgie."

Georgie frowned. "But I launched at a velocity of 2.24 meters per second at an angle of 53 degrees. I should have landed 10.3 seconds sooner and directly in front of the giant pumpkin."

"Go ask your Daddy, Georgie." Alex certainly wasn't going to get drawn into a discussion of headwinds and tailwinds and the additional safety buffers she'd implemented in the costume flight modules to keep kids from knocking into each other and going too high. Besides, Lucas was deluding himself with wishful thinking that Georgie was just memorizing words.

Georgie then giggled and said, "Daddy said I would scare you if I said this. Did it work?"

Alex laughed and shooed Georgie off. She glanced up and saw Lucas grinning. He mouthed, "Got you!"

Alex watched the kids zipping around to the various kiosks, shouting to each other and laughing, and realized she was genuinely happy. Her family. Her life. Not just her own child, but the others as well, and even the adults glowed happy and content, free of that rat-race, weary glaze that permeated other societies. There were still problems of course, because no society was perfect, but this felt close. Colony One was stable and would grow and thrive even without her.

A week later, Alex joined her daughter and the other techs in the underwater lab. Grace had beaten her there because Alex had been called off to a quick zoning meeting. Alex walked over and tapped Grace on the shoulder to get her attention.

Grace glanced over her shoulder with, "Hi, Mommy! Say hello to Henry." Grace had named that first octopus Henry and proceeded to name every other octopus that visited, as well as the dolphins. There was one octopus she named King Lark, who was not the biggest or the most dextrous, but Grace said he was their leader, and so rearranged Karl's name to make that one Karl's counterpart. The lab staff adored Grace, who adored them right back.

"Grace, tomorrow I want you to stay in school. You need the sunlight and human interaction," Alex said.

Grace gave a deep, exaggerated sigh, and groaned. Not arguing, she said, "The desks and lab lights are too bright. The octopi don't like it. Turn that stuff off."

"You know I'm down here to work, right? And those computers and screens are showing us data that we're using." Alex rubbed her daughter's head and kissed it.

"Move out of here then," Grace commanded. "We need natural light."

Alex noted how bossy her daughter was, with that self-centeredness of childhood. "Grace, learn to say please and consider other people's needs."

"But your lights are in the way."

Alex put her hand on her hip and tapped her foot, tilting her head and raising her eyebrow. She waited.

Grace sighed loudly again. "Please find a way to block the light from your workstations, Mommy."

"Ok, I will. But you have to learn the three new books I put in your list by the end of the day."

"But..."

"Don't make me change it to five books." Alex really had a difficult time being stern with Grace.

Grace pinched her lips together and frowned.

By the end of the day, a new one-way SEL window enclosed the lab desks, leaving the open-to-ocean area completely dark. Karl also rigged a two-way microphone and speaker combination so the sea creatures could hear Grace.

Grace spent most of each day sitting out in the dark area, socializing with the octopus-of-the-day, who was most often Henry. Sometimes she'd bring a children's book and read to them, with a dim flashlight pointed at the pictures. Other times, she'd play music or videos for them. Most often, she liked making shadow-puppets with her hands or using her stuffed animals to tell them stories. The dolphins squeaked back and the octopi flashed their skin-lights.

At first Alex and her three coworkers looked on this with amusement and crunched their numbers and did ocean measurements. But over time, Alex recognized that there seemed to be a pattern in the squeaks and lights that went beyond simple communication. Alex invited the world's top dolphin and octopi experts as well as several language specialists to come work in the lab.

Unfortunately, all declined; Colony One policies coupled with the Founder's adamant stance on the Earth's instability still curtailed immigration.

When Alex told Grace no one would come, her daughter had merely shrugged and said it didn't matter because she was going to learn their language. Alex responded by pointing out the best language books and recommending Grace learn a few other human languages so she'd have a foundation to work from.

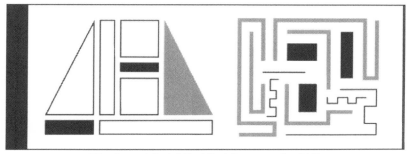

T plus 10:185:17:18   ~1π/15

"Alex, wake up!" the voice was loud, firm, demanding.

Alex blinked and triggered the lights, snapping awake. It took her a moment to realize she wasn't dreaming. There was a woman standing across the room, which shouldn't have been possible. Alex felt like she'd just barely fallen asleep in her island apartment, although she knew she'd dreamed of Halloween costumes.

"How did you get in here?" Alex checked her bioshield. The room alarm should have woken her. She checked it. Both her bioshield and her alarm were functioning normally.

The woman crossed over to the display wall and touched it. "I'm you, from a different timeline, from the future. Run the biology scans. I know you used to be Mary. I know you shot those girls when you rescued Caitlin. I know Sal fed you lasagne when you first met. I know Kuro Hamasaki shot you. I know the last thing you ever played on a piano was Claude Debussy's Deux Arabesques No. 1 and Milo heard you. Give me a HUD. I have things I need to share with you before I get pulled back to my own timeline."

Alex frowned and set her picobots to scanning the woman. Alex pushed herself out of bed and triggered her SEL clothing to a comfortable, martial-arts friendly jumpsuit. The woman could not have known all of those things. No one did.

The woman waited, the calm outward stance betrayed by an electric intensity and tension.

The scan completed, showing a perfect DNA match, for herself, only a

395

couple decades older.

The woman arched an eyebrow, "See? I'm you. Our timelines split the afternoon you slept with Jay. Do you have a child? Children?"

Alex crossed her arms. "Yes, a daughter. Grace Ember."

"Give me a HUD. Please, we don't have much time. Only three more minutes actually."

Alex gave the woman a guest HUD.

The woman talked while she typed with a fluency that could only have meant a lifetime of using the software. "When your daughter is about 8 years 6 months and 3 days old, an alien ship will be spotted. They are refugees. You have to feed them or they will die. They will be followed by a Resaund fleet. You must immediately, without mercy, without thought, destroy that fleet. If they are able to send a message back to their command, humanity will be destroyed. We cannot win. Alex, they walk right through SEL. You cannot save anyone but yourself."

She stopped talking for a moment and Alex realized her account was being accessed. Alex went to try and shut the woman out but realized that would just shut herself out.

The woman said, "I'm you. It's ok. You can trust me."

"The Earth?" Alex asked.

The woman shook her head once, sharply. "Run SEL around to hold the planet together. Lucas can give you a matrix for the band."

"When?"

"Varies by timeline. Cal Park is the right person to run Emergency Response. Hire really good epidemiologists. Come find me. Information is in the data I'm entering." She continued typing silently. She refocused on Alex again, and said, "I can't believe how young you look, so untouched. Kill that Resaund fleet. Don't let them send your location back. Don't..." The woman stiffened, swore, and instantly shrunk away to nothing as if being pulled away at the speed of light.

Alex immediately scanned the room. There was nothing. She recorded data for everything at the atomic level and shoved it into a newly created secure storage file. Then she sat down on her bed and waited a few minutes to wake up. She was truly awake. Then she replayed every detail in her mind. The woman's stance, her movements - all precisely matched Alex, and the hair, skin, and eyes reflected what Alex would expect her future-self to look like.

She pulled up her account and grabbed a report of everything that had been changed in the last hour, and only one file appeared. Alex didn't open that immediately, but instead went to her room's security footage. That had been erased and replaced with a note with her name on it, just as she'd done before to remove her time with Jay.

Alex returned to the file and tried to open it. It was encrypted with a password prompt. For the next hour, she tried every password she'd ever used.

None of them opened the file. Over the next month, she tried daily to open the file, but couldn't. She wanted to beat her future self to a bloody pulp.

Alex heard her bedroom door open and then heard the soft tiptoe footsteps of Grace.

"I know how to talk to Henry, Mommy." Grace announced loudly, pushing on Alex's shoulder to wake her. "But I need help displaying the lexicon. Give me someone to write the program?"

Alex blinked one eye open and peered at her HUD. "Ember, it's 4 a.m. Go back to sleep."

"If you set up the job announcement right now, maybe someone will be able to do it today." Grace stopped nudging Alex's shoulder. "Please?"

"Ok, ok, but only if you promise to sleep until 8."

"6." Instant renegotiation.

"8."

"7." Slightly more timid.

"8 or not at all."

"Ok. 8." Grace grumbled loudly at this injustice and turned and left.

Alex groaned, rolled over, and woke up enough to write a job announcement for a custom programmer with a specialty in graphics.

Two weeks later, Grace had her program and was busily entering data that she called Henry's lexicon. Alex walked into the dark room where Grace sat with her back to Henry, showing him her HUD. Alex was trying to think of a good strategy to get Grace to go out to the beach and play for a while. Her child was already starting to lose her tan, despite the sporadic evenings on the beach. She'd already finagled her way out of going to an exercise zone by jogging around the ocean habitat with Henry swimming alongside her. She'd talked to the personnel exercise coach and gotten the exercise waiver all by herself. Alex was so pleased that Grace had actually spoken to someone outside of this small social circle that she'd allowed it. "Hey, Grace, how's the communication going?"

"I need to add more words. Well, they aren't really words as much as emotions and concepts. It's taking a long time because our language is too inefficient."

"Show me?" Alex sat down next to her daughter.

Grace nudged Alex with her toe, "Say hi to Henry first. Don't just ignore him. He isn't just decoration."

"Hi, Henry. I'm sorry I ignored you when I came over," Alex said diligently, half-bowing to Henry. Henry's skin glowed.

Grace, who could see Henry from her own HUD, nodded in satisfaction, and flashed something in the special grid on her display. Henry glowed several rapidly shifting colors in response. Grace flashed a few more things and said to Alex, "I think I told him I'm going to be explaining stuff to you for a while."

"How clearly can you communicate?"

"Established things go pretty fast, but we both get stuck a lot. Henry gets frustrated. I think he's older than me even though they live less years."

Alex nodded. "Older than 5 years, huh?" Alex tickled Grace's side, and then peered at Henry, suddenly getting an idea. "Hey, if I wanted you to translate something for me, could you?"

"Maybe. What do you want to say?"

"About the Earth?"

Grace was aware of the Earth's limited human habitation lifespan, although she'd been so bored by Alex trying to show her the formulas and calculations that Alex had given up trying to explain it to her. Grace nodded. "Oh, sure. We've talked about the plastic islands. He's happy we're cleaning it up. He says some other stuff about the ocean floor, but I haven't been able to decipher that yet. He definitely understands he is on a planet."

"Does he understand about continents?"

"He knows the word, but I'm not sure we're talking about the same thing."

"How about our space station?"

"I've showed him pictures. They don't really understand technology. The dolphins get it, but they haven't been able to translate."

"The dolphins and octopi talk to each other?"

"And the squid and sea turtles. It's more of a common understanding than a common language."

"Can you tell them the Earth is going to have problems soon?"

"I've told them about the Earth. I keep getting back their word for seafloor. The dolphins say the same. It doesn't make much sense." Henry's skin lit up again in rapid color shifts. Alex put her hand up to the SEL window as her daughter flashed some patterns on her HUD much more slowly. "Henry asks if you are a sea turtle, but he asks that about everyone."

"Sea turtle?" Alex tapped her fingers on her chin, thinking. "Hmmm. Sea turtles live a really long time. Could he mean an elder? Maybe someone in charge?"

Alex watched as Grace closed her eyes and reviewed her memory. She wasn't quite as fast as Alex, because she probably hadn't figured out how to process information systematically yet and Alex was content to let her daughter figure that out herself. Alex's own method might not work best for her daughter anyway. After a full two minutes, Grace answered, "It's possible."

"Try telling him yes."

"Ok." Grace flashed a few things. Henry swam away. Grace turned to Alex, "Why did he go?"

"Let's wait a few minutes and see if he comes back. While we wait, why don't you show me your lexicon?"

For the next half hour, Grace displayed patterns and said what she thought they meant and why. Alex found it difficult to differentiate between the subtle curves and shapes made of almost identical hues and values. Concepts for things included variations for season. Ocean depth, for example, included constructs for visible light waves, salinity, temperature, pressure, tide, and geomagnetic location. These were altered by known presence of other sea life and time of the observation, within the solar year. To describe that place in the future, the image got a single bar of greenish-grey. One simple image conveyed everything of interest to not only find the exact place, but to safely travel to or circumvent the area.

The dolphin equivalent used minute changes in amplitude, frequency, and undertones to convey similar information. Abstract concepts were more challenging to decipher. Alex found the audio waveform visual representation even more confusing than the images. The meaning was in the change between their measurements, not the measurements themselves, so the same concepts might appear at completely different frequencies.

Henry came back. He was accompanied by King Lark, the older octopus. They were flashing their lights between them.

Alex did her best regal head-nod to King Lark and said to Grace, "I think you may have chosen his name very well." Alex turned around to sit facing the arrivals, who attached themselves to her SEL window.

King Lark began shifting colors directly in front of Alex. "What's he saying?" she asked.

"I can't read him that fast and I can't read both of them at the same time. I have to tell Henry to tell him to slow down." Grace fiddled with her interface, clearly getting upset.

"It's ok, Ember, take your time. They'll understand." Alex reached over and put her hand on Grace's arm to calm her.

"Ok, he just repeated the ocean floor again, but it doesn't make sense, there's a shift here." Her little finger pointed at some bluish green. "I don't know what that means."

"That's ok, Ember. What sort of things can you say? For instance, can you ask him if it's ok if I take them to space?"

King Lark kept flashing lights at Alex and Grace.

"There aren't any words for that, Mommy."

"Hmmm. How good is their eyesight? Do they see your videos well?"

Grace nodded. "Have to adjust the colors for down here though. At this depth, some wavelengths don't reach."

Alex rubbed her chin thoughtfully. "How about if I make a video that shows what we want to do and you fix the colors and show them? Would that work?"

"I think so."

"Can you tell King Lark to come back in 2 days?"

"Um." Grace fiddled with her HUD and flashed some lights. She watched the response carefully.

Henry and King Lark exchanged rapid flashes. Then King Lark, very slowly, very deliberately, lit up a few times, and then swam away.

Grace shook her head. "I don't know, Mommy. He just said ocean floor again. There's a bunch of embedded signals in it, but I don't know what they are." She pointed at part of one of the lights on her HUD. "That's ocean salinity and over here is temperature, but the numbers I think they translate to are within range."

"Well, I'll put together that video for us and we'll try again in two days. Meanwhile, I'll have our team look at the ocean floors. You did well, Ember. I'm proud of you."

Two days later turned into four because Grace forgot to account for some tidal shift in her translation, but this time they were ready with their video. In addition to the underwater lab team, Brian, Lucas, and Cal Park were in attendance, all sitting on the floor in the dark around Grace. Only Henry and King Lark showed up from the underwater kingdom.

Alex triggered the hologram which started with them in their lab, next to both Henry and King Lark, and shrunk them, expanding to show the ocean and ocean floor just beneath them, and then continents and the planet and Colony One's tiny habitat above. Then it reversed back to them and started forward, but this time, it showed a huge ball container around all of them and showed that being lifted up and getting attached to the space station. Then the image zoomed in on the ocean inside the habitat.

When it finished, Alex froze it at the end.

Henry and King Lark flashed rapidly at each other and then Henry flashed something slowly at Grace.

Grace said, "I don't know what that means. He hasn't used it before."

"If it were me, I'd want to see the animation again," Brian offered.

Alex replayed the animation, setting the pace slower, muttering, "At least he didn't say ocean floor again."

"We checked the ocean floors. We have nothing out of range," Cal said, reiterating what he'd been saying for the last three days. "Temperature, salinity, oxygen. It's all expected."

Henry flashed something else.

"They want to know when," Grace translated after a moment staring at her display.

Brian cleared his throat. "Politically, we can't do it until later when we take our entire island."

Lucas added, "I also want to run more simulations on Earth's mass and orbit to make sure Alex and I haven't forgotten anything."

"At least 'when' sounds like they are ok with us doing it. You have any way to say 'I don't know.', kiddo?" Alex asked.

"Um. Yeah. Sort of," Grace answered. "It would be hard to answer when anyway. Their time is defined by a lot of things and I don't think we could get it right anyway. I'm not that good at the nuances." Grace set her screen to respond.

King Lark lit up again.

Alex swore. "Even I know that one. Ocean floor."

Grace snorted. "See, Mommy? I told you that you could learn their language."

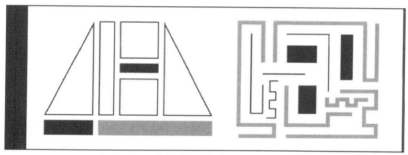

T plus 11:0:9:25   ~1π/30

Alex finished recording the thirty-fourth rescue pod message. She had so many languages to cover yet and already, she was beginning to wonder if her pronunciations and translations were correct. She stood up and stretched, rolling her neck and trying to loosen the muscles. She wanted to get fifty done before going to the pool to swim laps. She really hated sitting still for too long.

Her HUD flashed red entirely and an audible buzzer sounded in her ears. She cleared the alert and read the message. Grace's heart rate was elevated and her biometrics were showing extreme agitation. All five of her children were at the new coral reef grand opening and presentation, at Alex's insistence. Grace needed to get out of the undersea lab and her orphans needed some exposure to Colony One's environmental agendas. Alex had turned off the video feeds so she could focus on the current task.

Alex quickly reactivated Grace's video feed.

"I am not!" Grace shouted. "You should all go back to the United States! We don't want you here!"

"Grace, that's enough!" Nick commanded. He rubbed his thigh nervously, eyes quickly darting back down the tunnel where other people were slowly approaching.

"He started it!" Grace pointed at Brad.

401

"Everyone's so busy treating you like a Princess, you don't know how to be a person," Brad said, spitting at Grace and then sticking out his tongue. He followed this by calling Grace several words that Grace immediately started looking up. This search history flashed on Alex's display.

"I don't wanna go back," Peggy cried. "I wanna be a Princess."

"We're not going back," Tori said. She hugged Peggy close to her, glaring at Grace. "You're a princess to us, Peggy." Tori kissed the top of Peggy's head.

"You're so ignorant," Grace said, addressing Brad. "Zooxanthellae are smarter than you!"

Brad sneered at Grace. "You're a spoiled, rotten brat."

Alex cringed. She started toward her office door to go break up their fight, but then realized she couldn't without them wondering how she'd known about the fight.

Brad shoved Grace backward into the transparent SEL window separating them from the coral reef. Fish scattered at the sudden movement.

Grace rebounded and tried to punch Brad, but Alex's daughter didn't have a chance against Brad's street fighting experience and he was five years older than Grace. Brad easily dodged Grace and pushed her into the opposite window.

Grace hollered, although Alex knew it was humiliation, not pain. Grace's bioshield would protect her.

"Hey, now! What's this? Where are your parents?" A random citizen stepped between Grace and Brad, grabbing Brad's arm.

Brad instantly twisted free, forcefully elbowing the man in the ribs as he did so.

Unprepared, the man yelped in pain and bent forward. His hand moved as he activated his HUD.

Alex was impressed by how quickly Colony One's security team responded. She watched as officers arrived and secured her four orphans in SEL restraining bubbles. One of the officers recognized Grace and warned the other officers. They didn't put Grace in a restraining bubble, but instead politely invited her to accompany them, which she did, with a vindictive glare at Brad, who was beating on his bubble and shouting, although nothing could be heard due to the sound suppressors. Peggy, separated from Tori by the bubble, was crying. Tori looked like she might also burst into tears but her frozen, emotionless defenses were kicking in, and Nick had his arms crossed, but his eyes were panicked.

Quickly, Alex scanned back through Grace's video to find the start which seemed to be Brad complaining that he already had enough school for one day and that he didn't want to listen to a lecture on how baby coral could be moved to the new habitat. Grace, obviously mimicking Jay's environmentalist speeches, started explaining why the coral reefs were important and the conversation devolved from there. Grace was overbearing and condescending.

Her street kids responded as expected and soon the five were having a typical children's squabble.

Alex glared at the clock. What was taking security so long to call her? She paced like a caged tiger. On her HUD, her daughter was explaining and laying the blame entirely on Brad, and the two station security officers were listening intently and believing every word as Grace was able to speak clearly and sound like an adult.

After ten minutes of listening to Grace, one of the officers finally said, "We should call the Founder."

"We can't not call her," the other officer replied. "Tell you what. You call and I'll buy you a beer tonight."

"Drinks are free for citizens," Grace contributed, earning a disturbed glare from the first officer.

Alex noted Grace hadn't called her either and Grace still had full access to her own HUD. Her daughter certainly knew this mess was partly her fault.

The second officer, seeing this glance, said, "Ok, I'll make the call. You owe me."

Alex's HUD lit with an incoming call. She carefully relaxed her face and answered with the best calm voice she could muster. "Yes?"

"Founder, I'm sorry to disturb you, but we've had a slight problem with your four guests."

"Are they ok?"

"Yes, Founder, but I think you should come and speak with them before we release them into your custody."

"What happened?"

"Just a bit of a scuffle, Founder. One of the boys bruised a citizen. Nothing serious."

"I'll be right there. Thank you for calling me." Alex cut the phone connection.

When Alex arrived at the station security office a mere five minutes later, she requested a private conference room and her children. The officers brought Grace followed by the other four who were still secured in their bubbles. Alex dismissed the officers and removed the security bubbles. Peggy immediately flew into Tori's arms, and while Tori wrapped her arms around Peggy, her marble expression was securely in place.

"Brad started it," Grace began.

Cutting her off, Alex commanded, "Sit down, all of you."

They did, and Grace started again, and then Nick started to talk over her, and Brad jumped in. Soon the three were shouting over each other. Alex merely tented her fingers on the table and waited. Peggy's sniffles changed to full on tears again.

"Enough," Alex said. "You're making Peggy cry." Nick and Brad winced. Grace just lifted her chin and closed her mouth. "One at a time, I want to hear what happened. Nick, you start. You're the oldest."

Nick glanced over at Grace and then said, "Nothing. It was just an argument. Brad didn't mean to hurt that guy. He just startled him, is all."

"I see," said Alex, recognizing that Nick would downplay any incident to prevent repercussions on his family. She didn't blame him for not mentioning that Brad also shoved Grace. Nick couldn't know how Alex would react to an attack on her blood-offspring. "Tori?"

Tori remained frozen, apparently unaware of her surroundings, just like she'd been on that first day. It was her defense mechanism to keep her from being hurt. Alex wondered how long it would take Tori to start speaking again. When Tori didn't say anything, Alex continued, "Brad?"

Brad crossed his arms and scooted back in his seat. His gaze shifted to Nick and then he said, "It was just an argument. That guy just grabbed me. I was defending myself."

Alex nodded. "Peggy?" she prompted.

"I don't want to go back," Peggy sobbed.

"You're not going back, Peggy," Alex said. "We're a family now. We just need to learn how to get along with each other. What happened?"

Sniffling, Peggy answered, "Grace and Brad were fighting and a man tried to stop them and Brad hit him."

"Ok. Grace, your turn." Alex said.

Grace opened her mouth to correct the name, but Alex raised her eyebrow and Grace said instead, "Brad pushed me twice into the habitat for no reason."

"Hmmm. Should we pull up the security feed?" Alex asked.

Grace frowned and then repeated Nick, "We were arguing."

"All right." Alex sighed. "Families argue. That happens, but we need to talk, not resort to violence, to sort it out. Brad, you understand?"

Brad nodded.

Alex said, "Grace, school for two weeks. No leaving for any reason. You need to learn how to communicate with other kids. Focus on that."

Grace wrinkled her nose, but didn't complain.

Alex stood up. "Let's go get dinner. Brad, I'll apologize to the man you elbowed. I understand the instinct." Alex also planned to have a few words with security about treating Grace just like any other kid. Standard protocol was to bubble-restrain people and then sort out what was going on.

Later that night, Alex tucked Grace into bed and then instead of leaving, she sat down in the rocking chair next to the bed. "Ember, I need you to get along with them. They're your brothers and sisters now."

"But Mommy, they don't like me."

"They don't like anyone, Ember. People have been mean to them their entire lives. You need to take care of them anyway. You're scholastically much smarter than they are and know how we operate around here, but Ember, you can learn things from them, too."

"Like what?" Grace muttered.

"They know how to survive, Ember. I watched the security video. You were unintentionally condescending and insulting them. Brad overreacted, sure, but he's angry at the world. You have to expect it." Alex paused and then said, "Did you see how easily Brad escaped from that man's grip?"

Grace rubbed at her right temple and she closed her eyes, apparently recalling her memory.

Alex continued, "He's got some serious fighting skills. You should ask him to teach you. You may not need to know it, but if you ever do, it would be handy. Find out what else they know. You might be surprised. They're not stupid; they just learned different things. Try to be their friend and next time, don't edit the truth to suit you. Take responsibility for your actions." Alex stood and went over and kissed Grace on the forehead. "Nick will protect you if you let him. You need to listen to him when he tells you to do something."

Having given her daughter enough to think about, Alex left. She then went over to her other children's apartment and knocked. They wouldn't even consider bed for another hour or two.

Alex knocked and waited, hearing a movie in the background.

Nick opened the door, nodded once with resignation, and stood aside to allow her in.

Tori turned off the movie, but her emotionless face was intact. The two on the sofa were equally subdued. Not one of them had changed into their pajamas like they usually did. Alex lowered herself into one of the easy chairs and Nick sat next to the others on the sofa.

"Is this when you tell us you are sending us back?" Nick asked bluntly.

Alex answered in her best street-accent Spanish so they would understand she was one of them. "Nope. This is where I apologize for Grace's attitude and the Colony One security for treating you differently than her."

"But I pushed her," Brad said.

"Yup. I know. I watched the security video. Everything in Colony One is recorded. She didn't mean to be so condescending. She just doesn't know how to talk with people. I sure wish you guys would teach her."

"She talked with the police just fine," Nick said.

Alex sighed, not in frustration, but in agreement. "Yeah. Trying to weasel her way out of getting in trouble. I've spoken with our officers and told them Grace is not to be treated differently than anyone else in the future. Normal conversations about normal subjects, she can't do. She compared Brad to a zooxanthellae. What kid does that?"

"What's a zoo ah zan... anyway?" Brad asked.

"Zooxanthellae. It's the algae inside the coral," Alex said. Tori seemed to be relaxing just a little. "Grace shouldn't have said that and she should have obeyed you, Nick, when you told her to stop. I've told her she's to listen to you in the future. I know she doesn't act like a little kid, but she really is. She's younger than Peggy by three years and while she's pretty smart, she's still just a baby." Alex gazed at her four orphans, studying their postures. They finally seemed to be letting go of their fear of expulsion. "I meant what I said earlier. You're my family now. I'm not going to abandon you or deport you. Next time you have a problem with Grace, send me a message and I'll sort it out."

"Hello?" Mario Marino's gruff voice answered the trash phone Alex had sent him.

"Mario?" Alex was hiding in her private lab, with all security feeds set to show her quietly working on her HUD for the next half hour. It was a violation of security protocol and only her and Lucas knew how to do it with the picobots. Eventually, she'd need to deploy a picobot security backup to watch for altered video feeds, but that could come later.

"Alex. What's with the mystery phone? You have my secure line." Sal's brother sounded grumpy.

Alex peered at the time and then at the Earth time equivalent. It was only 10 p.m. in Atlanta, Georgia. He should be up. "This is for your ears only." Her picobots were operating the phone call and making sure he couldn't be overheard.

"Go ahead, but be quick. It's 4 a.m. I'm in London. What do you need?"

"I need a list of all family members and family friends, and I need you to prepare it yourself, personally," Alex said.

"What for?"

"List everyone you want to live if the Earth is ending. Everyone. Don't leave anyone out." Alex chewed on one of her fingernails, caught herself at it and stopped.

"Ok. When do you need it by?" Mario yawned loudly.

"As soon as you can get it done. By the end of the week at the latest."

"Ok. Are you coming to your birthday party this year?"

Alex hadn't been to one of her Marino birthday parties since the space station launch. The family carried on just fine without her. Presents were opened and redistributed without her pointless attendance. "No, and after you are done and send the list to me by a trusted family courier, if you need anyone added or removed, you need to let me know immediately."

"Hmmm. I thought that doomsday end-of-Earth stuff was nonsense."

"I can't wait anymore. I postponed as long as possible. Look, I don't want to scare anyone or make anyone panic, but you've known me from the beginning. You are one of the few people who can ask me a question and get the whole, honest truth, Mario."

"Uh huh." Mario's flat tone indicated how much he believed that. "How's that battery of yours work?"

Alex rolled her eyes. "Seriously? That's your burning question? I tell you the world is imminently in danger of absolute destruction and you ask about my battery?"

"Well..." Alex could hear Mario's shrug, if not see it.

"You've had the formula hanging in your study since Sal died." Alex's painting that Mario had refused to destroy was still hanging in Mario's house.

Alex heard the sudden intake of breath. "No. " There was a long pause and Sal's brother finally asked, "He knew?"

"Sure Sal knew. He worked with me on the business plans. Look, Mario, don't delay on that list. Get it done. It's the most important thing you could be doing right now. Everything else is irrelevant." Alex hung up and put her head in her hands, willing her knowledge to go away. It refused.

After a few minutes, Alex looked at her list again. Family first. All of them. Their friends. Jay and his family and friends and theirs. All employees and direct family who happened to be Earth-side. The entire Indian reservation, along with whoever was there. Every family with a park pass for the Indian reservation. Colony One's entire Pacific island and whoever was visiting at the time. Everyone waiting on citizenship and their families. The Hamasaki family and their friends. The seed bank. Some landmarks. Several of the best libraries and museums. How many people were inside the Louvre on a given day? How many people could she add and still have a sustainable habitat? She ran her numbers again. She couldn't save everyone, in fact, she could barely save any at all.

How many people could her space station really support? How many animals? The atmosphere oxygen was balanced by her picobots, but food - plants took time to grow. Could her picobots synthesize food? And space, that was a problem, not the space outside of the station, but the physical square meters per person and animal. She couldn't compromise the natural habitats; they were precariously balanced already. Her station finally had a magnificent honeybee population and while the honey was horrendously expensive due to the low quantity, honey would increase steadily. Honeybees were dying on Earth due to construction, agriculture, and pesticides. How cramped could she make people's homes for the foreseeable future and still have a society that wouldn't implode? How much height could she steal from inside every room before claustrophobia set in? And if she opted for less people, would they scream about the "useless flower field habitat" she was maintaining? Without it, the honeybees died.

She couldn't make these decisions alone. She scheduled a meeting with her key habitat scientists, along with Brian, Cal Park, and Lucas, for later that afternoon.

After the initial "we are just talking theoretically" lie during which Cal, Brian, and Alex exchanged haunted, knowing looks, the team settled in.

"We have a responsibility to all the species on Earth, not just humans," Cal said.

"Take people's pets, too," Brian said, "It will help with the trauma. We're going to have a lot of upset people."

Logan Malstrom, the eco-scientist for the general human habitat, stared at the spinning hologram globe hovering above the center of their table. "We should get more habitats up here. A desert comes to mind as does a northern hardwood forest and tundra. We could use some more maple trees and some of our species need the extreme temperatures to survive."

"We have a good set of habitats already. Why do we need more?" This was from Sharon Cerdas the lead eco-scientist for the montane rainforest that matched the Reserva Biológica Bosque Nuboso Monteverde in Costa Rica. Her habitat was stable and growing, a treasure of biodiversity, but she was constantly having to make adjustments to keep her environment safe. She was also routinely being asked to help her fellow lead eco-scientists. More habitats would certainly add to her already stressed workload.

"If the Earth were to undergo this supposed destruction, we lose everything. We have a fraction of a percent of the world's biologicals here," Logan retorted.

Juliana, Brian's secretary, asked, "Why can't we just create another planet and move everyone to it?"

"We can't destabilize our solar system," Lucas said, somewhat sharply. "Nor can we collect enough matter to support the entire human population."

Cal added, "We are most concerned with the survival of the human race and as many species we can save."

Juliana's eyes got wide, "You mean we're not going to save everyone? People are going to die?"

Alex inhaled, "It's not possible to save everyone. Our space station will only support so much life, and if we go over that, we'll all die. In fact, when we reach our maximum capacity, we're going to have to stop rescuing people. Very much like the Titanic, I'm afraid."

Brian frowned disapprovingly at Alex as tears formed in Juliana's eyes. "We have a responsibility to our families and friends. We're going to have a list of preselected individuals that will get picked up first."

Logan cleared his throat. "I don't want to say this, but doesn't that mess up our gene pool?"

Cal answered this before Alex could, "It does, but if we're very careful to do compatibility gene scans before reproducing, we can make it work."

Brian nodded. "We think it's best if the people who survive have as little grief as possible. If a mother is with her children, she can be happy for that. Our citizens need their family and friends rescued. We've always put our citizens first and we shall continue to do so. We're taking everyone, the old, the young, the men as well as women, without any regard for nationality or race. We're going to end up predominantly English-speaking because that's what we have the most of already."

"We'll still have people who have lost everyone they know and care about," Sharon rubbed at her temples. Then, observing Brian intensely, she said, "I'm glad this is only theoretical."

Brian winced guiltily; the truth was plain in his eyes. Alex wondered if they should have started with the truth. Alex pretended not to see this, and said, "Humor me. Our counselors and teachers are certainly going to have their work cut out for them, and we're going to need to assimilate all of these refugees into our society."

Logan observed, "Not everyone is going to want to become a citizen and you can't force them."

"True. We're destined to have a split population for a while. The refugee camp and Colony One. The refugee camp isn't going to be particularly pleasant, but we aren't going to let it devolve into chaos. We're going to have to create a lottery to bring families who want to become citizens into our training program. The benefits of becoming a Colony One citizen should be enough incentive to bring people into the future of the human race. They're going to have to learn to live by our rules."

"And our meat menu," Logan commented. "It will be a while before the cattle farm can provide enough meat for everyone."

Alex remained quiet. The cattle farm wouldn't support their increasing population.

"Do we have enough plants to provide food for everyone?" Sharon arched an eyebrow at Alex.

"We're going to end up with some synthesized foods, but ultimately, the real thing is better for its innate variety," Alex answered.

"How many people can we support?" Sharon pressed.

Cal provided the response this time. He'd worked with Alex on the numbers several times. "Right now, about 5 million, but it would be cramped."

Sharon choked out, "The world has almost 8 billion people on it."

Alex nodded. "That's what we're here to discuss. How can we make this space station support more people?"

After several more hours, they had a plan that would allow them up to roughly 19 million souls and their pets. Citizens were asked to prepare a list of family and friends under the guise of holding weekly vacation giveaways for people to come visit the station. They were told to list everyone they knew and mark people they'd prefer with bonus points.

Alex stared again at her own private list, which was terrifyingly small even now that was updated. Jay and Byron and their families and friends. Teachers and students from Kingsport Academy, including Ethan. She briefly considered leaving Ethan off, but that was a death sentence; the odds were against people waiting to be randomly rescued. The girl from the psychiatric hospital, a couple of the convicts from the prison, also the warden, Bill Stateman and his family and friends. She added the entire staff and student body of the yeshiva that funded her favorite library by Mario's restaurant in Atlanta. Most everyone she would have selected were already on someone else's list. Both Sal's brother and Kuro Hamasaki had provided their own lists.

Alex started looking at the world's population. They would need genetic variety. She started a second list, selecting people who were the top in their fields - scientists, athletes, performers, artists, musicians, doctors, teachers, military officers. She did a quick search and saw someone had already selected the Pope. She scanned down her list. It was a good list, with good genes saturating it. Privileged genes, she thought as she suddenly recalled digging through a trash can on the side of the street, scraping mold off an old bit of bread and eating it anyway. She had no idea where to find her old street friends or even if they were still alive. She deleted that privileged list and started over.

This time, Alex selected geographic locations, square kilometers in 20 of the world's worst slums. She then added humanitarians who would know how to speak those languages, and how to teach these people to fit into Colony One's vastly different society. Then she chose some of the world's most renowned instructors who would be able to balance these people's education level; she would not create a slave-class of people.

Alex added a fleet of psychological counselors and people who could help make her society cohesive. Then, she selected five random families from every country not already represented. It would be hard on them, but somehow, maybe, she could pull humanity together. Trauma, shock, culture, personal psychoses, and that would just be the main influx. What would she do about the people who felt entitled to power like Mario Marino and Kuro Hamasaki?

For a while, Alex watched individual lists from citizens roll in. It was one hell of a birthday present, she thought.

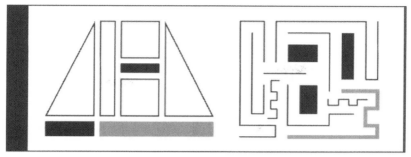

T plus 11:183:23:9   **~0π**

Alex kissed Grace's forehead, hugging her. Grace pulled free, saying, "I'm late. Henry gets upset if I don't get there on time." Grace had a following of octopi now, but Henry was by far her favorite. While usually solitary creatures, the octopi community really liked her daughter.

"Of course. Don't neglect your studies, Grace. As much as that language and lexicon are fascinating, you also need to be able to talk with humans besides scientists."

"Yeah, yeah," Grace muttered, with a dismissing wave of her hand as she ran off.

Alex shook her head, resigned. She supposed she'd've been just as precocious with different life circumstances. She was unconcerned about Grace's education, but her human interactions were suffering. Alex wasn't terribly worried about Grace's inability to talk to kids her own age and her daughter could talk with Karl and the rest of the oceanography staff without any problem, but that was still a very narrow social circle for a growing girl.

Alex went to the next room over to see if her four other charges were ready for school. She was pleased they had settled into their new lives over the last two years, but they were normal children, if ever there was a normal child. The social workers were content that the children were adjusting, although one of them had complained that the children didn't have an adult living with them. Alex pointed out that her apartment was right next to theirs and the walk from one to the other was less than most standard American households from upstairs to downstairs. They were in no danger of being without adult supervision.

Alex also still had secret video monitoring for each of them although she only checked on each of them every few hours. Brad was showing signs of depersonalization disorder, but he wasn't comfortable enough without Nick around for any therapy session, and he wouldn't discuss any of his problems in front of Nick. Alex and his teachers were working on building his confidence and independence enough to be able to get him into private therapy, and he was on a steady antidepressant medication. Now that Tori's drug addiction had been removed, she was mostly becoming their mother anyway, although Nick

411

remained the group's leader.

"Is Ember coming with us today?" Peggy asked as Tori was helping her into her backpack.

"Ember is headed to the lab today," Alex answered gently.

Peggy pouted. "How come she doesn't have to go to school and I do? I don't want to go to school. It's boring."

"Ember is ahead on her schoolwork and is learning how to speak to the octopi as her job today. You actually get to have a lot more fun. No playground in that lab Ember goes to." As it looked like Peggy was about to argue more, Alex added, "I suppose if you want, you could come up to the space station and hang out with me today. Hmmm. I'm going to be in meetings and lectures all day and it won't be much fun either." Which was unfortunately too true. "Your new friend Alice will miss you."

Tori glanced at Alex, took the hint, and said to Peggy, "Don't you want to have lunch with me and Nick and Brad and go to the beach with us after school?"

Alex smiled a thank you at Tori. "Yeah, I won't be back until late tonight. You'd definitely miss out on the beach too."

Nick, coming out of his bedroom with his books, firmly announced, "The four of us are going to school today, Peggy."

"But..." Peggy started, and Nick lifted his eyebrow at her, daring her to argue. Peggy frowned unhappily, but didn't continue.

Tori called out, "Brad, it's time to go. Come on!"

After another prompt, Brad made an appearance and grabbed his book bag. His hair was still uncombed, but Tori took care of that.

Alex walked the four of them to the school with a stop for breakfast, using the time to ask how they were doing, and giving them a chance to talk with her. She did this every morning, using the time as a mini-therapy session to alleviate any of their worries and problems.

Grace rarely joined them, usually grabbing a bit of fruit on her way to the lab. Alex reflected that she spent more time with these four than her biological offspring. When Alex left them at the school, she hurried off to the spaceport to catch the next shuttle. She watched the island fall away as they launched upward, enjoying the clear blue water near the island. Sadly, the massive trash island was still visible to the south, despite their cleanup efforts.

The zoning meeting dragged on and Alex checked the clock on her HUD. The upper right corner of the display showed Grace still in the lab, busily exchanging flashing images with Henry, although Alex had no idea what they were talking about. Alex cycled through her other children's video feeds. They were just leaving school and would go directly to the beach for their hour in an exercise zone. Alex was glad Peggy hadn't opted to come along; she would have been really bored after these six hours of meetings. Alex was barely avoiding a yawn herself. They were on yet another layout for a new restaurant district. Half of the attendees wanted it impressively big, while the other half wanted to increase the size of their stadium to include more fields.

"This would be easier if we just had more oxygen," one of the men grumbled with a significant glare in Alex's direction.

"We are converting space dust and debris into usable matter, but it takes time and our resources have to be shared with everyone," Alex replied calmly. "Everyone wants more space."

"We have more space. That massive empty housing district," the man persisted.

"We need that if something happens to the Earth." Alex kept her voice level, but her hand gripped her knee out of sight under the table. She'd been defending the empty apartments and buildings for six months. Most people still thought she was crazy. "That's nonnegotiable. You can't have it."

The man glared at her. "We can always add back to it if we need it. Like a bank loan. No need to hold up progress."

Alex rubbed at her knee and didn't reach across the room to try to shake some sense into the man. "There won't be time to repay it." After a brief pause, she said, "We've heard everyone's views on zoning. Perhaps it's time for a vote? Which would most of you prefer? The biggest stadium or the biggest restaurant district?"

Alex's HUD flashed red with an incoming urgent message. "Excuse me a moment," she said and switched on a privacy shield.

Cal's face appeared. His eyes were wide, panicked, and his face was flushed. "It's started."

There was no need for him to qualify what 'it' was. Alex swallowed as her stomach turned over. "Are you sure?"

"Absolutely no doubt. It won't be apparent on Earth for another hour yet; they think it's just another earthquake. I need your go-ahead to start the evacuations."

Alex inhaled. If he was wrong, the repercussions of the evacuations would be impossible to recover from. In her memory, she saw her future self stating that Cal was the right person. Exhaling again, she commanded, "Go ahead and start the evacuations. I'm on my way. Cal?" He blinked at her and Alex continued, "You are the right person for this. You've studied. Prepared. Done every simulation you could think of. You know more about what needs to be done than anyone else. You have my full confidence and support. Don't let anyone argue with you."

He nodded palely and shut down the connection. She lowered the privacy shield. To the people in the room, she said, "Go to your assigned Emergency Response center. You'll get instructions there." She didn't even wait to hear their questions. She was running. The prerecorded announcement appeared on her HUD, directing everyone to their posts. "Clear a path!" she shouted as she dodged through the marketplace. People moved out of her way, already heading toward their own destinations as instructed.

The main Emergency Response complex was already filling as people arrived and sat down at their stations to review the incoming data. "Talk to me," Alex gasped, skidding to a stop, in front of Cal.

"The super-volcanoes are erupting," Cal said succinctly.

"Which ones?"

"Most of them. It's a mathematical certainty." He pointed to the map of the Earth up on the main screen, striding over to it. "Massive earthquake here in the Bering Sea. St. Lawrence Island and Diomede have already been pulled underwater. The continental plates are finally shifting from the additional icecap water. Both Alaska and Russia along the Bering Sea are being pulled together. Akademia Nauk on the Kamchatka Peninsula is venting steam and ash. Social media is reporting that the dome buildup is visible to the naked eye. Columbia Generating Station in Washington has already declared an emergency and is shutting down due to earthquake activity." At Alex's slight head tilt, Cal explained, "That's a nuclear reactor. Luckily Bilibino Nuclear Power Plant was already shut down."

Alex glanced around. People were listening. Alex hoped they would fall back on their training and not panic.

Cal continued, "Phase 1 evacuations are underway. All the primaries are on their way here. The reservation is launching, but it's coming slowly so we don't destabilize the continent. Yellowstone hasn't erupted yet, but it will. Our Pacific facility has been shielded but I'm holding off on bringing that up to keep the water weight on the ocean floor semi-stable."

Alex nodded.

From the far side of the room, someone shouted, "We're registering earthquakes across North America!"

The reply came from the back center, "China's reporting scattered earthquakes too!"

The map up on the main screen updated with red dots and circles with associated magnitudes. Cal studied it. "Nancy, send out messages to Campi Flegrei in Italy and Catamarca Province, Argentina. We need data from their diagnostics to track the upheaval."

Alex noted with approval that the room wasn't chaotic at all like it had been during the earthquake-tsunami emergency. People knew where they were supposed to be and what to do for their piece of the massive plan.

Cal walked her through the expected progression of events. "It's not exactly one of the models I had prepared, but I'm pretty sure given the start point and cascading failures that it's close. I'll adjust the model as events progress." His eyes snapped to another red splash that appeared on the world map up on the secondary room screen and he strode off to consult with his team without even a brief nod to excuse himself.

As clearly as if the old Indian stood in front of her, Alex heard Soaring Eagle's voice say, "The desert rock weeps for the future." Alex went to attach herself to the evacuation team. She didn't want to miss a single person that was on her or Mario's lists. She took one of the free consoles and started verifying the individual pods and then detoured briefly to select and initiate one of the prerecorded message in all languages.

Alex's voice echoed in her ear, set by her picobots to her ears only. Jay would be hearing this message, as would everyone else on her list. "This is a prerecorded message from Colony One. The Earth is currently undergoing cataclysmic changes. You have been preselected to be transported to the safety of Colony One where a refugee facility will provide temporary housing. This safety pod has been programmed to respond to simple requests, such as 'pod, create bathroom' and 'pod, when will I arrive' and 'pod, create window'. Please take a few minutes to enter the names and probable locations of your family and friends on the keyboard in front of you and Colony One will attempt to rescue them."

Alex then verified the rest of the list. Everyone on her individual list was already in the air and headed for the station. Her HUD showed Ember safely in the Pacific island research facility. She sent a note to Grace to tell Henry they were evacuating and to tell her to keep her personal shielding at maximum. Alex automatically adjusted the shielding on her other four children. It was redundant but she couldn't help herself.

"Founder?" A woman touched Alex's arm and waited for her to look up before continuing, "We have requests for assistance from Russia, the United States, and Canada, and complaints from pretty much every European country about us kidnapping their citizens and violating air space."

Brian should be handling that. "Where's Mr. Kimberly?" Alex asked.

The woman bit her lip and stared at the floor. "He's the one who sent me to find you. He's meeting with Lucas."

"Ah. Ok. One moment." Alex raised a privacy shield and recorded, "This is Alex Smith, the Founder of Colony One. I regret we are unable to take your call at the moment. The Earth is undergoing catastrophic changes. The continental plates are shifting and we are expecting significant volcanic eruptions globally. Every effort is being made to provide assistance. Please have your citizens follow your local emergency plans, and secure your nuclear and chemical production and storage facilities." The less damage from nuclear and chemical contamination, the faster the Earth would heal. She lowered the privacy shield and sent the file to the woman standing next to her. "Have all incoming phone calls redirected and play them that message and hang up to keep the lines open."

"Yes, Founder." The woman nodded deferentially and departed.

Alex turned her attention to making sure the proximity programming was operating correctly. Anyone inside the same building as or within half a kilometer of preselected individuals would be automatically encased in a pod and lifted to safety. It was the only way to guarantee she didn't leave someone's baby behind. Pets were also contained and put in their own pod and rescued. When she was certain the evacuations were being handled correctly, she left to go to the refugee facility to make sure that was ready.

Alex started at the medical facility adjacent to and between Colony One and the refugee area. Refugees would not be allowed in Colony One areas without either becoming citizens or being a guest of a citizen according to the current tourist/visitor policies. People would be given medical treatment, housing, food, and access to their own exercise, recreation, and school facilities, but ultimately, they would need to integrate into Colony One. The actual refugee area was still empty - a lifeless, sterile environment awaiting impact.

The medical facility was the best she could provide. Alex met up with Kgomotso, who would be running the medical staff, with the expediency of sending him a message to meet her at the medical facility door. "How are you doing?" she asked him.

"I think we're ready for triage. I've got everyone sorted. They should all know what they are doing. Are we really expecting many people?"

Alex blinked at Kgomotso. "Hasn't anyone told you?"

"No. We're just following standard emergency protocols from the message that Emergency Response guy sent," Kgomotso replied.

Alex bit her lip. Their day was about to become brutal. "We are looking at roughly 18.5 million people in varying stages of health arriving at the station over the next 5 hours."

"What?!" he gasped.

Alex nodded. "I'm on my way to arrival reception next. Where's your team responsible for triage?"

"This way." Kgomotso stumbled off back toward the main hospital wing and Alex followed.

The 60 people milling around talking were obviously a mix of doctors, nurses, and staff, based on their selected SEL outfits that clearly marked them with white jumpsuits with profession-designating collar colors. Dark green for surgeons, green for doctors, blue for senior nurses, light blue for junior nurses, orange for trained medical staff, yellow for general staff. Everyone had a Colony One name badge.

They quieted when they saw Kgomotso and Alex enter the room. Alex spoke so that her voice would carry, "I need everyone responsible for triage to come with me to our new arrival facility in the next building over. Only red and yellow tag patients are to be taken to this medical complex." Those were the standard medical triage colors for people who needed immediate treatment or who would need observation. "You're to get the patients over here, drop them off, and get back to the intake reception. Do not stay here at the medical complex. Walking wounded and minor injuries are going to have to wait and should be told to go to their assigned apartments as directed by the other Colony One staff members. Tag their SEL I.D. bracelet so we can find them later." Alex paused to let that sink in, and then continued, "Black tag patients," those that were dead or going to die regardless of treatment, "Should be sent directly to the morgue. Families and friends may accompany their loved ones, but should be told to obey Colony One citizens at all times. No one gets onto the station without a SEL I.D. bracelet. Nobody, not even the wounded. If you can't immediately get or understand a name, use the John or Jane Doe sequence number. It's not your job to try to identify people or to help people find their loved ones. You're needed for medical activities only. Don't get distracted."

As Alex led the subgroup out through the convenient hallway to new arrival reception, Alex heard Kgomotso say, "We are looking at an impossible number of patients. We're going to do our best, but we're going to have to work calmly and systematically, putting our energy and time where it will do the most good. Yellows, er, general staff members, we're going to need you to make sure supplies are distributed and don't run out..."

Once at the arrival reception area, Alex found her staff also prepared. These wore Colony One stationer green jumpsuits and Alex changed her SEL outfit to match. Stars on their shoulders denoted seniority, giving them a militaristic ambience. Again, clear name badges adorned their shirts. Alex didn't include stars or a name badge on herself. She walked over to talk with the woman wearing the most stars. "Is everyone here aware of the check-in process?"

The senior intake administrator, a middle-age woman with greying hair, nodded and answered, "We take the people's names, addresses, and names of immediate family members, and issue SEL I.D. bracelets. If we can't get a name, for any reason, we issue them John or Jane Doe and the next number in sequence. We send wounded over to the triage area. We send the rest to the training area to view the material for how to use the HUD. Medical personnel are sent to the complex to assist. Multilingual people who can translate are asked to remain and assist. Everyone else we direct to their housing and tell them to wait there for further instructions. Families get solitary apartments. Couples and individuals get bunked four people to an apartment, and everyone goes in the next available apartment if they don't have one already assigned. We assure people that we will help them find their family and friends soon."

That speech was memorized directly out of Cal Park's guide. Alex vaguely wondered how calm the woman was going to be after checking in a million people. Alex nodded, and echoed Kgomotso, "Perfect. I need everyone to work calmly and systematically. Report any problems to dispatch." Speaking loudly so even triage people could hear, she said, "We'll get everyone a chance to eat and take breaks as we are able. Just do your best."

Alex had worked closely with Cal and Brian to set up a solid procedure for the processing and homing of refugees. Non-citizens would get signed in, be given a custom wristband and HUD, and assigned an apartment that contained beds, desks, and lockable cabinets. Families got their own apartments, while individuals and couples were set up in groups of four. All food was set up cafeteria style in a common area, next to a massive recreation area. The wristbands monitored their biological data, location, and the attached picobots also silently acted as birth control. Population control was critical to humanity's survival.

The first of the individual pods started to arrive. People seemed to fall into two categories: indignant or traumatized. Most had filled in the requested data entry in their pods on the way to the station and could be issued their wrist bracelets and living quarters without delay. Alex watched people arriving for a bit, looking for Jay in every new pod that arrived, even though she knew his likely wouldn't arrive at the station for another half hour. Several obnoxious fools were demanding to be taken back. She went over to handle it.

"Gentlemen!" she had to shout to get them to hear her over the din. "After the immediate crisis is over, we will be happy to provide transportation back to your homes, but right now, all of our citizens are busy. Until then, please accept our hospitality. We will get everything sorted out as soon as possible." She noted with admiration that her citizens were listening to her words and would use them for other people with the same complaints.

"But what is going on?!" one of them grumbled loud enough to attract others.

Alex didn't roll her eyes, although she wanted to. Just what she needed; someone inciting a mob-mentality this early in the event timeline. It was going to be bad enough without help. "The Earth is undergoing continental shifts which is causing earthquakes. You can view our news channel from your HUDs when you reach your temporary housing."

"I need a phone; my cell phone isn't working. I have to warn my family," one of the women said sharply.

"Put their name and address into our database. Our dispatch office is working on connecting people. Calls will come through on your HUD. If you would please come with me over to a brief presentation on how to use your HUD while you are here..." Was it lying to imply these people would get phone calls from anyone on Earth?

The man who had first spoken up stepped directly in front of Alex, invading her personal space and announced accusingly, "You're her! That crazy woman! You probably think this is some sort of apocalypse. You should be locked up! This is criminal. You can't just kidnap a bunch of people."

Alex did not grit her teeth in exasperation or give any indication at all of her irritation. This was only the very beginning of the refugees coming in now - the ones people specifically requested. "Sir, I am not kidnapping anyone. You will be free to leave as soon as the personnel are available to arrange it. In the meantime, please do not hold up our process. We are expecting a large number of people."

Alex saw her old schoolmate and antagonizer, Ethan Jaxon, arrive as his pod dissolved, leaving him at the end of the intake line, which was already snaking backward into a loud mass of unhappy people. He was missing his perfect haircut and his clothes reflected a low-middle class businessman. His exile hadn't been kind to him. Alex didn't want to deal with Ethan too. She decided she should head over to the medical complex where she could be more useful when the wounded started to arrive anyway.

Alex nodded to one of the security personnel waiting off to the side and the man came over. Security personnel were in full blue jumpsuits - a not-so-subtle American-police blue. "Help this man find his temporary apartment, please." She nodded at the man who was still standing in front of her, glaring.

"Certainly, Founder." The security guard turned to the man, "If you would please come with me, Sir, I'll be happy to assist you."

Before Alex could leave, though, her HUD flashed an incoming message from Cal. She ran up a privacy shield. "What's up?"

"We now have a critical number of nuclear facility failures." Cal spoke quickly. He obviously didn't have much time. "We're going to need to separate out people who have been overexposed to radiation. Lucas updated all our rescue pilots' software to scan people, but they've already picked up some. The radiation will contaminate our station and will infect our gene pool with mutations."

"How soon are they going to arrive?" Alex asked.

"Um..." Cal studied his HUD. "Earliest for the first one, maybe 30 minutes."

"Ok. Have Lucas reallocate space and mass for a flat apartment complex for 80 people, and put it adjacent to the arrival reception opposite the medical center. I'll finish all the connections and set it up." If she needed more space and atmosphere, she could take it from the refugee camp.

Cal nodded and cut the connection.

Alex spent a moment rubbing her temples and pondering how to best set up the separate area before lowering the privacy shield. She went over to the senior intake administrator and said to her, "We're going to start splitting some random people off for minor security screening. It might separate families, but assure them they'll be reunited." The administrator lifted her hand in front of her mouth and then rubbed her arm, unconsciously telegraphing her anxiety, no doubt trying to imagine how she could stretch her already sparse personnel. Alex rushed to assure her, "I'm going to run some stripes on the floor for the people who need to be additionally scanned and bring in another team for that processing so it doesn't impact your people too much. Just do your best to keep everyone calm."

The woman nodded and went over to one of her workers who was having some trouble getting one of the refugees checked in. Alex saw that the Marino's were starting to arrive. She didn't have time to try and sort them out. They'd get assigned to their own refugee section as they checked in, as would Hamasaki's people. A message arrived from Lucas and Alex again ran up a privacy shield and the two of them worked out a plan to keep the radiation contamination contained. It wouldn't be pretty, but it would be as humane as they could make it.

That's when the wounded began to arrive in shuttles, the lucky randomly-rescued people being brought in by trained Colony One pilots. Intake already had an appalling winding line of waiting people, which became chaos as the wounded arrived and started bypassing the long line. This first set included both broken bones from earthquakes and scorch-burns from Akademia Nauk's eruption. At least no one was complaining anymore about being yanked from their homes and life unexpectedly.

Alex helped with triage until she got a message from Lucas that her radiation holding facility was ready, and she went to finalize preparations there. She spotted Mario, Milo, and Luciano, as well as Rico and Emma. She waved in their direction but did not slow down. Jay and his latest girlfriend should also be somewhere in that line, but she didn't have time to look. When she was sure the radiation unit was set up to her satisfaction and the one-way door wouldn't allow people or radiation back onto the station, she went back to help with triage and quickly got pulled into surgery helping Kgomotso.

○ ● ❱ ❭ ● ❨ ❰ ●

Many long hours later, Alex again scrubbed her hands in the sudsy water, even though her picobots had already sterilized her head to toe for the countless time. Even with the help of medical staff that happened to arrive from Earth, the medical complex was overwhelmed. The morgue underneath the complex had turned into a mass grave of gently stacked bodies.

Every part of Alex's body ached from bending, lifting, pulling, and running. She spent a precious moment watching her daughter, who was calmly flashing lights at a dozen or so octopi, untouched by the catastrophe outside of her protective habitat-bubble. Her other four children were with their respective classes; the younger ones were watching a movie and the older ones were preparing meals for rescue workers. She glared again at the directive from Cal to report to the arrival reception for translation duty that flashed on her HUD and moved to obey.

At once, Alex saw the problem. Her refugees from the slums had arrived en masse. Lucas had simply lifted off the entire areas, complete with their housing, possessions, sewage, and weapons, and stuck these floating habitats underneath their refugee facility. The people were terrified and distressed. The Colony One citizens were trying to process these people into the official refugee living quarters. Alex's specially chosen social workers and counselors were long since processed and off to their own apartments. Alex cringed.

Alex set her picobots to record and amplify her voice across all of these habitats as well as the arrival reception and said, "You have arrived safely at Colony One. Earthquakes made your land unsafe and we moved you here to keep you alive. You can stay in your homes until we can move you and your belongings into better housing. Fresh food, clean water, and medical treatment will be provided. If you are missing a family member, please speak with one of the people in a green jumpsuit." She then repeated the message in the language of each of the habitats.

She then dug through the now massive database of people, seeking out her chosen counselors and sent them a message on their HUD that they were needed for translation and assistance back where they'd arrived. Hopefully they'd see the message and be able and willing to come help.

As Alex approached the registration area, she switched her costume to her standard station overalls. Alex then found the senior intake administrator, who was now looking extremely war-shocked, and tapped her on the shoulder to get her attention, and then raised a privacy shield around the two of them so they'd be able to talk. Alex set her voice tone as comforting as she could, and said, "Hey! Sorry about this nightmare. You've done so much already and I know this is just crazy insane."

"No one can even talk with these people. They don't understand us and we have no idea what they are saying. Security's had to confiscate a large number of weapons already. We can't even get their names."

"I understand. I'll issue them all SEL I.D. bracelets with John or Jane Doe and we can sort them out later. That'll cut down the immediate crisis, but won't help locate people. The destruction on Earth at this point means that their relatives that aren't here are going to be dead before we can find them anyway." Alex tried not to sound callous, but was certain it came across that way.

The woman's mouth dropped open. "How bad is it?"

While the woman had seen the wounded coming in, the overall impact wasn't being reported yet. Alex had a running video feed in her HUD which she was trying to mostly ignore. To function, she had to push her distress to the back of her mind. Alex asked, "How much truth do you want?"

"Just tell me."

"Ash and heat from super-volcanoes will cover the earth and kill the oceans. Water will be undrinkable for the foreseeable future. People who manage to get to stable shelters will probably starve to death before the radiation from nuclear meltdowns kills them. Our space station habitat can only support a certain precision-calculated population, and we either save ourselves and let the people on Earth die, or the human race becomes extinct. Eventually, the Earth will become habitable again, but it won't be within our lifetime, even if we can find a way to start cleaning up the radiation."

The woman paled.

Alex put her hand on the woman's shoulder. "We should have some people who can help translate arriving from the refugee population shortly. You're doing an excellent job. I could not have asked for anyone better. We need you."

Alex stayed to help with registration and translation. Even with the line moving steadily, it would be days before everyone could get even partially processed. Pods with healthy people were still waiting outside the station, while wounded were being brought in and sorted as quickly as possible.

The Indian Reservation was attached and in place, but still disconnected from the main station. The Pacific Island had yet to arrive, having been moved to a lower priority than the individual pods and random buildings where people were more likely to be terrified, but even those buildings were still waiting.

The last few rescue shuttles were arriving, having been given the order to return, based on Colony One's maximum station population calculations.

Everything was going as it should and only this one dreaded task required Alex's attention. Although she could have delegated it, and probably should delegate it, Alex simply could not subject anyone to the pending trauma. She needed her people strong, not broken.

Cal would handle their ecosystem. Lucas would finish connecting the rescued pods and buildings. Brian would handle Colony One politics.

Counselors and religious people moved among both populations, consoling and helping as much as they could.

The last few people in line had been picked up by her rescue workers. All had witnessed the destruction and had eyes glazed in shock. Her picobots were scanning them. The ones with too much radiation exposure were being flagged and the citizens who were sorting people were pulling those people aside.

"Sir, we're going to have to ask you to follow the blue dotted line on the floor there for an additional security check," one of her diligent citizens said, following the directions on her scanner. Many of this last group were being sent down the blue dotted line. The rescue pilot had ignored the restriction that had told him to ignore certain people and only pick up ones that scanned green on his ship's sensors. She certainly didn't blame him for wanting to save people. He wasn't the only pilot to do so.

The man being addressed was carrying a small girl who was not flagged, but who had moderate radiation exposure and the longer she stayed in the man's arms, the worse off she'd be. Alex swore under her breath, and fired off a summons for one of their counselors to come immediately.

Alex saw the counselor coming over and approached the man. "Sir, your daughter can wait with Carolyn. If you would please follow the blue dotted line, we're giving select people additional instructions and information. Your daughter does not need to and should not hear these. She'll be fine."

The counselor, who didn't know why people were being separated out, followed Alex's lead anyway, and promised, "I'll take excellent care of her for you." She looked at the young girl, who was maybe four years old. How she hadn't been overexposed to radiation was a miracle. "Your daddy needs to go take care of some things. We have some really tasty food. Are you hungry at all? What's your name?"

The girl blinked at the counselor warily. Her dad answered, "Her name is Mary. Her mom's gone." He hugged his daughter tighter. "I'm all she has. Please let her stay with me."

Alex smiled as warmly as she could at the young girl. "Mary, I really need you to go with Carolyn here while I talk with your Daddy."

Carolyn reached for the girl, who grabbed onto her father tighter.

Alex put her hand on the man's shoulder. "Sir," she pitched her voice very serious and gently commanding, eyes pleading, "I need you to give your daughter to Carolyn and come with me."

The man must have seen something desperate in Alex's eyes because he nodded and tried to hand his daughter off to Carolyn. Alex reached out and helped pry the girl off of him and passed her to Carolyn. Mary screamed and cried, but when Carolyn went to hand her back, Alex shook her head at the counselor. "Get Mary some food and clean clothes. I'll call you as soon as we're done."

Alex steered the man down the blue dotted line and followed him; they were the last that needed to go. Her picobots were screaming about her radiation exposure, and she directed them to block radiation. This cut off her connection to the station network and Alex shut down her now useless HUD, suddenly sharply missing the video feed showing her daughter still in the Pacific island research lab. It felt as if her right arm had been suddenly torn off.

When they were out of earshot of his daughter, the man whispered to Alex, "I won't see her again, will I?"

Alex swallowed and answered honestly, "See, yes. Touch, hold, hug, no. I couldn't let you keep holding her. Radiation exposure." To cross the additional shielding, Alex's picobots created sound for her voice based on her mouth's movement. They also relayed sound from each person based on their vocal cord movements.

Alex and the man went through the barrier that separated the radiation victims from the rest of the habitat. There was no way back until it was over. Alex pressed the button that completely separated their habitat.

"That's why I feel sick, isn't it?" he asked.

"Lethal dose, I'm afraid. I can't cure you."

"But my daughter?"

"She'll be ok. If you have any relatives or friends here, she can stay with them. If not, I'll personally see that she is placed with a nice family who will love and adore her and take excellent care of her. I promise you I will watch over her either way."

"I don't know," he sobbed. "I don't know who is here."

"We're gathering names and addresses for everyone and you'll have a chance to look through the list, as will everyone else. If there is someone here who knows you, you'll be connected."

"How much time do I have?"

"I can't say for sure. Hours or days. Not a week." For his particular case. Some would last longer. They entered a large room where comfortable chairs and sofas were scattered in a U-shape. Tables had computer terminals. And one wall had sealed cabinets. Many people waited. Too many, Alex tried not to weep.

The people milling about spotted her and before they could mob her, Alex walked to the front of the room, holding up her hands. "Everyone, I'm Alex Smith, Founder of Colony One." Her picobots were automatically translating where necessary. The room erupted into the noise of people asking questions, making demands, and shouting to get her attention. She kept her hands raised and waited for them to quiet. "I know you have questions and I'm here to answer them as well as to help you in any way I can. Please sit down." She waited until they sat down. One woman coughed into her sleeve and paled as she saw blood. She raised her hand.

Alex held out her hand, palm down. "I know you need medical attention. We'll get to that." She searched through the people until she saw a woman hugging her two children at her side. "Mrs.?" she asked.

"Carrisford," the woman replied.

"Would you please take all of the children into the next room over and watch them for me? There are toys and a playset for them. I'll speak with you afterwards." Alex watched as Mrs. Carrisford stood and nodded tiredly.

"I'll help," Mary's father said, "I already know what you're going to say."

"Thank you." Alex waited while all thirteen children were escorted from the room. Several people demanded to know what was going on. "There is no easy way to say this," Alex spoke softly, yet her voice carried. "You've all been exposed to a lethal dose of radiation and while I can't cure you, I will try to make your last days as comfortable as possible." She did not look at the door to the children's area.

"My son?" a man asked. His son had gone to the next room over to play.

"I'm sorry. Him too." Alex lowered her head and closed her eyes a moment. When she opened them again, she saw people next to the man had their hands on his back comforting him. "If you have family and friends that went along the other path as you boarded the station, they are going to be ok. If they have any radiation exposure, they will be treated and suffer no long term effects. You'll have a chance to speak with them shortly. If you want to tell them, you may, or if you want me to do so, I will."

She paused long enough for that to sink in, and then persevered. "You can expect nausea and vomiting almost immediately. Several of you have already thrown up. Diarrhea, headache, fever. This will be followed by dizziness and disorientation, weakness and fatigue. As the radiation takes its toll on you, you can expect hair loss, bloody vomit and stools, infections, and low blood pressure."

Alex continued, "I can and will give you any medication that you want to mitigate these symptoms. If you would like an assisted suicide, I will give you anesthesia and you will go to sleep and just never wake up. Parents, you choose for your children." Except the one whose parents had died on the way up to the station. That girl was probably in her early teens and had gone with the children into the next room. Alex was choosing for her, and that girl was destined for anesthesia before the end of the day, before she could experience any of the horrible side effects, before the reality of her parents' deaths could sink in.

Alex pointed to a door off to the left. "Down that hall are rooms where you can sleep and rest. The numbers on the door are how many beds are in the room." She pointed at the door they'd come in. "Down that way, you'll find private rooms with both computer terminals and a window to the station, where you can visit with your family and friends."

Alex crossed over to the side of the room with the counter and cabinets and triggered the panel to open the cabinets.

"Medical supplies. Take whatever you want, however much you want.

Assist each other. We will die with dignity and humanity, helping each other. Everything is labelled with recommended dosages and what they are for. You'll find everything from mild painkillers and anti-nausea patches to morphine and heroin and that last cabinet over there has hypodermics with a lethal dose of anesthesia in it."

Adding more instructions, she said, "Take a medical bracelet from this first cabinet and wear it. Please take a moment to enter your name, address, and personal details into one of the computers if you haven't already. It will help to connect you with your family and friends. If you need me, simply tap the bracelet and I'll come as quickly as I can."

Alex took a basket she'd prepared for herself that had some of each kind of medicine and went over to the woman who had coughed into her sleeve. "Nausea patch?" Alex held up a small square and stuck it to the woman's wrist when she nodded. Alex also gave her one of the medical bracelets. Alex recorded the woman's name and address as well as names of her family and friends.

Alex was thankful she could trust her people to take care of everyone and everything else. Jay and Lucas' Sara would see her children safe. She could focus on these pour souls.

Thirteen days later, everyone who had been in the radiation complex was dead. Alex incinerated the last corpse and kneeled, running the person's ashes through her fingers, even though she couldn't actually touch anything with her shielding. She was beyond tears, beyond hope. If she didn't have Grace to look forward to and take care of, she would have incinerated herself. She really needed to get her communication back online. She'd been so busy that she'd deliberately not tried to re-establish communication with the station. She had needed all her energy for the dying.

Alex glanced around blankly at the empty room. All that remained was to leave and destroy this last room, along with the ashes of good, kind people who, for the briefest moment in time, cared for each other and helped each other, the embodiment of all of humanity's best qualities. Nothing like dying to teach you how to live, one of them had said. Alex listened to the silence, hearing their voices, their concerns, their pain. Her heart felt like it was dead.

Resolutely, she dusted the ashes off her hands - more accurately, off the outside picobot shield protecting her hand. It wasn't necessary. That would also get left behind when she exited, but she felt like her hands might never feel clean again, even though she hadn't actually touched a single person. She didn't want Grace to wait a moment longer. Her daughter needed her. Her adopted orphans needed her. Her country needed her.

Alex pushed herself up to a standing position, every fiber in her body was

426

exhausted and drained, but as she stepped toward the radiation barrier exit, she realized she was desperate to hug Grace and hear her chatter about Henry and his fellow octopi, to hear about something other than the sorrow of dying. She wanted to hear Peggy complain about having to go to school. She wanted to see what kind of trouble Georgie was getting into. Life. Normal, everyday life. She could speak with Brian, Cal, and Lucas about station problems after she had some downtime. She was certain after these days being incommunicado, there were numerous problems that needed to be sorted out.

The long term problems - the culture shock of so many different people, transitioning refugees through the citizenship program, educating the masses of people from the slums, determining critical resources that had been overlooked and forgotten, and the sustainability issues caused by overpopulation - those things could wait. The emotional shock of losing the Earth and everyday life would take years to overcome, if it ever could be. Any immediate problems that had lasted these few days could surely last another day. Both the Marino and the Hamasaki families could survive another few days in the refugee camp.

Alex left the complex, leaving the contamination behind, and entered a person-sized transport ship. She turned off her additional radiation shielding. Her HUD activated as it connected to the network, although Grace's normal video feed didn't appear. Alex frowned. Their networks were likely overloaded. It would appear in a moment. Alex issued the command to send the radiation complex on a trajectory that would eventually throw it into the Sun.

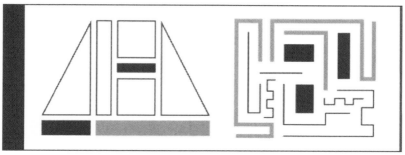

T plus 11:197:8:18   0

Alex navigated her transport over to the nearest part of the station and flew in through the shielding that kept the atmosphere in and the vacuum out. She was surprised to find herself on the far edge of the refugee camp, not at the crossover point between the refugee camp and the station. She pulled up a current map of the station. Everything had yet again been rearranged. The entire station's floor plan now spiraled to maximize natural light and visibility of the stars. While there were some dedicated places to view the Earth, those

427

had to be specifically sought out. The artificial atmosphere and sky currently mimicked a pretty clear blue, semi-cloudy day.

Walking paths sloped gently to almost follow the spiral curve, encouraging exercise, as people had to walk to get to the cafeteria for food. Multiple cafeterias, Alex saw on the map. Alex approved. She altered her clothing to nondescript jeans and a t-shirt to match the style of people she could see ahead walking between buildings. She supposed her pallor might make her unrecognizable, but she added a wig and baseball cap just to be certain.

Grace's video feed still hadn't appeared and Alex tried toggling to her other childrens'. Theirs didn't come up either. She tried calling Grace directly and the resulting "Person unavailable." made her stomach drop.

Alex created a privacy shield and called Cal, overriding his 'Do not disturb unless dire' setting.

"Founder?" Cal's voice sounded scratchy and tired. No video feed came up. "Are you back?"

"Yes, it's over. They're all gone. Cal," she bit her lip, terrified of the answer. "Where's Grace?"

"She's fine." Cal's video feed appeared. His hair was spiked at weird angles from his pillow, but he'd swapped his SEL clothing into a bathrobe. He looked as exhausted and beaten as she felt, possibly even more so. "At least I think she is. She should be. I needed the island's dome to protect some of the ocean or we'd have lost it all. We couldn't lift off with enough water and life to have a sustainable ocean with the biodiversity we need. Lucas helped me check the numbers."

Alex felt faint.

Cal went on, "We moved the whole island with the ocean below it southwest and expanded the dome out over the Coral Sea and some of the Great Barrier Reef. I couldn't save much of Queensland, as Lucas had to slice off the surface that already had too much radiation, acid water, and ash, but at least some of the Earth is protected. We'll have to keep rearranging it as the continents shift. Right now they've got just over 2000 square kilometers that's very oddly shaped."

Cal put his hand over his face. "I chose marine life over people, Founder. We have plenty of people, but only a little marine life. I'm sorry."

Alex was having a hard time breathing. "The communication, Cal? The communication. Why can't I contact her?"

"The entire dome had to be completely opaque to prevent radiation and to maintain the temperature. There wasn't time to establish a reasonable heat-exchange system, let alone a communication channel. We can't go down there and they can't come up here. Lucas says he can't create a teleportation door between us. I didn't even know that was a possibility. The dome is perfectly pressurized and stable as it is right now. We can't risk compromising that."

Alex's brain slowly translated this. Cal had trapped her daughter on a dead planet to save some fish. Alex swallowed. How had her future self not warned her? Maybe she should have been able to get into that file already? No, she knew the file's password now with absolute certainty. She should never have gone without communication for so long. Alex pulled up her phone registry. Jay was on the station, albeit in the refugee camp, but on station. How was she going to tell him she'd failed to save their daughter? Why hadn't she insisted Lucas focus on stabilizing that doorway technology instead of assigning all of those other tasks?

Cal tried to reassure her. "Oscar Straum is down there. He's the leading ecologist in that area, an expert on both land and the Great Barrier Reef. Saral Thrache is also there and you know he's one of our top SEL manipulators. Between the two of them, they can maintain the environment and keep it safe."

Alex cut the connection to Cal and bent forward, hyperventilating. Then she raised her head upward and screamed. The sound absorbed into the privacy shield, leaving her hollow and nauseous. She told herself that someone would step up and take care of her babies, but they were too young, too vulnerable, to be on their own. Numbly, she wiped away her tears, lowered the privacy shield, and started the long walk back toward her own lab. She would review all of the data herself and find a solution. Just because Lucas couldn't figure it out didn't mean she couldn't.

Alex was about halfway across the massive refugee camp when she heard a scream. Instinctively she turned toward the apartment building and made her way down the narrow hall. The rooms were barely habitable, just large enough for beds and desks, almost a caricature of school dorm rooms, and these were the ones with larger rooms for families. She followed the sound of weeping to a partially open door.

Inside, three young adult men were antagonizing a father, a mother, and a daughter. One held the mother, with a knife to her neck, to prevent the father from doing anything. The daughter clung to the father. Another of the attackers had his knife ready should the father try anything, while the last was digging through what looked like a school backpack.

Alex frowned, consumed by despair, anger, frustration, and sadness. Grace was trapped on a toxic, destroyed planet. Good people were dead, while these thugs decided to terrorize an already traumatized family. And Alex knew, with unequivocal mathematical certainty, that their habitat was overpopulated and the problems were nearly insurmountable.

As if she were floating outside of herself, Alex watched herself tilt her head at the gang, curiously devoid of emotion. She surrounded the three young men with her picobots and incinerated them. They vanished into bright flames and all that remained was dust. Alex didn't even care that one of the three was a Marino. The backpack fell to the floor and its contents, a couple schoolbooks and a teddy bear, fell out.

Alex would not let anyone destroy her home. The future of humanity depended on it. Alex saw herself glance over at the family and say indifferently, "This is my space station." She turned and strode off toward her lab.

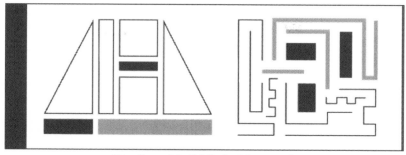

T plus 11:228:0:29   0

Interviewer: When did you know you were going to create a space station and your own country?

Founder: Do you think children should eat out of trash cans and be brutalized by the worst dregs of humanity?

Interviewer: I don't understand, Founder.

Founder: I have complete recall both visually and audibly. Sal suggested that I use this ability to do something I really wanted, and at the time, the only thing I wanted was a safe place. Food off a plate, not from a dumpster.

Interviewer: You're referring to Salvatore Marino?

Founder: Yes. He was a good man. Art lover. Savior of humanity.

Interviewer: But you created Colony One?

Founder: Sal suggested that I build a society where children would be safe. Our current situation is serendipitous.

Interviewer: Are children safe here? You executed three teens without trial, without following Colony One's investigation and forum process.

Founder: Innocent people will be safe, but we're overpopulated. Those teens were adults under our law and were fully aware of what they were doing. Security has confirmed this. Humanity can no longer tolerate crime. We do not have the space or the resources to provide rehabilitation and Colony One's way of life shall not be compromised.

Interviewer: Cal Park, the person who coordinated Earth's evacuation was such a criminal once upon a time, and without him, how many people would have died? Would he have survived under this policy?

Founder: He would have been executed. We're going to lose good people this way, but right now, we have no margin for error. Adapt to our society or die.

Interviewer: Is it true your daughter is trapped on Earth?

Founder: All five of my children are safely inside our Great Barrier Reef habitat. We will connect our habitats as soon as possible.

431

Interviewer: Would you let me write your story? I think many people would like to hear it and it should be documented for the future.

Founder: I suppose if I don't tell you, someone will make something up.

Interviewer: People should hear your story.

Founder: Ok then, I'll tell you and while it will be true, it won't be the whole truth because some of my memories belong to me alone. I'm only going to tell you the parts that mattered and only up until right now.

Interviewer: That's reasonable. You can't know the future.

Silence.

Interviewer: Where did the money come from to keep Green World afloat? Even if you add up the money you borrowed from Kuro Hamasaki and Mario Marino, and the money from antiques and art trading, you couldn't possibly have had that much money. It's basic math.

Founder: I'll tell you, but when you write my story, change it to writing novels to pay for the company. All authors dream of making lots of money by writing.

Interviewer: Anything else you want changed?

Founder: Hmmm. Now that I think about it, only one other thing. The rest can all be truth...

Made in the USA
Middletown, DE
10 January 2019